THE GREEN TIDE

Other great Warhammer 40,000 fiction featuring the orks

BRUTAL KUNNIN
by Mike Brooks

DA BIG DAKKA
by Mike Brooks

GHAZGHKULL THRAKA: PROPHET OF THE WAAAGH!
by Nate Crowley

GHAZGHKULL THRAKA: WARLORD OF WARLORDS
by Denny Flowers

GROTSNIK: DA MAD DOK
by Denny Flowers

DA RED GOBBO COLLECTION
A collection featuring the novellas *Da Gobbo's Revenge*, *Da Gobbo's Demise* and *Da Gobbo Rides Again* plus two short stories
by various authors

THE BEAST ARISES: VOLUME 1
An omnibus edition of the novels *I Am Slaughter*, *Predator*, *Prey*, *The Emperor Expects* and *The Last Wall*
by various authors

THE BEAST ARISES: VOLUME 2
An omnibus edition of the novels *Throneworld*, *Echoes of the Long War*, *The Hunt for Vulkan* and *The Beast Must Die*
by various authors

THE BEAST ARISES: VOLUME 3
An omnibus edition of the novels *Watchers in Death*, *The Last Son of Dorn*, *Shadow of Ullanor* and *The Beheading*
by various authors

THE GREEN TIDE

AN ORK OMNIBUS

MIKE BROOKS | JUSTIN WOOLLEY
STEVE LYONS | NATE CROWLEY

A BLACK LIBRARY PUBLICATION

'The Enemy of My Enemy' first published in *Inferno! Volume 1* in 2018.
Iron Resolve first published in 2019.
'Where Dere's Da Warp Dere's a Way' first published in *Inferno! Volume 4* in 2019.
Prisoners of Waaagh! first published in 2020.
'Mad Dok' first published digitally in 2021.
Warboss and *Catachan Devil* first published in 2022.
'Painboyz' first published digitally in 2024.
This edition published in Great Britain in 2026 by
Black Library, Games Workshop Ltd., Willow Road,
Nottingham, NG7 2WS, UK.

Represented by: Games Workshop Limited – Irish branch,
Unit 3, Lower Liffey Street, Dublin 1,
D01 K199, Ireland.

10 9 8 7 6 5 4 3 2 1

Produced by Games Workshop in Nottingham.

The Green Tide © Copyright Games Workshop Limited 2026.
The Green Tide, GW, Games Workshop, Black Library, The Horus Heresy, The Horus Heresy Eye logo, Space Marine, 40K, Warhammer, Warhammer 40,000, the 'Aquila' Double-headed Eagle logo, and all associated logos, illustrations, images, names, creatures, races, vehicles, locations, weapons, characters, and the distinctive likenesses thereof, are either ® or TM, and/or © Games Workshop Limited, variably registered around the world.
All Rights Reserved.

A CIP record for this book is available from the British Library.

ISBN 13: 978-1-83609-286-5

No part of this publication may be reproduced, stored in a retrieval system, or transmitted in any form or by any means, electronic, mechanical, photocopying, recording or otherwise, without the prior permission of the publishers.

This is a work of fiction. All the characters and events portrayed in this book are fictional, and any resemblance to real people or incidents is purely coincidental.

See Black Library on the internet at

blacklibrary.com

Find out more about Games Workshop
and the worlds of Warhammer at

warhammer.com

Printed and bound in the UK.

For more than a hundred centuries the Emperor has sat immobile on the Golden Throne of Earth. He is the Master of Mankind. By the might of his inexhaustible armies a million worlds stand against the dark.

Yet, he is a rotting carcass, the Carrion Lord of the Imperium held in life by marvels from the Dark Age of Technology and the thousand souls sacrificed each day so his may continue to burn.

To be a man in such times is to be one amongst untold billions. It is to live in the cruelest and most bloody regime imaginable. It is to suffer an eternity of carnage and slaughter. It is to have cries of anguish and sorrow drowned by the thirsting laughter of dark gods.

This is a dark and terrible era where you will find little comfort or hope. Forget the power of technology and science. Forget the promise of progress and advancement. Forget any notion of common humanity or compassion.

There is no peace amongst the stars, for in the grim darkness of the far future, there is only war.

CONTENTS

WARBOSS

MIKE BROOKS

DA KAST

ORKS

Waaagh! Gazrot

Gazrot Goresnappa, Da Snakebitten	Warboss, Snakebite
Old Morgrub	Warphead weirdboy, Snakebite
Genrul Uzbrag, 'Da Genrul'	Big boss, Blood Axe
Mag Dedfist	Big boss, Goff
Zagnob Thundaskuzz	Speedboss, Evil Sun
Skabrukk	Stormboy drill boss, Goff
Badzag	Skarboyz nob, Goff
Nuzzgrond	Trukkboyz nob, Goff
Skulsnik	Kommando kaptin, Blood Axe
Skrappit	Mekaniak, Evil Sun
Duffrak	Thundaskuzz's driver, Evil Sun
Rukknut	Shokkjump dragsta driver, Bad Moon
Uzgul	Beast snagga boy, Goff
Urlukk	Spanner, Deathskull
Gutzog	Spanner, Deathskull
Zukrod	Runtherd, Snakebite
Lootenant Kabrukk	Nob, Blood Axe
Lootenant Gubzag	Nob, Blood Axe
Skitta	Zagnob's fuel-mixer, grot
'Sarge'	Killa Kan, Da Genrul's attendant

Da GrotWaaagh!

Snaggi Littletoof	Da Grotboss, Chosen of Gork and Mork
Skrawk	Grot
Guffink	Grot
Kruffik	Grot
Snippa One-Ear	Grot
Lunk	Grot
Pukk	Grot
Wizza	Grot

Da TekWaaagh!

Ufthak Blackhawk	Big boss, Bad Moon
Nizkwik	Grot

HUMIES

Aranuan 25th Astra Militarum, 'Golden Lions'

Grozer Sudliff	Colonel
Armenius Varrow	Captain, Third Platoon
Deralee Bruja	Major
Sentra LaSteel	Tank commander, Seventh Company, *Golden Thunder*
Darrus Greel	Armour sergeant, Seventh Company, *Lion's Fury*
Kat Pallas	Driver, Seventh Company, *Golden Thunder*
Gravers	Gunner, Seventh Company, *Golden Thunder*

'Two Hands' Tayne	Loader, Seventh Company, *Golden Thunder*
Xanin	Sponson gunner, Seventh Company, *Golden Thunder*
Sanavar Deltis	Enginseer, Seventh Company
Elushka Bone, 'Old Bones'	Regimental commissar

Aranuan Citizens

Ama Junier	Planetary governor
Eza	Hunter
The Seer	Chief of Emperor's Gate

SKRAWNIEZ

Ilaethen Arhien	Autarch of Lugganath craftworld
Yria Nightsong	Farseer of Lugganath craftworld

The orkish mind is something that many of my esteemed colleagues will argue barely exists. They will maintain that the orks and their kin are little more than instinctive animals, carrying out the tasks and functions in which they have evolved to specialise without independent thought, somewhat in the manner of colonial insects. In this matter – as in so many others – it is in fact the magi biologis in question who are acting mindlessly.

Orkish society is considerably more dynamic than our own; my learned peers might deride it as chaotic, if they deigned to accept the truth of such a statement, but even that would indicate limited understanding on their parts.[1] *The simple truth is that an ork is far more capable than an unaugmented human of recognising when a situation is not to their individual benefit and taking action to remedy that fact.*

It might be argued that this cannot be true, since orks will readily throw themselves into perilous situations with little regard for their own safety, or indeed, in a combat situation, tactics. The key issue here is that this is a highly desirable state of affairs for an ork, for whom the outcome of a battle is of substantially less importance than experiencing said battle in the first place. However, should an ork 'boss,' 'big boss' or 'warboss' (the closest translations of their very loose command structure) not provide their followers with an appropriate level of excitement, combat or plunder – in other words, the things their followers desire – they can expect an attempted coup from within the ranks of those followers. This is a universally observed truth, wherever it has been possible to study the behaviour of orks with any degree of accuracy over a period of time.

If one compares this with the behaviour of, for example, the massed ranks of the Astra Militarum, for whom combat or even the potential of combat will provoke extremely negative physiological reactions, the difference is startling. Notions such as 'duty' might hold them to an undesirable course of action with poor outcomes; so too might fear of lethal censure by an officer such as an Imperial commissar, despite the fact that, should they act as a unit – as they have been trained to – the troopers could easily overpower and kill any such officer. The unaugmented human, enslaved to the whirl of emotions in their brain, is far more likely to go against their own wishes and interests rather than disobey a figure of authority.

For orks, that position would be unthinkable. So far as this xenos species appears to be concerned, although senior orks are larger than their subordinates, no ork – no matter how large – could

[1] I have separately catalogued seven hundred and forty-three instances of current recognised members of the Biologis holding or stating incorrect assumptions or observations about the orks and their related subspecies, which I have placed into the appendices of this work.

maintain authority over its fellows without providing them with what they want. Indeed, since orks gain in size the more they fight, being a large ork indicates that you fight regularly, and therefore following you is likely to bring any other ork into combat.

It would be an interesting state of affairs indeed if unaugmented humans were to show the clear, logical reasoning possessed by orks, and act on it accordingly...

– Extract from the works of Magos Kazadin Yallamagasa,
later known as the Biologis Diabolicus,
declared heretek in M38

DA BIT WOT COMES BEFORE DA FING

It was dark.

This was mainly because something was tied over Snaggi Littletoof's eyes, and therefore he couldn't see, but that was not a great deal of comfort. *He* certainly hadn't tied it there. Nor had he shoved the gag into his mouth, which foiled the efforts of even his needle-pointed teeth to bite through it, and condemned him to drool ceaselessly. He had not been the one to tie his hands behind his back, either, or attach them to something firm. He couldn't move, and he certainly couldn't escape. Not for the first time, he wondered what in the names of Gork and Mork a simple grot like him had done to deserve this.

Actually, there was probably quite a long list, now he came to think about it.

His eyes might be covered, but his ears were unstoppered, and he could tell from the acoustics that he was inside something: probably a hut, or maybe part of a wrecked vehicle. He was sitting on dirt, although that didn't mean that much in these circumstances. He could still hear noises from outside, but it sounded like the fight was over. He wondered who had won. He hoped that it was his side, assuming there was still a side to which he could claim he belonged.

Something *whoomped* softly, like a hanging swath of cloth being shoved aside, and Snaggi sat up a little straighter, trying not to tremble in fear. His experiences of such things were limited, but he was fairly certain that you didn't get bound, gagged and blindfolded just to then be offered a hot squig skewer and your pick of the battlefield loot.

His ears told him that someone had come to a halt in front of him, and his nostrils picked up the scents of bang-powder and smoke and shoota grease, but even had they been blocked too, some other sense still hinted at the *closeness* of another being. A moment later, hands were reaching around to loosen the gag, and it was pulled free.

Snaggi didn't say anything. If you'd been gagged, and the gag was then loosened, it probably did not mean that you were in a position where shouting for help was going to do you any good. Either help had already loosened the gag, or you were about to get asked some serious questions by those uninclined to help. Besides, who would help him?

Then the blindfold was pulled off, and he found himself staring at another grot.

Hope leaped in his fast-beating heart. They'd found him! One of his ladz had found him, and was about to get him away from all this...

His brain realised that he did not recognise this grot at about the same time that his eyes focused on the hulking shape that loomed further back, in the shadows of what was, he now saw, an ork hut. The hut was a crudely assembled but sturdy affair of looted scrap, fairly unremarkable as such things went, but the ork was something else. It was massive, one of the largest Snaggi had ever seen, and although its armour was painted in the black and yellow of the Bad Moons clan, that armour looked to be primarily composed of beakie bits.

'Dat fing out dere,' the grot said, snapping Snaggi's attention back to him. 'How's it work? How'd ya get 'ere, an' where'd ya come from?'

Snaggi licked his teeth nervously. If he was being asked this, then that implied he had some value: value that might evaporate as soon as he coughed up what information he had. He grinned at his captors, readying his mind for the battle of wits that would ensue.

'Tell me now, or I crush yer skull,' the ork rumbled, taking a tectonic step forwards. 'Ya ain't da only captive we got, yoo're just da one I'm askin' first.'

Orks were not given to idle threats in general, and Snaggi could immediately tell that this one was deathly serious: Snaggi's death, to be precise. He hastily revised his strategy from 'bargain for your life' to 'tell the scary ork what it wants to know and hope it then forgets about you.'

'Well,' he began hastily, 'dat's a bit of a long story.'

'Shorten it,' the ork suggested, folding its fingers into a fist that was roughly the size of Snaggi's entire upper body. 'Or I shorten yoo. By a head.'

'Yes, boss!' Snaggi gabbled, the honorific cutting in by reflex, even though he hated himself for it. 'So, uh...'

ONE

Warboss Gazrot Goresnappa had descended on the Imperial world of Aranua with all his forces and had, in the words of Major Saras, proceeded to give it such a thorough kicking that most of it didn't know which way was up any more.[2] The northern seas were now in xenos hands, including their promethium-extraction rigs. The main southern continent had been overrun, with neither high mountains, baking deserts, nor humid swamps providing any manner of meaningful defence against the invaders. Hive city after hive city had been taken. The populace either died in the fighting, were killed during the looting, or were enslaved.

Only one sizeable stronghold now remained: Davidia Hive, rising eight miles into the sky out of the blasted grey of Aranua's industrial heartland. It was a towering edifice of human engineering, and had stood in defiance of everything the galaxy could throw at it for seven millennia. Governor Ama Junier thought she should probably take some heart from that, but the simple fact of the matter was that up until now, the galaxy hadn't thrown orks.

And now here they were, virtually on her doorstep. She looked out of the window of her quarters. Above her, the sky darkened to a deep, deep blue. She could make out the curvature of the planet from up here. And yet despite the distance, despite the patchy cloud cover beneath her feet, if she looked down she could see the shifting mass of the orkish forces. There were so Throne-damned many of them!

'I take it there has been no word from the astropaths?' she asked carefully.

'No, ma'am,' Colonel Grozer Sudliff of the Aranuan 25th replied. His voice was level, but Ama could hear the tension within it. He was resentful of her question, because he would of course have informed her had there been any manner of communication to indicate that reinforcements were coming. However, unless she asked such questions, she risked looking like the clueless aristocrat she knew the general suspected her to be.

'And the tactical situation has not meaningfully altered?'

'No, ma'am.'

Ama sighed. An Imperial governor was supposed to lead and defend their

---

[2] The major was executed immediately following this statement, but that did not make it any less accurate.

world, but there was very little she could do in such circumstances. Colonel Sudliff had been in military command, and he had been pushed back and overwhelmed in short order. Not that Ama blamed the man for it: he would have needed to be the rebirth of Macharius himself to have succeeded against such odds, and Sudliff most certainly was not that. He was a solid and unremarkable man, born into an officer family. From there he had taken up a military position, which he held with no great problem until called upon in earnest, at which point he failed in a solid and unremarkable manner. Ama had needed to use every part of her wit and ingenuity to achieve the role of planetary governor when the previous incumbent had passed away, including the discreet assassination of three rivals. At least she'd had to do some thinking in her life.

Their options ranged from laughable to piteous. The might of the orks' ground forces dictated against any notion of a sortie or counter-attack, despite the fact that the remnants of Sudliff's troops were now holed up in the lower sections of Davidia, in cramped and unsuitable conditions. They had no Titans, no Knights, no super-heavy tanks: all the ordnance of that scale had either been destroyed or, to Ama's great displeasure, captured. Above Ama's head, the mobile, heavily weaponised agglomerations of scrap and junk that the orks used as warships, which had annihilated all merchant and military shipping that had stuck around to fight them, were patrolling, if 'patrolling' was the right term for 'moving unpredictably and haphazardly'. There were at least two warp-capable ships currently berthed in Davidia's space docks, but even the *Tennavar's Smile*, pleasure yacht of rogue trader Priam Huzinka, lacked the armour or weaponry to survive the orks' attention for long enough to get to the system's Mandeville point. There would be no escape off-world for Davidia's nobility, including Aranua's governor: at least, not unless an unheralded arm of the Indomitus Crusade arrived.

Ama tapped her fingers on the thick crystalflex in front of her. 'What do you suppose they're waiting for, colonel? They've barely hesitated before attacking a hive city up until now, by all accounts.'

'Can't say for sure, ma'am.'

Ama turned to him. Colonel Sudliff was the very image of the Imperial military: his hair was grey but still thick, and his mutton chop sideburns brushed the stiff, gold-embroidered collar of his dress jacket. His epaulettes sparkled, his creases were so sharp that he could have shaved with them, his boots were shined to a mirror finish, and his jacket's buttons were the maned heads of the animal that gave its name to his regiment, the Golden Lions. It was a shame his tactical wisdom was no match for his sartorial grandeur.

'Can you say at all?' she enquired. 'We await near-certain death at the hands of xenos invaders, colonel. I feel it is not unreasonable to hold some curiosity about what might be staying our execution, at least briefly.'

The colonel cleared his throat, and his usual direct – even impertinent – stare wandered from her face for the first time that she could remember.

'They seem to be building fires, ma'am. So far as we can understand these creatures, they... Well, if they were human, I'd say they were having a party.'

'A party.' Ama turned away from him to stare out of her window once more.

Darkness was falling on the ground far below, and she could indeed see the tiny sparks of light that must have been, if one were standing next to them, huge conflagrations. 'These creatures fall upon my world, they kill my people, and now they mock me by having a *party*?'

'If it please you, ma'am,' Sudliff offered, 'I doubt they're mocking you. These are orks – they're barely more than animals. Nothing that they do here will be considered with us in mind. They're simply doing it because they want to.'

'I know,' Ama murmured. She'd been underestimated, maligned, avoided, and outright threatened in her life, but never had she simply been *ignored*. 'If anything, that just makes it worse.'

TWO

'Get dose fires nice an' big! I want all dem humies to know we'z here, an' I want 'em shakin' in dere boots!'

Gazrot Goresnappa, also known as Gazrot Da Snakebitten, was without question one of the greatest orks to ever venture out into the galaxy and punch it in its face. A member of the Snakebite clan, he rose to violent prominence early in his life by regularly winning headbutting contests with smasha squigs. He had strangled the seven-headed serpent of Kryyk using one of its own necks, and had gone to the trouble of harvesting its venom glands, not to coat his blade or poison his enemies, but simply to add a bit of kick to his fungus beer. He quickly gained a strong following, based in part on his skill in combat, and in part on his propensity and ability to raise squiggoths of a size rarely seen. When he was slighted by Warboss Kurzan, Gazrot had ridden his herd right over the other ork's battlewagon, crushing it, and Kurzan inside it, in the process. After that, there had been little doubt in anyone's mind who should take the old warboss' place.

What this meant was that when Gazrot Goresnappa, close to ten feet tall in his hulking, fur-draped, smoke-belching mega armour, yelled at you to make a fire nice and big, you zoggin' well made that fire nice and big.

All around him, orks scurried to do his bidding, and the sight brought a smile to Gazrot's face. This was what it meant to be an ork! It wasn't like he was one of those self-important types, like the freebooter kaptins, or the Blood Axes that enjoyed mimicking the humie way of doing things. Gazrot didn't give himself fancy hats, or medals, or any other frippery. Gazrot just enjoyed a good scrap, and the more orks that followed him and did what he said when he said it, the more scraps he could win.

He'd very nearly won this one, which was why he was taking a moment to enjoy himself. There was one big humie camp left on this entire planet, so far as he could tell, which was the one looming above them all at this very moment. Gazrot would say this for humies: they knew how to build big. The 'city,' as the humies called it, must have been larger than any of the ships in his fleet, which was impressive in and of itself. It was taller than a mountain, with its summit lost in the clouds; it was practically a mountain in its own right, a gargantuan structure which wasn't just tall, but *wide*. Simply being near it would probably be enough to intimidate any normal creature.

Gazrot wasn't any normal creature. So far as he was concerned, the sheer size of this thing just made it more of an obvious and impressive target. He'd bring it down, just like his ladz had brought down all the others. Then the meks would strip out anything useful, and they'd get some of the fuel that Magzak's lot were pulling off the humie rigs in the big water to the north, and they'd build a whole bunch of new war engines, repair the ones that had been damaged, wait around a bit for a bunch of new boyz to show up – they always did, sooner or later – and then get back out into the stars in search of the next planet to conquer. That was life as it should be lived; that was the ork way.

In the meantime, though, he wanted to remind every ork exactly who it was that had led them here and crushed the humies. That wasn't him being self-important, that was just proper and sensible. It made it more likely that they'd do what he said, when he said it. Da Genrul had a humie word for that: 'dissipline'. Gazrot wasn't buying into any of that humie crap, though.

Da Genrul. Now, that was an ork who needed watching, Gazrot thought. Genrul Uzbrag was a typical Blood Axe, in that he liked the orks under his command to walk in straight lines and hit their heads with their hands when he told them to do something, and a whole load of other stuff he'd picked up from humies, and elsewhere for that matter. It didn't sit well with Gazrot, borrowing stuff from other species. What was wrong with being an ork, and doing things in the ork way, like Gork and Mork intended? Snakebites were traditionalists at heart, and Uzbrag's tendency towards innovation rubbed Gazrot up the wrong way. Still, there was no denying that the git was successful. He could clobber an enemy with the best of them, and sometimes his strange inventions and 'battle plans' actually worked surprisingly well. There was a reason he was one of Gazrot's favoured big bosses, but that didn't mean Gazrot trusted him. Although to be fair, he didn't trust anyone.

He certainly didn't trust Mag Dedfist. The massive Goff big boss was yelling at a bunch of his ladz to build the fires higher, which was all well and good, but Dedfist was a dour son of a squig who Gazrot reckoned wouldn't be content playing second shoota to him for much longer. One day soon, Dedfist would get it into his incredibly thick-skulled head to take a swing for his warboss, with the goal of taking his place. Gazrot had no intention of letting that happen, of course, but it wasn't like there were many options. He'd thrown Dedfist at the hardest knots of humie resistance, and the big Goff had gone through them without much pause, and certainly without taking any sort of noticeable harm. Dedfist had simply reinforced his own reputation with the boyz under his command, which wasn't going to do Gazrot any favours. No, when it came to it, he'd have to let Dedfist take his swing and then just stomp him flat into the ground, as tradition dictated.

He also didn't trust Zagnob Thundaskuzz, the Evil Sunz speedboss, but that was less because Gazrot thought that Thundaskuzz was gunning for him, and more because simply getting any concept into the speedboss' head was virtually impossible. You couldn't trust him to do anything other than accelerate off into the distance and kill things while going at an incredibly high speed, which, granted, was sometimes a very useful trait. It wasn't much good when you were trying to make sure the right bits of a Waaagh!

hit the enemy at the right time to cause maximum impact, though. Nonetheless, the Kult of Speed had a sizeable presence in Waaagh! Goresnappa, and Thundaskuzz had a correspondingly high amount of influence. He could neither be conveniently ignored nor disposed of, so Gazrot would just have to make use of him as best he could.

All of those were considerations for another time, though. Right now, the raging infernos that had been built had achieved the desired effect: namely, a whole load of orks were starting to congregate, wondering what was going on, and if there was going to be any food or, preferably, a fight.

Gazrot looked around, then tapped his shouty box to make sure it was working. It responded with a pleasing static squeal, which sounded almost exactly like a grot that had been stepped on. Dedfist had been watching him ever since he'd stopped yelling at his boyz to make the fires bigger, but now Gazrot could see the strange peaked hat of Da Genrul approaching in the midst of a big knot of Blood Axes, accompanied by the Killa Kan he called 'Sarge,' which followed him around with that ridiculous captured humie in a cage on its back. A rumble of engines and the stink of badly refined fuel smoke announced the arrival of Zagnob Thundaskuzz, resplendent on the back of his Deffkilla wartrike, and at the head of a veritable host of bikers.

Good. Let them all come. Let them see the might of the Great Goresnappa, Da Snakebitten, the ork who led them here. Let them be reminded who was in charge, and whose boot would be kicking their arse if anyone thought they fancied being warboss.

His own Snakebites were flooding in now, too: they didn't outnumber the other clans in his Waaagh!, but they were certainly the most numerous of any one faction. And of course, a truly great warboss didn't just have one clan behind him, he had many. They were all here, Bad Moons, Deathskulls and all, even a few freebooters hanging around the edges, but this was the main core of his force. Goffs for the really close-in fighting, Evil Sunz for the quick stuff, Blood Axes when you needed a sneaky git, and Snakebites to hold it all together: proper orks; true orks; orks you could rely on not to forget about the old ways, and how Gork and Mork wanted things done.

Still, for all the fact that Snakebites were undoubtedly the best clan, and that the war beasts his particular part of it bred were the biggest and stompiest around, there was something to be said for a bit of teknology now and then. No one had ever before seen a squiggoth the size of Tankbreaka, Gazrot's personal mount, but even that massive creature was dwarfed by the Mega-Gargant in front of which Gazrot was currently standing – *Da Kroolfang*. It somehow seemed even bigger than the massive human city, because that was just a *thing*, and things could be as big as they were: a planet was a thing, and no one would blink at that. The Gargant, however, was a giant effigy of Gork (or possibly Mork), and was shaped accordingly, with huge eyes that could fire energy beams, a gigantic bitey jaw, arms of death-dealing weapons, and a massive body which housed not only the infamous belly gun, but could also transport a whole host of boyz right into the thick of the fight, assuming any enemies were foolish enough to get close to such a gigantic machine of destruction. It was utterly titanic.

Gazrot had no doubt that some orks wouldn't like to stand directly in front of such a monstrous war machine, in case it made them look small by comparison. Gazrot had no such compunctions. He told the zoggin' thing what to do, where to go, and what to stomp: that made him the most powerful ork around. So far as he was concerned, the sheer size of the Gargant made him look *bigger*.

He flicked his shouty box again, and the resulting squeal-edged *thud* drew everyone's attention to him.

'ALRIGHT, LISSEN UP!' he bellowed, and the shouty box amplified his voice so magnificently that it was as though he were shouting directly into the ear of every ork present: every warboss' heartfelt desire. *'Now, I told ya all wot was gonna happen 'ere, right? We was gonna come down, give all da humies a right good kickin,' and take all dere stuff! An' we did it, didn't we?'*

His words drew a mighty roar of approval from the assembled orks. Out of the corner of his eye, Gazrot saw the crooked staff of Old Morgrub approaching, belting other orks on the head to get them out of his way. The weirdboy was the Waaagh!'s most senior warphead, at least so far as these things could be determined. He certainly seemed a little more grounded than a lot of the rest, although that was a bit like saying that one trampla squig smelled better than most of the others. Still, Morgrub had enough control over the power that built up within him to not explode too many heads by accident, and although sometimes he made less sense than a squig that had fallen in the fungus beer, he was capable of providing decent advice every now and then. Gazrot knew that his big bosses weren't fans of Morgrub's rantings, but that was just further evidence that, unlike Snakebites, they'd forgotten the ways of Gork and Mork.

'So now we got just one more fing to do,' Gazrot continued, as Morgrub finally clobbered his way to the front of the packed ranks of orkish faces, all lit up by the roaring flames. *'One more bunch of humies to stomp, and den all dis planet's ours!'*

That brought some cheers as well, but also some grumbling, because no more humies meant no more fighting. Well, actually it didn't mean that at all, because any ork could pick a fight with any other ork for just about any reason, including because both of them happened to want a fight, but that was just scrapping. That wasn't the full-throated bloodlust of the Waaagh!, where the orks all banded together and showed the other species in the galaxy exactly why they were the very best. A scrap was fun, without question, but it wasn't quite the same thing as charging into battle with the thunder of guns as your heartbeat, your mates beside you, and getting covered in someone else's blood, or ichor, or whatever turned out to be inside when you hit 'em.

'Once we're done 'ere, we'll get ourselves sorted out an' back onto da ships, den go an' find some uvver place to conquer!' Gazrot bellowed, to reassure his ladz. *'Dis ain't da end of the Waaagh!! Dis ain't even da beginnin' of da end! It might be da end of da...'*

He tailed off, because Old Morgrub was looking upwards with a strangely intent expression on his scarred, leathery face. Normally it took a lot to throw Gazrot off his stride, but there was something about the warphead's sheer focus that made him uneasy. Still not quite sure why he was doing it, and heedless of the impact such uncertainty would have on his standing amongst his boyz, he too turned and looked upwards to see what Morgrub was staring at.

THREE

Gork and Mork did not speak loudly to everyone. Many orks lived out their lives without ever really hearing the voices of their gods, save in the background roar of battle. For others – the weirdboyz whose heads exploded, for example – they spoke a bit *too* loudly. But for some rare orks, like Grand Warlord Ghazghkull Mag Uruk Thraka, the voices of the ork gods were their guidance, the fuel that powered the furnace of conquest and violence burning in their hearts, and which was crucial to their success at bringing others under their sway and dominating the galaxy.

Snaggi Littletoof knew in his heart that Gork and Mork were speaking to him, as well. The trouble was, he was a grot, and no one cared.

He'd tried to tell others about it, of course. The thing was, the volume of Gork and Mork speaking *to you* didn't seem to be anywhere near as important as how loudly you could talk about it to *other orks*. And when you weren't even an ork to begin with, that wasn't very loud at all. Snaggi was surrounded by hulking green giants, bellowing and roaring and kicking him without thinking – or sometimes thinking about it and then kicking him again, just to be sure – and not one of them was prepared to listen to the words of their own gods, just because they were coming out of the mouth of a grot. It was enough to make you sick. He'd had more than one hiding for 'bleedin' cheek' when he'd mentioned the gods, and he'd learned to keep his mouth shut now. More or less, anyway.

Still, he'd managed to get himself a fairly cushy little number, at least so far as things went for grots. No desperate clutching of an unreliable grot blasta and trying to get close enough to shoot some giant humie in a suit of armour, or a deadly-fast bugeye with four arms and knives for hands for Snaggi Littletoof, oh no. No, he'd managed to blag his way onto the Mega-Gargant known as *Da Kroolfang*, which was an awful lot of metal between him and anything that might want to kill him.

Of course, he wasn't a passenger. Snaggi and the rest of his little crew were under the theoretical oversight of Mek Zagblutz, a cantankerous old Deathskull with three eyes (two of them mechanical, but that was meks for you) and expectations of the level of work required from those under his command which were so high that Snaggi sometimes wondered if the old git had missed his proper calling as a stormboy drill boss. Right now they were greasing and polishing a collection of cogs and gears, the purpose of which Snaggi wasn't quite sure, but might have had something to do with turning the Gargant's head from side to side so its Gaze of Mork could incinerate whatever its kommander chose.

'Ow long d'ya fink it'll take to kill dat last humie city?' Guffink asked, scrubbing at a gear with his shiny-cloth. Guffink was hard-working and industrious, and generally made the rest of them look bad in comparison.

'Dunno,' Skrawk replied. The others waited for a moment to see if he was going to qualify that with anything else, such as musings on exactly what might cause a variance in the time taken, but nothing else was forthcoming. Skrawk wasn't much of a conversationalist.

'I fink it's da biggest dere's been yet,' Snaggi offered. 'So it'll prob'ly take longer.' He looked around to make sure no one was watching, then took a swig from his oil can. He spat it out hurriedly a moment later, because it tasted foul. It had done every time so far, but he made a point of trying it once a day, just in case one of the others had come up with a cunning plan to sneak some booze under Zagblutz's nose by putting it in a can. Snaggi wasn't going to risk missing out on some good stuff just because he got a mouthful of oil if he was wrong: that would have been cowardly, and that was not the way of Gork and Mork.

'See, I was finkin' dat,' Guffink replied amiably, 'but den I fort, well, as it's da last one, none of da ladz are off doin' anyfing else, are dey? So dere's a lot more boyz to kill it, an' dat means it might even be quicker!'

'"Da ladz",' Kruffik chuckled mockingly. Kruffik was big, at least for a grot, and liked to throw what weight he had around. 'Stop talkin' like yoo're one of 'em, Guffink. Any of 'em hears ya talkin' like dat, dey'll twist yer head clean off yer neck.'

'An' wot's it to yoo if dey did?' Guffink demanded, ceasing his polishing and rounding on the bigger grot. 'Eh? Why're ya so worried about wot an ork's gonna fink if he hears me talkin', Kruffik? Yoo ain't worried about *me*, I know dat much!'

Snaggi exchanged glances with Skrawk. This little exchange held the promise of livening up their work a bit.

'I reckon ya fancy yerself as an ork's runt,' Guffink continued, warming to his subject. 'Does that sound good, eh, Kruffik? Ya wanna do wot a nob says? Ya wanna carry his ammo around? Wanna polish his shoota for 'im? Workin' on a Gargant's not good enuff, is it? Ya wanna go pick up after a boss nob, den come back an' lord it over da rest of us like dat makes you all *important*?'

Snaggi was expecting Kruffik to belt Guffink round the face, but to his surprise the bigger grot just folded his arms and glowered. 'Yoo'z a snivellin' little whiner, Guffink, an' ya always have been. Yoo'z da one wot finks he's important – yoo'z as bad as Snaggi dere.'

Snaggi felt his brows rise, as he was unexpectedly drawn into this conflict. 'Wait a second, Kruffik, wotcha mean by dat?'

'Wot I *mean*,' Kruffik said, squaring up to Snaggi, 'is dat we'z all heard ya talkin' about da gods, Snaggi. We'z all heard ya saying dat dere talkin' to ya, like yoo'z somefing speshul. But ya *ain't*.'

Snaggi grinned toothily at him. 'Dat's okay, Kruffik. Yoo're just jealous cos da gods ain't talkin' to ya.'

'Dey ain't talkin' to *yoo* either!' Kruffik barked, his temper fraying. He reached out with one sharp-nailed finger, and jabbed Snaggi in the chest with it. 'Yoo're makin' it up to try an' make yerself sound important, so cloth'eads like Guffink 'ere might lissen to ya, an' do yer work for ya!'

Now, that statement wasn't born of any concern for Guffink, Snaggi knew. So far as ork kultur went – and grot kultur along with it – if you couldn't stand up for yourself, you got walked on. That was the way of the galaxy, and no one with any sense had any problem with it. The only reason Kruffik would object would be because he was jealous he hadn't thought of it himself.

The thing was, cunning plan though it might have been, that wasn't what Snaggi was doing. He wouldn't dare invite the wrath of Gork or Mork by claiming to hear their voices when he didn't. He knew exactly what he'd heard.

'Dey're talkin' to me right now,' he told Kruffik. 'Dey're tellin' me just wot to do.'

'Oh?' Kruffik's snort of derision was so forceful that it splattered snot all over his front. 'An' wot's dat?'

'Dis.'

Snaggi kicked him in the shin as hard as he could, which given he was wearing metal-capped boots, and Kruffik's shins were completely unprotected was, when everything was taken into account, pretty zoggin' hard.

Kruffik howled and hopped backwards, clutching his shin in both hands. Snaggi laughed at him, enjoying the other grot's pain, but Kruffik's rage quickly overcame it. Kruffik grabbed a wrench, a piece of dirty metal nearly as long as he was tall, and swung it in both hands, screaming as he did so. Snaggi stumbled backwards, fear replacing his amusement just as quickly as Kruffik's pain had disappeared, and ducked a moment before the wrench could connect with his head. The *whoosh* of air displacement hinted at exactly how heavy the impact would have been had the blow landed, but the force of the missed swing carried Kruffik around, off balance. Snaggi had no intention of letting him have another go, so he charged and put his shoulder into the other grot's ribs as hard as he could.

Kruffik let out a great huff of air, and they both went down onto the greasy plates of metal that formed the floor in this part of the Gargant. Guffink and Skrawk were cheering, as was the way of any grot when encountering a fight in which they were not a participant, but they weren't on anyone's side: it was just good old-fashioned appreciation of a brawl. Snaggi couldn't count on any help, even though it had been Guffink squaring up to Kruffik a few moments before, so he grabbed one of Kruffik's wrists in both hands and bit it as hard as he could. Kruffik howled and relaxed his grip on the wrench, dropping it completely, but Snaggi quickly realised that this was possibly a bad development for him. The wrench was big and clumsy, and although Kruffik would have clung to the weapon instinctively, it wouldn't have served him well at such close quarters. Now, however, the larger grot had his hands free to claw and strangle, and that wasn't going to go so well for Snaggi.

Snaggi went for his eyes instead.

Kruffik howled in pain as Snaggi's nails gouged at his face, but he flailed and thrashed and kicked so vigorously that Snaggi was thrown clean off him and landed hard on the deck again. He staggered up, looking for some sort of weapon of his own, but to no avail: Kruffik was too quick, and was already coming for him with fists balled.

A grot's punch would barely register to an ork, and even a human would probably shrug it off and swing one back with considerably more force, but they were plenty hard enough to another grot. Snaggi ducked the first and landed a pointy elbow into Kruffik's ribs, but then the other grot managed to get hold of him by the back of the neck and pulled him up sufficiently to send his next blow, with his other hand, right into Snaggi's gob.

Pain flowered, and Snaggi staggered backwards as the entire Gargant swayed around him. He spat out a toof, stumbled sideways, and caught at a lever of uncertain provenance in order to hold himself up. The last place he wanted to be was on the floor when his head was swimming, and Kruffik was still coming at him. Then an idea struck him, and he wrenched on the lever, trying to break it loose. Zagblutz's engineering wasn't always the most secure, and it would make a handy bludgeon...

The lever *moved*.

Kruffik stopped as something overhead *creaked*. It was a deep noise, one that reverberated around the Gargant's frame like an episode of particularly explosive flatulence in a squiggoth stall. It spoke not of the slight settling of a sturdy metallic superstructure, but of the beginnings of something more, something greater, something decidedly more emphatic than just a *creak*.

Very, very slowly, the ceiling began to move.

It was almost infinitesimal at first, only the faintest of shifts in shadow and light to suggest that something was happening. Then, as the movement became more obvious, more sounds sprang up. Scraping sounds, groaning sounds, the sounds of bolts and rivets *pinging* off from their fixings, the sounds of metal flexing in ways it was not supposed to flex, and tearing in ways it most certainly was not supposed to tear.

Snaggi didn't move. He was frozen in place by the fear that most commonly consumed a grot, which could be divided into two parts: firstly, that he was going to be crushed by something much larger and heavier than him; and secondly, that even if he somehow survived the current peril, he was going to be blamed for it.

'Oh, zoggin' 'eck,' Snaggi muttered weakly, as a thin crack of darkness appeared above him, and rapidly widened. That was the night sky, and one thing Snaggi was pretty certain about was that you weren't supposed to see *outside* a Gargant when you were *inside* a Gargant, unless you were looking through a window that a mek had specifically put there.

'Da head's comin' off!' Skrawk wailed, showing uncharacteristic perceptiveness and communication. 'Da zoggin' head's comin' off, ladz! Wot're we gonna do?!'

There was nothing they *could* do, of course – at least not to stop the landslide of metal which was even now carrying an untold tonnage of prime scrap, at least two high-power energy weapons, probably several orks, and quite possibly one very angry mekboy, forwards and then suddenly and quite terminally downwards. Snaggi managed to force himself to move and, along with the rest of his krew – hostilities abruptly forgotten – ran forwards to the front edge of the Gargant as the gigantic construction above them scraped onwards.

Snaggi got to the rail of what had been a viewing deck just as the ceiling began to tilt, and the head began to plummet. He looked over the edge and at first, of course, saw nothing but the underside of the Gargant's head. Then, as it fell and got smaller, he saw the rest of the Waaagh! spread out below, thousands of orks all gathered around blazing fires. They all seemed to be organised – insofar as orks were ever organised – into a loose semicircle around the base of the Mega-Gargant, and they began scrambling backwards as the head fell towards them. None of them were under it, but they'd been looking at something which had been...

'Oh, Gork's Green Grin,' Snaggi breathed, clapping his hand over his mouth. 'Da zoggin' warboss is down dere!'

For just a moment, Genrul Uzbrag thought that the enormous visage of Gork (or possibly Mork) falling off the Mega-Gargant was something Gazrot Goresnappa had orchestrated. He was still waiting for a squiggoth head to appear in its place, and Da Snakebitten to announce he'd created the galaxy's first Squig-Dread, or something equally ridiculous, when he realised that Gazrot's expression as he looked upwards at the massive hunk of falling metal was not one of triumph or pride, but one of confusion, rapidly overtaken by pissed-off comprehension.

Da Genrul had done enough yellin' back and forth in loud warzones to have picked up an understanding of what shapes an ork's mouth made when forming certain words, and so he was quite certain that he did not imagine that Gazrot said 'Oh zog' just before the Gargant's head landed on top of him.

Fire blossomed upwards, accompanied by roiling clouds of black smoke. Shards of metal were flung out, scything through the ranks and cutting down the ones at the front (mainly lower-ranking boyz, since any boss with half a brain kept a few footsloggers between him and Gazrot Goresnappa, just in case Da Snakebitten decided he needed to make an example of someone). A lot of orks cheered on general principle, since something loud and destructive had happened, and that was always worth cheering.[3]

Genrul Uzbrag's brows lowered, and not just because he was squinting against the cloud of dust and dirt blasted outwards by the impact. The presence of the warboss was the lodestone to which the rest of the Waaagh! was inexorably drawn: an invisible force, sort of like gravity, only not one the mekboyz could duplicate with a trukk full of spare parts, a free afternoon, and a plentiful supply of fungus beer. And now, in some way that Uzbrag could not quite verbalise even within his own head, that pull was gone.

Well, not gone, exactly. It was more...

...inwards.

* * *

[3] Exactly what had been destroyed was always an afterthought, since if you were still able to cheer, it wasn't *you*, and that was the main thing.

'You killed 'im,' Kruffik said, his tone one of bleak and utter dread. 'You killed da warboss, Snaggi.'

Snaggi's first instinct was to deny it. That was what a grot did: if something happened then you denied it, unless you were absolutely sure that the biggest ork paying attention was happy with it, in which case you claimed credit for it. He should deny that the lever had moved, and if it had definitely moved then he should deny being the one to have pulled on it; and if it was impossible to argue that he hadn't been the one who'd pulled on it then he should *definitely* blame Kruffik for hitting him so hard that he'd had no option other than to grab at the lever – no, better, that he hadn't even *realised* that he'd grabbed at the lever.

But he didn't feel like denying it. He could hear the great green voices of the gods, and the gods were telling him that he shouldn't be trying to hide this. Who could say they'd killed a warboss? Precious few! There were mighty beakies who'd never killed a warboss! There were flashy skrawniez who'd never killed a warboss! There were stompy metal gits with the glowy guns who'd never killed a warboss! So what if Snaggi couldn't actually *prove* that pulling on the lever was what had caused the Gargant's head to fall off? So what if it made no sense for Mek Zagblutz to have set up a lever that would make the head of his pride and joy fall off? Maybe the mek hadn't done it on purpose: maybe he'd made a mistake. Perhaps this was Snaggi's *destiny*.

He liked that.

'Yeah,' he said, tasting the word as it passed his needle teeth, relishing the thrill of danger as he admitted – no! Claimed credit for – killing Gazrot Goresnappa. 'Yeah, I did. I killed da warboss. An' ya know wot?' he continued, warming to the rebellious glow in his chest. 'Ya know zoggin' *wot*?'

He rounded on Kruffik and grabbed the horrified grot by the front of his rags.

'I ain't finished! I've had it wiv bein' kicked for fings I ain't done! Or even for fings I have! I've had it wiv bein' yelled at, and fightin' da squigs for me food! Dere's more of us dan dere are of dem! It's time for us grots to rise up, ya hear me? We're gonna show dese overgrown gits who da *real* bosses are round 'ere! An' if any of 'em don't like it...' He smacked the back of one hand into the palm of the other. '*Blam!* Dey're gonna get flattened, just like dat git down dere! Dis is just da beginnin'! Dis is da *Revolushun!*'

Far below, the orks of what had up until very recently been Waaagh! Gazrot weren't paying any attention to the tiny, animated figure screaming far above them.

They had suddenly acquired much more pressing concerns.

FOUR

Gazrot Goresnappa was given every opportunity to prove that he wasn't dead. Those orks who hadn't been crushed, incinerated by the explosion, or perforated by flying debris watched the fallen Gargant head expectantly, waiting for the warboss to angrily swat aside a piece of panelling or a broken strut and emerge from the wreckage, angry but largely unharmed, in an unquestionable sign of the favour of Gork and Mork.

As the smoke continued to billow out and the fires continued to burn, and there remained absolutely no sign that Gazrot was now anything other than an extremely flat green smear somewhere beneath the pile of metal, it began to dawn on the assembled mass that they were a Waaagh! which now lacked a warboss.

Some other clans might call the Blood Axes 'opportunistic'. They definitely called them 'sneaky'. So far as Genrul Uzbrag was concerned, those were just words used by orks angry that someone else had thought of something they hadn't.

'Dis is a sign!' he bellowed, striding forwards out of the mass of boyz to stand in front of them. He knew he was an imposing sight: a big ork with an axe-bladed choppa as tall as he was, which he could energise with a flick of a switch to envelop it in a crackling power field that would allow it to slice through pretty much anything. In his other hand he had a humie double-shoota, the sort carried by the really tough beakies in immensely thick armour. More than one ork had scoffed at him carrying a humie gun, but they hadn't laughed after Da Genrul had demonstrated its effectiveness: indeed, they hadn't been in much of a condition to do anything. Beakies were much tougher and shootier than normal humies, and Uzbrag saw no harm in nicking their stuff after he'd killed them.

'Wot sorta sign?' someone shouted.

'A sign from Gork an' Mork to say dat Goresnappa weren't da one to be leading dis Waaagh!' Da Genrul replied loudly, smacking himself in the chest. 'It should be *me*, instead! Cos I ain't fick enough to stand under a Gargant when its head's gonna fall off!'

'Oh yeah?'

Another disturbance in the green sea led to the mass of ork bodies parting, and the intimidating shape of Boss Mag Dedfist strode through, his mega armour hissing vapour as he came. Uzbrag immediately sized up his potential opponent.[4] Dedfist was broader than him, and very likely heavier even without the weight of his mega armour, but he wasn't quite as tall, and probably not as quick. On the other hand, if the massive power klaw that made up the left arm of his armour[5] managed to land a blow, that would probably be the last blow of the fight. The question would be whether he'd get the chance, or whether Uzbrag's choppa would strike home first. But then again, what about Dedfist's skorchas, the nozzles of which were mounted in the twin horns that jutted forth from the jaw of his armour? They could put even an ork as tough as Uzbrag right off his swing.

'Dunno what sorta fermented fungus beer ya been drinkin', but dere's no way dat *yoo* are da ork wot's gonna lead dis Waaagh!' Dedfist proclaimed, swaggering towards Uzbrag. 'Typical sneaky Blood Axe, wiv yer silly choppa, an' yer humie shoota, an' yer *hat*.' He sneered at Uzbrag's headgear, which lacked any of the horns, spikes, jawbones of large animals, or other accoutrements that would normally adorn such an item for a more traditionally minded ork. 'Ya ain't gonna be da one leadin' da charge, an' clobberin' da gits on da uvver end of it! Yer gonna be *hidin'* behind yer ladz!'

A collective ripple of anticipation and amusement rippled through the watching orks, because although fighting and talking were two very different things, that was very definitely fightin' talk, as in the thing you said in the full knowledge that the other ork was then going to try to punch you in the mouth.

Uzbrag's eyes narrowed, and his fingers tightened on the haft of his choppa. He could feel the anticipation of the orks around him: was he going to settle for clonking Dedfist around the head, a swift blow to establish his quickness and superiority of skill, or was he going to power up his weapon and go straight for a killing swing?

Neither, as it turned out, because someone else had something to say.

'Both of yoo zoggin' grots should go an' herd squigs!' a mighty voice bellowed at the top of its lungs. Both bosses turned, their violent intentions briefly postponed by the desire to see which other fool wanted his head kicked in, and were rewarded by the sight of Speedboss Zagnob Thundaskuzz standing upright on the back of his Deffkilla wartrike and staring balefully at them.

'Dat's strong words comin' from an ork standin' all da way over dere on his rokkit trolley!' Uzbrag retorted, to a general chorus of laughter. 'If ya got somefing to say, why dontcha come over here, an' say it to our faces?'

Shouts and hoots from the crowd accompanied that invitation, but they only rose in volume when Thundaskuzz actually *stepped off his wartrike* and began to shove his way through the assembled boyz. Speed freeks didn't get off or out of their vehicles without very good reason, and they generally weren't very impressed when they had to. The speedboss had his snagga klaw on one arm and a twin boomstikk in the other hand, with

---

[4] Any ork in a disagreement with another ork is a potential opponent.

[5] Also called the Dedfist, since Mag was of the opinion that if you'd found a good name you might as well get some use out of it.

a second such weapon shoved in the back of his belt. New mutters began to fly backwards and forwards, and Uzbrag heard a few quick bets taking place as well. If it came to a three-way punch-up, the logic seemed to go that Thundaskuzz's snagga klaw could strike from distance and then pull his enemy in for a proper goin'-over. Plus, everyone knew that speed freeks put all manner of chemicals into their blood to make themselves faster, didn't they? It wouldn't be a surprise if Zagnob could leave even Da Genrul in the dust when it came to reflexes.

'Goffs don't see nuffin' wot ain't in front of dere faces, an' Blood Axes can't be trusted to fight wot's in front of dere faces!' Thundaskuzz declared. 'When ya want somefin' done quick an' proper, who d'ya want doin' it?'

'SPEED FREEKS!' his loyal retinue of bikers yelled, waving their weapons in the air. One or two of the more excitable ones triggered their bikes' dakkaguns as well, which mowed down several of the orks in front of them and sparked immediate and violent retribution from the survivors, who turned around and began hauling the warbikers off their vehicles to give them a thorough pasting.

Violence, never far from the surface in any orkish gathering, bubbled up instantly, and rapidly spread out. The warboss was dead and there was no immediately obvious replacement yet, which meant that any sort of mass Waaagh! attack on the humie city probably wasn't going to be happening in the next few minutes. Given that, no ork was going to pass up the chance of a fight with his neighbour, as much to while away the time as anything else. If a bigger fight started, the survivors could always leave off and join it.

As slugga shots flew, punches landed, and choppas rose and fell, the three big bosses of the collection of orks formerly known as Waaagh! Goresnappa triangled up to each other, each waiting for someone else to make the first move. It wasn't that they didn't want to fight – all orks wanted to fight, it was the simplest, most primal instinct they had – but you wanted to make yourself look your best when you were scrappin' over rank. It was fine and proper to charge into humies or beakies or skrawniez before they knew you were there – although good luck with that against skrawniez, those pointy-eared gits always seemed to know something – because if they weren't paying attention then they obviously didn't deserve to even have a chance to stay alive, but it was a bit different when it was one ork against another, like this.

Being warboss wasn't just about hitting hard, it was also about being *tough*. You didn't want to make the first move, in case it looked like you were scared of being hit. So each one of them eyed the other two, muttering insults, and waiting for someone else to finally lose their rag and swing first. When they did, it was going to get extremely violent very, very quickly.

Or at least, it would have done, had all three of them not suddenly suffered a piercing headache and spontaneous nosebleeds.

'Wot da zoggin'...?' Uzbrag spluttered, wiping at his nose with the sleeve of his coat.

'It's Morgrub!' Dedfist spat, pointing with one finger of his power klaw at the figure of the old weirdboy, who was glowing with green energy. 'Dat bloody warphead's gonna blow everyone's skulls!'

Everyone knew that weirdboyz got all charged up when the orks around them were agitated. That was what made them such good weapons, because you could haul 'em into the middle of a fight, point them at the enemy, and hope that they'd be able to aim the power building inside them at the other gits instead of your own ladz. Even the mightiest sorcerers of other races would be hard-pressed to stand up to a weirdboy when he was surrounded by fighting orks, as at least one pointy-eared git would have been able to attest to, had Old Morgrub not burst his head open with a surge of pure Waaagh! energy during a duel. All that was left of him now was a funny-looking stone, which Morgrub had hung off his staff and sometimes licked when he wanted inspiration, or was bored.

The thing about Old Morgrub, though, was that he wasn't just any weirdboy, he was a warphead. Weirdboyz had a fairly short life expectancy, since the overload of Waaagh! energy could easily explode their skulls, but warpheadz were those who had survived for long enough to properly master their abilities, and were even more dangerous as a result. Whereas most weirdboyz were a bit uncomfortable with the building sensation of Waaagh! energy within them, and tried to avoid it, warpheadz couldn't get enough of it. They actively sought out any sort of fight simply in order to get charged up and let off a few blasts, which looked to be exactly what Old Morgrub was doing here. The problem was, he might just take a few dozen ork heads with him.

'Get 'im outta here!' Dedfist barked.

'Who're ya givin' orders to, ya git?' Thundaskuzz demanded, working the action on his snagga klaw even as he winced from the increasing pain inside his skull.

'Oh for Mork's sake, I'll do it me zoggin' self!' Da Genrul yelled, advancing on Old Morgrub with the intention of grabbing the warphead and hauling him as far away as possible from the massive ruckus that had broken out. However, before he could reach him, Morgrub threw back his head, spread his arms, and opened his jaws wider than would seem anatomically possible.

'Oh, zoggin' 'eck!' Mag Dedfist was heard to complain, as a pillar of lightning-wrapped green fire shot up into the air from Morgrub's gape, sizzling and spitting as it went. It rose straight and true, and as it did so it ignited the air around it, causing a titanic thunderclap that struck the assembled orks with a sound so loud it manifested as a physical force. The shockwave flattened boyz and rocked buggies on their suspensions; it kicked up dust and sent it spinning through the air in fractal spirals. It succeeded in stopping the fight in its tracks, which was a remarkable achievement in and of itself, and when everyone had turned around and picked themselves up off the ground, Old Morgrub was staring at them with eyes that were slightly too wide and a grin apparently directed somewhere slightly beyond every ork's left shoulder: or, indeed, the other way around.

No one moved, just in case it set Morgrub off and somehow singled them out for an exploding head. No ork minded the idea of dying, but there was such a thing as *style*. Dying with three different enemy weapons stuck in you and having left a trail of bodies in your wake was one thing; dying because a weirdboy hiccupped at the wrong moment would be just plain embarrassing.

'Da warboss is dead,' Old Morgrub said, in a sing-song voice like coiling serpents. His stare was discomfortingly unfocused, but carried the inherent threat that it might suddenly *become* focused, and on you, and that that would not be a good thing. 'Da warboss is dead. Long live da warboss.'

Dedfist, Uzbrag and Thundaskuzz exchanged glances. None of them had a great deal of time for Old Morgrub, but that was mainly because the old git had been Goresnappa's closest advisor, and the Snakebite had taken the warphead's deranged rantings as deep insights rather too often for their liking. On the other hand, Morgrub was a well-known figure within the Waaagh!, and even with Goresnappa gone his words would likely carry a great deal of weight.

Uzbrag decided to wait for a moment and see what Morgrub said. If the warphead spoke in favour of him, then clearly Gork and Mork wanted him to lead. If he didn't... Well, there was no point in heeding the ramblings of a demented old fool who couldn't tell a squig from a splatta kannon.

'I saw dis comin',' Morgrub declared. 'I saw a *lotta* fings.' He paused to lick the skrawnie stone on his staff, and giggled as a green spark earthed itself from the tip of his tongue. 'I didn't see who da next warboss would be...'

Da Genrul tensed, and felt the other two do the same. If Morgrub wasn't going to say their name, none of them had any current use for him.

'...but I did see how he will reveal himself,' Morgrub continued, still in that same sing-song voice. 'I seen it, right? A propha-see.'

It was difficult to hold the attention of a large group of orks, at least without that attention being focused on a fight. Morgrub was managing it, though.

'An' it's not gonna be by just duffin' up anuvver ork!' Morgrub said loudly, and although his gaze still didn't really light on anyone in particular, it definitely drifted towards the three bosses. 'Dat's not wot dis Waaagh! needs. We need an ork wiv *vision*.'

Everyone looked at each other, somewhat confused. Of the three obvious candidates who might step up to become warboss, none were missing even one eye, let alone both. Having vision didn't sound like a particularly specific requirement. What was the old weirdboy on about?

'A warboss ain't just da best fighter, he's gotta be da best *finker!*' Morgrub shouted. 'He's gotta lead da boyz to da best scraps, and da best loot! An' he's gotta do it quick, so we don't get bored!'

That was hard to argue with, at any rate, and there was a general nodding of heads and murmur of agreement. Few orks liked being cooped up on a ship. It was entertaining enough if there were any other ships to fight, because you could look out of a see-hole and see them get blown up, but it still wasn't really the same for the average boy with his slugga and his choppa. Unless some enterprising boss decided to go boarding, most of them just had to hang around and wait for the krews to do their thing.

'So da way we're gonna find out who da new warboss is gonna be, is like dis,' Morgrub said. He waved his staff imperiously, causing the various trinkets and gewgaws suspended from it on lengths of wire and leather to rattle together. 'Da Great Green spoke to me, an' it showed me somefing *speshul*.'

Now the old weirdboy's stare *did* focus, as ferocious and concentrated as the cutting-torch on a burna when the nozzles were closed down tight so it got all small and blue and mega-hot. He turned that stare on the three big bosses, so intense that Uzbrag could almost feel it pinning his thoughts to the back of his skull.

And then it wasn't just his own thoughts inside his skull any longer.

Everything went green. Not the green of an ork's skin, or a grot's skin; and not the green of leaves, or the green of mould. This was the proto-green, the greenest of greens. This was the green that came before, and the green that would still be hanging around after everything else had given up and gone. This was a green so rich, so vibrant and so powerful that nothing that actually *existed* could come close to it. It wasn't a colour that would submit itself to anything as mundane as simply being seen; it would mount an assault on optic nerves until it was the only thing left.

And out of that green emerged shapes.

Uzbrag was angry at them, at first – angry that they had ruined the green with their imperfection. Then he began to perceive what they were. Shootas and choppas, kannons and klaws, stikkbombs and just sticks with spikes through them, sleeted towards him faster than thought itself. With them came other shapes: the tiny forms of grots; hulking, angular Deff Dreads; massive, solid Stompas; enormous, towering Gargants; bulbous-headed squighogs; and most of all, the boyz. Ork after ork after ork whirled past, the vision giving Uzbrag enough clarity to realise that each and every one of them was slightly different, an individual. This was the Waaagh! itself, *his* Waaagh!, and every ork he saw here represented one of those around him. The Waaagh! knew its own, and it knew that it was strong.

Then the vision shifted. The centre of the strong green was overtaken by a weak, sickly grey, out of which emerged a towering shape. It was washy and indistinct, but Uzbrag recognised it after a moment: this was the one remaining humie city. The Great Green didn't know it so well as it knew the Waaagh!, but he could feel that it was showing him something important. The humies weren't a threat, they couldn't be a threat, but there was something he needed to do...

The vision lurched forwards, rushing towards the city, and then *through* it, *into* it, as though the walls themselves were inconsequential. Then it plunged downwards, not up to where the humie bosses would be, but into the city's half-abandoned guts. And there, buried so deep that it had been forgotten by any of the humies who came as close to mattering as a humie ever could, there was... something.

This was at the edge of what the Great Green could show him. It was something so different, so alien, that it was little more than abstract impressions in his mind. He got an image of glowy stones, like the one Morgrub had on his staff... of boots crossing a threshold... of stars... then, more certain again, of new planets, ones he had never seen before, with flames spreading across them and the vivid green following hard in the fire's wake... And behind it all was the laughter of Gork and Mork, laughter that filled the galaxy from edge to edge, laughter that charged him with fire, laughter that could kill whoever heard it. It was both the greatest thing Uzbrag had ever experienced in his life, and the most terrifying.

And then it was over.

Uzbrag shook his head, trying to get his bearings. Both Dedfist and Thundaskuzz were doing the same, like they'd just woken up from a bite from a dok's sleepy-squig. Had those gits seen the same things he had?

'Dere's a gate under dat city,' Morgrub said, his voice seeming to come from a long way away. 'Built by da pointy-eared skrawnie gits. If we find it, dat gate means we ain't gonna need to rely on da ships to move about! We can just go froo it, walk for a bit, an' den come out somewhere dere's a bunch more gits to stomp. An' after dat, we can do da same fing again, an' again, an' again!'

Da Genrul looked around. Most of the rest of the Waaagh! were looking interested, but without any indication that they had any idea what Old Morgrub was actually talking about. There was certainly no sign that they had seen what Uzbrag had seen. Was it just him, Dedfist and Thundaskuzz who had been granted the vision?

'So da ork wot's gonna lead da Waaagh! is da boss wot gets to dat gate first!' Morgrub declared forcefully. 'He's da one wot's gonna take the Waaagh! to da stars! He's da one wot's gonna turn planets green, one after anuvver! He's da one wot's gonna burn da galaxy down!'

Whether it was the concept of a new way of war, the method of Morgrub's delivery, or some leftover surge of Waaagh! energy that was bleeding off the warphead without him even realising it, his words resonated strongly through the assembled orks. A mighty cheer greeted his last words, as the Waaagh! forgot about kicking each other's heads in for now, and began to concentrate once again on the idea of doing it to everyone else instead.

'So dis gate!' Mag Dedfist bellowed, loud enough for everyone to hear him over the noise. 'It's under da humie city? Where?'

'Dunno!' Morgrub shouted back gleefully. 'Yoo're gonna hafta go lookin'!' He spread his arms, encompassing Dedfist, Uzbrag and Thundaskuzz all together.

'May da best ork win!'

FIVE

The proclamation ran through the camp like buggy fuel through a sick squiggoth. Every ork and grot was talking about it: how Old Morgrub had called down the power of the ork gods and they'd spoken through him in voices like thunder, declaring that this Waaagh! was the mightiest the galaxy had ever seen, and how it was destined to crush everything in its path; how the orks would rise and, through the power of their combined might, would conquer all other living beings and embody the Many-Fist Destiny of their species. No one questioned the veracity of the stories, or the fact that two different orks might be telling three different versions. The main thrust of the narrative struck right at the heart of every ork's beliefs, so it *had* to be true, and if it was broadly true, who cared about the details?

The only question left was which one of the three big bosses was going to take up the mantle of warboss. None of them had tried yet, and for very good and kunnin' reasons.

When it came right down to it, each one of them was still playing the odds as best they knew how. If Morgrub was right, and there really was a gateway made by the skrawniez somewhere under the humie city that could lead them across the galaxy in no time, then finding it first - and staying alive long enough to make sure that every other git knew you'd found it first - was the best way of piggybacking off Morgrub's influence and ensuring a seamless transition of authority from Goresnappa. These were concepts that orks understood without even really thinking about them.

On the other hand, if one of the other two gits got there first, you could still throw down anyway. It might be a bit messier, and a fair few of the more traditional Snakebites might take issue with how the warphead's propha-see had been ignored, but so what? Knock enough heads together, and sooner or later everyone would fall in line, or would be lacking enough head to complain about it any longer.

One upshot of the excitement around this novel way of deciding a leadership contest, and the general frenzied preparations as each big boss began organising the orks under their command to pursue their favoured method of attack, was that no one had thought to investigate exactly what had happened to make the head of the Mega-Gargant fall off in the first place and instigate this entire state of affairs. And what *that* meant was that Snaggi Littletoof, Guffink, Skrawk and Kruffik had managed to get out of and away from it without being hung up by their toes and beaten, fed to the gnasher squigs, used as target practice, or any of the other painful and likely fatal punishments that would normally have been enacted upon them under such circumstances. It helped that Mek Zagblutz had almost certainly been in the Mega-Gargant's head when it had fallen to its fiery doom, and since no ork really paid much attention to which grot was which unless they were supposed to be doing something for him, that meant they were probably out of the drops on that one.

Not that Kruffik seemed particularly confident on that front.

'We're gonna die,' he moaned, as the four of them scurried through the camp, dodging the feet of orks as they rushed hither and thither. 'Dey're gonna kill us for dis! An' it's all yoor fault, Snaggi!'

'Who's gonna care?' Snaggi demanded. When Old Morgrub had been blathering about the Great Green, the gods had spoken to him again! It had only been faint, a brushing at the edges of his consciousness, but it had been there nonetheless: he had seen the gate that the weirdboy had been talking about, surely a sign that he was favoured! He felt amazing. He felt invincible. He felt five feet tall, and as though he were weightless, yet as strong as a meganob.

A thought flitted across his brain. Was this how orks felt *all the time?*

'Wotcha mean, who's gonna care?!' Kruffik squeaked. 'Everyone! Everyone's gonna care! Of course dey're gonna care!'

'Why?' Snaggi asked him, swiping a screwdriver that no one seemed to be needing right now. 'Dere's a bunch of big bosses wot all wanna be warboss – ya reckon dey're gonna be mad dat I killed Goresnappa? Dey weren't gonna get to be warboss uvverwise!'

'Keep yer voice down!' Guffink hissed at him, and even Skrawk looked a little uneasy. 'Yeah, alright, maybe no one's comin' after us, but dat don't mean ya can just go shoutin' about it!'

'Shoutin' about wot?'

All four of them whirled on the spot, because that voice didn't belong to a grot. It was deeper, and more resonant.

It was Zukrod, the runtherd.

Zukrod wasn't much more than a yoof, with the green of his skin still relatively unscarred, and his build more lanky than bulky, but he'd not gone the way of some young orks and joined the stormboyz. Zukrod was a Snakebite, and he'd found his calling in the traditional work of a Snakebite: squigs and grots, and successfully beating them until they did what they were supposed to. That clan produced the most runtherds, and was widely reckoned to also produce the best ones.

'Nuffin'!' Kruffik said immediately, and anxiously. 'We weren't shoutin' about nuffin'! Did ya hear us shoutin' about anyfing? I don't reckon so, cos we weren't!' He grinned widely.

'Sounded to me,' Zukrod said slowly, 'like ya was sayin' somefing about da warboss. Da old warboss.'

'Nah, definitely not,' Guffink said, shaking his head vigorously. 'Why would we be doin' dat? We ain't been anywhere near 'im, or nuffin' like dat.'

'Sounded to *me*,' Zukrod said, flicking a switch which sent lightning sparking across the metal-toothed jaws of the grabba stikk he carried as a mark of his trade, 'like ya was talkin' about how ya *killed* da old warboss.'

'Dat's ridicul-arrgh!' Kruffik hastily corrected himself as the grabba stikk jabbed out at him, because a grot did not call anything an ork said or did 'ridiculous' if he wanted to remain in possession of all his limbs. 'I mean, dat's not wot was goin' on! We wasn't sayin' dat! How would we do dat?'

'Dunno,' Zukrod said. 'Maybe you was up in da Mega-Gargant, an' made its head fall off onto 'im?'

He grinned the toothy grin of an ork whose job it was to hurt grots, who really loved his job anyway, and who now had an excellent reason to indulge himself.

'Oh crikey,' Guffink whimpered, as Zukrod took a step forwards. 'You've gone an' done it now, Snaggi.'

'Dere's no point in runnin',' Zukrod chuckled. 'I'll only catch ya.'

Something snapped inside Snaggi Littletoof. He hadn't killed Warboss Gazrot Goresnappa just to let some jumped-up runtherd who probably wasn't even as old as him get all zap-happy with his grabba stikk. Fire flared inside his chest, the sort of fire that, once ignited, wouldn't be doused until it had consumed everything in its path.

He pulled the stolen screwdriver from his belt, clutched it in both hands, and took a deep breath.

'Waagh,' he muttered, and charged.

Zukrod wasn't expecting it. No ork ever really expected to be charged by anything: mostly, other stuff tried to avoid being charged by orks. Other than bugeyes, of course, and some of the tougher beakies, and a few of the pointy-eared skrawniez that moved real quick – oh, and those weird Chaos fings that glowed and gibbered and just sort of disappeared when you scragged or dakka'd them, instead of leaving a body behind like anything decent would – but *mainly*, other stuff tried to avoid being charged by orks. And if there was anything in the galaxy that an ork truly didn't expect to get charged by, then it was a snotling; but if there was anything *else* that an ork didn't expect to get charged by, it was a grot. After all, they were half the height, a quarter the strength, and perhaps an eighth the weight of an ork. What was a grot going to do?

In this case, the grot ducked under the jab of the grabba stikk, which was more reflex than actual aggression, since Zukrod's brain was still trying to come to terms with what his eyes were telling it, and stabbed the screwdriver right into the runtherd's left knee.

'Gahhh!' Zukrod howled, but an ork's pain threshold was high, and they could shrug off wounds that would incapacitate a human. 'Ya bloody little git! I'm gonna–'

He swung his grabba stikk two-handed, and Snaggi ducked under it.

'–tear yer–'

Zukrod swatted at the grot with the butt end of the haft, but Snaggi rolled to one side with an awareness and agility born of desperation.

'–zoggin' head off!'

Snaggi leaped athletically over a swing of the grabba stikk intended to take his legs out from under him, but Zukrod's body followed the momentum of the swing around. As the runtherd pivoted he lashed out with a kick, using the screwdriver-impaled leg, and it caught Snaggi square in the chest just as he landed. The grot flew backwards, landing in what might have been a pile of junk, or might have been some mekaniak's most prized possessions: it was often hard to tell.

'Right!' Zukrod bellowed, dropping his grabba stikk and limping towards Snaggi with his fingers outstretched. 'Try dodgin' me now!'

Snaggi was only too willing to try, but unfortunately his body had other ideas. It generally liked air if it was going to be doing anything athletic, and right now that was a substance in which it was distinctly lacking. He was unable to do anything much more than flail weakly as the runtherd closed in on him, with murder in his eyes.

Then, astonishingly, Zukrod staggered again as the electrified jaws of his own grabba stikk closed on his as-yet-uninjured knee. He collapsed sideways, convulsing, and the extra second or so's reprieve gave Snaggi the chance to haul himself back to his feet and lay eyes on his saviour.

'Long live da Revolushun,' Skrawk said quietly, releasing the grabba stikk's hold on Zukrod.

'No, no, don't do dat!' Snaggi wailed, but it was too late. Zukrod was already shaking his head and getting his wits back now he was no longer being electrocuted, and he was going to be up and dangerous again in a matter of moments. 'Gimme da stikk, gimme da stikk!'

Skrawk chucked it to him, and Snaggi caught it, fumbled it, nearly hit himself in the eye, then managed to get a proper grip on it at the second attempt. Zukrod was pushing himself up, letting his arms do most of the work of getting him back upright since one knee still had a screwdriver stuck into it, and the other had jagged tears in the scorched flesh.

Snaggi aimed for the runtherd's neck, and pulled the grabby-lever back as far as it would go.

The jaws snapped shut just under Zukrod's jaw, and the full charge of the stick flowed out into the young ork's body. Snaggi held on desperately as Zukrod began spasming, every one of the ork's muscles straining against itself, and made sure he didn't accidentally flick the switch that would turn the current off.

Zukrod screamed as his flesh began to burn, and his eyes began to melt, but Snaggi held on. He held on until Zukrod stopped moving completely, and was prone on the ground with froth bubbling out of his mouth.

'Ya killed 'im,' Kruffik whispered in horror. 'Ya killed an ork! A *runtherd!*'

'I already killed a warboss today,' Snaggi told him belligerently, looking around in case the little altercation had been seen, but no one appeared to be paying any attention. It was dark, and although orks and grots could see better at night than humies could, it wasn't their best time. The camp was still in an uproar as well, and there were shouts, and roaring engines, and any number of incidental scraps going on as orks got in each other's way and 'accidentally' picked up the wrong shoota.

They'd got away with it. Again.

'Dis is wot I'm talkin' about!' Snaggi hissed victoriously at the others. 'I said dat Gork an' Mork talk to me, didn't I? I said I hear dere voices! Look at dis! We just killed a runtherd, and nuffin' bad's happenin'! I'm da Chosen Grot! I'm gonna lead us outta slavery and into...' He paused, because he wasn't quite sure about the rest of that sentence, but the other three were looking at him. 'Somefing better!' he finished, as confidently as he could.

'Lead who? Us?' Kruffik objected. 'Dere's only four of us!'

'Dere's a lot more dan four of us in dis camp,' Snaggi said gleefully. 'Wot was dat ya said just now, Skrawk?'

'Long live da Revolushun,' Skrawk repeated.

'Exactly,' Snaggi said, puffing up his chest. 'It's time to spread da word! And da word is "Revolushun"!'

Within seconds, there was nothing to be seen except for a badly burned dead ork, with a hole in one knee that, until recently, had had a screwdriver sticking out of it.

LOTZ

'Whose Gargant is dat?'

The mekboy so addressed turned around and stared up into the face of Mag Dedfist. It was a fearsome face, scarred and brutal, and underlit by the pilot lights of the twin skorchas built into the horns that jutted from beneath his jaw. There were a number of possible answers to the question, and the mekboy chose the wrong one.

'Mine–'

A power klaw ignited and lashed out, sending the mek's broken body a good thirty feet through the air, before it landed in a boneless heap not far from an unattended stew pot. The mek's two spanner boyz, who'd been getting some of the excess gunk off their tools, looked at each other uncomfortably.

'Gonna ask again,' Mag Dedfist rumbled. 'Whose Gargant is dat?'

'Yoors, boss!' the brighter of the two spanners piped up. They were both Deathskulls, with blue paint adorning their faces and bodies in the hope of attracting good luck. At the very least, they managed to avoid the same bad luck that had befallen their mek.

'Dat's right,' Dedfist affirmed. 'Clearly yoo boyz've got good futures ahead of ya. Now go an' get it ready to stomp stuff. An' make sure da head ain't gonna fall off!' he bawled as an afterthought, as the pair of them scrambled away towards the brooding metal monstrosity. It wasn't quite the size of the Mega-Gargant which had spelled doom for Gazrot Goresnappa, but it was the largest one left, and had an impressive-looking array of suitably killy weapons.

'Yoo're gonna try to get dat inside da humie city?' Badzag asked dubiously. He was one of Dedfist's boss nobs, and headed up a bunch of skarboyz known as Badzag's Krushas.

'Course not,' Skabrukk replied, before Dedfist could answer. Skabrukk was the drill boss of Da Skyklaw, the Waaagh!'s largest mob of stormboyz. 'It's too big, ya zoggin' idiot. But it's got dead big gunz, so da boss is gonna use it to break froo da walls. Right, boss?' he added.

Dedfist clouted him across the face with the hand that wasn't enveloped in a power klaw. 'Did anyone say ya could talk for me, maggot-brain?' he demanded.

'No, boss,' Skabrukk replied, spitting out a couple of teeth that had been prematurely loosened. The other boss nobs who answered to Dedfist snickered at his misfortune, although not quite loudly enough to get a clobbering in their own right.

'Now, Skabrukk's right,' Dedfist acknowledged, with a glower at the drill boss. 'But dat don't mean he can just open his gob when someone's talkin' to me. We needs to get inside, an' da Gargants are da best tool for da job. Once da wall's been knocked in, we'll get da ladz together an' go find dis gate fing wot Morgrub's been gabbin' about.'

The assembled nobs nodded and muttered in the manner each thought was the most appropriate yet unremarkable way to signal their agreement. Boss Dedfist didn't like being contradicted, but he also had absolutely no time for sycophants. It was best to treat his pronouncements as common, orkish good sense, rather than some form of great insight.

'Dese humie cities've got fick walls,' Dedfist continued. 'It'll take da Gargants some time to get froo, so any uvver big gunz we can round up should give 'em a hand. Wot about da uvver two? Thundaskuzz an' Da Genrul? Dey tried to get dere hands on anyfing big or shooty, or bossed any of da ladz inta fightin' for 'em?'

'Don't fink so, boss,' Badzag replied. 'Thundaskuzz's gone off on 'is trike, and da Kult's gone wiv 'im. Dere's a bunch of trukkboyz who've followed 'im, but ya know what dose Evil Sunz is like – dey don't like big gunz, cos dey don't move quick enuff. It's mainly buggies an' some flyers an' dat. Nuffin' else could keep up!'

'Wot's 'e gonna do, drive round da city in circles 'till dey give up?' Nuzzgrond laughed, a little too loudly. He had a bunch of trukkboyz himself, and while hitching a ride to get into the middle of the fight faster was a perfectly acceptable thing for a Goff to do, he was probably a bit worried that Dedfist might think he was going to go off and follow Thundaskuzz on whatever form of high-velocity idiocy the speedboss was planning now.

'An' what about Da Genrul?' Dedfist demanded.

'Disapp... disappy... he's gone, boss,' Skabrukk managed. 'Some of the ladz were keepin' an eye on him, and said he went off south right after Morgrub said his bit. Most of da Blood Axes went wiv him, an' a whole loada grots, but nuffin' much dat was very stompy or shooty.'

Dedfist frowned, and scratched his chin. 'Wot's dat git up to?'

'Can't be much, can it, boss?' Nuzzgrond asked. 'He's not gonna get inside dat fing with a bunch of boyz an' grots. Or not quickly, anyway,' he added conscientiously, since it was a well-known fact that enough orks could do pretty much anything, given enough time and a suitable concentration span.

'Nah, I don't trust him,' Dedfist growled. 'He's a finker, dat one, and da only fing worse dan a finker is a finker wot's got a bunch of ladz followin' him. Da Genrul ain't gonna be leavin' da Dreads an' wotnot behind if he needed 'em to do wotever it is he's plannin' on doin'. So wotever it is, he's not tryin' to go straight froo da walls like a proper ork should.' He worked the action of his power klaw, the massive digits clanking against each other as his neurones fizzed and sparked. Finally, after several long seconds of deliberate cogitation, he raised the brutal weapon and pointed it. 'Skabrukk.'

'Me, boss?' Skabrukk asked uncertainly, wondering if he was about to get clobbered again for an as-yet-unrealised indiscretion.

'Ya see any uvver gits round 'ere called Skabrukk?'

'No, boss,' Skabrukk admitted, checking both ways just to be sure.

'Den I mean yoo. Yer stormies are a bit Blood Axe-y, ain't dey?'

Had it been any other ork saying that, Skabrukk might have taken issue with him. The members of Da Skyklaw were Goffs through and through, and liked nothing better than getting stuck into a fight as soon as possible. Indeed, much like Nuzzgrond's trukkboyz, they'd taken extra measures to ensure that they could achieve just that, although in the case of the storm-boyz it took the form of high-powered individual rokkit packs rather than a large and somewhat ramshackle vehicle. However, it was Mag Dedfist saying it, and Skabrukk had already taken one clobbering from him since his last meal, so he wasn't looking for another.

'Maybe,' he muttered, as non-committally as he thought he could get away with.

'Dere's no "maybe" about it,' Dedfist growled. 'Ya all walk behind each uvver in lines, ya do dat salutin' fing, ya all wear da same clothes as da rest of ya mob, an' polish ya boots, an' are basically all sorts of odd. Don't tell me ya ain't,' he added menacingly, 'cos I was a stormboy once, 'til I grew out of it.'

'Well, if ya put it like dat den I guess yeah, maybe we'z kind of a bit like Blood Axes,' Skabrukk admitted, shifting uncomfortably. 'But dat don't mean we're gonna go off an' join Da Genrul! Yoo'z da best big boss, boss, an' dat's da honest troof!'

'I didn't fink ya would, not even a stormboy would be dat stupid,' Dedfist declared, to another round of general laughter from the rest of his boss nobs. 'But I want ya to *pretend* to do dat, right? Get yer boyz, an' go an' see wot dat git's up to.'

'Ya want us to go an' *spy* for ya?' Skabrukk asked, bewildered. 'Boss?' he added hurriedly, a moment later.

It was a loaded question. Spying was grot work, or more accurately what grots just did in general, in the hope of currying favour with someone some-where. An ork might take a look at where the enemy was, simply to have some idea of which direction in which to charge or shoot, but he'd never dream of hiding his own presence in the process. Unless he was a Blood Axe, of course, in which case he might even be wearing clothes that looked a bit like whatever terrain he was in, and hang bits of bush off himself, and all sorts of other strange behaviour that only Blood Axes had any patience for.

Luckily for everyone concerned, Mag Dedfist was not simply an enor-mous ork with both a predilection and a talent for unbridled violence. He was also savvy enough to know how to get the orks under his command to do what he wanted without always having to beat it into them.

'Nah, it ain't spyin',' Dedfist said, laying a comradely power klaw on his subordinate's shoulder. 'Dis is *scoutin'*, an' dat's totally different. I want ya to go an' *scout* wot Da Genrul's doin', by lettin' 'im fink ya gonna join 'im. An' den I want ya to come back an' tell me wot he's up to, so we can scrag him if it looks like he's found a quicker way to get to da gate. Dat clear?'

Skabrukk, who was neither stubborn nor slow-witted enough to push his luck any further, nodded. 'Yes, boss. I'll get da ladz right on it.'

'Good,' Dedfist said, and turned away from him. 'Nuzzgrond!'

'Yes, boss?' Nuzzgrond replied promptly, having clearly learned from Skabrukk's hesitation on how not to respond to his big boss.

'Get yer ladz togevva an' do da same fing with Thundaskuzz. He might drink buggy fuel, but ya don't get to be speedboss wivout findin' da right sorta fights at da right sorta times,' Dedfist said. 'If it looks like he's got any clue how to get inside, ya come back and tell me, got it?'

'Yes, boss,' Nuzzgrond replied, doing his best to hide his disappointment. Nuzzgrond's mob would want to be right at the front line, watching the Gargants blow holes in the city walls and then piling into the breach, not driving around trying to find Zagnob Thundaskuzz and his convoy of speed freeks.

'We're gonna need to get da rest of da boyz up here, and have 'em hang around da Gargants,' Dedfist said, addressing his nobs as one. 'I dunno who da Snakebite bosses are, an' I don't much care neither. None of 'em is gonna be big enough to give me any lip, so unless dey've gone off wiv Thundaskuzz or Da Genrul for some reason, dey're mine now.' He turned and surveyed the humie city through the pair of dark-gogglez he'd had one of the meks build for him, his experienced eyes quickly and instinctively searching out the potential weak points in its massive form.

'Looks like dere's some sort of crack in it, over dere,' he said, pointing to where the hint of a darker fissure running more or less vertically down to ground level suggested some ancient structural damage from a hive quake. 'S'not anyfing da humies would've done on purpose, dey don't build like dat, not fings dis size. Dat's where we'll get da Gargants to shoot. Once dey've knocked a hole in da wall, I'll lead da Krushas in, wiv da rest of da ladz behind us.' His gaze tracked upwards, taking in the irregular sides of the hive, and the various outcrops that might be usable as gun platforms by defenders. 'I reckon da humies'll get some of dere gitz up dere to shoot down at us, so we'll need da stormboyz to go an' clobber 'em, maybe a coupla strafing runs from da fighta-bommas...'

'Boss?' Badzag piped up. The other boss nobs, recognising his tone of voice as one belonging to an ork who thought that what he was about to say could possibly be construed as being a bit foolish, but who was going to say it anyway, edged away from him.

'Wot is it, Badzag?' Mag Dedfist enquired, giving the boss of the Krushas his full attention.

'Boss, all dis...' Badzag began. 'I mean... Ain't dis a bit... Blood Axe-y?'

Everything went very quiet, or at least as quiet as it was reasonably possible for things to be in the middle of an ork camp preparing for battle.

'Wot did yoo say?' Mag Dedfist asked, very slowly.

'Ya know...' Badzag said, with a weak and ill-advised attempt at an ingratiating smile. 'All dese... taktiks, an' dat.'

'Taktiks?' Dedfist's bellow erupted forth like the wrath of a black-clad volcano. '*Taktiks?!* Who d'ya fink yer talkin' to, my lad?!' His power klaw shot

out and grabbed Badzag by the throat, and only the fact that its power field was not currently activated prevented the boss nob's head from coming clean off. 'Just in case ya ain't clear, let me give ya a quick lesson! What I'm doin' right now ain't *taktiks*! Dat's somefing wot Blood Axes and humies do, an' I never wanna hear it outta yer mouf again, got it? Wot I'm doin' is called a *plan!* An' do ya know wot da difference is between a plan an' taktiks, boyz?'

No one said anything, because all of them – with the possible exception of Badzag, who was in no position to answer right now – were smart enough to realise when Mag Dedfist was being rhetorical.

'A *plan* is how we make sure we kill da uvver gits,' Dedfist snarled into the oxygen-deprived face of Badzag, who was struggling hopelessly against the big boss' grip. '*Taktiks* is tryin' to make sure da uvver gits don't kill *us*, an' dat sorta finkin' is for cowards, an' grots!'

He released his hold on Badzag, who collapsed into the dirt, then hurriedly picked himself up again. You didn't want to be scrabbling around in front of the ork who might well shortly be warboss, even if – especially if – he'd just squeezed your head half off.

'Ya got yer orders,' Mag Dedfist growled at his nobz. 'Go an' get 'em done. When da sun comes up, I want all da ladz ready to go, an' I want to know wot's goin' on wiv dose uvver two gits who've buggered off an' seem to fink dey've got some sort of clever ideas!'

His nobz turned and hurried off, each one making the internal transition from meek subordinate who knew better than to speak out, to a feared boss who'd clout a lesser ork around the head for looking at him the wrong way. Dedfist watched them go, to make sure none of them were slacking, then turned and made for the Gargant into which the two spanners had disappeared.

'Now den, let's see what sorta gunz dis fing has...'

LOTZ

'Alright, ladz, put yer backs into it! C'mon, get dose shovels movin'! I wanna see dat dirt flyin,' an' if I don't den dere's gonna be heads rollin'! Ya hear me?'

Genrul Uzbrag leaned on the tall haft of his power choppa, and surveyed the excavations with satisfaction. For all the yelling and bawling he'd been doing to make the boyz think he was dissatisfied with their efforts, and that they'd better get a shift on, he was reasonably happy with the speed at which the trenches were being dug. It helped that most of the orks under his command were Blood Axes, and so were willing to put effort into things even if they couldn't see the immediate benefit to them, thanks to their respect for his authority. After all, Da Genrul was in charge, so it made sense that he knew best. Otherwise he wouldn't be in charge, would he?

Besides, it wasn't that orks didn't know how to dig, or weren't used to it. You had to dig the drops out somehow, wherever it was you'd set up camp; at least, unless you were near a handy natural cliff or ravine. Sometimes you had to find food underground, whether that was burrowing squigs or the more esoteric wildlife of whatever planet you happened to be on at the time. Blood Axes, in particular, were used to digging out trenches if there was any notion of protracted warfare that couldn't be won with a simple charge and stomping the gits on the receiving end of it. Any ork knew that the enemy would have a hard time shooting you if they couldn't see you, but only Blood Axes had really bought into the idea that you could make it harder for the enemy to shoot you *even if they knew where you were.*

So it was that to the eyes of most other orks, or humans, or indeed, many other species in the galaxy, what the boyz under Da Genrul's command were doing might seem a little unusual for orks, but nothing particularly ingenious. Digging in prior to a long siege of a city was hardly standard ork behaviour, but it made a certain amount of sense, given that they were in the wasteland where everything around the hive had long since been killed by industrial ash and toxic runoff. The nearest other humie buildings[6] were the best part of a day's march away, at the edge of this dead ground, so some other sort of shelter from speculative defensive shooting was probably a good plan.

However, that was not the point of the trenches: or at least, not the

[6] Or the remains of them, at any rate.

complete point of them. Da Genrul had different plans for them. Right now, however, he had yet another thing on his mind.

'Come on out, kaptin,' he said brusquely, pulling open the door of the cage strapped to the back of Sarge. Daggit, the gretchin pilot of Sarge, was one of the few grots who had managed to rein in his aggressive streak after being wired into the mini-Dreadnought: mainly because instead of getting his kicks through stomping on his former oppressors, the little runt got to hang around behind Da Genrul, feel important, and make affirmative noises like 'Yeah!' and 'Dat's right!' when Uzbrag was giving his orders.

Da Genrul didn't have Sarge following him around simply for the dubious level of support, though. That honour was because of who he was carrying.

Captain Armenius Varrow, formerly of the Third Platoon of the Aranuan 25th Astra Militarum regiment, the 'Golden Lions,' fell out of the cage and into the dirt, prompting general merriment in the orks around him. This wasn't anything new, since his sheer continued existence was the source of considerable amusement for the hulking warriors. They mocked his size, his lack of strength, the increasingly filthy uniform in which he was still dressed – basically everything about him.

Captain Varrow hadn't *intended* to be captured, of course. His regiment had been rotated to garrison his home world while it recruited to replace losses sustained against the forces of the Great Enemy near the Siren's Storm, and while the prospect of an ork invasion had obviously been a horrendous one, the 25th had nevertheless been eager not only to throw the xenos back, but also to prove themselves once more and blood the new recruits in the process. They had managed to stall the orkish advance at first, and there had been talk of it all being over by Sanguinala.

Then the problems started. Captain Varrow was leading the right flank of a pitched battle against the orkish aggressors on the Sacracian Heights, and everything seemed to be going well until it was very abruptly no longer going well at all. An advance by four platoons into what had appeared to be a mass ork retreat, caused by appalling casualties inflicted by sustained heavy weapons fire, was swamped when at least half of the apparent casualties got back up to attack Varrow's men as they advanced heedlessly into the trap. The heavy weapon teams were descended upon by orks borne aloft by crude, smoke-belching jump packs, the reinforcements ran into some sort of orkish flamethrower units, and his own command squad had been assaulted by orks wearing camouflage – camouflage! – who must have been waiting in place since before the battle had commenced. Varrow had killed two of those infiltrators, but when his power sword was knocked from his grasp he'd known the game was up. He had expected to die quickly and brutally, as had been the fate of his standard bearer and comms officer.

But that was not what happened. Either by luck or, he was increasingly being forced to accept, actual understanding and intelligence, the orks had neglected to kill him, the commanding officer. Instead, he had been subdued by frighteningly powerful hands, and bundled off to be presented, with considerable pride, to Genrul Uzbrag.

Now he was the Blood Axe boss' prize, halfway between pet and tactical advisor. Armenius Varrow knew, in his heart of hearts, that the Imperium would expect him to take his own life in order to deny any sort of satisfaction to the enemy. He countered those thoughts with the logic that, firstly, he had no easy manner in which to achieve this: the orks prevented him from coming into contact with any sort of weapon, and would in fact force-feed him if he attempted to refuse the food and drink they provided. Secondly, if he could escape, he could provide the Astra Militarum with unprecedented insights into the nature of orkish strategy and psychology, which could undoubtedly be used to fight them more effectively in the future. Thirdly, he could of course use his position to influence Uzbrag and suggest courses of action that would hinder rather than benefit him.

The only trouble was that Da Genrul was not, as a rule, easily taken in.

'Dis city,' Uzbrag said to him, managing to get the Low Gothic words out reasonably clearly, despite the presence of lips and tusks that were not designed for its syllables. 'You humies don't jus' build up, do ya? Ya build *down*, too. So dere's gonna be a lot of dis fing dat's below da ground, like one of dem...' He paused, and turned to look at the rest of the orks that made up what he referred to as his 'High Kommand'. 'Wot're dose fings where dere's only a bit of it above da surface, and ya can't see da rest of it?' Da Genrul asked irritably.

'Pot-squigs, sir?' suggested the ork known as Lootenant Kabrukk.

'...Not wot I was finking of, but it'll do,' Da Genrul conceded. He turned back to Varrow, who was trying to at least kneel upright on the ground, but struggling against the twin enemies of muscle wastage and malnutrition. 'One of dem. So, da uvver ladz are gonna try an' get in above ground, which don't seem like such a good plan to me, cos yer mates'll see 'em coming an' can shoot at 'em.'

The massive ork crouched down so that his head was roughly on a level with Varrow's, although his skull had to be about three times the size. Despite exhaustion, and the deadened emotional reactions brought on by being in the constant company of such horrors, Varrow could not suppress a shudder of fear. Orks had been bad enough when he had thought of them only as feral, albeit incredibly dangerous, green-skinned monsters. The fact that they could, at least in some cases, *think* and *plan* and even imitate Imperial mannerisms just made them all the more terrifying. Looking at Da Genrul and his High Kommand was like an obscura dream where Varrow's senior officers had morphed into crude, mocking monstrosities that sought to bring down everything he had ever loved and believed in.

'Dere's gonna be tunnels, right?' Da Genrul asked, his voice pitched low, and even, so far as it was possible for an ork, friendly. 'Tunnels goin' all froo da ground. Tunnels what'll get us *inside* da walls, if we find one an' follow it back. An' I reckon yer mates in dere will be so busy watchin' Dedfist's ladz, all bunched up an' obvious, and Thundaskuzz, who's gonna be drivin' round an' round lookin' for a way he can get all his buggies inside, dat dey won't be finkin' about what might be comin' from underneath 'em. Speshully when we're just sat 'ere goin' nowhere, from what dey can see.'

He leaned in a little bit closer.

'So, wotcha sayin',' kaptin? Ya reckon dere's tunnels comin' out from dat city?'

Captain Armenius Varrow did his best to steel his nerve. He was an officer of the Astra Militarum, from an unbroken line that stretched back to his great-great-grandfather, with assorted aunts, uncles and cousins thrown into the mix as well. His family was *bred* for command, it was their natural purpose in life. He was guided by the Emperor, his training, his years of experience, and the uplifting words of the *Regimental Standard*. He was capable of outwitting this fiend, no matter what manner of low cunning it had proved to possess.

'Keep digging all you wish,' he sneered into Uzbrag's face. 'You'll reach the planet's core before you encounter a weakness in an Aranuan city. We are a military people, and we build for strength and durability. If you want this city to fall, you'll have to charge into the teeth of its guns, along with your deluded comrades!'

There was a brief silence.

'Was dat a "yes" or a "no", sir?' the ork called Lootenant Gubzag asked, studying Varrow with suspicious eyes.

'I swear t'Mork,' Kabrukk put in, 'dese humies don't even know how to make sense in dere own language.'

A wide grin spread across Genrul Uzbrag's face, displaying far more teeth than Captain Varrow was comfortable with, no matter what he told himself. Da Genrul rose back to his full height once more, and beamed down at Varrow.

'It's a "yes". Dere are tunnels down dere. Keep the boyz diggin', an' we'll find one before long.'

Varrow's heart sank. It was true enough that Aranuan hives were ancient structures, which had settled deeper over millennia, not to mention been gradually buried as the ground level rose around them. Old sewage channels, thermal exhaust ports, even former access points: all of these might lie somewhere beneath their feet.

'Yeah, but wot if da humie's lyin'?' Gubzag asked.

'He *was* lyin'!' Da Genrul replied, exasperated. 'Wot he said meant "no"!'

'So how d'ya know he meant "yes", sir?' Kabrukk queried.

'Easy,' Uzbrag replied, with a smug glance down at Varrow. 'Humies are really bad at lyin' to fings wot scare 'em, an' dis one's one of da worst at it. He gets all sweaty, ya see? An' he can't look straight at me.'

Had he been a true hero of the Imperium, a Castellan Creed or a Commissar Cain, Captain Varrow might have come up with some manner of searing rejoinder that would have communicated his contempt for the entire orkish species, whilst simultaneously undermining Genrul Uzbrag's standing in the eyes of his subordinates as they witnessed how ruthlessly he had been mocked by a human prisoner. However, Armenius Varrow was no such fine specimen of humanity, and he could do nothing more than lower his gaze to stare miserably at the mud between his knees. The ork was right: he couldn't look straight at Da Genrul, and not because of hatred. He was scared. He was scared, and he did not want to die, and those facts disgusted him.

'Time for yer exercise, kaptin!' Uzbrag declared, reaching down to clamp one massive hand around Varrow's shoulder and hauling him up to his feet, where he managed to just about maintain his balance despite his treacherous body and the uneven footing. 'Off ya go. 'Ave a walk around, stretch yer legs. Can't 'ave you gettin' too stiff in dat cage, or ya might not last to give me any more advice!'

The High Kommand chuckled dutifully. Captain Varrow stared at his feet, at the fine boots he wore that were now spattered with mud, and also, he grimly suspected, with the blood of some of his dead men. 'Exercise time' was the most soul-crushing thing of all. Every ork in Da Genrul's warband knew of Captain Varrow, and would not harm him. Varrow had attacked one, once, in a desperate and fleeting attempt to provoke a noble death for himself, but he had simply been overpowered and had his face rubbed repeatedly into the mud, then been pelted with some sort of dung.

If he tried to pick up a weapon, he was disarmed. If he tried to attack an ork, he was humiliated. If he tried to escape, he was quickly fetched back. He was so inconsequential, so utterly unthreatening, that the cage in which he spent most of his time was not actually necessary for his containment: it was simply a way of ensuring that he was available at Da Genrul's pleasure, without the big boss having to go to the trouble of shouting at another ork to go and find his pet. This pseudo-freedom was, perhaps, the worst form of torture the orks could have devised for him, and it was made all the worse by the fact that Varrow honestly doubted it was anything more than a practicality for them.

All the same, if he was going to cling to any notion of escape, no matter how unlikely and self-deluding it might be, he needed to remain in some sort of physical condition. So he began to walk as he had been instructed, trying to work the kinks and strains out of his joints and muscles, just in case the moment ever came when he could be something more than a bad joke.

LOTZ

'Here they come,' Commander Sentra LaSteel said, holding her macro-binocs to her eyes. 'Dirty xenos scum. They've just rounded the northern spur.'

'What are they hoping to achieve?' Armour Sergeant Darrus Greel asked, from beside her. They were crushed up together next to one of Davidia Hive's ancient windows, one of very few that had ever been present at this low level. It was nothing more than a small arch of inches-thick crystalflex, scratched so badly by millennia of windborne particulates it was barely possible to see through it. However, lacking any form of reliable auspex, Sentra had taken up station here when she heard that a mechanised portion of the ork force had abandoned the foul camp on the city's eastern side and was traversing it to the north.

'The Emperor only knows,' Sentra replied, 'and I certainly don't care. There's a large chunk of the enemy's most mobile units headed our way, with no air support, no footslogger backup, none of those Throne-cursed Gargants. It's the perfect opportunity.'

She passed Darrus the macro-binocs, and he took a look for himself. He had to kick the magnification up to full, and the scratched and stained window eliminated any hope of seeing detail, but with the aid of the night-vision setting there was no mistaking the cloud of dust kicked up by the orkish convoy. He could just make out the multiple dark shapes covering the ground at what had to be a tremendous speed, although given the distance involved they still appeared to barely be moving.

'What are you thinking, ma'am?' he asked. 'A sortie?'

'You're damned right I'm thinking about a sortie, sergeant,' Sentra said. 'The north-west road gate's sunken, thanks to this place settling on its foundations, so it's not even visible from a distance. If we time it right, we can be out and in their midst before they realise we're coming. Those pieces of ramshackle junk might be dangerous to the footers, but we'll see how well they stand up to a few battle cannons without anything with more punch to ward us off!'

Darrus nodded, and handed the macro-binocs back. 'As you say, ma'am.'

Sentra knew that tone of voice, and she looked at him sidelong. 'I'm sensing there's a "but" lurking behind your lips, sergeant. Out with it.'

'Is that an order, ma'am?' Darrus asked politely.

'It damned well is an order, sergeant. Say whatever it is you've got to say.'

'Well, ma'am,' Darrus said, 'the colonel was quite explicit about the regiment's orders to withdraw into the city. He said nothing about us leaving it again, even if the orks presented a tempting target.'

'The colonel,' Sentra said, checking over her shoulder to ensure she could not be overheard, 'is somewhere up in the spire right now, probably nibbling on Genuvian quail's eggs and sipping two-hundred-year-old amasec with the governor. He's given up, and you know it.'

'I'm not arguing with any of that, ma'am,' Darrus said levelly. 'I'm just concerned about what's going to happen when he finds out that you've disobeyed an order. Or for that matter, what will happen if the commissar finds out.'

Sentra snorted. 'I'm even less scared of Old Bones than I am of Sudliff. She didn't execute the colonel for ordering the retreat – what's she going to do, declare me a coward for going out and fighting? Old Bones outlived her old regiment, she knows how the galaxy works. And don't give me any talk about "insubordination",' she added warningly, as Darrus began to open his mouth again. 'You said yourself, the colonel said nothing about us leaving the city again, either to say that we should *or* that we shouldn't. As a tank commander, I'm entitled to use my own initiative in an attempt to better the situation for our regiment, and the Imperium.'

Darrus shook his head. 'I can't say I'm comfortable with it, ma'am, but it's your call, not mine.' He sighed. 'Besides, I can't argue that the troops would like another chance to take it to the enemy.'

'We need to be out there, sergeant,' Sentra said firmly. 'The footers are far more suited to repelling an actual incursion than we are – we're better off thinning out the numbers of any orks that might end up making it in.' She pulled back from the window and dusted down her fatigues from where the aeons of dirt layered onto the wall had darkened the crimson. 'Let's get down to the bay and get our ladies running again.'

'Nothing moves faster than a secret' was an old Astra Militarum adage, and it proved well founded as the Golden Lions' auxiliary armour began to hurriedly prepare. At first it was just the Leman Russ battle tanks of Seventh Company – *Golden Thunder*, *Death Knell* and *Lion's Fury* – all of which came under the direct command of Sentra LaSteel. However, you couldn't start the engines of all three of your tanks without other crews becoming aware of what you were doing, especially when you were loading ammo hoppers as well. The bay, which during peacetime had been a holding area for land trains bringing supplies into Davidia and then exporting its industrial products to the Sacracia space port, had been half-full of silent combat vehicles and listless crews ever since the withdrawal had been completed. Not a one of them had trusted the locals not to interfere with their precious tanks, or even steal parts or ammunition for their own use, and so they had turned down the offer of billeting within the hive to instead make themselves as comfortable as they could on and around their mechanical charges. Anything that might break the tedium was seized upon, especially if it looked more interesting than the prospect of losing yet another game of snapper to 'Flash' Harvax of Second Company.

No one said the word 'sortie', of course. A couple of other commanders had shouted over to Sentra and asked her what she was doing, but she'd just given them a polite nod and continued her preparations without replying. She wasn't going to lie to them, because that wasn't the 25th's way. However, she certainly wasn't going to tell them outright what she was planning, because to give voice to a thing – at least to anyone beyond her own crews, whose opinions she might listen to, but whom ultimately were in no position to argue – was to give it a tangibility and form that could be challenged or countermanded.

Commander DeTay of Tenth Company was the first to join in. Only *Hammer of Aranua* was left of her command, but the battered old thing was possessed of the sort of indomitable machine-spirit that had seen it twice return to its own lines after it had been officially written off as a battlefield loss, and it coughed belligerently into life once more when appropriately coaxed. Not a word was exchanged between DeTay and Sentra, but there were faint smiles present on the faces of their crews as they worked to make their engines of war ready for another fight.

Flash Harvax was next, finally putting his deck of cards away and ordering his crews into action. Second Company's auxiliary armour unit was comprised of three Hellhounds – *Smoke Eater*, *Ash Kicker* and *Flame Rider* – and the stink of promethium in the air grew stronger as their inferno cannons were topped up. Then the two surviving Leman Russes of 16th had their netting pulled off, followed by the lone remaining Demolisher of First. All across the bay, tank crews that until a few minutes before had been the very picture of slovenly idleness were now once more moving briskly and with purpose.

Of course, no rousing of machine-spirits on that sort of scale was likely to happen without a member of the honoured Priesthood of Mars noticing. Sure enough, it wasn't long before Enginseer Sanavar Deltis was hurrying towards *Golden Thunder* with his hands tucked into his robe's voluminous sleeves.

'Cogboy's here,' Kat Pallas said in a low voice, without looking up from where she was attaching the newly refilled box magazine to Sentra's pintle-mounted storm bolter.

'Honoured adept,' Sentra greeted the enginseer, popping her head up from inside *Golden Thunder*, the Mars Alpha-pattern Leman Russ which was her command vehicle, where a moment before she had been swearing at the battle cannon's targeting auspex. 'What can we do for you?'

Deltis came to a halt and tilted his face – or what remained of it, given that it was now mostly cables, metal plating, and tiny lumens – up at her.

'There are an excessive number of possible answers to that question, Commander LaSteel, too many to be easily verbalised whilst making an efficient use of time, although the number of tasks that you could complete for me more efficiently than I could complete them myself is somewhat lower. However–'

'Forget it,' Sentra replied, then waved a hand before Deltis could inform her that the Mechanicus deleted nothing, certainly not data. 'I meant, why have you come here to speak to me?'

'Commander, the increase and manner of activity taking place suggests that you are preparing your vehicles for combat,' Deltis said briskly. 'I am here to enquire whether that is your intention.'

'Enginseer, are you aware of any orders being issued to the regiment's auxiliary armour units concerning preparations for combat?' Sentra asked, while Pallas tightened a bolt and tried her best to keep a straight face.

'I am not, commander.'

'And you are familiar with the command structure and protocols of the Aranuan Twenty-Fifth?'

'I am, commander.'

'Then it seems statistically unlikely, does it not, that we are preparing for combat?' Sentra asked. Beneath her, a sponson-mounted heavy bolter traversed a few degrees as someone checked its functions. Sentra deliberately avoided looking down at it, and stared at the enginseer instead, daring him to acknowledge that anything had happened.

'I see,' Deltis replied, nodding in as human a manner as he could still manage, since he had found that regular humans responded better to body language they could easily recognise. 'In that case, I will not offer to operate the road gate in order to assist the egress of any vehicles that might have been intending to leave the city to engage the hated xenos.'

Commander Sentra LaSteel had not got to her position in the Golden Lions without possessing an impressive tarot face, and without one would certainly not have been the veteran of many long nights opposed to Flash Harvax whilst still retaining ownership of at least some of her personal possessions. As a result, she was able to maintain a calm and composed exterior, despite her brain stripping a gear as she struggled to realign her expectations with her perceived reality.

'I'm sorry, enginseer,' she said, surreptitiously nudging Pallas to get her to stop staring. 'Would you care to expand upon your previous statement?'

'The vehicles of the Twenty-Fifth's auxiliary armour units are blessed in the eyes of the Omnissiah,' Enginseer Deltis said calmly, although Sentra had never really experienced a cogboy who got what she might call *emotional* about anything. 'Their purpose is to defeat His enemies, which in this case, are most readily embodied by the column of xenos vehicles approaching our position. Had the vehicles of the Twenty-Fifth's auxiliary armour units been intending to engage these xenos in combat, it is likely that they would have encountered resistance from the civilian operators of the road-gate mechanism, who might lack the necessary understanding of the Omnissiah's glorious purpose with regard to war. I would have been ready to explain these theological details and, if necessary, assume direct command of the gate's operating mechanisms in order to facilitate matters with the utmost efficiency.'

Sentra chewed her lip for a moment. 'Enginseer, I'm about to ask you a question, and in order to properly understand it and respond, you will need to access your lexicon of Aranuan slang.'

'Understood, commander.'

Sentra folded her arms. 'Are you taking the piss?'

There was a momentary pause, in which Sentra could almost swear she heard clicking noises coming from Deltis' head. However, after a moment the enginseer gave the binharic stutter that she had come to interpret, on the rare occasions it had occurred, as a chuckle.

'No, commander. Not unless you were attempting to deceive me with your responses to my original question.'

Sentra sighed. 'Fine, honoured adept, you win. I can't speak for anyone else here, no matter what they may or may not be doing, but I was certainly intending to give the xenos a taste of our cannons.' She laid a loving hand on *Golden Thunder*'s hull. 'It pains me to have these ladies cooped up in here when there's an enemy outside. We might not be able to engage them fully, but I'd rather be sent to a penal legion than let those scum ride around right under our noses without us bloodying theirs a bit.'

Enginseer Deltis nodded again. 'Then our intentions coincide, commander. I have been granted access to a part of the city's noosphere, and utilising this I believe I am able to monitor the xenos' progress with more accuracy than you. I shall ensure that the road gate is ready to operate at the correct moment, and I shall communicate this to you.'

Sentra smiled. 'That is much appreciated, enginseer. May the Machine-God bless you.'

'Thank you for your kind words, commander,' Deltis replied, with a slight quirk of his torso that could have been an attempt at a bow from a being whose spine no longer bent in the same manner as one composed of human vertebrae. 'I estimate that the most opportune moment for you to depart will be slightly in excess of seven minutes hence, although I shall update you with more detail as it becomes clear.' He turned and headed off towards the distant darkness of the road gate, a huge edifice of ancient metal at least three feet thick, and large enough that a medium-sized Battle Titan could have walked through it without having to duck its head.

'Right, the cogboy's onside, bless his circuits,' Sentra said in a low voice down into *Golden Thunder*'s crew compartment. 'That solves the problem of me having to pull rank on the door wardens. Pallas, is that ammo box secured?'

'Yes, ma'am,' Pallas replied, giving the bolt one last twist just to make sure.

'Good, I don't want it shearing off again. You go and tell Flash, get him to pass it on. Gravers!'

'Yes, ma'am?' the battle cannon's gunner replied.

'You go and give the good news to Commander DeTay,' Sentra said. 'I don't see the need to use a vox, even given how noisy it is in here. No point the brass getting wind of anything before they need to, right?'

'Yes, ma'am,' Gravers acknowledged, giving his weapon's targeting auspex one last ritual and rather hopeful thump.

Sentra caught the eye of Darrus Greel, currently checking the hull-mounted lascannon on *Lion's Fury*, and gave him a small smile. In just a few minutes, the 25th – or a part of it, at least – would have a chance to strike back at the foul enemy that had forced them to take refuge in this giant, stinking hive city.

And then, there would be a reckoning.

LOTZ

Zagnob Thundaskuzz had the wind in his hair squigs, a wrench between his teeth, and a song in his heart.

The song in question was the full-throated engine roar of his Deffkilla wartrike, the thrumming of its thick, nobbled tyres over the dirt and sand below him, and the howl of the jet engine powering everything along. His wartrike was the perfect blend of speed, power and killyness: it was tougher than a warbike, faster than a buggy, trakk or trukk, and while it might not have the sheer firepower of something like a boomdakka snazzwagon, it carried *him*, and that made up for it. The only thing better than driving really, really fast was driving really, really fast into a bunch of gits and charring them with the engine outputs, blowing holes in them with the boomstikks, or impaling one with his snagga klaw and dragging the unfortunate along behind him. So far as Zagnob was concerned, he was doing whoever-it-was a favour by helping them go faster than they probably ever had before; it wasn't his fault if they weren't up to it.

'See anyfing yet?' he bellowed at Skitta, his grot fuel-mixer, who was currently bracing a pair of make-bigger tubes against its eyes.

'Nuffin', boss!' Skitta squeaked. 'Dere's no doors!'

'How do dese gits get in an' out, den?' Zagnob muttered to himself, rubbing his chin. He glanced irritably upwards, to the blinking lights and faint reflections of whirling blades that signified where Da Red Barrun's flyboyz were keeping pace with his convoy in their deffkoptas. He was going to be incredibly displeased if this humie city could only be accessed by the air.

He forced himself to think, making his brain turn away momentarily from revelling in the speed and noise that surrounded him, and the never-ceasing black-hole draw of the horizon. Part of him wanted nothing more than to roar off into the distance, like all speed freeks, until he finally caught up with it and made the distance into his 'here'. However, the distance was a tricky quarry, and he hadn't caught it yet. On the other hand, it wasn't going away: it was always lurking there, within sight, but not as yet within reach. He had other ambitions he could fulfil in the meantime, if he could just concentrate on them.

Goresnappa had been alright as warbosses went: a bit of a traditionalist, like all Snakebites, but not to the point where he hadn't recognised the importance of having some fast-moving vehicles to surge around the enemy and clobber them from the side or rear. He'd led the Waaagh! to some good fights in his time, which was all most orks wanted from a warboss.

Zagnob was not most orks, though: he was a speedboss, the unquestioned leader of the speed freeks here, and held in high regard by any ork who had anything to do with driving a vehicle, or riding one into battle. Zooming into the middle of a scrap to show the rest of the boyz how it was done was all very well, but he chafed at how slowly everyone and everything else moved. It always took the Waaagh! too long to get to a fight, and then even when they found one, the speed freeks had to wait for the rest to get themselves sorted. It was an insult to him, to his machine, and to the Kult.

But what if Zagnob Thundaskuzz wasn't just speedboss, but the overall warboss? Well, that would be a different matter entirely. Then there would be a simple rule: any ork that fell behind, would get left behind. He would give the hordes of boyz the chance to build themselves a few trukks or wagons, of course, so they had a chance of keeping up, but the die-hard footsloggers could go their own way if they were going to deliberately persist in being so zoggin' slow. Then Zagnob could move at the speed that pleased him - really, really fast - and take on whatever enemy he found, as and when he found them.

In order to call the shots, he needed to become warboss. In order to become warboss, he needed to find this gateway that Old Morgrub had talked about, or at least be close enough to smack whoever did find it out of the way and claim it for himself. In order to find the gate, he needed to be able to get inside the humie city, and that was the thing that was currently stumping him.

There *had* to be a way in, though. The Waaagh! had kicked the humies' heads in and sent the survivors scurrying away to take shelter in this city: they certainly weren't anywhere else, so they had to be in there. Zagnob didn't reckon the humies could have airlifted everything back inside, not including all their big tanks and battlewagons, so there had to be a door that vehicles could use. He just couldn't *find* the zoggin' thing...

Something thundered, overhead. No, not quite overhead, Zagnob realised: it was coming from the upper reaches of the humie city, and it had the unmistakeable rolling quality of high-powered dakka. Humies had some appreciation for blowing stuff up with big guns, Zagnob would give them that. What was more, their guns usually made a satisfying booming sound, not like those fizzing energy wotsits the blue fishboyz used, or the nearly silent weapons of the skrawniez. You might as well not shoot at your enemy at all, if your gun wasn't going to make a good lot of noise while you did so...

'Dey're shootin' at us, boss!' Skitta wailed, as glowing projectiles began to arc down through the night towards them. Zagnob snatched the make-bigger tubes off the grot for safekeeping, then clipped it around the head so hard that said head cannoned backwards into the side of the trike.

'I know dat!' he bawled. 'Duffrak! Yoo seein' dis?'

'Yes, boss!' his driver said, over his shoulder.

'Gonna do anyfing about it?'

'Just wanna see where dey're gonna land, boss,' Duffrak replied, keeping his eyes on the sky. Zagnob grunted, but held his tongue. He'd given Duffrak the job of driving him around not only because he went very fast, but also because he generally managed to avoid driving into things by accident, and while Zagnob wasn't scared of a crash, crashing did mean that he had stopped going fast. He thought it was fairly likely that Duffrak would also be able to avoid getting hit by incoming ordnance. If not, then Zagnob would be giving a thorough kicking to anything of Duffrak that happened to be left afterwards.

He glanced over his shoulder at the loose wedge of vehicles following him: dozens and dozens of them, spread out in an attempt to avoid each other's dust clouds, because what was the point of going fast if you couldn't see how fast you were going? It might have been dark, but Zagnob's eyes were up to the task of picking out the different shapes and lines, and he could see the wide and varied scope of orkish vehicles that answered the call of his engine's roar.

There were sleek dragstas, low to the ground and aerodynamic, with the whirling gizmos of their shokkjump drives ready to be activated; the gun-heavy shapes of snazzwagons, their mek owners perched proudly behind their fearsome armaments and eagerly awaiting anything upon which they could unleash the full force of their deranged designs; megatrakk scrapjets, the now-wingless shells of aircraft whose fuselages had remained whole enough after a crash to be refitted for overland travel, armed with batteries of rokkits; the smoke-billowing kustom boosta-blastas, their oily fumes turning the night even darker; ramshackle squig-buggies, the grunts and squeals of their caged living ammunition loud enough to be heard even over the thunder of engines; and, of course, mob upon mob of warbikers, perhaps the most quintessential of ork speedsters. Zagnob had a certain amount of respect for any ork who threw in with the Kult of Speed, no matter how wild or outlandish their vehicle, but there was something simplistically appealing about a classic warbike's combination of high speed, ferocious firepower, and lack of obvious balance.

Even that wasn't the end of it. Da Red Barrun's deffkoptas were sort of like sky-buggies: they were not as fast or as heavily armed as the true flyers, the dakkajets and the burna-bommers and their ilk, but their pilots braved the air and its associated dangers such as flak, enemies, and unexpected avians without the protective surroundings of a cockpit, instead relying on their piloting skills and the favour of Gork and Mork to keep them from harm. And of course, back on the ground, there were the trukkboyz: Kult of Speed wannabes who lacked the know-wotz to build their own vehicle, or the teef to pay a mek to knock one together for them, but would cling onto the back of a transport simply to feel the wind in their faces and be able to jump out and clobber the enemy all the sooner.

Zagnob squinted. Trukks, like every other ork vehicle, were wildly varied in design, albeit broadly similar in terms of size and function,[7] and a good

[7] Every ork knew at what point a trukk stopped being a trukk and started being a battlewagon, although verbalising it might be another matter.

speedboss would know to whom every vehicle in a Waaagh! belonged, just in case he had to clobber the owner for beating him in a race. Zagnob had just seen one whose presence was unexpected, and it bothered him.

'Oi, Skitta,' he said, peering at a trukk that was powering up behind them. It looked like it was painted black, although it was hard to tell in the dark. 'Does dat look like Nuzzgrond's mob–'

The night erupted.

Flame and dirt kicked up, and one of the trukks following Zagnob's wartrike was abruptly and spectacularly rearranged into a blossoming flower of fire, shrapnel, and dismembered body parts. The humie artillery had finished its long arc down from the walls above, and was doing some proper krumping.

'Ya worked out where it's landin' yet?' Zagnob yelled at Duffrak, grabbing onto a handhold as the wartrike swerved to one side.

'Reckon so, boss!' Duffrak replied cheerily. 'But ya might wanna hold on for a minute!'

Hold on? Zagnob could have thumped his driver for such cheek. Oh, he certainly *was* holding on, but there was a difference between holding on because you, a speedboss, had decided to, and holding on because your driver had told you to. He had half a mind to–

Another explosion, and then another, and another. Night became day, briefly and repeatedly, and Zagnob caught momentary glimpses of the blue checks of Deathskull vehicles, the leering yellow crescent of the Bad Moons, and the fiery reds of Evil Sunz like him, all lit up in flashes of destruction as their neighbours were blown apart by the fury of humie vengeance.

He raised his face to the sky and howled in delight. He had the thunder of guns and the roar of speed around him, and that was all a speed freek needed in order to be happy. He would have preferred the presence of an enemy he could clobber as well, of course, but given they were all hiding behind those ridiculously thick walls, he would take this as a stopgap. How could anyone know they were truly living, unless there was the imminent possibility of being dead?

The mighty guns far above spoke once more, and a new rain of ordnance began to arc down towards them. The humies had altered their aim to account for their targets' fast-moving nature, and these shells were coming down in a curtain directly ahead. The only sure-fire way of avoiding them would be to stop dead.

There was no way that Duffrak was going to do that, and no way that Zagnob Thundaskuzz was going to tell him to, either. Instead, the driver raised one hand, and yelled one word.

'Skitta!'

The grot was also howling, with terror rather than with excitement, but it had enough brain space left around the edges of its panic to slam both fists down on the big red button that was its primary responsibility. Valves opened, and supercharged fuel gushed into the wartrike's system. It was a special brew, refined by the most skilled mekboyz and only available, let alone affordable, to important orks like Zagnob: mainly because he'd promised to kick the teef down the throat of any ork who provided it to someone else. It would burn out an engine in short order if used to excess, but when administered correctly...

The wartrike jerked forwards like a scalded smasha squig, flames as long as Zagnob was tall billowing from its jet outflow. They were almost flying now, getting huge amounts of air as they crested each ridge or bump in the ground; then the wheels would dig in again as soon as they touched down, and the acceleration would somehow increase. They were passing directly beneath the bombardment. Zagnob looked up and bellowed his defiance at it, at those rapidly growing miniature suns of blazing energy and high explosive that presumed to threaten him. Let the humies sling their dakka at him! If he had to die, then knowing the gits had needed to call upon their biggest guns in order to kill him was a decent enough trade-off. Zagnob wasn't sure what happened when you died, but if Gork and Mork were paying any sort of attention to him, he felt sure they'd think that being blown up while going really, really fast was a death you could have a laugh about.

The shells got lower and lower, causing the air to scream as it was torn asunder by their sheer speed and mass, and then–

–they were past.

The first shells ripped into the ground, inflicting yet more damage on it, but Zagnob Thundaskuzz's Deffkilla wartrike was out of blast range and gunning on into the night. Even Da Red Barrun's deffkoptas were taking evasive action in order to avoid being swatted from the sky as an afterthought; the rest of the ground convoy were either being blown to smithereens, had slewed to a shameful stop, or were engaging in a whooping diversion around the kill-zone.

'Waaagh!' Zagnob roared, a cry of simultaneous joy and challenge. The engine was cycling down again now, as the brief burst of acceleration granted by the speshul fuel began to wear off. Zagnob wanted to bring the sensation back, to feel his neck muscles once again at war with G-forces and air drag, but only a squigbrained fool pushed his machine harder than it could take. Any grot could achieve a brief burst of glory and then burn an engine out: the mark of a true speed freek was knowing exactly what line you could walk to get the most performance from your vehicle without leaving yourself coasting to an embarrassed halt atop a coughing pile of metal. He was alone, supreme and unchallenged in his speed and skill and daring.

'Boss?' Duffrak said. 'We've got company!'

Zagnob lowered his gaze from the heavens and looked ahead. Beams of light were splitting the night, but these weren't static searchlights, peering down from on high in search of targets for the big guns to let fly at; these jerked and juddered and shifted sharply, as the vehicles on which they were mounted bucked and bumped and bounced over the uneven terrain.

A wide, toothy grin spread across Zagnob Thundaskuzz's face.

'Looks like da humies have decided to come out an' play after all!' he chortled happily. 'Let's go an' welcome 'em to da party!'

'We're all on our own, boss,' Duffrak pointed out. He wasn't contradicting

Zagnob, merely reminding his boss of something which might have otherwise slipped his mind, but Zagnob was well aware of the situation.

'Da uvvers'll catch up,' he said, matter-of-factly. 'If we can't run rings around a bunch of zoggin' humies in da dark, den we don't deserve to be out 'ere at all.' He worked the action on his snagga klaw, hearing the satisfying *snik-snak* of its blades, and the hiss of gas as he twisted a valve to pressurise the harpoon attachment. Some of the humies liked to get a proper ork's-eye view of things by riding along with their heads and torsos sticking out of the top of their tanks, and while Zagnob could admire their enthusiasm for getting the wind in their faces like a proper speed freek, they made ever-so-tempting targets when they did so.

'Let's go an' have some fun,' he growled, and the wartrike leaped forwards once more.

LOTZ

'Ya can't rebel against da orks!' hissed the other grot. He was called Snippa One-Ear, for reasons that even Kruffik had not needed clarifying; he was very nominally in charge of the large collection of grots that Zukrod would have been leading – or prodding – into battle; and he was very obviously frightened.

'Why not?' Snaggi asked, trying to sound reasonable.

'Because dey'll kill us!' Snippa protested, tugging on his one remaining ear in fear. He and his mob were cowering in the shelter of a wrecked megatrakk, in the hope that everyone would forget about them until the coming battle was over. 'Dey'll probably kill us all just for ya talkin' to us about it!'

'Den wot've you got to lose?' Snaggi asked. 'If dey're gonna kill ya *anyway*, why not try an' get ya freedom?'

Several of the assembled grots looked at each other and nodded, with the confidence of those for whom the consequences of such actions were as yet only theoretical, but Snippa One-Ear was not so easily swayed.

'Dey *might* kill us for ya talkin' to us about it,' he argued, 'but dey'll *definitely* kill us if we try an' rebel! Dat's an important difference! It's like, numbaz an' dat.'

'Yoo're a coward,' Snaggi accused him.

'Yep!' Snippa replied, folding his arms and staring back challengingly. 'Of course I'm a coward! Grots are *s'posed* to be cowards! It's what keeps us alive! We don't get good guns, we don't get good armour–'

'We don't get *any* armour,' Kruffik put in.

'–right, dat,' Snippa agreed, without breaking his stride, 'an' da orks hide behind us an' let us get shot! Bein' a coward's da only way yoo're gonna get out alive!'

'So why do da orks hide behind us?' Snaggi asked, raising his voice so the entire mob could hear him. 'Dey're bigger dan us! *We* should be hidin' behind *dem*! Orks get armour! Dey get all da good weapons, so da enemies are scared of 'em! Dey get to ride around in trukks an' wagons, or on da back of squigs, so dey can get to da fight faster an' have less time gettin' shot at! Dey're da cowards, not us!'

'Wait,' Snippa said, frowning. 'Does dat mean dat you weren't tryin' to insult me when ya called me a coward, or–'

'Dat don't matter now!' Snaggi interrupted him, on the basis that momentum was more important that internal consistency. 'My point *is*, dat us grots get a bad deal! We get da *worst* deal in da history of deals wot've been done in da galaxy. We didn't even do da deal! Dere's not one grot here wot had an ork come up to him an say, "Hello little grot, would ya like ta get a gun wot a humie would larf at, an' a coupla bits of cloth to wear, and go an' stand in front of us when we try an' kill da rest of da galaxy?", is dere?'

'I wouldn't have said "yes" to dat,' Guffink said, shaking his head.

'Course ya wouldn't!' Snaggi agreed. 'Who would? Bein' a coward ain't gonna help ya get out alive, cos da orks always make sure we get da dangerous jobs! We just get told wot to do cos da orks are bigger, an' dey fink dat means dey can do wot dey want!'

'Well, it sorta does,' Snippa pointed out. 'Dat's how it works.'

'But it don't have to!' Snaggi said, appealing to the mob in general. 'Da orks *need* us! Dey don't know how to do half da fings dey want done, or if dey do, dey ain't got da patience for it! Dey've only got da patience to kick a grot if da grot don't do it like dey want it done. Wot dis Waaagh! needs is a warboss wot's gonna take grots seriously!'

'Dere's no ork in da history of all orks wot's ever taken grots seriously,' Snippa One-Ear objected. 'Now, I'll admit dat I ain't met every ork wot's ever lived, but I'm still pretty sure I'm right about dat. Dere's no warboss dat's gonna make life any better for us, so yer Revolushun's pointless.'

Snaggi grinned triumphantly. He was still riding on the wave of adrenaline that had engulfed him in the aftermath of frying Zukrod. He felt like he could reach out and touch the spire of the humie hive city, and maybe pull it down with one good tug. Gork and Mork were muttering away in the back of his brain, giving him the strength and the determination he needed to see this through, to change the face of the galaxy.

'No *ork* warboss is gonna make life any better for us,' he corrected Snippa, sticking his chest out.

'Yeah, dat's wot I said,' Snippa said, nonplussed.

Snaggi felt his grin slip a bit. 'No, wait, I meant...' He sighed. 'Skrawk! Bring in da stikk!'

There was a moment's pause, and then Skrawk shuffled in from outside with Zukrod's grabba stikk clutched in both hands. Snippa and the rest of his mob shied back from it in sudden and deeply ingrained fear, and Snaggi took the opportunity to take the tool from Skrawk and plant its haft firmly in the ground. It was taller than he was by some way, but so far as he was concerned, that just made him look more heroic next to it.

'Where did ya get dat?' Snippa wailed, trying to look all ways at once, as though expecting the grabba stikk's previous owner to emerge from the shadows, bellowing in rage.

'Took it from Zukrod,' Snaggi announced proudly. 'After I *killed* him!'

The jaw of every single grot in Snippa's mob dropped open, and every eye bulged.

'He's dead,' Snaggi persisted, keen to press his advantage with an audience who were suddenly hanging on his every word. 'Ya can go an' find him if ya want, just make sure no ork sees ya near his body, cos dey might get funny ideas about wot happened to him. An' I don't want ya takin' credit for wot I did!'

'You... *killed* him?' Snippa repeated, incredulously.

'He didn't just give me his grabba stikk cos he was feelin' generous!' Snaggi said. 'But I didn't just kill him – I killed da warboss too!'

He was expecting even more shocked reactions, but instead the grots in front of him just looked puzzled. A grot killing a runtherd, Snaggi realised, was vaguely possible for them to conceptualise: it was something that most of them would likely have dreamed of doing at some point, but they had lacked the courage, ability, or opportunity to do so. A grot killing a warboss, though, was outside of what they considered possible. It was ridiculous, like saying he had just eaten a battlewagon, or knocked a moon unconscious.

'I pulled da lever wot dumped da head of da Mega-Gargant onto him,' Snaggi said, trying to reframe events into something his audience could understand, and was rewarded with a few horrified expressions. 'Orks ain't so tough as all dat, ya just need to know how to squish 'em, or cook 'em, or wotever. If we put our minds to it, dere's no reason why da Revolushun shouldn't succeed!'

'An' wot are you gonna count as succeedin'?' Snippa demanded. 'Cos all I can see dat's likely is da orks stompin' us all flat!'

Here it was. His chance to finally verbalise what Gork and Mork had been telling him. His previous attempt at setting up the line had been kiboshed a bit by Snippa's reaction, but now Snaggi had a clear run at it.

'Success is gonna be when I become warboss!'

Laughter. Not just laughter, hilarity. Grots bending double, hands on their knees. Grots holding themselves up weakly on their neighbours. Grots rolling on the floor wheezing, most of the air they needed in order to simply survive stolen by their bodies' reactions to the utterly ludicrous notion of a grot being– No, not of a grot *being* warboss, because that was a concept too far, but of a grot *thinking* he could be warboss.

'Snaggi, dis is da best day of my life!' Snippa gurgled, from somewhere around knee height. 'I ain't larfed dis hard, *ever!* When I can get up, I'm gonna shake yer hand!'

'I ain't jokin'!' Snaggi shouted desperately. 'I mean it! I'm gonna become warboss!'

'But *how?*' someone shouted back, through splutters. 'Ya fink ya can outfight Dedfist, or outrun Thundaskuzz, or outfink Da Genrul?'

'I don't need to do any of dose fings!' Snaggi screamed angrily, levelling the grabba stikk at them all. 'I just need to get to dat gate wot Old Morgrub talked about, an' I need to get dere *first!*'

Silence fell, like the abruptly loosened head of a Mega-Gargant.

'Dat's wot da old warphead said, weren't it?' Snaggi asked quietly. 'I've heard wot everyone's been sayin,' an' more importantly, I *saw* it. Gork an' Mork showed me. Dere's a skrawniez gate of some sort under da humie city, and da big bosses are all runnin' around tryin' ta find it. Old Morgrub said da ork wot finds it first is gonna be warboss, an' Old Morgrub's got a lot of clout around here.'

'Yeah,' Snippa said a trifle hoarsely, pushing himself back to his feet. 'But he was talkin' about *orks*. An' you might've killed an ork, an' you might've dropped something really heavy on anuvver ork, but ya ain't an ork, Snaggi Littletoof.'

'Maybe not,' Snaggi admitted. 'But Old Morgrub's an odd sort. Are ya tellin' me dat if he finds a grot at da gate, dere's *no way* dat he's gonna say dat grot is da new warboss?'

A few mouths opened, and then closed again as their owners mulled this over. When push came to shove, there was no denying that Old Morgrub *was* an odd sort, even as warpheadz went. It was not, grot brains began to realise, completely outside of the realms of possibility. It wasn't *likely*, no one was claiming that it was *likely*, but it wasn't impossible.

For a group of beings for whom life consisted of a few painful certainties, mainly involving physical abuse and terrified death, 'not impossible' held a certain appeal that was hard to deny.

'Even if he does,' Snippa said slowly, 'dat doesn't mean da rest of da Waaagh!'s gonna accept it.'

'Course not,' Snaggi admitted, 'but dere's more Snakebites dan any uvver clan. Dere's no Snakebite big bosses, cos Goresnappa stomped any of his own clan wot got too big for dere boots, so da Snakebites'll probably back up wot Old Morgrub says, cos he's one of 'em. It's a long shot, but it might just work. Besides,' he added, 'I ain't just talkin' about gettin' to da gate. Dat's wot'll get dere attention, but we're gonna need to do uvver stuff to make 'em listen once we've done dat.'

'Wot sort of uvver stuff?' Snippa asked. He wasn't convinced yet, Snaggi could tell that much, but the very vague prospect of having someone in charge who might not send him to go and die somewhere on the simple basis of him being a grot was enough to pull him in for now.

'We're gonna need to be able to stop everyfing,' Snaggi said, lowering his voice to a more conspiratorial tone. Snippa's mob crowded in around him in order to hear, and he got a new flush of excitement and importance. 'We're da ones wot load da ammo, grease da gears, herd da squigs – all dat stuff. We need to talk to da riggers, da oilers, da orderlies, every other grot wot does somefing dat an ork can't do, or won't do. When da time comes, da orks are gonna have a choice to make.'

He took a deep breath.

'Dey can pay us grots some proppa respect… or dey can sit around with gunz an' vehicles wot don't work, while we head off on da first ever GrotWaaagh!'

LOTZ

Mag Dedfist was inspecting the weapons systems on *Gork's Hammer*, the Mega-Gargant he had commandeered as his own, when a flash of green light through the viewports arrested his attention. A couple of moments later, the metal of the hull above his head rang with multiple muffled impacts.

'Wot in da blazes?' the Goff muttered, then squinted in surprise as a howling shape plummeted past a viewport, clawing futilely at the air. 'Woz dat an ork?'

'Fink so, boss,' the spanner called Gutzog replied, pressing his face up against the viewport and trying to peer downwards. 'He can't fly, who-ever he is.'

A few more thuds and scraping noises came from above them, and Dedfist growled in irritation. He pointed at a nervous, oil-spattered grot who was hanging around the command deck with the attitude of one who was unsure if it would get in more trouble for leaving or for staying, and who had been on the agonised knife-edge of indecision for several minutes now.

'Yoo. Get out dere and find out why dere's boyz landin' on dis fing.'

'Yes, boss!' the grot squawked, and sprinted for the access hatch in the side of the head with the *flap-flap-flap* of its large bare feet. It desperately spun the opening wheel, then threw all of its body weight – such as it was – against the door, which barely cracked open. It backed off, desperation to please the warboss-to-be writ large on its face, and took a proper run up.

The hatch was tugged open from the outside just before the grot made contact with it, and the luckless creature's momentum sent it stumbling across the narrow gantry, and then over the edge to sail down into oblivion with nothing but a wailing cry of terror and despair to mark its passing. The ork who had pulled the door edged around it from the other side, casting an incurious glance in the direction of the falling grot as he did so, then pulled up short with one foot inside the Gargant's head when he clapped eyes on Mag Dedfist's hulking frame.

'Er... Hi, boss.'

'Wot da zoggin' 'eck is goin' on?' Dedfist demanded. 'Wot's da big idea?'

The ork was a beast snagga boy by the look of his crude armour, heavy, hook-bladed choppa, and a left leg which was a prosthetic from the knee downwards where a large squig of some sort had taken a nibble at him.

However, he was also a Goff, judging by the colour of his clothes, and in no way inclined to risk the displeasure of his big boss. He attempted an appeasing grin. 'Uh, not exactly sure meself, boss. Nob Badeye said he had a kunnin' plan, an' we all went to see Old Morgrub. Da boss – dat is, Nob Badeye, not you, boss – told Morgrub to jump us froo da humie walls so's we could get inside wivout waitin'. Morgrub called 'im a cheater, an' da next fing I know, we're all in da sky. Guess he must've jumped us up dere instead, to teach Badeye a lesson.'

Mag Dedfist's expression, which was never going to be accused of being naturally sunny, grew suddenly and unmistakably more thunderous.

'Not my idea...' the ork muttered hopefully, as Dedfist stamped towards him, even the sturdy plating of the deck beneath them flexing slightly under the weight of his massive armour and furious displeasure.

'An' where is Nob Badeye now?' Dedfist rumbled.

'Can't say for sure, boss,' the ork replied quickly, looking up at the big boss, who stood head and shoulders taller than him. 'Last time I saw 'im, he was headin' for da ground, proppa quick like. He missed da Gargant, ya see.'

Dedfist paused for a moment, the talons of his enormous power klaw flexing slightly as he considered this. Then he snorted dismissively, and prodded the other ork in the chest with his non-klawed hand.

'Get back out dere, and bring in any of da rest of yer mob wot landed on me Gargant. Den get down into da belly an' wait.'

'Wait for wot, boss?' the ork asked, then flinched backwards as Dedfist scowled at him. 'Just so's we know wot yoo're wantin'!'

'Wait until da doors open, cos dat's when yoo're gonna be chargin'!' Mag growled at him, and the ork beat a hasty retreat back outside to start hollering at any of his mates who had been saved from a fatal fall by the unexpected intervention of a giant ork-shaped metal head. Dedfist himself turned back to the spanners, who were watching him with a mixture of excited anticipation that they might be called upon to demonstrate the effectiveness of their creation, and fear that it was somehow going to be terminally disappointing, with emphasis on the 'terminally' part.

'Looks like some of me nobs have decided to play silly buggers,' Mag Dedfist declared, and the twin pilot lights of his jaw-mounted skorchas flared a little bit wilder, as if tuned to his mood. 'I ain't gonna hang around here an' wait for some jumped-up little zogger to sneak in like a bloody grot, finkin' dey can claim wot don't belong to dem! Sound da horns! We're gonna crack dat city open, an' I ain't waitin' for da sun before I get started!'

The spanner boyz grinned gleefully at each other, their excitement overriding their fear, and spun around in their seats. Each one reached up and grabbed a dangling loop of chain, then hauled on it with all their respective mights.

And the Gargant

ROARED.

It started as something felt rather than heard: a subsonic shake that began at the soles of the feet and rapidly climbed upwards, vibrating through limbs, shaking the spine, and dancing uncomfortably through and around internal organs. By the time it was resonating within the lungs, the ears had started to register its presence: first as a wave of pressure, and then as something that could more or less be described as sound, if sound was something that grabbed you by each side of your skull and headbutted you in the face. On and on it climbed, rising through the frequencies with the savage, uncaring grace of an apex ocean predator breaching the wave crests to snatch and crush a doomed warm, furry prey-thing between razored jaws, and then just when you thought it had reached its apex, it *kept going*. It was the throaty bellow of a volcanic eruption, it was the shuddering groan of a continent-sized sheet of metal being torn asunder, it was the tortured scream of a million overpowered steam whistles. It wasn't truly the voice of Gork, but it was, Mag Dedfist reflected, a zoggin' good imitation.

And it was not alone.

There were other Gargants in the Waaagh!, none quite so large as *Gork's Hammer*, but each one a malignant, brooding powerhouse of war in its own right. Beneath them were the Stompas: mini-Gargants that could scrag an Imperial Knight in a matter of seconds, and make a Warhound Titan think twice. Then there were the Morkanauts and Gorkanauts, the pride and joy of badmeks and outcast nobs, who preferred riding into battle within the thick metal hides of their own personal war machines rather than fixing up da boss' battlewagons, or leading a bunch of boyz. Their owners were still welcome, despite being somewhat antisocial even by ork standards, because anything big and shooty and stompy would have a place in an ork warband. There were dozens of Deff Dreads, fearsome hunks of scrap and weapons in their own right, each one equal to a whole mob of boyz in terms of durability and killing power. Even the Killa Kans, despite being smaller and lighter and undoubtedly more cowardly, were part of the Waaagh!'s mighty contingent of walkers. Every one, no matter the clan affiliation of the orks that built or crewed them, fitted in with Mag Dedfist's preferred approach to war: walk forwards, give 'em some dakka, then clobber 'em good an' proper.

They all raised their mechanical voices in answer to their overlord's call, stentorian bellows mixing with static-laden roars and fuzzed-out screeches. As they did so, the main body of the Waaagh! – the orks themselves – took up the shout. Mag looked out of the viewport and saw a mass of bodies swarming around the distant feet of the mighty war effigy in which he rode. He didn't need to dispense any orders: the Gargant's horns were instruction enough for the thousands of boyz around him, who knew that the time had come to pile headlong into the fight. Dedfist might not be warboss yet by the reckoning of Old Morgrub, but what say did the warphead really have in the matter? Da Genrul had got his bunch of finkers and oddboyz, and Thundaskuzz had the Kult of Speed, but the majority of the Waaagh! were here, and all too happy to follow Mag Dedfist's lead.

Still, the gate that Old Morgrub had talked about was supposedly somewhere inside the humie city, and Dedfist was going to be breaking down the walls anyway, to give the gits hiding in there a good kicking. He might as well find the gate while he was doing so, just to make sure there was no doubt in anyone's mind. Beating down challengers was entertaining enough, but Mag Dedfist was of the firm belief that the most important thing an ork could do was stomp the various other species of the galaxy into oily puddles, and orkish infighting was a distraction for which he had only a limited amount of patience.

'Looks like we got everyone's attenshun,' he said as the Gargant's roar died away, now supplanted by the answering cries from the rest of the warband. He even allowed himself to sound vaguely pleased, which he tried not to do too often, in case it gave his underlings the wrong idea. 'Alright, ladz, dere's a big crack runnin' a long way up da walls, pretty much straight ahead of us. Hit it wiv everyfing we've got. Dat's gonna be da quickest way in, an' I'm in no mood for waitin.'

The spanners hauled on levers and twisted dials with ferocious glee. Klaxons sounded, tinny and weak against the aftermath of *Gork's Hammer*'s true voice, but alerting the rest of the crew to what was about to occur. Behind them, the hatch creaked open again, and the first of what remained of Nob Badeye's mob began filing in. Mag Dedfist watched them hurry past out of the corner of his eye. The ork he'd spoken to was doing a good job of hurrying them along and bawling at them, a far cry from the meek and submissive display he'd put on when talking to Mag before. That was good: it was hard for a big boss to work out which of his underlings were decent commanders, since they all deferred to him (if they knew what was good for them). You couldn't get the measure of an ork until you saw how he was with his own mob, especially when their nob had just copped it. It looked like this one was the natural successor.

'Yoo!' Dedfist barked. 'Wot's yer name?'

'Uzgul, boss.'

'Yoo da nob now?'

Uzgul took a look at the others around him, then nodded. 'Yes, boss!'

Dedfist waited. He did not have to wait long.

'Yoo, nob? Dat's a zoggin' joke, Uzgul!' one of the others spat.

'Oh, an' ya reckon it should be *yoo*, Braggit?' Uzgul demanded, squaring up to him.

Mag sized them both up with an expert's eye. They were fairly evenly matched in terms of size and build, and there wasn't a great deal to choose between them on any other front either. Both had the traditional horned helmet of a Goff warrior, and both were thick with muscle. Uzgul had a simple choppa, a heavy hooked axe blade on the end of a thick metal pole, whereas his adversary had a more advanced sawtoothed chainblade that rumbled into fume-belching life as he pressed the activation switch – but that meant little. One would cleave deeper more quickly, while the other would cause much more damage if plunged into an enemy's body. At the end of the day, the nature of a weapon like that was of lesser importance than the skill of the wielder.

Neither ork went for their slugga. They were Goffs, after all, and beast snaggas to boot, and much preferred to settle things up close and personal. Each one swung at the same moment, while the rest of their mob backed away hurriedly, chuckling and whooping.

The command deck of a Gargant was far from a spacious area in which to have a fight, but that was of little consequence to a pair of Goffs: the purpose of a scrap was to win, and you couldn't win if you were out of reach of your opponent. Uzgul caught Braggit's in-swinging chainblade on the haft of his choppa and turned it aside, then mashed the butt end of it into Braggit's face to make room for a killing blow. The other ork staggered backwards, ducked the swipe that would have taken his head clean off, and tore his weapon up and across Uzgul's ribs, shredding fabric and flesh with equal ease. Dark blood flew, spattering against bulkheads and being turned into a fine mist in the air by the whirling saw-teeth of Braggit's chainblade. It was Uzgul's turn to stagger now – he emitted a grunt of pain as his torso was sliced open to the bone, and Braggit seized his opportunity. He lunged, looking to bury his weapon in Uzgul's chest and have its whining teeth chew through his opponent's body in a decisive blow.

He was too slow. Uzgul twisted aside and brought his choppa down on Braggit's arm, with enough force that the sturdy metal blade sheared right through muscle and bone, and left Braggit stumbling forwards with one fewer limb than he'd had a moment before.

'Ow! Zoggin' hell!' Braggit bellowed, turning on the spot, then raised his remaining hand as Uzgul drew his choppa back for another blow. 'Yeah, alright, alright. Da best ork won. Yoo're da boss.'

'An' don't yoo forget it,' Uzgul said, in a tone of deep satisfaction. He turned to the rest of them. 'Get movin,' we ain't got all day, an' ya don't want to be gettin' in Boss Dedfist's way! Down dose stairs, hup-hup-hup! Grubslakk, close dat hatch, dere's no one else out dere! Lugrukk, give Braggit his arm back. Yes, *an'* his choppa too! Braggit, see if ya can find a painboy to get da zoggin' fing stitched back on again, for Mork's sake. If it ain't ready by da time da boss gives us da signal, yer gonna be fightin' wiv one arm, so don't say I didn't warn ya!'

Uzgul's mob, as they now were, disappeared from the command deck with the efficiency common to any ork who knew that the quickest way to reach the next interesting fight was to get out of their boss' way as soon as possible. Dedfist could hear Uzgul harassing them all the way down the ladders that led into the Gargant's belly, but that wasn't uncommon: even having proven his worth through combat, Uzgul would still want to reinforce his new position in the minds of the others.

He turned back to the spanners, who had been watching the fight with the same eagerness as the mob whose leadership had been in question. 'Did I tell ya to stop doin' wot ya was doin'?' Dedfist demanded, scowling at them.

'No, boss,' Gutzog admitted, nudging his companion. The pair of them went back to work, doing all manner of teknikal things about which Mag Dedfist had no idea: but then, he didn't need to. A warboss didn't have to pay attention to mek stuff, any more than he needed to pay attention to painboy stuff, or runtherd stuff. Oddboyz weren't leaders – apart from the occasional exception like Mad Dok Grotsnik, or Da Meklord – they did what they were told, and the orks who were suited to end up as leaders – orks like Mag Dedfist – were the ones who did the telling. That was how ork society had worked for longer than anyone could remember, and Dedfist saw no reason for it to change now he was at the top.

Well. Nearly at the top. But that was just a matter of time.

Gork's Hammer shifted beneath him. The grumble of the mighty engines changed in pitch, the smokestacks thrummed as their output increased, and great cogs and wheels began to turn and grind together. Far below, even the least perceptive ladz were breaking into desperate sprints as they tried to clear a path in front of the titanic walker. Trakks and buggies coughed into life and pulled away.

The Gargant raised one enormous lumpy foot, thrust it forwards a couple of dozen yards, and thumped it back down again. The command deck rocked, but Mag Dedfist stood firm in his mega armour, and he grinned.

To either side, the rest of the Waaagh! was mobilising, following the lead of their new boss in his mighty transport. Engines roared, horns blared, and a few enthusiastic weapons barked into life despite the fact that they were not yet close enough to the humie city to achieve anything. More than that, Mag could feel power starting to surge up all around: power that was latent whenever orks were gathered together, and which only came to the surface when they were heading in a mass towards the enemy. This was the true energy of the Waaagh!, the connection that brought a warband together and transformed it from a rough collection of mobs and individual vehicles into a bellowing force capable of toppling entire worlds, even entire systems.

The attack was underway, and the power of the Waaagh! was his to command.

LOTZ

Captain Armenius Varrow had the beginnings, the very faintest beginnings, of a plan.

It was taking a lot of effort not to second-guess himself. This was hardly surprising, given the regular humiliation he had endured at the hands of his captors. He had lost a lot of his self-confidence, all of his swagger, and not a few teeth during his time in captivity with Da Genrul. All the same, he was from Aranuan officer stock, and while he might have shamed his family by being captured alive, Captain Armenius Varrow was not a man who would accept this fate. Men of lesser breeding might have capitulated mentally, but he had never given up.

Of course, there were those who might argue that by even answering Uzbrag's questions – especially since it had been established that Varrow was not good at deceiving the hulking xenos – he *had* given up. It was just Captain Varrow's good fortune that such naysayers were not present to further discourage him.

The orks under Da Genrul's command were certainly obeying their boss' orders. Soil was being rapidly and methodically shifted, with the same sort of haphazard efficiency that Armenius had noticed characterised so many of their endeavours. The brutes were noisy, argumentative, utterly slapdash, appeared to have little concept of danger and even less of safety, and yet they were undeniably, even terrifyingly, effective. He was uncertain whether his regiment, armed with shovels and pre-existing plans, and under the intimidating gaze of the regimental commissar, could have moved as much earth in so short a time. The orks had no plans, and very little in the way of instruction from their superiors – not to mention the fact that they occasionally stopped for a rowdy punch-up because someone had shovelled dirt into someone else's face, or stolen someone else's food, or they were all a bit bored – but still, somehow, the work was getting done.

The trenches were, as Da Genrul had intimated, only the start of what the orks were doing. Armenius could see deeper shafts running into the ground of Aranua, braced to keep them open. Crudely welded ladders disappeared into the depths, from which came the dull, repetitive sounds of tools biting into soil, mixed with grunts of effort and even the occasional raucous burst of what Armenius had realised, with some horror, was supposed to be singing.

He was on 'exercise time' again, and the horizon was starting to lighten with the dubiously welcome promise of yet another day in the orks' clutches under the punishing sun of this latitude, when the air began to shake with distant noise. He looked to the north, but could see little other than the artificial mountain of the hive city's bulk. Still, were those lights, off to the east? A veritable horde of lights? That must be where most of the rest of the orks' forces were. And although it was hard to tell at this distance, it looked to him as though they might be moving...

Heads came up, all around him. Noise died down and squabbles ceased, as every ork turned to look in the same direction. Diggers emerged from the tunnels, shovels and other earth-moving implements still clutched in their massive hands, their subterranean work temporarily set aside. A tension seemed to flow through the encampment, something that caught every ork up in its grip and held them.

For a long few moments, Armenius Varrow had the sensation that he was not in the middle of a large group of individual xenos, brought together by an affinity for warfare and violence, but surrounded by some sort of colonial organism, or perhaps a super-predator with one malignant and terrifying purpose running through every cell of its body, and those cells were orks. He had a sudden vision of what that might look like on a larger scale, if all the ork warbands across the galaxy were to come together with the same unity of purpose that he could sense in the air around him now, and was filled with unexpected gratitude for their belligerent nature and constant infighting. Armenius was a devoted servant of the God-Emperor, and he firmly believed that His light kept the Imperium whole and was what would guarantee humanity's eventual triumph over the myriad foes they faced, but there was still something sobering about the focus of these orks.

Millions of worlds and trillions of people though the Imperium contained, shielded though it was by the might of the Adeptus Astartes, the Adepta Sororitas and the Astra Militarum, and guided by the wisdom of the Master of Mankind though it might be, it was hard to see how his species could triumph if every ork forgot about internecine disagreements and came for them.

Those thoughts passed through Armenius Varrow's mind in a matter of moments, while the orks around him were still paying attention to whatever their comrades - or rivals, or whatever the appropriate term was - were doing in the north-east. As the surge of fear and disgust began to fade, or at least subsided back down to what had become normal levels for him, he realised that he had the opportunity he had been waiting for. None of the orks were paying attention to him! They were hardly reliable watch-canids most of the time, but there were so Throne-damned many of them that it had previously been impossible to escape every red, beady eye, even for a moment. Now, however, the psychic pull towards the violence that their kin were about to unleash might serve him well, if he was smart and quick.

Being smart and quick was by no means as easy for him as it had once been, given the privation to which he had been subjected, but Armenius was still able to propel his tired limbs towards a trench entrance and stumble down rough-cut steps into the earthworks. The ground was hard-packed under his feet – the result of being repeatedly trodden down by orks twice his weight or more – and he was able to hurry along at a comparatively swift pace towards the next target for his impromptu plan.

A shaft entrance.

It was deep, and it was dark, and he had no means to light his way, but Armenius knew better than to look a gift grox in the mouth. He could already hear orkish voices starting to grunt and grumble again above him, as whatever partial trance they had been in began to release them again. He might not get an opportunity like this again, and he really would be failing in his duty as a Golden Lion if he let it slip through his fingers. With any luck, he could evade the orks as they came back down: even if he were caught, he told himself guiltily, there was no indication that the xenos would inflict any particularly damaging punishment on him. He would simply be hauled back to Genrul Uzbrag once more.

The thought of that humiliation spurred him on, and he half-climbed, half-slid down the ladder into the depths below. He had seen how fast the orks worked, and there was every possibility that they would have already unearthed one of the various outflows or service tunnels that would be snaking out from the city. He could not stop them from finding them, nor could he stop them from entering them, but perhaps he could carry a warning.

Armenius was not overly familiar with the layout or structure of the Davidian underhive – such a place had been far beneath him, both literally and figuratively, when he had lived in the lower spire as a child of an officer family, before his life in service began – but he would have a far better hope of understanding signs and markings than the orks would. While they blundered around the maze-like structures of old tunnels and abandoned, half-demolished hab-domes which formed the meandering, largely lawless, and very nearly stable foundations of Davidia Hive, Captain Armenius Varrow would be heading towards help, straight as a las-bolt. He would bring word of the vile xenos' intentions, contribute to saving the hive from their subterranean treachery, and regain his honour.

Of course, even if Da Genrul's plan was foiled, that did not mean that the enormous offensive rumbling into action in the north would not endanger the hive as well, but Armenius could do nothing about that. If he had to put money on which was more dangerous – Genrul Uzbrag leading an unseen invasion through the tunnels, or an unknown ork at the head of an extremely obvious charge straight at the hive's main walls – he would be backing Da Genrul every time. The beast was a foul piece of work, but he had, in an odd way, earned Armenius' respect. Not *actual* respect, he hastily added to himself, nothing that meant the ork deserved anything less than utter annihilation by any means necessary or available, but the respect you might show a mighty carnosaur which had been brought to bay on a grav-bike hunt. You did not have to like something, or view it as anything other than a monstrosity, to appreciate the danger it posed.

He reached the bottom of the ladder, and cursed for a moment that he had not remembered to get his bearings before entering this stygian darkness, but he was still fairly sure that the city lay more to his right than to his left, in relation to the line of the trench from which he had descended. He blundered forwards, one arm raised above and in front of his face to prevent himself from walking head first into a bracing strut or similar obstruction, although most orks were at least his height, if not larger. Any tunnel down which they could walk would almost certainly be suitable for him as well.

More likely to bring him to his knees, he thought with grim humour, was the thick stench of the brutes that filled the unmoving air: although it was not, he had to admit, as foul a smell as he would have thought before he had spent time in the company of orks. Their odour was bitter and earthy more than anything else, albeit often flavoured with the chemical tang of their ballistic propellants, or engine grease, or something else's blood. However, overtly unpleasant or not, it was still strange and alien, and powerful enough that it lodged in his throat and made him feel as though some amorphous, barely corporeal being was making a spirited, if unsuccessful, attempt to strangle him.

He swallowed, and pushed onwards. Onwards and downwards, that was the key. If only he had been able to bring a lumen with him! But he was lucky to still have both his boots, let alone a light. He would simply have to make do with what he had, and pray to the Emperor that he found any breakthrough the orks might have unwittingly made into the underhive - and hopefully not by simply stepping unsighted into a hole and plummeting to his death or serious injury - before any returning orks found him in turn.

His raised hand encountered earth. Particles of it came away at his touch and fell into his upturned sleeve. He grunted in irritation and shook them out again, then felt upwards and ahead more cautiously. The last thing he wanted to do was to accidentally cause a cave-in: the thought of suddenly being buried beneath tons and tons of soft earth, unable to move and choking to death on the soil of his home planet, was a viscerally unpleasant one.

There was no mistake, even under the questing fingers of a more careful investigation. The downward-sloping tunnel along which he was travelling was closing in above him and, he found as he stretched his arms out, on either side. He could still make progress, but his headroom had disappeared. Soon, he was having to stoop a little. What was this? An ork might be able to fit into this space, but it would be a struggle, and why would they not have dug this section out to the dimensions further back, and further up?

Then he caught sight of something ahead in the blackness; or more accurately, he caught sight of something which made the blackness less black. Catching sight of something at all was noteworthy in and of itself.

Light.

And not just light. As he crept forwards, his mouth abruptly dry with nerves at the thought of being discovered, Armenius heard something over the hiss of his own breath, the faint rasp of the remnants of his clothes rubbing together as he moved, and the thunder of his heart in his ears. There were voices down here, but these were no ork voices, deep and guttural.

These were higher-pitched: harsh and choppy, yes, and certainly far from melodic or pleasing to the ear, but they lacked the depth or timbre of the warriors to whose presence he had become accustomed.

Gretchin. It had to be gretchin.

He had seen the little devils around, of course, but none of them – other than the thing inside the machine that carried his hated cage – dared approach too close to Da Genrul, and so Armenius had not had any real contact with them. They were sly-looking little beasts, with long and nimble fingers that seemed equally suited to theft or throttling. Every Militarum officer knew about gretchin, of course: they were poorly armed and had little in the way of armour, their marksmanship was only average and their general morale was considerably worse, but there were usually so Throne-damned *many* of the things that you could not simply ignore them. The orks would throw them ahead of the main advance to soak up gunfire and wear you down, before their more elite units[8] would steamroller right over their corpses to sweep away your half-exhausted troops who were now low on ammunition.

Armenius felt a momentary flash of pride as he remembered rank upon rank of the glorious Golden Lions, resplendent in their gold-trimmed crimson flak armour, each soldier bearing an M35 M-Galaxy Short-pattern lasgun, so very different from the ragged mobs of wretched gretchin he had seen driven into battle by whip-wielding overseers. Every one of Armenius' troops would give their life in service to the Golden Throne – officers like him, or the regimental commissar, would ensure that one way or the other. The Space Marines might be the las-scalpel with which the Imperium excised the canker of xenos or heretic incursions from the galaxy, but the Astra Militarum were the grist to the mill of conquest. It was through their glorious sacrifice that the Imperium's borders were protected, and its enemies worn down.

Now it seemed that there were a few more enemies in front of him, and Armenius had no intention of letting his life get ground between the millstones just yet.

The faint glimmer of stolen light from ahead of him illuminated a pickaxe that someone had carelessly left leaning against the tunnel wall. He picked it up, his fingers closing around the metal haft. It was heavy, but not unmanageable, even in his weakened state. It had to be a gretchin tool: an ork could probably shift more soil by just digging its fingers into the wall and making a fist. Presumably the smaller caste had been sent in to open up the first tunnels, and the orks followed along behind to widen them. That suited Armenius just fine. He stood little chance of troubling an ork with this tool – in his current condition, he would likely struggle even if he had his power sword in hand – but gretchin were small, and weaker than him, and easily spooked.

He crept towards the light and the sound of voices, both hands wrapped around the pick's comforting weight. He did not need to make an effort to move quietly, since the soil beneath his feet muffled any sound of movement, and his quarry was somewhat raucous.

---

[8] Anything that wasn't a gretchin.

He listened, concentrating. They were not far around the tunnel's next bend, so far as he could tell. All gretchin sounded alike to human ears, of course, but the time Armenius had spent around their masters had given him some unwanted insight into the ways in which the species' voices were subtly different. He was fairly sure he could pick out four different ones, layered over each other in the boisterous, squabbling manner that was the nature of orks and their kin. Four was a challenge, he thought, but as his grandfather used to say, *a Varrow never shirks a challenge.*

Armenius got as close to the tunnel bend as he could without giving himself away. There was a metallic clanging, as though tools had struck something made of a similar substance. He took a deep breath, and leaped into action for the first time in weeks.

To be entirely accurate, it was not a leap at all, since the headroom was not sufficient for anything like that. He realised even as he charged that the natural motion of a pickaxe, starting behind his own shoulder and brought forwards and down in an arc, was not going to work: he would hit the ceiling, and get his weapon stuck at best, and bring it down upon himself at worst. A Varrow always knew when to adapt, however, so he kept the pick down at his side, then brought it diagonally up and across his body.

The metal point embedded itself in the first head that turned towards him. The gretchin did not even have time to squeal in shock or terror as the tool punched up through its long jaw and drove through its skull into the brain, killing it instantly. It slumped, and its weight dragged the pick downwards. Struggling against it with muscles that had not been properly used in too long, Armenius found himself exposed and vulnerable, not to mention blinded as three more pairs of eyes with head torches blazing out above them turned towards him. He froze for a second, waiting for the sharp pain that would signify the end of his life as he was overwhelmed by the foul creatures, and his noble blood was spilled beneath Aranua's surface.

Instead, all three gretchin screamed in terror, and turned to run.

'Oh no you don't!' Armenius shouted gleefully, the sight of a fleeing foe catalysing his transformation from hopeless prisoner to avenging angel. He reached out and grabbed one by the ear, hurling it against the wall, then kicked the legs out from beneath a second. He managed to haul the pick free and dropped to one knee to hurl it two-handed at the last as it ran, and the agonised cry and suddenly falling light as it struck home indicated that he had found his mark.

That just left him with two of the little xenos to deal with, albeit now without the assistance of a weapon.

One jumped at him with a scream, its clawed fingers reaching for his eyes, and apparently now sunk so far into terror that it had come out the other side into the place where the drive to kill the thing that caused the fear outweighed the fear itself. Armenius swatted it aside into the tunnel wall, drove his knee into the jaw of the one that had been behind it – the things only came up to his breastbone, so it was not so great a feat of athleticism as it might have been – and felt something in his enemy's skull fracture, then grabbed the one he had just knocked aside and flung it again, this time bodily into its companion. They both went down in a hissing tangle of limbs, like an overlarge and intoxicated green spider, and Armenius seized a shovel that one of them had let drop.

'For Aranua!' he declared joyously, and began to batter them about their heads with it.

It felt so good to be able to once again vent the Emperor's wrath on xenos scum, after so long being forced to watch their kind walking shamelessly around as though they had a right to be on His planet! Each gretchin stopped moving after the first half a dozen or so blows, but he kept at it until he was panting and exhausted, which to be fair, was not that long after.

'Hah!' he shouted, and spat on the pair of bodies, then kicked the one upon whom he had performed an impromptu lobotomy, just for good measure. 'How do you like that?' However, his victory celebrations would have to be cut short. He had come here with a plan, and it would not do to jeopardise that by being caught by an ork when he was on the verge of success. He thought he had seen, in the swaying light of the struggle...

The head torches of the two last casualties had been crushed beneath the onslaught of his righteous strikes, but the one he had killed first still had a working lumen attached to the strap that ran around its head. He pulled it off the corpse and directed the beam to the opposite side of the tunnel, then suppressed a quite un-captain-like squeal of glee.

The gretchin had found a large piece of metal, roughly on the level of the floor of their tunnel. It was slightly curved, and disappeared down into the ground and into the wall, but just where the earth wall met the floor was a raised, round shape.

This was, unless Armenius Varrow was very much mistaken, some form of outflow pipe. And that was an entry hatch.

He set to work with the shovel feverishly, hacking back the wall and exposing the hatch. He had no qualms about what he was doing: the gretchin had already found it, and their masters would surely have the wit to work out what it was. There was no stopping them from getting into the system, so he would simply have to make sure that he got into Davidia ahead of them, carrying warning of their coming.

He was panting and his hands were blistered by the time he had uncovered the hatch and made enough space for it to be swung open. When he laid his hands upon the wheel and tried to turn it, and it did not move, his heart sank. The pipe had probably been buried for centuries at least, subsumed beneath the gradually accumulating soil; there was every chance that it would have rusted solid. This was little comfort, though, since the orks would undoubtedly find a way to get in, using high-powered weapons and explosives to which Armenius did not have access. Even if they brought the tunnel down in the process, Uzbrag would know it was here, and he would command it dug out again and opened. The beast had the capacity to be relentless, and was clearly invested in his plan. No, the wheel not moving for Armenius Varrow was no guarantee of safety for the people of Davidia.

He sat back on his haunches and prayed to the Emperor. It was a simple prayer, and while it might have technically contained more than *please, Lord of Terra, let me escape here alive*, that was certainly the dominant ingredient. He had no time for anything more involved, and the glow of triumph was being clawed back down by the fear of discovery and recapture. Da Genrul would notice that he was missing soon, surely, and then those laughing, hooting beasts would come for him once more...

He leaned forwards and tried again, gritting his teeth and putting everything his body had left into the effort.

The wheel moved.

It scraped and it groaned, but Emperor be praised, it moved! Armenius cackled with glee as he spun it, until finally something *clicked* and he was able to lift it up, pressing it back and away from him on protesting hinges to reveal an even deeper darkness beneath. It smelled awful – some form of effluent runoff, he presumed – but it was sweet, sweet freedom compared to the confines of his cage, bumping around on the back of that fiendish machine.

Armenius tied the headtorch around his skull and quickly scanned the dead gretchin bodies. The first one he had killed proved to have a simple firearm tucked into its belt, which it had never had time to even think about drawing thanks to the noble swiftness of his attack. It looked even cruder than a stub gun such as might be used by a downhive scummer, but Armenius was – with any luck – about to head into realms where such insalubrious specimens of humanity might lurk. Doing so without a firearm of any sort would be unwise; this piece of xenos hardware would serve for now, until he could get his hands on something more reliable. He knew that the Emperor would understand.

He took the shovel as well, since it would serve equally well as a bludgeon and a tool if he ran across any obstructions. Then, as well prepared as he could hope to be, Captain Armenius Varrow climbed into the pipe and closed the hatch again over his head.

It was down to him to save Davidia.

Da Genrul sighed. 'Nah, look, ya can't all be lootenants. How many lootenants do ya fink we zoggin' need? A major's more important. None of ya wanna be a major?'

The assembled orks shook their heads. Uzbrag narrowed his eyes.

'Is dis because "lootenants" has got da word "loot" in it?'

It was not often that burly ork nobs looked embarrassed, but this was one of those occasions.

'Mork's teef, da state of ya,' Da Genrul groaned. 'Dis is war, ladz, an' war is a serious bizness!' He hesitated. 'Well, it's zoggin' good fun most of da time, but dat's only because we do it proppa, unlike da rest of da boyz, who–'

He whirled around, his greatcoat flaring, and raised his double shoota, finger tightening on the trigger and ready to unleash high-explosive death at whichever fool was creeping up behind him. Then he grunted in recognition, and lowered his weapon again as a shadowy shape detached itself from the wall of his kommand bunker.

'Kaptin,' Uzbrag said, his tone just short of a remonstration, because while being cunning and sneaky was a good thing for a Blood Axe kommando, there was such a thing as trying to be *too* cunning and sneaky. 'Any news?'

'Da humie's gone,' Kaptin Skulsnik reported, saluting. His voice was low and unobtrusive, very different to most orks.

'About time,' Uzbrag said. 'I was beginnin' to fink we'd have to point it out to him. Did he kill anyone on da way?'

Skulsnik shook his head. 'Only some grots.'

'Bet he finks he's da big nob right now, don't he?' Da Genrul chuckled. 'Yer ladz tailin' him?'

'Yes, genrul. Waited until he was froo da hole, den went after him. He never even knew dey were followin.' I'm gonna go catch 'em up, an' we'll mark da way into da city for ya.'

'Good,' Uzbrag said, grinning. Let Mag Dedfist batter his head against the walls! Da Genrul had his own way of breaching the defences, unwittingly guided by one of the city's own.

He turned to his excessive number of lootenants, and spread his arms wide. 'Get da ladz togevva. We're goin' in.'

LOTZ

Sentra LaSteel had no idea what communication, if any, had passed between Sanavar Deltis and the civilian crew of the road gate. All she knew was that when *Golden Thunder* turned the corner to approach it with the remaining mechanised might of the Aranuan 25th behind her, the massive metal plates were grinding apart to allow them egress. One way or the other, Deltis had been as good as his word.

'Reckon we should get the cogboy a can of oil to say thanks?' Kat Pallas asked over the tank's internal vox, which was the only way Sentra, from her position in the turret cupola, was going to hear her. Pallas was the driver, and under her expert guidance *Golden Thunder* was practically as nimble and responsive as any Scout Salamander.

'Let's see if we make it through this alive, first,' Gravers replied, traversing the battle cannon a few degrees. He had checked its functionality before they had set off, but he always made another quick check once they were in motion. It was a personal superstition to which Sentra did not object, since it was better to find a fault before an engagement with the enemy than during.

'Positive as always, eh, Gravers?' said Two Hands, who was jointly responsible for both loading the battle cannon and operating the forward-facing, hull-mounted lascannon. Sentra had no idea why Loader Tayne was called 'Two Hands' – he indeed had two hands, both flesh and blood rather than bionic, and both apparently his from birth, so there seemed nothing remarkable there – and he'd already been in possession of the nickname when he had joined her crew. No one on her crew had ever asked, he had never explained, and so he was simply Two Hands to everyone. If someone from another crew expressed curiosity, Sentra tried to change the subject to avoid revealing that she had no idea why one of the people in whose charge she regularly placed her well-being had a nickname she could not explain.

'Are you expecting to live through this, then?' Xanin asked. He was one of the two sponson gunners, the most junior role on the tank.

'As the Emperor wills,' Two Hands said calmly. 'I'd like to blow holes in a couple of these xenos bastards before I'm done, but only He knows whether I'll get my wish.'

'Commander,' Greel's voice said into Sentra's ear over the vox. *'You're*

aware that we're going to be running out into fire from our own side? Some of the city's guns are shelling the ork column.'

'I know,' Sentra replied. 'For all the good it will do them. The orks are too mobile for the big guns to do much, curse their eyes. If we're out there as well, though, not only can we take them down one on one, but we might also be able to bunch them up or limit their manoeuvrability so the artillery can land more hits.'

'We know the orks aren't fools, commander, and nor will they hang back and engage us at range. They'll head straight for us.'

'Which is why we're bringing Flash,' Sentra said with a smile, looking over her shoulder at where Flash Harvax's three Hellhounds were rumbling along in a line. Flash himself was not visible: crewing a Hellhound was dangerous enough as it was, given the truly terrifying amount of highly volatile promethium present in the vehicle to power its turret-mounted inferno cannon. Poking one's head out of the turret while jets of burning liquid were gouting around changed the designation from 'dangerous' to 'suicidal,' and while Harvax was a man who seemed to have been behind the door when fear was handed out, he was a little too fond of his own face to have any desire for it to be burned off by a malfunction, misfire, or particularly strong gust of wind.

'I wasn't aware that we were capable of stopping him from coming.'

'We weren't, but you know what I mean,' Sentra admitted. She cast a knowing glance over at *Lion's Fury*, the turret of which was also firmly locked down. Darrus Greel was a cautious man, and preferred being surrounded by armour plating. For her part, Sentra would duck inside if the going got too hot and the air too full of shots, but she preferred to rely on the evidence of her own eyes as well as her auspexes when determining the next course of action for her engine of war, and those that followed it.

The road gate was coming up. Sentra took a deep breath through her respirator, tasting the rubber and cloth and plastek, and held it as they crossed the threshold. She had worn the respirator out of habit ever since the action against the so-called Plague Children on Hammus XIII, a heretic uprising that had been unquestionably foul, but thankfully brought to battle and eradicated before it had got too large or powerful. Her previous loader, Amman Duznik, had died choking on his own blood after failing to fasten his breathing equipment properly when the hull had been pierced. Sentra's first demand of Two Hands had been that he demonstrate to her that he could fasten a respirator securely with his eyes shut.

Orks had no known history of using biological weapons - hateful brutes although they were, there was at least a certain honesty about the way in which they made war - but in some strange way, Sentra would have felt more naked going into battle without her respirator than if she had lacked her uniform. Gravers was not the only one who had a personal superstition, rooted in practicality though they both might have been.

'Lights,' she commanded, and the tank's powerful lumens snapped to life, spearing out through the blackness to illuminate the gritty earth and occasional tenacious shrub that constituted the landscape for miles around Davidia Hive. Sentra could *feel* the hulking presence of the hive directly behind her, a gigantic shadow looming into the sky that was simply too large to think about directly. She had seen bigger mountains in her travels across the galaxy, but none that stood so alone, rising up sheer from the ground without slope or foothills. And Davidia Hive was just one of innumerable hive cities across innumerable worlds in the Imperium: masterworks of engineering, and constructed not for some galaxy-spanning great purpose, but simply to accommodate the people that inhabited the God-Emperor's domain.

Sentra realised, once again, how humanity was destined to rule the galaxy. What other species could match their industry, their creativity, the sheer size and scope of their achievements? No matter the outcome of this battle, whether or not she and her crew survived, she could take comfort from the knowledge that the xenos aggressors would never truly triumph.

She keyed her headset to broadcast to all the vehicles with her. The time for any sort of vox silence was past: the brass would learn of their sortie soon anyway, and communication was more important than secrecy now they were outside the walls.

'Heads up and look alive, everyone, they'll be on us within moments,' she declared. The night erupted into light and noise not far to the north, as shells fired from above began to detonate, hopefully taking some of the orks with them. 'There's no space or time for fancy tactics, and you all know how to do what you do best. Keep them at distance if you can, keep out of Flash's way if you can't, and give 'em hell!'

A chorus of cheers answered her, as the various tank commanders and their crews responded to her with vigour. Sentra raised the macro-binocs to her eyes and peered through the darkness, trying to make out signs of the enemy – the lights were more so that Pallas had some idea of what terrain she was driving through. Robust and powerful though a Leman Russ might be, it would still be little use against the Imperium's foes if it ended up on its side because the driver had steered it into an unseen ravine.

It was hard to make anything out, what with the brilliant flashes of ordnance that were even fiercer through her night-vision scope, but in the gaps between detonations Sentra thought she could just make out a single vehicle, jinking and swerving through the low dunes. She frowned in concentration, and... yes! That was no after-image of her own side's weaponry she could see, but the distinct glow of a crude-but-powerful ork propulsion system. It looked to be a trike of some sort, as ramshackle as anything she had seen in the orks' forces.

'Gunner, target, forty degrees,' she said. The turret began to traverse beneath her, as Gravers set his auspex to the hunt.

'Throne, it's moving,' her gunner muttered a moment later. 'Target acquired, gun laid. Loader, high-ex.'

There was a *thunk* as Two Hands cycled the correct autoloader. 'High-ex up!'

'Firing.'

Sentra closed her eyes as the battle cannon spoke, to prevent herself being blinded by the flare in her macro-binocs. The noise of the discharge was muffled by her responsive headset, which was all that stood between her and permanent, profound deafness, but it was still loud, not to mention the shudder of it reverberating through her bones.

'Round out,' Gravers intoned.

'Miss,' Sentra reported. Her macro-binocs had picked the ork vehicle up again, some way past where dirt was still pattering back down in the aftermath of Gravers' shot. 'Fire again.'

'Target acquired,' Gravers replied. 'Probably. Gun laid. Loader, high-ex.'

'High-ex up!'

'Firing.'

Golden Thunder lived up to her name again, and once more spat devastation out into the night. And once again missed, Sentra noted with rising anger, as another explosion failed to even clip the elusive, fast-approaching ork vehicle.

'Round out. Sorry, commander,' Gravers said. 'Whatever's steering that thing is either a genius, or suffering some sort of seizure.'

'Well, we are about to be in a target-rich environment,' Sentra declared, as more and more blurs of movement appeared in her sights. The rest of the ork convoy had been lagging behind this front runner, but they were visible now, and by the Emperor and all the primarchs, there were a lot of them. Few, if any, would be a match for a single vehicle in her thrown-together squadron one on one, but orks never came one on one. They came in a mass, combining reckless speed with disproportionate firepower. You might total one with a single shot, but there would be two more behind it, and three more behind those. Before you had managed to take them all out, their guns would have wrecked something important with either some sort of physics-defying blast, or a simple hail of high-calibre bullets too ferocious for even cast plasteel to resist.

The rest of her vehicles opened up. For a moment, Sentra thought they had now all realised what Gravers had been firing at, but the shots were looping far longer: they were targeting the main group of xenos vehicles, leaving the trike unmolested. She wasted a second considering whether she should order it destroyed as some sort of object lesson, but decided against it. This was not an official operation, after all, and her authority over these dregs and remnants came more from seniority and respect than any true command structure. If the trike continued to evade Gravers and got close enough to be a menace, Flash's Hellhounds would incinerate it.

Her vox crackled, followed by the warning chime of a direct command override. This was not a call that she could choose to ignore.

'LaSteel, what in the name of Terra are you doing?!'

It was Colonel Sudliff himself. Sentra was almost impressed. She had not expected him to be paying such close attention to ongoing developments on the ground, let alone know her name.

'Engaging the enemy, sir!' she called. And then, because there was a principle at stake, 'Gunner, target thirty degrees.' The trike was still zigzagging, but it appeared to have changed overall course to head towards *Golden Thunder*. That suited Sentra just fine. The turret ground back a little, still doing its best to track the trike, but Colonel Sudliff was not satisfied with her reply.

'You had no such orders! Withdraw to the city at once!'

'With respect, sir,' Sentra said, as Gravers informed Two Hands that nothing in the horde they were facing would require armour penetration, and so he should continue to load high-explosive unless specifically informed otherwise, 'you can court-martial me if I make it back alive.'

'For the Emperor's sake, LaSteel! I have no interest in court-martialling anyone, I just want my tank crews alive for when we need you!'

'You need us now, sir!' Sentra insisted doggedly. 'We can do more good here and now than we can cooped up behind the walls!' The battle cannon roared, but it only took a glance to confirm that it had missed once again. Not that she could truly fault Gravers for it: the trike was hard enough to keep in her sights from second to second with her macro-binocs, let alone trying to draw an accurate bead on it with a weapon. The orks were firing back now, their mismatched and somewhat haphazard weaponry roaring gleefully away, almost loud enough to drown out the whoops and cheers of the drivers, gunners, and passengers.

'LaSteel, since you have clearly abandoned all respect for authority, it appears I must appeal to your glory-hunting nature,' the colonel's voice said in her ear, acid dripping from his tone. *'The main orkish rabble is currently launching an offensive against the hive's eastern boundaries. I had intended to order the armour out to take them in the flank and give them something to think about, rather than let them bring their full force against the walls. However, since you have chosen to engage in this* skirmish *instead of waiting for deployment orders, I can do no such thing. If you would* care *to disengage and actually contribute to the defence of the hive, rather than attempting to drown your own feelings of inadequacy in cordite and promethium fumes where you are, I do not believe you will have trouble in locating the conflict.'*

The connection went dead as *Golden Thunder*'s battle cannon thumped once more, and the lascannon stabbed a lance of light out with a similar lack of effect. Colonel Sudliff had said his piece, and he had no interest in further communication. Sentra's gut roiled with fury and fear. Fury, because how dare he accuse her of hunting glory when she was only trying to fight the Imperium's enemies, exactly as she was supposed to? Fear, because she had thought that she was discharging her duty in an honourable manner – far more so than she could have expected when stuck inside Davidia – but now she had learned that a major battle was about to commence, and she was not able to be present. What if the lack of the 25th's armoured units was the telling factor that allowed the orks to break the hive's walls? She knew the likelihood of that was low, given the sheer amount of the xenos present compared to the low number of tanks, but nonetheless–

'Incoming!' Greel yelled over the vox, and Sentra jerked in shock as something swooped down out of the blackness above her with a whirr of rotor blades, then blasted off a bunch of explosive rockets that screamed through the air and detonated somewhere behind her. She had not realised that the orks had flyers with them!

'Bring the bastards down!' she screamed over the vox, slapping off the safety of her storm bolter and elevating the twin barrels. The orks were flying without lights – of course – but now she was looking for them instead of concentrating on the ground force, they were easy enough to make out. She opened fire, sending a double line of bolt-shells roaring upwards even as *Golden Thunder*'s battle cannon boomed out again. The heavy bolters in the sponsons were opening fire as well, now the orkish vehicles were coming closer, but her pintle-mounted weapon was the only thing they had with any real degree of fire upwards. What she would give for a Hydra or two! But their anti-aircraft capability was gone, lost in the battle of the Sacracian Heights, and so it was only weapons like hers that stood a chance of bringing their flying enemies down.

No air support, no footslogger backup, none of those Throne-cursed Gargants. It's the perfect opportunity. Those had been her words to Greel, but they had not been accurate. The orks might not have their over-boosted aircraft overhead, but they had air support of a sort. Sentra scored a hit, the mass-reactive round detonating on impact and tearing the flimsy ork vehicle nearly in half, and she let out a cry of savage triumph as it fell in flames, but her storm bolter alone was not going to be enough.

The chatter of other pintle weapons joined hers, as some of her fellow officers risked venturing beyond the armoured shells of their vehicles to help her swat the xenos from the skies. These rotor-bladed flyers lacked anything much in the way of armour, but in the manner typical of orks they punched far above their weight: one unleashed a volley of its rockets, which struck home almost certainly more by luck than judgement, and the Demolisher *Glorious Storm* detonated with concussive force. Sentra counter-rotated the cupola, leaving Gravers to find his own targets, and fired at the veteran tank's killer. It dodged her shots, but Darrus Greel was luckier: her second-in-command stitched fire down the flying machine's flank, and it too began to fall from the sky.

Sentra instinctively tracked its descent to see where it was going to land, and a shock of horror ran through her like a physical force.

'Oh no...' she whispered.

The wrecked ork flyer crashed down onto *Ash Kicker*, the second of Flash Harvax's Hellhounds, and its remaining rockets went up. A moment later, the Hellhound did too.

It was like an early sunrise, if the sun were close enough to scorch your eyebrows off. Sentra jerked backwards instinctively, jarring her spine against the far side of the turret, as furious heat washed over her, flash-drying the sweat on her skin and burning the air out of her mouth. *Smoke Eater* was gunning along in front and escaped the blast, but *Flame Rider*, following along in its comrades' wake, was inside the radius before it could take evasive action. For a moment Sentra clung to the hope that it might be sturdy enough to weather the hit and keep going, but it was not to be: before the first spasm of *Ash Kicker*'s death throes had even finished, *Flame Rider* went up as well, in another titanic explosion that engulfed a Scylla light tank and took that with it.

Sentra looked over at Greel. Her sergeant was open-mouthed with horror at the unintended consequences of his actions, and frozen in place with his hands still locked on his pintle-mounted storm bolter, the weapon idle in his grasp.

'Commander!'

That was Xanin, yelling over the vox-net. Sentra turned away from the blazing wreckage and her stunned subordinate, just in time to duck as *Golden Thunder*'s hull rang with the impact of heavy ballistics.

It was that Throne-damned trike! She got a brief glimpse of it roaring past, still unscratched by gunfire, and now it was between her and her colleagues the sponson weapon couldn't target it for fear of hitting their own. The massive ork perched on the back of it seemed to be laughing at her.

Then it gestured with one arm, and *something* flew out to impale Sergeant Darrus Greel, commander of *Lion's Fury*.

'No!' Sentra screamed, in terror and fury. Greel's eyes went wide, wide enough for her to see the whites, even through the darkness and across the distance between the two of them, and then a cable snapped taut and he was plucked from his turret. His body skidded across the ground, ricocheting off *Death Knell*'s tracks with bone-snapping force, and then he was gone.

And then the rest of the orks were on them.

At point-blank range, even the orks' erratic driving styles could not save them all: battle cannons might not be able to traverse low enough to hit a target directly in front of the vehicle on which they were mounted, but hull and sponson weapons had far easier kills to make. The night was lit up again as ork vehicles blew apart or went up in flames, but there were so many of them, *so* many of them, and only *Smoke Eater* remained to bathe them in burning promethium.

The left-side sponson heavy bolter exploded as something potent landed a hit, and *Golden Thunder* rocked on its tracks, coughing to a halt. Sentra spun the cupola around, hoping to at least partially cover them from that side, closing her ears to screams below that might have been panic or might have been pain, and were probably both. A larger vehicle roared up, a wheeled troop transport. *No footslogger backup,* Sentra thought desperately, firing the storm bolter, but although she cut down two of the hulking orks crammed into the machine, her firepower was not enough. The rest leaped across the gap, or tried to: three fell short, clawing vainly at the air and the Leman Russ' side, and at least one went under the wheels of its own machine. Those remaining, perhaps half a dozen of them, made the jump, and their boots thudded down onto her tank.

The closest one raised a massive two-handed cleaver above its head, and swung it down at her with a roar of rage.

Sentra had already drawn her sword. It was an antique power weapon, presented to her by Major Saras in honour of her actions in an engagement against the aeldari two decades ago, when *Golden Thunder* had loosed the shot that brought down a Wraithknight. She activated the power field with a flick of her thumb, and raised it to block the blow.

In terms of sheer strength, she was utterly outmatched. The ork was taller than any unenhanced human she had ever seen, and far broader. However, not even brute strength could always be a match for technology.

The crackling edge of her blade sheared straight through the heavy metal head of the cleaver, sending half of it clattering away over the tank's hull behind her, and the rest swiping harmlessly down past her nose as the ork's swing did not encounter the resistance it was expecting. The ork itself made a noise that was hard to interpret as anything other than dull-witted surprise, right before Sentra cut it off at the knees.

Muscle, sinew, and bone – even as sturdy as that which belonged to an ork – provided no more resistance to her sword's disruptor field than metal had, and her vicious swipe ended with dark blood spattering across *Golden Thunder*'s armour plates, and the ork toppling sideways with its lower limbs abruptly truncated.

Sentra did not see the next blow until it was too late. It was a blunt impact that caught her under her upraised arm and lifted her bodily out of the cupola, and the sharp pain that accompanied it suggested that it had cracked a rib or two in the process. She slid across *Golden Thunder*'s hull, her own desperate grabs no more effective than the orks' had been, and fell.

She managed to avoid spitting herself on her sword, but the impact jarred every bone in her body. She was on the opposite side of the tank to where the failed boarders had landed, but that was of little comfort to her. She scrambled to her feet, wincing and cursing, and looked up.

Guffawing orks primed their club-like grenades, and dropped them into the hatch out of which she had just been forcibly removed before she could unholster her bolt pistol and even make an attempt at shooting them down. The detonations within were near instantaneous. There was no chance that any of her crew would have survived if even one of the grenades had gone off, let alone three or four.

Sentra LaSteel gritted her teeth, fumbled for her sidearm, and prepared to sell her life as dearly as possible.

The rapidly approaching roar of an untuned engine grabbed her attention. She turned to her right just in time to see a red-painted bumper, across which was stretched a gibbering gretchin lashed in place with chains, and then the world was dark and spiky, and went away completely.

LOTZ

Zagnob Thundaskuzz bellowed with laughter, and reeled his snagga klaw back in. The humie that had been on the other end of the line was long gone, jarred free by one too many impacts, although it had been looking far from healthy even before that. Humies were so frail! One good hit would usually do for them, and if you chopped anything sizeable off them then they just keeled over and bled to death, instead of looking around for a spare like an ork would.

He fired his boomstikk at the nearest humie vehicle, but its armour was up to the job. Zagnob supposed it made sense that humies would surround themselves with armour given they were so breakable themselves, but it still wasn't much fun. He clapped Duffrak on the shoulder, leaned forwards, and pointed at his intended target. 'Burn 'em out!'

'Yoo got it, boss!' Duffrak replied cheerfully, opening the throttle. The wartrike jumped with a sudden burst of speed, then the battle skewed around them as Duffrak threw the vehicle into a skid and rammed the throttle half-closed again. The jet engines, burning hot and fierce, were concentrated down into potent spear of heat that ripped along the humie tank's flank. Paint blistered, metal softened and sagged, and–

BOOM!

–ammo cooked off, yielding yet another explosion to add to the many that had already lit up the night. A few stray bits of metal from it *spanged* off the rear of the wartrike, and one or two dug into Zagnob's arm, but he had more important things to do than pay attention to minor scratches. The stricken tank was already behind him, as Duffrak expertly wrangled the controls to bring them around and get them moving again, and Zagnob took a moment to take stock.

The humies were being overwhelmed and outmanoeuvred, as was usually the case when they went up against the Kult of Speed. Oh, tanks hit hard when they hit, but the ladz knew a thing or two about steering in a way that made the enemy miss most of their shots, which was a totally different thing to dodging, because dodging implied you were scared of getting hurt. Making the other gits look silly by missing, though, that was perfectly fine orkish behaviour.

One of the trukks was obliterated by a point-blank hit from one of the big turret guns, and pieces of boy flew everywhere, but Rukknut's dragsta fired its shokk rifle as it went past, and the weapon's weird warp tek simply ripped a piece of armour the size of three orks off the tank's flank. Then Skrappit's snazzwagon skidded up, and Skrappit himself emptied the magazine of his mek speshul into the tank's exposed interior, and his grot hanger-on chucked in a flaming bottle of Mork-knew-what, and that was the end of that. The ladz hadn't even planned it, because planning was for gits and Blood Axes. This was just orks acting in perfect synchronicity, effortlessly complementing each other while also really sticking it to the humies.

Zagnob sighed as a buggy and a trakk collided head-on, and the drivers scrambled over their own machines in their eagerness to come to blows over whose fault it was that they had both stopped moving. Well, it wouldn't be a proper scrap if some orks didn't end up fighting with each other as well. If orks stopped doing that then they'd be like those blue fishboyz that made really shooty stuff for orks to steal – at least, Zagnob assumed that was the reasoning, as they certainly didn't try very hard to hold onto it when you got up close to them – and who thought everyone might want to be on their side. Apparently, you could trick them by saying you wouldn't fight them, and then they'd actually be really surprised when you *did* fight them. Zagnob had no qualms about that sort of low cunning. Anyone who believed that an ork wasn't going to fight them deserved everything they got, and while anything other than heading for the enemy straight-on might technically be cowardice – or Blood Axe thinking[9] – sometimes it was so funny that it didn't count.

'Wanna go back round for anuvver pass, boss?' Duffrak called.

Zagnob surveyed the scene, his expert speedboss eye understanding the swirling, explosion-ridden mess of mass vehicular combat with the same ease as a painboy understood what bone went where. 'Nah. Reckon these gits are pretty much done. I'm more interested in where dey came from, cos dat's wot's gonna get us inside.'

'Dere tracks ain't gonna be hard to follow!' Duffrak said eagerly, gunning the engine again, and sure enough the dirt ahead was all torn up by the myriad of humie tanks which had recently passed over it. The rest of the Kult of Speed fell in behind Zagnob's wartrike once more, leaving the pitiful and largely flaming remnants of the humie convoy in their dust. There were fewer orks than there had been, of course, but that was the way of war. The best went on to the next fight, and the ones that didn't, didn't: at least, unless the rumours were true, and when you died Gork and Mork gave you a new body and sent you back to fight again. Zagnob wasn't sure about that, because he certainly couldn't remember being anyone other than Zagnob, but that in itself was comforting, in a way. If he hadn't been anything before Zagnob, then he was unlikely to be anything after Zagnob. Being dead and stuck in your own body unable to move at all, let alone go fast, was the worst thing he could think of, so with any luck he just wouldn't even know he was dead. And if you weren't going to know you were dead, why was being dead anything to be afraid of?

---

[9] Essentially the same thing.

All the same, he wasn't in any hurry to stop being Zagnob, because being Zagnob was a lot of fun, so he was glad to see Da Red Barrun's remaining deffkoptas roaring away upwards to go and have a highly explosive conversation with the big guns that had been shelling them all. The tracks Duffrak was following were heading in more or less a straight line for the massive bulk of the humies' city wall, so the guns probably wouldn't be able to shoot at the Kult soon in any case, but a little bit of extra help never hurt.

They crested a rise and hit a firmer, more defined surface: one of the humie roads, which snaked away through the dust and bushes to... somewhere else, Zagnob had no idea where, but presumably there had been another lot of humies at the far end of it, before Waaagh! Goresnappa had come here. More importantly, however, it was a big road, which probably meant that the end of it which terminated at the humie city had room for a lot of vehicles to get in and out at once, and *that* was excellent news for the Kult of Speed.

Of course, he realised as they chicaned through a couple of bends and the base of the wall in question came into view, it would be just like the humies to have shut the gate behind themselves after they'd left.

It was a massive thing, certainly tall and broad enough to walk a couple of Stompas through side by side when fully open, if he was any judge. But it wasn't open, and Zagnob needed it to be open if he was going to get inside and find Old Morgrub's special gate, and that was a problem which was going to take more than a bit of acceleration to solve.

Zagnob *hated* problems like that.

'Wot's da plan, boss?' Duffrak called.

Zagnob grunted. It galled him, but he was going to have to do the thing he liked least.

'Slow down a bit. Let's let da uvvers catch up.'

Duffrak obediently throttled back, without making any sort of comment. As a speed freek himself, he was going against his instincts too, but he knew better than to provoke Zagnob by saying anything. A speed freek who had to slow down would be edgy and prone to lashing out, and Zagnob's snagga klaw was too sharp to trifle with.

The rest of the Kult did not take long to join them, and near the front was the exact vehicle Zagnob had hoped to see: Rukknut's shokkjump dragsta, a low-slung machine that ran half on high-grade fuel and half, from what Zagnob could work out, on a simple and stubborn refusal to accept the limitations imposed by standard physics.

'Don't fink da humies are gonna open dat for us!' he yelled across at Rukknut, who stared back at him with the impassive, blacked-out gaze of his road gogglez, which he wore to protect his eyes from hazards like flying grit and bits of dead humie. 'Need ya to shokk froo it, den open it from da uvver side! Reckon ya can do dat?'

'Sure fing, boss!' Rukknut said, grinning so widely that it looked like his head might fall off. Any dragsta driver would jump – quite literally – at the chance to show off what his machine could do, and Rukknut was no exception. Zagnob had no idea what Rukknut and his grot gunner would find on the other side of the gate, but this was his first plan for getting the zoggin' thing open. If it didn't work, he hadn't lost much: only Rukknut.

The dragsta's engine screamed as Rukknut floored the pedal, since the shokkjump only ever worked if the machine was going pretty much flat out. Zagnob watched as it pulled away, saw the spinny wotsits on the back begin to rotate faster and faster, saw the blue lightning begin to crackle and sizzle around the rotating orbs, saw the guns on either side of the gate open up in a fruitless attempt to score a hit on the vehicle racing towards them, saw Rukknut raise his hand and then slam it down on his dashboard just before the dragsta reached the gate–

KRUMP!

'It weren't meant to do dat, was it?' Duffrak asked dubiously, as the dragsta abruptly became both the widest and the shortest vehicle outside the walls, and the rest of the Kult of Speed cheered lustily in the manner of orks who had just seen a spectacular death inflicted on someone who wasn't them.

'Nah,' Zagnob grunted. That was the problem with fancy mekboy stuff. If it worked, it worked really well, but if it didn't work when you needed it to, you were rarely in a position to be able to go back to the mek in question afterwards and have words with him about how many teef you'd paid him for the work, and whether he'd like to keep any of the ones currently gracing his own gob.

'We gonna shoot our way froo, den?'

'Nah,' Zagnob repeated, with a sigh. Much as he would have loved to bear down on the massive edifice in a cloud of dust and engine fumes and blow it to smithereens with the enthusiastic application of some dakka, he doubted that approach would work any better. The entrance had the look of something that was considerably thicker than your standard humie vehicle armour. If he'd had a couple of Stompas on hand to pound it with deffkannons and supa-gatlers, that might have been a different matter, but all the walkers were on the other side of the city. It was going to take more than a few rokkits to get through this, Zagnob knew in his bones.

'Skrappit!' he bawled over the din of engines, twisting around until he laid eyes on the mek. 'Get yer wheels over here!'

Skrappit's boomdakka snazzwagon heeled over, bringing Skrappit himself alongside Zagnob. The mek grinned, and patted the multiple barrels of his mek speshul lovingly, and probably absent-mindedly. Zagnob resisted the urge to trigger his snagga klaw and knock the smug git from his gunner's perch. So what if his buggy was shootier than Zagnob's wartrike? It wasn't as fast, *and* he didn't have something capable of dragging an enemy along behind him.

'What's up, boss?'

'Need to get dat fing open,' Zagnob said, indicating the gate. 'Dere's gotta be some sorta controls on dis side, and since yoo're one of da best meks around–'

'Hang on, hang on. *One of* da best?' Skrappit repeated incredulously.

'Well, yeah,' Zagnob said, his voice as innocent as a snotling skipping through a mushroom field. 'I mean, dere's Skarbag–'

'Dat zoggin' Snakebite? He won't touch nuffin' what ain't been built by orks! He ain't gonna get ya froo humie tek!'

'Or dere's Wurznik–'

'Wurznik?!' Skrappit's eyes actually bulged with indignation. 'He ain't just unreliable, he's *shoddy!* He built da dragsta dat just wrecked itself!'

'Well, dat could've just been driver error,' Zagnob said reasonably.

'Driver error, my arse!' Skrappit barked. 'If ya told Wurznik ta get ya froo dat gate, he'd probably only make anuvver, ficker gate come across on top of da one what's already dere!'

'Sounds like a tricky job, dunnit,' Zagnob tutted. 'Ya sure yoo're up to it?'

'Humies don't know nuffink about elektrik an' dat,' Skrappit said loftily. 'Dey do all dere wirin' da same way! No imaginashun.' He slapped himself on the chest, twice. 'You get rid of da guns so I don't gotta worry about da gitz shootin' at me while I'm workin,' an' I'll have dat gate open before ya can say...' he pulled a complex-looking tool out from his belt, '...eudatrikamital polaroconverter.'

Zagnob mentally attempted the first couple of syllables a few times, and fell flat on his metaphorical face. 'Yeah, alright, square deal.' He racked the action on a boomstikk, raised his snagga klaw, and gestured for the advance.

More detailed instructions were not necessary. The Kult of Speed would drive up to the gate and would immediately and automatically shoot back at anything which dared to shoot at them. The sheer volume of firepower at Zagnob's command might not have stood a chance of punching its way through the obstacle in their path, but it would be more than sufficient to take out the fixed weapon emplacements, even with an approach to aiming that went something along the lines of pointing the gun vaguely in the right direction, pulling the trigger, and letting Gork and Mork take care of the rest. Now suitably motivated, Skrappit should have no problem in 'convincing' the gate's controls to do what he wanted, and then the way would be open for Zagnob Thundaskuzz and his convoy to race onwards, in search of the path to the stars.

'But, boss,' Skitta piped up, as the roar of engines rose up around them again, 'can you even *say* "eudatrikam–"'

Zagnob casually kicked out backwards and sent the grot head first into the fuel tank's cover. There was an audible *clang*, and Skitta slumped bonelessly to the deck.

'Shut up, Skitta.'

LOTZ

It was time for the Waaagh! to show what it could do, and it turned out that what it could do was level a truly stupendous amount of dakka at the walls of the humie city.

Mag Dedfist grinned with glee as the Mega-Gargant's gut buster belly gun boomed out yet again. The kickback from the massive weapon rocked even the mighty war machine on which it was mounted, but Gargants were built to withstand such forces. A moment later, the resulting explosion blew a chunk of wall the size of a Stompa into smithereens, and the skullkrusha mega-kannon mounted on *Gork's Hammer*'s right arm spoke in turn, further damaging the humies' rapidly weakening defences. They were right up close, pretty much point-blank range for a war machine this size, and not even recoil was going to ruin the aim by enough to count.

The city was an 'ard case, there was no doubt about it, but Mag knew that it was weakening. It didn't matter how thick your wall was: give a few Gargants a go at it, and it would fall before long. The sun was only just coming up, and Mag was already fairly sure they could be inside before the middle of the day. The humies' only chance would have been if they had enough dakka of their own to keep the Waaagh! away from their walls, but that did not appear to be the case. Oh, some of the ladz at the front had run into and over those buried explosives the humies liked to put down, and everyone behind had had a good laugh as they got blown into the air, but once one lot of boyz had gone over them, it was safe for everyone else: and besides, that was why they'd started sending grots forwards first, instead. When it came to actual kannons and the like, the city didn't have anywhere near enough for the job. They'd krumped a couple of Stompas, and a gunwagon or five, but the Gargants were protected by kustom force fields, and simply shrugged the impacts off.

Not that Mag was willing to chance it. He'd ordered the flyers in, and fighta-bommas and dakkajets had taken out most of the humies' gun emplacements in short order. The stormboyz had taken care of the rest, bounding upwards on their rokkit packs and either killing whatever humies were crewing the guns, or simply whacking a bunch of stikkbombs down the huge barrels and letting everything sort itself out. Now the humies had no way of fighting back, at least until the wall was well and properly broken down and ork and humie could come face to face.

That was what Mag was waiting for. As soon as the way was open to the interior, he would leave the Gargant's command deck and lead the charge in. In the meantime, there was no point being down on the ground and hanging around directly in front of the point being targeted by the biggest guns in the entire Waaagh!, especially given how inaccurate a lot of them were. Besides, Mag had not reached his lofty position of command without a certain amount of low cunning, despite his no-nonsense Goff approach to things, and he was well aware that any ork looking to put himself forward as another candidate for warboss might arrange for some sort of 'accident' involving heavy artillery if Mag was standing too near the breach. Mag certainly couldn't envisage any ork having the guts to challenge him directly: Thundaskuzz and Da Genrul were definitely about to back down right before Morgrub had said his piece, no question about it, or if the fight *had* gone ahead then the gits would have undoubtedly ganged up on him – so some sort of duplicitous treachery followed by, 'Oh no, Mag's dead, wot a shame, guess I'll 'ave to be da leader now,' was the only way he could see it playing out.

'Hit it again,' he growled, his eyes fixed on the widening breach in the humie walls.

'Da gut buster don't reload dat quickly, boss,' said Urlukk, the spanner that wasn't Gutzog. He flinched sideways as Mag rested the Dedfist on his shoulder.

'Den make it happen *quicker*,' he said, in a tone that brooked no argument. Urlukk nodded hurriedly, then picked up one of the speaker tubes and began bawling instructions and invectives down it in roughly equal measure.

'Nuffin' else coming at us from da humies?' Mag asked Gutzog. 'Nuffin' on da scopes?'

'Not a fing, boss,' Gutzog replied, slapping his instruments in case that made them reveal a secret which they had until that moment been keeping to themselves. 'Dey ain't comin' out from behind dere walls.'

Mag grunted thoughtfully. 'Humies are tricky gits, an' dey know better dan to just sit dere and wait for us to get at 'em. Where's dere tanks and trakks? We didn't stomp 'em all before dey ran away da last time. Surprised dey ain't done a Thundaskuzz an' come out to hit us in da flank.' He frowned. The only thing worse than an enemy doing something you didn't expect, in Mag Dedfist's mind, was an enemy *not* doing something you *did* expect. Granted, that was generally because it meant they were then going to be a sneaky git and do something you *really* didn't expect at some later point, but–

Something dark flashed past the Gargant's viewing window, and he looked up sharply. 'Wot was dat?'

'Someone fallin' off da top again?' Gutzog asked, following his gaze.

'Nah, dis was movin' upwards,' Mag growled, flexing the talons of the Dedfist (having remembered to move it off Urlukk's shoulder first). 'Besides, dere's no one out dere now.'

Clank.

'Ya sure about dat, boss?' Gutzog enquired, looking up towards the noise. 'Cos dat sounded like–'

'I know wot it sounded like!' Mag barked, striding towards the access hatch. Was this the humies' cunning ploy? Had they sent one of their own bosses, or some sort of kommando-equivalent, to try to take him out? Well, he'd like to see them try! In fact, he absolutely would: he didn't imagine the fight would last that long, but it might amuse him for a few moments. Watching a Gargant under his command utterly pulverise something the humies had built was quite gratifying, but it felt like something a Bad Moon would do. Mag Dedfist didn't take the same sort of delight in outsized guns and the destruction they wrought, no matter how impressive. This was only a stopgap until he could get up close an' personal with the enemy, so if the enemy had been obliging enough to come to *him*...

He pulled open the access hatch and found himself looking at Skabrukk, the stormboy drill boss.

'Wot da zoggin' hell are *yoo* doin' here?' Mag demanded, although at least Skabrukk's still-fuming rokkit pack explained the fast-moving shape that had gone past the viewing port. 'I told ya to go an' see wot Da Genrul's up to!'

'We did, boss!' Skabrukk said quickly, with the harried grin of an ork who could see a power klaw attached to a bad-tempered big boss in front of him and a long fall behind him, and who had no intention of finding out if his rokkit pack would save him from a combination of both. 'We went an' checked on him, just like ya said! But da git's gone!'

'Gone?' Mag repeated. 'Just him, or all his boyz as well?'

'All of 'em, boss! Dey'd dug a bunch of holes in da ground, but dere didn't seem to be anyone in 'em. Or if dere was, dey'd gone down deep. We didn't follow down far,' he admitted, sheepishly jerking a thumb towards the rokkit on his back, 'cos, well, ya know how dese fings get caught on stuff if ya ain't in da air...'

'Down deep...' Mag Dedfist muttered to himself. What was Uzbrag up to? It would be just like Da Genrul to hide from humie guns, but the vast majority of the humie attention was going to be on Mag himself, and the massive wave of orks under his command. How was hiding underground going to benefit the Blood Axe and his crafty underlings?

Unless...

'Gork's teef!' Mag bellowed in fury, as realisation dawned. 'Dat sneakin' git! He's *cheatin'!* He ain't goin' froo da walls, he's goin' *under* dem!'

'Is dat cheatin'?' Skabrukk asked, perplexed.

'Of course it's zoggin' cheatin'!' Mag roared. 'Dat's no way for an ork to behave! We go froo walls! Or over 'em, over 'em is fine if necessary. I'd even accept goin' *around* one, dependin' on how long it takes, but *under?* Dat's outrageous.'

Skabrukk wisely kept his mouth shut.

'How long has he been gone?' Mag demanded.

'Dunno exactly, boss, but it took us a bit longer dan usual to get back cos Grukk Gitstoppa's rokkit was on da blink, an' yoo was a stormboy once, ya know how important it is to maintain unit co-hee-shun...' Skabrukk tailed off in the face of Mag's glare, which imparted in a wordless yet utterly expressive manner how very much he did *not* understand the importance of that.

'Well, anyway, den it took me a bit to find out which Gargant ya was in, cos it's kinda loud down dere an' no one could hear wot I was askin' 'em–'

'Never mind, I get da picture,' Mag said in disgust. 'Zoggin' good scout *yoo* are. Never send an ork to do a grot's job, I guess. Get back out dere an' get Da Skyklaw togevva,' he continued, ignoring the look of chagrin that crossed the drill boss' face, 'and be ready to move when I give da word. I was gonna try an' make dat hole bigger, maybe get a few of da wagons in wiv us, but if Da Genrul's long gone den dere's no time to waste. He ain't gettin' to dat gate before me, ya hear?'

'I hear ya, boss!' Skabrukk replied loyally. He saluted, which garnered a dirty look from Mag, but drew attention away from how he had very nearly objected to the insinuation that he was worse than a grot. 'I'll get goin,' den, an' see ya on da ground!' He backed off, jumped into the air and fired up his rokkit pack, and corkscrewed off in a plume of choking black smoke before he could be blamed for anything.

Gork's Hammer shook again as the gut buster fired once more. Mag Dedfist barely glanced in the direction of the humie city, but slammed the hatch shut and turned to the two spanners.

'I'm goin' down dere an' I'm goin' inside. Yoo gitz coming?'

Gutzog and Urlukk looked at each other. Stomping humies sounded fun and all, but different things appealed to different orks, and what two orks who had helped build a Mega-Gargant wanted more than anything was to sit inside it and laugh their heads off while killing anything that came within a five-mile radius. What was more, each one was realising that with their former big mek gone courtesy of the Dedfist, and Mag himself about to depart, *Gork's Hammer* was going to be in need of a kommander - you know, to look after it until Mag came back - and that was not a position that could be shared.

Mag watched them for a second as their stares became glares, then growled in irritation. 'Fine. Stay up here like da zoggin' grots ya are. But if dis fing lands a shell on me while I'm down dere, an' it don't kill me, I'm comin' back ta knock both yer heads off yer necks!'

He left without waiting for a reply, clumping down the ladder that descended from the head. He passed teams of sweating boyz hauling on levers and pumping on pistons to move the massive arms and keep coolant flowing; he passed loaders ramming new shells into breeches as fast as they were kicked out, or feeding gigantic belts of oversized rounds into enormous hoppers as tall as they were; he passed grots clambering everywhere, oiling joints and adjusting bolts, greasing cogwheels and furiously shouting readings from gauges to junior spanner boyz. Then he was in the proper guts of the machine, climbing down past the closed-off section that housed the rear end of the gut buster, where shells the size of warbikes were loaded into the mighty kannon. Beneath that was the belly, where the boyz who had blagged a lift inside the enormous walker would mill about until it was time for them to pour out and overwhelm whatever had been beneath the Gargant's notice, or as a counter-offensive if enemy troops tried to force their way inside to bring it down from within.

The boyz in question in the belly of *Gork's Hammer* were Uzgul's mob and

Badzag's skarboyz. Uzgul's orks were swaggering and posturing, and definitely trying to give the impression that they were not at all intimidated by the hulking, scarred warriors with whom they were sharing the space, with their extra-large helmet horns and black-painted choppas. The skarboyz, in contrast, were pretending to ignore the new arrivals, and treating them as beneath their notice. No ork was going to stand for that for very long, no matter the situation, and Mag was certain that if he had not arrived, violence would have broken out inside the Gargant before long.

However, he had plans for violence to break out *outside* the Gargant, and he swatted one of Uzgul's lot out of his way just to get everyone's attention. It might mean risking getting a shell dropped on his head by some nob looking for quick advancement, but better that than letting a Blood Axe get to the goal first.

'All dese uvver gits are in a zoggin' rush, an' doin' all sorts of cheap stuff tryin' to get inside dat city first, when everyone knows it should be me wot gets to dis gate da skrawniez built and becomes warboss!' he announced loudly. 'So here's da plan. We open dese doors, we charge froo da hole da Gargants have just made in da wall, we kill any humie who gets in da way, an' we find dat gate before anyone else does. Got it?'

A selection of nodding horned helmets indicated that the boyz had indeed got it. That was the sort of plan that Goffs could easily understand: charge at the enemy and do them over, and sort the less important stuff out afterwards.

'Good,' Mag said. 'If any of ya sees da gate before me an' points me at it, ya can be big boss when I'm in charge. If ya get some idea about havin' Morgrub say dat *yoo're* warboss instead, I'll rip ya in half. Sound fair?'

Heads nodded again. None of them had any intention of challenging Mag Dedfist for anything right now. Getting a bit of reflected glory by making themselves useful to him, on the other hand, sounded like a good idea. And if things went well, then who knew? At some point down the line, maybe one of them might find himself in front of Mag and telling him to go for his klaw, or similar. They knew this, and Mag knew this, but Mag couldn't kill all of his potential future competitors, because that would mean killing most of the Waaagh! And besides, any warboss who didn't want a couple of big bosses around him to keep him on his toes and in top fighting condition was an insecure warboss, and probably not worth following.

'Get dose doors open, den!' Mag instructed. 'We've got humies to scrag.'

Someone – either one of Badzag's boyz or an obedient grot who had heard the order – pulled the correct lever, and the doors began to grind open. The Gargant's interior was immediately filled with dust as the choking air outside flowed in. Mag inhaled, and smelled gun smoke and rokkit propellant, the ozone afterstink of kustom mega-blastas and their ilk, and an awful lot of powdered humie building material. He lumbered into the closest he could come to a run in his mega armour, and the rest of the boyz formed up around him, their previous rivalry forgotten. All that would matter now would be who could kill more of the enemy.

They ran over broken ground: first the chewed-up dirt of the planet's surface, pocked with craters where mines had exploded or ordnance shot at the walls had fallen short, and then the rubble of the walls themselves. What had once been a thick dark crack in the city's wall was now a gaping crevasse, and the sheer amount of destruction unleashed by the Waaagh! had left a carpet of debris that extended out from the target area for a hundred yards or more. It got thicker and higher the closer to the wall Mag got, and with a lot more hanging around as particulates in the air, it was like running through gritty mist.

Other orks fell in with him: ones he recognised, such as Da Skyklaw, and ones he didn't, like a bunch of Deathskull lootas, and a big mob of boyz in Snakebite colours, all furs and squig hides. A veritable tide of grots came scuttling along in their wake as well, presumably survivors from the mine-clearing mobs.

It might seem suicidal to run headlong into the breach of a defended city, but Mag knew the business of close combat like few others. Any humies on the other side of the wall would not be pressed up against it in a position to make it a choke point: they would be further back, fearful of the bombardment that had caused this damage, and wary of the wall collapsing on them. Once there were orks inside the walls the gap would be held, and more and more would flood in like a tide. The key was to make sure that the first orks through were the toughest and roughest of the bunch, to take whatever the humies could throw at them and still stand their ground.

That was why Mag was at the front. There was no ork, either on this world or aboard any of the kroozers orbiting it, who could stand up to him. He would be first through the walls, and the entire Waaagh! would know that it was him who drove the humies back.

The gap was directly in front of him now, a black chasm of uncertainty. The weak grey half-light of the pre-dawn was being filtered out by the smoke and dust from the bombardment, so the only illumination as Mag plunged in was from the pilot lights of his skorchas. It lit up the dull grey expanse of rubble that shifted beneath his feet, and reflected back off the angular, broken surfaces on either side of him. There was no resistance here, of course. If he'd been facing orks, they would have swarmed out as soon as the walls had been breached, but that was not the humie way. Although of course, if it had been orks inside this city, they wouldn't have been cowering behind the walls in the first place...

Something blocked his path: a length of metal the width of a grot's body, perhaps a piece of rebar that had either somehow survived the onslaught of the wall around it being blown away, or that had fallen here. Mag didn't know, and didn't care. He activated the Dedfist and punched through it. It sheared and shattered under the impact, and he tramped onwards. It couldn't be much further now. Even cowardly humies could only make their walls *so* thick.

There. He sniffed, and over the dusty scent of pulverised rockcrete and the permanent chemical tang of his skorcha flames, he could just make out a new smell. Stuffy air, air which had not been moved by a natural wind for centuries, if not millennia; the scent of humie gunmetal, which was a sharper, thinner smell than the good strong stink of an ork shoota; and most prominent, humie sweat.

Humie sweat, and humie fear.

Mag grinned. The enemy knew what was coming, and they were scared. Well, he would show them why, on this occasion, they had got things exactly right.

The breach had narrowed now, even the mighty weapons of the Waaagh! having had less effect the further into the wall they had got, and it was not more than a couple of orks wide. Or, as it turned out, approximately one Mag Dedfist. He saw the glimmer of light ahead of him, and accelerated as much as he was able to.

A flash of ruby red from ahead, and then another: thin lines that burned tiny blooms of heat damage onto surfaces never intended to be exposed to the air as they struck the sides of the breach. The humies couldn't see him quite yet, but they could hear him coming.

'Hold!' a humie voice bellowed in response to the stray shots.

'WAAAAAGH!' Mag replied, and burst through the final gap into the humie city beyond.

A blizzard of las-bolts came at him as soon as he emerged, but they splashed harmlessly off his thick armour plate. Mag retaliated by triggering his skorchas and his kustom shoota at the same time, letting rip with all the firepower at his command.

The humies had set up a few defensive emplacements of sandbags, crates, and what looked like a couple of buggies without any guns – what was the point of a buggy without any guns? – in this space, which seemed to be a wide, tall roadway that followed the line of the exterior wall, with another branch running off into the city's interior a little further along. The closest barricade disintegrated under Mag's opening volley, such makeshift protection proving no match for the shells of his kustom shoota, and those defenders who escaped that fate were roasted by the flames that washed over them. Humies scattered, some burning and some simply terrified. It made no difference to Mag: he plunged into them, the Dedfist swinging and crackling with power, and cut them down.

Then the boyz behind him arrived.

Badzag's skarboyz were next, thundering through with their own raucous war cries, and heading left where Mag had gone right. None of them were a match for him in terms of size, toughness, or equipment, but there were many more of them, and the defenders they charged only managed to bring down a couple before they were overrun by the massive orks. Uzgul's mob didn't want to be outdone, and went straight ahead, into the teeth of increasingly desperate las-fire.

Mag heard the deeper coughs of heavier guns opening up, and looked across to see a bunch of humies manning larger versions of the guns that beakies carried. That was the sort of thing that might actually trouble him, so he waved his power klaw in that direction.

'Skabrukk!'

Da Skyklaw soared out of the breach and into view, skimming along the ceiling and, in at least one case, misjudging it slightly and bouncing off in a shower of sparks. However, their angle of attack was successful: the humies didn't manage to get their guns elevated in time, and the stormboyz descended on them in a hail of flame, sharp edges, and well-polished boots.

A humie ran at Mag, yelling in anger. It looked like one of their bosses, to judge by its fancy clothes – lots of gold bits, and a rack of medals like Da Genrul had made for himself – although it was not noticeably bigger than any of the others, and so still only about half his size. Its weapon was a fancy-looking long, thin-bladed choppa, which it wielded in a two-handed grip that made it at least look like it might know what to do with it. Mag found the notion of a humie trying to scrag him so entertaining that he decided not to roast this enemy as it closed with him: after all, humies who actually *wanted* to fight were a rare bunch, and the tendency should probably be encouraged. He set his shoulders, flexed the talons of the Dedfist, and waited.

The power field on the humie's choppa activated just as it made its first swing, either because it had been trying to take him by surprise, or because it had only just remembered to turn it on. It made no difference, since Mag easily knocked the blow aside with his power klaw, nearly tearing the weapon from the humie's grasp. Many of its kind would have backed away at that point, overawed by his sheer strength, but this one recovered itself and came at him once more, its face screwed up with concentration.

'Good on ya,' Mag told it conversationally, parrying its attacks again. 'But I got somewhere to be.'

He thrust the Dedfist forwards. The point of one talon punched through the humie's carapace breastplate with a noise like a boot breaking the ice on a puddle, and the humie sagged around it, the weapon falling from its hands with a clatter. Mag hurled it off to one side, sending a spray of blood along with it, and turned to see who was next.

As it turned out, who was next was a tank.

It wasn't a proper tank, not the sort that the humies normally brought to a fight, but it was a vehicle on tracks with a gun on the top, so by Mag's understanding, that made it a tank in humie terms. It was rumbling up from further along, perhaps only just getting here. Maybe the humies hadn't been able to get all their remaining forces organised in time, and so they were still arriving in dribs and drabs. You wouldn't get that with orks: they would all have already been as close to the enemy as possible, just waiting for a chance to have a go at them.

Mag charged.

The tank saw him coming, and its weapons opened up, but it didn't seem to have quite got itself ready. One of the las-blasts spat out by the turret gun clipped Mag on the shoulder and actually burned through his armour, but by the time it had got to his flesh, it did little more than sting. Then he was on it.

He reached out with the Dedfist and tore through the metal, grabbing the hull gun and wrenching it out in a shower of sparks. He shoved his kustom shoota into the gap he'd just created and pulled the trigger, pouring rounds into the interior, while reaching up with his other arm to shear the multi-barrelled turret gun off halfway along its length. It tried to fire again a moment later, over his head since it couldn't lower enough to reach him, but the lack of a full barrel must have caused some sort of catastrophic error. The base of the gun exploded, taking half the turret with it.

Mag laughed. More and more orks were pouring through – the lootas were in now, and chewing up any remaining cover with hails of fire from their deffguns, which more than made up for in quantity what they lacked in accuracy – and whatever hopes the humies might have had of stopping the incursion had been smashed almost before they'd begun. Now all Mag needed to do was press on into the depths, and find–

The crowd of grots had followed in hard on the orks' heels, which was odd in itself, given that Mag hadn't seen any runtherds prodding them along. They were running through the remnants of the fighting, paying as little attention to it as they could, and heading for the passage that led away from the walls and towards the centre of the city. And… was one of them holding a grabba stikk?

Mag absent-mindedly uppercut the tank with his power klaw, flipping it over onto its side with a tremendous crash, and glowered as the last grot disappeared from his view, surging ahead with very un-grotlike eagerness. Something strange was going on here, and Mag Dedfist was a Goff, which meant he had a profound and innate distrust of the strange.

'Oi!' he bellowed, his roar of command cutting through the gunfire, explosions and screams. Any ork not actively involved in scragging a humie looked around to see what had provoked their big boss' anger, and Mag raised the Dedfist to point with one of its talons.

'Follow dose grots!'

LOTZ

'Zoggin' 'eck, zoggin' 'eck, zoggin' *'eck!'*

Snaggi's plan had been simple. For him and his ladz to get in he needed the orks to blow a hole in the humie city's wall, and thankfully that was exactly what that squigbrained lump Mag Dedfist had intended anyway. Once that was done, the brave grots under Snaggi's command would race ahead – and crucially, downwards – while the orks got stuck into the humie defenders. Snaggi had never seen an ork who was willing to pass up a fight for any other goal, and he hadn't imagined that would change here. Dedfist would get to scraggin', and would either lose interest in Old Morgrub's gate, or would forget about it until he had run out of enemies, which, given the size of this place, should hopefully take some time even for him.

Unfortunately, Snaggi had forgotten to take a few things into account.

The first was that although Mag Dedfist was not what you might call a *finker*, he was possessed of a certain stubbornness that ran right through his train of thought. He was not easily dissuaded or distracted from something on which he had set his sights, and the problem with this enormous humie city was that the gits were literally everywhere. Mag could walk in any direction and find enemies, so he could head for wherever he thought this gate might be and still get a fight of some sort.

The second was that grots running ahead without a runtherd actively driving them onwards was an odd enough occurrence that even orks would notice it. Now Snaggi and his ladz had a suspicious Mag Dedfist somewhere behind them, doing his best to hunt them down to find out what in Gork's name was going on, and that was not where you wanted Mag Dedfist to be.

The third, and most immediately pressing thing, was that running ahead of the orkish advance meant encountering humies *whom the orks had not yet scragged.*

'Didn't ya fink of dis?' Kruffik wailed, desperately pulling the trigger on his blasta. By chance – or perhaps due to Snaggi's inspirational presence, which Snaggi decided was an explanation he liked far better – the shot hit its intended target, and one of the humies that had been firing at them staggered and dropped with a hole in its chest.

'Waaagh!' Snaggi yelled, firing his own blasta one-handed, while the other hand firmly clutched the grabba stikk he had taken from Zukrod, and which had rapidly become his symbol of office as the leader of da Revolushun.

Another humie dropped, and although it was arguable that Snippa One-Ear had fired in the same general direction at roughly the same time, Snaggi had no problem with claiming the kill as his own. 'Take dat, ya gitz!'

The humies, who were a somewhat more ragtag bunch than usual, had first retreated from the onrushing grots, then had apparently realised what they were facing and started fighting back. Now, however, the massed fire of grot blastas seemed to have dissuaded some of them once more. Half kept advancing, roaring in anger and firing, but the rest were backing off again and looking for cover. Their surroundings were not what Snaggi would have usually thought of as a 'humie place': less shiny metal and straight lines, more ruined and grubby, with dripping pipes, faltering lights, and patches of stuff that might have been slime and might have been some sort of organic growth. Maybe that was why the humies were less neat and tidy, too.

'C'mon, boyz, we've got 'em on da run!' he yelled, hoping that it would become a self-fulfilling prophecy. He thew the zap-lever on the grabba stikk, activating the charge around its metal-toothed jaws, and charged forwards. Gork and Mork had spoken to him: they had singled him out as the grot who was going to lead his kind to freedom, who was going to rise above the orks and become the first-ever grotboss. What did he have to fear?

Well, none of his ladz following him and thereby leaving him an isolated and obvious target, for one thing, but happily it seemed that was not going to be the case. A high-pitched cry of 'Waaagh!' went up from several dozen grot throats, and his own personal green tide surged after him, screaming and yelling and firing their blastas.

Had all of the humies either come to meet them, or backed off, taken cover and started firing, things might have gone badly. As it was, the humies' lack of discipline was fatal. The ones behind couldn't get clear shots, thanks to their more aggressive mates who were in the way, and a couple of the ones who drew their own weapons and ran to meet the charge of Snaggi's Grot Brigade actually went down from accidental shots in the back: at least, Snaggi assumed they were accidental, since humies did not tend to take the ork approach to marksmanship of 'if you get in the way of my gun then it's your own stupid fault.' The aggressive ones managed to cut down one or two of Snaggi's brave ladz each, but they lacked the numbers to really make an impact, and point-blank blasta shots combined with stabbas in the ribs ended the fight within a matter of seconds.

Snaggi himself caught a humie by the neck with the grabba stikk and chuckled with glee as its hair stood on end and the flesh melted off its face. He opened the jaws again and it dropped, stinking of burned hair and charred meat.

The rest of the humies wanted no part of it. They turned and ran, firing wildly back over their shoulders as they did so. The Grot Brigade hunkered down on the other side of the cover that the humies had just abandoned, braced their blastas, aimed, and fired. Grots might not have good guns, Snaggi reflected as humie after humie toppled head over heels, but they knew how to send a slug in the right direction, unlike orks. That just made it all the more outrageous that orks kept all the best guns for themselves, and this was a strong candidate for the first thing that was going to change when he became grotboss.

'See?' he told Kruffik confidently, puffing out his chest. 'Nuffin' to worry about. Da gods are wiv us!'

Kruffik looked at him dubiously for a moment, but apparently concluded that there was no obvious evidence to the contrary. 'Alright. So which way now?'

Snaggi paused, while his loyal followers looted the dead humies for whatever weapons they had been carrying. These ones had not generally been armed with the zappy light guns most humies had, although there were still one or two of them. In fact, they had weapons much more like ork ones, albeit on a smaller scale. The human he'd fried with the grabba stikk had one slung over its back on a length of chain, and Snaggi reached down to disentangle it, then inspected it. It looked like a twin boomstikk, but on a scale far more manageable for a grot than the massive, hulking things orks like Zagnob Thundaskuzz carried around.

'Ya know, dis ain't half bad for humie work,' he mused, cracking it open and peering at the shiny shells within. A further quick rummage revealed a pouch of spare shells on the humie's belt, which he appropriated with glee. 'When I become grotboss, I reckon we should take a buncha humies as slaves an' get 'em to make guns for us! Dey've got da sizin' down right, look–'

'Snaggi!' Kruffik hissed at him, breaking his reverie. 'Which way?' The other grot pointed a taloned finger back in the direction from whence they had come, and Snaggi was about to tell him that no, of course they weren't going back *that* way, when he heard the distant bellow of ork war cries, and the guttural cough of shootas. Mag Dedfist, or some of his boyz, were catching up to them.

'Yeah, yeah, alright,' Snaggi muttered, closing his eyes – mostly, anyway, since no grot trusted other grots enough to properly close his eyes around them, lest he be hastily relieved of anything he once thought he owned. 'Just need to talk to da gods.'

The trouble was that regardless of talking to them, listening to them, attempting to interpret his surroundings as signs of their intentions, or any other method that Snaggi could think of, the gods were being remarkably close-mouthed about exactly where he could find this gateway. They had been clear about his destiny as grotboss, there was no doubt about *that*, but it seemed that Gork and Mork were not giving out any easy answers with regards to Old Morgrub's little puzzle.

There were two possible explanations for that, Snaggi thought to himself as he wondered how long he could wait for guidance until it was definitely time to run in any direction that presented itself. The first was that the gods knew he could do this, and didn't need any help: in effect, any choice he made would be the right choice, because this was his destiny. The second was that Old Morgrub was nothing more than a squigbrained madboy who had made this whole charade up, and Snaggi's destiny was entirely separate from finding this gate thing the skrawniez might or might not have left here.

The more he thought about it, the likelier the second explanation seemed. Snaggi had killed Gazrot Goresnappa before Morgrub had said anything about this gate: in fact, the old warphead had probably come up with the idea as a desperate attempt to keep some form of control over the Waaagh!, since his pet warboss was no more. Yes, that was it: Morgrub knew who was responsible for Goresnappa's death and was therefore the obvious candidate to take over, and he knew Snaggi talked to the gods, and he knew that therefore Snaggi would have no need of his advice. This was all just a ruse! No wonder Snaggi didn't know which way the gate was: there was no such thing! He must have imagined that part of the vision, led astray by Morgrub's words in the aftermath of it. Morgrub was just a fraud, trying to buy time until he could come up with–

'Snaggi!'

'I'm workin' on it!'

'No, Snaggi, *look!*'

Snaggi properly opened one eye, then gasped in amazement. A green glow was building in the air in front of the Grot Brigade, crackling with power that earthed itself in the ground beneath their feet and caused little clumps of pale fungus to spring up wherever it touched. The surge of Waaagh! energy coming off it was invigorating, and Snaggi abruptly felt as though he could lift a humie with one hand.

'It's da gods!' he breathed in delight. 'Dey've come to show me da way!'

The curtain of power divided and parted, and Old Morgrub stepped through.

'Yoo boyz lost?' the warphead asked conversationally, leaning on his trinket-bedecked staff and showing a lot of teef in a wide grin.

The assembled grots glanced at each other nervously. Being addressed by an ork in a manner that was not preceded by some sort of kick and an expletive was an unknown experience for most of them. Being spoken to in a tone of voice that bordered on friendly, or at least as friendly as an ork could ever get, was utterly alien. And this was not just any ork: this was Old Morgrub, Gazrot Goresnappa's advisor and the closest thing to a senior weirdboy you got in that strange, non-hierarchical and often head-exploding bunch of oddboyz.

'Snaggi's lookin' for da skrawniez' gate!' Guffink piped up from somewhere to Snaggi's right. Snaggi immediately wanted to clock the other grot around the head with the grabba stikk, but he didn't feel that using the tool of their oppressor for its original purpose rather than turning it on orks or humies would go down that well with the ladz, so he nobly resisted the temptation in the interests of grot solidarity.

'Is dat so?' Morgrub asked, raising his eyebrows. He sniffed the air, then licked that shiny stone he'd taken from a skrawnie weirdboy. A fat spark jumped from it to his tongue, and he grinned even more widely. When combined with his stare, which permanently seemed slightly vacant, even Snaggi had to admit to himself that the warphead was rather unnerving, and that was without including the possibility that he might explode however many heads were in the vicinity if he got overexcited.

'I reckon ya might wanna try goin' dat way, and downwards,' Morgrub said, pointing ahead and to the left as Snaggi looked at it. Snaggi nodded – that was also the direction he had just decided was obviously the best way, but it was good to have his instincts backed up.

He raised the grabba stikk. 'Grots! Onwards!'

The Grot Brigade surged forwards once more, slightly fewer in number than they had been, but now battle-hardened and newly equipped with weapons taken from vanquished foes. Most importantly, Snaggi now knew that he had the favour not only of the gods, but also of Old Morgrub. The warphead knew of Snaggi's plan and approved of it – as of course he would have to, seeing as how Gork and Mork had granted Snaggi their favour – and so Snaggi could rely on Morgrub's influential backing when the time came to declare himself as grotboss. None of the orks would dare to oppose him then! It was exactly as he'd always said: his destiny was calling, and it was calling him ahead, and to the left, and downwards.

Old Morgrub backed into some shadows and watched the grots go, then looked around. The first of Mag Dedfist's lot were already piling into this chamber, and the one at the front – Skabrukk, a part of Morgrub's Waaagh!-energy-addled brain threw at him – was roaring along on his rokkit pack and seemed to have caught sight of the stragglers.

'Over dere!' the stormboy drill boss roared, pointing. 'Dat way, dat way!'

A mighty bellow announced the arrival of Mag Dedfist himself, mega armour spewing fumes as he thundered along. Well, Morgrub thought, the grots knew which way to go, and that meant that Dedfist did as well, since he hadn't got bored of following them yet. It was probably better this way: Dedfist, with typical Goff stubbornness, wouldn't appreciate the thought of being led by the nose.

Morgrub concentrated, doing his best to ignore the splinter in his brain where the presence of the skrawniez' gate nagged at him, and the background roar of the Realm of the Gods. He could feel where the different parts of the Waaagh! were, thanks to the concentrations of energy that ebbed and flowed around the masses of orks, and after all this time his mind was so finely attuned that the different forces stood out to him like beacons.

Sadly, not all of them were where they should be.

'Gotta do everyfing myself,' he muttered, wrapping himself in power and disappearing again.

LOTZ

Captain Armenius Varrow was cursing everything.

He cursed his own body, which was weak and trembling after exertion that, although rigorous and extended, would never have troubled him before his incarceration. He cursed his lungs, which appeared to have more holes than a Masali cheese, judging by the way they seemed to let oxygen slip through their metaphorical fingers instead of forcing it into his bloodstream. He cursed the designers and builders of the Davidian undercity, who had created such a warren of tunnels and service vents, and he cursed the governor and every single official beneath her who had abandoned this part of the city and let it degrade into dirty, poorly lit squalor with thoroughly inadequate signage. Most of all, he cursed the orks that had driven him to such desperate measures, and since he was a soldier, he had quite an extensive lexicon of profanity on which to draw.

However, despite all the challenges that faced him, despite the towering odds against him, he was triumphing. His progress had not been particularly fast, and nor had it been without mistakes or backtracking, but he was getting there. He had managed to interpret the peeling, damaged, acid-scarred or lichen-obscured paint marks and metal plaques intended to give an indication of where in the system a person was, and rather than getting lost in that system, or even wandering the wrong way further out into where the tunnels and sewers terminated, he was getting closer to civilisation.

Or what passed for civilisation at this depth, anyway.

Armenius wiped a sweaty hand on his damp and stinking trousers, and took a new hold of the firearm he had procured from the gretchin. It barely even qualified for the word 'gun' in his mind, but 'firearm' probably worked: it was a word that he felt could more reasonably apply to such a primitive creation. He had no idea if the weapon would shoot, even less – if it was possible – if he could aim it with any accuracy, and none at all whether it would blow up in his hand, but it was all he had. At the very least, the thing *looked* imposing. It was nothing in terms of size when set against an ork gun – and Armenius had seen more of them, and at far closer range, than any human should have to, so he knew what he was talking about – but it still had a ludicrously large bore by the standards of the Imperium, and was basically a roughly made hand cannon.

He might need all the intimidation he could muster, for the inhabitants at this depth were unlikely to be welcoming to outsiders, or, for that matter, even to each other. Armenius had heard tales of the underhive, and knew it as a place of lawlessness, and likely of heresy, where mutation and deviancy ran rife. Contaminants and pollutants twisted human biology into mockeries of its true form, which was no more than those who chose to live down here deserved. Even worse were the ones who tried to leave and move upwards into the hive, as though they could be tolerated in any form of decent society. A nobleman like Armenius knew that the menial labourers of the main hive – Plasteel City, as it was nicknamed – were the sort of talentless dullards who were only good for working in the forges and on processing-plant lines, collecting refuse, and picking up a lasgun and obeying the orders of their betters in the planetary defence force or Astra Militarum. However, they were still human: they had the appropriate number of correctly shaped limbs, eyes, and other appendages,[10] they lacked mutations and the curse of witchery, and they worshipped the Emperor. None of those things were certain down here.

He trudged forwards, his nose by now almost inured to the fresh scents of putrescence and effluent that were stirred up with each step. It was astonishing what a man could get used to after even a relatively small amount of time exposed to something. After all, had he not got used to being surrounded by monstrous, murderous xenos? Although perhaps that was a greater indication of his own steely nerves rather than the hardiness of his species as a whole. How many of his fellow officers would have managed to remain unbroken in the face of such horror? Precious few, he thought fiercely.

It took someone not only of the correct breeding, but also of resolute moral fibre, to maintain their composure when under such pressure. Not only had Armenius continued to deceive and lie to his captors when interrogated, but his spirit had sufficient fire left to attempt this bold escape plan. Even more than that, he had overcome the limits of his own body, inflicted by the orks' mistreatment of him, *and* also multiple dangerous xenos foes in order to get this far. And he was doing it not just in the interests of his own freedom – no, he could have sought that at any time – but to save the last bastion of human civilisation on Aranua from its doom. He had picked his moment to strike, waited until his actions would have the maximum effect. This was worthy of a medal, an honour, perhaps a promotion! Although of course, Colonel Sudliff would have to actually defeat the orks and rebuild the Golden Lions before there was much that would be worthy of having Major Varrow command them.

There was light up ahead, reflecting off the walls of what looked like a junction, and it was not just the soulless, intermittent light of the few surviving lumens in this tunnel system. It was flickering, that much was true, but not in the haphazard, binary on, off, on again of a faulty fitting. This was a flowing flicker, the natural shifting and ebbing that came with flames.

Fire. A small fire, such as one might build for cooking or warmth. Where

---

[10] Barring industrial or battlefield accidents.

there was fire in the depths, there would be people. Or at least, things that looked like people, Armenius reminded himself. He was not out of the minefields yet, not by a long shot.

He debated how to approach. Should he sneak closer until he had some idea of who – or indeed, what – might be lurking around these flames, and whether he wanted to attract their attention at all? Or should he openly announce his presence, so they did not mistake him for some stalking predator come to snatch them away into the darkness? He was under no illusions that he had any great capacity for stealth left in him, for his legs were weary and he was unused to this manner of terrain. He would be unsurprised if locals knew how to pick out echoes and the faint slosh of water and sludge underfoot in this environment of strange acoustics, and would know he was coming well before he had any notion of who they were.

Openness it was. He was a captain of the Golden Lions, damn it, and although his uniform was torn and soiled it was still distinguishable to anyone who had any idea what an Astra Militarum officer looked like. He was not trying to rob these people, he was trying to help them: no one else was going to be bringing news of Da Genrul's intention to infiltrate Davidia Hive by this route!

'Ahoy, the fire!' he called, then cursed his voice as it cracked and broke. He tried again. 'Ahoy!'

The words echoed and tumbled away along the large pipe through which he was walking, towards the light ahead of him. Nothing happened for a few moments, other than his next few trudging steps forwards, lit mainly by the head torch he had appropriated from the dead gretchin. Then a harsh ratcheting sound met his ears: the noise of a shotgun being racked.

'Oozat?'

For a single heart-stopping second, Armenius thought he was back in the orks' camp. Then reality asserted itself once more, as his ears reminded his brain what they had actually heard, rather than what it feared they had: this voice did not belong to an orkoid, no matter how slurred its Gothic was. It might have roughly the pitch of a gretchin, but it was definitely human. The surge of relief he felt at hearing another human voice for the first time in... he truly had no idea how long... was enough to make him stumble forwards at a greater pace. He might even welcome being threatened at gunpoint, if it were only one of his own kind who was doing it.

'A friend!' he called hopefully, although he did not put his gun away. That would be foolish.

'Ain't got no friends down here,' the voice replied. 'Specially not one who don't know to keep his voice down!'

'Fine,' Armenius said, somewhat more quietly. 'But friend or not, I have no intention of harming you, if you can say the same.'

'Well come on slow then, Fancy Talk, an' keep yer hands where I can see 'em when ya get 'ere. Assumin' you've got hands,' the voice added, suddenly suspicious.

'Yes, two of them,' Armenius said, almost giddy with delight at exchanging words with another human. He was coming up on the junction now, close enough for the slight curve of the pipe to no longer hide it from him. It was a confluence of four pipes, with a small fire burning off to one side that was contained within a metal bin, to keep it out of the layer of sludge on the floor. On the other side of the fire, backed into a corner where nothing could come at them from behind, was–

A monster.

Armenius' reflexes began to twitch his arm up, ready to risk the wrath of the double-barrelled shotgun his soldier's instincts had already identified without even thinking about it, until his brain managed to once more decipher the unclear signals from his senses. That was not a hideously deformed or mutated skull; rather, it was the chitinous head of a giant arachnid, hollowed out to form a crude hat or helmet, with the huge mandibles protruding forwards like the galaxy's most threatening pair of eyebrows. What Armenius had taken for a misshapen body in fact looked relatively normal at second glance, and was instead wrapped in some form of hairy pelt that had thrown off his original perception. The two hands that held the shotgun certainly seemed human enough, as did the wizened face that peered out from beneath the spider-helm.

'Oo'z you, then?' the underhiver demanded. 'No more steps, not just yet – not 'til I've had a look at ya.'

'I am Captain Armenius Varrow, of the Aranuan Twenty-Fifth,' Armenius said. 'The Golden Lions?' he added hopefully, when the expression scrutinising him offered no glimmer of recognition.

'Oo're they?' the other person said, looking him up and down.

'You've not heard of the Aranuan Twenty-Fifth?' Armenius asked, appalled.

'Dunno. What's an Aranuan?'

'I– What– *You* are an Aranuan!' Armenius spluttered. 'As am I, as is everyone in this hive!'

The underhiver cocked their head. 'That a fancy word for "person", then?'

Armenius did his best not to scream in frustration. Of all his luck, which had been tremendously foul despite his dogged determination to make the best of it, the first person he encountered had to be this simpleton! He should have expected nothing better from an underhiver.

'Do you know what this planet is called?' he tried.

Eyes that glittered with reflected firelight narrowed suspiciously. 'What's one o' them?'

Armenius gritted his teeth, and tried to recalibrate his brain to something better suited to his current situation.

'Do you know what an ork is?'

'Never heard of him. An' if I ain't heard of him, then I ain't hunted him, an' if I ain't hunted him, he don't exist.' The underhiver cackled, a curiously lilting and high-pitched sound which was nevertheless soft, and did not carry far. Armenius wondered, for a moment, what kind of life a person had to lead in order for even their laugh to be modulated so as not to draw attention from beasts that lived in the shadows, whether those beasts wore human shape or otherwise. Not a life he would care for, he felt sure, despite the fact that his own had hardly been short of misery in the recent weeks and months.

'Orks exist,' Armenius said. He intended his voice to sound firm and authoritative, striking a tone that would make even the most sceptical, backward downhiver reconsider their position on something. Instead, the words came out weary and haunted.

The underhiver's head tilted back the other way. 'Seen that look before. That's the look of someone who's gone through hell. Or might still be there. Fine then, Fancy Talk, orks exist. What are they, an' why should I care?'

'They're... monsters?' Armenius ventured uncertainly, suddenly unsure how to describe the xenos threat to someone who lacked the comprehension of what a planet was, let alone which one they were on. 'Big. Green skin, tusks. Fierce, tough.'

'Ow many legs?'

'...Er, two?'

'Two?' The underhiver frowned, insofar as their expression could be made out under their spider-helm. 'Two arms, as well?'

'Yes.'

'You sure you've not just seen some people what looked a bit green? There's a family down by the Great Send what's got a bit of a green cast to 'em, on account of–'

'No!' Armenius shouted, his frustration boiling over. 'No, they are not *people!* They're aliens! Xenos! They are a blight on the cosmos, and I was captured and I have escaped, and they are coming, do you understand me? *They are coming!* I have to warn everyone!' He raised the firearm, not to threaten the underhiver with it – for their shotgun's barrel had not moved away from him, and Armenius had no intention of risking it – but to display it, crudely hewn barrel pointing at the ceiling. 'You see this? I took this from one of them!'

'Lemme see that,' the underhiver said immediately, their eyes flashing to it. They held out one hand, although the other kept hold of their shotgun.

'I'm not giving you my gun,' Armenius scoffed. 'You can see it well enough from there!'

'No, I can't,' the underhiver said calmly. They crouched down slowly, and set the shotgun down, then held out their hand again. 'There ya go, Fancy Talk. I've put me own gun down. Gimme yours. Lemme see it.'

There was a curious intensity to them, and the way their eyes had not moved from the gun in Armenius' hand. He walked closer, growing in confidence as he did so. He was larger than this person, and considerably younger. Weathered and toughened by their life they might be, but if it came to a quick and desperate grapple over a weapon, he might actually have a better chance than trying to win a shootout with a gun of such uncertain provenance. Once he was close enough to feel the warmth of the flames from the fire, he allowed the firearm to be taken from him.

'Hmm,' the underhiver grunted, weighing the gun in their hand. They turned it over, back and forth, then ran a finger down the barrel. They sniffed it, screwed up their face at whatever they smelled, then stuck their tongue out.

'Oh, I really wouldn't–'

They licked the back of the chamber in which the rounds were stored, but instead of recoiling in horror as any sensible person surely would, merely pursed their lips as though in thought.

'This is new,' they said.

'Well, I don't know about that–'

'Not in age,' the underhiver snapped, looking up at him. 'This is *new*. Not seen one like this before. Not this size, not this weight, not this build, not this taste. That's not cordite being used as propellant, neither. No, I ain't never seen a gun like this, an' I've seen a lot of guns in my time.' They chuckled again, high and soft as before, but their eyes were cold and hard. 'Something strange about you, something strange about this. Ya don't last long here if ya don't respect the strange.'

Armenius felt like he was being weighed and judged by this odd person in their spider-helm and rat-cloak, and he found himself straightening his shoulders. It was preposterous: what right did this underhiver have to judge *him*, a captain of the Golden Lions, and from a noble family to boot?

Circumstance, that was what.

'Alright, Fancy Talk,' the underhiver said after a few moments more, and handed the gun back to him. Armenius took it with relief, which was an odd sensation to experience when receiving a piece of xenos technology – in the loosest sense of the word – but his world was now very small, and very dark, and somewhat tunnel-shaped. He knew what this gun was, and where it came from, and what it meant, and that was something he had to hold on to.

'Alright?' he repeated, hopefully.

'Maybe there's somethin' down here I don't know about,' the underhiver said, picking their shotgun back up. 'So what're you tryin' to do about these monsters, these orks o' yours?'

Armenius' knees almost gave out, and not just from fatigue. He had found another human, and although that human had no real idea what was going on, or what the danger was that threatened them all, they seemed willing to help!

'I need to get uphive,' he said immediately. 'I need to get in touch with the people in charge, and tell them that the orks are trying to invade from down here. They're digging in from outside. I got away and I got ahead of them, but they'll find their way in sooner or later.'

'The people in charge, eh?' the underhiver said. They licked their lips, and squinted. 'Alright. I know the way. You seem kinda in a rush, Fancy Talk. Wanna get goin' right off?'

'Yes,' Armenius breathed. 'Oh Emperor, yes!'

'None o' that!' the underhiver snapped. 'You don't take His name in vain!'

Armenius opened his mouth to protest, stopped, opened it again to ask how this person even *knew* about the Emperor when they didn't know what a planet was, and in the end thought better of that as well. He probably could find his way uphive on his own, eventually, but his new companion's accoutrements were testament to just a couple of the potential perils that lurked down here, so alienating someone who had just agreed to guide him seemed foolish.

'Of course,' he said, politely. 'My apologies. It won't happen again.'

The underhiver grunted, and began belting things onto themself: packs, tools, and all manner of other paraphernalia.

'What do I call you?' Armenius asked. *What name do I shout if a spider bigger than I am is about to pounce on us?*

'Eza.'

'Eza.' Armenius nodded. 'And, uh, I don't mean to be rude, Eza, but just so I know, you understand… are you a man or a woman?'

'Hah!' Eza chuckled once more. 'Don't matter. There's only two things what matter here, Fancy Talk – are you alive, or are you dead? If you're the first, and you're not careful, you'll end up the second before long.' They paused for a moment, then spat. 'For that matter, if you're the second, and you're not careful, you can end up the first. Or somethin' that looks a bit like it, and walks a bit like it, but don't sound or smell right.'

Armenius wasn't sure how to respond to that, so he said nothing. Tales of underhive revenants had made for enjoyably spooky ghost stories when he was a child, but now he was down here with nothing for protection but a firearm for which the term 'dubious provenance' was probably being charitable, and an ancient hunter wearing a spider's head over their own, such things no longer seemed so harmless.

Eza finished their preparations and straightened up, took their shotgun in both hands, nodded at Armenius, and took the tunnel leading off to the left of the one from which he had emerged. Armenius followed gratefully. He was a man used to a command structure, and although as captain he had made his own decisions, that had still been within the framework of orders coming from above. Being on his own for so long had worn him down, and so having someone else make the decisions for a while – even decisions so simple as which way he was supposed to walk – was almost blissful.

He did not let down his guard completely, of course. It was possible that Eza was leading him into some sort of cannibal ambush. However, his options were few. The one thing Eza could not do was lead Armenius to somewhere *more* isolated. Armenius might never make it to the main hive, get a chance to vox the colonel or the governor, make his report, or receive his due reward. However, the more people he met and told about the subterranean ork threat, the greater the likelihood that someone somewhere who actually knew what was going on would hear the news, and take action.

For now, that would have to do.

Kaptin Skulsnik and his Guttas came from the shadows, from the same tunnel out of which Armenius Varrow had emerged, but they moved far more quietly, and they did not announce themselves by shouting ahead. There were ten of them, their green skin smeared haphazardly with mud to mimic the play of shadows in a dark, poorly lit environment, and the blades of their weapons dulled to minimise reflection. They spread out near-silently, sniffing the air, examining the ground for tracks or other tell-tale marks in and around the semi-liquid sludge. Skulsnik drew his knife down across the wall twice with a faint scraping noise, scoring through the centuries-old patina of dirt and into the surface beneath to leave a large 'X'. Further back the way they had come, his sensitive ears could just make out the faint susurration that spoke of a loud noise at distance. Other orks, even other Blood Axes, were not as subtle or stealthy as kommandos, but they didn't need to be. They were well on the path now, and it would not be long before they could abandon trailing the humie, and start to choose their own route.

In the meantime, however, the Guttas still had a job to do.

'Dat way,' Skulsnik said softly, and the kommandos pressed onwards, tracking the humies deeper into the hive.

LOTZ

'I fink I got it!' Skrappit shouted. The humies had inconsiderately not left a control panel on the outside, so the mek had battered and burned his way into the wall in an effort to find the wiring that operated the road gate. Now, head and shoulders into a ragged hole excavated with a tightly focused burna flame and a sturdy choppa blade, he finally sounded hopeful.

'About zoggin' time,' Zagnob Thundaskuzz muttered. The Kult was getting restless, and it was all he could manage to keep some of them from tearing off into the dawn. They'd swiftly taken out all of the humie guns, and now there was nothing to do except that mortal enemy of the speed freek: waiting. So far, Zagnob's authority and the promise of an imminent scrap with whatever humies were inside was winning out over the lure of the distant horizon, wind in their faces, and dust in their teef, but he could feel the mood changing. Speed freeks lived for the rush of acceleration, and orks – speed freeks in particular – rarely had much notion of delayed gratification.

He looked around and his eyes lighted on the black-painted, spiky shape of a Goff trukk he had seen earlier. 'Oi, Nuzzgrond! Dat you?'

'Yeah.' The nob's horned helmet poked out around the slabs of metal welded onto the side of the vehicle in an attempt to give the occupants some sort of shelter from gunfire until they could get into a position to jump out and apply their choppas to the enemy. 'Wot's da hold-up?'

'Skrappit's doin' somefing mekish,' Zagnob said dismissively. 'He'll be done any minute. Wot're yoo boyz doin' here wiv us, den? I fort yoo'd be hangin' around wiv Dedfist, seein' as how yoo're his pets an' all.' He laughed nastily, just to put a point on it, and several of the other speed freeks within earshot chuckled merrily as well, enjoying a bit of trash talking when they heard it.

'We ain't no ork's pets!' Nuzzgrond barked, glowering back at Zagnob from beneath his helmet's rim. 'Followed ya cos we fort dat maybe yoo'd know a quicker way into da city, since ya like speed an' dat, but I'm startin' to fink we should've stuck with Mag!'

'Hmph.' Zagnob simply sneered at the nob, mainly because he didn't have that good of a comeback. Mag Dedfist was a plodder, but he was a plodder who'd been left with access to an awful lot of dakka, and heavy-hitting war machines. It wasn't unfeasible that he might have managed to batter his way inside by now, through sheer brute force and ignorance. Not that

Zagnob wanted to let on to that, just in case the ladz with him decided that Nuzzgrond had a point. Besides which, even if Dedfist had managed to get in somehow, he wasn't going to have found an entry like this, through which the Kult of Speed could easily get all of their vehicles. All Zagnob needed was for that zoggin' mek to hurry up and do what he'd been so confident he could do...

'No, I def'nitely got it!' Skrappit called happily. There was a flash of light and a sizzle of electricity which coincided with a yelp of pain from the mek, and nothing else happened.

For a few seconds.

Then, the massive doors began to shudder and shake, and a deep metallic groan rang out. It was sufficiently loud to cut through even the low thunder of idling engines, and every driver, gunner and passenger looked up eagerly, their various squabbles and arguments forgotten. Orks could easily get distracted, it was true, but it might only take one thing to refocus them. For speed freeks, the prospect of being able to drive really fast at an enemy and fill them with dakka would do it every time.

Zagnob had ordered the wrecked shokkjump dragsta to be dragged and shunted out of the way well before now, because he was a canny speedboss with the kind of vision and preparedness that marked him out from his underlings. As a result the route in was clear, and as soon as the doors were wide enough apart, warbikes began to zip through with their dakkaguns already blazing.

'Right!' Zagnob shouted at Duffrak. 'Let's get–'

He didn't have to finish the sentence, because Duffrak had already opened the throttle. The Deffkilla wartrike lurched forwards with a howl of engines, and immediately collided with a megatrakk scrapjet which had clearly had the same idea. The impact jolted Zagnob loose, and he fell over the side of his kommand platform, landing on the scrapjet with a thud. The fuselage was roasting under his hands, the cool of the Aranuan night having done little to leech away the excess heat from the trakk's abused engines.

'Fink yer some sort o' brain boy, do ya?' Zagnob bawled at the scrapjet's driver, raising his snagga klaw. 'Get dis fing–'

'Boss!'

The high-pitched squeal came from Skitta, and Zagnob looked around just in time to see the grot waving helplessly as Duffrak, oblivious to his speedboss' predicament and eager to make up for lost time, accelerated away towards the widening gap in the doors. The wartrike jinked around a buggy, squeezed through a space it had no right to get through, and was lost from view. A moment later there was an almighty rending noise as other ork vehicles smashed into each other, each one trying to be the next through into the interior.

'Zoggin' idiots!' Zagnob snarled. He rounded on the scrapjet driver, who largely consisted of a manic grin and a pair of goggles. 'Wotcha waitin' for? Get us inside!'

The driver howled with glee and fed power to his engine with a howl of turbines. The immediate way in front of them was blocked by a pair of buggies that had come together and were now interlocked by their twisted chassis, but it seemed the scrapjet pilot had a solution for that.

Granted, the solution involved firing his rokkit kannon at point-blank range.

Zagnob yelled in alarm, and ducked instinctively as pieces of machine flew everywhere. Then the scrapjet's nose-cone drill hit what was left in their way, and the vehicle chewed through the wreckage without slowing. The huge, widening gap of the gate loomed up, through which was coming intermittent bursts of gunfire, but nothing in any sort of volume that would trouble the assembled speed freeks. Whatever resistance the humies had mustered within had either been blown apart by the opening volleys of the first few warbikes inside, or had never amounted to much in any case.

They screamed through the gates, flanked on one side by a trakk mounting nothing more than a giant skorcha as a weapon, and on the other by the trukk containing Nuzzgrond's mob. Zagnob caught a glance of the chaos that had ensued within, and grinned with glee.

It was a giant road tunnel, as wide and as tall as the gates themselves, and the sort of place that could have been held quite effectively if enough firepower had been concentrated here. Unfortunately for the humies, that had not happened. A few crushed corpses bore silent witness to the doomed attempts to defend the tunnel, with only one smoking warbike wreck beside them in exchange for their sacrifice. The fight here was not completely over yet, though: a searing flash of light grabbed Zagnob's attention, and he saw three of the spindly walkers the humies used advancing out of a side passage. Their concentrated firepower took out another bike as it roared past them, the rider going too fast to adjust his trajectory in time to get any shots off before he died.

The skorcha trakk accelerated ahead and strafed the walkers with flame, but to no apparent effect. Nuzzgrond's trukk, on the other hand, slewed to a halt and disgorged its black-clad contents. The Goffs piled in, swarming the larger constructs and hacking at fuel lines and hydraulic cables with their choppas, firing their sluggas into any available opening, and clamping tankbusta bombs wherever they could. One was crushed beneath a giant metal foot, and another had his skull split by a feverishly waving kannon as one of the machines thrashed about trying to defend itself, but it was over in a matter of seconds. Nuzzgrond might not be a true speed freek, but he and his boyz knew choppa work well enough.

They were past the fight in a moment, barrelling on into the tunnel so fast that the regularly spaced lights the humies had placed overhead blurred into one flickering line of illumination. Zagnob looked up and caught sight of his wartrike ahead of them, where Duffrak was clearly going full throttle unless and until he received an order to the contrary from behind him: an order which would never come, given Zagnob was all the way back here. He half-turned to look at the scrapjet driver, and pointed with the hand with which he was not clinging on to the fuselage.

'Get after dat trike! I want–'

He never got a chance to finish the sentence, because something leaped at him.

It came from the side in a blur of red, the motion expertly judged to intersect with the scrapjet's progress despite the speed at which the vehicle was travelling, and with the sort of bound that could not have been powered by any form of natural limbs; at least, not unless it was one of the bugeye monsters, and Zagnob was fairly sure he would have noticed if any of *those* had been kicking around. It landed on the scrapjet directly in front of him with a clank of metal-on-metal as its feet magnetically locked to the hull, and Zagnob met the gaze of several metallic eyes within the depths of its hood.

Cogboy, his mind informed him within a split second: one of the humie mekboyz, who seemed just as prone to altering and upgrading their bodies as their ork counterparts. They exhibited rather un-humie individualism in that respect, despite their tendency to act as mindlessly and predictably as buzzer squigs about other things. Zagnob had already seen how enhanced its physical capabilities were in comparison to its weaker, squishier kin, and it was safest to assume that any part of it might be a weapon, so he was already ducking out of the way when it raised one arm to point at him.

Ruby red light beamed out, narrowly missing Zagnob's left shoulder. He heard a bellow of pain from behind him as it struck the scrapjet driver, which was abruptly truncated. That was probably a bad sign, at least for the driver: the only reason that any ork hurt badly enough to yell out in pain was not just going to switch to yelling in anger once the pain had stopped was because they were dead.

Zagnob swung his snagga klaw at the cogboy's legs, but the humie pistoned its left leg up and down within a moment, trapping his klaw underneath it with another metallic clang. Zagnob gave it a heave, but the cogboy had him trapped fast, and his attention was rapidly attracted to the arm weapon redirecting to point at his face. He grabbed where a wrist would have been on a normal humie and twisted, and the cogboy's next shot sizzled wide of him again.

Two metallic tendrils whipped out from the cogboy's back. One snaked down Zagnob's free arm, trying to anchor it in place for the humie to tug its weapon arm out of his grip, while the other wrapped around his neck like a constricting serpent. Zagnob tensed his neck muscles against it, daring it to try to suffocate him, but he was at a severe limb disadvantage: the humie's arm that he did not have hold of flashed out, slamming a metal fist repeatedly into his face.

It was painful, yes, but it was also infuriating. This humie cogboy had the zoggin' cheek to gobsmack him? Zagnob tightened his grip on the wrist of which he had hold, and felt metal begin to crack and bend beneath his fingers. There was a gun in there somewhere, and guns could do annoying things like explode if you squeezed them too hard, but he wasn't going to tolerate this any longer. He wasn't exactly getting much use out of his hand at the moment anyway...

Something *crunched* in a way that apparently went beyond an ability to easily repair, because the cogboy bleated mechanically and yanked its arm back, but left the hand - and the gun built into it - behind in Zagnob's grip.

He dropped the scrap and tried to hoist his other hand free, but the humie's magnetic clamp of a foot had him pinned.

There was a jolt accompanied by a tremendous juddering shriek, and a spray of sparks from his left. The scrapjet was still powering along, but it had veered into the tunnel wall, and was now scraping along against it. The friction and heat could easily cook off any remaining wing missiles on that side, which would cause an explosion that... Well, it would be hilarious, but also probably lethal. Dying in a big bang was far from the worst way to go, but Zagnob Thundaskuzz hadn't got this close to Old Morgrub's mysterious gate to be blown into squigfood by accident, so he needed to get himself free.

The cogboy's head snapped around, and it clearly saw an opportunity. Its body twisted strangely, joints moving in ways that no bipedal vertebrate should have been able to manage, and Zagnob found his snagga-klaw arm wrenched up off the scrapjet's fuselage, only for his entire body to be pivoted around and his face rammed against the wall by the cogboy's remaining hand.

'Gaaaah!' he bellowed, as the side of his face began to be abraded away by the metal panelling. He kicked out, and scored a hit against whichever leg it was that was still supporting the cogboy, but it wasn't enough to snap the limb. His face was agony, and he didn't have time to muck about. The skin on that side was gone and the muscle tissue was being worn away fast; it would be down to the bone of his skull within seconds.

However, the snagga klaw on his right hand was free again now, albeit being held harmlessly away from the cogboy by the humie's unnaturally angled other leg. But it didn't necessarily need to be pointing at the git for it to be useful.

Zagnob triggered the firing mechanism in his klaw and felt the slight kick of it run down his arm as the grapnel shot up and away. It caught on something a moment later, and the sudden, extreme force exerted on his shoulder, as his momentum courtesy of the scrapjet was brutally arrested, might have dismembered a being from a less hardy species. However, orks were as tough as they came, and Zagnob Thundaskuzz was one of the toughest orks going.

In this case, he was going upwards.

He was plucked skywards, or at least ceilingwards, and the cogboy came with him, its magnetic clamp foot having been insufficient to keep them both rooted to the scrapjet. That saved its life, at least for the moment, because they were only just clear when the scrapjet's remaining munitions detonated and turned it into a high-speed fireball.

Not that the cogboy appeared at all grateful for Zagnob's timely intervention, since it still seemed intent on trying to kill him, but it was finding that more difficult now. The humie still had more limbs than Zagnob did, but it had lost its leverage. Zagnob wrapped his legs around its waist and yanked backwards with his left arm, ripping the mechanical tendril gripping it out from the socket where it attached to the humie's back, then grabbed hold of the one still around his neck. The cogboy squealed mechanically and clawed at his face with its hand, but it wasn't enough to prevent Zagnob from tearing that tentacle loose as well.

The humie wasn't done. Its feet came up behind Zagnob, knees and ankles twisted and bending unnaturally, in order to sink metal claws into the flesh of his back. He bellowed in pain and headbutted it. The impact was a single extra spark in the pre-existing agony that was his head, and barely worthy of notice to him, but something within the cogboy's hood cracked as his forehead connected with it. It burbled again, even its cry of distress sounding less precisely formed than before, and some sort of fluid squirted out over him. Suddenly it was not clinging to him any longer, but trying to get away. Zagnob aimed a punch at it, but it somehow slithered out of his grip and dropped, wailing.

It landed on the floor beneath just in time to be hit by the spiked ram of a boosta-blasta, and disintegrated into an assortment of limbs, various mechanical fluids, and surprisingly little blood.

Zagnob sighed and lowered himself down again with the snagga klaw, making sure all the gits coming his way saw him and knew to steer to one side, then went in search of one particular part. He found it just as a boomdakka snazzwagon pulled up alongside him.

'Alright, boss?' Skrappit the mek shouted gleefully. 'Told ya I'd get us inside, didn't I?'

'Dat ya did,' Zagnob admitted, wincing. Speaking was wreaking merry hell with the ruined left side of his face. 'Now give us a lift, me trike's gone an' zogged off cos I got busy killin' dis git.' He held up the cogboy's head. The statement was not technically true, of course, but Zagnob would salute a grot and call it warboss before he admitted that he had *fallen off his own vehicle*. That way lay mockery and humiliation.

He tossed the cogboy's head underarm to Skrappit, who caught it. 'Can ya do anyfing useful wiv dat?'

'Reckon so,' Skrappit said, prising one of the cranial plates off and peering inside. 'Should be able to get us froo any more doors, for one fing.' He produced a bunch of wires from his belt, and began plugging them in with the happy air of one for whom true joy could only ever be found alongside the risk of electrocution.

'Good, now move over.' Zagnob hauled himself up alongside the mek, and Skrappit's driver took this as his cue to floor the accelerator once more. The snazzwagon leaped forwards with a squeal of tyres, and Zagnob made sure he remained upright, because Gork take him if he fell off this zoggin' thing as well.

'Da tunnel's forkin'!' the driver bellowed, after they'd been going for a few seconds. 'Which way, boss?'

Zagnob peered ahead of them. Both possible routes had the humies' lights running along the ceiling, like the one through which they were currently travelling, but the fork to the right appeared to have a greenish glow to it as well.

'Go right!' he yelled, and the driver hauled on the wheel to obey. It seemed that the rest of the Kult had already made the same decision, judging by the black tread marks and haze of fumes down that tunnel, so if nothing else, Zagnob reckoned he had a good chance of catching up with that wretched

Duffrak if they went this way. It looked like he wasn't the only one who had naturally gravitated to green, which only made sense, because what ork wouldn't?

As they whipped past the other entrance, Zagnob narrowed his eyes. 'Hang on, wot's dat?'

'Wot's wot?' Skrappit asked, looking up from his work.

Zagnob peered backwards. The other tunnel mouth was already behind them and out of sight, and even his finely honed ability to see things and interpret them in a split second had not been fully up to the task, but he could have sworn something had been lurking in the shadows back there. Something that might have looked a bit like an ork, trying not to be seen, and holding a staff from which dangled various oddments and trinkets.

That made no sense. There were no orks on foot on this side of the humie city, and no ork would stand by quietly and let a cavalcade of vehicles go past without trying to blag a lift, or at least cheering and firing whatever weapon it had to hand.

'Wot's wot?' Skrappit repeated.

'Never mind,' Zagnob said, turning back to face the way they were going, like a proper speed freek should. 'Prob'ly nuffin.'

But that did not prevent the uncomfortable and decidedly un-orky feeling of unease in his gut that something was going on which he did not fully comprehend.

LOTZ

Governor Ama Junier was tired. Throne, but she was tired. Sleep was both a distant lure, taunting her with its unavailability, and an enemy to be shunned. How could she sleep when Davidia Hive, the seat of her authority and the last known redoubt of humanity on this planet, was under attack by orkish invaders? To sleep now would be to give in – to acknowledge that there was nothing she could do, to admit her uselessness, because who could sleep if they had any hope of influencing the outcome? And simultaneously, she could *not* sleep, even had she tried, because her brain whirled around and around over the same simple but insurmountable problems.

Too many orks. Too few defenders. Too little time.

'What is the situation?' she asked, approaching the main tactical hololith with a slow pace that she hoped indicated deliberation and calm, rather than an effort to not fall over her own feet out of weariness. 'Have the orks breached the main city?'

Colonel Sudliff turned towards her. Even through the haze of utter tiredness, Ama could tell that the man was puzzled. Puzzled might actually be a good thing, she decided, with the strangely floaty thoughts of one in the grip of overwhelming fatigue. Puzzlement indicated something other than abject acceptance of their doom.

'No, governor,' Sudliff replied, his tone of voice mirroring his expression.

She frowned, and surreptitiously put out one hand to steady herself on the edge of the hololith table. She ignored the binharic cluck of disapproval from the Mechanicus adept lurking on the fringes of the room to make sure everything ran smoothly, and that none of the Golden Lions' high command damaged anything too valuable to the Omnissiah with their uncomprehending prodding.

'Please explain,' Ama said, hoping for once that he would take it as snootiness, since the alternative was admitting that she had absolutely no brainpower left to work anything out for herself.

'I'm not sure I can, governor,' Colonel Sudliff admitted, turning back to the hololith. He tapped something, and the overview of the hive, with its many turrets and spires, expanded to focus solely on the lower regions. 'The orks came in at ground level on opposite sides of the hive. A main force incursion here' – he gestured, and a section of the eastern wall turned red – 'where they exploited an existing weakness in the hive structure, and overwhelmed the defenders we were able to station there.'

'Why were we not defending this weakness in greater force?' Ama demanded.

'A matter of logistics,' Sudliff said. Ama glowered in a way that she hoped expressed her refusal to be fobbed off by such dissembling, and the colonel coughed uncomfortably. 'We simply had too few defenders, spread out to cover too many areas. The orks could have hit us anywhere along the eastern flank, and they will pass up an obvious weak point as often as not, so we had no way of knowing they would attack there. We tried to reposition other units to bolster defences once they had committed to the attack, but at that level of the hive, the infrastructure of roadways and the like is... somewhat lacking. By the time reinforcements arrived, the xenos had already established a beachhead.'

Ama sighed. 'And the other side?'

'A breach through the north-western road gate by a high-speed mechanised force.' Sudliff tapped something else, and a smaller red icon flashed up. 'They somehow managed to override the gate controls after Commander LaSteel disobeyed direct orders, left the hive to engage them on their approach, and got our armoured reserve annihilated.'

'How long has it been now?' Ama asked.

'Twelve hours, give or take,' Major Deralee Bruja replied, from the other side of the hololith table. She was a tall woman with rich umber skin, and cheekbones that looked sharp enough to cut anyone who got too close to her. Ama had no idea if the Lions' second-in-command was more tactically astute than Sudliff, but she certainly did a better job of looking like a leader. Sudliff resembled any number of the stuffy, aristocratic officers Ama had dealt with as she fought and clawed her way into power – the sort who relied on nothing more than his rank and his bloodline to get things done. Major Bruja looked like she could land in the underhive in rags, snap a bunch of orders at the first group of gangers she saw, and have a reasonable chance of being obeyed.

'I'm confused,' Ama admitted. 'Have the city's defences held better than expected?' Sudliff was right about one thing, at least: the lower parts of Plasteel City, at ground level and below, had been abandoned to dereliction, and only the routes up from the road gates were maintained with any care. With such a warren of pre-existing shafts, vents and full-blown transit routes to follow up from their breach points, the orks should have had their pick of options to rise through the hive and slaughter everyone in their way. The defenders did not even have enough bodies to place one solitary soldier at every potential entry point, let alone resist with any sort of strength.

'Plasteel City's defences have not been tested,' Colonel Sudliff informed her, which at least explained his look of puzzlement. Ama couldn't wrap her own head around it, either.

'They have not?'

'No, ma'am,' Sudliff confirmed. 'Our intelligence is limited, of course...'

Ama did not think she imagined the grimly amused glance Major Bruja shot her.

'...but all the reports we have been able to gather are suggesting that instead of ascending, the orks are going *downwards*,' the colonel concluded, apparently unaware of his subordinate's wordless humour.

Ama swallowed, barely able to believe what she had just heard. 'They are... not coming for us?'

'So it would seem,' Sudliff said, spreading his hands with the air of a man who had no answers, and was not inclined to question the mercy of the Emperor too closely.

Ama was not of a similar mindset. If there was one thing she had learned on her long path to planetary governor, it was that something which looked too good to be true usually was.

'Why?' she demanded. 'They have always previously targeted the highest population densities, the greatest concentrations of our troops. These monsters live for fighting and slaughter. What is in the depths of this hive that can attract them away from us?'

'We don't know, ma'am,' Major Bruja said simply, although her tone indicated that she did not share her commanding officer's relief at this state of affairs. Ama met her eyes, and suppressed a smile. Yes, Deralee Bruja was a very different breed of officer to Colonel Sudliff. Ama would have enjoyed the chance to match wits with her over a regicide board and a few glasses of amasec, under different circumstances.

'I want to find out,' she heard herself saying.

'Ma'am?' Sudliff asked, in the special tone of voice that the military reserved for when they had just heard a high-ranking civilian say something that sounded incredibly foolish, and were waiting for confirmation of exactly how foolish it was before committing to any definite response.

'Colonel, I am aware that I can make no strategic or tactical demands of the troops under your command,' Ama said primly. 'However, I feel most strongly that tempting although it is to hide up here and hope that the xenos have somehow forgotten about us, it is not the behaviour of loyal citizens of the Imperium. If the orks are not killing us then it is because they have found something better to do, and that notion is more terrifying to me than the thought of them breaking in here right now and slaughtering us all.'

Colonel Sudliff harrumphed and grimaced, and studied the hololith as though he could pull an answer for her out of its delicate web of light. However, it seemed that he could not, any more than he could totally dismiss her words. He looked at Bruja.

'Major, your thoughts?'

'The governor has a point, sir,' Bruja replied, straightening her spine and shoulders with the automatic reflexes of someone who would probably have a reasonable chance of coming to attention even while asleep, should a superior officer walk into the room. 'Even if we should die, the Imperium may be able to retake the planet, but only so long as the orks leave us a planet to retake. Who can say what manner of devilry they might be up to in the depths? There are thermal shafts that sink deep into the planet, and these beasts revel in destruction, after all.'

'They're barely more than animals,' Sudliff muttered.

'Are you telling me that the Golden Lions have been mauled and beaten back by *animals*, colonel?' Ama asked sharply. 'That is hardly a glowing reflection of your command!'

It was a strong statement, and not one that she would have ordinarily made. But Ama was tired, and it was hard to corral her thoughts before they slipped through her lips, and she very definitely had a bad feeling about the notion of orks choosing not to kill her people. The galaxy did not just... *let you off.*

The flash of Sudliff's eyes suggested to Ama that had she been one of his officers, or even a colonel from another regiment, he might have responded violently to such words. However, even an Astra Militarum colonel would think twice about taking any sort of action against a planetary governor, so long as the governor was not actively interfering in military matters, which Ama was not doing. She was simply trying to prod him in the direction she wanted, and her weariness had robbed her of any subtlety.

'Very well,' Sudliff said, through gritted teeth. 'It may be a fool's errand, but Emperor knows that the loss of a few bodies won't have any impact on our ability to withstand an assault if it should come. My main concern is that sending anyone down to reconnoitre might simply attract the bastards' attention, and draw an attack onto us which might not otherwise have occurred.' He looked at Bruja. 'Major, put the word out. I want volunteers only. Standard suicide mission detail – anyone earmarked for the penal legions gets their record scrubbed if they come back with useful intel, anyone without a mark against them gets promoted if they live, full honours and hero's bonus to surviving family if they die.' He flapped his hand. 'Make it happen.'

'Sir.' Major Bruja saluted, turned sharply, and left.

'I acknowledge the logic of your thought process, ma'am,' Sudliff said stiffly into the resulting silence, 'but I hope you're prepared for what this might bring down on us.'

'I am planetary governor, colonel,' Ama replied, trying to focus on the hololith. It was so damned complicated! So many domes, chambers, and tunnels... but the red icons indicating hostile activity definitely seemed to be converging inwards and downwards, so far as they could tell. 'I cannot govern a planet which no longer exists, and I have no illusions that the orks will not blow it up if they can find a way to do it. Nor do I have any trust that their infernal ingenuity will not be up to that task. Do you?'

Colonel Sudliff sighed, and closed his eyes.

'No.'

LOTZ

Eza led Armenius steadily through the darkness for hours, not always upwards, but never downwards. As time wore on, their surroundings grew gradually less wretched, although still hardly anything that Armenius would not have classed as 'wasteland.' Still, he began to appreciate the subtle differences in the underhive environments. A thermal shaft bringing up heat from far below not only raised the ambient temperature enough to bring him out into a sweat, but also attracted swarms of flying insects which then got tangled in the webs of orb spiders as big as his hand. However, the dry heat led to less fungus growth: it clustered around the dank corners instead, and where moisture in the air condensed onto cooler metal surfaces, and was fed on by molluscs with jagged shells that looked oddly rusty. Armenius tapped one with his finger, and found to his shock that it felt like metal.

'Iron snails,' Eza remarked, watching him. 'Absorb the metal they crawl over, then strengthen their shells with it.'

'Fascinating,' Armenius murmured. He pointed at another group of slimy creatures further up the wall, which were as long as his forearm, and strobed gently through greens and yellows. 'And them?'

'Glowslugs,' Eza said with a shrug. 'Harsh poisonous, so don't go eatin' one, Fancy Talk.'

'Hadn't intended to,' Armenius replied weakly, eyeing the creatures, and trying not to imagine what depths of starvation he would have to sink to in order to view one as an appetising meal, or indeed, as a meal of any sort.

'Good,' Eza said, their voice conveying enough surprise at Armenius' apparently good sense that Armenius felt he should probably take offence at it. What was he going to do, though? He was still reliant on the hunter's guidance to get him to where he wanted to go, so there hardly seemed any point in sticking his nose in the air and wandering off in a huff. He fell in behind Eza again, and took some comfort in the fact that his instincts not to trust anything organic which glowed appeared to be correct.

It was not long after the iron snails and glowslugs that they found the first signs of human habitation: or at least, the first signs that Armenius recognised, since Eza had already been muttering to themself about more tracks than usual, or how no one had harvested that growth of fungus lately. To begin with, there was a light far up and to the left when they emerged into an old hab-dome. It was the steady pale burn of a lumen, not the strobing pulse of a glowslug, and Armenius expected Eza to head straight for it. When the old hunter kept picking their way forwards, however, Armenius cleared his throat quietly.

'Should we not be talking to whoever lives up there?' he asked.

'No one lives up there,' Eza answered, without even turning around to see what he was referring to. Armenius looked back, and the lumen light was gone.

'Then what was–'

'Nothin' we want to concern ourselves with,' Eza said shortly, and Armenius decided to hold his tongue. The underhive was a strange place, and he did not need to poke into every corner and secret it held. Many of its residents would not be as accommodating as Eza, whose assistance had in any case only been procured by the sight (and smell, and apparently taste) of a gun they did not know, and what that might mean in terms of an unknown threat. Armenius just needed to get a message uphive, and leave the underhive to its ways.

They had to climb out of that dome, up what had once been a wide and undoubtedly grand staircase, but which was now simply a collection of trip hazards lined up one after another, a seemingly endless array of crumbling rockcrete, loose slabs and missing sections. Eza navigated their way up with the casual ease of one who had gone that way many times before, and Armenius swiftly realised that following in their footsteps was the fastest and safest way to travel. Once at the top, however, he found that the tunnel by which they passed through the wall between this dome and the next was well traversed, even to his eyes.

'Oh yes, we're gettin' close now,' Eza said, when he remarked on the footprints in the dust. 'Not far to go.'

That was music to Armenius' weary ears, and especially to his even wearier feet, but confusing as well. They had not yet reached the kind of population density he would have expected close to the wall – actually innumerable walls, barriers and blockades – that prevented the lawless folk below from passing up into Plasteel City without the permission of the hive's security forces. Everything he had learned of the depths suggested that the upper levels of the area designated as 'underhive' were not that dissimilar to the lower areas of Plasteel City itself in terms of quality of life, the main difference being that while both theoretically came under the purview of the governor, only in the latter was there much chance of laws actually being enforced.

When they came out into the next dome, Armenius was not prepared for what he saw.

This was undoubtedly a populated area. The hab-blocks and old factorum buildings which had been nothing but abandoned ruins in areas lower down were occupied, with lengths of cloth, pieces of scrap metal, or boards of freeze-dried fungus starch covering up holes in the architecture to give those who lived within some semblance of privacy. Lights split the darkness here and there: not just the ancient lumens in the ceiling up above, coaxed into life with prayer and semi-understood mechanical knowledge, but handheld devices, or those worn on the head like his own pilfered xenos tech, and cookfires, flickering warmly beneath pots or the skinned carcasses of some downhive creature judged fit for consumption.

Under normal circumstances, Armenius Varrow might have regarded such a place as a nest of scum and vermin, undoubtedly fallen far from the light of the Emperor and in all likelihood crawling with heretics and mutants. After so long with nothing but orks for company, however, the sight of a settlement populated by his own kind was enough to bring tears to his eyes. Humanity! Glorious, smelly, flawed, beautiful humanity! This was what he had been fighting to defend; this was what he was still defending now, through his quest to alert his superiors to the danger posed by the Blood Axe force.

'Checkpoint,' Eza said quietly, as they approached the first building. 'Try not to look dangerous, an' let me do the talkin,' lest the guardians take a dislike to ya.'

'Guardians?' Armenius blinked, his eyes still not yet having readjusted to the level of light they were approaching, dim though it was by the standards of the surface. He made out a crude barrier drawn across the road, and two figures standing by it. Their helmets were little more than beaten metal, coming together into a point above their heads, but the weapons they held were long-barrelled lasguns which looked deadly enough. The settlement's security then – either some form of community force, or muscle for whichever gang leader had taken this place as their own. He swallowed, and prepared himself for a potential shakedown, not that he had anything of value they could take.

'That you, Eza?' one of them shouted, half-raising his weapon.

'Shangai,' Eza called back, and the two guardians relaxed again. 'Got someone with me, but don't alarm yourselves about it – he's harmless.'

Armenius bristled at that, but refrained from disputing it. He was supposed to be trying not to look dangerous, after all. Granted, he was carrying a massive handgun, but someone walking the Davidian underhive *without* a gun was probably much more worthy of fear.

'Outsider, eh?' one of the guardians said with a contemptuous sniff as Armenius drew closer. He was a wiry man, his skin dark as shadow, with a tuft of beard on the end of his chin. 'Where're you from, stranger?'

'Found 'im down in the tunnels, when I were huntin' spider-spawn,' Eza replied, without letting Armenius speak. 'Got tales of monsters, he has, an' says he needs to speak to the people in charge.'

'Monsters?' the other guardian said dubiously. She was far paler than her companion, and only had one eye, which was a brilliant green and was studying Armenius intently. 'What manner of monsters?'

'Eh, no one knows monsters like Eza,' the first guardian said, waving them through. 'If you think he needs to be heard, he needs to be heard. Get in with you, then.'

'C'mon, Fancy Talk,' Eza said, beckoning, and Armenius hurried after them, with a quick nod to the guardians which he hoped conveyed professional respect.

Armenius had no idea what manner of reaction he would have garnered within the settlement had he entered it on his own, but his companion seemed to be attracting most of the attention as they walked through. People hailed Eza, often with the same 'shangai!' greeting they had used with the guardians, called out to enquire about their health, or whether they had slain anything impressive lately. The spider-helmed hunter replied to all such greetings with a dusty chuckle or a few quick words, but did not slow their pace.

'What is this place called?' Armenius asked in a low voice, as he hurried after Eza.

'Emperor's Gate,' Eza replied, mere moments before waving and replying to a young woman leaning out of a window above them.

'Why is it called that?'

'Oh, you'll see,' Eza replied, looking back at him and flashing a grin. 'At least, assuming the direguards let us in.'

'Direguards?' Armenius frowned. 'More guardians?'

'Dontcha know nothin,' Fancy Talk?' Eza demanded. 'The guardians keep us all safe, the direguards keep the seer safe.'

'The seer?' Armenius' stomach clenched. Should he have paid attention to his instincts about mutation and heresy? Was this a stronghold of witchery?

'Aye, the seer,' Eza said, as though it were unremarkable. 'She and her council are the people in charge, an' that's who you said you wanted to talk to. Dontcha have seers where you're from?'

'I think we maybe call them something different,' Armenius said cautiously. It did not necessarily mean anything: everyone knew that underhivers were a suspicious bunch, and would be just as likely to swarm and mob a sanctioned psyker to burn them as a witch as they would be to follow a witch and proclaim them as a prophet of the Emperor. It could be that 'seer' was simply a title used for a leader with great vision in a more metaphorical sense.

And if not? If the leader of Emperor's Gate was actually a witch? Well, Armenius still had his duty to perform. If dealing with a witch was the only way to get a message uphive, then so be it: he would just have to direct the Emperor's cleansing fury here afterwards, in the form of a few flamer teams.

'Here we are,' Eza said quietly, as they turned a corner on what appeared to be the settlement's main street. 'Now, you remember what I said about not lookin' dangerous?'

'Yes.'

'That goes double for now.'

They rounded the corner, and Armenius came to halt in utter shock.

He had expected a large, impressive building: perhaps a former office of the Administratum, from the time when this level of Davidia had been in use by such officials. He had certainly *not* expected the sight that met his eyes.

It was a huge arch, which Armenius had only not seen previously due to the cluttered nature of other buildings getting in the way and his low angle of vision. The structure must have towered over a hundred feet high in total, right up towards the roof of the hab-dome, but it was not its scale that so shocked Armenius, for he had seen the Spatian Gate on Thracian Primaris.

'What... is that?' he managed.

'*That* is the Emperor's gate,' Eza said, with a hint of smugness. Then they hastily raised their hands. 'Shangai!'

Their voice was a little more hesitant this time, and Armenius understood why when the shadows cast by the portico and columns of a nearby building disgorged two warriors.

Armenius disliked them immediately. Each carried a heavy autorifle with a bayonet slung under it which was so long as to practically be a sword, but it was not their armament which set his teeth on edge. Their helms were of a similar conical shape to the guardians at the barricade, but these fully enclosed the wearer's head behind an impassive mask broken only by eye slits. From the crest of the helm fell a long tail of what looked like hair, although presumably not attached to the scalp of the wearer. Their flak vests and the ballistic plates added over the chest were orange, but the helms were painted black, and the design made them look positively inhuman.

And combined with that damned gate...

'What is it made of?' he asked. When Eza did not answer him immediately, he repeated himself more urgently. 'The gate! What is it made of?'

'Not now,' Eza muttered. They moved forwards and engaged the two warriors – direguards? – in hasty conversation, with the occasional jerk of the head back at him. Armenius paid no attention, and gave no mind to not looking dangerous. His eyes tracked back and forth along the gate's length, taking in the seamless construction, the pale surface on which no dirt or dust seemed to have collected, and... were those markings on it, set into the substance itself? Armenius was too far away, and the available light too dim, for him to make it out for sure.

'Right, what were you gabberin' on about?' Eza demanded, turning back to him as the direguards disappeared into the building from which they had emerged. 'That's the Emperor's gate, like I said.'

'What's it made of?' Armenius repeated, not looking away from it.

'Damned if I know,' Eza said, with a shrug. 'Legend says it can't be marked or harmed, though all of us know better than to try. I mean, why would you want to mark it?'

'No human made that,' Armenius said, feeling the certainty inside him crystallise as he verbalised it.

'Well of course we didn't!' Eza laughed. 'The Emperor made it! It was His gift to us.'

'His gift?' Armenius was trying hard not to sound too sceptical, since he knew better than to openly scoff at underhivers' beliefs when he was in the middle of their town with an important message to deliver and only a questionable xenos firearm for protection, but his credulity was being stretched. The damned thing was making him uncomfortable just by its proximity. 'How do you know it's from Him?'

'Because long ago, He would send His great warriors through it.'

That voice did not belong to Eza: it was softer, and feminine. Armenius turned, and nearly recoiled at what he saw.

This black helm was more ostentatious than those belonging to the direguards, with a forward-curling ridge at the top, and large eye-lenses that were opaque, at least from the outside. Shiny chunks of metal ore had been affixed to it in an arrangement which was either haphazard, or deliberately – and, Armenius felt, aggravatingly – asymmetric. The newcomer wore robes of the same shade of orange as her guards, and a polished, oval stone sat over her breastbone.

'Shangai, seer,' Eza said, bowing.

'Shangai, Eza,' the seer replied, the sightless eyes of her helm turning towards them for a moment.

'What do you mean, the Emperor sent His warriors through this gate?' Armenius demanded. 'And what's this "shangai" thing you keep saying?' He knew that he should not ask such questions, he knew that he should just get on with his mission and have done, but even his great weariness was not enough to fully blunt the anger edging its way up to muster between his teeth. And to think Eza had told him not to take the Emperor's name in vain!

'It is the greeting of the Emperor's warriors, passed down to us through the generations from those who witnessed their last arrival here,' the seer said calmly. 'The Emperor sent His warriors to scourge the world of the unworthy. Our ancestors escaped His wrath, and we have lived in accordance with His values ever since.'

Armenius looked around, and properly took in what he saw for the first time. There were people here, for sure, but where were the signs of faith and devotion? Where were the aquilas? Where was the stake at which heretics would be burned? Why was everyone wearing a polished stone of some size or colour, somewhere on their person? The Imperial creed varied from planet to planet, he knew this: you could not expect the inhabitants of a feral world who interpreted the Emperor as the sun in the sky, or those of a mighty munitions factory in which they churned out shells through processes of which they had no true comprehension, to worship in the same manner as a cardinal world where the Ecclesiarchy ruled all. Even so, this was a perversion of faith worse than he had ever seen. Did these people still count as faithful? Was it enough to hold the name of the Emperor in reverence, if nothing that you did held any relevance to how He was to be worshiped?

Focus, Armenius. Nothing has changed. This is no worse than when you were given latrine supervision detail when the colonel caught you at his amasec. Just hold your nose, do what needs to be done, and get out the other side.

He opened his mouth to speak, but a flicker of movement caught his eye, away beyond the so-called Emperor's gate.

Green movement.

It was instinct, at this point. Armenius whirled, raising the weapon he had carried for so long in his right hand, and fired.

The concussive noise was tremendous, and the recoil brutal for someone used to the smooth whisper of a laspistol. It felt like the bones of his wrist had been pulverised, but it was not that which knocked him off his feet. That was Eza, tackling him down to the ground, as the seer screamed and stumbled away from him, and her direguards ran forwards with the barrels of their autorifles coming up to target him.

'You stupid *mon-keigh*!' Eza shouted into Armenius' face, their own face screwed up in rage and fear and sorrow. 'You've killed us both!'

Armenius ignored them, so much as it was possible to ignore someone on top of you. He did not even pay attention to the direguards as they placed themselves between him and their charge, and took aim at him. He shoved Eza out of the way enough to look in the direction he had fired, desperate to at least see whether he had been correct before he was killed by these damned heretics.

A cluster of green bodies was gathered around one of their own number on the ground, looking down at it. One of those still upright was holding a twin-jawed pole considerably taller than it was.

'Orks!' Armenius howled, pointing desperately. 'Look, Emperor damn you! *Orks!*'

The xenos looked back up and at him, and Armenius saw once again the red eyes and pointed green ears that had haunted so many of his dreams of late. Grots rather than orks, it was true, but where grots went, the orks followed. How had they got here so fast?

That was not important right now. Grots had little stomach for a fight. If Armenius could only direct the fighters of Emperor's Gate towards them, the little bastards might be scared off or killed, and he could get away before their larger cousins arrived.

The grot with the pole raised it into the air and howled something. Its companions – and there were a lot of them, Armenius realised with a sinking feeling, and the guns they held looked less like the rough firearm in his own hand, and rather more like Imperial hardware – echoed its cry.

Then the entire mass of them, in contravention of every piece of information or experience Armenius possessed about their mentality, charged.

LOTZ

Ilaethen Arhien waited, and the host of Craftworld Lugganath waited with him.

The webway was neither warm, nor cool. It was not a natural place, did not *feel* like a natural place, no matter how many millennia had passed since it first laced its way through and between and under the galaxy, halfway between the material universe and the realm of the immaterium. It was a lesson that something did not become natural merely because it had existed for a very long time, even by the standards of the children of Asuryan. Ilaethen had trodden the surface of countless worlds in his life: beautiful maiden worlds, still unspoiled; the far-flung Exodite worlds, simple and severe; and, far too many times, the lost worlds that had been invaded and devastated by the warlike lesser species. Even those last, though they might be wrapped in the fumes of war, though the air might taste of smoke and death, though the very ground might shake from the thunderous tread of monstrous war machines and the impact of colossal munitions, still felt more natural than the webway.

The fact that the webway had become a second home for his kin despite this was not a reflection on their affinity for this place. It was instead a testament to what had been inflicted upon them by usurpers, raiders and predators. The galaxy had been in flames since the Fall, and the younger, hungry species wished for nothing else. Other craftworlds still had some hope for the future, still entertained notions that even if they could no longer rule the stars, they might at least be able to set their own boundaries and live within them, safe from fear or threat.

Lugganath's people knew this to be folly. There was little for the aeldari out there save for bloodshed, sorrow, and a reminder of how they were fading from power. However, that did not mean that the material universe could be ignored completely. After all, damaged and lost though much of it now was, the webway still spanned the galaxy, and was accessible from innumerable points. If Ilaethen's people were to be kept safe, then they had to ensure that no one accessed the webway other than aeldari. Theoretically, that should be impossible in any case, but Ilaethen had learned long ago that comfortable theories rarely stood up well to the indifference of an uncaring galaxy.

He shifted his gaze to Yria Nightsong. The farseer stood tall and sombre, her shaved head revealing the smooth planes of her skull and orbited by wraithbone runes. They meant little to Ilaethen, who had never progressed far along the Path of the Seer. The Path of the Warrior had always called to him, but his self-control had sufficed to see him turn away from each aspect after he had studied it. Now he walked the Path of Command as an autarch, one of the hands that guided the blade of Lugganath's forces. However, he did not dictate where the blade should be deployed.

He raised an eyebrow slightly, the miniscule movement as clear as words to someone such as Yria, whom he had known for centuries. *The runes remain unchanged?*

Her lips pursed. *They do.* He could read the regret in her face, though it would have been an impassive mask even to some of his own kin, let alone an alien. Her expression cleared, and she looked directly at him. *This course is necessary, although it saddens me.*

He inclined his head a fraction, once. *As it does me.* Ilaethen had no regrets about killing those who threatened what remained of his people's way of life, but it was a rare occurrence indeed when such an action cost no lives of Lugganath in return – and Lugganath had no lives to spare. Every engagement that could be foreseen was weighed to a nicety by their seers to determine the benefits, and the price. Which were the threads of fate that could most efficiently be severed to bring about the desired result, or stave off the greatest disaster? How likely was it that the act of engaging would itself spark disaster?

Some foes were largely predictable, albeit implacable: the brutal Imperium ploughed forwards and drowned the galaxy in its own blood, throwing their brief lives away to achieve short-sighted dominance. Common ground might be found with them in the most desperate of situations, against foes the mon-keigh perceived more horrific than the aeldari, but in the end their shallow, bitter hatred of anything even remotely different from themselves would lead them back to violence and treachery. The reawakened ancient enemy of the Great Dynasties were even worse: near-mindless machine bodies, led by those few who retained some semblance of wider comprehension. Ilaethen was not certain which was worse: the tragedy of so many lives being lost to a species that did not realise its time was past, or the possibility that they might yet truly rise again. The swarms of the Great Devourer were predictable, certainly, but that did not mean that they could be easily stopped. Against such hunger, foresight was of little use other than guiding the children of Asuryan out of its reach.

Then there was the foe against whom the forces of Lugganath had mustered; a foe whom the foolish underestimated, and of whom the wise were wary. Predictable in their lust for violence and conquest they most certainly were, but even the arts of the most skilled seers sometimes availed aeldari warriors little in terms of how that violence was going to play out, moment to moment. How such beasts might gain access to the webway was unclear, but the runes seemed certain that they had the capacity to do so, and that could not be tolerated.

Ilaethen sighed. He had learned, in years past, that the mon-keigh had a saying: 'no battle plan survives contact with the enemy.' It was emblematic of their species, in that it made excuses for failure before such an event had even occurred. Ilaethen himself had planned, overseen, and executed whole wars that had fallen within acceptable and predictable parameters, from the timing of the first raid to the climactic and crucial slaying of the enemy general.

But when it came to the orks, he conceded that the mon-keigh might have a point.

There was nothing for it now, however. In a way, he was glad that Yria's runes had not changed, despite the losses which were sure to follow. He could feel the hot, heavy beating of his blood in his chest, rising up to ensnare his mind. Lugganath had roused for war, and once so roused, war could not easily be set aside.

Ilaethen's people might be as at home in the webway as they were in their craftworld, but the craftworld still bound them with some ties that could not be broken.

LOTZ

'For da GrotWaaagh!'

Snaggi Littletoof screamed his war cry, and it was taken up by the loyal ladz all around him. He had been guided here, right to the gateway, by the knowledge of Gork and Mork – and, alright, a bit of a hint from Old Morgrub, but he was a warphead so that was practically the same thing – and he wasn't going to let a bunch of humies get in his way now, especially since one of them had shot Kruffik. Snaggi wasn't going to miss Kruffik at all, but it was the principle of the thing. Besides, always good to let the underlings think you might care if they died.

'Get 'em!' he bawled, and his mob, the first members of what would surely come to be one of the most feared warbands in the entire galaxy, surged forwards with screams, and yells, and the crack of gunfire. They had crept past the humie guards to get into this settlement, and slit a couple of throats when needed in order to remain unseen, but the time for subterfuge and concealment was over. Snaggi aimed the humie boomstikk one-handed and pulled the trigger with a joyous grin: the recoil nearly jarred his shoulder out of its socket, but by the gods, what a *noise* it made! Not as much kick as an ork shoota, but at least that meant he had some hope of shooting straight with it.

Most of the humies panicked and ran, fleeing from the righteous wrath of Gork and Mork's chosen like the cowardly gits their species were when they didn't have superior numbers, or some of those well 'ard beakies in their supa-armour. A few chose to stand and fight, which was zoggin' foolish of them, because they weren't enough to have a hope of standing up to the GrotWaaagh!. One of Snippa One-Ear's mob bought it, courtesy of a rattle of small shells from a humie wearing an orange vest and a weird helmet that looked a bit like those the skrawniez wore, if it had been built in the dark by a grot who had only heard a rough description of one. That was not enough to turn back the green tide, however, and the humie and its mate both fell as grot gunfire tore into their bodies. The second one was still moving when Snaggi reached it, and he gave it a good old zap with the grabba stikk until its flesh was smoking and it had stopped spasming, to make sure it was properly dead.

'Secure da perimeter!' he yelled at his troops.

'Uh, wot?' Skrawk asked, scratching his head. Snaggi sighed, and bopped him on the skull – but gently, because Snaggi decided that a future grot-boss would favour correction, not punishment.

'Spread out, an' make sure da humies don't get near da gate,' he clarified, pointing at the enormous arch of that weird bone-stuff the skrawniez made things out of. It wasn't actually bone – at least, he had never found a bit of it which had been any good to eat, and Mork knew he had tried – and it wasn't metal, and you couldn't do a zoggin' thing with it that was any use, but it was hard-wearing, he'd give it that. Bloody skrawniez, they had to be all special and have their own thing that no one else could have, didn't they?

'But dey ran away!' Snippa pointed out.

'Dey're easily scared, but dey'll be back soon, an' wiv a bunch of dere mates,' Snaggi said grimly. 'Dey built dere town around dis fing, dey've gotta fink it's important. I ain't havin' any humies around to get in da way when da rest of da Waaagh! turns up an' we show Old Morgrub dat it's da grots wot got it done, am I right?'

The ragged cheer which went up suggested that he was indeed right, and his mob spread out with their weapons aimed at the surrounding buildings and streets.

'Snaggi?' Guffink said quietly, after a few seconds of fierce concentration had passed.

'Wot?'

'So we keep da humies from gettin' dere gate back, I unnerstand dat...'

'Yeah?'

'How're we gonna keep Mag Dedfist from takin' it off us? Only he's a lot bigger dan da humies, an' he's basically got all da boyz from da Waaagh! wiv him wot weren't in Stompas an' dat, an' he weren't dat far behind us last time we checked...'

Snaggi sighed. 'Ya just gotta put yer trust in Gork an' Mork, Guffink. Dey know dat I'm dere chosen one, an' Old Morgrub knows I'm dere chosen one, so when Morgrub sees us wiv da gate, dat's gonna be an end to it.'

'But I'm just sayin,' wot if Mag gets here first? Like, before Old Morgrub? Or wot if he don't listen to Morgrub? I'm just tryin' to fink dis froo, an' dere's a lotta very-ubbles.'

Snaggi frowned at him uncomprehendingly. 'Very-ubbles?'

'Yeah, it's somefing Zagblutz used to say. Fink it means "stuff wot changes a lot".'

Snaggi opened his mouth to deliver a stinging retort, something that would leave Guffink shamefaced for questioning the will of the gods. The problem was that the will of the gods, which Snaggi knew to be true, was nevertheless struggling to hold up in his mind against Guffink's ragged logic, despite the fact that the deliverer of said logic was currently investigating the contents of one nostril with his finger.

Intellectually, yes, *intellectually* Snaggi knew that he was the chosen one of Gork and Mork, because, well, he had to be, didn't he? He had dropped the Gargant's head on Gazrot Goresnappa, and grots didn't get to do something as momentous as that without the favour of the gods. It was logical, it was sensible, it was bleeding obvious.

However, Snaggi's brain also possessed the intellectual knowledge that Mag Dedfist was perfectly capable of arguing against the logical, the sensible, and indeed the bleeding obvious; and what was more, that Mag Dedfist was big enough and mean enough that he just might *win*.

'S'gonna be fine,' he said. 'Cos…'

He paused, searching for inspiration. What he found instead was dakka. And while dakka might serve in the stead of inspiration for a lot of orks in a lot of situations, it was not what Snaggi was hoping for right now given that it was not any of his ladz who were the cause of it.

'Yoo hear dat?' Snippa One-Ear asked, perking his remaining ear up as the sound of shots began to ring out. It was joined a moment later by the roar of a mass of orkish voices, coming from the same direction from which they had entered the town, which meant it was highly likely that Mag Dedfist and his boyz had managed to follow Snaggi and his mob here after all, despite the distance they had tried to put between them.

'Nuffin' to worry about!' Snaggi said, as confidently as he could manage. 'Dey're just gonna take care of da humies for us!'

His head jerked around as a new noise reached his ears. This also contained elements of dakka, but the hearing of a grot was sensitive to more than just gunfire, and Snaggi could make out the throaty roars of many, many engines.

'Speed freeks,' Guffink whispered. 'But Mag didn't have any buggies an' dat wiv him, did he? Dey all zogged off with Speedboss Thundaskuzz.'

'Dat's comin' from a different direcshun!' Snippa wailed. 'Dat *is* Thundaskuzz! Da git must've found a way to get da buggies inside!'

'Well, den da two of 'em can scrag each uvver for all I care!' Snaggi spat, hastily reloading his boomstikk. It was just his luck that that oil-drinking gearhead had managed to make it here as well! Honestly, you would have thought that Gork and Mork might see their way to giving their chosen one a slightly easier time of it, but perhaps that was the way of things. Greatness was forged through challenges, and Snaggi Littletoof was about to experience the greatest challenge of his existence to date.

Still, at least Da Genrul hadn't made it this far. Snaggi had heard that the Blood Axes had been digging holes around the south end of the humie city, for whatever reason Blood Axes had for doing anything, so it wasn't like they were going to be showing up anytime soon–

A building exploded, directly in front of him.

The harsh bark of shootas rang out, and humie voices could be heard screaming and shouting. It wasn't Mag's lot responsible for this – not unless some of them had circumnavigated the town to attack it from two sides at once, which was hardly a Goff strategy, given that Goff strategy usually extended to 'hit 'em really hard, an' if dey ain't dead, hit 'em again.'

It seemed that Da Genrul had arrived with a typical lack of fanfare, and an equally typical application of violence.

'Snaggi?' someone whispered.

'Look, we're no worse off dan we was,' Snaggi managed.

'Yes we are!' Snippa hissed. 'Last time dese gitz were at each uvver's froats, we weren't standin' between dem an' wot dey wanted to get to!'

A humie appeared, running full pelt away from the Blood Axe onslaught, with three orks in pursuit: it was, Snaggi realised with a start, the one who had shot Kruffik. One of the orks threw something blunt, perhaps a small chunk of what had recently been building, which clocked the humie on the back of the head. It fell headlong, clearly dazed, and something spilled from its grasp which looked very much like a grot blasta, but it still flailed weakly to try to get up and keep moving. Snaggi levelled his boomstikk to shoot it, but the purposeful look of the Blood Axes moving up behind their quarry made him reconsider. It seemed like these orks wanted that humie alive for something, and it was a foolish grot who killed something on the rare occasion an ork wanted it alive. Even if Snaggi was going to become grotboss and lead the entire Waaagh!, it didn't make sense to push his luck before that had been confirmed, did it?

Then Da Genrul hove into view, one hand on the haft of the power choppa balanced casually on one shoulder, the other clutching his beakie-made twin shoota, and with Sarge the Killa Kan clumping along behind him on its piston-driven legs. One of the other orks hauled the dazed humie upright and turned it to face Genrul Uzbrag, whereupon it promptly began to wail.

'Ah, kaptin,' Da Genrul said genially. 'Good to see ya again. I fink exercise time is over, don't yoo?' He knocked on Sarge's hull, and the Killa Kan obediently turned around to present an empty cage.

The humie howled and thrashed and wept, but nothing it did could prevent it from being stuffed into the cage, and the door closed and locked. With that done to his satisfaction, Uzbrag at last deigned to notice Snaggi and his ladz.

'Who left dis buncha grots here?' Da Genrul asked, nonplussed. Another building collapsed some way behind him, and a handful of fleeing humies found that the shadows into which they were desperately running contained kommandos with sharp knives and sharper grins.

'Uzbrag!'

Snaggi was not certain if he was relieved or alarmed by the bellow that rang out and dragged Da Genrul's attention away from him. On the one hand, it meant he did not have to face down the Blood Axe big boss there and then. On the other hand, it meant that Mag Dedfist had not fallen down a hole, or been blown up by his skorchas malfunctioning, or even, outside possibility though it might have been, been killed by a humie, and *that* meant that the Goff was going to be trying to lay his own claim to the gateway.

'Dedfist!' Da Genrul retorted with a grin. 'It's kinda impressive how ya can be so fick dat a wall can't stop ya!'

'We'll see who's larfin' when I take ya head off!' Mag Dedfist bellowed, advancing from the far side of the gate with the thunderous tread of a mega-armoured ork in a great hurry. He pointed at the nearest of Snaggi's ladz as he passed them, causing them to shrink back from him in fear. 'Dese your grots den, muckin' about an' messin' fings up?'

Uzbrag cast a puzzled glance at Snaggi. 'Nuffin' to do wiv me.' He shrugged the power choppa off his shoulder. 'Now, we can all see dat I got 'ere first, but since I can already tell dat ya ain't interested in fings like dat, d'ya wanna get down to it now, or wait for Thundaskuzz to show up?'

'Thundaskuzz?!' Dedfist guffawed. 'Wot makes ya fink dat git's comin'? He's still drivin' around in circles lookin' for a door, cos he don't have da brains to make one of his own!'

'He might not have brains, but all dat time clankin' around in yer armour means *yoo* don't got any ears,' Da Genrul said smugly, and looked meaningfully to his left.

The howl of engines had already been growing louder, but it rose to a crescendo as a Deffkilla wartrike screamed between two buildings and screeched to a halt in an extended skid that crushed one of Snaggi's ladz who didn't manage to get out of the way in time. Zagnob Thundaskuzz, who now had rather less face than the last time Snaggi had seen him, glared down at the other two big bosses from his platform and worked the action of his snagga klaw with an audible *klik-klak*. He was not alone, either: his convoy of heavily armed and lightly armoured vehicles pulled up behind him, with the bad nature of speed freeks compelled to stop.

'Who let da runts in?' were Zagnob's first words, his surprise at seeing Snaggi and his mob standing around the skrawniez' gate apparently greater than his desire to exchange unpleasantries with his rivals.

'I figured dey were his,' Mag Dedfist rumbled, pointing at Da Genrul.

'Ya need to stop tryin' to fink, cos ya clearly ain't any good at it,' Uzbrag scoffed. 'Alright den, boyz, we're all here again, an' nuffink's been settled, so where's da warphead? Or am I gonna have to do dis da old-fashioned way, like Gazrot would've wanted, an' beat some sense into da pair of ya?'

He flicked the switch on his power choppa to activate the crackling energy field around its blade, an action that was reciprocated by Mag Dedfist and his power klaw. Zagnob Thundaskuzz racked the action on his double boomstikk, and eyed the pair of them, waiting to see who he should plug first.

'Alright, alright, stand back dere! Let me froo!'

Some of the orks who had gathered around to see the three big bosses go at it began to shift out of the way, which was not a particularly orky thing to do, unless the ork demanding that you do so might just make your head explode if you didn't. The shape of Old Morgrub emerged, his staff still rattling with trinkets and his eyes slightly too wide and slightly too vacant as ever.

'Well done!' he cackled, shaking his staff until it rattled. 'Yoo all got here! So, who got here first?'

'I did!' Snaggi shouted, leaping into the gap while Da Genrul was still taking a breath.

Every single ork head turned to look at him. For the first time in Snaggi Littletoof's life – quite probably for the first time in history – a grot found himself the centre of orkish attention.

It was... not entirely pleasant.

Options capered through his brain like a snotling after too much fungus beer. He could run. Just turn and run. None of them would pay any attention to him: they would all go back to their quarrel, because grots simply weren't worth paying attention to. If any of the three big bosses saw him tomorrow, they wouldn't even remember him.

Or, another possibility, he could quickly size up which of the three he thought was most likely to win, then declare that he'd claimed the gate for him. If his chosen fighter lost then he could still disappear with the same chance of anonymity, and if he turned out to have backed a winner then there might be something in it for him.

Something... Like a half-chewed humie leg. Or a shiny rock that the ork didn't want.

Neither of those options were acceptable. Not because he had an outsized and unrealistic appetite for glory and recognition, no: it was because Gork and Mork had spoken to him, damn it all, and they had made it very clear that he was their chosen one. *He* was supposed to lead the Waaagh! *He* was supposed to turn things around and bring grots to their rightful place on top! This was bigger than his own individual thoughts and fears: this was about *destiny*!

'I am Snaggi Littletoof!' he shouted into the silence. 'I killed Gazrot Goresnappa when I dropped da Gargant head on him! I killed Zukrod da runtherd wiv his own grabba stikk! Gork an' Mork have spoken to me, an' told me dat I'm gonna be Da Grotboss!' He pointed behind him at the huge arc of the skrawniez' gate. 'An' I found da gateway first! Dat *proves* it!'

There was a further silence, as the assembled orks considered what they had just heard. Then Da Genrul looked at Old Morgrub.

'Yoo're a Snakebite, Morgrub, ya know about runts an' stuff. Ya know dis little git?'

Morgrub's eyes swivelled towards Snaggi, without the rest of his head moving. They roved over him for a few moments, and then the warphead opened his mouth to deliver his judgement. Snaggi squeezed the grabba stikk tighter, waiting for the vindication and acclamation which would surely emerge.

'Never seen 'im before. Kill 'im if ya want, he's in da way.'

Snaggi's mouth dropped open. How could– But he– This wasn't *fair!*

'Enuff said,' Da Genrul grunted, raising his twin shoota. 'Zog off, runt.'

Light flickered. Not the lights far above in the dome's ceiling, dirty and yellow and very, very humie in their tone. This was cold and clean, and seemed to banish shadow, leaving anything it touched illuminated with a clarity that was not exactly bright, but which hurt the eyes nonetheless. It cast stark, unpleasant shadows on the ground.

And it was coming from directly behind Snaggi.

He turned away from the confused expression washing over Da Genrul's face, something pulling at him hard enough to look away even from his own impending death. The arch, which until now had been nothing more than hollow, if still imposing, was now filled from edge to edge with a shimmering veil of light. It was not bright, but nor was it hazy, or lazy, or faint, or gentle. It shifted from steel-grey to ice-white, and from chilly blues to a cold green that was no kin to any shade of orkish skin.

'I knew it'd work!' Snaggi heard Old Morgrub cackle behind him. 'Get enough of us here, an' I knew dey'd come to protect da doorway! Dey can't let us get in, ya see? Dey're too scared, cos dey know I've got me stone, an' if we *do* get in, dere's nowhere we can't go!'

Snaggi frowned. There seemed to be… shadows behind the light? How did that work? Snaggi was not the most well versed in exactly what light did to make things look the way they looked, but he was pretty sure that you only got shadows if things were standing *in front* of the light.

'Oh,' he heard Old Morgrub add, 'ya might wanna take a step back for dis next part.'

The light parted, and death flowed out.

LOTZ

Everything had gone according to plan, even if Genrul Uzbrag said so himself.

Kaptin Varrow had played his part perfectly, almost as if he were one of Uzbrag's own, rather than a captive. The key thing to outwitting humies, Da Genrul had come to realise, was that they were always incredibly eager to assume that they were more intelligent than you were. They would often fall into even reasonably obvious traps, simply because they could not wrap their heads around the idea that an ork was capable of laying one.

For that, Uzbrag supposed the Blood Axes should be thankful to the other clans. There were certainly some warlords here and there who had a grasp of grand strategy – Ghazghkull Thraka was as cunning as any Blood Axe, despite being a Goff, but then Ghazghkull was the Prophet of Gork and Mork – but in general, most orks, even warbosses, just reacted to what was in front of them. That was often still enough to scrag humies, since they seemed to expect orks to be slow and lumbering, but it wasn't what you might call 'taktiks'. No, for forward planning and sideways thinking you usually needed a Blood Axe, and the fact that the rest of the clans didn't bother with such niceties just made it all the easier to hoodwink a humie.

It had taken a bit of effort to get everyone into the tunnels – Sarge the Killa Kan had been especially tricky – but it was worth it. Uzbrag's ladz had followed the trail laid down by Skulsnik's Guttas, and didn't even get too distracted on the way. They didn't have any vehicles with them, no buggies or trakks or flyers or Deff Dreads, and nor did they have any mek gunz or other fancy bits of big dakka, but Da Genrul knew that those things were not essential, when it came down to it. He had mob after mob of ladz, ranging from the masses of regular boyz who wanted nothing more than to empty their sluggas and shootas into an enemy, and then maybe get a bit of choppa work in too, to the more specialist mobs like the tankbustas with their rokkit launchas and high explosives, and the burna boyz who could and would immolate anything that moved. He had meks, and painboyz, and runtherds, and every one of them had the sort of orkish ingenuity that would one day bring the galaxy to its knees. The gubbinz he had left behind could be replaced, given a bit of time and a few resources.

All he needed was orks. Everything else would take care of itself, sooner or later.

The humies down here barely counted as opposition. Uzbrag's military mind almost despaired of how pitiful this town's defences had been. Had the humies not known he was coming? Well, of course they didn't know specifically, that was sort of the point of sneaking in via the tunnels rather than battering his way in through the walls, but did they not even know that there were orks outside, who might theoretically get *in*side at some point? Honestly, Da Genrul had expected better than this of humies. They might be a bit naff in a fight most of the time, but normally they at least knew that there *was* a fight. Skulsnik's ladz had slit the sentries' throats, and no one else noticed the Blood Axes until they were blowing up buildings and letting rip with dakka.

It was convenient in a way, though. He hadn't even had to go searching for the skrawniez' gate, since Varrow had led him directly to that as well, and the lack of resistance from the humies meant there was no argument that he had got here first. Not that it seemed to make any difference, since Mag Dedfist was utterly incapable of accepting that Uzbrag was the better ork. As for Zagnob Thundaskuzz, Uzbrag was surprised he had even managed to remember the gate for long enough to get inside and try to find it, let alone actually succeed.

As it turned out, however, the gate might not have been what the three big bosses had been led to believe. Which just showed what you got if you were foolish enough to trust a weirdboy.

'I knew it'd work!' Old Morgrub cackled as the gate lit up with strange lights. 'Get enough of us here, an' I knew dey'd come to protect da doorway! Dey can't let us get in, ya see? Dey're too scared, cos dey know I've got me stone, an' if we *do* get in, dere's nowhere we can't go!'

Uzbrag glowered at him, hoping for some sort of additional explanation that actually made, y'know, *sense*, but it seemed that was too much to hope for. Morgrub just licked the stone he had taken from that skrawnie weirdboy, and giggled as it sparked on his tongue. Uzbrag considered shooting the grot at which he was still aiming his beakie shoota, but the runt wasn't even looking at him any longer, and shooting a grot in the back was so pathetic that it wasn't even funny. Besides, Uzbrag had more pressing concerns than disciplining one runt with ideas above its station, so he rapped on Sarge's hull to get the Killa Kan to pivot around on the spot.

'Look at dat!' Da Genrul ordered the cowering Kaptin Varrow in humie-speak, pointing at the shifting lights in the gateway. 'Wot's goin' on?'

Varrow's eyes went wide as he beheld what was going on, but he appeared to be either unable or unwilling to communicate exactly what 'that' was. Uzbrag growled in frustration, and spun his power choppa to loosen his wrist up for whatever was about to go down. In the process of doing so he accidentally split the skull of one of the grots which had been surrounding the gate (for reasons he still had not quite puzzled out) and was now fleeing away from it (for reasons which were at least a little more understandable, at least bearing in mind the general mentality of grots).

'Oh,' Old Morgrub said conversationally, to the assembled orks in general, 'ya might wanna take a step back for dis next part.'

Uzbrag opened his mouth to ask the old git what he meant by that, but was brought up short when it became obvious. The shimmering curtain of light filling the giant archway began to boil – Uzbrag had not seen light boil before, but he couldn't think of a better term to describe it – and figures stepped out of it.

They were tall and slim, lithe and athletic, clad in figure-hugging armour of dark shiny cloth and hard orange protective plates. Their weapons were long and slender, all organic curves and smooth edges, not like the blocky, angular equipment of the boyz. They were possessed of the sort of fluid grace that reminded Uzbrag of a buzzer squig swarm: no movements were sharp or jerky, everything was smooth from one moment to the next, almost as though a small body of liquid had taken flight with a callous disregard for concepts like gravity. However, whereas buzzer squigs lacked intelligence, and their apparent unity simply came from a shared instinct to head for the nearest food source and avoid threats, each of these beings was obviously under the control of a conscious mind.

Well, and they were solid, rather than being made up of thousands of tiny bodies, but Uzbrag thought that distinction was fairly self-evident.

He knew what they were, of course. He had fought and killed them before, or at least things that looked and moved a lot like them, although he remembered those ones being a bit spikier. Given the context of where they were, and what they were emerging from, it was a fairly easy conclusion to draw.

'Skrawniez!' he bellowed, for the benefit of any of his mobs who were a little slower on the uptake, or did not have a sufficiently good view. He raised his beakie-shoota to open fire.

The skrawniez beat him to it.

The first ones out let rip with a hail of their slicy-disc things, the sort of ammunition that could take your hand off if you weren't careful. Uzbrag felt a *thump* from his chest and looked down to see three of them sticking out, all in a neat little row, where they had cut through the fabric of his greatcoat and embedded in the breastplate of the armour he wore beneath it.

'Oi!' he bellowed, outraged. 'Dat nearly got me!'

He opened fire, and he was not the only one. The skrawniez had been their usual annoyingly speedy selves and got their shots in before the ladz could react, and orks were already fumbling their shootas as arms fell away, or falling over as a leg got sliced off, or even just toppling backwards because a few internal organs had taken the brunt of the volley. However, there were still a lot of orks on their feet, or who were more angered than incapacitated by whatever had hit them, and they all had guns. The whisper-sounds of the skrawniez' slicy-discs slipping through the air like a rippy-fish through water were drowned out by the cough and roar of sluggas, shootas and big shootas getting their own back. Agile and elusive though the skrawniez were, and surprisingly tough though their flimsy-looking armour might be, there was only going to be one outcome. Slim bodies fell, ripped apart by munitions that prized efficacy (and a great deal of noise) over elegance. Trying to get into a dakka contest with a Waaagh! at close range was never a good idea.

Unless, of course, you brought tanks to a gunfight.

Uzbrag obliterated the closest skrawnie with a volley from his beakie-shoota, then blinked in surprise as the gate lights darkened once more. However, this did not resolve into another wave of skrawnie infantry: instead, the light slid apart and flowed around the twin-scythe prow of a floating vessel, its heavy guns already spitting death as it *thrummed* over the heads of the skrawnie troops who were still standing.[11] Uzbrag fired upwards into its hull as it passed over him, but his shots simply glanced off in showers of sparks without even leaving a scratch. A door at the rear hissed open as though in response to his attack, but his attempts to shoot through it were foiled by some sort of force field.

However, at least it seemed that the skrawniez inside were not content to let the tank's gunners have all the fun. A whole bunch of them jumped out clutching pistols and chain-choppas, and they were even wearing a shade of dark green, unlike the orange vehicle in which they had been riding. Uzbrag nodded in approval: it stood to reason that even skrawniez might behave in an appropriately orky manner if they wore green.

They landed like a thunderbolt in the midst of Da Genrul's ladz, their helmets spitting flashes of light even before they hit the ground. Boyz fell howling, clutching their eyes or their necks, and the skrawniez gave no time for the rest to sort themselves out. They plunged in with blade and pistol, decapitating and eviscerating. Slicer ammo punched through ork torsos in a fine spray of blood and went on to strike other victims; spindly chain-choppas met the trunklike limbs of boyz and prevailed in a shower of gore, leaving the bewildered amputees toppling sideways, or lacking a weapon with which to parry the next blow that was aimed for their necks.

'Now *dat's* more like it!' Uzbrag exclaimed with feeling. Blood Axes might think tactically, but he enjoyed a good scrap up close as much as the next ork: in fact, probably more than the next ork, since he was more likely to win. He raised his power choppa and pointed at the skrawnie mob.

'Officerz! Get 'em!'

The skrawniez had done a lot of damage to the boyz, striking hard and fast before their victims could react, and pressing the attack to prevent their victims from getting themselves organised and applying boot leather to the problem. What this situation needed was a bit of leadership by example, which was exactly what was about to arrive in a flurry of shiny medals and grimy choppas.

Da High Kommand was five of Genrul Uzbrag's most hard-bitten nobs: four lootenants led by Zorlag, who had finally accepted the rank of major, wielding choppas that probably weighed as much as a skrawnie, and clad in the best 'eavy armour that teef could buy. They were outnumbered two to one by the pointy-eared gits, but chain-choppas that had ripped apart lesser orks glanced off them with skittering noises, and it was skrawnie blood that flowed when they struck back. Uzbrag would be the first to admit that orks didn't move as smoothly as some of the things they clobbered across the

[11] And also over the troops who were no longer standing, but not all of those had heads left.

galaxy, but that didn't mean that they were slow. They were certainly fast enough to chop a skrawnie in half if they let their guard down for half a second, and that was what the major's power klaw had just done.

Still, one of the skrawniez was on a different level to the rest. It flowed aside from strikes and ducked under point-blank shots, always avoiding harm by the narrowest of margins, then lashing out and leaving death in its wake. One of the lootenants took a swing at it, a diagonal downward blow which should have been unavoidable, should have left the skrawnie as nothing but two asymmetric pieces in a pool of its own blood. The lootenant in question was Kabrukk, one of the biggest and strongest under Da Genrul's command, and a towering piece of ork-flesh. The green-armoured skrawnie almost looked like a grot when set against him, so different were they in size and bulk, and it didn't dodge the blow.

It caught it.

Kabrukk had the briefest of moments to register what had happened, and for shock to spread over his face as he realised that the haft of his weapon was held fast in the clutches of the skrawnie's own power klaw. The skrawnie held him there for a moment, making a point of demonstrating its strength in a manner that Uzbrag found almost admirable. Then it flowed into motion again, using Kabrukk's choppa to hoist itself off the ground and deliver a back-flipping kick into his jaw. Kabrukk staggered backwards, teef flying, and the skrawnie fired a volley of slicers into his neck before its feet even touched down again. Kabrukk's head began to slide off his shoulders, and Uzbrag had seen enough.

'Dat one's mine!' he bellowed, holstering his beakie-shoota, and spinning his power choppa to make the point and attract its attention. The tank the green skrawniez had arrived in was still dakka-ing its way through his ladz, but a series of concussive explosions sent it rocking and announced that the tankbustas had found their range. Then dark shapes soared through the air in long rokkit-propelled arcs, and the ladz of Mag Dedfist's stormboyz known as Da Skyklaw landed on it. Uzbrag thought he could probably leave that to others to handle: this git looked like a challenge, and it had been too long since he'd had a proper fight.

The skrawnie nob heard his yell, and its strange crested helm whipped around to focus on him with insectoid lenses. It decapitated another boy with an almost casual backswing of its chain-choppa, and sprang towards him.

Uzbrag stepped to meet it, bringing his power choppa around in a two-handed swing at chest height. The skrawnie's helmet guns, which had flared as though about to fire, disappeared from view as it threw itself into a graceful roll and evaded his blow by the width of a grot's promise. Uzbrag let his momentum carry him around, and he aimed the point of his weapon at the skrawnie's chest as it came back up to its feet. His enemy nodded once, as though in recognition of a worthy adversary, then attacked again.

Gork's teeth, but it was fast! It had two obvious weapons, the chain-choppa and the power klaw, but the klaw also had that slicer-thrower built in, with which the skrawnie let rip at the slightest opportunity. Then there were its helmet guns, which were not going to have enough punch to seriously trouble an ork as big and tough as Uzbrag, but certainly had the potential to throw him off his swing at a critical moment.

Finally, there was the skrawnie itself.

It had already demonstrated the surprising amount of sheer strength contained in its skinny body, and it was not above throwing elbows, kicks or knees at an opportune moment. None of those blows in and of itself would put Uzbrag down, but the skrawnie was not going for one big hit to take him out. It was trying to wear him down, to bleed him from several cuts, debilitate and disorientate him before moving in for the kill. It was a good strategy, like Uzbrag had seen beast snaggas utilise when faced with massive prey animals, enemy war beasts, or even vehicles.

However, he was none of those things. He was Da Genrul, and he was *always* one step ahead.

He ducked his head, and the needle-thin slivers fired by the skrawnie's helmet guns glanced harmlessly off his reinforced hat rather than embedding in his flesh to provide the conduit for the laser sting intended to follow. He whirled his axe-headed power choppa two-handed, an almost casual move that parried and blocked strike after strike from his enemy's klaw and chainblade with the head or the haft, then struck back with a blow that left a long, deep gouge across the skrawnie's breastplate. The skrawnie leaped into the air to deliver a spinning kick to Uzbrag's head; he caught the git's shin a hand's breadth from his ear, then wrenched it around to slam his enemy bodily into the ground by its leg.

He lashed out with his power choppa again as the skrawnie raised itself back to one knee, and the force of his blow ripped its parrying chainblade from its grasp. He turned the motion of that strike into a second one, bringing his weapon around to raise it overhead in both hands, then slashing downwards.

The skrawnie's power klaw flashed up and caught the haft before the axe head landed, just like it had done with Kabrukk.

Uzbrag wrenched backwards to pull the skrawnie towards him, and lashed out with a knee at what was now its head height.

The skrawnie's helmet guns discharged into his thigh at the exact same time that he connected with the snout of its helm. Something cracked, and it wasn't his knee. Uzbrag bellowed in pain as the sting flashed up his leg like fire, but the skrawnie had caught the worst of the exchange. It was flung backwards, and it flailed ungracefully for the first time as it tried to get its legs back under it. Its ruined helmet fell away from its head to reveal sharp cheekbones and the ubiquitous pointy ears of its kind, as well as slightly glazed eyes and a nose from which a trickle of blood was running.

'Come on!' Uzbrag roared, stomping unsteadily towards it. 'I don't need two workin' legs to scrag ya, ya little git!'

To its credit, the skrawnie nob didn't do what a lot of enemies would have done in this situation, in that it didn't turn tail and leg it. It probably could have outpaced him, unsteady on its feet or not, given he was limping now, and there were few things in the galaxy as fast as a skrawnie which had decided that it did not want to be caught. Instead it came to meet him one more time, power klaw extended and spitting slicy-discs, a snarl of rage twisting its lips.

Some of the slicers lodged in Uzbrag's armour again, but none of them found a weak point, and he ducked away from the rest. The blow he'd delivered to the skrawnie's head had clearly scrambled its perceptions: he was on top of it before it realised, and his choppa swept around and up to take its power klaw off at the elbow.

Even then, with one limb missing and blood gouting, the skrawnie did not cry out. It simply hissed with rage and malice, and reached for his eyes with hooked fingers.

Uzbrag's arm was longer. He grabbed it by the throat with his free hand, and tightened his grip. The skrawnie's eyes bulged for a second. Then its vertebrae snapped, and it went limp. Uzbrag nodded in satisfaction, turned around, and hurled its corpse back towards the gateway. He was hoping to send it right back through, which he thought would be quite funny, or if not, maybe take out one of its mates on this side. Instead, it bounced off the prow of another one of those floating tanks.

There were now several of them, Uzbrag noticed with the closest he ever really came to concern. There were also a lot more skrawniez than the last time he had looked. In fact, the pointy-eared gits were everywhere, pushing the boyz back as they came. The ground was awash with orkish blood, and the skrawniez were fighting with grim determination, paying little attention to their own losses.

'Dey really want dis, don't dey?' Skulsnik observed, arriving at Uzbrag's elbow. His knives were wet with skrawnie blood, and he'd lost an eye to someone else's blade since Da Genrul had last seen him.

Uzbrag cast a glance in the direction of Old Morgrub. The warphead was not hard to find: his chilling cackle rang out as his mouth opened wider than should be possible, and then he vomited a tide of green fire which washed over the nearest mob of skrawniez and melted them where they stood.

'Dat git knew dat somefing like dis was gonna happen when we got 'ere, an' he said nuffink,' Uzbrag observed angrily. 'I ain't got no problem wiv a scrap, dat's all good, but I ain't havin' a zoggin' weirdboy finking he can lead me around like a squiggoth! We're gonna have words wiv him once we're done 'ere.'

'Sounds good to me, genrul,' Skulsnik agreed.

'In da meantime, we'd best take care of dis lot,' Uzbrag said, shaking his head. 'Dey're all the same zoggin' size! How're ya s'posed to know which one is da boss?'

A new sound rolled out across the battlefield. It was a war cry, but it was not the voice of a mortal creature: no lungs of flesh and blood had produced that bellow of pure rage, hatred and bloodlust. It was like a furnace with a thirst for vengeance, or a volcano out for blood. It was fire and destruction given form and thought.

The light in the gateway parted once more, and *something* strode out.

It was titanic, a bipedal monster taller than any ork. High, jagged crests rose on either side of its head, and its body was molten red, glowing with heat and hate. It bore a gigantic rune-encrusted sword in its right hand, its left hand dripped with blood, and when it opened its mouth to roar again the very air trembled as the white-hot heat of its innards gusted forth.

'Never mind,' Uzbrag said. 'Found 'im.'

LOTZ

Ilaethen Arhien felt the war song rise in his blood as the Avatar of Khaine strode out of the webway portal and into the midst of their foes.

The decision to rouse the craftworld's shard of the Bloody-Handed God was never taken lightly. The presence of the avatar, and the psychic echoes it carried of Kaela Mensha Khaine's rage, inspired their warriors to greater deeds and ever more tenacious ferocity when they faced their foes. However, there was always a cost to such an impact: great deeds were not heroic if they led to portions of Lugganath's forces being overextended or exposed, and ferocity was a poor substitute for strategy. As was always the case for the asuryani, strict mental discipline was essential if they were not to be swept up and carried away by the sheer intensity of the experience.

Ilaethen felt it now, as he soared above the battle on the wings he had been gifted by the Temple of the Nine Winds, banking close against the ceiling of the dome and effortlessly evading the wild and sporadic attempts of the orks to shoot him down. His blood raged with the desire to crash down and wreak havoc on the filth that heaved beneath him, to slaughter them and drive them back, and save his people from their belligerent menace. However, his focus was laser-sharp, and as unyielding as chains of adamant. This was a desperate fight with no scope for error, and little room for manoeuvre. His tactical insight was needed from this vantage point, and when he did commit to the battle himself, it had to be in a surgical strike of great value.

The avatar ploughed forwards, the Wailing Doom in its hand sweeping back and forth, seeming to torment the very air through which it cut. Orkish lives were reaped as though they were wheat to a harvestman's blade, and the asuryani formed up behind the avatar in a wedge that drove into the thickest concentration of the foe. Ilaethen's lips twitched into a grim smile behind his war mask, but he was not unaware of the dangers posed by such an offensive. They had to hold the webway gate, they *had* to. If they could break the enemy and drive them away, then this aggression would serve their purpose. If not then it might simply weaken their defence, should the orks show the tactical wherewithal to circumnavigate the fiercest fighting and strike for their target. Assuming the gate *was* their target, that was.

He focused his thoughts, reaching out for the mind of Yria Nightsong. He lacked any great psychic gifts, but she was powerful and skilled enough to hear him if he called for her.

+Have you determined the crucial thread?+

There was a momentary pause, and then he heard her voice in his head. It was as though she were standing next to him, but this psychic communication also allowed him to feel the frustration in her soul.

+No. These beasts are a tangle of potential futures, and many could rise to ruin now the gateway has been opened.+

Ilaethen frowned.

+Now the gateway has been opened? We have widened the scope for disaster through our actions?+

+Widened the scope, but lessened the severity. You know that all our actions can change the weave of fate. Not acting unless the orks breached the webway was too great a risk, for there was one who held the power and the desire to do so, and it could have brought disaster. Now more of them have the potential to affect our future, but many would do less damage, and the creature who previously posed the greatest danger is now a lesser threat. If the orks do not believe it to have a unique power, they are less likely to follow it.+

+But we should still prevent them from gaining access to the webway.+

+Of course. Some things are immutable.+

The orks had, of course, noticed the arrival of the avatar, and most were surging towards it. Their species was drawn to conflict as though each and every one of them followed the Path of the Warrior, and Ilaethen momentarily considered what that might be like. How would it feel to know that this Path was all that you would ever need, and that to tread it could bring no disaster beyond your own death? If the aeldari abandoned their rigid discipline and all followed the Warrior Path then they would be extinct within a century or two, for they could not replace their populations at a rate that would permit that scale of warfare. There were always more orks, however, and Ilaethen had never seen a sign that any of them cared anything for the survival of their species. They did not care, and did not have to. Whatever nature or altered biology had given rise to them had ensured that they remained untroubled by the wider concerns of the universe.

Ilaethen Arhien, who agonised over minute details of defence and war, who keenly felt the loss of every spirit that fell in battle and was laid to rest in Lugganath's infinity circuit, felt the twin blades of envy and hatred pierce his heart. Envy, for a life so uncomplicated; and hatred, for the destruction they wrought with it. And hatred too, for himself, for envying these beasts.

+Ilaethen! Beware!+

Yria's warning to him came a moment before even his comparatively dull psychic abilities felt a swelling of raw, brutal power directly beneath him. He banked to one side, seeking to evade whatever crude sorcery an ork psyker was directing at him, but no bolt of power came lashing upwards. Instead, his head was enveloped by agonising pain, and his vision faded into the glowing darkness of a stygian blue.

His mastery of the wings of a Swooping Hawk was such that he could fly while blinded, of course, but to fly blinded whilst also in great pain, and above an enemy intent on shooting him down, was another matter entirely.

He cut into a tight circle, hoping to avoid collision with any tall objects. His path through the air was predictable, it was true, but how much difference did that make when his foes' shooting was so erratic in any case?

'Yria!' he whispered, resorting to messenger waves rather than attempting to focus his thoughts. Not only would it be more difficult to do so while in such pain, but the psychic resonance of it might bleed across to her.

He felt the surge of her will, and then he was blinking rapidly clearing eyes as the alien malignancy was blown away like foul air banished by a fresh breeze. His keen vision, now returned to its full power, swiftly picked out the ork responsible for his brief incapacitation, since it was staggering to one side and slapping itself in the head as it dealt with the psychic backwash of having its conjuring severed. One of the beasts' psykers had been the strand of fate which sent the craftworld down this path, and although Ilaethen could not be certain that it was this one, it was clearly a dangerous foe.

He tucked his wings, and descended like the wrath of Asuryan himself.

None of the orks saw him coming. He threw himself into a forward somersault at the last moment before he touched down, to give his star glaive extra momentum, and the keen-edged weapon bisected the ork psyker down the middle. The two halves of its body dropped away from the path of his blade, the damage too severe for even its unnaturally rugged constitution to have a hope of surviving. The orks around it gaped in shock for the moment it took them to register the arrival of the winged warrior in their midst, and Ilaethen punished them for it.

They wore black, and although no ork shunned melee combat, it was the black-clad ones who seemed the most brutally and enthusiastically skilled at it. Ilaethen's long-handled blade swept out and took the heads from three of them before they could react. Then they piled into him, crude blades raised high and simple firearms blasting.

He could not dodge all their attacks, and nor could he block them all, but he could block some and dodge others. One ork might find their weapon's swing touched aside by the gentlest of nudges from the haft of his star glaive, and then that its blade had buried itself in the torso of one of its fellows. Another might fire two shots at his body only for Ilaethen to have jinked from side to side in the time between it pulling the trigger for the first and second time, and two other orks on the far side of him now had new holes in them, while Ilaethen had thrust the tip of his glaive through the shooter's throat. He danced among them with the same grace and skill as one of the children of Cegorach, and left a trail of destruction as he went. He broke bones with kicks, he swept out legs and bowled his enemies over with calculated blows from his wings, and always his glaive was flashing, like the light of ancient stars.

There were some twenty orks around him when he began. When he stopped moving, less than ten seconds later, none had more than a few breaths of life left, and for some it had already departed. For his part, Ilaethen had one wound on his left arm, where he'd had no option but to take a glancing blow from his last enemy a moment before he killed it.

A trio of wind riders screamed by overhead, their jetbikes' weapons discharging razor-edged shuriken into another mass of orks, scything down nearly half with one run. Ilaethen dipped the tip of his glaive in a salute to them and leaped skywards once more, fighting down the urge to give himself over to the lure of the avatar's aura and launch himself headlong into the nearest foes. He could ill afford to get bogged down fighting the rank and file of the orks' troops, despite the damage he could do to them. He was not invulnerable, and to be an autarch was to know your own worth without arrogance or undue humility. Few indeed were those individuals who could master the Aspect Paths without being subsumed by one, and their value to a craftworld was nearly incalculable. Only the certain elimination of a grave threat to his home would justify the loss of Ilaethen's life: any lesser prize would be a folly.

Once aloft, he took in the shape of the battle once more, and saw that it was far closer than he would have wished. This once-abandoned gate was buried deep beneath a mon-keigh city, and the orks had not cracked the structure open to a sufficient extent to bring their great machines of war within; but although not the smallest, the gate was far from the largest, and its dimensions meant that the host of Lugganath had not been able to deploy their mightiest weapons either. The presence of a Wraithknight would have surely secured the outcome, but it had not been possible to bring any of the craftworld's few remaining specimens through. This battle would be carried by troops and vehicles, and while the aeldari had far superior quality and finesse, the orks had greater numbers and sheer brute force on their side.

Ilaethen saw one of their filthy four-limbed war walkers, belching noxious black fumes and painted in ugly splashes of brown, clanking towards the main concentration of asuryani. Its bulky weapons thundered, but lacked the accuracy to trouble its targets. A support platform's D-cannon shot wide, missing the Dreadnought but ripping a momentary hole into the warp through which a group of luckless orks were sucked; a hail of shuriken from the Guardian teams was more accurate, but their shots failed to find anything critical such as power couplings or hydraulics. The Dreadnought's claws sizzled and sparked with energy as they powered up, ready to rend flesh.

The avatar intercepted it.

Both were metal, but the living metal of the avatar's body moved with a smoothness and swiftness that the clumsy engineering of the orks could never hope to match. The edge of the Wailing Doom sheared off one of the Dreadnought's claws with a noise that sounded like souls bring ripped from their bodies, then the great daemon of the aeldari plunged its weapon to the hilt into its enemy's body.

The Dreadnought wobbled, but although the pilot was surely doomed, orks were nothing if not hardy. Even when outmatched, and with what remained of its living body now pierced by a blade longer than an aeldari was tall, the Dreadnought's operator still had the will to strike back one more time before death claimed it. Its weapons blazed in a point-blank barrage that thundered into the avatar, and triggered an explosion so bright that even Ilaethen had to turn his eyes away for a moment.

When he looked again, the Dreadnought was smoking wreckage on its back.

The Avatar of Khaine was still standing, and the bright rents on its chest which revealed its internal fires were already healing over. It reached out with one hand and ripped the Wailing Doom from the Dreadnought's chassis, then raised it above its head with a bellowed challenge.

A volley of shells ripped out of the orks' ranks and smashed into the avatar. It had little appreciable effect other than enraging the daemon further, but Ilaethen could track the shots' origin, and his eyes narrowed behind his war helm as he made out what was approaching. It was another hulking metal shape, in dull black rather than brown, but although similar in size to the avatar's recently vanquished foe, this was not another war walker. This was perhaps the largest ork that Ilaethen had ever seen.

Its bulk was certainly greatly increased by the massive armour it was wearing, but there was no mistaking the fact that even beneath those thick metal plates, this was an ork of massive physique. One arm ended in the still-smoking barrels of the gun - more like a small cannon - which it had just fired, and the other in a gigantic three-pronged power claw. Two flame-tipped horns jutted forwards from beneath its jaw, and vomited fire ahead of it as it closed the distance. The avatar saw only another victim, and raised the Wailing Doom, ready to discharge a bolt of ravening energy from it at the onrushing ork.

Which might have been why it did not see the other ork until it was attacked from behind.

This was another huge ork, although neither as bulky nor as heavily armoured as the black-clad one. It wielded a massive axe with a powered head, and buried the blade deep into the avatar's side with a guttural bellow. Molten metal flew from the force of the blow, and the avatar staggered from this unexpected attack. It lashed out with the Wailing Doom, but the ork had already disengaged and ducked away, the avatar's white-hot blood spitting off the blade of its axe as it was purged by the power field. The avatar whirled, scattering burning droplets from the wound, and the other ork crashed into it.

It was a titanic clash, for this was not an ork commanding a war walker through a system of levers and crude bionic impulse links, but a massive, battle-hardened creature in full control of its own body. Its speed and economy of movement were almost frightening to witness, the very peak of the orkish culture of violence. Its first blow knocked the avatar down to one knee; its second was an almighty backhand which sent the daemon sprawling with its face caved in on one side.

Ilaethen tensed, and prepared to dive. He was unsure if the blade of his star glaive had either the length or the keenness needed to penetrate this ork's armour, but it was a foe that could not be allowed to live.

+Ilaethen. I have found the original beast - the one who brought these events to pass, and who must be stopped.+

Ilaethen blinked. +But the avatar-+

+Kaela Mensha Khaine can look after himself, Ilaethen.+

Ilaethen closed his eyes. He knew better than to doubt his farseer. He focused his thoughts once more.

+Guide me.+

Yria laid her casting over his eyes, and it picked out a single ork, lighting it up in his vision no matter where it moved. Ilaethen beat his wings once, and dived towards it.

Whether by chance, psychic awareness, or some form of bestial intuition, the ork detected him coming. Ilaethen felt its gaze lock with his for a moment, before green energy wrapped itself around the ork's head and blazed at him. He threw himself into a shallow roll and felt the blast scorch by him, leaving him untouched. The ork's eyes widened as it saw him evade its attack with the speed of thought, and raised the staff it carried as though to ward him off. Ilaethen saw something dangling from it that sparkled with a familiar light, and realised to his horror and anger that the creature was carrying a waystone as a trophy! He readied his star glaive to strike, to avenge the unfortunate spirit who had been denied the tranquillity of their craftworld's infinity circuit...

...and the ork disappeared.

One moment it was there, then there was a flash of green light, and it was gone. Ilaethen pulled up as his star glaive slashed through the space where the beast had been, but this was no illusion: it had used its power to transport itself away, somehow.

+Ilaethen! It is here! It–+

A brief, bloody vision seized Ilaethen. He was looking through lenses, not of his own helmet, but of a seer's ghosthelm. An unbearable pressure built within his head before he could react, a nuclear core of ferocious green energy which slammed outwards. He felt his head explode, cracking the ghosthelm with the sheer violence of it–

–and he was back in his own body as the psychic bleed from Yria Nightsong's communication died along with her spirit.

Ilaethen howled with grief and rage, his fury and sorrow further amplified by the presence of the avatar. One of Lugganath's greatest farseers had been slain by the trickery and foul sorceries of the orks, and he now wished only to slaughter them all. Thoughts of holding the gateway or defending the craftworld were washed away by bloodlust: he simply wanted to kill.

Had his perceptions not been so clouded by his emotions, he would have noticed the orks before they struck. They were a small group, arrayed as though ready to pounce upon the psyker who had just fled, but they were content enough to bury their long blades in an aeldari autarch instead. Ilaethen's star glaive killed one of them, but it was a death-blow reflex. The last thing he felt was the rough kiss of an ork's blade opening his throat from behind.

LOTZ

Armenius had sobbed. He would be the first to admit it.

He had been *free*. He had broken away from the orks and managed to liberate himself through nothing more than his own wits, cunning, and combat skills, which had remained undimmed despite his captivity. He had slain the filthy xenos in his way – only gretchin, admittedly, but he could hardly be blamed for that – and come up with a workable plan on a very limited timescale. He had navigated his way into Davidia's lowest reaches, successfully interpreted the frankly appallingly signed maze of tunnels until he found a local, and then impressed upon them the importance of his mission in order to secure their assistance.

He had been so close, *so* close to being able to transmit a message uphive and inform his superiors about the orkish threat from beneath (and once he had done that, he would also have found a way to let them know about the disgustingly heretical levels of xenos influence on the population down here). He had been within touching distance of acclaim, recognition, a promotion, and a return to as much safety as could be found on a planet overrun by an orkish Waaagh!, even one which currently lacked an overall leader. Had the orks united again and pushed upwards then Armenius Varrow would have been at the forefront of the defence, leading troops inspired to new levels of loyalty and ferocity by his heroism.

Instead, he had been betrayed. He *must* have been betrayed, even if he was currently unsure exactly who would or could have betrayed him, or why. Eza? The hunter had been eager to help once Armenius had coolly and calmly explained the situation in terms their somewhat primitive mind had been able to grasp. Had they been *too* eager? Were they simply a xenophile, eager to see humanity brought low by any alien race? Had they left a trail for the orks to follow, guiding them up into the hive? It spelled disaster for them and their community, of course, but such was the way with heretics of all stripes: they had no concept of the certain misery which awaited them should they turn their backs on the light of the Emperor. If they did, they would never do it.

And so, Armenius had wept. Not because of the horror of being imprisoned once again, of course – he would bear that with the same stolid resilience with which he had greeted all orkish blandishments so far – but because he had been unable to warn his comrades in the Golden Lions of the threat. What hope did the hive have without him?

Then the gate opened, as Armenius had feared it might from the moment he laid eyes on it, and horror surged forth.

Armenius read the *Regimental Standard* religiously, and he was well aware of the menace of the perfidious aeldari: or at least, as well aware as any reasonable officer of the Astra Militarum could be without delving into areas of knowledge best left to the Inquisition. He had recognised the heretical influences on the people of this hab-dome, and he knew what the true identity must have been of the 'warriors of the Emperor' who had come through that gate in ages past, or however the so-called seer had described them. All the same, seeing them in the flesh was another matter entirely. It shook him so badly that he actually attempted to communicate with the dull beast-machine to whose back his cage was strapped.

'Move!' he wailed, hammering desperately on the hull of the Killa Kan known as Sarge as the first aeldari warriors let loose a hail of shuriken from their weapons. 'Retreat! Run away! Get us *out* of here, you overgrown bloody grot!'

Sarge did no such thing. Instead, it opened fire with the hefty weapon serving as its right arm, which looked a bit like a heavy stubber if a heavy stubber had been designed by a member of the Mechanicus with an unshakeable conviction that bigger and louder was definitely better. Armenius covered his ears and howled as the racket thundered into his head, but Sarge was not yet done with his torment. The Killa Kan activated its speakers, bellowed *'WAAAGH!'* at the top of its tinny lungs, and lurched towards the enemy with quite un-grotlike enthusiasm. The massive saw blade on its left arm whined up to cutting speed, but Armenius had little faith in its chances of survival. He would not have liked to take on Sarge on his own, even if he had his power sword back, but this was the aeldari: their melee troops moved like quicksilver, most likely through a combination of disgusting xenos biology and foul alien sorcery, and their weapons made a mockery of armour plating. They were no match for the massed lasguns and overwhelming vehicular superiority of the Astra Militarum, of course – the *Regimental Standard* was very clear about that – but set against the crude, clanking hordes of the orks? It was scalpel against sledgehammer, and while Armenius' money might have been on the sledgehammer in the long haul, he had no wish to be strapped to the back of something making itself an obvious target for the scalpel's first incision.

They said that necessity was the mother of invention, in which case desperation was surely its father. Armenius gripped the bars of his cage and appealed to one of the beings in the galaxy he would have normally considered least likely to help him, without even going into how unlikely it would be for him to actually make such an appeal under virtually any other circumstance.

'Genrul! Genrul! *Help!*'

Sarge was Da Genrul's... pet? Bodyguard? Icon bearer? Armenius had no idea what the relationship between the two actually was, or even if he had a suitable lexicon for understanding it. The important thing was that the Killa Kan rarely left Uzbrag's side, and it was not unreasonable to assume that, given the wily Blood Axe kept Sarge around for some reason, he would not want it to run off and get itself destroyed.

Da Genrul was looking upwards as a grav-tank of a design the Imperium classed as a Wave Serpent thrummed overhead, and then began to disgorge melee troops that fell into the orks' ranks – insomuch as they had ranks, which they essentially did not – like particularly lethal, dark-green hail. At no point did he pay any attention to Armenius' increasingly panicked shouts, nor to the fact that Sarge was disappearing in the direction of the aeldari.

'Emperor preserve me,' Armenius whispered, as shuriken began *spanging* off Sarge's shoulders, razored shards of death pinwheeling away. The Killa Kan might have sufficient armour to stand up to the aeldari's basic weaponry – if monomolecular-edged killing discs could be said to be 'basic,' which they were by the standards of these foul xenos – but Armenius certainly did not. If Sarge turned to flee now, or if the aeldari got behind it, Armenius was a sitting waterfowl. He hardly thought that one species of xenos would recognise him as a captive rather than a willing collaborator with another species, let alone that they would care. The aeldari were heartless, aloof and arrogant, and known for the cruelty they inflicted on others, apparently for no reason other than the enjoyment it gave them. He could expect to be used for target practice if he was lucky, or as a living vivisection lesson if he was less so; nothing more.

...Better the daemon you knew?

He reared up as far as he could within the confines of his accursed cage, pressing the side of his face against the bars which formed the roof of it in order to get the best view he could of what Sarge was up against. It did not make for comforting viewing.

The aeldari did not hold to the human idea of ranks any more than the orks did, but there was at least a greater sense of organisation to them, fluid although it was. Armenius' experienced eyes picked out several distinct groups of warriors arrayed in front of the gateway, laying down fire from their shuriken catapults and the occasional support weapon, the latter mounted on their floating anti-grav platforms. Most wore the sort of orange-and-black combination he had seen on the inhabitants of Emperor's Gate, but these were the original, not human aping distorted by decades, centuries or even millennia of faulty memory. Every warrior's armour fit like a second skin, emphasising the slenderness of their build and belying the unnatural strength and resiliency Armenius knew them to possess. Every trained soldier of the Astra Militarum was aware that the aeldari were decadent, simpering aliens with no stomach for a fight, but also that you should never turn your back on one until you were certain it was dead, and preferably in several parts. It was well known that the treacherous xenos would wait until your back was turned to launch an underhanded attack with the last of their strength, instead of accepting their inferiority and dying with good grace.

Sarge was heading straight for the greatest concentration of them, with no coordinated support from the rest of the Waaagh!, and precisely zero tactical awareness. It was going to get them both killed, and so far as Armenius was concerned, the loss of a captain of the Aranuan 25th would be a greater blow to the Imperium than the death of one Killa Kan would be a gain.

'Left! Left, you brute!' he bawled, hammering on that side of its chassis as one of the support weapons began to swivel towards them. 'Big gun! Big gun *bad!*'

It was probably too much to hope for that the grot inside Sarge's shell was actually listening to him, or for that matter could understand his words. However, whether through luck, an unlikely communication between a man and a lower lifeform, or even the divine intervention of the Emperor Himself, Sarge veered to the left just as the aeldari weapon fired.

Armenius had no idea what it was – some sort of unholy beam weapon which caused the very air to vibrate – but the important thing was that it missed. Sarge lumbered on unharmed, which meant in this instance that Armenius remained unharmed as well, and the large weapon on the Killa Kan's right arm tracked towards the weapon. Say what you wanted about grots, and Armenius certainly would given half a chance, but they tended to have a deal more accuracy to their shooting than their larger cousins. Large-calibre shells tore up the ground, ripped through a couple of Guardians who happened to be in the way, and then made a mess of both the support weapon's platform and its operator, who collapsed with at least three holes the size of Armenius' fist through their body.

'Hah haaaah!' Armenius cackled with relief, then ducked down hastily as another stray round whined and ricocheted past his head. At least, he hoped it was stray; if the aeldari cowards had got it into their heads to shoot at a helpless captive simply trying to stay alive, there was little hope for him. 'Saints' blood, what is wrong with you?' he yelled, just in case. 'I'm a prisoner!'

His protestations did nothing to help: the whine of shuriken catapults accelerating their ammunition met his ears a moment before another storm of blades clattered off Sarge. One deflected back off the bars of Armenius' cage, and sliced through the already-ragged left sleeve of his coat before tinkling away to Emperor knew where. He hissed in alarm, and examined his arm: a thin red wound and a trickle of blood met his wide eyes. Throne of Terra, he hadn't even felt it! Mercifully, this was little more than a scratch, but he immediately checked himself all over in case he had been dealt a more serious wound without realising. The stories of soldiers caught by an aeldari volley and falling apart into pieces without their nerves even registering that they had been hit suddenly seemed far more feasible.

He appeared to be otherwise unmarked, at least by the aeldari, although he had no guarantee for how long that state of affairs would continue. Sarge was nearly on the xenos now, and its saw blade was whining up to truly obscene speeds as the pilot sought to get to grips with its enemies and live out a gretchin's deep-seated desire to bloodily dismember other beings whilst being insulated from any reprisal. Armenius heard the whine of chainblades – a thin, eerie sound, very different to the guttural combustion-engine roar of orkish weapons of the same sort – and realised that the aeldari were going to be doing their utmost to make those reprisals stick, regardless of the Killa Kan's intentions.

He felt more than heard when combat was actually joined: the rhythmic thunder of Sarge's steps hesitated for a moment longer than usual before the next impact, and its chassis tilted as its saw arm swung out. Armenius felt the juddering run through its body as the hideous weapon connected with a living body, and the spray of gore thrown out behind the Killa Kan into his field of view left him in no doubt as to the result. The aeldari were almost certainly fleeter of foot than the war machine to which Armenius was unwillingly strapped, but they were locked in place by their apparent determination to defend the gateway, and so they could not retreat before it, as they were known to often do when the noble armies of the Imperium tried to bring them to battle. Armenius could understand the xenos' rationale – they appeared to use this gateway, and others like it, to move around the galaxy somehow, and no one in their right mind would want their private highway infested by orks – but his superior tactical mind could see how it would be their weakness. The aeldari made war by striking hard, then fading away from counter-attacks. If their initial assault here did not debilitate the orks, they would be easy meat for the brute strength of their enemies.

Sarge's chassis rang with the sound of multiple impacts as aeldari close-combat Guardians struck back, seeking weak points with their blades. One flowed into view, its weapons drawn back in preparation to strike, and Armenius withdrew as far and as high as his cramped cage would allow.

'Don't hurt me!' he begged, waiting for the leaping lunge that would thrust the blade with its spinning, diamond-edged teeth in through the bars to spit him and rip out his innards, as the xenos recognised a hero of the Imperium.

The aeldari did not even look at him, so far as he could tell from its forbidding helm. It slashed at Sarge's body, throwing up sparks but causing no other damage that Armenius could discern, from his admittedly imperfect vantage point. Sarge was not satisfied with the blood it had shed so far, and its saw arm swung again. Armenius felt it connect once more, and then something landed wetly on top of the Killa Kan, just above his head. He looked up, and recoiled in horror as a pair of legs with no torso attached dropped past him.

The body followed a moment later, and clung to the bars of his cell.

It was a hideous, incongruous sight: the upper half of an aeldari Guardian, its battle helm unmarked and its body armour shining and splendid, until you got to the waist, at which point it became ragged fabric and even more ragged flesh, and a blood-soaked mass of gradually sagging viscera. Yet still, the foul xenos had found the strength and wherewithal to wrap one of its arms through the bars to arrest its fall, and was reaching in with the shuriken pistol in its other hand.

Armenius did not know for certain whether it was seeking to shoot Sarge in the back in a last gasp of desperate defiance at its killer, or attempting to execute him either as an orkish sympathiser, or simply as a human that it thought might, unlike the metal monstrosity carrying him, be within its capability to slay. Probably the latter. Well, he was going to prove the cowardly creature wrong.

He twisted as far away from the pistol's barrel as he could, seized the aeldari's wrist in both hands with a strength born of desperation, and began slamming its hand against the cage's solid floor. The aeldari hissed something at him, but Armenius let his rage take over and bellowed in anger as he continued his assault. After four, five, six such impacts, the pistol finally tumbled free of the aeldari's grasp. Armenius pivoted and lashed out with his foot, kicking it in what would have been its face had it not been wearing a helmet. The aeldari was knocked backwards and, stunned by his mighty strike, lost its grip on his cage. It dropped out of view without a further sound. Perhaps his blow had even killed it: broken its neck, perhaps?

More importantly, he now had a weapon.

He snatched the shuriken pistol up before Sarge's erratic movements could send it skittering over the floor and out through the bars, but even in his desperation he made sure to keep his fingers away from anything that might function as a trigger; the last thing he needed was to accidentally shoot himself with a xenos weapon designed for slicing through flesh and bone. He managed to get hold of it without incident, and arranged it into something approaching a ready position in his right hand, although it was poorly designed. The grip was too thin to feel properly secure, and what looked like the trigger-stud was a little too far forwards for his index finger to reach comfortably. Give him a regular-issue laspistol any day. However, needs must.

Sarge roared, its speakers emitting a static-edged screech of distortion and anger, or possibly pain, and the Killa Kan broke into a run. It lumbered off, away from the aeldari with which it had been locked in combat a moment ago. Armenius saw their receding figures, and hastily tried to hide the plundered pistol behind his body in case they got the wrong idea. What was going on? Had the gretchin pilot suddenly been overwhelmed by the fear common in its unarmoured kin and elected to flee? Had a chance blow caused some form of malfunction, sending it pelting away despite the wishes of the xenos nominally in control?

It didn't matter. What mattered was that another support weapon was swivelling towards Sarge as it ran, and this time the Killa Kan paid no attention to Armenius' frantic thumping and bellowed instructions.

The weapon fired.

Something below Armenius exploded, or possibly *im*ploded, and Sarge fell sideways.

The impact threw Armenius against the bars of his cage as they hit the ground, drove the breath from his lungs, and numbed the arm on which he landed. He kept hold of the pistol through a heroic effort of will, but his situation had drastically worsened. High up on Sarge's back, he had been lifted above the main level of fighting, and shielded from the worst impacts for as long as the Killa Kan had been facing its enemies. Now, the machine was immobilised, spluttering weakly, and missing at least one leg from what he could make out. Now, Armenius was an easy target for any pointy-eared aeldari wretch who wanted to get a metaphorical feather in its figurative cap by putting a murderous end to the career of perhaps the greatest captain of the Aranuan 25th.

Well, placing your faith in the Emperor of Mankind was a good and devout thing to do, but there came a time in every hero's life when he had to take a stand and strike out for himself. That time had come for Armenius.

He levelled the pistol at the crude lock on the door of his cage. High-velocity, razor-edged aeldari rounds against poorly forged ork steel. There could surely only be one winner in that contest, and it was the man inside the cage, who would be free again within moments.

On the other hand...

Armenius was as good as anyone at judging angles, but he was no artillery captain or Basilisk gunner. He *thought* he could point the pistol and fire it in a way which meant that any ricochets would spin harmlessly off – or harmlessly to him, anyway, which was all that mattered – but could he be sure? This was a xenos weapon, after all, and the aeldari were notorious for scoffing at concepts such as regular physics. And orkish metal: who could judge how that would react? It would be a poor service to the Imperium if Armenius were betrayed and slain by the same device he was attempting to use to gain his freedom, should a shuriken rebound in an unexpected manner and lodge itself in his heart, or neck, or bowel. He did not appear to be the centre of anyone's attention at the moment, so perhaps he should just–

An unearthly roar rang out, and a monstrous shape strode out of the still-shimmering aeldari gateway.

An avatar.

Armenius did not delve too deeply into xenos lore, of course he didn't, but there were some things you could not help but hear about once you had risen to a certain level within the Astra Militarum. There were whispers that ran around the officers' mess, whispers that you kept away from any member of the Commissariat as though your life depended upon it, because it probably did. Armenius had heard rumours of soulless metal men and how they could suck away the power of even the most potent psykers: which might not be such a bad thing, all things considered, had they not also been rumoured to blast Imperial citizens and troops into their component atoms. He had heard rumours of how some of the Traitor Space Marines which plagued the Imperium might not be the unnaturally preserved remainder of the great betrayal in ages past, but might actually be *new* traitors, turned from Chapters currently thought to be loyal.

And he had heard tales of the great metal daemons of the aeldari: gigantic molten figures of hatred and death, an alien war god incarnate.

That was what he was looking at now, and it drove all thoughts of caution from his mind. The thunder of its voice reached down into his soul and crushed it with white-hot fingers, and the momentary touch of its glowing eyes upon him as it scanned the battlefield withered his courage like a plant flash-burned by fire. Nothing mattered any more except *getting away from that Throne-damned thing.*

He pointed the shuriken pistol at the cage lock again and, his vision blurred by terrified tears, pressed the firing stud. The weapon thrummed slightly in his grasp, a faint but powerful vibration, and spat a stream of shining rounds. The lock was ruined within half a second; the bar to which it was attached was severed as well, before Armenius was able to coax his finger off the firing mechanism. He kicked out: the remains of the lock dropped away, and the door fell open with a clang.

He scrambled for it, this new promise of freedom, his insides so twisted by fear and hope that the combination reached up his throat and threatened to strangle him. He clawed his way out, still weeping, and ran. He ran away from the gunfire and bloodshed; he ran away from the alien gateway to a terrifying, unknown realm; and most importantly he ran away from the fiery metal daemon with its sword that sang a song of ruin as it swept through the air. He ran with a strength born of terror, ducking and cowering as ork shootas stitched glowing lines towards the gateway and the aeldari sent streams of whisper-thin shuriken back. He rolled desperately to one side as ork vehicles roared past, their drivers and gunners paying no attention to him in favour of targeting the gateway's defenders. He ran on, between the buildings of Emperor's Gate, keeping away from the shadows which he knew all too well might hide Da Genrul's kommandos from his view.

He ran towards the side of the dome opposite the one by which he had entered, praying as he ran that he might find an escape there. Orks were still streaming in from either side, but one lone, running human was of no interest to them compared to the battle. All the same, he did not slow once he had left the fighting behind him. He would not stop until he had escaped the dome completely.

Or, as it turned out, until he came upon a dark tunnel leading through the dome wall which was not disgorging orks, and ran into a thicket of lasgun barrels.

'Don't shoot!' he shouted, raising his hands and blinking into the light of photo-lumens, and making sure to avoid triggering the shuriken pistol. 'Don't shoot!'

'Who goes–' a voice began, and then stopped in shock. 'Captain Varrow?!'

'Who's that?' Armenius said. It was a human voice, and it knew his name, but his insides were wound far too tight by now to give in to anything approaching relief. This could be a mind-reading witch with their armed escort of underhive scummers, or, or...

'Captain Varrow,' a new voice said, and Armenius' throat tightened as the speaker stepped out in front of the lasguns and into the dim light of the dome, sufficient for him to see the peaked cap, the black greatcoat, and the iron-grey hair. Commissar Elushka Bone.

Throne, he would almost prefer the mind-reading witch to Old Bones.

'Commissar,' he said, his feet coming to attention without receiving a conscious instruction from his brain, although his hands remained raised in dim acknowledgement of the gun barrels still trained on him.

'You are recorded as lost in action, captain,' Bone said, her voice as sharp as a flensing knife. 'What are you doing here? And by the God-Emperor, what is happening in there?'

'The orks took me prisoner, commissar,' Armenius said. 'The suffering I've endured, I...' He swallowed back the emotion that threatened to choke his words. Just living through it had been bad enough – now he actually had to verbalise it to another human, it all came crashing back in even more intensely than before. 'They managed to gain entry to the hive, and I escaped.' He declined to mention how he had already escaped once, but then been captured again: even in his ragged-nerved state, that did not seem a sensible thing to admit. 'Commissar, there is... *something* down there. I believe it's a heretical aeldari construct, one of their infernal devices which allow them to move around the galaxy. The orks are trying to enter it, I think, and the aeldari have, er, emerged. To fight them.'

Bone looked at him, then past him. The expression on her face quite plainly said that she would have no intention of believing him were she not able to see the flashes of explosions and hear the rumble of gunfire, and was still having doubts about it despite those details.

The avatar roared again, and Armenius flinched despite the fact that it was far more distant now than the first time. You simply did not hear the voice of an alien god and remain the same man afterwards.

'We were aware of the orkish incursion,' Bone said, almost absently. Armenius could see explosions reflected in her dark eyes. 'Colonel Sudliff ordered a team of volunteers to gather intelligence on what is occurring.'

'Very sensible,' Armenius said, nodding like a fool.

'I have executed the colonel for cowardice,' Bone said, her eyes boring into him. 'We are not here to gather intelligence. We are here in full force, under the command of myself and Brevet Colonel Bruja, to destroy the enemy.'

'Ah,' Armenius stammered. 'E-even more sensible?'

'You say you were captured by the orks, and that is why you are still alive?'

Armenius breathed out. At last, he would get to deliver his hard-won information! 'Yes, commissar! Their warboss was killed, and I have discovered that the three largest remaining orks are in a struggle for dominance. They are an Evil Sun named Zagnob Thundaskuzz, a Goff called Mag Dedfist, and a Blood Axe known as Genrul Uzbrag, or simply Da Genrul. Our tactics should be varied depending on which of them gains supremacy, but we could capitalise on their current disarray by–'

'We need explosives,' Bone interrupted, turning to look at the soldiers in the tunnel. 'Send three teams to drill them into the ceiling from the dome above. All other units will advance on the xenos. Should we fall, the explosives are to be detonated. We'll drop a few thousand tonnes of rockcrete on these bastards and see how much they like that.'

'Commissar,' Armenius said, feeling his tentative footing begin to slip away. 'Should we not–'

'Armenius Varrow, you were captured by the enemy and have undoubtedly aided them,' Bone said, cutting him off again. She still was not looking at him. 'You are, even now, holding a prohibited xenos weapon. You should have taken your own life rather than let yourself be corrupted in this manner.'

Armenius swallowed. 'But commissar, I can–'

'I will now correct your error.'

Armenius just had time to register that Elushka Bone had drawn her bolt pistol from its holster and levelled it against his forehead, before he was incapable of registering anything, ever again.

LOTZ

Mag Dedfist was pissed off.

He'd done everything he was supposed to. He'd obeyed both the vision, and Old Morgrub's explanation of it. He'd smashed straight through the walls of the humie city with the sort of speed and violence that would be expected of the very best of the Goffs, and slaughtered everything in his way. That should have been an end to it.

It was those zoggin' grots, that was the problem. He hadn't trusted it when he'd seen them racing off as though they had a mind of their own, rather than doing whatever it was a runtherd told them to do. It turned out that he'd been right to be suspicious: the little gits had scampered off ahead of him, almost as if they were trying to find Morgrub's gate in their own right. If he hadn't bothered with following them, and had forged his own path instead, he was certain he would have got to the gate quicker. Instead, Da Genrul was already there, looking as smug as a squig in a feed trough.

All that effort, and for what? Back to where he'd started, facing down Uzbrag and Thundaskuzz, with Old Morgrub giggling in the background. That was the last time he paid attention to anything a weirdboy said, even if he *was* a warphead.

Mag's mood hadn't even improved much once the gateway had opened and the skrawniez had come pouring out. They were thin gits that broke easily. It was like punching a tent: no real resistance, and a similar lack of satisfaction from the inevitable collapse which followed. Still, Mag rampaged around for a bit, blowing them apart with his kustom shoota and clobbering them with his power klaw, trying to get at least some enjoyment from the whole situation.

Then he heard the hot-git yelling, and his day got a lot better.

Mag *knew* about hot-gits. If you got the skrawniez really riled, sometimes they showed up with one: a big metal skrawnie, only it wasn't really that scrawny any more, which blazed with heat and carried a massive choppa or spear. He'd seen one once, back when he was nothing more than a boy with a shoota. It had torn through a battlewagon like it was made of sticks, and he'd actually admired how killy it was, although he never got close enough to have a go at it himself.

That was going to change today.

The hot-git wasn't hard to make out: it was about three times the height of a regular skrawnie, and when it moved, the dark, dull red of what passed for its skin cracked open to reveal the white-hot fire within. They were made of metal, Mag had heard, although he wasn't sure how that worked. Typical skrawnie nonsense, he reckoned.

Still, it seemed that this hot-git was just as good at scrapping as the one he saw all those years ago. It cut down half a dozen boyz with one sweep of its massive blade, and when a trio of squighog boyz pelted towards it, all whooping and hollering, it fired a blast of *something* from its choppa that atomised the middle rider in the time it took for Mag to blink. That was enough to send all three squigs squealing away in terror, with the two remaining beast snaggas on their backs yelling and cursing futilely. Mag laughed at them as they careered past him, then swatted aside a skrawnie that had got too close, and set off towards this most worthy of foes.

A Deff Dread got there first: a rare Snakebite Deff Dread, cobbled together by one of the few mekboyz the clan produced. Skrawnie cutty-discs rattled off its armour with no effect, and its power klaws were just charging up for some proper scragging when the hot-git jumped in to ruin its fun. That huge choppa took off one of the Dread's klaws, as clean as you like, then the hot-git rammed it straight through the main chassis.

The pilot was no cowardly squig, and fired off all his weapons at point-blank range. The explosions – or possibly the hot-git's flaming blood – must have cooked off the rest of the machine's ammo stores, because there was a massive bang. However, in the aftermath of it, the Deff Dread was in a smoking heap on its back, and the hot-git was still standing. Not only was it still standing, but it was *healing*: the damage was already scabbing over, as dull metal skin replaced the blazing innards which had been exposed. It ripped its huge choppa out, held it above its head, and roared what could only be a challenge.

Mag grinned. An enemy that healed that quickly would be *very* fun to fight. It would last for ages!

He took general aim with his kustom shoota, and let rip. The hot-git was so large that he couldn't really miss, and his shells slammed into it. They did little except anger it, and Mag practically felt its eyes land on him, so powerful was its gaze. The very air around it was shimmering from the heat it was giving off. This was going to be a fight to remember.

He lumbered forwards into a run. Mega armour didn't make an ork any faster, but it certainly added momentum – enough momentum to give even this massive thing some problems. The hot-git levelled its choppa at him and furious energy began to build around the blade. Mag gritted his teeth: he had no idea if he could stand up to the sort of blast that had destroyed the squighog nob, but he wasn't going to give this bloody skrawnie monster the satisfaction of seeing him flinch or dodge. Goffs met the enemy head-on, no matter what was thrown at them...

And then Genrul zoggin' Uzbrag appeared from *behind* the hot-git, and laid into it with his power choppa.

The energised blade bit into the hot-git's side, and molten metal spilled out. The hot-git roared in pain and anger, and spun around to take a swing at Da Genrul, but Uzbrag was a typical sneaky Blood Axe, and was already running like he was some sort of grot.

Mag was furious. He'd waited *years* to have a crack at one of these, and now Da Genrul wanted to steal his thunder? It was outrageous is what it was. He wound up all that rage into his klaw arm, and expressed it with a cataclysmic punch that connected with the hot-git's chest.

This was satisfying. *This* had substance. The aftershock shuddered back up Mag's arm as he made contact. The blow sounded like an explosion in a furnace, and the hot-git was driven down to one knee by the force of it, bringing its monstrous head more or less level with his own. The hot-git began to bring its choppa around, but Mag was too quick: he dealt it a thunderous backhand across the face, sending it sprawling with its head caved in on one side.

The hot-git roared through its broken mouth, but Mag could sense that there was pain there as well as rage. He took one more step to stand over it, raised his klaw, and drove the talons of it down into the hot-git's chest. The monster roared again, even louder, and Mag bellowed in triumphant answer as he sank his weapon deeper and deeper, searching for its heart.

However, the zoggin' thing apparently didn't have one.

Both of its hands came up to clamp around Mag's power klaw. He just had time to notice that one of those hands seemed to be dripping with blood before he felt the tremendous heat seeping through the thick metal around his arm, and the damned stuff began to *soften*.

It was shock more than pain that caused Mag to jerk his arm backwards, but the power klaw didn't come with him: the metal attaching it to his armour melted away, and his weapon remained in the hot-git's grasp, and still partially embedded in its chest. He swore violently as molten bits of metal dropped onto his arm, and swore some more as the hot-git plucked his power klaw out and tossed it aside, then flowed back up to its feet and took up its massive choppa once more.

Mag Dedfist began to wonder whether having an enemy who healed so quickly was such a good thing after all.

Still, he'd hurt it, and hurt it good. He raised his kustom shoota again, ready to give the hot-git another salvo, at least make it walk through pain to get to him. Gork and Mork couldn't fault him if he died fighting this monster; it would be a death to be proud of.

The hot-git took a step forwards, and then a harpoon smashed through its neck and came out the other side in a spray of molten metal.

'Gotcha!' Zagnob Thundaskuzz bawled, as his snagga klaw took the hot-git in what probably counted as its throat. 'Hot-git' was certainly the right name for it – he could feel the heat coming off its body from here, although to be fair, the torn-up side of his face could feel a lot of things at the moment, down to and including minuscule air currents. He expertly clamped the harpoon chain to his wartrike's chassis, because while Zagnob might not pay much attention to a lot of extraneous detail in life, he understood weight and balance and momentum. Trying to bring this thing down himself would simply see him falling off his own vehicle for the second time in one day.

'Come around!' he yelled at Duffrak, and pulled out one of his twin boomstikks. It coughed twice, sending bolts as thick as a humie's fist into the hot-git's chest and spattering more of the molten metal which seemed to serve the thing as blood. Duffrak obeyed his order, expertly skidding into a turn, then hammering the engines up again and taking off in a new direction. The hot-git, which had just taken one lumbering step after them, was taken off guard and off balance: the harpoon chain jerked tight and the wartrike shuddered to a halt, but the skrawnie beast was tugged off its feet.

'YES!' Zagnob cheered. 'Drag it! Drag it!' This would be his greatest success yet as speedboss, if he could ride through the battle dragging *that* behind him.

'Tryin',' boss!' Duffrak assured him, but the hot-git's weight was simply too great: the tyres were spinning and sending up smoke, but not getting enough purchase.

Time for special measures.

'Skitta!' Zagnob ordered imperiously, pointing. The grot screamed, and hammered the red button once more. The engines howled even louder, and there was the slightest of lurches. They were doing it!

Then Zagnob saw Mag Dedfist coming up behind the hot-git, raising his kustom shoota to take aim at the back of its head.

'Oh no ya don't,' Zagnob muttered. He grabbed his other boomstikk and opened fire. The first shot missed; the second hit Mag in the shoulder, staggering the Goff backwards. Zagnob broke his weapon open to reload, but the hot-git reached up with one hand that was glowing with heat, and took hold of the chain...

The chain softened and snapped. The wartrike, no longer tethered to its metal anchor, lurched forwards so violently that Zagnob had to hang on desperately to avoid tumbling off. There was a wet splattering noise as they went into, through, and over a brawling ruck of boyz and skrawniez at full speed, but while this would normally have brought a smile to Zagnob's face, now he could only think about the prey that had got away.

'Back dat way!' he yelled at Duffrak, who hauled the steering bars around obediently. 'I want anuvver crack at dat fing!' They swerved around, dodged a plummeting skrawnie sky-bike that crashed and exploded close enough to spray them with shrapnel, and accelerated towards the hot-git again. It was now back on its feet, and it drew its arm back, then threw its massive choppa overhanded.

The weapon whirled through the air faster than Zagnob would have believed possible, and slammed straight through his wartrike, point first, pinning it to the ground. Duffrak was impaled; the vehicle itself came to a dead stop.

Zagnob himself did not. He was catapulted directly forwards, flying through the air towards the creature that had just wrecked his ride.

Perhaps the hot-git was not expecting Zagnob to have the presence of mind to turn his unexpected flying lesson into an attack, but no one and nothing had faster reflexes than an Evil Sunz speedboss. Zagnob lashed out with his snagga klaw, and hammered the warboss of all punches straight into the hot-git's face.

And it went *down.*

Molten blood spattered up Zagnob's arm, but the pain was as nothing compared to the triumph that rushed through him. He'd done it! He'd taken out the biggest, baddest skrawnie in the place!

The ground came up to meet him, but not with any intent to congratulate. He landed hard, and skidded through dust and rubble to come to an undignified halt at the base of a half-ruined wall.

'Waaagh!' he bellowed, fighting his way back up. 'Dat's wot I'm talkin' about! 'Ave it, ya great big–'

The hot-git was getting up again.

'Oh, zoggin' 'eck,' Zagnob said with feeling. What did it take to put this thing down properly? He broke into a run, hoping against hope that he could land another punch before it rose to its full height and he was reduced to taking gut shots.

Mag Dedfist had recovered himself and was lining up a shot again, but the hot-git seemed to have its own ideas. It reached out behind it, still on one knee, and opened its hand. The choppa with which it had killed Duffrak – and more importantly, Zagnob's wartrike – shuddered, then freed itself with a screech of metal-on-metal, and flew through the air towards it.

Mag saw the huge weapon coming, and managed to get his mega-armoured bulk out of the way. The choppa settled into the hot-git's hand with a *thunk*, it extended it towards Zagnob, and the air above it began to shimmer with heat...

...and Da Genrul buried his power choppa into its shoulder, knocking its arm and sending a bolt of ravening energy scoring across the ground instead of straight into Zagnob.

Da Genrul ducked under the hot-git's blade as it swung around for him once more, but he felt the heat of it as it passed rather closer to his head than he would have liked. He retreated again, wary of his injured leg, and looking for an opening: there was no point rushing in against this enemy, one who could end you with one shot–

Zagnob Thundaskuzz pelted up behind it and clobbered it with his snagga klaw, drawing another howl of ire, which just showed how much sense Evil Sunz had.

'Wot da zog do ya fink ya doin'?' Mag Dedfist roared at Da Genrul, as the hot-git rounded on Zagnob. The Goff was punching his kustom shoota, which had apparently jammed.

'Tryin' to kill dat fing!' Uzbrag told him angrily. 'What do *yoo* fink I'm doin'?'

'Dat's mine!' Mag bellowed.

'Yoo had yer shot, an' ya missed!' Uzbrag retorted. 'Tell ya wot, let's *all* scrag da zogger, an' sort everyfing else out afterwards!'

Mag opened his massive mouth to argue, then looked over at where Zagnob was desperately scrambling away from the massive choppa as it swung down and buried itself into the ground, and shrugged. 'Wotever. First decent plan yoo've ever had.'

Da Genrul spun his power choppa. 'Alright den. Let's do dis.'

Mag wrenched his malfunctioning kustom shoota off through sheer brute force, then picked up what turned out to be the severed arm of a Deff Dread, which he wielded like a club. Uzbrag nodded at him, and they charged.

'Waaagh!'

Zagnob had just landed another blow, tearing through the hot-git's right knee. It staggered, but managed to grab Thundaskuzz with the hand that wasn't holding its choppa. The Evil Sun howled in pain as the hot metal closed on his shoulder and began to burn him, but only until Mag Dedfist clobbered the hot-git on the back of its head with his makeshift bludgeon.

The skrawnie beast toppled forwards, releasing Zagnob and throwing out its hands to break its fall. Da Genrul swung his power choppa again, and felt the shudder as the blade bit into the hot-git's side. Consistent damage, that was the key: they had to keep hitting it, faster and harder than it could heal.

'Keep at it!' he yelled. 'If we work togevva, we can–'

Zagnob raised his snagga klaw to take a shot at the hot-git's neck, but Mag shoved him aside. The Goff grinned so widely it could be seen even above the massive metal underjaw of his armour, and lined up his own blow with his salvaged weapon.

The hot-git's choppa speared right through his mega armour, transfixing him.

Mag howled in pain and staggered back, the Deff Dread's arm falling from his grip and landing on his own head. The hot-git was exposed, and Zagnob had the perfect opportunity to take its head off with his snagga klaw before it could protect itself, but he swung at Mag instead, punching through the Goff's armour and burying the twin prongs of his weapon in Dedfist's chest. Mag went down, and Zagnob whooped in joy and revenge.

The hot-git staggered up, reached out, and clamped one hand around Zagnob's head while he was still cheering over the fallen Mag. Zagnob's howls of pain were muffled by the massive metal fingers as they began to cook his brain inside his own skull. Uzbrag brought his own power choppa back for another blow, but the hot-git's choppa leaped out of Mag's corpse at its gesture and landed in its hand again, and its backswing took Da Genrul in the chest.

It was, by some freak of chance, only the flat of the blade, but that didn't prevent him from being knocked a couple of trukk-lengths away by the blow, and he felt something inside him break from the force of it. He struggled up again, leaning on the haft of his power choppa, just in time to see the hot-git run Zagnob Thundaskuzz through as well.

'Zoggin' idiots,' Uzbrag muttered. 'We could've taken it!' Well, there was only one thing for it. It was still a bit busted up, so if he got really lucky...

Uzbrag's ears twitched, and he became aware of a new noise, audible even over the thunder of battle going on around him. All orks knew the sound of boots on the ground, but these weren't orkish boots.

It sounded like the humies had decided to join the party properly at last.

They poured into view from between the buildings beyond the hot-git, yelling and whooping like they were orks themselves, although Uzbrag reckoned they had a better chance of scaring themselves than anyone else. A whole mob of them opened up with their zappy light-guns, firing indiscriminately into the battling orks and skrawniez. Notably, a lot of the shots hit the hot-git.

'Whoops,' Uzbrag said. 'Yoo didn't want to do dat, humies.'

The hot-git never seemed to be anything less than furious, but this new attack appeared to stoke its rage to new heights. It flung Zagnob's body off its choppa with a scream, and stormed away from Uzbrag and towards these new irritants, stomping Mag Dedfist underfoot as it went. If there had been any life left in the big Goff's body, it undoubtedly fled when half his chest was flattened.

It probably would have been bad enough for the humies if it had only been the hot-git heading for them, given how terrified they sounded as it approached with their shots bouncing harmlessly off it. However, a few of the boyz nearby decided to pile in as well, and more surprisingly, a large chunk of the skrawniez seemed to get caught up in the hot-git's anger. They moved with deadly swiftness, following in its wake almost like boyz tailing a Deff Dread into the heart of a fight.

'Oi!' Da Genrul shouted. 'I haven't finished wiv yoo yet!' But the hot-git took no notice, and began slaughtering humies by the handful, while they desperately brought up bigger and bigger guns to shoot it with.

'Well, I ain't chasin' ya,' Uzbrag muttered, poking at his ribs and wincing. 'When yoo're zoggin' ready, eh? Coward.'

He turned around, and realised that they'd won.

LOTZ

If there was one good thing about being a grot, Snaggi thought, it was that enemies would usually pass up the chance to shoot at you if they could shoot at an ork instead.

The orks sometimes didn't give them a choice, of course. Many a mob of grots had been prodded into place on a battlefield by an enterprising runtherd with a good knowledge of when to duck, precisely so that the enemy would literally have to go through Snaggi's kin in order to get to the orks behind. This was just another example of how unfair the galaxy was, given that most of those grots didn't want to be there in the first place, and the orks universally *did*.

However, in this case, when Snaggi threw himself onto the floor and covered his head with his hands, the skrawniez didn't waste their time and ammunition on him and his ladz. Snaggi heard the first volley whisper by overhead and bite into the orks behind him, which under the circumstances was about as good an outcome as he could have expected, given that Da Genrul had been about to shoot him. Of course, that didn't mean he could be complacent.

'Run for it!' he yelled, and the grots with him scattered. Since they had been surrounding the gateway, that basically meant each one of them ran directly away from it, and the terrifying warriors it had just disgorged. Granted, that meant they were running towards the orks they had just been defying, but the orks quite literally had bigger things to think about. Kicking a cheeky grot was something they could - and indeed, did - do any day, whereas mixing it up with a bunch of skrawniez was a far rarer opportunity. Snippa One-Ear abruptly became Snippa No-Face when he ran headlong into the blade of Da Genrul's power choppa, which the Blood Axe was spinning to warm himself up for the fight to come, but if Snippa couldn't look where he was going then the git only had himself to blame.

'Wot's da plan now?' Skrawk asked, as a small group of them dived for cover in a humie hut. The former occupants had clearly already decided that staying put around this many orks was a bad plan and had legged it, so there was no one to pop up with a gun and an inconvenient attitude to property ownership.

'Da plan is not to die,' Snaggi said firmly. 'Dat's da first an' most important part of it, an' look! Dere's already gits out dere who ain't even managin' dat.'

Two orks collapsed a short distance away from where the grots had taken cover, their heads sliced clean in half by the skrawniez' cutty-discs. Snaggi shook his head, and tutted.

'See? Dat's wot ya get when dere ain't proppa leadership. Da big gits can't even follow a simple plan.'

'An' supposin' we manage to not die, is dere any more to da plan?' another grot asked. He was one of Snippa's old lot: Snaggi thought his name was Lunk, and already had him pegged as a potential troublemaker.

'Only fools rush in,' he said loftily.

'Waaagh!'

'Well, an' Goffs,' he amended, as the black-clad part of the orkish forces charged into the teeth of the skrawniez' guns with typical enthusiasm, if such a word could be said to apply to orks who were never happy with the quality of the fight once they found it. 'But anyway, my point is... Look, dere's loads more skrawniez comin' outta dat gate, so da sensible fing is to wait an' see wot happens, right?'

'Not sure dat "wait an' see" is a great battle cry for da GrotWaaagh!, dat's all I'm sayin',' Lunk muttered. Snaggi scowled at him, because he was fairly sure that that was not, in fact, all that Lunk was saying.

'I'm gettin' da feelin' dat yer castin' aspershuns over me leadership qualities,' he said menacingly, standing up to his full height and glowering at the other grot. 'Wotcha got to say to dat, eh?'

'Wot've I got to say?' Lunk repeated. He rose up to his feet as well, out of the instinctive crouch he had been in, and folded his arms. 'I reckon... I reckon dat ya ain't no ork, Snaggi Littletoof, an' ya haven't got da faintest idea wot da best fing to do is, dat's wot *I* got to say.'

Snaggi laughed loudly and falsely, and pointed at Lunk. 'See? Dis is da sort of finking we've got to deal wiv, ladz! No, I ain't an ork,' he continued, staring fiercely at Lunk, 'an' I'm proud of it! Wot good am I gonna do, goin' around pretendin' to be an ork? Ya gotta get dis idea dat orks are better dan us just cos dey're bigger outta ya head! Dey ain't *kunnin'*! Both da gods have got space for kunnin', but da orks mainly focus on the "brutal" part, cos dat's wot dey're best at! But just fink about it for a second! Wot if ya could get proper orky brutal, but wiv grot kunnin? Dat's wot da GrotWaaagh! is gonna be about, ladz! *We* give da orders, *dey* do da fightin', everyone wins, an' everyone's happy! Well, except whoever it is we're fightin',' he admitted, 'but who gives a zog about dose gits?'

'Da orks ain't gonna follow a grot wot don't wanna rush in,' Lunk said stubbornly. 'I ain't seen no sign dat da gods talk to ya, Snaggi, no matter wot ya say.'

'Yeah?' Snaggi wanted to give Lunk a taste of his boomstikk, but that seemed like a very orky thing to do. 'Is dat so? Well alright den. Da gods are still tellin' me dat we should get to dat gate an' get froo it, but dey're also tellin' me dat if we was to make a run for it now, it'd be a very bad fing for us, an' we should wait.'

Guffink poked his head around the door frame. 'I mean, dere's a lotta fightin' goin' on out dere right now, so I ain't sure dat's much of a prediction, Snaggi.'

'No, just wait,' Snaggi said. 'Just wait.' He fixed Lunk with a stern look, and dared the universe to prove him wrong. Damn it all, *he* knew that the gods were speaking to him! And yes, okay, most of the time they definitely wanted him to go and get stuck in, but it wasn't his fault if the gods had a slightly inflated idea of what he could manage. Gork and Mork were used to dealing with orks, after all, it only made sense that they might get a bit mixed up now they had shifted their favour to a grot–

A blood-curdling roar split the air. Snaggi, despite knowing that something awful was coming, jumped so much he nearly dropped the grabba stikk.

'Yeah,' Guffink managed weakly, as a gigantic daemon of molten metal holding an enormous choppa emerged from the gateway. 'I fink dat counts as a bad fing.'

'I really don't wanna be stuck in here wiv dat!' Skrawk wailed. 'Snaggi! Can we get outta here?'

Snaggi swallowed, and tried to maintain his composure. The big glowing fing wasn't coming towards them, at least – it seemed to be heading in the general direction of Mag Dedfist's lot, which really drove home Snaggi's point about not rushing in – but Skrawk had the right idea: this really was no place to be hanging about. The traditional grot thing to do in such circumstances was to do a runner back the way you'd come and try to avoid any runtherds you might meet along the way, but Snaggi was not going to run from his destiny. He'd led them here, by Gork and Mork, and he was not going to turn around now. He was going through that gateway, and Old Morgrub *was* going to acknowledge Snaggi Littletoof as Da Grotboss!

He caught a glimpse of Da Genrul running off towards the skrawniez' monster, and snorted in grim amusement. Well, that should take care of one of his rivals, at least. Mag Dedfist was certain to get stuck in as well, if he was anywhere nearby. With any luck, the three of them would scrag each other. However, there was still one other pretender who needed taking care of.

'Anyone see Thundaskuzz?' Snaggi asked, trying his best to see through the scrapping going on directly in front of them.

'Da speed freeks have split up,' Guffink said, pointing to a trio of warbikers hurtling towards a group of orange skrawniez and unloading their dakkaguns into them, and then at what looked like the boomdakka snazzwagon of Skrappit the mek, exchanging fire with a floaty-tank. 'He could be anywhere.'

'But he ain't gone froo da gate?' Snaggi said.

'Nuffink's gone froo da gate from dis side, uvver dan some dakka,' Guffink replied, shaking his head. 'Da skrawniez have got it closed up tighter'n a painboy's stitch job.'

'Dat's not usually very tight,' Skrawk pointed out. 'Dere's often quite big gaps.'

'Yeah, dat's why I said dey've done it "tight*er*", not "tight *as*". Obvious, innit?'

So, there was still a chance to be first, Snaggi thought, ignoring the bickering of his underlings. That was the goal. He'd got *to* the gate first, but none of the orks had cared about that: not even Old Morgrub, who had clearly gone deaf to the will of the gods. However, surely no one could argue with

Snaggi's claim to the title of warboss if he actually went where no grot had gone before, and made it *through* the gate first.

He was going to need more than just his own legs to do that, though, because while Snaggi was quite fond of his own legs – certainly enough that he wouldn't want anyone to take them off him – he was not overly confident in their ability to get him through the gate before any of the skrawniez could shoot him. Luckily, the sort of ingenuity which had made him an obvious choice for grotboss had not deserted him.

He looked at the grots with him. Five in total: Skrawk, Guffink, Lunk, and two more by the names of Pukk and Wizza.

'Follow me, ladz,' he said boldly, and scampered back out into the fight.

He didn't wait to see if they were following him. Rather, he led the way and made it obvious by so doing that he expected them to follow him, and hoped that reality would just sort itself out accordingly. Somewhat shockingly, reality obliged: at least, if the squeals of alarm from behind him when explosions went off nearby were anything to go by. Snaggi experienced another surge of pride. What other grot could boast such loyalty from his fellows? Even a runtherd couldn't manage this sort of thing without some well-placed threats.

Of course, even the most loyal of followers needed to see some sort of results if they were to continue placing themselves at risk at their leader's behest, which was why Snaggi was grateful that it was not far to what he had identified as their objective.

The wartrakk was still upright, but that was more than could be said for its crew. The driver was slumped over the controls, missing most of his head thanks to some typically cowardly long-ranged skrawnie pot-shotting. The gunner was nowhere to be seen, but a spray of dark blood over the weapon platform suggested that he had not just nipped off to get a nice juicy squig for a snack.

'Right, we're gonna take dis, an' we're gonna drive it straight at dat gate,' Snaggi said, patting the trakk on its flank as though it were a smasha squig that needed soothing. 'Blast right froo dem skrawniez, an' make history! Dat'll really show da orks wot grots can do. *An'* it means we get out of here,' he added, looking meaningfully at Skrawk.

'Well, yeah,' Skrawk managed, 'but only by drivin' straight at da gits wiv da big guns!'

'Ah, but we've got a big gun now, too!' Snaggi said, pointing at the double big shoota on its mount. 'If Lunk stands at da bottom an' yoo sit on his shoulders, yoo can dakka 'em before dey get us, can't ya! An' if Pukk pushes da pedals an' Guffink steers, we can drive it no trouble!'

'Wot about yoo an' Wizza, den?' Lunk demanded, seeming less than happy about being Skrawk's seat.

'Wizza's gonna be da spare, ready to fill in if one of ya...' *dies*, Snaggi's brain supplied, but he shunted it away. 'Needs a rest,' he finished, daring any of them to disagree with him. 'I'm Da Grotboss, so I'm gonna be directin' ya all, right? Now get to it!'

The driver was pushed unceremoniously off his seat, and they arranged themselves as Snaggi had instructed. Lunk was still grumbling, but Snaggi pointed out that at least Skrawk was the smallest of them, so he swallowed his complaints and let the other grot climb up on him. Then Guffink pressed the starter button, the engine roared into life, and they were ready to go.

Grots, driving a trakk! And Snaggi Littletoof, standing proud right behind the driver's seat, with a boomstikk in one hand and the symbol of his kind's oppression in the other! It was like a moment out of legend. It was a moment that deserved to *become* a legend. Snaggi Littletoof deserved to become a legend.

Well, he was on his way.

'Forwards!' he yelled, and Pukk stamped on the go pedal.

The trakk's engine roared, and it lurched away in a shower of gravel and surprised cursing from its crew. Snaggi swayed, but managed to remain on his feet: it would not do for Da Grotboss to be sent tumbling at the moment of his greatest triumph (to date). Lunk nearly didn't manage it, but was held up by Skrawk's death grip on the big shoota. However, said death grip involved clamping his fingers on the triggers, and the twin weapon sent a ragged burst of fire ripping upwards into the air.

It was an appropriate enough way to mark the start of their progress towards glory, but it was going to attract attention. A few ork heads turned towards them as the guns went off, since orks were always attracted to the noise of dakka, and Snaggi felt the slight bite of anxiety in his throat. He knew in his heart that there was absolutely no reason why grots *shouldn't* be driving a trakk, especially since the previous owners had come to a sticky end through no doing of his or his ladz, but he was not quite sure whether the orks would feel the same way about it.

Well, he was committed. He might as well make sure that the orks saw the grot who would soon be giving them their orders.

'To da gateway!' he yelled at the top of his lungs, striking a pose and gesturing with the grabba stikk as they raced across the ground.

'We're already goin' to da gateway!' Guffink protested, not looking around from where he was wrestling with the handlebars.

'Yeah, I know,' Snaggi said, out of the corner of his mouth. 'I'm tryin' to be inspirashunal.'

'Uh, boss?' Wizza said tentatively.

'Wot?'

'Shouldn't we be goin' a bit faster? Only dese fings normally get ahead of da boyz, but some of 'em are catchin' us up...'

Snaggi looked over his shoulder, sudden uncertainty seizing him. Sure enough, there was indeed a mob of orks charging after them, and they were getting closer. That didn't seem right.

He looked over the side of the trakk. It *felt* like they were going fast, but then Snaggi had never ridden on a trakk before, so maybe he had been deceived. Other evidence, such as the gradually closing bellows of 'bloody cheeky grots!' and the like, certainly seemed to suggest that it was his perception which was in error, rather than the world.

'Pukk!' he barked. 'Wot's da problem? Why ain't we goin' faster?'

'Da pedals are well stiff, boss!' Pukk panted, from somewhere just past Guffink's crotch. 'I fink ya need ork legs to press 'em down proper!'

Snaggi cursed everything. Why did ork meks make vehicles that only orks could drive? That was just inconsiderate. Luckily, he had a plan for just such an eventuality. 'Wizza! Get up dere an' help wiv da pedals!'

'Yes, boss!' Wizza replied, scuttling forwards. If that was partly just to get that bit further away from the orks catching them up, well, at least Snaggi knew how to motivate those under his command.

It took Wizza a couple of moments to negotiate his way past Guffink, but when he managed to do so the effect was immediate: the trakk lurched and accelerated, and the outraged shouts of the boyz behind them got angrier, but began to fade as the trakk pulled away.

'Hah!' Snaggi gloated, abandoning any ideas of being an inspirational figure, in favour of outright mockery. 'Yeah, zog da lot of ya!'

A roar of engines grabbed his attention, and he looked away from the receding footsloggers to see other red-painted vehicles pulling alongside them. And then pulling past them, because two grots together might manage to make a wartrakk go faster than a bunch of orks on foot, but they still couldn't match up to an actual ork in control of a vehicle. Snaggi caught a brief glimpse of a confused expression on what was left of the face of Zagnob Thundaskuzz as his Deffkilla wartrike overtook them, and then the speedboss was gone.

Heading for the gate, with a bunch of others behind him.

'No!' Snaggi yelled desperately. 'Dis was my idea, ya zoggin' great gits! *My* idea!' Why did he have to be cursed with *grots* taking his orders? All he'd needed was one decent ork driver and he'd have been away! He fumbled with his boomstikk as the gate drew closer - but not quickly enough, not for him - and wrestled with the idea of shooting Zagnob Thundaskuzz in the back. On the one hand, it was undoubtedly a very bad idea, but what did he have to lose at this point?

Well, head, legs, arms, potentially fingers one by one...

He was still caught in the web of indecision when light erupted near the gate: not the strange, cold, shimmering light of the gate itself, but good, strong, green light. It faded away almost immediately to reveal the shape of Old Morgrub, right in amongst some of the fanciest-looking skrawniez. One of the skrawniez drew a blade which flickered with darkness, and Snaggi thought for a moment that the warphead had had it, but Morgrub had already raised his staff and was bellowing something, and then heads exploded all around him.

It hadn't been planned - it couldn't have been planned, not least because that would have involved Zagnob Thundaskuzz having a concept of something more to do a few moments into the future other than 'continue to go fast' - but the speed freeks chose that moment to open up with their weapons. The remaining skrawniez around the gate, the ones who hadn't followed their big glowing metal friend, did not do well in the next few seconds. The Kult of Speed were no more accurate than most orks, but by Gork and Mork, they made up for quality with quantity. The skrawniez had no defence against the hail of fire that swept across them, and nowhere to hide from it. Only one of their big floaty guns got a shot away before its crew was gunned down, but to give the skrawniez due credit, it ripped a hole in the world for a moment and pulled two warbikes through into whatever lay beyond, turning them into a crumpled mess as it did so.

'Zoggin' 'eck!' Guffink exclaimed, twitching the handlebars and jerking them slightly further away from the rapidly diminishing rip in reality. 'Dat fing's dangerous!'

It certainly was, but it hadn't hit Zagnob Thundaskuzz, and the speedboss was nearly at the gateway now. Old Morgrub had somehow survived the barrage which had killed the skrawniez around him, and Snaggi waited for the warphead's eyes to light up with that green fire again, and for him to call down the Foot of Gork, or explode some more heads, or do *something* to prevent Thundaskuzz from getting through.

No such thing happened, but the Evil Sunz speedboss did not roar through the skrawnie gate as Snaggi had feared. Instead he veered off to one side, heading for the massive scrap that seemed to be shaping up around Mag Dedfist, Da Genrul, and the hot-git.

Snaggi punched the air in delight with the hand that held the grabba stikk. He should have known that the gods would intervene on his behalf! Thundaskuzz was too interested in a fight to claim the destiny which was Snaggi's by rights, showing the typical lack of forward thinking with which orks were cursed. This was why it should be grots in charge!

'Alright, ladz,' he gloated. 'Straight on! We've got dis in da bag!'

A moment later, he frowned. If he went through the gateway like this, on the trakk, then technically he wasn't going to be the first. That honour would go to Pukk and Wizza, working the pedals, since they were at the front. Should he order them to stop?

As it turned out, the gods had taken care of this as well. Unfortunately for Snaggi, this took the shape of one skrawnie who wasn't properly dead yet managing to claw his way back up behind the disappear-kannon, and activating it.

Snaggi threw himself clear of the trakk, but the rest of his crew lacked his superb reflexes, given as how they were stupidly holding onto things, or had another grot sitting on their shoulders, or what have you. The disappear-kannon ripped open the world again, and a swirl of unnatural colours that made Snaggi's head hurt to look at engulfed the trakk. Snaggi felt it pulling at him, and he scrabbled desperately in the dirt and dust as he landed, trying to get a grip on it. He felt himself starting to slide backwards...

...and the awful tugging sensation ceased. He looked around. Half a front wheel, crumpled; a few trakk links, buckled; someone's leg, without even a decent boot on the foot for him to take. That was all the kannon had left of his ride, and his ladz.

Thin, vicious, green rage surged through Snaggi's body. He scrambled back up to his feet, and levelled his grabba stikk at the skrawnie who had so insulted him.

'You!'

The skrawnie's helmet was emotionless, of course, but Snaggi could practically feel the fear his shout had engendered in the wearer. Some might have thought that the shakiness as it started to line the kannon up on him was due to the hideous injuries it had sustained, but Snaggi knew better: it was terrified of him! And with good reason, for he was vengeance incarnate. He charged towards it, determined to punish this pointy-eared git who had dared to destroy Da Grotboss' wartrakk... and also his ladz, but Snaggi could find new ladz anywhere, whereas trakks tended to have ork owners who were not inclined to part with them.

He had a moment's warning as the business end of the disappear-kannon glowed, and threw himself to one side. The weird krumpy-light missed: something behind him got chewed up and vanished, but the gods were still smiling on Snaggi Littletoof! Everyone knew that the skrawniez were good at shooting, didn't they? It must have been the favour of the gods which saved his life.

The skrawnie didn't get another chance to defy the gods. Snaggi fired the boomstikk into its face, splintering its helmet's faceplate – *he* didn't miss, because he was better than any skrawnie – and then latched onto its skinny neck with the grabba stikk. The skrawnie spasmed as he zapped it with the grabba stikk's full force, then fell bonelessly to the ground when he opened the jaws again. Snaggi whooped in triumph, then stopped as he noticed the skrawnie's chest was still moving up and down. How much did it take to kill one of these gits? He racked another shell into his boomstikk, and took aim.

A big green hand came down on his gun.

'Leave it,' Old Morgrub said. The warphead reached down and plucked the injured skrawnie off the ground, holding it by the neck with one hand. 'We're gonna need one of 'em alive.'

'Wot for?' Snaggi asked.

'Weirdboy stuff,' Morgrub said, with a wink. 'Look at da gate.'

Snaggi did so, and his jaw dropped open in despair. 'Wot? *No!*'

It was closed.

Well, it wasn't *closed*, you couldn't really close something that was just an arch. However, the weird light which had filled it had disappeared, and it was once more just a curve of stone-like stuff with nothing but clear air in the middle.

'I can open it again wiv dis git, don't worry about dat,' Morgrub said. 'An' yoo'll go froo first,' he added. 'I'll make sure of dat. Yoo've proved yerself to da gods.'

Snaggi gaped at him. 'Really?!'

'Oh yeah,' Morgrub grinned. 'Now we just gotta wait for somefing.'

Snaggi squinted. On the other side of the gate, he could just make out what looked like the hot-git piling into a bunch of humies in the distance, with the small shapes of other skrawniez around it.

He looked around. 'Where are all da uvver skrawniez?'

'Dead,' Morgrub said happily. 'Or on da way to it.'

Sure enough, the rest of what had once been Waaagh! Goresnappa were mopping up the few remaining skrawniez, and looking around for what to do next. Snaggi's chest swelled with pride. They would look towards the gate, they would see him standing next to Old Morgrub, and they would–

'Attennnnnnnnnnn-SHUN!'

And they would see, Snaggi realised with a sinking feeling, the limping but unquestionably still alive figure of Da Genrul.

LOTZ

Da Genrul's leg was giving him grief, and his ribs were none too happy either, but he was still armed and upright, and quite definitely the largest ork in the vicinity since Mag Dedfist got stomped. All around him, orks were polishing off the skrawniez that had not followed the hot-git off on its rampage. They'd given the Waaagh! a good scrap, Uzbrag would admit that, but when it came down to it, nothing could beat orks in a straight-up fight.

He was ignoring the fact that there was still dakka going off behind him. So far as he was concerned, the Waaagh! had won *this* fight, given that the skrawniez appeared to have given up on it and run off to start scragging humies. If they came back again, they could call it a new fight, and start over.

His eyes lit on Old Morgrub, standing near the gate, next to that ridiculous grot who'd given Uzbrag some lip earlier. The gate itself, he noticed with displeasure, now lacked the shimmering light through which the skrawniez had come. Uzbrag was no expert in artefacts created by the pointy-earz, but he had an inkling that you couldn't just step through it at any point and have it work. Had that zoggin' warphead dragged them all under this giant humie camp just for his promised gateway to the stars to stop working?

Kaptin Skulsnik and the Guttas materialised at Uzbrag's left elbow.

'Want us to do 'im over, boss?' Skulsnik muttered. 'We were gonna stick 'im earlier, but da git went all green an' disappeared on us. We scragged a fancy flyin' skrawnie instead, tho.'

'Leave 'im for da moment,' Uzbrag replied in a low voice. 'If he can get da gate open again, he's still got a use.'

'Gotcha, boss.'

Da Genrul inhaled. Time to take control.

'Attennnnnnnnnnn-SHUN!'

Only the Blood Axes really knew what he was yelling, of course, but the eyes of the rest of the Waaagh! gravitated to him nonetheless. Uzbrag felt their gazes land on him, and could tell that the various nobs and kaptins were weighing him up, deciding whether now was the time they wanted to make a bid for leadership themselves. He glowered around at them, meeting each pair of eyes that dared to hold his gaze, and watched them drop, one after another.

Apparently not, then.

'Mag Dedfist is dead!' Da Genrul bellowed. 'Zagnob Thundaskuzz is dead! I'm warboss now, an' yoo're all a part of Waaagh! Uzbrag! You got it?'

A cheer went up. Orks didn't like uncertainty, and fun though the race to get here had been, everyone felt better now they only had one warboss to worry about displeasing. Uzbrag stomped towards Old Morgrub, secure in the knowledge that the Waaagh! was behind him. Let the warphead try something funny now he didn't have two other big bosses to play him off against!

'Wot's dat for?' he demanded, pointing at the half-dead skrawnie that was limp in Morgrub's grasp.

'For da gate,' Morgrub replied. He gave Uzbrag a sly grin. 'Assumin' ya still wanna go froo it?'

Uzbrag drummed his fingers on the haft of his power choppa, and gave the matter some thought. He looked over at where the fight was still going on, skrawniez against humies, accompanied by screams, flashes of light and explosions: all the good stuff. A lot of the ladz were starting to shuffle in that direction as well, drawn by the incessant lure of a fight they weren't part of. Most of them were looking at him, waiting for the new warboss to give the order for them to pile in.

It was the order Gazrot Goresnappa would have given. It was the order Mag Dedfist would have given. As for Zagnob Thundaskuzz, he wouldn't have given an order so much as set off for the fight at top speed and expected everyone to follow him. It was the expected order.

So maybe, Da Genrul thought, it was an order he shouldn't give.

'Ya see dat over dere?' he yelled, pointing at the fight. 'Ya see dat? Dat's skrawniez an' humies kickin' da snot out of each uvver! An' ya see dat big fing with da massive choppa? Dat's a hot-git! It's dead fighty! It killed Mag Dedfist and Zagnob Thundaskuzz! Didn't get me, cos I'm *smart!* An' I bet ya all want to go an' get stuck in, am I right?'

Another cheer greeted these words, as was to be expected. It was easy to get orks to cheer, if it sounded like you were promising them a fight.

'Well,' Uzbrag said. 'I've got a better idea.'

That statement was met with confused blinks. Better than *a fight?* This was a concept the Waaagh! had not encountered before. Da Genrul had to get them back onside quickly, but he reckoned he knew how to do that.

'See, we've been fightin' humies ever since we landed on dis planet!' he shouted. 'An' it's been fun an' all, but it gets a bit samey after a while, dunnit? Maybe we should go an' find somefing else to clobber? An' yeah, dat hot-git's well fighty, but da fing about dat is, it came out of *here.*'

He pointed at the gateway.

'So I reckon dere's more of 'em on da uvver side! Maybe a lot more! We could have da best scrap of our lives if we go froo dis gate! We could find all sorts of interestin' fings to give some dakka to! So whaddya say, ladz? Dere ain't many humies an' skrawniez left. It's almost a shame to ruin da fun for 'em, an' it wouldn't be a challenge for us to finish 'em off. Let's leave 'em to it, an' go an kick da rest of the galaxy's faces in instead!'

It turned out that orks could grasp the concept of something better than a fight, so long as it was a *bigger* fight. Another cheer went up, and the Waaagh! began to pile forwards eagerly.

'Over to yoo,' Uzbrag said smugly, turning to Morgrub. 'Can ya ackcherly get it–'

He stopped. Morgrub had one hand around the skrawnie's head, and the gate was filled with shimmering light again.

'Oh. Alright.' Da Genrul shrugged. If the warphead hadn't been able to do what he'd promised, way back before they'd even got inside the walls, Uzbrag could have blamed the failure on him and had the full support of the Waaagh! in taking Morgrub out of the reckoning for good. As it was, it looked like they were good to go.

Or were they?

Uzbrag eyed the curtain of cold light and took another look at Old Morgrub. The warphead hardly looked trustworthy at the best of times, so it was difficult to work out what he might be thinking. All the same, Uzbrag had seen various force fields and the like at work, and he was aware of the notion that sometimes you could get through something in one direction, but definitely not the other. Might this be a trick to get Uzbrag out of the way, so Morgrub could turn this into a WeirdWaaagh! under his command?

That grot with the grabba stikk was looking expectantly at Old Morgrub. Da Genrul came to a decision.

'Oi, you!'

The grot turned towards him, its mouth opening almost as though it was going to answer him back, but it never got the chance: Uzbrag's boot connected solidly with its midsection, and sent it sailing through the air. It wailed, still somehow holding onto the grabba stikk, hit one side of the arch, and ricocheted off it through the lights and out of sight. Old Morgrub practically bent double laughing, which at least showed the old weirdboy still had something approaching a normal sense of humour somewhere.

'Huh,' Da Genrul grunted. 'Reckon it works.'

'How d'ya know, boss?' Skulsnik asked.

'Well, da grot didn't bounce off and catch fire, or just disintegrate into little bits of wotnot,' Uzbrag said confidently. 'It went froo, so it's all good.'

'Yeah, but goin' froo might've killed it,' Skulsnik pointed out. 'Da skrawniez are well strange.'

'Eh, it's a grot,' Uzbrag said dismissively. 'Goin' froo *might've* killed it, but lotsa fings'll kill a grot wot won't kill an ork. I'm warboss now – can't let a little fing like gettin' killed stop me.' He raised his power choppa. 'Come on, ladz! It's time to take da Waaagh! *to da stars!*'

He charged. And Waaagh! Uzbrag charged with him.

DA BIT WOT COMES AFTER DA FING

The ork frowned.

'Ya didn't shorten dat at all. And ya ain't explained how ya ended up *here*.'

Snaggi grinned hopefully. He had been hoping to impress his captor with his obvious ingenuity and leadership potential. 'But I told ya wot ya wanted to know, boss!'

'No, ya didn't,' the ork rumbled, picking up a large and extremely dangerous-looking hammer with an axe head on the back of it. 'Guess we'll ask da next one.'

'No! No, wait!' Snaggi yelped. 'I fort it was obvious! I mean, dat is,' he added hastily, aware that he had just implied the ork wasn't intelligent enough to understand what he'd been saying, 'it's da skrawniez! Ya gotta have a skrawnie to get froo da gate!'

The ork paused, the hammer halfway raised. 'A skrawnie?'

'Yeah!' Snaggi confirmed, nodding furiously. 'Da tunnels are wot dey use to get around! Dey're da ones who can turn da gates on an' off! So if ya wanna get in, yoo're gonna need one!' he added, helpfully.

The ork studied him carefully for a few seconds. Snaggi did his best not to squirm, but it was difficult. Not only was this ork massive, he also gave off the impression of being quite smart, for an ork. That was not a combination with which Snaggi felt particularly comfortable.

'We did see wot looked like a skrawnie hangin' around just before we nabbed dis git, boss,' the other grot said. Snaggi glared at him. So this was the traitor who'd captured him! He'd make sure to get his revenge, assuming the ork didn't hammer him flat.

The ork nodded. 'Right, skrawniez it is.' He leaned down, until his face was a few inches away from Snaggi's. Given the ork's head was roughly the same size as all of Snaggi, this did not do much for Snaggi's general state of mind.

'Yoo're my grot, now,' the ork rumbled. 'Ya do wot I say, when I say it, or I feed ya to me squig. Ya got dat?'

Snaggi hated himself, but there was nothing he could do. He nodded his head. 'Yes, boss. An,' uh, who're yoo? Just so I can say, if someone asks who me boss is.'

The ork's face split into an entirely unpleasant grin. 'I'm Ufthak Blackhawk, an' I'm da big boss around 'ere.' He straightened up again. 'Nizkwik, show dis one wot to do. I'm gonna talk to Da Meklord.'

Snaggi watched the massive ork thud away, each step like a Deff Dread's, then turned his attention to the other grot.

'So, yoo're Nizkwik, den?'

'Dat's right.' Nizkwik untied Snaggi's hands and smirked at him. 'I'm da grot da boss kicks least! An' he's never fed me to his squig!' He squared up to Snaggi, trying to make himself look taller, even though they were the same height. 'So I'm not gonna have any trouble outta ya, am I, Snaggi Littletoof?'

'No,' Snaggi said, shaking his head. He waited until Nizkwik had turned his back before sticking out his tongue.

Yet.

Orks, grots, squigs, skrawniez: it made no difference. Gork and Mork had spoken to Snaggi Littletoof, and if he knew one thing for sure, it was that his destiny would *not* be denied...

CATACHAN DEVIL

JUSTIN WOOLLEY

----- DEPARTMENTO MUNITORUM FORM 8712/AM/R03 -----

ASTRA MILITARUM OPERATIONS REPORT

CORRESPONDENCE NUMBER: OR-12710735626

TO: High Command, Task Force Devotion of Pangea
CC: Departmento Munitorum – Office of Records – Correspondence Department
Office of the Supreme Commander Ultima Segmentum
Officio Tactica Logistics Division
FROM: Major General Niko Nillom, Officer Commanding Gondwa System Defence
SUBJECT: Gondwa System Defence Update
ENCLOSURES and REFERENCES:
1. Pangea Subsector Reference Chart
2. Gondwa System Defence Force Breakdown and Distribution Report
3. Final Casualty Report from the Purging of Karst
4. Request Form for Priority Two Transfer of Additional Reinforcements (Seventh Submission)
5. List of Approved Devotional Prayers for Upcoming Purge of Gondwa VI

In the name of the most Holy Emperor of Mankind I, (insert name here) MAJOR GENERAL NILLOM, submit the following report on (insert relevant operation name) THE GONDWA SYSTEM DEFENCE.

Following my last official report (see OR-12710735501), after successfully purging the planet Karst in the Regmenta System (see reference 1 for planetary location), the defence of the Pangea Subsector turns to the Gondwa System, specifically the planet Gondwa VI – jungle world status: minor agricultural/intermediate resources, planetary standard classification: C-.

My headquarters unit along with the newly deployed Skadi Second Infantry have arrived on Gondwa VI, where the greenskins have landed after retreating from Karst. Gondwa VI's unusually active and fluctuating magnetic field causes difficulty with sensor scans from orbit and with vox communication on the surface; additionally the thick jungle that covers the majority of the planet makes visual reconnaissance all but impossible – as a result the number of xenos present is unknown. Despite this, I have no doubt the Skadi Second Infantry, although a relatively new regiment, are up to the challenge. Support is en route from the Catachan 57th Jungle Fighters, who are currently in warp transit. Refer to references 2 and 3 for current force breakdown and the casualty report from the battle for Karst, where the Catachan 57th assisted in ridding the planet of the ork menace.

I would also like to draw your attention to enclosure 4, where, despite my utmost confidence in the Skadi Second and the Catachan 57th, I have submitted a seventh request for additional reinforcements to the Officio Tactica.

The Gondwa System has known the threat of orks before and has overcome the green-skinned xenos numerous times, and I have no doubt that with the blessing of the Emperor we shall do the same again (see reference 5 for approved devotionals). All the Emperor's warriors, from myself and my staff officers down to the troopers who wield the Emperor's fury on the battlefield, are ready to purge the greenskin threat from Gondwa VI and continue the holy work of pushing them from this subsector of Imperial space. Our courageous Astra Militarum troopers are prepared to face the enemy, they are ready for the battles to come, and they stand in good spirits for war.

- - - - - END COMMUNICATION - - - - -

CHAPTER ONE

TORVIN

Trooper Ted Torvin was not in good spirits for war. He hadn't been in good spirits since he'd received the official notice of his tithing some – what was it now? – five months earlier.

Congratulations and blessings of the Emperor upon you, citizen. By glorious providence and Divine hand, you, along with 50% of the population of your hive subsector, have been drafted into the Skadi Second Infantry Regiment of the Astra Militarum. You are called upon to serve the most Holy Emperor of Mankind in defence of the Imperium and humanity. Be thankful and give praise that your life will now have meaning alongside the billions of others who fight valiantly and die with distinction to maintain the purity and safety of the glorious Imperium. Through battle you shall live forever in the Emperor's eyes and the light of the Golden Throne shall shine on you eternal.

One month after being tithed, Torvin had been shipped off for eighty days of basic training on Skadi's moon of Edda and then had endured almost two months in transit through the warp aboard the Imperial Navy transport *Shadow of Radiance.*

Now he had arrived on another world, an idea that seemed absurd or at least like some kind of elaborate ruse. Yet the fact was undeniable. The pressing wet warmth that permeated even here, inside the thick stone walls of an Ecclesiarchy chapel, was a heat and humidity that never occurred on Skadi, which was far enough from its star as to be perpetually in icy winter. Still, even with the inescapable alien heat; even after flying over the dense jungle, seeing it spreading away in all directions in myriad shades of green such as he had never imagined; even with the constant smell of damp ground and decaying vegetation, so thick he felt as if he were drinking it in through his nose – even with all that, he didn't feel like he'd travelled to a planet far, far from his own.

Conceptually, he knew he stood in the upper levels of Karoo City on the jungle world of Gondwa VI, but it didn't quite feel real. It didn't feel as though he'd been uprooted from the only home he'd ever known and deposited light years away. It seemed to him as if he'd remained perfectly still and the entire galaxy had pivoted around him.

Torvin looked around at the richly adorned chapel. It was a long space of alcoves and echoes. The rows of intricately carved wooden pews had been stacked against the walls to clear space for an entire Astra Militarum company to roll out their sleeping mats. Both the task force headquarters unit and the Skadi Second Infantry had occupied the vast Ecclesiarchy building soon after their arrival on Gondwa VI. The priests of the Adeptus Ministorum had praised the troopers of the Skadi Second and blessed them in the name of the Emperor with chanting and incense, but their scowling faces made it clear they were less than pleased with the Imperial Guard commandeering their place of worship as accommodation.

With its stone walls, high arched roof and enormous frescoes, the chapel was immediately familiar to Torvin. It was much like those on Skadi and, he imagined, much like those on countless other Imperial worlds. The focal point of the building's design was the huge stained-glass window at the far end of the long space. Stretching from the floor to the cavernous roof, it depicted the Holy Emperor adorned in golden armour, His head rimmed with a halo of light and a flaming sword in His hands. Perhaps it was the familiarity of that image that made Torvin feel as if he could somehow still be at home; everywhere across Imperial space the Emperor was there, the great unifier of them all.

Despite all that was familiar, there were many depictions around the chapel Torvin did not recognise: saints and martyrs native to Gondwa VI or the surrounding worlds. Names he did not know but whose deeds, he was sure, the children of Gondwa VI could recite by rote. One wall bore an impressive fresco of the thick green jungle, and striding out of it were enormous figures in blood-red armour: Space Marines of the Adeptus Astartes. Had those true angels of the Emperor once set foot upon this planet? The thought that he was on a world where the Adeptus Astartes had fought was enough to convince him he was indeed far from home. Nothing like that had ever happened on Skadi. He wasn't on his frozen backwater any longer.

Around him, the troopers of his platoon sat on their bedrolls or stood putting gear into their packs, preparing equipment, delicately cleaning their lasguns in readiness. They chatted cordially. Some even laughed. How could they laugh at a time like this? When they were awaiting word about their orders from command. When they were waiting to learn how and when they would be sent out into the unknown jungle to engage the orks.

Slow-witted savage animals who somehow understand how to piece together the most rudimentary and barely functioning technology. Stupid, unsophisticated and lacking all but the ability to charge straight to their deaths at the hands of stalwart Imperial Guardsmen. They may seem imposing at first glance, larger than a human and more muscular, but appearances are deceiving. Their muscle is more plentiful but still weaker than a human's, and though it may seem improbable from their size, do not shy away from them even in close combat as a human is stronger and can best them with a bayonet to the throat.

That's what their briefing on the greenskins had said, but immediately after it had finished, as they filed out of the briefing room on board the *Shadow of Radiance*, Torvin had heard veterans of the regiment, as few as there were, chuckling and speaking to each other.

'Stupid is right,' one of them was saying, a corporal Torvin didn't know, 'but I sure as Throne won't be lettin' any of 'em get close enough that I have to stab the bastards.'

'I know,' another of the grizzled few answered. 'I saw one of the greenies, half its jaw missing and all, grab hold of Trooper Hafden's arms and rip them off still holding his lasgun. Hit them from a distance, I reckon. Las right between those red eyes from as far away as possible.'

'Weaker than a human,' the corporal continued, muttering as they moved away, 'that's some gold-plated crem right there.'

It was well known that from the time a new Imperial Guardsman arrived on their first battlefield, their average life expectancy was little more than fifteen hours. Torvin knew he would be tossed into his first battle soon and could just about hear some enormous clock ticking down the minutes to his inevitable doom.

He stared down at his equipment, laid out on the stone floor before him. He knew he'd humped all this down from the drop-ship but it suddenly seemed like a lot and he wasn't exactly sure how to fit it all back in his pack. Torvin looked up and saw Frent, the vox-trooper from his squad, screwing a long antenna onto the vox-transmitter he would carry as part of his load. Not far away, a heavy bolter team was loading metal boxes with lengths of belt-fed ammunition. At least he didn't have to heft around all that gear too. Take the small mercies, as his father would say. Though, a large mercy would be more welcome, like if the orks just decided to give up and leave Gondwa VI. From everything he'd heard about the greenskins, there was no warping chance that would happen.

'Oi, Torvin.'

Torvin turned to see his squad's corporal, Algarn, approaching. Algarn was a tall, thin man with a face all sharp lines and angles, and the white hair common to their icy home world.

'Yes, corporal?'

'What are you doing?'

'I'm packing my gear ready to move out,' Torvin said. 'Like Sergeant Troovey ordered.'

Algarn looked at his laid-out gear and empty pack. 'You know you got to fit all this gear in your pack, trooper?'

'Yes, corporal,' Torvin said. 'I was just making sure I had everything first. That's what they told us to do in basic training.'

'Right,' Algarn said, looking at Torvin's shiny new kit, carefully arranged on the floor, 'and you've got everything, do you?'

'Yes, corporal.'

Algarn sniffed. 'That so, is it?'

'Yes, corporal,' Torvin said, but he was suddenly less sure than he had been a moment ago. 'I think so, corporal.'

'Got all your kit then do you?'

Torvin had now progressed to completely unsure. 'I...'

'We're more'n likely heading out to shoot some orks, you know that don't you, trooper?'

'Yes, corporal.'

'And what, by the Throne, are you going to shoot them with, Trooper Torvin?'

'Uh, my las...' Torvin's voice trailed off. 'Oh.' He looked around, saw his lasgun still propped up near the door where his squad had left their weapons. It was the only one there.

'Yeah,' Corporal Algarn said. 'Gonna need that to dispatch the Emperor's fury ain't you?'

'Yes, corporal,' Torvin said.

'I know I told all you new recruits that looking after your socks and boots is even more important than your lasgun,' Algarn said, 'but that don't mean you can leave it behind.'

'Yes, corporal. Sorry, corporal,' Torvin said, his face growing hot as he moved off to retrieve his weapon.

Torvin carried his lasgun back to his equipment, chastising himself for being such a fool. The punishment for misplacing a rifle during basic training had been seventeen lashes. Back then, the instructors had drilled it into every recruit: if you want to be one of the few that survives those first fifteen hours, you better remember your training; the Emperor blesses those that remember their training.

Torvin placed his lasgun down beside his pack where it would be impossible to forget it again. Then he began stowing away the rest of his equipment, wishing as he did so that he could stow away his fear just as easily. Everything the Astra Militarum had determined he needed to be an effective instrument of the Holy Emperor's will went into the pack: lasgun maintenance kit including sacred cleaning oil and cloth freshly blessed by the tech-priests; two spare lasgun power packs; three days' worth of nutrient-rich synthetic food rations; *The Imperial Infantryman's Uplifting Primer*; one roll of toilet paper; water canteen; holy purifying tablets; two pairs of socks (spare); one undershirt (spare); two pairs standard-issue underwear (male, spare); one raincoat; Guard-issue medi-pack including blessed tonics (small); sleeping bag and canvas tarpaulin; razors (x2); shaving foam, toothbrush and toothpaste; and a mess kit including plate, cup, bowl and the combination spoon, fork, knife generally referred to by the troopers of the Skadi Second as a FRED – a Fragging Ridiculous Eating Device.

The rest of his equipment, including his helmet, flak armour and webbing – containing another lasgun power pack, utility knife, bayonet and primary water canteen – he placed to the side, knowing he would need to don these prior to moving out. Last of all, he took out the only thing he carried not issued to him by the Astra Militarum: a small printed pict. He wasn't sure whether he was permitted to carry it with him out on a mission, but he was going to. He couldn't leave it behind. He'd only been a trooper in the Astra Militarum for two months but that had been long enough to learn many important lessons from the veterans: never volunteer for anything; troopers exist to hurry up and wait; if it isn't yours, don't touch it; and the only time it's good to ask for permission is when you want the answer to be no.

He'd seen other troopers with personal items such as talismans hanging from their belts or tucked into their helmets. Some had images of saints or other iconography threaded onto the dog-tag chains around their necks.

There were some with picts or letters from home, but these were few and far between. Letters were rare for the simple reason that most of the working population of Skadi could read only the barest amount necessary to do their jobs -for most that meant knowing how to read the shift clock in the mines - and they could write even less than that. Picts were even rarer than letters because it was only wealthier families that could afford a picter. Torvin was just going to follow the lead of the other troopers and assume he could carry the pict with him as long as it was kept hidden, particularly whenever Commissar Redvin was around.

He looked down at the image in his hand. Melina. She smiled back at him from the past. Torvin had never known anyone who smiled as much as Melina. Most people on Skadi had never smiled a day in their life. Though to be fair, life in the mines beneath the ice never gave anyone much of a reason to smile. But Melina smiled. On their icy home she had been his source of warmth. They would have been married last week. Now they would never be married. Even though he kept repeating the mantra that his training would keep him alive, Torvin had the sinking feeling that his fifteen-hour life expectancy would more than make sure he would never see his home world, let alone Melina, ever again.

'Fourth Platoon, bring it in.'

The thunderous voice of Lieutenant Olga Gernson, Torvin's platoon commander, boomed out from her heavyset frame, bouncing off the stone walls of the chapel like the blast of a frag grenade. Torvin saw her striding down the length of the nave wearing her helmet and flak armour, which only served to make her seem more massive than she already was. The troopers of the Skadi Second - even those not in her platoon, since her reputation was almost as big as her stature - called her Olga Ogryn because how anyone, woman or man, could grow that monstrously large without some hint of abhuman in the family, no one knew. Of course, no one would say this to her face or within earshot of an officer, or worse still a commissar, but there was no doubt she knew of the name and didn't seem too concerned. Torvin quickly slipped his pict of Melina into his shirt pocket.

'I said, bring it in, troopers,' Gernson roared again, apparently dissatisfied with the lacklustre pace displayed by her platoon. Fourth Platoon moved to meet her where she'd stopped, taking a knee around her. This was it then, Torvin supposed, they were about to get the assignment the platoon had been promised. They were about to head out for glorious battle in the name of the Emperor, and Torvin's clock was about to start ticking.

'Right,' Gernson said, 'hurry up and get your kit squared away, we're about to move out. Our first operational objective will be to hold Outpost Four, a watch station on the approach to Karoo City. We'll be relieving a local militia, maintaining a presence there and engaging any greenskins sighted because it's a vital location for tracking enemy movements. There have been orks spotted in the area. Apparently, this planet's magnetic field is a bastard on comms and any monitoring is shot to crem because of that. Plus, all these blasted trees they've got here make it Throne-damned hard to see from orbit. So it's old-fashioned boots on the ground to keep a lookout for the enemy. If we see them inbound, we send up a signal flare and then we start killing xenos.' Gernson turned to Sergeant Troovey. 'I expect the platoon to be boots out in one hour.'

'Yes, ma'am,' Troovey replied.

Gernson nodded to him and then turned her gaze back to the troopers of Fourth Platoon. 'Carry on, troopers,' she said before walking away. Torvin had half expected some words of encouragement or support, but he supposed that was it. He returned his attention to packing.

'Here ya go.'

Torvin looked up from his equipment to see Corporal Algarn. He was holding out a data-slate. Torvin took it, turning it to look at the screen.

DEPARTMENTO MUNITORUM FORM 87390-B/MSG

CORRESPONDENCE REQUEST

'You and the other newbies got a chance to write home if you want,' Algarn said. 'Tell anyone that cares you're about to see combat for the first time, that you're thinking of them as you fight for the Emperor. Whatever. I don't give a crem what you write, just hurry up about it.'

'Thanks, corporal,' Torvin said.

'Just hurry up.'

Torvin looked down at the data-slate. He immediately knew it was Melina he would write to, but he suddenly didn't know what to say. He looked up to see Algarn still looming over him like a dark cloud. It was even more difficult to think with the tall, perpetually annoyed corporal hovering overhead.

'Could you just give me a minute, corporal?' Torvin asked. He watched Algarn's eyebrows raise and immediately regretted the words.

'Warp no, trooper,' Algarn said. 'I'm not giving you a Throne-damned minute. I need you to write whatever soppy crem is going to gush out of your green-arse face to your rich mummy and daddy so that I can get the other fodder around here to do the same before we move out. Throne-damned "give me a minute." I'll give you my boot up your standard issue, Torvin, that's what I'll give you.'

'Sorry, corporal.'

Torvin looked back to the slate. *Note that all correspondence is monitored and reviewed,* it read. *Any information about active operations will be redacted. Any heretical or blasphemous content will also be redacted and may be grounds for punishment up to and including death.*

He filled out Melina's details in the recipient section of the form and then wrote a quick message. With the warning that everything he wrote would be read, he obviously couldn't tell her about the fear that had gripped him knowing that his life was very likely to end within the next day. Even leaving out his fears, nothing he wrote would be sufficient to explain the hole that had opened in him after losing her. He scribbled something down, constantly aware of the ever-present impatience of Corporal Algarn. Reading back over what he'd written, his message seemed particularly inadequate. *My dearest Melina, I hope you are well. I am very likely soon to face the orks in battle. It is thinking of you that keeps me strong. I will miss you always. Ted.*

They seemed such hollow words but there was no time for anything more; Algarn was already holding his hands out and clicking his fingers for Torvin to hand back the slate. He filled out his details at the bottom – name, rank, serial number – and then submitted the message.

Trooper Torvin, T. your request for correspondence has been submitted. The Departmento Munitorum will forward message once a servo-skull at your relevant regimental headquarters has checked and approved form X7132bDe/P01. Expect message receipt at destination between three and seventy-two standard weeks.

Corporal Algarn snatched the data-slate from Torvin's hand and moved off to find other recruits who had yet to see it. Algarn obviously considered this a pointless exercise. He must have been ordered to get the unit writing home from someone up the chain of command. When he was younger, back on Skadi, Torvin had once overheard one of the nobility talking about the message he'd received from his brave daughter, who had been tithed and was fighting some alien menace elsewhere in the galaxy in the name of the Emperor. He remembered quite clearly how her father had said she'd spoken of the glory of war against the abhorrent alien and how she'd felt the Emperor at her back. Torvin wondered now whether she'd actually felt the same as he did: alone and afraid, but not wanting to admit as much in any monitored correspondence. It suddenly seemed obvious to him that messages home from the Astra Militarum were not at all for the troopers on the front line. They were to make everyone else feel safe and proud.

Torvin finished closing up his pack and placed it ready beside his webbing, armour and lasgun. He wandered over to where a group of other troopers from his squad sat speaking to each other. They had all completed their soldierly duty of hurrying up, and now came the waiting. Trooper Ernest Norsten, Trooper Freya Gorm and Trooper Henrik Gernt, like Torvin, were all freshly minted Imperial Guardsmen, having been tithed at the same time and completed their basic training together.

'Has she even seen combat before?' Trooper Norsten was saying.

'Who's that?' Torvin asked, trying to catch up on the conversation.

'Lieutenant Gernson,' Norsten answered. 'She's all blast and bluster but no one seems to know if she's actually been in combat.'

'None of us have,' Gorm interjected.

'Yeah,' Norsten said, 'but we're troopers, she's a lieutenant – be nice to know our platoon leader knows something about what to do when the crem starts flying.'

'So why don't you go on and ask her then?' Gernt said; the implication that this was a terrible idea was obvious.

'Crem no,' Norsten said, 'I don't have a bastard death wish. She'll probably snap me over her knee.'

'Yeah, so she can probably do the same to the greenskins,' Gorm said. 'She's the lieutenant either way so what does it matter?'

'I hope we find out quickly,' Norsten said. 'I hope the orks attack when we're holding this outpost because I can't wait to kill some xenos. I'm going to snuff a dozen I reckon.'

'Yeah, all right.' Gorm rolled her eyes. 'You're sure to be a hero of the Imperium.'

'Maybe I will,' Norsten continued. 'They'll be remembering my name on Skadi. We ain't got many heroes but they'll be remembering me. Norsten the Ork Slayer. Probably get two dozen if I can get to the front rank. Can't wait.'

Norsten turned to Torvin, who had been quietly listening. How Norsten had the audacity to say Lieutenant Gernson was full of bluster while he sat there talking about becoming some legendary war hero was beyond him.

'What about you, Torvin?' Norsten asked. 'How many orks are you going to slay?'

'I haven't really thought about it,' Torvin said, which wasn't exactly a lie. He had done little but think about being in combat with the orks and how he might survive, but he hadn't thought at all about how many of the xenos he was going to kill. He'd just assumed the answer would be zero.

'Haven't thought about it,' Norsten echoed to the other troopers around him. 'Everyone's thought about killing xenos.'

'Sure,' Torvin said. 'I'll probably kill some orks.'

'Don't sound very sure about that,' Norsten said. 'Are you some kind of xenos-lover?'

'Norsten!' Gorm jumped on him, her voice a harsh whisper. 'Don't even joke about that.'

'Maybe I'm not joking,' Norsten said. 'I've seen Torvin moping about, and I saw this too.'

Torvin was too slow to react when Norsten lunged forward and plucked the partially exposed pict from his top shirt pocket.

'Hey!' Torvin called, trying to grab it back, but Norsten had already turned away and was looking at the pict of Melina.

'Who's this then?' Norsten asked. 'This the reason you're afraid?'

'Give it back, Norsten,' Torvin pleaded. 'It's important.'

Torvin grabbed at the pict again, but Norsten moved it out of range of his grasping hand.

'First tell us who she was.'

Torvin sighed. 'Fine, her name is Melina. Now give it back.'

'Your girlfriend?' Norsten asked.

'We were supposed to get married,' Torvin said. 'Now let me put it away.'

'She's cute. Nice smile,' Norsten said. 'Shame you'll never see her again.' He looked at Torvin. 'Why do you bother carrying this? You're an idiot if you think you're ever getting back to Skadi. Let me help you get in the mood for war.'

Norsten grabbed the pict with both hands, making ready to tear it down the middle. With a reflex action Torvin jumped at Norsten, slamming him back against the cold, hard stone of the chapel floor. Straddling him, Torvin grabbed at the pict, trying to pull it free of Norsten's grasp. Perhaps because he'd caught Norsten by surprise, Torvin managed to rip the pict free. He squeezed it in his fist as he pulled his arm back ready to punch Norsten square in the face. He never had the chance to follow through as a large boot struck him in the side, kicking him off the shocked Guardsman.

'What's this Throne-damned crem, troopers?'

Torvin rolled over, winded by the blow. He looked up to see the boot was laced to the foot of Sergeant Troovey. Troovey, second-in-command of the platoon, was a man almost as large as Lieutenant Gernson and there was no question about whether or not he'd seen combat during his Imperial Guard career. He was one of the few grizzled veterans who'd been transferred from other regiments to join the newly formed Skadi Second Infantry. His face was criss-crossed with scars and his eye had long ago been replaced with an augmetic after it had been torn from its socket by some multi-limbed, thick-shelled xenos on a faraway world.

'Sorry, sir,' Torvin stammered.

'Did you just call me sir?' Troovey asked. 'I'm a sergeant, not an officer. Don't call me sir, I work for my Throne-damned living. Now, you gonna answer me? What the crem is going on?'

It was Norsten who jumped in. 'Torvin here was getting worked up because I was telling him he'll never get back to Skadi, sergeant. We were talking about killing orks and he doesn't seem to want to, he's acting a coward.'

As if that word were a beacon calling out across the universe, Torvin saw someone even worse than Sergeant Troovey approaching: Commissar Mave Redvin. Like all commissars, Redvin wore a black peaked cap adorned with a shining gold aquila. Her polished breastplate was adorned with a decorative skull and, over that, her black greatcoat with gold epaulettes and red lining hung down to swish around her feet as she walked with slow, purposeful steps towards them. Even Sergeant Troovey remained silent as she approached.

'A coward here is there, sergeant?' Commissar Redvin asked when she reached them.

'Not in my platoon, commissar,' Sergeant Troovey said. 'I can assure you of that.'

'What's the concern then?' Redvin continued. 'Your platoon is about to move out, we do not need a breakdown of discipline before you've even left.'

'No, commissar,' Troovey said, turning his attention to Torvin and Norsten. 'These two are just so keen to start fighting greenskins they're taking it out on each other.'

Commissar Redvin looked at Norsten and Torvin. 'Well, troopers, you make sure you save your fighting' – her eyes fixed on Torvin with an almost supernatural sternness – 'and your bravery, for the enemy.'

Torvin swallowed. 'Yes, commissar,' both he and Norsten said, in almost perfect unison.

'Good. Carry on, and good hunting,' Commissar Redvin said as she turned to walk away, her greatcoat swirling out behind her. 'The Emperor protects.'

'Sergeant, I–' Norsten said once Redvin had moved away to inspect the rest of the troopers around the chapel, but Troovey quickly interrupted.

'Shut your crem hole, last thing I need is a commissar up my arse.' He pointed directly at Norsten's face. 'You listen good. No trooper really knows how they're going to react until the crem starts flying out there, so you save your accusations of cowardice and just worry about pointing your own lasgun where it needs to go. Now finish packing your gear.'

'I'm already fin–'

Sergeant Troovey glared at Norsten.

'Yes, sergeant,' Norsten said.

Sergeant Troovey walked away and the troopers sat in silence. Torvin wondered whether Norsten was right. Was he a coward? He'd never considered himself a coward before he was tithed but since then it hadn't seemed far from the truth.

Back on Skadi, after he received his notice of tithing, he'd considered taking Melina and running away with her. It wouldn't have been hard to vanish in the labyrinthine squalor of the lower hive. But he couldn't ask that of Melina, and he didn't want to live as a deserter either, constantly knowing the Arbites would be searching for him. The punishment for desertion from a tithe was death on sight. If the choice to be a deserter made someone a coward then the truth was simple: Torvin was too afraid to be a coward. He looked at Commissar Redvin strolling down the lines and the troopers all around her quieting down, standing taller, looking like strong soldiers of the Imperium. Perhaps that was the irony of the entire Astra Militarum, he thought – every single Imperial Guardsman is too afraid to be a coward.

CHAPTER TWO

TORVIN

Torvin leant back and waved frantically at his face as something, some huge insect as big as his fist, flew close by. Seemingly unconcerned by his attempts to fend it off, the insect investigated him momentarily, circling his head, sounding like the buzz of a Valkyrie engine as it passed his ears. Apparently finding nothing of interest it flew away, darting between dense mossy trees and hanging vines to quickly disappear into the jungle. Torvin returned his attention to where he was going just as a springy branch, bent forward by Trooper Gernt in front of him, whipped back to slap him broadside across the cheek.

'Throne damn it,' he muttered as he raised his lasgun, bayonet fixed to the end, and slashed at the jungle.

New branches, vines and leaves seemed to fill the space in front of him with every step even if he tried to follow the path Gernt and the other troopers were cutting through the trees. When they'd looked out at the jungle from atop Karoo City it had certainly seemed thick, but this was even worse than he'd expected. He could be only steps behind Gernt and barely be able to see him through the green. When he looked up, the canopy completely blocked the sky and the diffuse light that filtered down was tinged with a yellow-green hue. Even the ground beneath his feet was only visible some of the time. More often than not he was pushing through ferns and monstrous ground-covering plants with leaves almost as wide as he was tall, his legs out of sight below the knees. It was like trudging through the worst blizzard back home on Skadi, but this was a living blizzard of reaching creepers and enormous flat fronds that couldn't be waited out.

He might have complained about blizzards on Skadi but what he wouldn't have given for the freezing touch of wind-whipped snow right now. The jungle heat made everything about this worse. It was a damp, concentrated, energy-sapping heat that made every step of lugging his pack and lasgun more difficult. He was sweating profusely, his fatigues drenched through. Then again, he didn't know how much of that was his own salty sweat and how much was the moisture from all around him. Every leaf was wet. The ground was soft enough that his boots regularly sank sole-deep or further. The air itself was saturated to the point he thought it might have been easier to swim.

Now, after hours of slogging through the dense vegetation, the jungle was, mercifully, beginning to thin somewhat. They were finally emerging from the valley and drawing close to the location of Outpost Four, strategically very important for the early warning it would offer of any ork forces attempting to move on Karoo City.

'Contact!'

The call came like a las-shot from somewhere ahead of him.

'Contact two o'clock, fifty yards!'

Torvin wasn't sure whose voice it was; he thought it might have been Norsten's. The shout was followed, almost immediately, by the unmistakable ringing crack of lasgun fire. The jungle ahead was lit with flashes of orange-red as streaks of las illuminated the dense green of the jungle, burning through foliage and blasting chunks from trees. Torvin stood and watched. Shouts echoed around him, from troopers ahead and behind. Calls from Sergeant Troovey and Lieutenant Gernson to get a positive ident on the enemy even as other troopers seemed to fire blindly ahead. How many times had he been part of a contact drill during his basic training? Fifty, a hundred, more? They had repeated common battle drills so many times they were supposed to be ingrained, automatic reactions, so that on the battlefield there would be no need to think. *Reaction to ambush (far), reaction to ambush (near), reaction to indirect fire, reaction to chemical or biological attack,* or, exactly like this, *reaction to enemy contact (visual, direct fire).* They had trained each situation so many times, the instructors assured them muscle memory would kick in in combat, no Guardsman would need to consciously consider his or her actions, and no one, Emperor forbid, would freeze.

But Torvin had frozen.

The lasgun fire continued. The shouting continued. But Torvin was rooted to the spot, unable to move as if he'd become just another part of the jungle. Something slammed into him from behind, knocking him stumbling forward. Torvin turned back to see that Corporal Algarn had charged into him, shoving him forward with his shoulder. Algarn had been last in the platoon's marching file but had moved up quickly at the contact call. His face was furious as he looked at Torvin.

'Get your lasgun up and move into suppressing-fire position, Torvin!' he roared.

Torvin stared at the corporal. He knew Algarn was speaking to him, but it was as if the words had no meaning.

'Torvin!' Corporal Algarn roared again.

Still, Torvin stared at the senior trooper, unable to process anything; everything seemed as meaningless as the eruption of fire in the trees ahead. Algarn growled at Torvin and then moved on through the jungle, barking at other troopers to get into better positions, to fan out, to move up, to do as they were Throning-well trained to do.

After what was probably only thirty seconds, maybe a minute, Torvin heard Lieutenant Gernson roaring for them to cease fire, a sentiment echoed by Sergeant Troovey. The barrage of las-rounds slowed. Several stray bolts continued through the trees.

'I said cease fire!' Lieutenant Gernson shouted, that finally being enough to bring silence to the jungle. 'Circle up! Defensive perimeter! Whoever called that contact, get here now!'

Now that the gunfire had stopped it was as if Torvin's mind had snapped back to reality; his brain had returned from warp knows where it had gone and slammed into his head with the realisation that he'd been completely left behind and that he hadn't done a Throne-damned thing in that whole situation. He hurried forward to his platoon and dropped to a knee beside Trooper Gernt, raising his lasgun and pointing it defensively out into the thick jungle growth.

'I called the contact, lieutenant,' Norsten said, moving up to where Lieutenant Gernson and Sergeant Troovey stood in the centre of the platoon's defensive ring.

'What happened?' Gernson asked.

'I definitely saw movement in the trees,' Norsten said, 'something green, I swear it on the God-Emperor Himself. I thought it had seen us, so I called an immediate contact rather than dropping and reporting a sighting. I think I hit it too, at least someone did.'

Sergeant Troovey looked from Norsten to Lieutenant Gernson. 'Well, we can be sure it weren't no ork, ma'am.'

'We can?' Norsten said.

Sergeant Troovey turned to look at Norsten. 'Yes, trooper. Notice how there wasn't nobody returning Throne-damned fire? Orks would've been shooting back, wouldn't they?'

'Uh, yes, sergeant. I suppose so,' Norsten said.

Lieutenant Gernson looked at Norsten. 'All right. Norsten, take Gorm and scout out there, see what it was. Quickly now. The rest of you, keep your eyes open.'

Torvin watched Norsten and Gorm move out in the direction Norsten had first called contact. The jungle out there had been shot to pieces – burned leaves, singed vines and other organic debris lay scattered across the ground, and many of the thinner trees had been hit and cut through, lying flat or having fallen and landed propped up against larger trunks. Norsten and Gorm stayed low, creeping out into the trees, slashing at the foliage with their bayoneted lasguns to clear the way. They soon vanished from sight. It wasn't long before they re-emerged though, and they were carrying something. They moved to where Lieutenant Gernson and Sergeant Troovey waited, and Torvin saw the two troopers had a four-legged animal slung between them, Norsten holding its forelegs and Gorm its rear. They dropped it on the ground at Lieutenant Gernson's feet like a house cat delivering a gift to its owner. The animal was a large green-coated creature with long tufted ears, three eyes and black spots over its coat. It had been ravaged by lasgun shots.

'Well,' Sergeant Troovey said, 'at least it's green.'

'Sorry, lieutenant,' Norsten said, 'it must have been this I saw.'

Lieutenant Gernson took a moment. 'Must have been,' she said eventually. 'I'm not going to berate any trooper for a false contact in this festering place, especially because, like the good sergeant said, at least it's green. It's tough to see your hand in front of your face out here and I know we're all eager to kill some orks, but let's try to get a positive ident before we blast half the jungle, shall we?'

'Yes, ma'am,' Norsten replied.

'Right,' the lieutenant continued, 'everyone form back up to move out, and keep ready because if there are any orks around, we've made a warping hell of a racket.'

Fourth Platoon collected themselves into formation again and continued their march through the jungle, the excitement of their false contact with the enemy dying down. As Torvin moved off he saw Corporal Algarn walk up beside him. He swallowed, keeping his eyes front, trying not to make eye contact.

'All good then, Torvin?' the corporal said.

'Yes, corporal,' Torvin replied.

'That so, is it?'

Oh, Torvin thought, it's going to be this again.

'Yes, corporal.'

'See,' Corporal Algarn said, 'if I'm not mistaken, in the middle of that contact you were just standing around like you were taking a piss, maybe daydreaming about something more fun to do with your junk.'

'Lucky it wasn't a real contact I suppose, corporal,' Torvin said, trying to smile, hoping that he could make light of the situation and Algarn would leave him alone.

'Well, see that's the thing,' Algarn said. 'I didn't know it wasn't a real contact and if I don't know somethin' then you can bet your crem you don't know it. If that was a real contact, you should've been up there laying down suppressing fire. Because if you're not doing that then there's a chance one of those troopers directly engaging the enemy gets wasted. You don't want to be responsible for getting a fellow Imperial Guardsman killed, do you, Trooper Torvin?'

'No, corporal.'

'No, I didn't think so. You're lucky we don't have a commissar attached to us on this little outing because imagine if Commissar Redvin had seen you just standing there. She would have shoved her bolt pistol so far up your backside, you'd taste the bolt coming out on your tongue. So here's what's going to happen, Torvin. Because I'm a nice guy, I'm not going to tell anyone about what you did back there, as long as you sort yourself out before we really get in the crem and you wind up getting someone killed. You freeze in combat and get your own arse blown off I don't really give a crem, but I could be the trooper you're supposed to be covering, so do your damn job.'

'Yes, corporal. Sorry, I just–'

'You just what, Torvin?' Algarn snapped. 'You going to give me an excuse?'

'No, corporal. I don't know what happened. I just froze up.'

'Yeah, you did. Don't let it happen again.'

Corporal Algarn began to move away, dropping back towards the end of the column.

'I just don't want to fight, corporal,' Torvin said just as Algarn was leaving, immediately regretting it when the corporal about turned and hastened to move in front of him, cutting him off and stopping them both.

Algarn stared at him with a new fierceness. Torvin swallowed. 'I'm just not sure why I'm here,' Torvin continued. 'I'm not sure I'm a very good soldier.'

'You are here because you were tithed, Torvin, and you'll be a good soldier because that's what the Emperor and Imperium demands of you.'

'I was supposed to be an Adminstratum scribe like my father,' Torvin said. 'We lived above Skadus Hive, recording quota information about the under-ice mines. I'm not meant to be here.'

Corporal Algarn stepped forward. He grabbed the front of Torvin's flak vest and pulled him in close so that they were almost nose to nose. 'I said I was a nice guy, Trooper Torvin. I didn't say I would abide blasphemy. You are out here to kill the xenos. You best accept that and, Emperor knows, you best want to do it. You are bordering on heretical here, trooper. Keep your mouth shut and your lasgun up, and when the time comes you will pull that trigger and you will enjoy the euphoria of doing the Emperor's work. Forget your life on Skadi, Torvin. From now on, killing orks is the only thing that matters.'

CHAPTER THREE

NOGROK

'Krumpin' humies is the only fing wot should matter to you, Nogrok,' Warboss Kazkorg Gutstompa said in his guttural snarl, picking Nogrok out of the gathered warband and staring at him, his heavy green brow furrowed and his red eyes daring him to keep asking questions.

Warboss Gutstompa wasn't the biggest warboss Nogrok had ever seen. His old boss, Warboss Ripspitta, had been taller, by at least a couple of snotlings, and he'd been wider too with a bigger head, which meant he was probably loads thinkier. Still, Gutstompa was more than big enough that Nogrok probably shouldn't be getting on his bad side – though it was hard not to get on a warboss' bad side because they usually only had one side and it wasn't a good one. Where most warbosses had the meks fit them with an imposing power klaw or kit them out in a colossal suit of armour, Gutstompa had instead elected for two massive hydraulically assisted boots to be riveted directly into the thick green flesh of his legs. He wasn't called Gutstompa for nothing.

Gutstompa had called the whole warband together in the middle of the small humie town they'd attacked the day before to explain what they were going to do next. Nogrok might have just been one of the boyz, especially in this new warband, but now that Gutstompa was laying out his plan he couldn't help speaking up. He'd always seen better ways of doing things. At least Ripspitta had listened to him, even if he didn't always follow what Nogrok thought would be the best taktiks. He'd known Nogrok and his kommando boyz had something to offer. Nogrok wasn't saying that if Ripspitta had listened to him back on that desert planet things would have gone better, but maybe if he had listened, him and pretty much the whole warband wouldn't have got proper krumped by the humies and left Nogrok and his crew to get stuck with Gutstompa and these thieving Deathskulls gitz.

'Yeah, I get it, boss,' Nogrok said, 'but I woz just wonderin' why.'

A low growl rumbled from somewhere deep in Gutstompa's throat. 'Dat's the problem with you Blood Axes, ain't it? Always wondering. We gonna attack dat humie base, Outpost Wotsit, coz the humies keep guardin' it. If the humies keep guardin' it den dey must think it's important, ain't it? So we gonna take it off 'em.'

Nogrok considered a moment. 'I s'pose that makes sense.'

'Of course it makes sense, you zoggin' git! I is warboss, whatever I say makes sense coz I say it does.'

'So,' Nogrok said, continuing well beyond when any reasonable ork boy would have shut his mouth, 'I can take my kommandos and we can do a recon-o-sance mission. We'll sneak in da jungle and see where da humie base is weakest. Then you can smash in there.'

Warboss Gutstompa stared at Nogrok, the cogs in his brain slowly churning through fungal soup, mostly surprised, like the rest of the warband, that Nogrok was still speaking. 'Wot?' the massive ork said eventually.

'Just helpin' with da plan, boss.'

'Helpin' with da plan?' Gutstompa said. 'Wot is all dat unorky sneakin' ya on about? I don't care 'bout no sneakin' and I don't care 'bout you helpin' with da plan. I 'as already got a plan. We gonna go up to dat humie outpost, we gonna line up, den we gonna yell Waaagh! and we gonna charge the humies and krump dere faces in. Den, after dat, we might yell Waaagh! again.'

'Boss, I is–'

'Oi!'

Nogrok turned to see he'd been interrupted by Warboss Gutstompa's second-in-command, Nob Gruk Jaggedteef – another ork who was vastly larger than Nogrok. Jaggedteef had moved through the gathering of orks to stand right beside him.

Looming over Nogrok, Jaggedteef smiled, revealing teeth that had been filed into vicious serrations. Nogrok had just enough time to think how much Jaggedteef was a stupid Deathskulls git before the nob's immense green fist flew forward and connected with his face.

When Nogrok opened his eyes he was lying flat. He sat upright. His thick spongy veins pulsed with runaway ork rage. The furious drive to fight filled him, made his head feel hot, and all he could think about was smashing that zoggin' Jaggedteef git right in the face. He'd smack him back in his stupid jaw and crack those rough teeth off, and then he'd use them to buy a new choppa, and then he'd use that choppa to smash him in the face again. He would have done it too, except he had to wait for his eyeballs to realign so that he could zoggin' see straight. That and, he soon realised, he wasn't in the street with Gutstompa and the rest of the warband any more. He was back on the second floor of the ruined building he'd occupied with his kommando mob.

''Ere look, Nogrok's awake.'

Nogrok looked in the direction of the voice. He saw too many versions of the same orks, so he slapped himself hard on the side of the head. That seemed to straighten something out and he could suddenly see again. The multitude of orks coalesced down to the five kommandos left in his mob: Grimguk, Ruktug, Nukka, Urkgob and Flik. There used to be more but not since everything went wrong on that desert planet. He'd managed to get some of his mob away though because he was a proper kunnin' ork. Sneaked off like ghosts they had. That's what some of the humies had called them once, ghost orks.

'Wot 'appened?' Nogrok asked.

'Jaggedteef smacked ya,' Flik replied.

'I know that bit,' Nogrok said, 'I was dere when dat 'appened. Wot after dat?'

'Gutstompa talked about takin' dat humie base,' Grimguk said. 'Said we doin' it when the sun comes up. Dat was it. We carried ya back up 'ere coz ya weren't wakin' up.'

'Attackin' in the day?' Nogrok said, shaking his head. 'Git. We should get 'em in the dark. You been keepin' watch?'

'Course,' Grimguk said. 'Like ya told us.'

When Gutstompa's warband had attacked this humie town they'd managed to wreck just about every building. Some they'd blown up on purpose with direct rokkit attack, others by accident with rokkits meant for somewhere else. Some they'd smashed in the windows, doors and even walls with wild choppa swings. There were even buildings completely levelled after some overexcited ork boyz forgot that trukks have brakes – that had happened more than once even in this minor skirmish. Out of all the buildings they'd destroyed, this was the one Nogrok had told his kommandos to grab because the ruined second level provided good views down the main street while still having some walls left to take cover behind. It was the best place to keep watch for any humie counter-attack. Then they could be down there fighting as soon as they got here.

'Oi, you up dere, ya zoggin' bloody Blood Axe bloody zoggin' gitz?'

The thick, slowly slurring voice came rolling up from the level below. Nogrok heard the sound of heavy footfalls on the stairs and clambered to his feet, turning to see a couple of the fightiest Deathskulls gitz staggering up to the second level, fungus beer sloshing merrily from the enormous cups they held in their hands. Snaga and Flogga stumbled up the last few steps and, because they went everywhere with him like a couple of well-trained squigs, Nogrok was unsurprised to see Gruk Jaggedteef, similarly clutching a flagon of fungal beer, thump up the stairs behind them.

Jaggedteef smiled his pointy grin at Nogrok.

'Heard ya been sleepin,' ya puny git. Dat right? I knocked ya flat, did I?'

Nogrok sniffed. 'I was just restin' up,' he said. 'Need to be proper sharp for attackin' da humies.'

Jaggedteef let out a small growl. Nogrok knew Jaggedteef didn't like him.

'I don't like you, Nogrok.'

See.

'I don't like none of you Blood Axe gitz. You all humie lovers aren't ya?'

'Yes, Nob Jaggedteef,' Nogrok said. 'We love humies all right. We love killin' 'em.'

Jaggedteef's growl intensified. His large flagon of fermented fungus shattered as his large hands squeezed in an effort to contain his temper. Nogrok also knew Jaggedteef absolutely hated the way he always managed to deftly evade his insults, brushing them off and not giving the big nob the rise he was looking for. Jaggedteef wanted nothing better than an excuse to fight him. He wanted Nogrok to utter anything that might come across as a challenge to his authority so that he could kill him and be done with it.

'Stop lookin' at me wiv ya weirdboy eyes, Nogrok.'

'Sorry, Nob Jaggedteef,' Nogrok said, 'I ain't got any others.'

Jaggedteef wasn't alone in being freaked out by Nogrok's eyes. He'd always had one perfectly normal eye and one that was green instead of red, and as much as orks weren't afraid of much, they could be unnerved by the smallest things. As such, his fellow boyz had always been wary of Nogrok and steered clear of him most of the time. Maybe that's why he'd ended up as a kommando, an outsider from the beginning.

'Wot are you lot doin' up here anyway?' Jaggedteef asked. Nogrok had no doubt he was trying to find something he could use to krump him.

'Keepin' watch,' Flik said. 'Like Nogrok told us.'

Jaggedteef turned his attention to Flik. Orks usually showed little in the way of emotion apart from anger, hatred, rage and, sometimes, fury, but Nogrok saw contempt all over Jaggedteef's face. Flik was small. A runt, really. Plenty of orks started off a bit scrawny and they either died or survived by being particularly crazy or particularly good at specific types of killing. These orks soon got big enough that no one even remembered they started off small, but unfortunately for Flik, he was proper small. In fact, it wasn't rare for other orks to call him a stinkin' grot when they first saw him, which he took relatively well – at least it would seem that way at the time. Nogrok found it useful having a smaller kommando; it meant he could get him to squeeze into places the rest of them couldn't, but really it was a zoggin' surprise Flik hadn't been krumped by some bigger ork long ago. Then again, Nogrok supposed he was one of them that was good at a specific type of killin'. Flik's type of killin' was hidin' in tiny places and jumping out to slit throats – usually the throats of those who'd called him a grot. Maybe he'd be a risk when he got bigger, but Nogrok would deal with that later; until then he was handy to have around.

'No one's talkin' to you, snotling,' Jaggedteef said to Flik. Flik's face hardly moved but Nogrok saw the hardening of his tiny red eyes. Jaggedteef had gone on Flik's list, but Flik would have to get in line to have a crack at cutting this nob's throat.

Jaggedteef turned back to Nogrok. 'What are you tellin' your gitz to keep watch for anyway?'

'Humies,' Nogrok said, thinking that even for a thick-headed nob like Jaggedteef that should be obvious. 'Case they come counter-attackin'.'

Jaggedteef snorted a short laugh. 'Watchin' for humies. Real orks don't need to keep watch. We always ready for a fight. Who told you to do that anyway? I'm da nob. You just a bunch of unorky Blood Axe gitz. Don't know why Warboss Gutstompa decided to bring you lot along. You got done in by humies on dat last planet – still got sand in me boots from dat place – why we want to keep a bunch of you what got beaten? You got all your thinkin' 'bout taktiks and special gubbinz and you still got smacked didn't ya? What is this gubbinz anyway?'

Jaggedteef moved to where Nogrok's equipment was stacked against the low wall.

'Dat's my gubbinz,' Nogrok said, stopping himself before he added, *you thievin' bloody Deathskulls git,* knowing that was exactly what the nob wanted.

Jaggedteef ignored him, pushing over his neatly piled gear with his foot – at least it was neat for an ork in that it was all in the same pile in the same place. The large nob bent over and picked up a pair of goggles with dark green lenses. He dangled them in front of his face.

'Wot're dese puny things?'

Nogrok looked at him. 'Night-seein' goggles,' he said.

'Wot you need night-seein' goggles for?' the nob asked.

'Coz I'm a kommando,' Nogrok said. 'Then I can do killin' in the dark and wotnot. Could ya put 'em down?'

'Why?' Jaggedteef said. 'You worried I gonna break 'em?'

Nogrok didn't reply.

Jaggedteef dropped the night-seein' goggles on the hard stone floor. Nogrok saw one of the lenses crack and felt a rush of heat to his head.

'Wot?' Jaggedteef said. 'It were an accident.' He lifted his boot and slammed it down on the goggles. They crunched beneath his heel, smashing beyond repair. 'Oops. Had another accident.'

Anger flared in Nogrok. He had to struggle against his very nature, every one of his ork cells calling for a fight, but he managed to hold himself back.

Jaggedteef smiled. He could probably smell the desire for violence pouring off Nogrok, but there was nothing Nogrok could do right now; his instinct to fight was hard up against his instinct to submit to the bigger ork. Jaggedteef turned to Snaga and Flogga.

'You boyz come and take whateva ya want.'

Jaggedteef's two lackeys came over and began rifling through all of Nogrok's stuff – everything he'd managed to scavenge over the years. The bits he'd bought from mekboyz and, worst of all, the loot he'd managed to collect from the humies they'd fought against before. Snaga picked up Nogrok's 'urty syringe. That had cost Nogrok a fortune in teef because Deathskulls painboyz were just as greedy as any of the other Deathskulls gitz. It was loaded full of a thick, purple liquid that the dok had said would knock out most orks and at least sap the strength from one as big as a nob. He was saving that for a special occasion. Thankfully Snaga, because he was thick, didn't realise the value of it and tossed it back onto the pile. The loss of the night-seein' goggles was bad enough – though he knew he had another set of them somewhere that, while they weren't quite as good, would do the job – but then he saw Flogga grab his most favourite thing.

Nogrok had deliberately tried not to look at it because he didn't want to draw the other orks' attention to it, but now Flogga had spotted it. The Deathskull picked it up and slid it out of the leather sheath. He held the knife up. It was almost as long as the ork's forearm, massive for a humie blade. It gleamed, still shining just as it had when Nogrok had plucked it off that dead humie. The humie must have cleaned it and he'd never managed to draw Nogrok's blood with it before Nogrok killed him. It was a Catachan knife, a long-bladed, half-serrated fang of cold steel.

It was nothing as special as some of the humie weapons – their big fists, or those nice loud chainswords, or those glowy swords that some of them had. Didn't matter to Nogrok though. He liked this better than all of them. This was a real cutta, simple and sharp. Plus, Nogrok liked the humies it came from, those Catachan ones – they were good for fighting against, and the way they sneaked around to do their killing, most orks thought it was nonsense, but Nogrok knew it was proper good taktiks.

'Cor,' Flogga said, eyeing the blade as he turned it in front of his face. 'Look at dis.'

'Give me dat,' Snaga said, lunging forward to try to grab the Catachan knife from Flogga, but the other ork was too quick at turning and holding it out of reach.

'Zog off,' Flogga said, 'dis mine.'

'I wanna look,' Snaga said, lunging again, but again Flogga moved it out of reach.

'Nah,' Flogga said, 'I know you wanna pinch it and you ain't havin' it.'

Snaga bared his teeth. 'I said give it.'

'Oi,' Nogrok said, unable to contain his rage that they were fighting over who was going to take his prized possession. Plus, these two at least weren't as big as Jaggedteef. 'Dat cutta is mine, you zoggin' gitz. Ain't none of you havin' it.'

Flogga and Snaga turned on Nogrok, suddenly unified once again. They had been on the verge of beating each other senseless over this new-found prize, but now they seemed to have remembered there were Blood Axe gitz here they could fight instead.

'Ain't yours no more,' Flogga said.

'Yeah, ain't yours,' Snaga said. 'It's ours.'

'Mine,' Flogga said.

'Yeah,' Snaga continued. 'Dat's wot I said, it's ours.'

Flogga looked sideways at Snaga but decided to deal with that problem later. He brandished the long-bladed Catachan knife and pointed the curved tip at Nogrok. 'Unless you can take it back, this cutta mine now.'

'I killed da humie I took it off,' Nogrok growled. 'I'mma kill you to get it back.'

Jaggedteef thumped forward towards Nogrok. He was at least a half again as tall as Nogrok, which meant he was intimidatingly large. You didn't get to be a nob without being big and tough, and then when you got to be a nob you got even bigger and tougher. That's what made it so hard to get rid of them, so hard for other orks to work their way up.

Jaggedteef stopped when he was close to Nogrok, standing over him, a menacing slab of green. He snarled, his thick green lips pulling back from his protruding tusks and teeth that had all been snapped, cut and filed into points seemingly as sharp and just as serrated as Nogrok's Catachan knife. The nob swung his heavy fist but, unlike out on the street, this time Nogrok anticipated it and dodged back out of the way. Jaggedteef's hooked punch sailed through the air in front of him. The nob's face showed momentary confusion as he was surprised by how quickly Nogrok could move, but this expression soon slid back into anger.

'This ain't your fight, Jaggedteef,' Nogrok said. He called past the nob to Flogga and Snaga. 'Why you gitz need a nob to do your fightin' for ya?'

They growled and snarled at Nogrok but didn't reply.

'They my boyz you threatenin' to kill,' Jaggedteef said. 'You don't get to kill my boyz.'

'You forgettin' Warboss Gutstompa put me in your mob too, didn't he,' Nogrok said.

'So wot?'

'So don't that make us your boyz too? Why you tellin' them to take my gubbinz? Why you tryin' to krump me?'

'I said you don't get to kill my boyz,' Jaggedteef said. 'I didn't say nothin' 'bout *me* killin' my boyz. If I wanna kill some of me own boyz I will, you included – 'specially you, coz you is a humie-lovin' Blood Axe git.'

Jaggedteef swung his fist again. Again Nogrok managed to dodge. But this time Jaggedteef wasn't going to relent in his attack. He swung his other stone-mallet fist. This time Nogrok couldn't get completely out of the way. He had to stick his own arm up to try to block the strike. Nogrok took the force of Jaggedteef's blow on his forearm but by Gork and Mork the nob was strong. The fist slammed through Nogrok's guard. There was a crunching in his arm that made his hand go all wobbly, and then Jaggedteef's punch connected with the side of his head. Nogrok felt the inside of his head go wobbly too and took several stumbling steps backward. He was readying to hit back when Jaggedteef kicked him in the stomach sending him arcing back across the room and sliding along the ground.

'I ain't gonna kill ya, Nogrok,' Jaggedteef said, 'but you needs to learn dat I am da biggest and I am da 'ardest and I am the nob. Get at 'im, boyz.'

Nogrok rolled over to see Flogga and Snaga hurrying towards him. The two Deathskulls began kicking him repeatedly. Nogrok thrashed on the ground, trying to strike at the other two orks, but there was little he could do as their kicks slammed into him. He growled and covered his head, knowing that was the bit he needed to keep from getting busted too badly.

'Keep out of it, the rest of you Blood Axe gitz,' Nogrok heard Jaggedteef roar as Flogga and Snaga rained large-booted kick after large-booted kick into him. 'Or you'll get more of a krumpin.'

The other kommandos must have moved into action, but Jaggedteef's threats were apparently enough to keep them from intervening.

As Nogrok lay on the ground being repeatedly booted by Jaggedteef's little snotling pets, his anger grew and roiled inside him. Nobz might be big and tough and keep getting bigger and tougher, but Nogrok was going to find a way to tear Jaggedteef down. An outright stand against a massive nob like him with his loyal gang of boyz would just get him krumped like this again, probably get him killed dead next time, but he would find a way.

He was a kommando. He was a ghost ork. He knew loads more about taktikal killing than these Deathskulls gitz. He'd show them. He'd find a way to get his cutta back from that git Flogga and he'd find a way to shove it right through Jaggedteef's eye and into his gitty brain. Then, after he'd taken Jaggedteef's place as nob he'd show them all how good at killing a Blood Axe was. He'd start with any of these other Deathskulls gitz who deserved it, then he'd get onto killing the humies.

CHAPTER FOUR

NOGROK

Nogrok held up his hand, indicating for the kommandos behind him to stop. They weren't far from the edge of the trees now. He could see up ahead where the jungle thinned out and opened into the much brighter clearing around the humie base. Nogrok crouched low in the thick, damp undergrowth, letting himself sink into the green foliage. He slipped off his pack, feeling a recurrence of anger when he noticed the empty spot where the sheath of the Catachan knife was usually buckled to the side. *Thievin' Deathskulls gitz.*

He flipped open his pack and retrieved his long-seein' goggles. He'd got these from that Catachan humie too. Those Catachan humies didn't have as much stuff as other humies, but what they did have was good. They knew how to use it too. He'd fought against humies that had all kinds of flashy armour and helmets and rode around in tanks and whatnot, but they were just like Bad Moon gitz – all flashy gubbinz with no idea how to use it.

Some humies he'd fought against had even run away, and not like a taktikal running away either, just proper running away like they were scared or something. But those Catachan humies, they wouldn't run away. They didn't run anywhere. They crept up all stealthy like, coming out of nowhere to slit throats and cause carnage. Some humies had called his kommandos ghost orks, but the Catachan humies were the proper ghosts. That's what his kommandos were going to be like. Let the other orks call them unorky or whatever, Nogrok knew doing stuff the way of Mork was just as good as doing stuff the way of Gork. Mork was proper kunnin', so why shouldn't an ork do that? If they weren't supposed to go sneaking around in the jungle, then why did Gork and Mork give orks green skin? That was ready-made camouflage that was.

After Nob Jaggedteef and his zoggin' gitz had come through, stole all his good kit and kicked him around, Nogrok had gathered his kommando mob together.

'We gonna kill dem gitz?' Flik had asked.

Nogrok shook his head. 'Nah. We'll get our chance. Forget about those gitz for now. We gonna go do our recon-o-sance of the humie base even if Warboss Gutstompa ain't got the brain to know it's good taktiks. Get your kit, we movin' out.'

As the kommandos gathered their equipment, loaded up their packs, strapped on their choppas and sluggas, and left the humie town to disappear into the jungle, Nogrok didn't tell them that even though he'd said to forget about those Deathskulls gitz, he wasn't going to. He couldn't forget. Those Deathskulls were all the zoggin' worst and he was going to get even. Mostly he wanted to kill Flogga for pinching his knife, but Snaga too, and of course Jaggedteef. He just had to plan it. They'd need to be sneaky about it.

The kommandos had moved through the jungle as swiftly as they could while keeping noise to a minimum. It had taken them a long time to learn how to move silently. Nogrok might have believed there was just as much Morkiness in an ork as there was Gorkiness, but most orks couldn't help but make a racket when they thundered along, especially through a jungle or forest where there was loads of stuff to step on and break, or plants to swoosh through, or trees to push over just for the fun of it. Plus, most orks couldn't keep their mouths shut long enough to be sneaky.

Nogrok had made his kommandos practise keeping silent as they moved. At first, they'd been appalled by the idea that they had to train, not seeing the point in doing something when they didn't actually need to. That just seemed like swinging a choppa around and pretending to kill a humie when they could just go out and swing their choppas at actual humies instead. But once they started to see results, started to realise they were getting better at being sneaky – which Nogrok assured them was the point of being a kommando – they kept their training up, and now they were proper good at stealth.

Nogrok was happy to be in the jungle. The last planet they'd been on was all hot and sandy with open space everywhere, not the most ideal for sneakin', but this new jungle planet, this was where he knew his kommandos would be at their best.

Nogrok looked back and saw Flik and Nukka kneeling down amongst the trees. He could just make out the shape of Ruktug further back and Grimguk and Urkgob should be back behind them. Nogrok signalled for them to stay where they were while he scouted ahead. He left his pack where it was, taking just his long-seein' goggles and the slugga hanging from his side, and crept through the thinning jungle towards the edge of the clearing.

He watched each step, showing patience near miraculous for an ork, putting his heavy foot down slowly, heel first, and rolling forward such that he could stop if anything beneath his sole began to snap or crack. He kept low, eventually dropping onto his stomach and crawling forward until he reached the treeline.

Up ahead, the jungle had been cleared in a wide area and at the centre, higher than the surrounding wilderness, was the humie outpost. Nogrok immediately saw why the humies kept defending this base – it was the best place to see anyone coming into the valley towards where the big humie city was. There was a lot of cleared space all the way around the outpost too, so that any attack from the jungle would be spotted well before it reached the outpost. There was a low rockcrete wall and then a high wire fence about halfway into the cleared area which would slow down any attack and give the humies in the base a good chance to start shooting before anything got to them.

Nogrok held his long-seein' goggles up to his eyes to take a better look at the humie outpost. It was built from rockcrete, just like the outer wall, with what looked like only one thick metal door and no windows. The walls were tall and flat, made so they would be hard to climb. Walking along the top, moving in pairs, looking out towards the jungle, were humies.

These humies wore flashy armour and helmets, and carried those las-shootas they liked so much. Nogrok continued scanning the walls and saw several big shootas spaced along the top pointed out towards the clearing. That's where the most dakka would come from. If Gutstompa would actually listen to him, Nogrok would be able to go back and report about the base's defences, but he was sure the warboss and the rest of the warband were going to just blindly charge out of the jungle and try to smash their way through, getting shot at the whole time.

Nogrok moved the long-seein' goggles back along the top of the wall and then stopped, moving them back again. One of the humies was looking towards him. Nogrok watched as the humie fumbled at his side and then lifted up some long-seein' goggles of his own, pointing them right towards Nogrok.

Nogrok smiled. He'd been proper sneaky and didn't know whether the humie could see him or not. Maybe it was because he was still annoyed at those Deathskulls gitz, but he decided to have some fun with the humie. He stood, lowering the long-seein' goggles, and moved forward a couple of steps, enough that he was out of the trees and knew the humie would definitely be able to see him. He grabbed his slugga, pointed it at the humie, mimed shooting and then stepped back into the trees, dropping low and vanishing.

Nogrok chuckled to himself as he moved back to his kommandos. He hoped he'd given that humie a bit of a scare with his brainological warfare. When he reached the other kommandos, he called them over, keeping his voice low as he spoke to them.

'Gutstompa's gonna attack from this way,' Nogrok said. 'There's walls and fences, and the humies have got shootas up on the roof. It looks better to attack from the sides – there ain't as much room there but a small mob like us can get in easy. We're gonna wait for Gutstompa to charge in and while they are gettin' krumped and the humies are distracted, we attack. We'll be able to get in close and actually kill some humies instead of just runnin' into humie dakka like those gitz will.'

With that, Nogrok threw his pack back on and he and his mob of kommandos moved off, back into the dense jungle, to flank the humie base and await the main attack from Gutstompa's warband. It didn't take long and as Nogrok and his ghost orks were creeping through the jungle, he heard the roaring of the warboss.

'WAAAAAAGH!'

Gutstompa, it seemed, was sticking with his plan.

CHAPTER FIVE

TORVIN

Trooper Torvin was on his second watch.

His first had been a graveyard shift the night before, Fourth Platoon's initial night manning Outpost Four. The tall lumen towers around the area had been alight then, blasting white luminescence out over the clearing surrounding the outpost. The enormous globes were bright enough to illuminate the space around them as if it were day. The ground was lit more than enough to see anything that might be approaching - either heading for the outpost or looking to move into the valley towards Karoo City. The treeline had still been dark, though, and the jungle beyond had blended into a single plain of vast blackness, a looming unknown beyond their tiny patch of safety. Now, in the daylight, Torvin could see the individual trees around the clearing, but beyond that the jungle had simply gone from vast unknown black to an undulating green blanket that spread out to the horizon without end. He'd hoped it would all seem better in the morning, but the jungle still gave Torvin just as much of a feeling of crushing insignificance as it had the night before.

He walked the thin battlement that ran along the top of the outpost. There wasn't much to Outpost Four; it provided the bare minimum necessary for a watch station and minor fortification. A small windowless, colourless fort with thick outer walls that formed the rampart atop which Torvin stood. There was an open central section, with thick metal doors on both the north and south sides, and stairs that provided roof access.

Straight corridors ran off to the east and west providing access to a small barracks, a rudimentary mess, a less than adequate number of amenities for a full platoon of troopers, a small communication and control room with vox-link back to Karoo - and emergency flare launchers in the event Gondwa VI's magnetic behaviour interfered with that - and an armoury that didn't seem to have been restocked with weapons or ammunition in the last few years, though Torvin had noticed there was a larger than necessary stockpile of demolition charges. Outpost Four was a small enough facility that the outer wall, the wire fence, the defensive ramparts and even the constantly manned heavy bolter emplacements didn't make Torvin feel particularly well fortified.

Trooper Norsten, unfortunately assigned as Torvin's partner for this shift, chattered incessantly as they walked the rampart.

'How long do you reckon until the orks attack?' Norsten was saying. 'Hopefully not too much longer.'

'Hopefully they don't attack at all,' Torvin said in reply. 'We don't actually want to have to defend the outpost, you know.'

'It's inevitable,' Norsten said. 'I'm looking forward to it. By the time we've fought them off, my name will be etched in Skadi's history.'

Torvin muttered sounds of inattentive agreement as he kept his eyes trained on the edge of the jungle. For someone so keen to get into battle with the greenskins, Norsten did not seem to be too concerned with keeping watch for them. Torvin, on the other hand, could think of very little other than the fact that the vicious orks, who, by all accounts, were not as easy to kill as the Departmento Munitorum would like him to believe, were definitely out there lurking in the jungle, gathering their numbers to take this world.

Of all mankind's abhorrent alien enemies, the orks are surely the most cowardly. They mass in great warbands and use their sheer weight of numbers to defeat their foes. Their numbers are their only strength and they use them like the cowards they are, knowing they cannot defeat you, a warrior of the Emperor, without attempting to overwhelm you. Never fear though, steadfast Imperial Guardsmen with lasguns in their hands and prayers on their lips are more than a match for any number of the green tide who would throw themselves against you.

'I was the best shot in our training group,' Norsten was saying as they walked, 'did you know that? I'll hit the greenskins as they come out of the trees. It's not even that far.'

Norsten turned, likely because Torvin had not mumbled an affirmative response, and realised only then that Torvin had stopped. 'What?' Norsten asked.

Torvin squinted his eyes towards the trees. There had been a brief flash, almost like the sun had been at just the right angle to reflect off something. He stared at the distant treeline, watching to see if there was anything there, looking for signs of movement. The trees waved in the gentle breeze. Some of Gondwa VI's native birdlife took flight over the jungle canopy. Threatening grey clouds rolled through the distant sky.

Torvin was about to forget it, chalk it up to his ever-fraying nerves, when he saw it again. It was smaller this time, but it was there: a flash low in the scrub at the treeline. He felt a growing tension, a knot of unease in his stomach. He grabbed at the magnoculars that hung from his webbing, almost forgetting he had them with him, and hastily fumbled them up to his eyes.

Torvin focused on the spot he was sure he'd seen something, ignoring the range information, wind velocity and terrain topography that appeared around his view. There was a thicket of fernlike plants grown dense around the edge of the clearing where they found access to sunlight more readily than deeper in the jungle. Torvin watched them, holding the magnoculars as steady as he could to avoid the amplified movements of his trembling hands. There was something there. He could see it now. Some shape low to the ground. Perhaps some equipment had been left there and maybe there was something on it, a tag on a backpack or the like, something that moved just enough in the light breeze to catch the sunlight and reflect it back at him. Torvin was just about ready to believe that theory when the ferns shook with a sudden overwhelming movement that took him by surprise.

The shape on the ground rose out of the plant cover almost as if it were unfolding, opening up, a flower unwrapping itself to show its petals to the sun. It took a split second longer than it should have for Torvin to realise what he was looking at.

It was an ork.

The creature emerged from where it had been hidden among the leaves. An actual greenskin. Torvin had never seen one before, but he didn't need briefing notes or *The Imperial Infantryman's Uplifting Primer* to identify this creature. What else could it be? Every child on a million worlds knew about the big-headed, green-skinned brutes that ravaged the galaxy, and now Torvin was looking at one.

From this distance he couldn't be sure exactly how tall the ork was – about as tall as an average human, maybe a little bigger? Torvin quickly scanned the trees, but the creature seemed to be alone. There was no sheer weight of numbers, no green tide like he had been led to believe. The ork just stood there, looking back at him.

More surprising than seeing an ork alone, staring out from the edge of the jungle, was that the greenskin was clutching magnoculars of its own. Then, when it lowered them, Torvin saw black lines painted in slanting stripes across its face. Even the two tusks that protruded from its mouth had been wrapped in black cloth. The clothes it wore were sewn together from patches of various shades of green. The cracked and worn leather of the ork's belt and the empty bandoleer slung over its chest had been darkened. By the Emperor, Torvin thought, as realisation struck, this ork – this brutish, savage, apparently stupid beyond measure ork – was wearing camouflage.

While Torvin stood, stunned by what he was seeing, the ork pulled an oversized pistol from the holster at its waist. It lifted it, pointing it straight at Torvin, and smiled. The thing was smiling at him. It raised the gun once with a motion like it was firing and then it lowered the pistol. Torvin felt a rush of cold move through him: fear or adrenaline or both, he didn't know.

The ork stepped back into the trees, keeping its beady eyes on Torvin as it retreated into the green dark of the jungle, human and ork watching each other until eventually the camouflaged greenskin vanished from sight. Torvin's breathing was fast and shallow. His heart was thundering in his chest, and he could hear the whooshing of blood through his ears. It was only then, when the ork had disappeared and Torvin had lowered the magnoculars from his eyes, that he managed to speak.

'What is it?' Norsten was saying, in a tone that implied it wasn't the first time he'd asked.

'Ork,' Torvin said, though it was little more than a tiny croak.

'What?' Norsten said.

Torvin turned to look at him. 'An ork,' he repeated. Then he finally managed to say it loud enough to get the reaction he thought it deserved. 'There was an ork in the trees!'

Norsten's face drained of colour just the smallest amount as he rushed over. He held out his hand, clicking his fingers for Torvin to pass him the magnoculars. Torvin did so without comment.

'Where?' Norsten said. 'I don't see anything.'

But Torvin had turned away. 'Sergeant Troovey!' he called. 'Sergeant!'

Sergeant Troovey was down the other end of the battlement but turned at the call of his name and, apparently recognising the desperation in Torvin's voice, jogged quickly towards him.

'What is it, trooper?' Sergeant Troovey asked.

'I saw an ork in the trees.'

Troovey looked at him as if in evaluation. 'Where?'

'Down there, southern treeline, about midway along.'

Troovey turned to Norsten, who was still studying the edge of the jungle through the magnoculars. 'Norsten?'

'I can't see anything, sergeant.'

'You sure you saw an ork, Torvin?' Troovey asked.

'Yes, sergeant, absolutely positive. The thing was looking at me. It was wearing Throne-damned camouflage!' Torvin felt himself getting more animated. Why weren't they doing anything?

'Pass me the magnoculars, Norsten,' Troovey said. Norsten handed them over and the sergeant spent a not inconsiderable amount of time scanning the same area of trees before he eventually passed them back. 'Torvin,' he said. 'Orks don't sneak around the jungle wearing camouflage. I don't know what you saw but it wasn't an ork. I don't know if you're taking the piss out of Norsten here, I know you two don't exactly get along, but let's not report another false contact.'

'Sergeant–' Torvin started, but Troovey cut him off with a raised hand.

'Enough,' Troovey said. 'Orks don't sneak around, trooper. They couldn't sneak up on a blind, deaf and Throne-damned dead ogryn. Keep about your watch and keep a look out for the real sign of orks – a tide of green monsters roaring and charging out of the jungle.'

In that moment, a roar of 'WAAAAAAAAGH!' filled the air. At first it was a single booming voice, but the call was soon taken up by a multitude of more guttural cries, and a tide of green monsters came roaring and charging out of the jungle.

In a single moment the jungle changed from an ominous but still landscape – darkness hiding the possibility of enemies – to an eruption of sound and movement: no longer the possibility of enemies but the horrific certainty of them. The trees shook. The smaller bushes and ferns were torn from the ground in sprays of dirt as the heavy feet of the greenskins smashed through them. Ork after ork after ork pounded from the shadows, pummelling the jungle floor to compost. In the blink of an eye, so fast that it might have been shockingly comical if it weren't so terrifying, hundreds of the xenos piled into the clearing around Outpost Four.

'Something like that, sergeant?' Torvin said, mostly out of pure shock.

'WAAAAAAAAAAGH!'

The horde of greenskins roared again, and with this second reverberating war cry and with the commotion of them stampeding from the trees, flocks of the native jungle birds took flight, clouds of them fluttering into the sky desperately fleeing from the xenos' charge. Lucky bastards. What Trooper Torvin wouldn't have given for a pair of wings at that very moment.

These orks were not, unfortunately, only holding magnoculars. They had massive axes and long-bladed swords of jagged steel which they waved wildly over their heads. Some of them wielded revving chainswords, dented and rusty. Others carried chunky rifles with thick cylindrical barrels, long rocket launchers, or huge belt-fed guns.

Neither were they wearing camouflage like the first ork he'd spotted. Instead, they wore mostly bright colours, makeshift armour of yellow and red decorated with patterns in black and white, though without doubt the most common colour was blue. Blue clothing, blue helmets, blue paint splattered across their weapons and faces.

'Contact!' Norsten shouted from beside Torvin.

'You cremming think, trooper?' Sergeant Troovey roared at Norsten. 'This is not when you call a blasted contact. This is when you Throne-damned start shooting!'

Norsten looked at the sergeant. Troovey leant towards him and screamed, mouth open and spittle flying. 'Fire!'

The whine-crack of lasguns finally burst forth from the rampart around the outpost as the men and women of the Skadi Second Infantry, Fourth Platoon beat back their shock and began unleashing the fury of the Emperor on the greenskins.

Sergeant Troovey hurried off towards the stairs down into the outpost, his voice booming over the sudden cacophony. 'Defensive positions! All troopers to defensive positions!'

Torvin gripped his lasgun as he dropped to take cover behind the battlement wall. He watched more members of the platoon sprint up the stairs to join the firing line, hastily loading rifles or strapping on helmets.

Torvin heard the drumbeat thrum of a heavy bolter emplacement, increasing in volume as other emplacements joined to release a triumphant chatter of fire. He watched the heavy bolters turn on their mounts, the arms of the Guardsmen manning them shaking violently with the rapid pounding shots as they ran lines of fire over the front ranks of the orks, the white phosphorus tracer rounds leaving streaks of light even in the daytime.

Orks charged across the cleared ground to the rockcrete wall and wire fence. Some way back from the fence a booming shower of dirt flew into the air, parts of an ork soaring skyward along with it. Further down the line of orks another explosion sprayed a dozen of the smaller orkoid creatures, the ones they called grots, up in a circular pattern of squealing gore. The xenos had reached the defensive minefield but even as the ground burst under them, there were far too many for the mines to stop. When orks were blown limbless by the explosives more just trampled over them to take their place in the charge.

Behind the rampaging orks, back in the jungle, the motion of the trees became more extreme. Torvin watched as they shook aggressively from side to side, many of them falling, their tops disappearing from the canopy. Smoke billowed out in thick plumes and even over the sounds of shooting, the clanking and grinding of messy mechanical motion could be heard. Soon after, groups of bipedal mechanical walkers decorated with ork-skull motifs came thundering out of the jungle on rickety legs, their spinning saw blades cutting through tree trunks as they swung around seemingly at random, several of them even hitting each other and causing showers of sparks to spray into the air. Torvin could only describe these things as scrap-metal cannisters on legs, albeit massive cannisters with guns and several arms, each with a saw blade or a clanking claw. Several more walkers, apparently based on the same two-legged design but even larger, came stomping out of the trees moving faster than the smaller walkers and using their hydraulic arms to slam them aside if they got in their way.

Torvin had slid down with his back to the battlement wall, clutching his lasgun to his chest. He was vaguely aware of the commotion around him as the troopers of the Skadi Second were shooting out at the advancing horde. Shouts filled the air, gunfire, explosions, mayhem. Torvin had been afraid of the moment he would get into battle and now it was here, and it was even more frightful than he'd imagined. The sound of battle drowned him until he was unable to do anything but cower.

Beside him, Norsten was also crouching below the battlement wall, but at least he was facing the correct direction and popping out of cover to fire his lasgun towards the approaching orks. Torvin was doing none of these things. He shrank into himself, hiding from the chaos.

'Come get it, you greenskin bastards!' Norsten was shouting. 'Come get it!'

Torvin squeezed his eyes closed and whispered prayers to the Emperor. He'd never doubted the Emperor's protection of humanity before, even when he'd received his notice of tithe. But now, as he faced battle for the first time and wild brutish aliens charged towards him, he didn't know whether the Emperor would hear him. Perhaps that was why Imperial Guardsmen died despite having the God-Emperor of Mankind on their side: the Emperor couldn't hear their prayers over the cacophonous madness of battle.

'Focus fire on the fence line!' Sergeant Troovey was yelling from somewhere nearby. 'Hit the ones at the fence!'

Torvin knew that meant the orks had reached the protective fence that ringed the outpost about halfway to the trees. He realised then that maybe he did want to see what was coming. Maybe not knowing what was coming was making things worse. He needed to force himself to face the greenskins.

After a number of steadying breaths Torvin turned, popping his head up above the battlement, and immediately caught sight of an ork rocket spiralling through the air towards the wall, trailing grey-white smoke in a twisting aerial display. He briefly registered troopers scattering to take cover and then a sudden, monumental explosion filled every one of his senses.

Torvin felt sudden blistering heat on his skin as he watched rockcrete debris spray across the rampart. He coughed and spluttered as the acrid aroma of burning explosive filled his nose and the taste of thick dust settled on his tongue. His ears rang with a high-pitched squeal. He turned to see the impact point a short distance down the battlement. A small area of the protective wall had been blown inward and several Guardsmen lay sprawled out on the ground. He couldn't recognise them, but it was not for lack of trying; their faces, smashed to pulp by rock and burned away to black, were unrecognisable. Torvin's stomach reflexively jerked. He felt acidic bile rise up the back of his throat and despite attempting to hold it back, he ejected vomit in a spray across the stone.

Dazed, he felt something strike the side of his helmet. At first, he thought he'd caught a glancing blow from an ork round but as he turned, he saw Corporal Algarn squatting down next to him. He seemed angry. Torvin stared at him blankly and Algarn smacked him in the side of the helmet again. Torvin realised then that the corporal was shouting something.

'Fire your weapon, Trooper Torvin!' Algarn screamed at him. 'Turn around and do it now!' Algarn grabbed Torvin roughly by his fatigues and spun him to face the advancing greenskins. Lifting him, he even positioned his lasgun on top of the wall. The corporal leant down until his mouth was merely an inch from Torvin's still-buzzing ear. He shouted, 'Throne-damned shoot!' and smacked him on the back of the helmet once again.

Perhaps it was the shock of the shouting or being struck on the helmet, but Torvin's finger snapped back and his lasgun cracked. Once this first las-shot appeared in the air, joining his weapon to the stampeding orks below, it suddenly became easier. He was terrified but now the fight was something he was part of, not just something that was happening to him.

Torvin squeezed the trigger again, and again, and again. His situational awareness returned and he took in the battle before them. The orks had breached the fence and were streaming across the clearing towards the base of Outpost Four. The walking cans were struggling with the wall and had drawn the attention of the heavy bolters, their explosive shells ripping into the ork walkers with concussive force. Several of the contraptions stumbled and fell, their armour punctured by sustained heavy bolter fire.

The larger walkers had much less trouble. Torvin watched as the first of them collided with the wall, staggering back like a confused animal that had crashed into a glass door. But with the roar of some orkish engine and with a pillar of black smoke ejecting into the air, the walker charged again, this time smashing its way through the wall and continuing on even as heavy bolter rounds sparked off its armour in bright yellow sprays.

Ork bodies littered the clearing, hundreds of them, and more joined them with every second as the xenos charged fearlessly into death, running towards the far superior position of the Imperial Guard. Still, it didn't matter how many of them died. There were always more.

Torvin fired down into the mass of green, ducking as return fire pinged off the wall around him, but this time he managed to clamber up again and keep shooting. He didn't know whether he'd hit any orks. His shots blended with all the others lighting up the battlefield, an onslaught of las-fire that was doing nothing to halt the ork advance. There were too many. He could already see that. They would not be able to stop them reaching the outpost.

Torvin heard a scream and turned in the direction of the sound. Trooper Gorm howled, gripping at her shoulder as she sank back against the wall, blood spraying from the stump where her arm had been. An ork round had all but torn the limb off, leaving mangled meat hanging from her shoulder by strips of white sinew and strands of red muscle. She was staring at it, trying to push it back up like somehow it might reattach itself. Torvin felt what minor resolve he had gained begin to flood out of him again.

'They're coming from the trees to the east too! They're using smoke!'

The shout came from the eastern end of the rampart, not far from where Torvin and Norsten were hunkered down. Torvin turned to look and saw the panicked face of Trooper Heim, another of those he'd gone through training with, appearing from around the corner. Behind him, Torvin could see a thick grey cloud billowing up, obscuring the jungle to the east. 'We need support over here! They're using Throne-damned smoke to cover their advance.'

Lieutenant Gernson thundered along the rampart past Torvin and Norsten. She shouted orders in all directions. 'You,' she called, pointing to Trooper Heim, 'if the orks are attacking from that side too then get your cremming arse back over there and stand your ground! I'm coming!'

'Yes, ma'am,' Heim said, turning nervously and moving back around the corner to the eastern wall.

Gernson turned to those around Torvin facing the main attack. 'Pick your targets,' she yelled, her voice reverberating from her massive frame to bellow down the line. 'Don't just blindly fire! Pick a greenskin and put it down!' She moved off in the direction of the east wall, continuing to fire off orders more rapidly than the Guardsmen could fire las-shots at the orks below.

Torvin turned his attention back to the mass of orks charging wildly across the clearing. It was not an encouraging sight. The first of the greenskins were reaching the base of the outpost wall. The Guardsmen all along the battlement began to fire almost straight down, massacring those below. Beside him, Norsten continued to shout as he unloaded the Emperor's own fury into the aliens. At least they had the height advantage. The top of the outpost was almost twenty-five feet off the ground and the Guardsmen should be able to annihilate the greenskins while they tried to climb. Torvin hoped that advantage would be enough because the orks sure as crem had the numbers.

'Hit the little bastards with the ladders!' Sergeant Troovey called as he moved up the battlement. 'The grots! Shoot the Throne-damned things!'

Torvin saw them soon after Troovey began roaring these orders. Throughout the green mass, partly hidden by the larger orks around them, many of the smaller creatures known as grots were carrying long wooden ladders that looked so rickety and poorly constructed, they might not support the weight of a human let alone an ork, but that was not a theory Torvin wanted tested. He began firing at the ladder-bearing grots. As he did, he could tell the battle was intensifying on the east side of the building. Lasgun shots continued to crack and heavy bolters continued to fire intermittently, but the booming sounds of ork weapons grew even louder and so did their howling, roaring, hooting battle cries. Troopers were shouting warnings.

'There's ropes on the walls!'

'They're coming over the top!'

'Where? I can't see crem!'

Then the screams began. Shouting troopers were cut off midway through calling out warnings with gurgling cries. When Torvin braved a look in that direction, the air was still thick with impenetrable smoke, which had now begun to float across the outpost. He couldn't even see the corner of the building any more. As he watched, he saw a dark shape appear in the smoke, a silhouette that resolved into a figure – a Guardsman.

Trooper Heim, his uniform bloodied and his helmet askew on his head, came bursting from the smoke. He wasn't even holding his lasgun. He was just running. His face ashen. His eyes dinner-plate wide. He was running for his life, and it didn't last very long. A boom came from behind him and his entire body lurched forward. His feet were lifted off the ground as his torso burst open in an explosive display of blood, gore and jettisoned ribcage.

Behind Heim, Torvin saw an ork emerge from the smoke. The greenskin wielded a fat-barrelled pistol. It was an ork much like the one Torvin had spotted in the trees – not the same one exactly, but another dressed in makeshift camouflage. The greenskin fired its pistol and Torvin heard the shot whistle past his head. He didn't dare turn to see who it might have hit.

Torvin raised his lasgun too slowly, as if he were moving through water. But with the repeated cracking of a laspistol firing three shots in quick succession, the ork jerked. Black burn wounds of instantly superheated flesh appeared on its shoulder and chest, and then a final one blew the side of its skull into cauterised chunks. Somehow the creature still stood, wavering on its feet. Sergeant Troovey charged past, lowering the pistol he'd just fired and opting to raise a chainsword. He brought it down in a howling strike to hit the ork in the neck. With an arc of red and green gore he decapitated the greenskin.

Sergeant Troovey turned to Torvin, Norsten and the several other speechless Guardsmen around them. 'You lot,' he barked, 'the greenskins are on the wall down here, move up with me. We're going to hold them off while the rest of the platoon maintains fire on the primary ork force. Weapons up.'

'No,' Norsten said from beside Torvin.

'What did you just say to me, trooper?' Sergeant Troovey said, but when Torvin turned to look at Norsten he saw he wasn't really speaking to the sergeant. He was muttering to himself.

'No,' Norsten repeated. His face had gone pale. There was no hero of the Imperium in his boots now. 'No, no, no, they're not supposed to get this close. We're supposed to shoot them from a distance.'

Sergeant Troovey glared at Norsten. 'Throne-damned recruits!' he roared. 'Get your Emperor-damned arse up and move! Do it now!'

Troovey grabbed Norsten and dragged him along, getting him to move despite Norsten appearing not even to notice. Somehow Torvin managed to get himself to follow.

'Hold here, weapons up,' Troovey ordered when they'd moved down the rampart a short way, nearing the edge of the smoke. It was starting to clear slightly and Torvin could make out shapes moving in the grey.

Norsten did as ordered, raising his lasgun and aiming it into the smoke, but he immediately began firing. 'No!' he yelled as he fired blindly into the smoke cloud. 'We have to keep them at a distance!'

'Crem it!' Sergeant Troovey yelled. 'Wait for a target, Norsten, we've got friendlies in there!'

But Norsten wasn't listening, at least not to Sergeant Troovey; he was listening only to whatever voice had cracked free and was rattling around in his head. 'No! No! If we see them, they're too close! We have to keep firing!'

Torvin had frozen during the battle. The mayhem and fear had got to him. He had slid down the wall in terror and projectile-vomited up his entire breakfast ration. But what he saw in Trooper Norsten was even more severe. One moment he had been killing orks with confidence, maybe even enjoyment, and the next he had descended into lunatic ravings. His eyes were wide with panic but also distant, as if his mind had been evacuated and left only utter terror to run his body. He continued firing into the smoky haze again despite Sergeant Troovey's protests.

From somewhere in the smoke came a bellowing ork war cry.

'WAAAAAAGH!'

The shapes moving in the smoke were coming closer to them now, turning from misty shadow monsters to clearer figures, wide-shouldered and menacing. Torvin gripped his lasgun, squeezing it tighter than his training told him he was supposed to, but if he loosened his grip at all he was sure the weapon would shake out of his grasp entirely. The frontmost figure burst from the smoke, yelling as it came.

'We've lost the east side!'

Torvin was surprised to see the hulking shape resolve into Lieutenant Gernson. She was splattered with blood, both human and ork. Olga Ogryn was roaring orders as she came.

'Prepare to hold h–' The lieutenant jerked as the flash of a las-shot struck her in the shoulder. Her thick flak armour absorbed some of the beam, but her flesh was still burned black beneath.

'No!' Norsten was screaming. 'We have to kill the xenos!' And he fired again. And again.

'Norsten! Hold your fire!' Sergeant Troovey screamed, but it was too late.

Norsten's second shot hit Lieutenant Gernson in the chest, vaporising the flak armour there and opening her flesh to the ribs. The third shot struck her in the centre of the throat, blowing her windpipe into a cavernous black hole and all but decapitating her. She dropped.

'Shit!' Troovey turned to Norsten. The Guardsman, still immeasurably lost to reason, continued to fire at Gernson's already dead body.

'I got one!' Norsten screamed. 'I got one!'

Sergeant Troovey smashed Norsten in the side of the head with the hilt of his chainsword, knocking the trooper to the ground.

'That was the lieutenant!' Troovey screamed at him.

Norsten, splayed out on the floor, his smashed cheek bleeding profusely, looked in the direction of Gernson's body. 'What?' Some sense seemed to return to him, though his eyes went wide again. 'Oh Emperor! Oh Emperor!'

Troovey lifted his laspistol and pointed it at Norsten's face.

'No!' Norsten cried out. 'Sergeant, I'm sorry. It was–'

Troovey executed Norsten with a single shot.

None of the Guardsmen had time to react. Thundering from the smoke came the screaming, wild faces of maniacal greenskins intent on murdering humans.

'Fire!' Sergeant Troovey roared.

Torvin did so. He was submerged in the carnage of battle so far that it had begun to drown out everything else. He felt disconnected from himself, as if all he could do was copy those Guardsmen around him. They fired and so he fired.

They hit the orks coming through the smoke with a dense stream of lasfire. Most of the orks ran at them with melee weapons drawn, hooting and howling, and the Guardsmen cut them down. One large ork who continued charging forward despite taking several lasgun shots to the stomach had almost reached them.

Now Torvin felt his panic rising again. This was the closest he'd been to one of the orks. He could see the shining red of its eyes; the scratches on the hooked tusks in its wide, roaring mouth; the muscles that bulged in its raised arm as it prepared to swing a large-bladed axe, gouged and rusted but certainly sharp enough to cleave a human skull in two. What he didn't see was any of the supposed weakness these creatures had compared to an Imperial Guardsman in hand-to-hand combat. Still, with a bestial bellow of his own, Sergeant Troovey dashed forward to meet the creature.

Troovey swung his chainsword and took the ork's arm off at the elbow before the monster had the chance to swing. Then he thrust forward and jammed the ripping teeth at the tip of the chainsword into the ork's chest, mincing through flesh and bone.

Some of the orks coming behind this first wave still had their rudimentary rifles and pistols drawn and began firing in return. Here, facing orks already on the rampart, the Guardsmen had nothing to take cover behind. A trooper next to Torvin was thrown back when an ork round hit him in the chest. Another Guardsman nearby was struck in the forehead. His skull ruptured like a dropped melon, blood and gore spraying in all directions; a warm spatter of it struck Torvin on the cheek and he had to blink some of it out of his eye. Apparently, he had not freed himself entirely of his breakfast, as he felt thick acidic bile rise into his throat again. This time he managed to swallow it back down.

'Keep them off the ramparts!' Torvin heard Corporal Algarn shout.

Torvin glanced back to the defence against the main attack – only for a moment, but long enough to see the rickety ork ladders were on the wall and that, despite Algarn's plea, they weren't going to keep them off the outpost for long.

Sergeant Troovey hacked at an ork with his chainsword before turning to the Guardsmen defending the attack from the east. 'Fall back, close up.' He turned to Torvin. 'You, come with me and watch my back.'

Troovey moved back along the rampart towards the stairs. Torvin was only too happy to follow, but as the first of the orks clambered up over the main wall he was sure this retreat was only an illusion of safety.

'Algarn,' Troovey called before he headed back down into the outpost, 'the lieutenant is dead. I'm going to contact Karoo. Hold this Throne-damned wall.'

Torvin followed the sergeant as he loped down the stairs, clearing the steps two at a time. They turned and headed for the communications room. The door was ajar and Sergeant Troovey hit it at a run. Inside, perched over the vox-console and calling desperately into the microphone, was Trooper Revna, one of the platoon's vox-operators. She was repeating the same message.

'Karoo City, this is Outpost Four, do you read? Over.'

'Can you get through?' Sergeant Troovey asked. 'Anything?'

'Negative, sergeant,' Revna said, 'not a thing. It's got to be that magnetic interference. I can't get word to Karoo City.'

'Sergeant Troovey!'

The shout drew Troovey back out of the comms room. Torvin, not really knowing what he was supposed to be doing, followed. Corporal Algarn was descending the stairs. His normally sharp, clean fatigues were covered with sweat, blood and other fluids of unknown origin. His face was harrowed. 'We can't hold them,' he said, 'they're overrunning us already.'

'Numbers?' Troovey said.

'Ours or theirs?' Algarn replied.

'Ours,' Troovey responded quickly, 'how many left?'

'Some, but it'll be none soon enough.'

'Emperor damn it.' Troovey turned to look at Torvin. 'We're going to the armoury to get the distress flares. Let's go.'

But as they made to move forward, an explosion rocked the outpost from above. Dust and debris billowed down the stairs and a concussive wave threw Algarn off his feet. The sounds of cheering and roaring orks could be heard from above, and the sound grew suddenly louder as greenskins appeared through the dust at the bottom of the stairs. They were already pouring into the outpost. Algarn tried to gather himself and get to his feet, but he wasn't fast enough. One of the orks shot him in the back with a booming pistol, the sound reverberating inside the space.

More orks descended the stairs. The armoury with the emergency distress flares was on the other side of the group of snarling greenskins and Troovey and Torvin weren't getting past. They were now cut off from their only chance at letting Karoo know they'd been attacked. Torvin knew any help sent would be received much too late for them anyway – every Guardsman in the outpost would be dead in minutes – but now they couldn't complete their primary mission, their whole reason for being stationed out here: they couldn't alert the Imperial forces. The orks could pour down into the valley and Karoo City would receive no early warning.

It seemed the same thoughts had just gone through Sergeant Troovey's mind. He turned to Torvin. 'Torvin, go out the north door, head into the jungle and get to Karoo. Tell them Outpost Four is lost to the orks and the city is under threat.'

'Sergeant–'

'Go,' Troovey said to him as he lifted his chainsword. 'And you better Throne-damned make it!' The sergeant turned and screamed as he charged at the group of orks. 'For the Emperor!'

Torvin ran. He sprinted through the outpost, bashing his way through the heavy door, and was suddenly outside again. He didn't look back at the cacophonous sounds of battle behind him as his adrenaline drove him across the clearing. It was quieting down. No, that wasn't quite true. There were ork war cries still filling the air, and the sounds of their blasting, overly loud weapons, but what he couldn't hear any more was the crack of lasguns firing or the shouts of Guardsmen. He didn't want to think about what that meant. He reached the treeline without being shot at and plunged into the semi-darkness of the jungle. This time he ploughed forward unconcerned with the vines and branches that whipped and scratched at his face. Thorned plants tore at his uniform and he slipped and staggered through the thick, wet leaves around his feet.

He ran.

He ran for as long as he could, gulping air against his burning lungs.

He had to get to Karoo City.

CHAPTER SIX

TORVIN

The reliquary room of the Karoo City chapel had been requisitioned as headquarters for the operation to purge Gondwa VI of the greenskins. It was from here that the command staff dictated the orders Guardsmen like Torvin would carry out across this world. Now, Torvin waited outside.

Corporal Steig, attached to Gondwa System Defence Headquarters, had escorted Torvin straight here after his arrival back in Karoo City. Now, outside the door, the corporal kept looking over at him. Torvin knew why. He'd seen his reflection in every window they'd passed. His face was haggard, scratched, bruised and still covered with streaks of dried blood. His uniform was wet and torn, mangled almost beyond recognition. He looked like an old wrung-out sponge. He'd plunged headlong through the jungle on a desperate dash back to Karoo City for nine or ten hours. He was dehydrated, starving, almost passing out on his feet. The corporal was either surprised Torvin was still alive or dreading ending up looking the same way.

Corporal Steig knocked on the door.

'Come.'

He pushed the door open part way and stuck his head inside.

'Yes, what is it, corporal?'

'A message, sir,' the corporal said. 'From Outpost Four.'

'Go ahead then.'

'Well,' Steig said.

'Yes, hurry up about it.'

'It's just there's a Guardsman here with the message. It seems vox is down.'

Torvin heard the exasperated sigh from inside. 'Come in then, we're almost done. You'll have to wait.'

'It's just–'

'You'll have to wait, corporal.'

'Yes, sir.'

Corporal Steig gestured for Torvin to enter. Torvin gingerly did so. Inside, Major General Niko Nillom, commanding officer of the entire defence of the Gondwa System, Colonel Estrid Grimsson, commander of the Skadi Second, Commissar Mave Redvin and a small handful of other staff officers were gathered around a central table on which a large paper map had been unrolled. None of them so much as looked at Torvin.

The golden images of saints and martyrs, and heavy bound books of devotional prayers to the Emperor of Mankind, had been pushed to the sides of the space, leaving it looking like a war room overdecorated with religious clutter. Perhaps command thought if they planned their battles here, amongst such a plethora of iconography from the Cult Imperialis, the Emperor would bless their endeavour to purge the greenskins from this world and might even offer divine intervention should they need it. The officers leant in around the table as if discussing grand strategy, as though the fate of the entire Imperium depended on the decisions they made in this moment. The stocky, almost plump Major General Nillom was reading from a data-slate.

'All right, three more items,' the major general said, taking a sip from the cup of amasec on the table in front of him before wiping his bushy moustache. 'First, how is discipline, commissar?'

'Discipline is sufficient at this stage, major general,' Commissar Redvin replied. 'We are yet to have any incidents that couldn't be rectified with minor floggings.'

'Excellent,' Nillom said. He referred to the slate in front of him again. 'Ration distribution, Colonel Grimsson?'

'Up to date, sir,' the colonel responded. 'The troops have enough protein gruel for three days.'

'Good, good.' Nillom checked something off his list. 'Speaking of rations, I'm getting a little peckish myself.' He turned to the staff officers, looking over them for the lowliest rank. He settled on a lieutenant present. 'See if you can't organise us something, lieutenant. Some of that local pastry-wrapped meat if it's still around.'

The lieutenant nodded and hurried away, no doubt to pass the orders down the chain.

'Right,' the general said, 'on to the final item on the agenda. The most serious topic for discussion in today's meeting. It appears the Skadi Second regimental standard on display outside the chapel has been damaged. It was likely torn in transit, but I will not have that on display to the population of Karoo City until it is repaired. We are here to rid their world of the greenskins, but we are also representing the Astra Militarum, and we will not do so with shoddy standards. Can I leave this with you to be rectified, Colonel Grimsson?'

'Yes, sir, of course.'

'Excellent. Now, this message,' Major General Nillom said as he turned to where Torvin stood beside Steig near the doorway. His eyebrows raised as he looked at Torvin for the first time. 'You're in quite a state, trooper.'

'Ah,' Torvin managed. 'Yes, sir.'

'What's your urgent message then, trooper?' Nillom asked.

'Sir,' Torvin said, 'I'm Trooper Torvin, with Fourth Platoon.'

Nillom stared at him as if waiting for him to continue. When he didn't, the general's forehead creased into deep furrows of annoyance. 'And what does that mean to me?'

'Sir,' Colonel Grimsson said, 'that's Lieutenant Gernson's platoon.'

'Yes, yes, of course,' Nillom said, but Torvin was more than confident the general had no idea who Lieutenant Gernson was. Nillom took a sip of amasec from the clear cup in front of him, which looked to Torvin to be some kind of expensive crystal, and leant towards Colonel Grimsson. 'And just quickly remind me what they were doing again?'

'Sir, Fourth Platoon was sent to man Outpost Four,' Grimsson said.

Before he'd been tithed to the Imperial Guard, when stories of the mighty Astra Militarum had been told on Skadi, Torvin had thought the high ranks of the Guard must be men and women on par with gods. They seemed as lofty and far above common humanity as a warrior of the Adeptus Astartes. But now, faced with this short, heavily moustached man who barely knew what was going on in the operation he was supposedly running, his assessment of the deities of the Astra Militarum was rapidly changing.

'Ah yes, yes,' Nillom said, 'one of the watch stations.'

'Yes, sir,' Colonel Grimsson agreed, 'but Outpost Four is one of the watch stations on the main approach to Karoo City, the one at entrance to the valley.'

At this Major General Nillom's eyes grew slightly wider before narrowing, signs of concern touching his face that he quickly acted to quell. He ran his hand over his moustache. 'Why aren't you there then, trooper?'

'That's why I've come, sir,' Torvin said. 'Outpost Four has been lost to the orks. I think I'm the only survivor.'

'What?' the general blurted. His words began to splutter out from under his moustache. 'How? How can that be? Why weren't we alerted via vox?'

'It's down, sir,' Torvin said, 'the interference from the planet I think.'

'Well, yes but what about the backup?' Nillom asked. He turned to Colonel Grimsson. 'There's a backup isn't there?'

'Yes, sir,' the colonel replied, 'flares, sir.'

'Well,' Nillom said, returning his attention to Torvin, 'what about the flares?'

'The ork attack overwhelmed us so quickly they were inside the outpost before we could do that, sir.'

'How did you survive then, trooper?' Commissar Redvin asked, her words slow and deliberate. 'If your entire platoon was lost, how are you standing here?'

'Sergeant Troovey sent me, commissar,' Torvin answered. 'When he knew the outpost was lost, he sent me to warn you, to report what had happened.'

'It sounds to me like you fled,' Commissar Redvin said. 'I overheard your fellow troopers calling you a coward before you left. Did you flee, Trooper Torvin? Did you desert your post?'

Torvin felt his extremities go cold – the kind of sudden, acute fear that had struck him when he'd first seen that camouflaged ork in the trees.

'No, commissar.' Torvin knew his voice was wavering. 'Sergeant Troovey ordered me to fall back to Karoo City and warn you that we'd lost the outpost and the orks could attack the city without warning.'

Commissar Redvin stood from the table and moved towards Torvin. With a practised flourish she flicked her long black greatcoat aside and drew her ornate gold-inlaid bolt pistol from its holster with one smooth movement.

Torvin found himself staring at the polished gunmetal end of the weapon, his eyes drawn to the dark circle of the barrel, a sunken black eye looking back with the glint of a loaded bolt inside.

'According to Astra Militarum regulations the penalty for desertion is death. The penalty for cowardice is at the discretion of the commissar but is also up to and including death. As a commissar of the Officio Prefectus I am hereby authorised to pass summary judgement and carry out the sentence of execution.'

'Ma'am,' Torvin spluttered, 'I swear on the Golden Throne, on the Emperor Himself, I was ordered to leave the outpost and return here. If I was a deserter, why would I come back?'

Commissar Redvin did not lower her bolt pistol, but she had not yet pulled the trigger.

'Now, now, commissar,' Major General Nillom said. 'I'm sure there's no need for an execution. There's no evidence that Torren here is lying.'

Torvin opened his mouth to correct the general's pronunciation of his name but then thought better of it. He shouldn't draw any more attention to himself.

'I agree, sir,' Colonel Grimsson said. 'It's more important that we move quickly to act on this intelligence and resecure such a vital watch outpost from the enemy. Thank you, trooper.'

Commissar Redvin lowered the bolt pistol, which allowed Torvin to relax slightly, but not all that much because the commissar's eyes seemed just as threatening as the pistol barrel. 'Very well,' the commissar said, 'but I am in charge of drill and discipline in this regiment and I will be investigating the conduct of this trooper further.' She looked to Corporal Steig, who had done a far better job than Torvin at vanishing into the background. 'Corporal, arrest this trooper on my authority and have him locked away.'

Corporal Steig moved to Torvin. When the corporal faced away from Redvin he gave Torvin an apologetic look, but Torvin knew he would not disobey an order from a commissar, especially one that seemed to reach for her bolt pistol so easily. He took Torvin by the arm and led him out of the room.

He had felt guilty about it, knowing the fate that had befallen the rest of his platoon, but Torvin had been happy to be away from Outpost Four. He was happy to have survived. But now it seemed he had jumped, or as he'd tried to explain, been ordered, out of the frying pan and into the fire.

CHAPTER SEVEN

ALDALON

Colonel Haskell Aldalon was the first to exit the Devourer drop-ship, stepping off even as the ramp was still lowering. The ancient hydraulic mechanisms of the ship droned loudly, the moan of a machine-spirit that had served the Imperium for millennia, ferrying men and women to battlefields across the galaxy. Aldalon landed softly, almost soundlessly, on the space port landing pad. He took a moment to let his body acclimatise to the gravity of the world, bending and straightening his legs. It was close to that of the artificial gravity on board an Imperial Navy void-ship. In fact, as always, the artificial gravity had been subtly adjusted en route to match that of their destination and prepare them for the gravitational acceleration they would feel on planetfall. Still, there was always a subtle difference to the pull of actual gravity. Actual gravity made him feel denser, more real. He much preferred the heaviness of solid rock underfoot to the simulation created by the technological machinations of the Adeptus Mechanicus.

It wasn't necessarily that he distrusted the Mechanicus, but more that, like all those from his world, he had been taught from a very young age to put his faith in cold steel and cold wits. He flexed his right hand, feeling the fingers and thumb of his ever-present power fist open and close with servo-assisted strength. The fist's disruption field hummed with a familiar low-frequency buzz. Aldalon had the tech-priests of the Cult Mechanicus to thank for his trademark weapon after all; he couldn't bemoan them and their mysterious ways too much, even if all those he'd met had seemed off-putting at best and repulsive at worst.

Aldalon walked across the landing platform away from the drop-ship. Whenever they landed on a new world, he always ensured he was the first to step onto it. That was how things were done on Catachan, the world that had forged him. He might have been a colonel, in command of the entire Catachan 57th Jungle Fighters Regiment, but he would not lead from behind like Imperial Guard officers from other, softer worlds. His leadership philosophy was the same as that of all officers from Catachan. It was a philosophy of first and last. As regimental commander he would be first when required. First to step onto a new world, first to charge onto a battlefield, first to launch the ambush, first over the wall. He would also be the last when required. Last to eat, last to sleep, last to leave.

On the death world of Catachan only the hardest survived into adulthood, and of those that survived only those with a will of rockcrete made it into the storied ranks of the Catachan Jungle Fighters. Of the Jungle Fighters themselves, it required a body and mind harder than ceramite to climb the ranks like Colonel Haskell Aldalon had done. On Catachan there was no beginning as an officer, regardless of your family heritage. Every single member of the Jungle Fighters began as a trooper and worked their way up. On Catachan every rank, like every scar, like every breath, was earned.

The colonel walked to the edge of the landing platform, a massive circular pad large enough that drop-ships like the Devourer class or even small merchant voidships could land. He looked over the edge. Karoo City was spread out below, or at least stacked below, level upon level, like a pyramid punctuated by needle-thin spires, steeples with arched windows and hab-blocks grown tall with ad hoc construction over the years. Behind the city, looming over it like a watchful guardian, was a rocky, granite-faced mountain that rose, like the city itself, from the canopy of the jungle.

As with almost all Imperial cities the highest levels of Karoo City were home to the upper classes – the rich, the nobility, the merchants. Those for whom life in the Imperium was bearable and, in some cases, even comfortable. The architecture around the landing pad reflected this fact: he saw hab-blocks with large, multiroom apartments and among them even stand-alone residences, whole houses belonging to wealthy families. The next levels were primarily divided into sectors for the Ecclesiarchy, the Administratum, the Mechanicus.

Then with each descending stratum the quality of life likewise descended until, Colonel Aldalon had no doubt, you reached the lower levels, down beneath the canopy of the jungle, whose inhabitants scratched out a living from the squalor, men and women labouring in hidden workhouses and factorums or trudging out daily into mines or quarries. It was always that way. Always the same. Those at the top looked down, figuratively and literally, on the workers below them. The lofty heights of this world, like all worlds, was held up on the backs of the toiling masses.

Aldalon looked away from the city. It did not bother him. It was the way of things on Catachan so why should it not be the way of things everywhere? The strong would survive.

He took a deep breath. Even here in the upper reaches of the city, high above the green canopy, he could smell the damp, musty odour of the jungle. The native plants and animals may have been different, but the smell of every jungle was the same: the fresh wet leaves on those trees who'd won the battle for height mixed with the heavy rot and decomposition of the flora that had lost, fallen to the forest floor to fertilise the soil for those that would try again. The jungle was just like the city – a battle for height, an impossible battle to crawl out of the dark for most.

Aldalon turned at the feeling of someone approaching. Sergeant Learna Sappa moved to stand beside him. He hadn't heard her footsteps, but she was a Catachan Jungle Fighter and so this was unsurprising. Sergeant Sappa was staring out over the jungle landscape as well.

'It's nice to be on a world covered in green again,' she said without looking at him. 'Better than the desert dust of Karst.'

Colonel Aldalon grunted something of an affirmative reply. Karst had been a battlefield on which they'd won, but personally he had lost. She knew this. She should understand it better than any other. He'd already told her not to speak of Karst.

'Looks a little like Catachan, don't you think?' Sappa said.

'It looks a little like home, yes,' Aldalon said. 'It doesn't sound like home though.'

Sergeant Sappa looked at him. 'No?'

'No.' He turned and began walking away. His troops of the 57th Catachan Jungle Fighters were disembarking the drop-ship and he needed to go and find whoever was in charge here. 'There's not enough screaming.'

CHAPTER EIGHT

ALDALON

Having left the Catachan 57th to get themselves squared away, Colonel Aldalon walked down the long chapel, past rows of Imperial Guard soldiers barracked inside. They looked up at him as he passed, hastily stiffening in respect for not only his rank but also the red bandanna he wore tied around his honestly ridiculously large bicep.

The Catachan Jungle Fighters were legendary among the Astra Militarum. In stories told to children they were almost as lauded as the Adeptus Astartes themselves, in a lot of ways maybe even more so, because the men and women of Catachan were just that – men and women. Everything they did, every storied battle they won, they did without all the advantages of the Emperor's Space Marines.

Aldalon did not acknowledge the troopers around him in return. He had little time for soft-world Guardsmen, and these were worse than most. A new regiment apparently: the Skadi Second Infantry, a force who'd not seen combat from a world he didn't care to learn anything about.

Around him, the chapel was resplendent with stained glass, painted frescoes and imposing statues of Imperial saints, but Aldalon did not stop to take that in either. He walked to the reliquary room at the end of the chapel, where he'd been told Major General Nillom, commanding officer of the Gondwa System Defence, would be waiting. One of the Skadi Second corporals, standing outside, snapped a hasty salute before opening the door for him.

Aldalon entered the room without waiting to be announced. The occupants turned and a short, round man wearing a stiffly pressed uniform bearing the single pip and aquila epaulette of an Astra Militarum major general stood from a seat at the table.

'Ah, Colonel Aldalon I presume. I am Major General Nillom. You and the Catachan Fifty-Seventh have my thanks for joining us on our blessed mission to cleanse this world of the greenskin threat.'

'Just going where we're told, sir,' Aldalon replied.

'Yes, of course, but you have my thanks none the less. I am very pleased to have warriors of your calibre with us and I have no doubt your expertise in jungle warfare will prove most useful here. Please' – Nillom gestured towards the table – 'join us. We were just discussing our next steps in ensuring the orks flooding through this subsector are finally stopped on this world. I understand you've met at least some of these greenskins in glorious battle already?'

Aldalon nodded as he moved to the table. 'Karst.'

'Yes, some of the warband the Imperial forces pushed back from Karst appear to have joined forces with the warband pushing through the Gondwa System. They have a nasty habit of doing that, the greenskins, don't they? Please, have a seat, colonel.'

'I'd prefer to stand.'

'Very well,' Nillom said. Aldalon saw the general take note of his power fist. 'I've read some of your dispatches. The troopers call you "Hell Fist" don't they?'

Aldalon nodded.

Major General Nillom smiled. 'Do you ever take it off?'

'Have you ever put one on?'

The commissar sitting at the table rose so quickly that the legs of her chair squealed on the polished stone floor before the whole chair fell back behind her. 'What insolence! You may be a colonel, but you are still addressing a major general of the Imperial Guard!'

Aldalon turned to look at the commissar and her blustering, red face. His face, as always, could have been carved from stone.

'I have never had the misfortune of being attached to a unit from Catachan, but I know your reputation,' the commissar spat. 'Do not think I will accept ill-discipline from any member of the Astra Militarum, Catachan or not!'

'If you are aware of our reputation, commissar' – Aldalon let a controlled hint of disdain creep into his voice as he used her title – 'then you will know that those of the Commissariat fare better if they take a gentle touch with us.'

'Are you threatening me, colonel? My powers over the Imperial Guard are not limited by rank, you had best remember that.'

'And you best remember that we Catachans are the real Imperial Guard, not some children playing at soldiers.'

'A holy bolt pistol makes no distinction, colonel.'

'All right,' Major General Nillom said, 'that's quite enough. We are all feeling a little heightened with the task ahead of us. A task I'd like to focus on, if you please, commissar.'

'Very well,' the commissar said, though Aldalon did not miss that she pushed her greatcoat aside as she lifted her chair back onto its feet and sat, keeping her bolt pistol exposed.

Aldalon grunted for Nillom to continue.

'Good. Introductions then,' Nillom said. He indicated the commissar. 'You've met Commissar Redvin. This is Colonel Grimsson, commander of the Skadi Second. And this is Governor Erwin Misom, planetary governor of Gondwa VI.'

The general did not bother to introduce the handful of other, lower-ranked staff officers around the room or, of course, the servitors mindlessly tapping at data-slates or shuffling paper. That suited Aldalon fine; the fewer people he had to deal with the better.

Aldalon quickly evaluated the others at the table. Commissar Redvin, it was obvious enough from their first interaction, was a prototypical commissar, used to keeping conscripts in line but likely nothing but a leash on the throat of real fighters. Colonel Grimsson looked bland enough that she could have been any officer from any soft-world. That wasn't to say she wasn't an effective regimental colonel, but she would have a lot to prove to earn the respect of the Catachans. Lastly, Governor Erwin Misom: the man looked like a wet swamp weasel. His dark hair was parted in the centre and slicked down in what must have been a local style, but it did little other than accentuate how thin his skull was. He wore a tunic inlaid with gold braiding and had gold rings on almost all of his fingers.

Aldalon did not judge the unfamiliar dress or customs he encountered. He had seen clothing, heard music and listened to slang language as varied as the worlds he'd visited. What he did judge, though, was how this man positively dripped with wealth and extravagance – things that, as a Catachan, he could not help but equate with weakness.

'Your arrival is very well timed, colonel,' Major General Nillom continued. 'The Skadi Second have been doing an admirable job in defence but we have very real concerns about an attack on the capital.'

It was Planetary Governor Misom who spoke next. His voice was nasal and high to such a theatrical extent that Aldalon was sure he must have been doing it on purpose. Aldalon doubled down on his first assessment. This man was weak-bodied, and likely weak-willed as well, and though Gondwa VI might have been a jungle world, it was nothing like the death world of Catachan. This man could never have been governor there. Aldalon would be willing to bet Misom would not have lived past five years old. At five years old, Haskell Aldalon was already killing Catachan death cobras and had survived not one but two bouts of noxious blood fever.

'The lower levels of Karoo,' Governor Misom was saying, 'where the commoners live, are quite far below the jungle canopy. I'm told the jungle approaches to the city there are quite dense and difficult to monitor. Plus, Gondwa VI's magnetic field apparently causes all sorts of problems with communication and monitoring. We have outposts set up around the city to keep watch instead, you see.'

'I read the briefing,' Aldalon said, wanting to hurry this along.

'The outposts have flares to signal that an enemy is approaching should vox communication fail,' Misom continued.

'That was in the briefing too,' Aldalon said. 'Contrary to rumour, Catachans can read. Has there been any change to the situation worth actually mentioning?'

'Well,' Governor Misom said, holding his hand to his chest in mock shock. 'I was simply trying to be helpful.'

'We've lost Outpost Four to orks,' Major General Nillom said. 'One of the main watch stations. The first task for you and your Catachans will be to take it back. Send your regiment to take back Outpost Four before any ork forces decide to appear out of the jungle right on the doorstep of Karoo City. While your troops are securing Outpost Four, we can discuss how you think we can push the orks back through the jungle and try to flush them off this world.'

'No,' Aldalon said. 'I'll be leading the troopers to take back the outpost. Has intelligence changed since the briefing I received?'

'No, colonel,' Nillom said, 'intelligence has not changed, but I was hoping you could help plan for a larger offensive.'

'We will,' Aldalon said, 'but it is the Catachan way that I lead the first battle here. Based on your intelligence I'll only need two squads. My second-in-command, Lieutenant Colonel Hurn, and the rest of the regiment will remain here. Besides' – Aldalon closed his power fist until the fingers began to grind together and spark with energy – 'I need to kill some orks.'

CHAPTER NINE

ALDALON

Colonel Aldalon walked down the wide stone steps from the chapel. In front of him, milling about the atrium, waiting for word of their mission, were the men and women of the Catachan 57th. They wore jungle-green camouflage, though most of them sported only tank tops and several were bare-chested. All, regardless of rank or gender, had their heads shaved to the skin leaving only a short mohawk over their scalps. Many were tattooed with skulls, Imperial aquilas or symbols of home. The curling shape of a Catachan Devil – the terrifying truck-sized scorpion creature native to Catachan – was always a favourite. What better to remind a Catachan of home than a monstrous living killing machine? Those of a higher rank – corporals and sergeants – shunned rank slides on their uniforms, instead opting to have their rank cut or tattooed directly into the flesh of their arms. All of them, even those without tattoos, were scarred, carrying the signs of battles past or simply wounds picked up during a life on Catachan.

Each of the soldiers sported a red bandanna, the symbol of the Catachan Jungle Fighters. How they wore it differed – most over their head or around their forehead, some tied around an arm like Aldalon's, or hanging around their neck – but all wore it proudly. And though they wielded varying weapons – auto-pistols, lascarbines and flamers among others – they each carried a long-bladed Catachan knife, a weapon that was just as much a symbol of who they were as the red bandanna.

They looked up as their commanding officer emerged from the gothic archway. They did not snap to military attention as he approached – there was little pomp and ceremony within the Catachan Jungle Fighters – but he did not need to call for their attention or reprimand them for not listening; their conversation stopped instantly as he began to speak.

'All right,' Aldalon said. 'We have our first objective. I'll be taking Lieutenant Trast and two squads to reclaim an outpost the Skadi Second have lost to the greenskins.'

'My squad will volunteer.'

Aldalon turned to the voice, but he already knew who it was. Sergeant Sappa had raised her knife in the air. Aldalon scowled, but the sergeant continued.

'As we're a new squad I'd like the opportunity to cut our teeth early.'

Aldalon ground his own teeth. 'Fine.' He could not make a display of telling a willing new squad leader they couldn't get into combat, regardless of how he felt about it. 'Sergeant Sappa, Sergeant Dram, your squads be ready to move out. We hit the jungle in thirty minutes. The rest of you will bunk here in the atrium, I don't expect we'll be gone longer than a couple of days. Lieutenant Hurn will be acting CO in my absence. Carry on.'

The Catachans dispersed. Those that would be moving out began to ready themselves, checking equipment and strapping on packs, applying camouflage paint to their exposed skin.

'Sergeant Sappa,' Colonel Aldalon said before the sergeant moved away to do the same, 'a word.'

Dark-skinned, tall and thin, Sappa moved with a grace that hid her strength. She was a force to be reckoned with, Aldalon knew that, but that wouldn't stop him from berating her. He eyed her sternly as she approached.

'What do you think you're doing interrupting me like that?'

'Sorry, sir,' Sappa said, but Aldalon knew she wasn't. 'My squad is just itching for a fight. We didn't see much action on Karst and after my promotion I'm keen to get some unity in the squad.'

'You'll get your time, sergeant,' Aldalon replied.

'Will I?'

'Watch it, Learna,' Aldalon said.

'Tell me,' Sappa said, 'is this about Brant?'

Aldalon let out a growl. 'I told you not to bring it up.'

'We are all Catachan Jungle Fighters,' Sappa said. 'All of us have earned our place here, you don't need to protect me any more than the others.'

'I'm not protecting you.'

'You always taught me that unit cohesion is key to the Catachan way. I need to fight with my squad to get that.'

'You got your way,' Colonel Aldalon said, 'you're on the mission. But I'm telling you not to ambush me like that again.'

'But, colonel,' Sappa said, with the audacity to smile, 'you taught me how to ambush too.'

CHAPTER TEN

TORVIN

Ted Torvin sat in the corner of his dank cell leaning back against the cool stone. It was musty and warm in the box they'd locked him in, the only respite being to slump against the damp slime dripping down one wall. Across the semi-dark space, which wasn't even wide enough for him to lie down, he watched a drop of water run along a line of mortar between heavy stones, struggling to continue as long as it could before being absorbed into the grout.

Torvin knew what that felt like. He'd battled his way through life, done the best he could to survive despite being dragged into the Astra Militarum. Sure, he'd had a few missteps, he'd be the first to admit it. He wasn't made for war, but he had, he'd swear to the Emperor Himself, done the best he could.

Now, despite following his sergeant's orders to leave the outpost and get word of the greenskin attack back to Karoo City, he'd been locked up for cowardice and desertion in a tiny dungeon beneath the chapel, a cell normally reserved for heretics and traitors. He thought about his father's stalwart advice – what was the small mercy he could take from this? He wasn't dead, at least.

Torvin opened the top pocket of his shirt, glad he'd slipped the pict of Melina in there before he'd gone on his watch shift at the outpost, and that the troopers who'd patted him down for weapons hadn't bothered to rummage through his pockets in detail before they tossed him in here. He pulled the pict out and looked at it. Melina was still staring at him with those same pretty blue eyes, still smiling that wide smile. He wondered if she was smiling now. Part of him hoped she was, and yet another part of him hoped she wasn't. Selfishly, he hoped she hadn't smiled at all since he'd left Skadi.

The heavy metal lock on the door unbolted with a sliding thunk. Torvin hastily tucked the pict away and when the ancient hinges squealed, the figure in the doorway was not one of the troopers bringing him food as he thought it might be. Instead, standing in the doorway in her long black greatcoat with its broad shoulders and her peaked cap of office pulled down menacingly low was Commissar Mave Redvin. Torvin climbed to his feet as swiftly as his joints, stiff from his time in the cell, would allow.

'Commissar,' Torvin said.

'Follow me, trooper.'

Commissar Redvin turned and walked away with the supreme confidence of one who knew her instructions would be followed.

And she was correct. Torvin, despite knowing it would lead nowhere good, followed the commissar from the cell. 'Where are we going, commissar?' he asked as he trailed behind her, trudging back up the steps from the small Ecclesiarchy dungeon. The commissar did not answer. 'If you're going to execute me, you could have done it before making me walk up all these stairs.'

Commissar Redvin stopped in mid-stair climb and turned to look back at Torvin. He was suddenly unsure why he thought making a joke to lighten the mood might have had any possibility of working on a commissar.

'Like the Holy Emperor we all serve I am going to offer you the path to divine salvation,' Redvin said. 'I am going to provide you the means to prove you are not a coward. I trust you will welcome that opportunity?'

'Yes, commissar,' Torvin replied. 'May I ask how?'

Commissar Redvin held him with her rockcrete stare. 'Have you ever heard of the Catachan Jungle Fighters?'

CHAPTER ELEVEN

TORVIN

When Commissar Redvin led him back to the reliquary room, Trooper Ted Torvin found himself, once again, in the company of officers so far above his rank he felt as though he should be craning his neck until his head spun. He recognised several of the faces: Colonel Grimsson was there and of course he recognised Major General Nillom, who turned as he and the commissar entered, but there was another man in the room he didn't recognise. He was a huge, dark-skinned man with shoulder-length dreadlocks on his otherwise shaved head. His muscular arms were as sharply defined as the granite mountain behind Karoo City. He wore a flak vest over the equally intimidating muscles of his chest and Torvin noticed that even now, inside the regimental headquarters, he wore a green power fist, actuators visibly sliding inside it as he flexed the fingers. His other hand looked to be bionic.

There was something else Torvin noticed: tied around his power fist-wielding arm was a red bandanna. He was a Catachan Jungle Fighter. When Commissar Redvin had asked whether Torvin had heard of the Catachan Jungle Fighters he'd almost laughed. She might as well have asked whether he'd heard of Cadia, or Armageddon, or hell, even the Adeptus Astartes.

There were countless worlds across the Imperium and most of them, like his home world of Skadi, hardly anyone had heard of, but there were those few so legendary that their names were known everywhere Imperial culture reached across the unfathomably large galaxy. The death world of Catachan was one of them, and the warriors that hailed from it were equally famous. Like many throughout the Imperium, Torvin had considered them almost mythical, maybe just propaganda inventions, but now he was face to face with one.

Together with the other officers in the room, the Catachan turned to stare at Commissar Redvin and Trooper Torvin as they entered. His face showed little change, but Torvin could almost feel the contempt radiating off him like a cold breeze. He wasn't sure if it was directed at Commissar Redvin or himself, or maybe both of them. The man's eyes flicked quickly between the commissar and Torvin, and then he sniffed dismissively. Oh, the derision was definitely for both of them.

'Thank you for waiting,' Commissar Redvin said. 'Colonel Aldalon, now that you're ready to depart you'll be taking this trooper with you on your offensive to retake Outpost Four.'

'What?'

The shocked words came from both Colonel Aldalon and Trooper Torvin in perfect unison. Torvin quickly pulled himself in line. He was lucky he hadn't been shot by the commissar once before and he didn't think he'd survive giving Redvin a second excuse to pull her bolt pistol. He hadn't meant to say anything, but the shock had bested him. Still, he was surprised the same had happened to the granite-faced Catachan colonel. His expression had cracked as well. But just like Torvin, as quickly as it had broken, Aldalon returned to his straight-faced glare.

'Not an option, commissar,' Colonel Aldalon said. 'Catachans work alone. We certainly don't take soft-worlders with us.'

'Trooper Torvin is the last survivor of the platoon that was stationed at Outpost Four and is a Guardsman like any other. He'll be going with you to both prove his worth to the Emperor and to assist you in your mission,' Redvin replied.

Colonel Aldalon looked from Commissar Redvin to Trooper Torvin again. As much as he tried not to, Torvin physically recoiled under the penetrating power of Aldalon's glare. He wished he could disappear, or at least declare in no uncertain terms that this wasn't his idea and he had no intention of going on a mission with the Catachan Jungle Fighters, where he was sure he would just get in the way.

Colonel Aldalon continued to stare at Torvin for much longer than was comfortable before he spoke. 'This may be a Guardsman, commissar, but not all Guardsmen are created equal.'

Torvin felt the full force of Aldalon's disdain. There was no misinterpretation; Colonel Aldalon did not think Torvin, maybe not even Colonel Grimsson or the major general himself, worthy of classification in the same Astra Militarum as himself and the Catachan Jungle Fighters.

'Besides,' Aldalon continued, 'I fail to see how having a member of a defeated unit is of benefit to me or my mission.'

Commissar Redvin didn't answer Colonel Aldalon directly but instead turned her attention to Major General Nillom. 'Major general, having local knowledge of the area and detailed first-hand experience of the outpost and its surrounds can only be a good thing, and Trooper Torvin here, by order of the Commissariat, must be permitted to prove he is not a coward worthy of a bolt-round or a place in the penal legions. I consider this an excellent opportunity to accomplish my duty to enact disciplinary realignment on Trooper Torvin while also aiding our broader mission here on Gondwa VI.'

Colonel Aldalon raised a single eyebrow at Commissar Redvin.

'Very well, commissar,' Major General Nillom said. 'I cannot say I agree with your suddenly dropping this on myself or on Colonel Aldalon, but you will have your wish.' He turned to Colonel Aldalon. 'Colonel, you will take this trooper with you on your mission.'

The Catachan remained silent for long enough that Torvin began to grow uncomfortable. Even Nillom started to fidget. Eventually the colonel's power fist opened and closed.

'Fine,' he said. 'I can see no reasonable way out of this. If that's all, sir, we'll be moving out.'

'Yes, thank you, colonel,' Nillom said. 'That will be all. The Emperor protects.'

'The Emperor protects,' Aldalon responded before heading for the door. He growled a single word as he walked past Torvin. 'Come.'

Torvin threw one last look at the higher-ups in the headquarters room. Major General Nillom had returned his attention to a data-slate in front of him as if the whole thing had been a distraction from something more important, probably what colour the drapes should be in his regimental bedroom. Commissar Redvin smiled at him. It was not a warm smile of Emperor's blessings. It was the smile of something about to eat him. He hurried from the room after Colonel Aldalon.

'Sir,' Torvin said as they left, trailing the enormous man. 'I was only at Outpost Four for a day before the orks arrived. I don't know how much help I'm going to be.'

Aldalon growled again. 'You think I don't know that, trooper? Just keep your mouth shut and follow me. That is a task far simpler than holding an outpost against ork attack, or is it something too onerous for you Skadi Guardsmen as well?'

'Uh,' Torvin replied, 'I can do that, sir.'

'Obviously not,' Aldalon said without looking back at him. 'The first part of my instruction was to keep your mouth shut.'

'Yes, sir,' Torvin said. 'Sorry, sir, you asked a question is all and I wasn't sure...' Torvin let his voice trail off as Aldalon stopped.

The Catachan colonel turned his massive bulk to face Torvin, a deep rumbling growl building in his throat again. Torvin swallowed and suddenly wished for something that would have been unfathomable just a few hours before. He was pretty sure he would have been much better off if he'd stayed at Outpost Four with the rest of Fourth Platoon.

CHAPTER TWELVE

ALDALON

Colonel Aldalon stopped and listened. The jungle was quiet. There was the sound of insects buzzing incessantly and occasional birdsong, but there were none of the noises that permeated the jungles of Catachan: the shrieking of huge spur-winged megaraptors swooping and circling each other in mating season fights; the sounds of hidden predators thrashing in the undergrowth as they tore the flesh from still-living prey; the screams of humans ravaged by deadly, flesh-necrotising plant poisons or whichever of a hundred other deaths had proved their undoing.

On Catachan it was often the silence you had to be afraid of. The deadliest things moved in silence. They crept or slithered, or dropped from above to end your life before you were even aware they were coming. Aldalon held his hand up in a fist and then extended a finger and made a circling motion. Two squads of Catachan Jungle Fighters moved in towards him, emerging from the dense green as if appearing from nowhere, following his hand signal to assemble on him. They took a knee as they reached the colonel but kept their weapons up and at the ready.

The troopers weaved between trees and moved through hanging vines and underbrush as if they were incorporeal, hardly making a disturbance – after all, the deadliest things from Catachan moved in silence. The same could not be said of this Trooper Torvin they'd been forced to bring with them. He brought up the rear of the troopers, mostly because he seemed to have a hard time keeping up, but even despite being slow he slogged through the jungle pushing aside branches and wading through ground cover with easy-to-spot movement and sound that would carry. Aldalon might as well have been forced to drag a tank along behind them. He watched Torvin thunder in and drop into a kneel, holding his standard-pattern lasgun as if it were a death cobra that might spin around and bite him. Aldalon shook his head before turning his attention to the gathered Jungle Fighters.

Sergeant Sappa and her squad had formed up on one side, and Aldalon mentally checked them off: Devi, Ryhorn, Fletcha, Braker, Whirler, Setarn, Grast and Himrod. He did the same for the troopers in Sergeant Dram's squad: Krall, Wetwer, Crusel, Tacter, Thorn, Grath, Krill and Holler. Aldalon ensured he knew the names of every member of his regiment – from the newest recruit to his most hardened veteran. With the two squads, himself, Lieutenant Trast and the dragged-along soft-worlder that made twenty-one of them.

Intelligence was sketchy on the enemy force holding Outpost Four. Torvin claimed the initial attack had been at least five hundred orks and there were at least half that number remaining. Based on reports of ork sightings in the briefing and Aldalon's experience of Guardsmen's overestimation, he put the number in the initial attack at more like a couple of hundred, with maybe a hundred left, probably less. They'd do some initial recon to be sure, but it seemed likely that it would be twenty Catachans against somewhere in the order of a hundred orks. He could take Torvin out of the equation because that soft-worlder wouldn't contribute worth a damn and Aldalon would be sure he wasn't getting in the way – one way or another. So, twenty Catachans against a hundred orks. Not the best odds for ordinary Guardsmen, but for Catachans fighting in the jungle with guerrilla tactics, it was just an ordinary workday.

'We're somewhere between thirty minutes and an hour out from the objective,' Aldalon said, keeping his voice low so that it didn't carry through the dusk air. 'We make camp here before it gets dark. I want a standard perimeter defence with supporting fire-lines. Sappa's squad east side. Dram's squad west side. Orks tend to wander about rather than send out official patrols. They're haphazard at best and they're unlikely to roam this far, plus they'll make even more noise than Torvin here so we should have warning, but I want full concealment anyway – let's not take chances. Lieutenant Trast and I will scout ahead while you prep this position. Move out.'

With well-drilled practice the troopers of the 57th Catachan Jungle Fighters kept low, moving just as silently as ever as they fanned out into the thick jungle. Sergeant Sappa's squad did as instructed, taking position to cover the eastern arc. Sergeant Dram's squad did the opposite, moving to the western flank. Each trooper knew the precise distance they needed to position themselves from the others.

The Catachans kept visual contact as best as they could as they set up defensive positions, but it was difficult in the dense green of the jungle with its all-consuming plant life. They would lose visual contact as night fell but were well within range of sound signals using clickers and other coded techniques almost indistinguishable from the sounds of the jungle.

The Catachan troopers carried only small packs; some had only a tiny haversack slung over one shoulder. They each pulled out a camouflaged tarpaulin, which they pitched angled low to the ground, barely above the height of the undergrowth, and secured with dark green cord to nearby trees. They stashed their gear inside, which now that their simple sleeping equipment was erected amounted to little more than a single water canteen and ammunition. They moved plant cover and fallen debris to conceal the tarpaulins even further until they were all but indistinguishable from the surrounding jungle, and then they slipped inside, weapons at the ready, eyes out into the jungle.

Aldalon watched the soft-worlder as the Catachans went to work. They'd left him alone; no one from Catachan had time for incompetence. Their world quenched them to be the hardest humans in the galaxy. They would not bother helping this fragile example of their species. It was not callousness. At least not deliberately. It was the way they had all been raised as a necessity for survival.

On Catachan you did not associate with the weak because the weak would get you killed. Every one of its inhabitants knew they had to rely on those around them to survive, and there could be no fractured links in the chain. One shaky foundation and the structure would collapse. Children of Catachan learned early to distance themselves from those they perceived as liabilities. Not only that, but it also wasn't uncommon for those seen as dangerously incompetent to disappear or to turn up dead with no witnesses.

Torvin stood around like a lost lamb wondering where his flock had wandered off to. Then, in an effort to perhaps seem like he knew what he should be doing, the liability walked a short way into the jungle and dumped his massively overstuffed pack onto the ground. Aldalon watched as he opened it and began pulling out an unimaginable amount of unnecessary equipment: spare socks, spare clothes, ration pack after ration pack, handbooks and manuals, toiletries; he even had one of those useless Munitorum multi-tools for eating with, for Emperor's sake.

Finally, Aldalon was relieved to see him reach in and pull out his sleeping tarpaulin. Unfortunately, he also pulled out one of the bulky Departmento Munitorum-issued sleeping bags. So many things he didn't need. Aldalon had instilled in the Catachan 57th the three Ws. They were all they needed. Weapons, water and will. As Torvin unfurled his sleeping kit, Aldalon took a quick look at where he'd positioned himself, right in the middle of Braker and Whirler's fire-lines. It was unlikely they'd have an ork incursion, but if they did, Torvin would probably get shot in a friendly fire incident. He considered letting it go but then he sighed. Emperor damn it. He was getting soft in his old age.

'Sergeant Sappa,' Aldalon called and moments later she emerged from the jungle, materialising from her concealed position. Aldalon saw Torvin do a double take. Sappa had been less than twenty yards away but had been all but invisible until she stood and began moving towards Aldalon. Torvin's face made it clear he had no idea where the troopers were now that they had hidden themselves. Seeing Sappa appear was like a phantom passing through a wall and solidifying right before his eyes.

'Yes, sir?' Sappa said as she approached.

Aldalon lifted his chin to gesture in the direction of Trooper Torvin. 'That one. Sort him out, will you?'

Sappa looked to where Torvin threaded thin rope through the metal eyelets of his tarpaulin and then stood, searching the area around for somewhere to tie off as if he hadn't planned the location of his shelter at all.

Aldalon smiled with mock encouragement. 'He can be in your squad.'

Sergeant Sappa looked for a moment like she was going to argue before seeing the colonel's raised eyebrow and thinking better of it. 'Yes, sir.'

'Good, find somewhere for him to sleep behind the perimeter where he isn't going to get himself shot.' Aldalon turned to Lieutenant Trast, who was waiting nearby. 'Ready, lieutenant?'

Trast nodded. 'Always ready, sir.'

'All right.' Aldalon flexed his power fist habitually. 'Let's get the lie of the land. Might get to dispose of some greenskins if we're lucky.'

***

Colonel Aldalon and Lieutenant Trast moved away from the Catachan position in the direction of Outpost Four with Aldalon leading the way. None of the troopers would question the colonel's decision to undertake this scouting mission himself; they were well aware of his idea of leadership. First into the fray. Still, he knew it wasn't tactically sound for the two highest-ranking officers on a mission to move out together on a recon. He would have sent Trast anyway. He had the best surveillance equipment and was an expert scout and tracker. But he could have sent him on this recon with any of the other troopers. The truth was Aldalon wanted to be doing something. He wanted to distract himself with the thrill of guerrilla warfare, that constant invigoration of danger and deceit; and, if they happened to encounter any orks, he was keen to show them why he was called Hell Fist. For Colonel Aldalon, the greenskins had a lot more to answer for than just being xenos scum.

Aldalon moved a short distance into the dense, wet trees before stopping and turning back. From here the Catachan troopers were all but indistinguishable from the jungle. The wall of thick green was disturbed only by the movement of Sergeant Sappa as she stood over Trooper Torvin, trying to get that useless soft-worlder to pack up his equipment and move to a more suitable location.

To most people, even the small percentage of this world's population who actually ventured out into the jungle, the location would have looked like any other – all but identical to the maze of mossy trunks, hanging vines and thick ground cover all around them. But Aldalon picked out the unique aspects of the spot immediately, taking a mental picture to remember where his troops were hidden. Several fallen trees, one on the ground and two others fallen in the same direction but propped up in the V-shaped branch attachment of a larger tree. A rare section of ground where the plants were thin enough to see damp, brown dirt. A collection of vines that hung in a looping pattern he would recall. He turned, confident he could find this place again, and began advancing slowly through the jungle, full stealth movement, and non-verbal and subvocal communication only.

The pair of Catachans moved through the trees for close to an hour, every movement slow and considered to disturb as little vegetation as possible, every step measured and controlled to avoid even the slightest noise. As the jungle began to thin, Aldalon gestured with palm down to indicate they needed to move even slower, and though they were already making barely a sound it was time to move silently – Catachan silent.

Aldalon stayed low as he crossed a creek of quietly running water and crested a small rise on the other side. He stopped, knelt and turned to where Trast was moving a short distance behind him. He pressed the transmit button for his vox. Both he and Trast wore throat mics that allowed whispered voice communication.

'Orks ahead,' Aldalon whispered.

Trast nodded. 'I hear them.'

Shouting was coming through the jungle. Angry shouts in deep, thick voices. Barked orders in simple Low Gothic, almost childlike – if children spoke in booming growls and snarling reverberating shouts, and if they were thick-muscled green monstrosities. The sounds were greenskins doing what greenskins did. The sounds of arguing and infighting.

'Move up,' Aldalon said. 'Get a count.'

Aldalon and Trast worked their way through the thinning jungle until they reached the treeline at the edge of the clearing. In front of them was their objective, Outpost Four. The air in the jungle was always thick, dense with smells of damp earth and wet, decaying leaves, but the clearing was filled with the stench of death. Not just any death though – this was the sickly-sweet aroma of ork death; of rotting, festering fungal organs. A smell both disgusting and satisfying. Aldalon could see thick, viscous ork blood on the tree trunks and dripping off leaves as it was thinned with water. All along the treeline were the scars of battle on the natural world, trees shredded by bolter rounds and scorched with the ultra-heat of lasgun fire.

The remains of the dead started here, greenskins cut down even before they'd made it out of the jungle during their attack on the outpost. In the heat, they'd already begun decomposing. Aldalon moved around one, crouched down beside it to examine it. The creature had fallen on its back, a rusty axe still clasped in its grip. Its chest had been opened in a cavernous hole and most of its insides had been ejected in a spray pattern on the jungle undergrowth behind it, a direct hit from a heavy bolter round. Its eyes were still open, but the red irises were vacant of life and stared straight up at the canopy overhead. It had three blue lines painted over its face in diagonal slashes. Deathskulls. A cursory glance at other bodies confirmed Aldalon's thoughts. Most of the rest were Deathskulls too.

Aldalon moved right to the edge of the jungle, ignoring the rest of the ork bodies in the trees and taking in the scene ahead. On top of a hill was the outpost itself. It hadn't taken long for the new occupants to stake their claim – a large blue ork skull had been sprayed on the outer wall. Around the outpost, maybe fifty yards from the building, was a protective fence of razor wire and a low rockcrete anti-vehicle barrier.

Or at least there had been. In front of where Aldalon and Trast crouched in the trees, a large section of the fence had been flattened and the rockcrete smashed through in sprays of debris. Aldalon could immediately tell what had been responsible for the damage because several of them had not made it much further. There were three of the smaller ork walkers they called Killa Kans and even one large Deff Dread on the ground. They were covered in ragged holes having soaked up enough heavy bolter fire to put them down.

The ground between the trees and the fence was cratered in areas where orks had tripped ordnance in the defensive minefield. Elsewhere, the soil had been chewed up by bolt-rounds and burned by las-fire.

Then there were the rest of the bodies. From just ahead of them, cut down quickly like those he'd already seen, to a mass green grave at the fence where they'd obviously been held up and mowed down, and then stretching all the way to the base of the high outpost wall, were hundreds of dead orks. The xenos had done what they always did. They'd charged straight at the enemy and, despite the outpost's far superior position and defensive infrastructure, Aldalon knew from having faced the greenskins before, they'd probably enjoyed it.

Large sections of the outpost's defences were still standing: the lumen towers looked undamaged and operational, and they would need to come back and see whether the greenskins had figured out how to turn them on or whether they were automated. A night approach would be greatly aided if those weren't on. Although the battlement wall had been damaged, blasted in by probable rocket attacks in several places, all but one of the heavy bolter emplacements along the rampart seemed to be in place.

'The greenskins charged straight across the minefield,' Trast said from beside Aldalon.

Aldalon nodded. 'The schematics in the briefing showed the minefield laid out in a standard segmented pattern. Doesn't look like they've triggered them all. We can use that.'

'Outpost still looks defensible,' Trast said.

Aldalon nodded again. The orks had obviously used their numbers to overrun the Imperial forces as was their usual approach, but surely even the most inept Guardsmen could hold that outpost against this many orks charging through a clearing of mines, throwing themselves at the vehicle barrier, razor wire fence and then the high wall? It would have been a frontal swarm of green targets.

Scattered amongst the ork dead were small, human forms. The Skadi Second Infantry, all of them but for the one they'd been forced to bring with them, had been tossed over the side of the outpost wall and left in a messy pile at the base. Uniforms soiled with dried blood, tangled limbs both attached and detached from their bodies, decapitated heads. Aldalon may not have thought much of soft-world Guardsmen but the sight of xenos scum treating dead humans with less dignity than they deserved still caused a rise of anger. It was then that he noticed something else. To the east of the outpost, where the treeline and fence were closer, the fence looked to have been breached much more cleanly. A rumble of distaste rose in Aldalon's throat.

'Emperor's Throne,' he muttered beneath his breath.

'What is it, sir?' Trast asked.

Aldalon pointed to what he'd seen. 'Look there, the greenskins flanked them.'

A major frontal offensive was expected but then a smaller force had moved in from the side to take advantage of the distraction. Aldalon saw from Lieutenant Trast's expression that he too understood the implication.

One of these green bastards is a little smarter than usual.

'Get your count,' Aldalon said.

Trast nodded, pulling his magnoculars from his webbing. He took a moment and then lowered his magnoculars. 'Half a dozen up on the rampart. Another group of ten I can see inside the outpost through the breach in the south wall. I think we're safe to estimate sub-one hundred.'

'Confirmed. Let's head back.'

The two Catachans continued on for a short while before Aldalon heard voices. Gruff voices. Ork voices. Twigs snapped, leaves crunched and undergrowth swished as it was pushed aside without care. Aldalon shot his hand up in a fist and then sank as low as he could without going prone, still wanting to keep his eyes above the undergrowth. The sound was coming closer, the muted ork chatter solidifying into understandable words.

'Why is we doin' dis anyway? When I said I wanna krump I mean I wanna krump humies not krump trees.'

'We is doin' it coz the boss said we 'ave to do it.'

Aldalon signalled for Trast to come closer. The lieutenant, staying in a crouch, moved slowly and silently until he was beside the colonel, both of them remaining completely still behind a large, fernlike plant.

'Simultaneous takedown,' Aldalon whispered.

Lieutenant Trast looked concerned. 'Sir,' he said, 'I think we should leave them be. Maintain concealment and let them pass. I'm certain we can keep out of sight.'

Aldalon looked at Trast. His face betrayed the fact that he wanted to berate the lieutenant for arguing with him, but he kept his voice low. 'Pincer, I'll go right, you go left.'

Despite the colonel's obvious displeasure, Lieutenant Trast tried again. 'Sir, you're normally happy for my input. In this case I think we should keep the initiative.'

Aldalon pinched his lips in angry frustration. Normally he might take his lieutenant's advice, but not today. The two orks were approaching.

'Ain't nothin' gonna be out 'ere.'

'Just shut up and keep lookin.'

'I'm lookin'. I'm lookin' at trees.'

Aldalon looked at Trast. 'Your objection is noted. Two-man pincer, silent takedown. You're left. I'm right. On my mark. Clear?'

Trast nodded. 'Sir.'

Aldalon waited, watching in the direction of the ork voices. He soon caught sight of the movement he was looking for. Off to their two o'clock. The orks were moving with such disdain for any sort of noise or movement discipline that the entire jungle, from the smallest rotting leaf to the trees extending out of the canopy, seemed to gyrate from side to side with their every step.

He soon caught sight of the greenskins themselves. There had only been two voices and he quickly confirmed it was two orks. They moved abreast, trampling through the dense foliage, the blue on their clothing, weapons and skin standing out as completely unnatural against the green all around them. They were going to walk straight across in front of them.

Aldalon looked sideways at Trast. His lieutenant was right: if they dropped to the ground, those idiotic creatures would stomp by without a single look in their direction. Still, Aldalon gritted his teeth. The only thing he could think of that would be better than keeping the initiative right now would be the chance to murder an ork. He gestured for Trast to move forward. And, like a good solider, Trast didn't argue again. He followed his orders, slowly drew his knife from the sheath at the back of his belt, and headed off to the left.

Colonel Aldalon moved like a predator of Catachan, a venomous spine-backed blood-leech or a neurotoxin-wielding death viper stalking prey, terrifyingly quiet. He advanced in an arc around the path of the approaching orks to be ready to attack from the right-hand side. He dropped into a crawl, creeping forward inch by inch until he was positioned beneath one of the large, wide-leafed ground-covering plants, lying in wait for his moment to strike.

Orks were not creatures well suited to patrol. They had the intelligence of a fencepost and attention as changeable as the wind, and whenever they were sent out in groups of more than one their discipline was sure to deteriorate into arguments and fighting relatively quickly. In fact, Aldalon would not have been surprised if a single ork managed to start fighting with itself if left alone long enough. The two orks seemed completely unaware of the purpose of what they were supposed to be doing, trudging along shouting at each other and paying no attention to the jungle around them. Not only were they not keeping watch they were obviously oblivious to the nearby danger of Catachans lying in wait.

'Nah, I is gonna krump more humies than you, ya git,' the ork on Aldalon's side was saying.

'Zog off you is,' the other ork snapped back. 'I krumped loads of dem in their town.'

'Dey weren't even fightin' humies, some of 'em was so tiny,' the first ork said. 'Back on dat stinking-hot sand planet I krumped loads more humies than you and I is gonna do that again.'

Aldalon had called for a silent takedown, a common approach when the Catachans wanted to maintain the element of surprise. According to standard operating procedure he and Lieutenant Trast should wait until the orks had passed and then carefully move out of concealment before swiftly attacking from behind, drawing their razor-sharp serrated Catachan knives across the tough, ropey flesh of the greenskins' throats. Dropping to the ground with them to soften the fall of their bodies and, particularly in the case of orks, removing their heads to make sure the deed was done. Sometimes death had a bad habit of not sticking to orks as well as it should.

But as he watched the greenskins Aldalon felt fury boil inside him. Thumping blood rushed his ears. The hot urge to fight filled him. He wanted to kill these orks. He wanted them to die. He wanted all orks to die. Aldalon had called for a silent takedown. He had ordered Trast to do that, but instead of following his own orders, Aldalon, as if the fury inside him were guiding his movements, rose from his prone position directly in front of the two xenos and charged at them in sudden, roaring rage.

Aldalon had been so well camouflaged that as far as the orks were aware, a charging, shouting, power fist-wielding human just seemed to appear in front of them, and they were both momentarily shocked into stunned silence. Ork brains were not wired for carefully attentive patrols – but they were wired for fighting. The greenskins' surprise lasted only a moment before Aldalon's charge triggered something deep inside their genetic coding, the singular instinct for an ork to match aggression with aggression.

Aldalon saw the moment their wide eyes changed. The red marbles shoved into the green dough of their faces lit up like it was only fighting that switched them on. The two orks' brows crunched down in anger, their teeth bared, and they roared. But Colonel Haskell 'Hell Fist' Aldalon gave them no quarter for their brief moment of inaction and he fell on the first of the orks as it was grabbing for its weapon. Aldalon had charged his power fist while he had been lying in wait and now it crackled with energy as he squeezed its knuckles tightly. He struck the ork in the face with all his servo-assisted might.

As far as non-genetically enhanced humans went Aldalon was strong, and with the strength amplification of the power fist he hit hard. Hard enough to cave the ork's face in beneath the blow, its skull fracturing, red blood spraying in a fine mist in all directions. But it was the disruption field of the fist that added even more damage. In the carnage of the strike it was too small to see, but as the fist impacted, the high-frequency energy that arced around it began tearing the molecules of the ork apart. Like a microscopic shock wave moving ahead of the massive gauntlet, the energy caused atoms to vibrate so aggressively that they burst apart. Flesh erupted. Muscle fibres shredded. Bone disintegrated. With this added destructive power, Aldalon's forceful punch ploughed through the ork's head until the creature's brain was crushed beyond even a greenskin's ability to heal.

Seeing Colonel Aldalon's mad attack, Lieutenant Trast scrambled to his feet to engage the second ork. Even as its colleague's brain was being crushed into mushroom soup the second ork was already in motion. It lifted its slugga and aimed it at Aldalon's head. Aldalon leant back out of the way as the ork squeezed the trigger. Trast slammed into the ork with a shoulder charge. The slugga fired with an overly loud boom, but the shot flew overhead into the thick jungle canopy.

The ork stumbled but recovered quickly to spin and take aim at Trast. Aldalon's power fist shot out and clamped on the ork's slugga, squeezing and crushing the chunky barrel. The ork tried to fire, but the crushed barrel caused the rudimentary pistol to backfire, shattering the slugga and sending jagged metal spraying back and embedding into the ork's arm. The ork howled, not in pain but anger, ripping the destroyed weapon from Aldalon's power fist and swinging it at his face. Aldalon brought his fist around to block the blow. The ork swung its arm back for a second strike, but Lieutenant Trast appeared and drove his Catachan knife hilt-deep into the ork's throat, the end of the sharp blade protruding out the other side.

Aldalon slammed his power fist into the ork's face, not fully charged with crackling energy this time but enough to send the creature sprawling onto its back in the wet, green undergrowth. Aldalon dropped onto it, straddling it on his knees. He punched the ork in the face once, twice, three times. He opened his power fist and slammed it down over the ork's busted face, grabbing its skull.

Aldalon squeezed. Letting out a primal growl he clenched his fingers. The power fist that perpetually wrapped his hand responded, and with its amplified strength it crushed the ork's head, folding both sides of the greenskin's skull together like an empty ration tin. Red and green ichor leaked out from the ork's mouth, eye sockets and nostrils. Its arms and legs twitched spasmodically before falling still. Colonel Aldalon looked up, huffing deep heaving breaths.

Lieutenant Trast stared at him. He didn't say anything, but he didn't need to. The question was written across his face: *what in the Emperor's name was that, colonel?*

CHAPTER THIRTEEN

NOGROK

Nogrok sat on the battlement wall dangling his legs over the side as he looked out at the jungle. He and his kommandos were always the only ones keeping watch. Sure, Gutstompa had been sending a few boyz out on patrol, but none of them had any idea what to do. They just wandered around the jungle, where you couldn't see your own mitts in front of your face, making a racket. It was getting dark now, but Ruktug had found a switch that turned on the big lights so the whole area around the outpost was lit up like the middle of the day. Weren't no humies going to be sneaking up on them now.

Nogrok could hear the rest of the warband inside the outpost, what was left of them anyway. They'd been celebrating their victory over the humies ever since they killed the last one and chucked it over the wall by looting everything they could. Warboss Gutstompa wanted them to find all the dakka they could before they attacked the humie city.

Nogrok looked down at the clearing littered with bodies. He did a quick calculation: there were loads of dead boyz out there and that meant there was probably that many loads less in the warband now. He shook his head. Stupid Gutstompa. He had wasted too many boyz taking this tiny humie base. None of the nobz or warbosses ever cared how many boyz they lost when they fought. Neither did Nogrok to be honest, but he knew that if they wanted to attack that humie city down in the valley they needed more boyz than they had. If Gutstompa had just listened to him Nogrok reckoned his taktiks would have got half as many orks dead. That would have meant, like, half loads dead.

Nogrok had lost two of his kommandos during the attack. Urkgob got messed up by the humies' big dakka that was just shooting like crazy into the smoke. Just bad luck that one. Mork rolled his dice and got a dead 'un. Grimguk, on the other hand, got blood crazy and went charging into the humies like all of the Deathskulls gitz and got himself krumped. Serves him right for not doing taktiks.

Below him, the stack of humie bodies was beginning to smell. Humies smelled disgusting when they were alive but once they were dead and starting to rot, they smelled heaps better. Nogrok inhaled deeply through his wide, flat nose, savouring the odour. Dead humie smelled good, like a years-old squig pit. He was gonna make more of that smell.

Nogrok turned at the sound of metallic thumps behind him: hissing, squealing hydraulic steps. Warboss Gutstompa was coming up the stairs. When the massive ork reached the rampart he saw Nogrok and his brow descended in a scowl. He took a swig from the cup in his hand, his huge green fingers almost engulfing the whole thing.

'Evenin',' boss,' Nogrok said, even though what he wanted to say was *evenin', you stupid git.*

The warboss' reply was a rumbling growl in his throat. 'Wot you doin', Blood Axe? Why ain't you–' The warboss paused, waited, then let out a long rolling burp. 'Why ain't you drinkin' to our victory and getting loot like I told ya?'

'Just keepin' watch for any humies coming for a fight.'

'Why you always doin' that?' the warboss snarled. 'We don't need you doin' that. We gonna go get the fight.'

'Humies love to do a counter-attack, boss,' Nogrok said. He stopped himself from asking whether the warboss knew what a counter-attack even was.

'Counter-attack. Dat sounds like some dumb humie stuff. You humie-lovin' Blood Axe git. Orks only care about one type of attack, and dat's proper attackin.''

'The humies will want this base back. They gonna attack soon coz they know loads of your boyz 'ave been krumped.'

Warboss Gutstompa's red eyes thinned. 'Wot you talkin' bout loads of my boyz got krumped? Who you think you are? Some krumped countin' git? I ain't had loads of my boyz krumped.'

'Uh,' Nogrok said, gesturing to the clearing in front of them.

'Wot? Dat's not loads. Dat's only heaps. Besides, we got more boyz on the way now we've got hold of this humie base. You wait an' see. More boyz'll show up. And soon, after we krump even more humies and take dat city down there, my warband is gonna become a proper Waaagh! before you even knows it.' As if suddenly remembering who he was talking to, the warboss growled again. 'I don't 'ave to tell you nothin' anyway. You just do as I say.'

More heavy footsteps sounded on the stairs – not quite the pounding thumps of Gutstompa's hydraulic legs but loud enough that it had to be a big ork – and moments later Nob Jaggedteef, the second largest ork in the warband, came onto the rampart.

'Boss,' Jaggedteef said as he spotted Gutstompa. 'I sent two boyz out on a patrol round the jungle and they ain't come back.'

'Probably off drinkin' then,' Gutstompa said.

'Nah, boss,' Jaggedteef said, 'the next patrol of boyz found 'em. They been krumped.'

'Wot?!' Gutstompa said, displaying much more emotion than when he'd looked out at all the dead ork boyz littered over the approach to the outpost. 'Was there fightin' I missed out on?'

'Ah, I think so, boss, maybe just a little bit. Didn't look like they krumped each other,' Jaggedteef said.

'Was it humies?' Gutstompa asked. Nogrok didn't miss the sidelong glance he gave him as he asked this.

'Dunno. Da 'eads was squished pretty good. Must be a big humie if it was.'

Gutstompa growled again. He was always grumblin' and growlin'. 'Dem sneaky humies sneakin' round in da jungle. Dey think they is proper kunnin'. Stupid gitz. Don't know how to do a proper fight.'

Nogrok thought about humies sneakin' around out there in the jungle. He'd seen orks sneaky-killed when they were on that sweaty, gritty desert planet. He wondered whether it could be the same humies they'd faced then, those Catachan humies. Secretly, he hoped it was. They were his favourite humies. They was proper sneaky humies. Jaggedteef said the other boyz had had their heads squished. That sounded like it might be the Catachan big boss. He was like a proper warboss with his big bit of power fist kit. Nogrok never got a chance to fight that power fist humie back then, but maybe, just maybe, if those same humies were here on this stinky, wet jungle planet he'd get his chance to try to kill the power fist humie this time.

'Right then,' Gutstompa said, seeming to come to a decision. 'Jaggedteef, send out two more boyz wot can see if dey can find any more humies sneakin' about. I wanna find dem and show 'em a real fight.'

'Boss,' Nogrok said.

The huge head of the warboss turned to Nogrok. The corner of his dark green lip twitched up to reveal the roots of his sharp yellowed teef. His red eyes shone with scorn and one of his pointed ears twitched with barely contained agitation. Warboss Gutstompa was giving Nogrok the look of contemptuous anger that instantly closed the mouths of most orks, those conditioned by instinct to the greenskins' overall guiding principles of bigger is better and might makes right – but, as should already be quite clear, Nogrok was an outlier when it came to ordinary orkiness.

'I ain't talkin' to you, Nogrok,' the warboss said, attempting to ignore him by turning back to Jaggedteef. 'Is that clear, Jaggedteef? Find me those stinkin' humie gitz.'

'Sure is, boss,' the nob replied. 'I'll send a couple of my best boyz out. I'll send Flogga and Snaga. They proper good at killin' humies. If dere really is humies hangin' around out dere those two'll find 'em.'

Flogga and Snaga, Nogrok thought, those thieving gitz. They weren't good at nothing. Patrols weren't gonna do anything anyway. The humies already knew they were here – that's what Nogrok had been trying to tell Gutstompa. The humies would launch a counter-attack any time. They needed to stay here being ready. Anyway, Flogga and Snaga would probably go out there and the same thing would happen to them. They would get proper smashed. That humie warboss with the power fist would use it to crush their stupid git heads in too. Flogga was the zoggin' git that stole his favourite Catachan knife, and Nogrok wanted nothing but to see him dead, but he wanted to be the one to kill him. Plus, if that git went out in the jungle and got himself krumped then Nogrok would never get his good cutta back.

'Boss,' Nogrok said, trying to get Gutstompa's attention again. 'Boss.'

Gutstompa growled and spun to look at the Blood Axe kommando like a parent completely fed up with question after question after question. 'What?' he shouted. 'What do you zoggin' want? Why you always got to talk to me, you Blood Axe git? I dunno why I ever picked you and your mob up.'

'Dat's what I said,' Jaggedteef added, unnecessarily if you asked Nogrok.

'Boss, I just want to point out, sendin' out a two-ork patrol is exactly the same as what you did last time, and they got krumped.'

'Are you sayin' I'm a dumb git?' Gutstompa said.

'Nah, boss, not at all.' Yes, though, absolutely completely. 'I just thought I'd suggest some taktiks to get the humies to come to us.'

'I don't need nothin' from you,' Gutstompa said. He looked at Jaggedteef. 'You know what to do when I get sick of listenin' to this git, Jaggedteef.'

Nogrok turned to see Jaggedteef's large fist plummeting towards his face once again. It slammed into the bridge of his nose and Nogrok felt something crunch before his oddly shaped fungus brain slammed into his thick but porous ork skull. Nogrok slumped to the ground in a floppy heap of green flesh, dazed but not completely unconscious yet.

'Should I just kill 'im?' Jaggedteef asked.

'Nah,' Gutstompa said. 'He is a proper git but what 'e did attackin' this base from the side was real kunnin' stuff.' Gutstompa threw Jaggedteef a sharp look. 'Don't you tell 'im I said dat.'

'Nah, course not, boss.'

Gutstompa was quiet for a while as he stared out at the clearing between the outpost and the edge of the jungle. 'Oi,' he eventually said to Jaggedteef, 'you reckon that's heaps of dead boyz or loads?'

That was when unconsciousness took Nogrok.

CHAPTER FOURTEEN

NOGROK

This time when Nogrok came groggily back to consciousness, opening one eye and then the other, he was looking up at the light blue sky. It took only a moment to realise he was lying flat on his back on the rampart. He knew exactly what had happened. That Jaggedteef git had thumped him again.

He sat up quickly, this time not with the urge to immediately fight back like before – though he did have that urge, he just had something else more important on his mind. As he suspected, Jaggedgit and Gitstompa were gone, and if those two giant zoggin' gitz were gone then Jaggedteef would have already sent Flogga and Snaga out on their patrol to try to find the humies – and Nogrok wasn't going to miss this opportunity to be rid of them.

Nogrok descended the stairs into the noise and stink of an outpost meant for less than fifty humies but occupied by double that number of unwashed, drunken, rowdy orks whose satisfaction with having done some fighting was wearing off and who were all growing itchy for another bloody good fight – even if that meant it needed to be with one another. He was jostled around in the overcrowded space, ignoring aggressive pushes and insults hurled at him in attempts to provoke a response worthy of a brawl.

Eventually he spotted Flik. The small ork was similarly ignoring shouted insults, though these were a little more well earned as Flik, with his small stature, had decided that the quickest way to navigate the throng of orks was to just run over the top of them, jumping from shoulders to shoulders to head. Nogrok called to Flik, who turned to see him and changed direction, kicking off the back of one ork's head, and made it across the crowd to him, dropping back down to the ground.

'Boss,' Flik said, 'where ya been?'

'Up the top,' Nogrok said, purposely choosing to exclude the part where he'd been knocked out by Jaggedteef again. 'Listen, you 'eard anythin' about Flogga and Snaga goin' out on a patrol?'

'Yeah, those gitz left not long ago.'

Nogrok turned and began pushing his way through the crowd to the exit. He had his slugga on his waist and his second-best cutta hanging from his belt; that was all he was gonna need.

'Nogrok,' Flik called after him. 'Whatcha doin'?'

Nogrok ignored Flik as he hurried outside. As he passed a mekboy who had his head deep inside a busted Deff Dread, Nogrok grabbed a tin of black grease from the bench-top, twisted the lid off and plunged his fingers inside. He let the tin drop and then drew his fingers in chaotic slashes across his face, drawing thick lines of goopy black. He pulled out his cutta and plunged into the jungle on the hunt for Flogga and Snaga.

It wasn't a hunt that was overly challenging. The two orks were some way in front of him but not far enough that it was difficult to pick up their trail. In fact, as he moved through the dense jungle, as swiftly as he could while maintaining quiet, he knew he could have followed these stupid zoggin' gitz even if they were halfway across the planet. They had ploughed forward, slashing and crashing their way through the trees in an obvious path of orkish destruction. Of course, the trail could have been made by any of the groups of orks Gutstompa and Jaggedteef had sent out on patrol, except for one thing that made it real obvious he was following the path of Flogga and Snaga: he could hear their dumb voices. Not only were they speaking to each other, boasting and arguing without giving a single thought to trying to keep quiet so the humies didn't hear them, but also the zoggin' idiots was even shouting out for the humies like they thought they was trained squigs what might come when they were called.

''Ere, humie humie humie,' Nogrok could hear Snaga yelling into the jungle. 'Come out, come out, wherevers you at.'

'Yeah,' Flogga called soon after, 'we got a nice surprise for you, some real tasty food that is for humies and definitely not for orks.'

'Dat's right, humie food 'ere and not orks wot gonna krump ya.'

Nogrok drew closer, keeping low, using camouflage and concealment and all the silent movement he'd practised to remain undetected by the patrolling pair, not that they would notice much. Once, when moving towards them, he'd grown a little complacent and stepped on a large rotten tree branch that was hidden under a pile of dead leaves. It broke in two with a sudden, loud crack. Nogrok froze in place. The sound had pinged through the jungle, splitting the normal sounds with its brief intensity right in a lull when Flogga and Snaga had stopped speaking or calling out. Nogrok expected the jungle around him to burst with shots from the orks' shootas and for him to burst right along with it. Nogrok waited, listening for the response.

'What was dat?' Flogga asked.

Nogrok slowly lowered towards the ground, hoping he could avoid enough of their shoota shots to fight back. He gripped the dirty leather-wrapped handle of his slugga where it was holstered at his waist.

'What was wot?' he heard Snaga reply.

'Dat noise?' Flogga said.

'Wot noise?'

'Dat one.'

'Dat's you talkin,' ya git.'

'Nah, listen,' Flogga said. He paused, listening. 'I can't 'ear it now.'

'Yeah,' Snaga said. 'Dat's coz you weren't talkin.'

'Never mind. Come on.'

The two orks moved away. Nogrok shook his head. How were these two gitz higher up the warband food chain than he was? Still, that wouldn't be a problem for long. He was about to make sure of that. The only food chain they would be part of was fertiliser for some jungle plants. Nogrok had crept after the pair of orks again, trailing them further out from the humie outpost, waiting for the perfect opportunity to strike. His Gorkish desire for revenge, the desire to smash these two gitz in the backs of the heads as loudly as possible right now was, as always, difficult to ignore. But Nogrok focused on the Mork in him.

With patience almost beyond belief for a greenskin Nogrok followed Flogga and Snaga through the jungle for close to two hours. Eventually, Nogrok's proper good kunnin' was rewarded when he overheard Snaga.

'Oi,' the ork said, 'look at dis.'

'Wot?' Flogga said as he came over to where Snaga had stopped.

The two of them were looking down at something on the ground.

'It's an ork,' Flogga said.

'I know it's an ork, ya git. I'm an ork. Wot's 'e doin' 'ere? Is dere another warband 'ere?'

'I don't know. I ain't an expert on warbands.'

'You ain't an expert on nothin.''

'Let's just see if 'e got any gubbinz,' Flogga said.

'I found 'im,' Snaga said. 'You go see if dere's any other gitz like dis around.'

'Whatever,' Flogga replied, 'I'll look over 'ere.'

Flogga wandered a short distance away, looking around for any other ork bodies to loot. Snaga bent down, searching the corpse in front of him.

Nogrok watched Flogga for a moment, making sure the ork was paying as little attention as he hoped, and then crept, with even greater care than he had shown so far, towards Snaga.

Nogrok moved like a shadow, a green, parthenogenetic fungal shadow. A ghost ork. When he was almost within striking range, he slowly slipped his cutta from its sheath, very aware that soon he was gonna have his good Catachan cutta back. This cutta was practically blunt compared to that one. Still, it would be sharp enough for this.

He gently pushed aside the curtain of ropey vines drooping down from a branch overhead – the last cover before Snaga was right ahead of him. Nogrok led with the point of his blade, slipping it through the vines first and following with his body. When he was a step away from initiating the kill, Snaga's head snapped up and he turned to look behind him. Some orkish instinct had triggered at the last moment to tell him either he was about to get into a fight or about to get killed.

Nogrok, with no choice now, leaped on Snaga's back, wrapping one arm around the ork's face, covering his mouth as best as he could as he brought his cutta blade up to Snaga's neck. Snaga twisted, trying to shake Nogrok off like a squig mounted for the first time desperately trying to dislodge its grot rider. But Nogrok hung on.

He felt the serrations of his cutta bite into Snaga's throat and he maintained pressure, dragging the blade and opening a cut across the larger ork's windpipe. But Snaga's hands flew up and grabbed at Nogrok's knife arm, managing to hold it at bay. Snaga's strength proved too much for Nogrok and he managed to pull the knife blade away. Nogrok cursed. He'd managed to cut into Snaga's neck but not enough for it to be fatal, probably not even enough to take him down; it was barely bleeding. Nogrok was also well aware that this silent takedown kill had been neither silent nor resulted in a kill. Plus, with Snaga stumbling under him he hadn't even managed the takedown part.

As Snaga continued to thrash beneath Nogrok, he eventually stepped too far and tripped over the dead ork, causing him to slam heavily to the ground. Snaga lost his grip on Nogrok's cutta arm and Nogrok took full advantage.

He jammed the tip of the blade into the side of Snaga's neck. As Snaga desperately tried to buck and writhe, Nogrok used a sawing motion to rip his blade out the front of Snaga's throat.

The result was a torrent of hot red blood that gushed onto the ground, sprayed further by Snaga's gurgling gasps. Nogrok maintained his grip over Snaga's mouth until the ork's thrashing eventually stopped. Nogrok knew that had not gone well and he was certain Flogga had heard, and sure enough the second ork called out.

'Oi,' Flogga's voice called through the trees, 'wot you doin' to dat dead 'un?'

Nogrok didn't move, and neither did Snaga because he was, thankfully, dead. When there was no reply Flogga called out again.

'Snaga? Wot you doin,' ya git?' Flogga paused. 'Right. I'm comin' over.'

Nogrok climbed off Snaga and moved to the side, keeping low. He readied his knife. Just as he hoped, when Flogga breached the thick foliage the first thing he saw was Snaga's body on the ground in a pool of dark blood. That sight was enough to keep him from noticing Nogrok, wearing camouflage and crouching low in brush nearby. Flogga held Nogrok's Catachan knife in his hand. It was beautiful. Nogrok couldn't wait to get it back.

'Humies!' Flogga called. 'Get out 'ere.'

Nogrok couldn't help himself. 'Nah, not humies.'

'Wot in the name of Gork and Mor–' Flogga started as he turned in the direction of Nogrok's voice, but Nogrok erupted from his concealed position to take advantage of the other ork's confusion.

Nogrok slammed shoulder first into Flogga and despite the other ork being larger, Nogrok hit with enough force to send him sprawling onto his back. Nogrok jammed his blade, still wet with Snaga's blood, hard up under Flogga's chin, and slammed it into his head.

Flogga's wide eyes showed recognition as he grunted, gulped and gasped against the steel blade shoved up into his jaw, through the roof of his mouth and into his brain. Nogrok was glad. He wanted him to know who had done this. He wanted the git to know this was payback. He reached across and grabbed the Catachan knife from where it had fallen to the ground nearby. He held it up in front of Flogga's face.

'Dis is mine, you thievin' Deffskulls git.'

Then he turned his grip on his reacquired favourite cutta so that it was pointed at Flogga's face. He lifted the knife and drove it hard into Flogga's right eye, slicing through his eyeball with a squelch, feeling it grind against the thick bones of his eye socket, cutting its way through skull with its sharp edges and plunging straight into Flogga's stupid gitty brain. That was two Deathskulls gitz he wouldn't have to worry about any more. He yanked the Catachan knife free and wiped it on Flogga's shirt. He held it up, smiling, and saw his black-striped face reflected in the shiny blade.

CHAPTER FIFTEEN

TORVIN

Torvin had spent several nights on Gondwa VI now and none of them had been comfortable. The night on this world seemed just as hot and thick with humidity as the day.

Back home on Skadi, when the sun dropped below the horizon the temperature plummeted, resulting in nights that were bitterly cold. Of course, this presented challenges of its own, but at least inside the hab-blocks and houses citizens could huddle around the warmth of a geothermal-tapped vent, a powered heater or a coal hearth if they lived in the lower levels not blessed with electricity. You could wear thermal layers beneath your clothes, wrap yourself in blankets or animal furs to seal in your body heat. It was possible, despite the dark ice and howling winds outside, to warm oneself. Here though, there seemed to be no escape: day or night the heat was oppressive and inescapable. There were only so many layers of clothing one could remove.

Initially, Torvin had slept in the high-ceilinged chapel with the rest of the bunked-down Skadi Second. At the time he had considered this uncomfortable, lying on a bedroll over the hard stone, the heat of the planet amplified by the hundreds of warm bodies sharing the space, the air filled with the grunts, snores and smells of soldiers. Then he'd slept at Outpost Four, which had been much the same but with his sleep interrupted by his watch schedule, and of course then the orks had come. After that, it had only got worse when he was sent to the Ecclesiarchy cells beneath the chapel. There he'd been locked into a stone box for the treatment of heretics, a space where he couldn't even lie down, and had been forced to sleep propped against the slimy wall with his legs tucked up. Rest had been difficult to come by in that place. He would wake regularly as one part of his body or another went numb beneath him or succumbed to the pressure of the stone and demanded he adjust his position. He hadn't thought sleeping conditions could be worse than that, but now, here he was in the jungle.

The Catachans were lying in their concealed positions; half of them would sleep while the other half kept watch and then they would switch. Torvin had been told in no uncertain terms that he was just to stay in his position, eat something and then sleep; that he should keep silent and not do anything stupid.

That didn't bother him in the slightest. He was exhausted. He felt like he'd barely had any rest since he'd been on this Emperor-forsaken planet and the Catachans had moved at an absolutely relentless pace. Still, as he slipped beneath the tarpaulin, he quickly realised this was even worse than his dungeon cell. Sure, he could stretch out here but when he did, he felt nothing but damp plants and sticky mud beneath him. More than once he was sure he could feel things crawling against his skin and there seemed a constant swarm of flying insects that invaded his shelter and buzzed around his face.

It wasn't just this humid, wet, crawling bed that made this night worse than all the others, though. It was actually trying to sleep in the jungle. He'd looked out from the outpost at the crushing darkness of the jungle unable to determine what might be in there, but now he was part of it, right in the darkness and the fear. As night fell, the thick blackness was all around him. He could see barely a few yards and in the dark, the sounds of insects buzzing and chirping and things moving through the dense foliage seemed a hundred times louder. He didn't know what animals or dangerous creatures crept through these trees at night, but one thing he did know was that there were orks out there.

Torvin may have been struggling but he could see the Catachans were not. They had settled down in the mud and bugs and darkness like it was a soft bed - but no, that wasn't quite the right metaphor. The Catachans would scoff at the idea of a luxurious place to sleep. They were not behaving as if they were in plush surrounds, they were behaving as if they were exactly where they were - in sticky, wet jungle; they just loved it. They were jungle animals themselves.

From the darkness to Torvin's right came the sound of two sharp clicks. At first Torvin tried to ignore it, thinking it was some insect or bizarre jungle creature. It was probably best if he didn't look; there were doubtless things out there it was better not to see. Or maybe he should look. He didn't really know which was worse. But when the clicks sounded again, in the same deliberate rhythm - twice then a break, twice then a break - he turned in that direction.

He was shocked to see a Catachan trooper emerge from the darkness. He hadn't heard any sign of his approach. He was holding a small box in his hand, a thin piece of domed metal on top. When the trooper pressed his thumb down, the metal popped in and out, click click. It was obviously some kind of signal the Catachans used to draw attention without having to speak, a signal that seemed to fit into the sounds of a night-time jungle. Torvin didn't know the trooper's name - he hardly knew any of their names because they hadn't bothered to introduce themselves. Torvin was under no illusions about how the Catachans felt about him. He wondered if it was any consolation to them that he didn't want to be here either.

The trooper signalled and it took a moment for Torvin to realise the signals were directed at him. He made a series of hand gestures at Torvin, moving fingers, his fist and then pointing out into the jungle ahead of them. Torvin stared, completely lost as to what the trooper was trying to say. The Catachan noticed the lack of comprehension on Torvin's face and sighed, setting his jaw in annoyed frustration. He moved through the undergrowth to where Torvin remained hunkered down in his concealed position beneath his camouflaged tarpaulin.

'Emperor-damn soft-worlder,' was the first thing the trooper said to Torvin, which was the standard greeting the Catachans had for him. 'Don't they teach other Guardsmen hand signals?'

'Yes,' Torvin said, suddenly feeling a desire, after the constant disparagement he'd heard from other Imperial Guard regiments, to defend himself and by extension the rest of the Astra Militarum, 'we learn hand signals, but clearly different ones to what they teach on Catachan.'

The trooper grunted. It seemed to Torvin he had no response, but it certainly wasn't a sound of acceptance. 'I said I'm going out into the jungle. I don't expect to be long and that means don't shoot me when I come back. If you know which end the las-bolts come out of that is.'

'Whatever,' Torvin said.

The Catachan trooper actually smiled and gave a single breathy laugh. Torvin hadn't yet got a read on how serious the Catachans were. They seemed ready to murder him in his sleep and each and every one of them had a look in their eyes which made them seem capable of snapping into psychosis at any point. Or maybe they were just trying to scare him. As Torvin watched the trooper move away in the dark, he swallowed. He hoped they were just hazing him, but he felt a very real undercurrent of fear that they absolutely weren't.

Just as he'd said, it didn't take long for the Catachan Jungle Fighter to return. Torvin had his head down, using the ring pull to crack the seal and peel the lid off a standard-issue Imperial Guard nutrient gruel ration.

As an Imperial Guardsman you will consume the Imperial Guard nutrient gruel ration, available in sixteen ready-to-eat flavours designed for easy field consumption. The Imperial Guard nutrient gruel ration contains all nutritional requirements for a fighting member of the Astra Militarum and has a shelf life of one hundred and sixty standard years. Note: if Imperial Guard nutrient gruel rations are consumed as a soldier's sole source of sustenance for longer than five consecutive days, adverse effects have been observed including but not limited to headaches, stomach upset, birth defects and heart failure.

Torvin used his FRED to dig out a semi-solidified spoonful of nutrient gruel and ferry it to his mouth. He chewed – a somewhat useless gesture on the already porridge-like paste – and swallowed, working his tongue to try to determine the flavour. It was a little like the boiled purple cabbage and fermented fish soup commonly eaten as a traditional meal on Skadi. He looked at the lid, which declared this nutrient gruel to be Garthar Roast Chicken flavour. With no idea where Garthar was or what a roast chicken was supposed to taste like, Torvin couldn't tell how good the flavouring was, but if he had to make an educated guess he'd say not very.

The sound of clicking from the jungle ahead of him drew Torvin's attention. Now that he was attuned to it, he easily recognised the sound. It came from somewhere in the darkness of the trees, getting progressively louder as it drew closer. Torvin put down his meal – for want of a better word – and picked up his lasgun from where it lay beside him, just in case.

He watched the darkness ahead of him. Click click. His eyes traced the lines of what trees he could see in the crushing black. Click click. His eyes strained, trying to catch a glimpse of movement, desperate to confirm that the sound really was the returning Catachan trooper. Click click. He saw a flicker and pointed his lasgun in the direction of the shifting shadows. The shape of the Catachan trooper emerged as if the thick darkness itself had coalesced into his form.

The trooper looked at Torvin. 'I said not to shoot me, soft-worlder.'

Torvin looked down and then relaxed his white-knuckled grip on the lasgun. 'Sorry.'

He realised his sudden nervousness was unwarranted, foolish even. If the orks somehow knew they were out here, they wouldn't announce their arrival with coded clicking; they'd announce their arrival the same way they always did, with roaring, howling war cries and a mad charge crashing through the trees.

Torvin watched as the trooper moved towards his position. It took Torvin a moment to realise he had something slung over his shoulders. When the trooper was close enough for Torvin's night-adjusted eyes to make out details, he saw that it was an animal of some sort, a long dark-scaled serpent-like creature, but one that had four pairs of legs along the length of its slender body, a lizard of some type.

The trooper lifted the creature from behind his head and placed it on the ground. He slipped the vicious Catachan knife from the sheath at his waist and beheaded the lizard with a quick, businesslike chop. With eight similar motions he removed the creature's legs. Lifting the lizard by the tail, the trooper ran the point of the blade down the length of the belly and then smoothly scooped out its innards with another run of the knife. A series of cuts at the tail and he took hold of the skin, pulling swiftly to rip the scaly surface layer from the white flesh, dropping it on the ground with the pile of still-warm internal organs.

After a cursory rinse with water from his canteen, the trooper cut the meaty body in half and tossed one half to another Catachan trooper who had emerged nearby. Then, the trooper who had been hunting lifted the lizard to his mouth and bit into it, using his teeth to tear into the raw stringy flesh. It came away in strips that he hastily gobbled down. As he was chewing he looked up at Torvin, who was staring at him. With a mouth full of raw lizard flesh he gestured with the remaining meat and spoke quietly.

'You want some?'

Torvin shook his head, looking down and spooning more of his gluggy Imperial Guard nutrient gruel ration into his mouth. The trooper moved closer, crouching and moving in beneath Torvin's shelter. He leant his face in close enough that Torvin could see the mashed lizard flesh between his teeth as he spoke, still chewing on the recently caught animal.

'What is that?' the trooper asked, looking down at the ration tin and the bland grey sludge inside.

Torvin was surprised. He'd thought this was one of the Catachan 57th's veteran soldiers. He certainly looked that way with the greying hair on his temples and the latticework of scars that covered his face and body. 'It's an official Imperial Guard ration,' Torvin said, 'the ones we're supposed to eat.'

The trooper reached out and snatched the tin from Torvin's hand. He turned it in his grip, looking it over, and without warning plunged two fingers into the contents, scooping out a small amount and licking if off to taste it. He worked his mouth and then made a face of disgust. 'I've never actually tasted one of these.' He tossed the tin back to Torvin, who caught it awkwardly. 'Won't be doing it again neither.'

'I thought they were standard-issue for all Imperial Guard,' Torvin said.

The Catachan trooper laughed. 'In case you haven't figured it yet, we Catachans ain't standard Imperial Guard. How many of those tins you got in your pack?'

'I don't know,' Torvin said, 'nine or ten.'

The trooper shook his head. 'Why would I carry all that extra weight around?' He lifted his partially eaten raw lizard. 'You can get food anywhere.' He took another bite. 'I'm going back to my hole. Enjoy your... whatever that is.' With that the trooper moved away into the dark.

Well, Torvin thought, sure, he'd watched a Catachan catch, kill and eat some raw jungle lizard that may or may not have been highly toxic, but at least he'd had something resembling a conversation with one of the Jungle Fighters. It hadn't just been a Catachan berating him for being a soft-worlder or an incompetent Guardsman or any of the usual things they said to him.

Torvin jumped as the trooper reappeared, spilling some of the nutrient gruel he was lifting to his mouth. He had emerged suddenly from the dark again.

'Oh, and by the way,' the trooper said. 'Just leave your lasgun alone. You've been put here so you don't have to guard anything. Don't touch your weapon again, soft-worlder. You might hurt yourself, or worse, one of us.'

The trooper vanished again. Torvin wiped the spilled Garthar Roast Chicken-flavoured nutrient gruel from his shirt and sighed; that seemed more like it.

Torvin had settled down to sleep, or at least attempt to sleep, when he next heard the voice of Colonel Aldalon.

'Circle up.'

Torvin tentatively emerged from his concealed position, his 'hole' as that other trooper had called it. He saw the power fist-wielding shape of the colonel. When his eyes adjusted, Torvin saw Aldalon was covered not just in camouflage but also in random splatters of blood, almost slightly luminescent in the dark. Ork blood. Torvin had seen enough of it in the battle over Outpost Four to recognise it. He watched the other Catachan Jungle Fighters emerge from their holes and so, guessing it was best if he followed orders too, he climbed out from under his tarp and joined them. Once the two squads were assembled, kneeling in an arc in front of the colonel, Aldalon spoke.

'We've had a run in with the greenskins,' Aldalon said. 'Took down a pair on patrol but we may have alerted others to our presence.' Torvin saw the way Lieutenant Trast looked sideways at Aldalon, but he wasn't sure what that meant. 'They probably won't notice a couple of their boyz not coming back from patrol but eventually they'll realise there's probably something in the jungle worth fighting. We're moving up the mission timetable and going on our first raid on the outpost now.'

Torvin swallowed. He had no idea whether that included him, but he didn't particularly want to go back and face the orks that he'd only just escaped from last time through right-place-right-time luck.

'Lieutenant Trast will accompany Sergeant Dram's squad. I will accompany Sergeant Sappa's squad. The first raid objective is still the same as outlined before we left. Sergeant Dram's squad to take east-side perimeter around the outpost, Sergeant Sappa's to take west. Our objective is to disable as much of the still-active security as possible. That includes cutting power to external systems like the lumen towers and any perimeter motion detectors, cutting tripwires, and mapping an approach to the outpost. I want to collect unexploded ordnance from the minefield too. Plus, we'll whittle down the ork numbers by taking out any patrols or sentries wandering too far from the outpost. You know what to do. Standard perimeter raid on a fixed position. Soften them up. Clear?'

The Catachans nodded. Torvin didn't know what to do, but he wasn't going to say anything. He still wasn't even sure all this included him, and they didn't just want him to stay here and not get in their way.

'Good,' Aldalon said. 'Break down camp, gather your equipment. We move out in fifteen.'

Torvin watched as the Jungle Fighters moved quickly and quietly, dismantling their carefully constructed concealed positions. They were just as deliberate at replacing the leaves and branches from their shelters back into the jungle as they were when they had built them. They scattered the foliage around, not wanting to leave any trace that they had been here at all.

It was a testament to the skill of the Jungle Fighters that the area was almost entirely unchanged from before they had arrived. As much as he didn't think their attitude towards Imperial Guardsmen from other worlds was entirely fair, he had to admit, if the Skadi Second Infantry had trudged through the jungle and camped here, there would be signs everywhere, flattened foliage, cut branches, firepits and probably even whole swathes of felled trees.

Torvin couldn't believe they were going on a raid now. Had the Catachans managed to get any sleep? He sure hadn't and Emperor knew, he was exhausted, barely able to stand. Did these Jungle Fighters ever need to rest?

'You too, soft-worlder – break down and get ready to move out.' Torvin turned to see Sergeant Sappa watching him. 'You deaf?'

'No, sergeant,' Torvin replied. 'I just wasn't sure whether that included me.'

'Colonel Aldalon put you in my squad, didn't he?'

'Yes, sergeant.'

'Well, my squad is going on a perimeter raid on the outpost,' Sappa said, 'so break down camp and gear up.'

'Yes, sergeant,' Torvin said. 'And sergeant?'

Sappa stopped as she was walking away and turned back. 'What?'

Torvin suddenly regretted speaking but swallowed down the lump in his throat and continued. 'My name isn't soft-worlder, it's Torvin.'

Sappa rubbed the bottom of her nose with her forefinger and then sniffed before turning and moving off to pack up her own camp and get her equipment.

Torvin moved as quickly as he could, doing his best to return the jungle plants he'd used as cover for his scrape to some approximation of where he'd found them. He thought he'd done a reasonable job, but he didn't miss the raised eyebrows and looks of derision from the Catachans watching him. He rolled his wet tarpaulin and stuffed it into his pack along with the rest of his equipment. It took him longer than the rest of the Catachans to finish. Sergeant Dram's squad had already moved out when he was ready and looked up to see Colonel Aldalon, Sergeant Sappa and all her squad waiting.

'Right,' Sappa said, 'let's move. Soft-worlder, you're just ahead of me.'

The squad, Colonel Aldalon in the lead, moved off into the dark, wet jungle.

After an hour of moving steadily forward, trying to advance as silently and carefully as the Catachans, Torvin saw Colonel Aldalon ahead. He'd brought them to a halt. Once he caught sight of Sergeant Sappa, the last in the line, he indicated with a circling finger for the squad to rally up.

'Devi, Whirler,' Aldalon whispered, 'you two, scout ahead but do not engage. I want to know if the lights are on and how many greenskins are on the rampart.'

The pair of troopers nodded and then headed into the jungle. Without being asked, the rest of the squad moved into defensive positions. Torvin did what he'd grown accustomed to already and sat down out of the way.

As he waited, Torvin pulled the pict of Melina from his pocket and unfolded it. The darkness in the jungle was thick now; the brighter of Gondwa VI's two moons had sunk below the hilly horizon and so there was almost no light penetrating through the canopy. Torvin unclipped a pouch on his webbing and pulled out his small, finger-sized flashlight. He clicked it on, shining the light down on Melina's face. She smiled at him, but now, her smile didn't seem so comforting.

In a shocking instant the flashlight was slammed from his hand in a mighty swat. Torvin reeled back, beginning to stammer out words of shocked surprise, but anything that might have escaped his throat was cut off as a powerful, mechanical grip closed around his neck. From the gloom, Colonel Aldalon had seized Torvin with his power fist.

Torvin grabbed at the power fist in a futile gesture to try to free himself as Aldalon squeezed and lifted him to his feet. Torvin spluttered against the crushing force engulfing his windpipe. The colonel slammed him back against the trunk of the closest tree. Torvin's legs dangled beneath him, tangling in hanging vines as he kicked.

Aldalon's face was a mask of rage. Torvin half expected lightning to fire from his mouth like some furious deity, but it was only furious words that emerged. Still quiet to maintain stealth, but that was perhaps even worse.

'What do you think you're doing breaking light discipline, you putrid little idiot?' Aldalon snarled. His free hand appeared bearing his Catachan knife, and it was suddenly pressed against Torvin's cheek, hard enough that it began to cut a line from mouth to ear. 'We are near the outpost. Well within range of wandering greenskins and you dare turn on a light. You do something as stupid as that again, you dare endanger my troops again, and I'll kill you.'

The power fist opened and Torvin dropped, choking, to the ground. He tried to whisper an apology, but managed nothing but vapid gasps. Around him the other Catachans had turned to look at the confrontation, but none had moved from their positions, except Sergeant Sappa.

'Sir,' she said, her voice low so as not to carry, 'go easy on him. He's just a soft-worlder. Perhaps we should leave him behind.'

Aldalon growled. 'Our orders are to bring him, so we bring him. I put him in your squad, so you get his head right.' Aldalon reached down with his power fist and picked up the flashlight from where it had fallen into the mud. He squeezed, crushing it between servo-driven metal fingers, the light flickering out, then dropped it in front of Torvin. Next, he plucked the pict off the ground and held it up to look at it. He turned his eyes to Torvin. 'Who is this?'

'Melina,' Torvin managed against the burn in his throat. 'We were to be married.' He swallowed, trying to push down the pain. 'Before I was tithed.'

Aldalon looked at him and then knelt. He slammed the pict up against Torvin's chest, forcing him to catch it. 'You are a Guardsman,' Aldalon said in his low rumble. 'You exist to kill xenos. If it isn't abundantly clear, I don't want you here. You are soft, but you better become hard very quickly or one way or another you will die.' He pointed to the pict still pinned to Torvin's chest. 'As soon as you were tithed, your life was over. Accept it. There isn't room for anything but war any more.'

Torvin sucked in a painful breath. 'What's the point then?'

'What?'

'What is the point of fighting,' Torvin said, 'if we aren't fighting for those we love?'

'The point,' Aldalon said, 'is to kill orks.' The colonel stood. 'The only thing you need to love any more is the Emperor and a fresh lasgun power pack.' He turned and walked away.

Torvin sat where he'd been dropped. He looked at the pict of Melina before folding it and putting it back in his pocket.

'Listen, soft-worlder,' Sappa said. 'My father is harsh but fair, you better listen.'

Torvin looked in the direction of the fading colonel. 'Aldalon is your father?'

Sappa nodded. 'I took my mother's name, wanted to make it as a Jungle Fighter without relying on him or his reputation. He's right though. Get your shit together or you'll have more to worry about than orks.'

CHAPTER SIXTEEN

ALDALON

The rain had started twenty minutes earlier as little more than a misty drizzle that drifted down and barely made it through the treetops, but it had intensified now into a powerful jungle downpour. It hammered through the canopy, slamming aside the initial shield of leaves like lasgun fire through simple ork armour. It pounded down on Squad Sappa of the Catachan 57th Jungle Fighters as they drew nearer the outskirts of Outpost Four.

'It's getting wet fast,' Sergeant Sappa said. 'We'll need to be careful with footing.'

Aldalon watched as the soft soil, always close to saturated anyway, turned to slushy mud and then became spotted with dark, ankle-deep puddles rapidly growing in width and depth.

'It'll mask our approach,' Aldalon said as heavy drops thundered down, leaving them drenched beneath the torrential shower. 'I've been on worlds as varied as you can imagine. Landscapes of lifeless rock and dust, worlds entirely covered with water or volcanoes, or cities that float on gas where there's no real planet at all, and you know what's always there?'

'What's that?' Sappa replied.

'Rain,' he said. 'Or something like it at least. In some places it's constant, in some almost non-existent. Sometimes it's acidic or methane instead of water. But there's always rain. Something falls onto the planet to wash it clean. At least as much as possible in this galaxy. The rain's on our side, sergeant. We are here to clean this place.'

Aldalon looked at Torvin, the soft-worlder. As the useless trooper's foot sank into a deep puddle he stumbled trying to pull it free, crashing forward and catching himself on the trunk of a thin tree. The whole thing shook and all that useless equipment he carried rattled around noisily in his pack.

Aldalon growled. Movement could be difficult in the rain, sure, but apparently it was more difficult for some than others. He should have squeezed harder on the soft-worlder's throat, should have killed him. How long until the imbecile drew attention to them? If they'd been facing any enemy but the orks he might have already alerted them.

Why in the God-Emperor's name did the rest of the Astra Militarum have such insufficient training in everything other than how to fill out paperwork? How had the Imperium stood against the constant barrage of foes if it was men like Trooper Torvin manning the defences? But Aldalon knew how.

It was because there were men and women from Cadia, men and women from Armageddon and Krieg and Elysia, and men and women like him, from Catachan.

They would hold the line for the Imperium when all the Trooper Torvins, Major General Nilloms and Governor Misoms folded.

After a short time Aldalon brought the squad to a halt again. He pulled out his small command data-slate. Apart from the few pieces of uniform he wore, trousers and a flak armour vest, there were only four pieces of equipment he carried that were officially issued to him by the Departmento Munitorum: his throat vox-mic, his plasma pistol, his power fist and his command data-slate.

His data-slate contained mission briefings, maps and intelligence reports, and was constantly uplinked to regimental headquarters when in the field – or at least it was supposed to be. He knew the magnetic field of this planet was reported to cause ongoing issues with communications. He was sure that would be blamed for his inability to get a signal back to Karoo City, but the truth was the uplink functionality on this thing barely worked on any planet, magnetic interference or not.

He checked the time: ten standard minutes until when he'd ordered Lieutenant Trast and Squad Dram to begin the raid. He would synchronise with them. If they were discovered and the orks attacked in response it was best they engaged the xenos on two fronts simultaneously.

'Trast and Dram will be waiting on the eastern side of the perimeter,' Aldalon said to Sergeant Sappa. 'There was a smaller breach through the fence there, a flanking attack.'

Sappa nodded. 'The soft-worlder confirmed your theory when I questioned him about it. There was a smaller group of orks that attacked from the east. He'd seen an ork in the trees too he said, an ork in camouflage.'

Aldalon knew none of those back at headquarters had believed Torvin, but despite him being from a useless, poorly trained regiment, Aldalon was not so quick to dismiss the soft-worlder's claims. All evidence suggested the orks had undertaken a concealed surgical strike to breach a heavily defended position already focused on a massed siege from another direction.

'Intelligence indicates at least some of these orks are the same ones we faced before,' Aldalon said.

'On Karst?'

Aldalon took a long breath. 'Yes, on Karst.'

'You think it's them, don't you? The orks who killed Brant.'

Aldalon was quiet. He'd been right beside Brant when the attack had happened on Karst, an ambush from orks even he hadn't seen lying in wait. One of them had pounced on Brant, slit his throat before he had a chance to react, an ork wearing camouflage. An ork that had later faded away in the heat of battle, but he remembered him – an ork with one red eye and one green eye.

'Ghost orks,' Sappa said. 'Apparently that's what other Guard regiments call them.'

'They'll be ghosts when we're done with them,' Aldalon said.

Devi and Whirler soon returned, confirming that the Outpost Four perimeter lumen towers were lit, casting bright light over the entire circumference of the clearing around the outpost. The minefield, tripwires and perimeter defence guns were within the range of that bright light. There was no way for an approaching enemy to breach the trees without a near certainty of being spotted. The lights were likely on a centralised timing switch – on at dawn, off at dusk. He doubted the orks would think to operate them if they were manually controlled. That made the first objective clear at least. They would need to find the power line into the outpost and cut it.

Aldalon swiped at the surface of his data-slate, stopping on the plans of the outpost he'd been provided with by the planetary government. They were old, dating from the time of the outpost's construction just short of a century earlier. He just had to hope they were still accurate. According to the plans there was a power transformer on the north side of the outpost, but it was hidden behind the outer wall. What he could see that was useful was the dotted path of the underground power line running into the facility. It extended in a north-east direction, almost impossible to find without these plans.

Aldalon keyed his throat mic. 'Trast, do you copy?'

The response was nothing but hissing static.

Aldalon looked to where Trooper Grast, the vox-trooper for Squad Sappa, waited nearby. Aldalon tapped his head, signalling for her to come to his position.

'Can you raise Lieutenant Trast?' Aldalon asked, keeping his voice low.

Grast slipped on her headset, checked the channel, then keyed the transmit button on the side. 'Squad Dram,' she said quietly but clearly, 'this is Squad Sappa, do you read? Over.'

He waited but Aldalon could tell from Grast's face that there had been no reply. Besides, he could hear the harsh spray of static coming from the trooper's headset.

'Squad Dram, this is Squad Sappa, do you read? Over.' Another pause before Grast looked at Aldalon. She shook her head. 'Sorry, sir, nothing.'

'Fine,' Aldalon said, 'carry on.'

The trooper nodded and returned to her position. Aldalon knew Lieutenant Trast would not attempt an incursion to deactivate any of the outpost's defensive systems and acquire some explosives from the minefield while the area was lit so prominently by the lumen towers. Aldalon would have to lead Squad Sappa around the north side of the outpost and cut the power. This was not an unexpected outcome, but it would alert the orks to their presence in the area.

Aldalon knew he'd probably already given up the initiative with his unrestrained attack on the orks before. He couldn't let himself give in to anger like that again. He was more disciplined than that. Still, cutting the power to the outpost would certainly give away their intention to attack, but it had to be done.

Aldalon called over Sergeant Sappa and showed her the image of the outpost plans. 'We're going to move in around the north and cut this power line here. Split your squad. Defensive sight lines here, here and here. Pick whomever you want to go in and dig for the power line.'

Sappa looked at him. 'You got your entrenching tool, sir?'

Aldalon scowled.

'What?' she said. 'I'm joking.'

Sappa moved away to prepare the squad. Aldalon growled as he watched her leave. Since when had he raised someone who made jokes?

The jungle around the north side of the outpost proved to be thinner than that on the westerly approach. Aldalon watched as Sergeant Sappa spread her squad out into twin extended file, keeping the distance relatively large between each trooper thereby presenting a more difficult target to spot moving through the thinner jungle than a close-packed knot of soldiers. He hadn't needed to ask her to do this. She was well trained. Of course she was, he had ensured it. No daughter of his would be anything but the most well-trained Jungle Fighter. She had taken her mother's name to avoid comparisons to him; that did not bother him, and he knew the truth of any accusations of nepotism from those who did know she was his blood kin.

There was no advantage to being the child of the great Colonel Haskell 'Hell Fist' Aldalon, no prestigious shortcut to the upper ranks. In fact, the truth was he was harder on his children than any other trooper on Catachan. He trained them harder, pushed them harder. He thought that had been the advantage he had given them – the best preparation for the life of war they had ahead of them. It had not seemed so for Brant. He had failed him.

Aldalon moved at the back of the squad, forcing himself not to take the lead. Learna had asked for her and her squad to get the combat experience she felt they needed, and he couldn't deny her that. She was right. She was a newly promoted squad leader in command of a new squad. Several of them were veterans of the 57th. She needed to earn their respect. And even with those veterans in the squad, none of these particular soldiers had operated as a squad together in the past. She was right to want to take control; she had to establish her leadership and the squad needed cohesion. So, Aldalon stayed at the back and let her take command. Besides, it meant he could watch the Emperor-be-damned soft-worlder in front of him, make sure he didn't completely ruin their mission.

From his position as the rear soldier Aldalon saw the halt signal passed back through the squad. He stopped, dropping to his knees and reflexively pulling his plasma pistol from where it was holstered at his waist. The next signal relayed down the lines of troopers was an ears-out signal – be silent, listen, someone in the squad has heard something.

It took only a moment for Aldalon to hear it too. Stomping feet and ork voices. They'd stumbled on a greenskin patrol – though it was probably more accurate to say the greenskins had stumbled on them. From the sounds of the footsteps, and the number and volume of the voices, there were more in this patrol than the two Aldalon had encountered earlier. It was difficult to say but Aldalon estimated there were at least ten in this group. Perhaps they'd learned their lesson; perhaps they knew there were enemy forces around now and were increasing numbers. The order came down the line from Sappa, passed in hand signals – down, take cover. She was going to hide from the orks, let the patrol pass. They would keep hidden until they had at least managed to disable the power. Good call. It's what Aldalon would have done. At least it's what he would do if his anger did not overrule him.

The Catachans went into full concealment, taking cover in the vegetation around them. Despite the jungle being clearer here it was still plenty dense enough for them to vanish. It took less than a minute and they were gone from view. Gone from view and silent.

The ability of the Catachans to disappear was almost otherworldly. It was almost like they became more than part of the jungle, black holes in the vines and leaves that sucked in their surroundings to keep them concealed. All of them were black holes, except for Trooper Torvin, who Aldalon could see was making an attempt to hide but, as far as Aldalon was concerned, might as well have been a supernova. Aldalon could see his helmet, not at all camouflaged, above the fern he had hidden behind.

By the sounds of their voices and their crunching, bulldozering footfalls, the orks were drawing closer. Would the greenskins see Torvin where he was half hidden amongst the dark green? Likely not, but Aldalon could not bear such a poor display of jungle warfare in his presence.

Aldalon pulled his clicker from a pocket on his trousers and thumbed down the small sliver of metal. It click-clacked but Torvin did not look in his direction. He tried again, clicking twice in quick succession. Still, the stupid soft-worlder did not look towards him.

'Torvin.' Aldalon kept his voice low but hissed the trooper's name in his direction. 'Torvin.'

Finally, Torvin looked back. Aldalon gestured for Torvin to get down. Obviously what Aldalon thought was a fairly obvious signal was not so obvious, because the Emperor-damned soft-worlder stood up. He stood up like he thought Aldalon was calling him over. Aldalon almost leapt out of his skin to tell him to get back down or to smash him back down himself with a swift power fist strike to the top of the head. He managed to restrain himself though and instead continued his wild waving.

'Get down,' he hissed again, but with the orks almost on them he knew he was keeping his words too quiet for them to carry. The idiot trooper finally got the meaning of his wild hand waving, or perhaps he managed to read his lips, because he suddenly realised what he'd done. In his haste to return to his hiding space he stepped backwards, tripped on something hidden in the undergrowth and stumbled, his feet tangled beneath him and his pack full of useless gear weighing him down. He dropped. Aldalon squeezed his eyes shut at the noise, sending a silent prayer to the God-Emperor that the orks hadn't heard.

'Oi!' The gruff voice of an ork immediately told Aldalon that this particular prayer would go unanswered. 'What was that zoggin' racket?'

'Dunno.'

'Well go and 'ave a look, ya git.'

The orks were in sight now. Aldalon's quick count gave thirteen of them.

These were not wearing camouflage, instead clad in the blue of Deathskulls. One of them, the top half of its face painted in blue, its armour decorated in the chequered pattern the greenskins commonly wore, split from the main group and moved in the direction of Torvin.

At least the soft-worlder seemed to have found, or at least fallen, into cover. Aldalon watched as the ork drew closer to Torvin; it seemed to be sniffing the air as if it were some animal searching for prey, which he supposed was exactly the case. The greenskin moved closer to Torvin's position, its gaze falling on the spot where the soft-worlder was hidden.

'Break cover! All engage!'

The shout came from Sergeant Sappa. She'd obviously considered the squad compromised as the ork was just about to find Torvin.

'Humies!' the orks shouted.

To his credit, at least Torvin started shooting. Leaning out from his location behind the fern, he sent las-shots streaking towards the ork that had almost found him. The first shot missed wide, bursting a small tree, but Torvin's second shot hit the ork in the leg. It was not enough to kill the greenskin, but it dropped to the ground as it struggled to draw the oversized pistol hanging from its belt. Aldalon charged from his nearby position.

The blue-faced ork turned to face Aldalon as he charged madly out of concealment. The ork's eyes went wide as it saw the power fist coming towards it. Aldalon hit hard and the ork's blue-painted face became a red-painted face as the front of its skull caved in and bright ork blood exploded out like a bursting firework.

For a split second, there was quiet. It always seemed to happen that way. A shot rings out and a Guardsman drops or a xenos is splattered across whatever ground they are fighting on, and there comes a moment of near tranquillity – like the universe is pausing, taking a deep steadying breath to ready itself for the violence to come.

The fraction of a second passed in a loud exhalation and carnage ensued. The crack of Catachan lascarbines rang out, subtly different to the sound of Torvin's more standard-pattern lasgun, quieter by virtue of being smaller and less powerful. And those shots were answered by the roar of ork firearms. There was nothing so consistent to the sound of ork weaponry. Each cracking, blasting, booming shot was different, but they all had one thing in common – they were louder than necessary.

'WAAAAAAGH!'

The war cry, now so familiar to Aldalon after years of meeting greenskins in battle, was hollered into the air as the orks, unsatisfied with a near-proximity firefight, charged in to engage in what they liked best: up-close hand-to-hand combat. This was their natural advantage and Aldalon knew, in the jungle environment with so many blocked sight lines, the Catachans would not be able to avoid melee. They needed to thin the orks' numbers as much as possible while they had even a slight distance on them.

The greenskins had dropped their pistols and rifles in favour of their brutal swords and axes as they thundered in for a charge. Catachans were deadly when they had their knives in hand, but against the strength of greenskins, and lacking the element of surprise they so often operated with, they were still at a disadvantage. In his peripheral vision, Aldalon saw the rest of Squad Sappa closing back towards him and Torvin.

'Cut them down,' Aldalon called.

The Catachans continued their barrage of las-fire at the orks and, as they drew in range, those Jungle Fighters with hand flamers sprayed cones of superheated promethium at them, melting the green skin from their bones. The Catachans did their best to drop as many of the orks as possible before the moment when they would need to draw their knives.

The Catachans moved as they fired, closing ranks, and by the time the xenos reached their lines at least four more of the orks were dead. That left eight orks against the ten Catachans. Better odds. Aldalon's power fist crackled as it drew energy, and he felt the thrill of the imminent fight rise within him. As the orks came upon them Catachan steel flashed in the dark. The Jungle Fighters paired up or fought in threes, standard operating procedure for fighting the stronger orks. One Catachan would engage an ork directly and fight defensively as the second or third attacked from the side or struck as the greenskin showed an opening.

Aldalon noted the soft-worlder was still hiding behind his fern. So be it. Aldalon didn't want him in the way anyway, and he didn't want to worry about that fool's safety. All he intended to worry about was adding some more ork lives to his growing collection.

The red mist descended over Aldalon's eyes. Orks were strong, certainly stronger than a human, but Catachans hadn't gained their reputation for nothing. None of them backed down. They dodged, parried and lunged forward with their knives, covering each other and fighting in teams. Aldalon, of course, had an advantage that left him stronger than any of the orks. His charged power fist disintegrated ork flesh and easily shattered their bones. He swung so hard at the first of the xenos to come for him that he decapitated it with one clean strike to the side of the neck.

Beside him Aldalon saw Trooper Setarn cry out in agony as an ork axe sliced across his abdomen. He clutched desperately at the blood and organs that spilled, but Aldalon instantly knew there would be no saving him. Especially when the ork's axe came back across to lodge in his neck and finished the job. Aldalon's rage boiled up again. There was at least one Catachan dead. There should have been zero. He looked around for his next target.

He turned to see one of the larger orks charging at Sappa. For some reason she was away from the main group of Catachans, away from the support of others. She dodged to the side, slashing at the overcommitted ork as its momentum carried it past her. Her razor-sharp Catachan blade sliced through flesh on the side of the ork's neck but not quite deep enough to be fatal, certainly not to the resilient xenos. The ork spun and lashed out with its axe. Sappa was quick enough for the blade to sail past her, but the hilt and balled fist of the ork struck her in the shoulder, sending her tumbling back. The ork began to reposition for another blow, the killing blow.

The red mist of battle rage cleared and Aldalon was running to his daughter. Even in the dark, the ork's axe seemed to shine as it rose over the greenskin's head and despite the xenos moving in apparent slow motion as Aldalon's adrenaline slammed through his veins, he too seemed to be moving as if through thick resin. The axe came down with a thunk before Aldalon could reach the ork. He smashed his power fist into the side of the creature's head and it crumpled to the side. He looked down at the axe still in front of him, expecting to see it splitting the skull of his only daughter, his last remaining child, and yet it was only stuck in the jungle mud. Sappa had rolled aside and risen smoothly; her Catachan knife was buried in the ork's guts.

Her eyes flashed at him. The anger he knew to be a daughter's disappointment and rage at her father rather than battle fury or annoyance at her superior officer.

'What are you doing? I had it covered. You don't come to the rescue of other troopers so don't do it for me!'

'Focus on the battle, sergeant.'

'You never protected Brant like that!'

Aldalon spun to her. 'And look what happened to him, Learna!'

Learna went quiet. 'We are Catachan,' she said. 'Death in battle is our destiny.'

Aldalon gritted his teeth, furious at himself for that crack in professionalism. 'I said focus on the battle, sergeant.'

She turned away, hurrying back to where a pair of Catachans fought an ork. Aldalon watched her go. She was right. There was no retirement for a Catachan Jungle Fighter. They fought for the Imperium as long as the Emperor deemed them worthy, and then they gave Him the ultimate sacrifice. Aldalon had always known this. He had known it when Brant and then Learna had been selected to become some of Catachan's finest. It hadn't bothered him then. In fact, he had felt honoured that both his children would continue his proud legacy for Catachan. Why then did it bother him now? Had he lost his edge?

Brant's death did not feel like the ultimate sacrifice for the God-Emperor of Mankind. It felt like Aldalon himself had given the ultimate sacrifice – a piece of him was gone. He may as well have been dead and yet he was still here to fight on for the Imperium. A dead man walking but for the sliver of life remaining, and that sliver of life was with him now, in battle, in the same grave danger that Brant had been.

The soft-worlder's words came back to him. *What is the point of fighting if we aren't fighting for those we love?* Aldalon growled under his breath, scowling at his own thoughts. Love. There was no room for love in a Catachan Jungle Fighter.

CHAPTER SEVENTEEN

TORVIN

Torvin remained in cover behind the large fern, crouching down in what concealment it offered, though he was certain any orks that cared to search would find him. One thing was clear though, he wasn't frozen in fear this time.

He was aware of the situation in front of him, able to follow the ebb and flow of the carnage rather than feeling completely overwhelmed by the very thought that he was in combat. He'd even shot at the orks as they charged, and he'd hit at least two of them that he was sure of. He'd only grazed the first one in the leg, but he was certain it had been his las-round that had blown open the chest of another, leaving a cauterised crater. It wasn't fear that held him in place this time. Instead, it was horrific fascination – not at seeing the snarling, hulking orks again, but the Catachans.

This was nothing like the combat he'd seen when the orks took Outpost Four. In that battle the Guardsmen of the Skadi Second had been defensive, conceding ground to the xenos as they backstepped with desperate defensive parries, trying to position themselves to maintain as much distance as possible. They had lunged forward to strike at the greenskins only when a perfect opening appeared and even then, if they managed to hit their target the orks had barely seemed to notice.

They may seem imposing at first glance, larger than a human and more muscular, but appearances are deceiving. Their muscle is more plentiful but still weaker than a human's, and though it may seem improbable from their size, do not shy away from them even in close combat as a human is stronger and can best them with a bayonet to the throat. What a load of crem was right.

In the battle over Outpost Four, the Skadi Second had always appeared as men fighting monsters. They faced down the greenskins with the constant sense that they were at a vast disadvantage and the fight was not one in which they hunted for victory but in which they fought to survive.

This was different. The Catachans fought like bloodthirsty maniacs. They fought like he was sure the Departmento Munitorum propaganda was intended to make all Guardsmen fight. They slammed into the orks as if they honestly believed these monstrous greenskins were far weaker than them. Torvin knew that wasn't the case. The Catachans understood this enemy better than most; they had fought them before, some of them more times than they could remember. They knew the physical advantages the orks had over humanity, it was just that they didn't care. They didn't fear them.

As one Catachan trooper charged, screaming, long knife raised over his head, he was met by an ork screaming too, axe raised in turn. Torvin already knew the Catachan Jungle Fighters were nothing like other Imperial Guardsmen, but here, watching them, he saw them for what they were. Covered in black and green paint, displaying their red clan colours with their bandannas, they were rippling-muscled insane jungle-dwelling killers, howling as they charged their enemy with a complete absence of anything that might resemble rational fear. They were human, but there was nothing in that moment that separated them from the greenskins they fought.

While all the Catachans were occupied fighting like beings possessed, one of the orks rounded the fern, gaze fixed on Torvin, bloodlust shining across its beady red eyes.

'Help!' Torvin said as he clambered to his feet. 'Need some help here!'

He knew it sounded pathetic but what else could he do? He couldn't take on an ork alone.

The greenskin came for him. This was it then; this was the moment he found himself in true, up-close, heart-pounding, sweat-sharing melee combat with an ork. This was the moment he would die in service of Emperor and Imperium light years from Skadi, Melina and everything he'd ever known.

It was entirely by reflex that he lifted his lasgun. He didn't have time to get a shot off and hadn't fixed his bayonet, which he realised might have been useful at that moment, as cursory as using any weapon against this beast might have been, but when the ork growled, swinging its chipped and pitted machete-like blade down at him, Torvin managed to get the body of his lasgun in the way.

He held the rifle out in front of him with two hands, one near the butt and one wrapped around the barrel, awkwardly catching the strike. The ork's strength sent the blade well into the lasgun until it came to a stop embedded in the rifle's body. The force slammed Torvin's hands back towards him until the rifle was across his chest, the curved end of the ork's weapon stopping an inch from splitting his forehead right down the centre. The greenskin growled and leant forward, pushing down against Torvin's guard. It was truly close to him now. When it exhaled in a sharp huff, Torvin felt the hot, stale breath on his face.

'Break!'

The shout came from somewhere over the ork's shoulder. It was Sergeant Sappa; she was coming towards him at a rapid pace.

'Torvin, break now!'

Torvin didn't immediately understand her meaning, but some synapses in his brain connected and he let go of his lasgun and dived to the side. The ork stumbled with the sudden removal of the resistance but quickly righted itself.

Sappa's shout had not only alerted Torvin to her presence but alerted the ork as well. It spun, swinging its blade in a wide horizontal arc. Sappa ducked, anticipating the strike. Unfortunately, she had not anticipated that the lasgun would remain stuck to the ork's blade. The butt of Torvin's lasgun clipped her on the cheek, and she staggered. It was only a glancing blow, nothing that would result in anything more than a purpling bruise, but it had thrown off her attack.

Sappa used her right hand, her knife hand, to catch herself on the wet jungle ground. The ork stomped down with a heavy black boot, pinning the serrated blade of her Catachan knife into the soil. She had no choice but to release it, an act that clearly pained her more than any ork strike to the face. She rolled and regained her feet.

The ork shook its blade, trying to free Torvin's lasgun. When the weapon didn't budge, it grabbed at it and tried to pull it off. Torvin watched as Sappa pulled another knife from her belt, this one much smaller than her Catachan blade. She probably used it for cutting and eating food.

She lunged at the distracted ork, who was still battling at trying to free its weapon from the clutches of Torvin's lasgun. Her quick strike hit the ork's upper arm. The greenskin growled and, as if the wound had given it more energy, it wrenched the stuck lasgun off its machete.

As Torvin collected himself he watched the ork return its attention to Sappa, freshly freed blade ready. The ork smiled a devilish grin, its nose crinkling. For her part, Sappa showed nothing but the famous Catachan stoicism as she faced it down, her eyes burning. She brandished her weapon, which seemed little better than a fancy butter knife, before her, and Torvin was almost certain this was what had made the ork smile.

His heart pounded. His stomach dropped. He couldn't let Sappa take on the ork alone. Torvin dashed for where Sappa's knife had been left in the muddy ground. He grabbed it and turned back to see the ork rush at Sappa using its size and strength in an attempt to overwhelm her.

Sappa back-pedalled, wildly swinging her tiny knife, but the ork closed the distance and smashed into her, sending her sprawling to the ground. Knowing this was his opportunity, Torvin stabbed the Catachan blade as hard as he could into the ork's side.

The ork wasn't wearing armour on the side of its torso, just a thick vest over its front and back, and the sharp blade penetrated flesh. Torvin could feel the thick, gristly muscle resisting and the scrape of the blade as it met hard ork ribs. Even as finely honed as the knife was, and as hard as he tried to stab it in, the blade made it less than half its length before slowing to a stop. Still, half a Catachan knife embedded in its side was more than enough to draw the ork's attention. As the greenskin turned, Torvin yanked hard on the blade's hilt to pull it free. The serrations ripped and tore as Torvin managed to get the knife back out, sending a thick ooze of blood down the ork's side.

The creature roared and swung at Torvin, who reflexively dropped to his knees. That brutal blade whipped across above his head. From behind, Sappa jumped onto the ork's back, wrapping her arms around its neck. She held on as the ork tried to shake her loose. She lurched back, knife gripped hard, and then stabbed the greenskin in the side of the throat, pulling back again with a spray of blood and then stabbing once more.

The ork slammed its fist back at Sappa with a desperate strike to knock her free. She fell back and landed heavily on the ground, appearing dazed. The greenskin lifted its blade to drop a powerful blow, but Torvin launched into action again. He sliced at the ork's machete-wielding arm before it could swing and his blow landed squarely where he'd been aiming. The Catachan knife with its razor edge cleaved almost all the way through the ork's wrist. The greenskin lifted its arm as if unsure what had happened and why it suddenly couldn't swing its sword. It seemed confused at first, staring at its hand hanging by thin strands of tendon and twisting muscle, the whole mess dripping with ichor.

'End him now,' Sappa said.

Torvin stabbed again with the Catachan knife, jabbing it into the ork's stomach. Here it slipped in much further, squelching into the creature's fungal organs.

'I said end him!' Sappa roared at Torvin. She was up on her feet again, grabbing Torvin's arm. She pulled, getting Torvin to drag the knife back out. She forced his arm up and slashed the knife into the side of the ork's neck. With their awkward two-person strike the blade did not penetrate far, but Sappa began a sawing motion. 'Cut its head off!'

As the ork thrashed, Sappa forced Torvin to hold strong and continue to saw back and forth. Warm xenos blood sprayed over Torvin's face, in his eyes, on his lips. Sappa stayed with Torvin, her hand on his as they cut into the ork's neck, slicing and ripping through muscle and flesh, grinding and crunching through bone, until eventually, as they hacked through dense ork vertebrae and cut the last of the green flesh, the creature's head came free and dropped, as did its large body, to the jungle ground.

Torvin stared down at the bloodied knife in his hands; he could feel the warm splatters up his arms and on his face. He turned to look at Sappa. She nodded at the knife in his hands. 'Keep that for now,' she said. 'I've got another.'

Around him, just as he had reflected, the Catachans fought not to survive but to win, and so they did. The orks lay dead on the ground, all of them shot on their approach or killed in hand-to-hand combat by the wild, bestial attacks of the Jungle Fighters. The Guardsmen had not gone without casualties, though. There were two of the Catachans who had fallen, given their lives for the Emperor in this place.

'Soft-worlder!'

Torvin turned. Colonel Aldalon was storming towards him and while the battle with the orks may have been over, the look on Aldalon's face showed he still felt he had a target. He reached Torvin and without hesitation slammed his power fist into Torvin's chest. The colonel had restrained himself, not charging the fist with flesh-disintegrating disruptive energy and holding back the weapon's full strength, but he still hit hard enough to send Torvin sprawling, gasping and painfully winded, to the ground. The colonel stood over the top of Torvin, bending down and pointing at him aggressively in rage and disgust.

'What did I tell you about getting my troopers killed, you Emperor-damned fool?'

Torvin stammered a reply which was little more than rasping whining sounds as he fought against his spasming diaphragm.

'Why in all the warp can't you stay hidden?'

Torvin sucked in as much air as he could against the pain in his abdomen but as he tried to speak, he instead broke into a fit of coughing.

Torvin expected to be murdered right there where he lay, but he saw some of the rage drain from Aldalon's eyes, replaced instead with disappointment and contempt. He shook his head. 'I shouldn't expect any better from whatever planet you're from.'

'I thought... I thought you were calling me over.'

Instead of responding Aldalon turned away in disgust. 'Sergeant Sappa,' he said.

'Sir.'

'I told you to babysit this soft-worlder and keep him from doing anything stupid. Take him back to camp while the rest of us go on to cut the power.'

'You can't–' Sappa said, seemingly about to grow animated but managing to restrain herself. 'Colonel, that is my squad. I should be leading it. I'll send Torvin back to camp with someone else.'

'You've got your orders, sergeant,' Aldalon replied, unblinking.

For a moment, longer than Torvin thought most people could, Sappa stared down Colonel Aldalon. 'Fine,' she said, turning to Torvin. 'You're with me, soft-worlder.'

Torvin followed Sergeant Sappa into the jungle. She moved with purpose into the dark and he struggled to keep up and not lose her in the dense black. She still moved in close to silence despite the fact that Torvin could barely see in front of him. He knew he, on the other hand, was stumbling forward, crashing through leaves, branches and vines, but he had no choice if he didn't want to lose sight of her and be left completely lost in the wilderness. He had no idea how she knew where their camp would be, but she seemed more than confident of their direction. After ten minutes of moving, Torvin broke into an almost-run to catch up and speak to her.

'I'm sorry,' he said. 'I was doing my best.'

Sergeant Sappa stopped and Torvin almost ran into the back of her. She turned on him, hissing her words. 'We move in silence. Are you as much of a slow learner as my father thinks you are?'

He didn't speak for the rest of the journey, not that Sappa ever gave him the opportunity to.

After a long time passing through what seemed to be unknowable, unrecognisable surrounds, Sappa finally halted and turned to him. 'Find your hole and hunker down,' she said, her voice low. 'It's just over there.'

Torvin looked around, suddenly recognising the location he'd set up his tarpaulin in concealment before they'd moved out. Sappa wandered off without giving him any further instructions, so he dropped his pack, pulled out the tarp and began setting up somewhere to sleep again. This time, once he'd erected his low, tentlike roof, covered it in branches and leaves, and shuffled inside, pulling his gear in with him, he found, despite everything, he was exhausted enough to fall into a quick, heavy sleep.

CHAPTER EIGHTEEN

NOGROK

As an ork, Nogrok did not have much awareness of his own psychology and probably didn't realise that happiness was not an emotional state greenskins could achieve. They came close to some equivalent during the heat of battle, a state of rapturous delight brought about by fulfilling their fundamental evolutionary purpose, but they were never truly happy.

Though they felt driven to kill, and felt satisfaction in the moment of the kill, the thing they were fighting was suddenly dead after that and they immediately felt the urge to kill again. There were always more things that needed killing. This inbuilt instinctual desire made fighting and killing for the ork species more like a blissful drug they were constantly suffering withdrawal from than an actual conscious choice or reasoned pursuit. This state of constantly seeking their next dose of the closest they could come to satisfaction was what drove the greenskins' constant expansion through the galaxy on the hunt for more things to fight. This was why, despite waging epic wars on a galactic scale, they never seemed to have any strategic goal. For the orks, the act of fighting was the goal.

So, when Nogrok considered himself quite happy sitting on the rampart of Outpost Four examining the sharpened edge of his recently reclaimed Catachan cutta, it was more accurate to say that he was momentarily content. Even for orks like Nogrok who, for whatever genetic reason, weren't quite so beholden to the addiction, there was still the constant gnawing draw to be satisfied. Nogrok had been occupying himself with good taktikal thinking about the next kunnin' step in his plan to get rid of Nob Jaggedteef, when his thoughts were interrupted by the raging shouts of Warboss Kazkorg Gutstompa somewhere in the building below.

His booming voice was so loud that it carried outside, clearly understandable over the almost constant noise and shouting of the population of orks who were still holed up here waiting impatiently to be given their next opportunity to fight something. Nogrok knew those Deathskulls gitz were ready to burst. They had taken to even more constant and prolific infighting than usual, part of the reason Nogrok and the other Blood Axe kommandos spent most of their time on the roof.

Whenever the urge to fight got too overwhelming for one of the Deathskulls, if they happened to spot one of the Blood Axes it would be them they directed their frustrations at. They'd fight one of their own klan if they had to, but it was better to seek out some git from another klan. It wasn't cowardice that drove Nogrok and his mob to the roof, it was simple maffs about self-preservation. Almost the entire warband were Deathskulls and it didn't take a mekboy genius to figure that meant bad odds for living.

'Why do I keep missin' the krumpin'?!' Warboss Gutstompa was shouting, his anger obvious from his volume and tone. Nogrok had heard the rumours, of course; rumours spread through an ork warband faster than a squig escaped from a milkin' pit. Another patrol of boyz had not returned, this one loads bigger than the ones and twos that had been goin' out before. 'I am boss,' Gutstompa was continuing. 'I should get to fight whenever a fight 'appens.'

Nogrok rolled his eyes, looking back out at the jungle around them. Warboss Gutstompa didn't seem to understand that if you weren't there when the fighting happened then you wouldn't get to be part of the fighting. If he wanted to fight so bad, he should go out on a patrol. Nogrok ran his finger along the edge of his knife. Actually, that would be great – maybe he could sneak out and kill Gutstompa just like he did with Flogga and Snaga. Probably not, but it was a nice thought.

Nogrok was watching the jungle when, without warning, the clearing around the outpost was plunged into darkness.

'Oi, did anyone else go blind or was it just me?' Nogrok heard Flik ask from nearby. 'Wait, nah, someone just turned out the lights, innit?'

Nogrok's eyes were adjusting quickly as well.

'What now?!' Gutstompa roared from down below and was soon thundering up the stairs to the rampart. The imposing shape of the warboss looked out at the suddenly dark scene. He looked around and his eyes fell, predictably as far as Nogrok was concerned, on him and his Blood Axe kommandos. 'What you Blood Axe gitz been doin' up here?'

Nogrok stared at him. 'You think dat was us?'

'Of course I fink it was you, you always doin' stuff.'

More orks, including Jaggedteef and his gitz – what was left of 'em anyway, Nogrok thought to himself with pleasure – paraded up to the roof level of the outpost to see what had happened with the lights. Jaggedteef's eyes landed on Nogrok as well.

'Wot did you do, you git?'

'Zog off,' Nogrok said. 'We ain't done nothin'. We was just sittin' up 'ere and the lights went off.'

'Who did it then?' Gutstompa asked, which surprised Nogrok because he thought it seemed obvious, though he'd always known Gutstompa was much better at stomping guts than he was at thinking.

'Humies innit,' Flik said. 'Dem humies out dere are cuttin' da lights so we can't see 'em comin'.'

Nogrok nodded. His mob knew what was what. 'That's right. It's da sneaky humies out in the jungle. Same ones wot was in the desert against us. That's wot they do, sneak about turnin' lights off and whatever. Gettin' ready to attack.'

'Dat ain't right.'

'Why da humies wanna fight in da dark? Can't even see what ya krumpin.'

The comments came from some of the orks who'd joined them on the roof. Nogrok wouldn't go as far as to say they were frightened, but they were confused. Most orks weren't like Nogrok. When Nogrok saw the humies do something, he wanted to learn about it; most of the orks couldn't comprehend what they were even doing. The idea of the humies sneaking around out there, attacking without being seen, it was too much for their fungus-mush brains to handle.

'Stupid gitz,' Gutstompa boomed. 'Why don't they fight proper?'

Nogrok looked at the furious confusion on Gutstompa's face – his brain was just as mushy as all the others.

'They are fightin' proper,' Nogrok said. 'Like proper humies is all, not like proper orks.'

Jaggedteef rounded on Nogrok. 'You always was a humie lover.'

'I ain't never said nothin' about lovin' humies,' Nogrok said. 'I'm just tellin' it like it is. You expect 'em to fight us like we wanna fight 'em. That ain't what they gonna do. Why would they?'

'We should send all our boyz out there, boss,' Jaggedteef said to Gutstompa, pointedly ignoring Nogrok. 'Dey won't expect that. Charge at 'em with a proper loud Waaagh!'

Nogrok huffed and this time when Jaggedteef spun towards him, he could see the nob was ready to storm him.

'Look,' Nogrok said, 'you think I'm a humie lover but I ain't. I just think we should learn from 'em.' He turned to Gutstompa. 'Boss, Jaggedteef's way of fightin' the humies hasn't worked, has it? They been pickin' us off while we is here waitin' for your reinforcements, and if you send all the boyz out there then they is gonna take the humie base back while we is gone, which is the whole thing they want anyway. I say we need to fight 'em the same way they fight us. If the humies ain't gonna fight like orks then we are the ones wot need to change.'

Jaggedteef had heard enough. He moved towards Nogrok, his eyes seething. 'You tellin' me my way ain't workin'. You sayin' I is stupid, you Blood Axe git.' It was predictable that Jaggedteef would respond in this way, rushing towards Nogrok ready to attempt to knock him out again or maybe krump him properly dead – so predictable that Nogrok already had his Catachan knife raised before the nob had even started moving. Nogrok whipped the blade up, the point directed right at the face of the larger ork. Jaggedteef stopped himself just short of being run through with the savage serrated knife.

'You raisin' a weapon at me. Dat's grounds for a proper dead krumpin', Blood Axe.' But Jaggedteef paused as he took in the blade being wielded in front of him, grimacing at what he saw, not out of any fear of the fact that Nogrok had a weapon, but because of which weapon it was. The nob's red eyes peered out from beneath his furrowed brow, examining the knife in Nogrok's hands before his eyes moved to meet Nogrok's. 'I know dat cutta.'

'Oh, dis little thing?' Nogrok said. 'Yeah, dis one my favourite cutta. Lost it for a bit but I got it back now.'

Jaggedteef growled. 'Flogga had dat cutta.'

'No,' Nogrok said, unable to keep the fury from his voice. 'Flogga pinched this cutta from me, now I got it back.'

'I seen Flogga take dat cutta on the patrol dat him and Snaga ain't come back from. How did you get dat cutta back?'

Nogrok smiled, knowing his refusal to answer would drive Jaggedteef to boiling point.

'I said, how did you get it back, you zoggin' git?' Jaggedteef roared. 'You killed me boyz!'

Jaggedteef batted Nogrok's blade aside and grabbed at the smaller ork's throat. Nogrok struggled but the nob was far too strong.

'You killed Flogga and Snaga ain't you? Dat's why you got dat cutta back?'

'I got it back,' Nogrok managed to rasp through the nob's crushing grip on his windpipe, 'coz it was mine. You gonna kill me for gettin' back wot was mine? Dat's between me and Flogga. Ain't got nothin' to do with you, nob or not.'

Nogrok had chosen his words carefully. He knew all orks loved fighting and killing and being brutal, even with each other, but they did have a kind of code. When there was a disagreement, orks were generally left to settle their differences without interference from others.

In this case, the orks watching this showdown understood the basic chain of events. Nogrok had hunted down and killed Flogga because Flogga had stolen his knife. That was fair game as far as they were concerned. Now Jaggedteef was annoyed that Nogrok had killed one of his boyz and was gonna krump him. Fair enough that was, too. The part that worked in Nogrok's favour was that ordinarily if one of the boyz attacked a nob out of nowhere, they'd not only have to deal with the nob but probably a load of his boyz protecting him too. Here though, Jaggedteef was attacking Nogrok and if Nogrok managed to kill Jaggedteef in self-defence then that was just how it went for the nob.

Nogrok lashed out with his knife, bringing it back around to slash at Jaggedteef's face. With his free hand Jaggedteef caught Nogrok's wrist, stopping his swing in mid-arc. Jaggedteef scowled at Nogrok. His voice was as serrated as Nogrok's knife.

'I been waiting to krump you.'

Nogrok glared back. Jaggedteef's grip tightened around his throat and the nob lifted Nogrok off the ground; still Nogrok managed a brief reply before the passage of air into and out of his lungs was completely exhausted. 'Same.'

Nogrok had his Catachan blade back but that didn't mean he'd done away with the other cuttas he had. He'd purposely kept Jaggedteef's gaze on the massive blade. It was imposing and easily held attention, especially the attention of orks, whose only interest outside of killing things was the weapons used to do it. While Jaggedteef was distracted, Nogrok slipped a second knife from his belt and rammed it upwards. Jaggedteef did not have a third arm with which to catch this strike. Nogrok drove the blade straight up under Jaggedteef's chin. It punched easily through the soft flesh there and continued upwards, cleaving his tongue in two and then piercing the roof of his mouth, coming to a stop only when the hilt slammed into the underside of his jawbone.

With his eyes wide from shock, Jaggedteef's grip on both Nogrok's wrist and throat relaxed. Nogrok dropped, anticipating the outcome and landing on his feet. The nob grabbed at the knife sticking out from the bottom of his head. With no hesitation Nogrok launched forward. Jaggedteef swiped at him, but at the last moment Nogrok changed direction.

Nogrok had thought this through many times. To get to be a nob you had to kill a nob, but killing a nob was easier said than done because they were, by definition, bigger and stronger than other orks. The answer had been clear to Nogrok for a while. To kill a nob, you needed to remove those advantages. He'd long needed an opportunity to get Jaggedteef in a fight no one would interfere with. He'd needed to be ready, to have a plan in place. And he did.

Nogrok slashed at the back of Jaggedteef's knees, cutting through the sinewy strands of tendon beneath his green skin. Jaggedteef's legs collapsed, and he dropped with a jolt to his knees.

Nogrok kept moving, circling quickly around Jaggedteef. That was the first issue dealt with – the nob's size. A growl escaped Jaggedteef's scowling face as he pulled Nogrok's knife free from his jaw and used it to slash at the Blood Axe moving around behind him. Nogrok managed to hop back and arch his body so that Jaggedteef's wild swing passed in front of his stomach.

Nogrok might have cut the nob down to a more manageable size, but he still had the second issue to deal with – Jaggedteef's overwhelming strength. Even wounded as he was, a single strike from Jaggedteef would be enough to end this fight. Nogrok knew there would be no holding back at simply knocking him unconscious this time. Jaggedteef would pummel him into fungus paste.

Keeping his eyes on Jaggedteef, who was turning quickly to track him for another attack, Nogrok reached into the pocket of his trousers and pulled out the next step in his plan. His 'urty syringe. If the painboy git who'd fleeced him for it was right, it should make Jaggedteef no more stronger than Nogrok himself was. Nogrok gripped the 'urty syringe tightly. He could only afford one dose with the zoggin' daylight robbery price the painboy offered it for, and so he'd only get one shot at this. If he messed it up, he was as good as permanently knocked over.

Nogrok waited for Jaggedteef to lash out at him again. He jumped back, the knife Jaggedteef had pulled from his own jaw once again sailing past Nogrok. Close, but not close enough. Nogrok took his chance and launched forward, extending the 'urty syringe as he did so, leading with the long pointed needle. He landed the blow right in the flesh of Jaggedteef's back. The end of the needle hit and at first Nogrok thought it had pierced easily, but then he saw the needle had snapped clean off near the body of the syringe. He heard snickering from somewhere in the watching crowd. Zoggin' painboy, it had to be; he'd zoggin' well sabotaged the needle.

'Stupid git,' Nogrok swore under his breath.

Jaggedteef swung and this time Nogrok was hit hard with a backhand that sent him flying across the rampart. He slammed into the battlement wall with a brain-loosening crunch. He dropped to the ground, barely conscious but lucid enough to know that he'd dropped his Catachan blade, but that he was still holding the syringe.

Jaggedteef clambered to his feet, stumbling once as his right knee gave out again, but he managed to stand eventually and stalk awkwardly towards Nogrok. He reached out and grabbed Nogrok around the throat again, snarling.

'Now I'mma show you why they call me Jaggedteef,' he said. He opened his mouth, revealing every one of his filed teeth. He leant forward and bit down hard on Nogrok's left ear. He pulled his head back and ripped the lobe completely off in a tearing spray of blood. He spat the torn flesh onto the ground. 'Bit by bit.'

Jaggedteef opened his mouth again, ready to chomp down on Nogrok's other ear. Nogrok moved quickly, shoving the syringe into Jaggedteef's mouth and jamming it as far back into the nob's throat as he could. He slammed his other hand on the plunger at the rear of the syringe and injected the purple goo directly into Jaggedteef's gullet.

He didn't get very far before Jaggedteef bit down with all the tremendous force of his massive jaw muscles, cutting the syringe in two and shattering the glass cylinder. Half the purple 'urty stuff inside sprayed out onto the ground, but at least the other half had gone down Jaggedteef's throat. The nob coughed and spluttered but maintained his grip on Nogrok's throat with one hand while he grabbed at the broken syringe in his mouth with the other. He pulled it clear and spat out purple slime, dragging his fingers along his tongue to clear off shards of glass. Nogrok struggled to break free from the still-superior strength of the nob.

Nogrok watched Jaggedteef's face. The nob's eyes widened as he felt the change, his sudden inability to squeeze Nogrok's neck into a squig noodle. In place of the usual potent rage in Jaggedteef's eyes, Nogrok saw panic. It seemed he'd stumbled upon perhaps the one thing in the galaxy that could strike fear into the heart of an ork nob: the loss of their terrific strength.

Nogrok struggled hard, mustering all the strength he had, and managed to kick against Jaggedteef, breaking his grip. Jaggedteef was accustomed to fighting with brute strength, overwhelming his victims in seconds. He had no idea how to win a fair fight.

Nogrok slid to the side, ducking out from under the nob's imposing frame. He darted for where his Catachan knife had fallen to the ground, grabbed it, and turned back to Jaggedteef. He had to be quick, before the effects of the 'urty syringe wore off. The nob lashed out at Nogrok with a hooking punch, a swing that would ordinarily have levelled Nogrok, but he raised his free arm in an attempt to block the strike. The two orks' forearms connected, smashing against each other. Nogrok braced himself and, as he'd hoped, stopped Jaggedteef's blow.

Jaggedteef, on the other hand, was shocked at the result and stared, stunned at the fact that Nogrok was not splattered across the rampart.

Nogrok took the opportunity to jab his Catachan knife into Jaggedteef's stomach. He dragged the blade all the way across the huge ork's torso. When he reached the opposite side, Nogrok pulled the weapon free; as the serrations caught, he extracted not only his blade but also a large percentage of Jaggedteef's internal organs. With a slurping sound and a stench not unlike an overfilled ork toilet, Jaggedteef's guts spilled across the rampart of Outpost Four.

Jaggedteef stared down at his insides, seeming to take a moment to notice that they were now on the outside. He grabbed at them, attempting to shove them back in so he could get on with the fight. Orks could survive some horrendous injuries. Given the correct care Jaggedteef might have even been able to survive complete evisceration of a third of his insides but, as he stumbled forward trying to collect his guts, Nogrok made sure no one would have the chance to patch him up by leaping forward with the Catachan knife again. This time, he stabbed the nob right through the eye socket and into his brain not once but six times, ripping the ork's brain into mush. As Nogrok pulled his blade free for the last time, panting his exertion, he stepped back and let the body of Nob Gruk Jaggedteef drop with a thump.

'Told you I'd get you, you git.'

The orks were quiet. Nogrok hadn't expected celebration from the onlooking Deathskulls – he was a Blood Axe after all – but still, that had been a proper fight and a nob had been krumped, and that usually drew more of a reaction than silence deader than Jaggedteef. Nogrok looked around. Most of the greenskins just looked shocked. Nogrok's eyes eventually fell on Warboss Gutstompa. Jaggedteef had been one of his most trusted nobz, but the warboss didn't seemed overly concerned that he was dead. If he was weak enough to have his guts spilled on the floor, then he wasn't worth being a nob after all.

'You fink you is a nob now?' Gutstompa asked.

Nogrok shrugged. 'I killed one, didn't I?'

Gutstompa walked over to Jaggedteef's body. The warboss nudged the fallen nob with the end of his enormous armoured foot. 'Yeah. Looks like you killed Jaggedteef, but it weren't a proper fight, was it.'

'What?' Nogrok said. 'I killed 'im, ain't I?'

'You had to give 'im that purple juice, didn't ya,' Warboss Gutstompa said, returning his attention to Nogrok. 'Needed to weaken 'im or whatever, didn't ya. I can't 'ave no nob of mine be an ork wot needs to weaken stuff 'fore they fight.'

'I killed 'im,' Nogrok said. 'Since when does it matter 'ow I did it? Ain't no rules 'bout fightin.' Winning's winning, ain't it? Nothin' wrong with usin' Mork's own kunnin.' Ain't that right?' Nogrok directed this last question to all the watching greenskins. 'I said' – Nogrok spoke louder when they didn't answer – 'you kill a nob, you get to be a nob, ain't that right?!'

'Yeah.'

'S'pose.'

'Nah, not when you couldn't beat 'im one-on-one.'

'Nogrok cut 'is guts out still, didn't 'e? Proper good dat was.'

A flurry of voices fired up from the crowd, most in favour of Nogrok's statement, but many not. Gutstompa eyed Nogrok. He growled, a sound of annoyance but also of resignation.

'All right,' Gutstompa said, 'dis is it then. I still think you is unorky the way you did in Jaggedteef, but you did do 'im in, I can't say you didn't. So, you needs to do somethin' else to prove you got wot it takes to be a nob in dis warband. What you gonna do?'

'Killin' humies is orky, ain't it?' Nogrok asked.

'Yeah,' Gutstompa said, 'course it is. Proper orky.'

'Right and none of you lot 'ere 'ave even killed a humie since we been waitin' 'ere. If I go and kill a humie then I get to be a nob, and I get to do things my way.'

'Yeah, all right. You go out dere in da jungle and kill a humie and bring me back its 'ead and you can 'ave wot you want.' Gutstompa smiled. 'But you gotta go alone.'

'Fine,' Nogrok said. He stared at Gutstompa. 'I is best alone.'

CHAPTER NINETEEN

NOGROK

Nogrok lived up to the ghost ork nickname as he moved wraithlike through the jungle. With refreshed camouflage paint and his fungus brain focused on the task, carrying nothing but a small – by ork standards at least – slugga hanging from his belt, and his Catachan knife gripped in his hand, he had set out to find and kill one of the humies that had been sneaking around the outpost.

Nogrok was a sneaky ork, much more naturally inclined to subterfuge and the kunnin' arts than most greenskins, so he was always going to find his way to the kommandos, those orks that appreciated that type of thing. But even when he was surrounded by other orks who wanted to be sneaky, it was from the humies that he'd learned how to be *proper sneaky*.

He knew it was the Catachans out here, the best humies at being sneaky. At least he hoped the humies were Catachans. Killing one humie didn't seem like much, but killing one Catachan was a big deal – a bit like killing a nob. They were always together, always doing good taktiks, and they were proper tough. The thought of trying his kunnin' skills against the Catachans was too good to pass up.

He'd get to show Gutstompa too. He'd prove he could do what none of them had managed to do and kill one of the Catachan humies and bring his head back to show the big git. Nogrok had killed one of them before and he'd do it again.

He wasn't sure where the humies were, but he knew they had to be close. They'd cut the lights to the humie base and Nogrok knew what that meant: an attack was coming, and the humies had to be close enough for that. They'd be hiding in the jungle somewhere nearby.

As Nogrok moved around the edge of the jungle on the northern side of the outpost he found, a short distance into the cover of the trees, a series of holes and a trench cut into the ground, as if someone had been trying to dig something up. Near one end of the trench Nogrok looked inside to see a thick cable buried underground. He crouched down to take a closer look and could see the cable had been cut through.

It didn't take a mekboy to realise this cable ran straight to the humie base and must have been the power for the big lights, and probably everything else there too. The humies had been here. Nogrok wouldn't be able to track them through the jungle. He knew the Catachan humies wouldn't make it that easy, but he knew the direction they were probably heading – back towards the humie city in the west – so Nogrok started in that direction, moving as fast as he could without making too much noise. He was the hunter now. He had to catch up to the humies.

All he needed was one.

What he found was two.

Maybe it was luck or maybe Mork was smiling down on Nogrok. Nogrok had revered Mork much more than Gork for as long as he'd existed, always praising him to other dumb gitz who thought Gork was best, so it was about time Mork finally did something for him.

He'd been hunting less than an hour when ahead of him, barely visible in the dark foliage, he spotted two humies. They spoke quietly, trying to stop their voices from carrying, but Nogrok was close enough to hear.

'Thorn,' one of the humies said, 'I can hear your movement from up there. I told you to move back to camp with sound discipline.'

'Lieutenant,' the other humie said, 'the orks will never hear us. They'll be too busy stomping around and yelling at each other.'

'I don't care, trooper, I told you to go silent, so you go silent.' The humie's voice sounded like a nob trying to keep from blowing his top. 'You're a Jungle Fighter so act like one. We don't get complacent. Doesn't matter if you're worried about the greenskins or not.'

'Yes, lieutenant.'

'Good. Hold here to put some distance between us, then move with full sound discipline.'

'Yes, sir.'

The nob-humie moved away and Nogrok could see the other humie waiting where he was. Nogrok smiled. That humie had been part right and part wrong. He might not have been moving through the jungle as quietly as Nogrok knew the Catachan humies could, but he wasn't exactly being loud either. He was probably right that most orks wouldn't have noticed him.

Nogrok had seen some of those Deathskulls gitz so wrapped up in an argument over whether one of them had bet the other one two bags of teef or three bags of teef that he could throw a baby squig further than the other one, that both of them failed to notice an actual explosion as humie bombers flew over the top of them and dropped massive bombz. He was also wrong, though, because Nogrok had heard him. Nogrok had heard him and so that humie should definitely be worried about greenskins. That humie should be worried about him.

Nogrok moved with all the stealth he'd learned, his Catachan knife held in a steady grip in front of him. He moved slowly, sidestepping to manoeuvre around behind the humie, keeping his eyes fixed on the shape in the darkness.

Nogrok slowed as he saw the humie move. He was only a few steps from him now. He paused, stopping midway through parting a drape of hanging vines, when he realised the humie was lifting a weapon. In a flash of light he saw the humie had a small burna pistol in his hand, and Nogrok stiffened as he thought the humie was about to spin and shoot incinerating fire in his direction. Instead, the humie used the pilot flame on the end to light a cigar.

Nogrok relaxed. He was a little disappointed. He'd been ready for the challenge of killing a Catachan Jungle Fighter, but this one was not on his game. Still, that wasn't going to stop Nogrok from cutting his head off. Like Warboss Ripspitta used to say, you snooze, you get krumped.

In any normal jungle the thick vegetation concealed a lot, especially from the air, where it was difficult to see through the thick cover of the tallest trees – the canopy on Gondwa VI was even worse, an almost impenetrable blanket of rolling green when viewed from above. But Nogrok was sure Gork and Mork could still see him. Moving up on this humie so stealthily as to be undetected was kunnin' enough for Mork for sure, and what came next was brutal enough to please Gork. Nogrok was an ork that managed to please both aspects of orkiness in a way that few truly mastered.

Nogrok crept up behind the smoking humie in silence – not ork silence, which was often far further from noiselessness than they thought, but actual, proper silence.

He readied his blade, took that last stride quickly, and launched with a motion so fast that it would have impressed a Catachan coiling death cobra.

Nogrok clamped one green palm tightly over the humie's mouth to stifle any noise. The humie grunted in shock and attempted to call out, but Nogrok was already drawing his blade across the humie's windpipe and his muffled shouts ended as gurgling red bubbles pouring out his gouged-opened neck. Proper kunnin' attack.

Next came the proper brutal bit. Nogrok pulled his Catachan knife free and plunged the blade into the humie's back. Again and again and again. He relished the slice and tear of the blade going in and out, in and out, ripping the humie's flesh and insides to shreds.

The humie flopped to the ground. Nogrok was unsure exactly when he'd died, but he was proper krumped. Nogrok slammed the knife down on the humie's neck with a strike powerful enough that it sheared straight through muscle, sinew and spine. He grabbed the short-cropped humie hair and tugged, pulling the humie's head off.

Nogrok lifted the head to stare at it. The humie still looked shocked. *Should have been paying attention, shouldn't ya!* A trickle of blood pattered down from the ragged neck onto the jungle ground. Nogrok sheathed his Catachan blade and stuck his fingers out beneath the trickle of warm crimson blood. He let some splatter onto his fingers and then painted it in stripes over his face. He bent down and picked up the bloody cigar from the ground. It had gone out in the blood and mud, but Nogrok stuck it between his teeth anyway and walked off through the jungle back towards the humie outpost, where Warboss Gutstompa would be waiting, as would Nogrok's promotion.

As dawn approached, light began returning to the jungle. Nogrok moved through the trees, passing the spot he'd prepared before he'd left to kill the humie just in case he had to kill something else.

It didn't surprise Nogrok when he emerged from the treeline and immediately came face to face with six Deathskulls boyz waiting for him. He'd expected Gutstompa to do something like this.

'Mornin,' Nogrok said, 'you lot goin' on patrol?'

The frontmost Deathskull and the largest of the boyz was Grink, one of Jaggedteef's most loyal gitz and a wannabe nob in his own right. Grink growled under his breath. 'Nah, not patrol, just waitin.'

'Oh yeah, and wot ya waitin' for?'

'You obviously, ya git,' Grink said. 'I thought you was supposed to be smart.'

'Not smart,' Nogrok said, 'just sneaky. Bit like Warboss Gut-stompa's tryin' to be sneaky sendin' you out 'ere.'

'I ain't said Gutstompa sent us,' Grink added hastily, but orks, as a species who existed solely for war, were terrible at lying.

'Course Gutstompa sent ya, none of you bloody gitz do anythin' without Gutstompa shovin' his mitt up your rump and wigglin' ya about like a puppet.'

Grink's face bloomed with anger. 'You goin' the right way for a krumpin'! We out 'ere coz of wot you did to Jaggedteef.'

'No you ain't. You think you shoulda been next in line to be nob after Jaggedteef, Grink, and coz I krumped dat git you is worried I is gonna take 'is place. Dat's why you 'ad no problem comin' out 'ere to krump me when Gutstompa told ya to. Probably told ya you would be made nob when I was a dead 'un, right?'

Grink's face almost glowed in the still-purple early morning light, though he said nothing. He said nothing because Nogrok was right.

'And the rest of you gitz,' Nogrok said, gesturing at the remainder of the Deathskulls boyz, 'you is 'ere coz you'd rather 'ave Grink as ya next nob 'stead o' me.'

None of them said anything. Most of the clumps of fungus they called brains raced with the amazement that Nogrok had figured everything out so fast, like he was a weirdboy or somethin.'

Grink growled again. 'Whatever. Let's just get 'im.'

The Deathskulls ran at him and Nogrok turned and ran back into the jungle.

'The git's runnin' away!' Grink roared.

Nogrok's feet pounded against the ground. He ripped through ferns, blasted through branches and batted hanging vines aside with reckless abandon. It wasn't easy to run from a bunch of Deathskulls wanting a scrap, but he had to fight the Gorkiness and stick with Morkiness right now. He had to reach his preprepared spot with enough time and with enough distance between him and the Deathskulls.

He kept going, putting himself at a safe remove before stopping. He turned back. Grink and his boyz were approaching. Nogrok pulled the detonator from his pocket. He'd spent a bunch of his teef on the 'urty syringe he'd used on Jaggedteef, and this was what he'd spent the rest on. When the Deathskulls reached the location where he'd buried the explosives, he pressed the big red button on the detonator.

Nothing happened.

He pounded the button a series of times with his thumb but there was still nothing. Zoggin' stupid mekboy had sold him a dud! As bad as painboyz those mekboyz. Hard to know whether this one had done it on purpose like that zoggin' painboy had or whether it was just a standard mekboy balls-up. Either way he supposed it didn't matter. The bloody thing didn't go boom.

Nogrok chucked the detonator towards the approaching orks in frustration. It hit one of the Deathskulls on his blue-painted forehead and bounced straight off. Nogrok pulled his Catachan knife, readying himself for a fight. He wouldn't be able to hold off six other orks – that's what the zoggin' mine was supposed to do – but he wasn't going to go down without a scrap.

Nogrok watched as the Deathskulls charged, planning which of them he'd take down first, when shapes dropped from the jungle canopy. Ork shapes. Camouflaged shapes. Flik, Nukka and Ruktug, the remaining Blood Axe kommandos, leapt from the treetops and landed on the rear three orks, slamming them into the ground and quickly cutting their throats, sawing through far enough to make sure they were dead.

At least Nukka and Ruktug managed to drop their targets to the ground; it was a little more difficult for Flik, who didn't quite weigh enough, but he made up for it with the vigour he used in cutting his ork's throat. As the front three orks turned to see what had happened behind them, Nogrok was already running forward. He slammed into Grink, running him through with his Catachan blade before pulling it out and slashing at his face, almost cutting the top half of his head off. The last two orks found themselves suddenly outnumbered four to two. They were put down with a quick, no-nonsense kommando slaughtering.

'Thanks, boyz,' Nogrok said.

'No worries, boss,' Flik said. 'We overheard Warboss Gutstompa tell that lot to come after ya, make sure you didn't come back. Couldn't stand for dat.'

'I was thinkin' he'd do something like that,' Nogrok said. 'I had a plan. Probably woulda been better if I killed 'em all meself, then I coulda dragged all the 'eads back an' really showed Gutstompa.'

Flik looked from Nukka to Ruktug and then back to Nogrok. 'Still can do that, boss, we ain't gonna say nothin'. Just make it look like ya killed 'em all yourself.'

'Bit sneaky ain't it?' Nogrok said.

'Well, we's kommandos ain't we?'

Nogrok nodded. ''Spose so.'

'What was yer plan anyway, boss?' Flik asked. 'How was you gonna krump all of them boyz?'

With a concussive blast that shook the foundations of the jungle around them, rattling tree trunks, dislodging branches from the canopy overhead and causing the local birdlife to burst into flight for miles around, the ground where Nogrok had buried his remote mine erupted in a blooming dome of dirt, mud and plant life, showering debris down on them and peppering the undergrowth all around.

'Huh,' Flik said. 'Shoulda done that earlier, boss.'

Stupid zoggin' mekboyz.

CHAPTER TWENTY

NOGROK

Nogrok walked up to the humie base dragging a sack along behind him. A myriad collection of orks watched from the rampart, staring down over the battlement at Nogrok crossing the clearing alone. Warboss Gutstompa was among them. Nogrok had spotted him before leaving the treeline, but now he made sure not to look up at him. He wouldn't give the giant git the acknowledgement. The observant among the orks noticed the sack Nogrok pulled with him was made from torn and mouldy ork-sized clothing decorated with the distinctive blue of Deathskulls and they suspected what was coming. Most didn't, though, because they were about as observant as a pile of squig turds.

Nogrok reached the outpost and pushed his way through the crowd of orks that had gathered, shoving their way forward to see whether or not the Blood Axe had managed to kill a humie after all.

'Oi! Ya get one?'

'Nah, no way 'e did, stupid git.'

'What's in the bag then, you git? Callin' me a git!'

'I ain't callin' you a git, I'm callin' 'im a git.'

Nogrok ignored the orks, who parted far more easily for him than they ever had before. He hoped it was because they suspected he was about to become a nob and not because they were eager for him to get up to Gutstompa to see the monstrous warboss put those mechanical legs of his to good use in squashing him.

Nogrok climbed the stairs to the roof of the building, lifting the sack so that its contents didn't knock against each step on the way up. Gutstompa was there to meet him as soon as he emerged at the top.

'Ya made it back then?' the warboss grumbled, not at all disguising how bloody disappointed he was.

'In the green flesh, boss,' Nogrok said, then lowered his voice. 'No thanks to you.'

'Wot?'

'Nothin',' Nogrok said. 'Here ya go, I got a present for ya.' Nogrok reached into the sack and pulled out the head of the humie he'd killed. The Catachan humies never had much hair so he had to pull it out upside down with two fingers in its dried-out mouth and his thumb on its chin. Nogrok tossed the head towards Gutstompa. It hit the ground and rolled, wobbling, coming to rest against one of Gutstompa's overly large shining metal boots.

The warboss reached down and picked up the decapitated humie head, examining it as if to make sure Nogrok wasn't trying to trick him.

'If that ain't enough for you to give me Jaggedteef's place as a nob then here, dis should do it.' Nogrok turned the sack upside down and six ork heads plummeted out and rolled across the ground, the six heads of those Deathskulls Gutstompa had sent to kill him.

Gutstompa's wide jaw pulsed as he ground his teeth. 'Fine. You's a nob. Nogrok Sneakyguts.'

All around him, orks bellowed at the promotion of a new nob.

'WAAAGH! Sneakyguts! WAAAGH!'

CHAPTER TWENTY-ONE

TORVIN

Torvin woke in chaotic confusion.

His body had yanked his consciousness back to the surface in a panic as it suddenly found itself unable to breathe. Torvin thrashed, his groggy mind thinking at first that his hastily erected tarpaulin had collapsed on him, but he quickly realised there was too much weight on him – the weight of a person.

Torvin's tarpaulin shelter was torn off him, draped branches, carefully arranged vines and all. A Catachan trooper was standing above him. The jungle had turned to lighter greys and desaturated greens as night neared its end. It was light enough for Torvin to recognise that the trooper towering over him was the same one who had caught and eaten that lizard-like creature before they had left for that ill-fated mission to cut the outpost lights.

'What are you doing?' Torvin stammered.

'They call me Poison Guts, did you know that, soft-worlder?' the trooper said, leaning close to Torvin's still-startled face. 'Holt 'Poison Guts' Fletcha.' Torvin saw the flash of a blade before his face; it was coated in a viscous slime that dropped from the top along the sharpened edge. 'Why do you think they call me that?'

Torvin swallowed. 'Probably something to do with what I'm guessing is poison on your knife.'

'Yeah, it's an easy one, ain't it?' He turned the blade admiringly. 'One stab in the guts from this and you'll be on the ground seizing, shaking and frothing bloody bubbles from your mouth in five minutes. Dead in six.'

'That doesn't sound great.'

'No, it's pretty much the worst way to go.'

Torvin nodded, not knowing what else to say.

'There's another name you should know too,' Poison Guts continued. 'Trooper Mort Setarn. He was my friend and you got him killed. Those orks would never have found us if it wasn't for you. You're a risk to all of us. Give me a reason why I shouldn't plunge my poison dagger into your belly right now?' Poison Guts leant forward even closer until their foreheads were almost touching. 'One reason, soft-worlder, that's all – you got one?'

Something shifted in Torvin. He almost felt the realignment within him, the flick of a switch. He pushed himself up until his forehead pressed into Trooper Fletcha's. He spoke through teeth gritted so hard it was lucky they didn't crack. 'Go on then,' Torvin snarled. It wasn't anger, at least not just anger; it was something much more complex than that. There was fear and hopelessness and anger and desire. 'Do it then. Do it!'

Poison Guts Fletcha pulled back from Torvin, surprised. He hesitated and it was long enough for Torvin to swing his head up, slamming his forehead into Fletcha's nose. Torvin felt a crunch beneath the blow, a sound that just a week earlier he might have found disconcerting but now found somewhat satisfying.

Fletcha reeled back, blood spurting from his nose, his top lip already swelling. Torvin grabbed for the Catachan knife that Sappa had given him. His hand found the handle and he swung it at Fletcha with an anger-fuelled viciousness. Though Fletcha was rattled by his suddenly shattered nose, his Catachan instincts flared, and he dodged back. Torvin's knife blade slashed through the space in front of him, catching Fletcha on the forearm. The tip dragged a long red line through the skin.

Fletcha's disadvantage lasted only a moment before he brandished his knife in a fighting stance. His eyes locked on Torvin's. His body was coiled like a spring, ready to release its potential energy for combat. Torvin knew he was going to die here, but he didn't care any more. The life he thought he was going to lead was gone. Ted Torvin accepted he was already dead, and that made all the difference.

He charged at Fletcha with at least some of the fearlessness he'd seen in both the orks and the Catachans. Fletcha watched him come. He took a backstep – not from fear, but to put himself in a better position. He did not swing his poisoned blade, at least not yet; he swung his fist. It connected with the side of Torvin's face, knocking him stumbling. But Torvin was not deterred. He slashed with the knife again, a wide deadly arc, which Fletcha twisted to avoid, but Torvin again drew a line of blood, this time across the Catachan's shoulder. Torvin watched, ready to try to fight as Fletcha rose again, but it was not a scowl of anger he saw on Fletcha's face. It was a smile. His front teeth stained red with the blood that flowed freely from his nose, he smiled.

'That's enough.'

Torvin looked to the voice and saw Colonel Aldalon watching on. Fletcha looked at his commanding officer as well, and for a moment Torvin wasn't sure what he was going to do. Then he pulled a cloth from his pocket and wiped the poison from the blade of his knife. He looked back at Torvin and nodded, as if in acknowledgement. Torvin, so shocked by this change, nodded in return.

Torvin looked back at Colonel Aldalon expecting a scowl of reprimand, but instead the colonel was eyeing him with a face of passive granite. The colonel looked down at the blade in Torvin's hand.

'Clean that and then put it away,' Aldalon said. 'We don't draw blades on each other.'

'He was going to kill me,' Torvin stammered.

'You'd be dead if that's what he really wanted,' Aldalon said. 'From where I was standing, he didn't look like the one who wanted to kill.'

CHAPTER TWENTY-TWO

ALDALON

Colonel Aldalon watched the jungle. Dawn was breaking over the canopy, but little light had penetrated its depths yet. At best the shadows were slightly less than at their darkest, tinged green with what light could fight through the dense upper layers.

Objectively, their raid on the outpost had been a success. Aldalon and Squad Sappa had managed to cut power and disable the lumen towers. Lieutenant Trast and Squad Dram had used the cover of darkness to recover a generous supply of explosive ordnance from the minefield. They had achieved their objectives and yet it had been far from good enough. Squad Sappa's skirmish with the orks had resulted in two casualties and then, on rendezvous, Trast had informed him that Thorn was missing. Instead of preparing for the next phase of their mission Aldalon had to send Trast and a small party out to find a missing trooper. He ground his teeth with frustration. Not good enough for the Catachans.

Most people would have been unable to discern movement out there in the trees, between the mossy trunks, twisted limbs and gnarled vines, but most people were not Catachan, and even then, most Catachans were not Haskell Aldalon. He knew Lieutenant Trast was returning before even the Jungle Fighters watching the perimeter.

Aldalon moved to where Trooper Ryhorn was on guard. The trooper turned to look at the colonel, expecting some instructions or an order. Instead, Aldalon kept his eyes on the trees. After a moment he spoke.

'Here they come.'

Trooper Ryhorn looked at Aldalon in surprise and then looked out at the jungle, thinning his eyes in time to catch sight of Lieutenant Trast emerging from the trees. He raised his eyebrows as he looked back at Aldalon, even more impressed by his commanding officer than usual.

Trast approached and nodded. Behind him, Trooper Crusel was carrying a body drooped over his shoulders. He bent in front of Aldalon and gingerly set the corpse on the ground. There was no doubt it was Thorn: he was wearing Thorn's uniform and had a Catachan red bandanna tied around his bicep. The thing that made it more difficult to identify him was the fact that he was missing his head.

Aldalon looked up at Crusel. 'I'm going to assume you didn't just leave a piece behind, trooper?'

Crusel shook his head. 'No, sir. Whatever did it took a trophy.'

Aldalon sniffed.

'He was tail-end, sir,' Lieutenant Trast said. 'Last time I saw him I had to give him a dressing down over sound discipline. It's possible he was taken by the orks.'

'We would've heard that wouldn't we, sir?' Crusel asked. 'The greenskins make a hell of a racket. Unless it was the ghost orks.'

Aldalon turned to Crusel. 'What did you say, trooper?'

'Uh, the ghost orks, sir,' Crusel said. 'You know the stories about ork kommandos. No way orks could move that quietly unless they were dead.'

Aldalon wanted to agree. He wanted to be certain there was no way an ork could sneak up on a Catachan Jungle Fighter and ambush them. He would have believed it once too. But the image of that ork attack on Karst jolted to the front of his mind once again. A whole squad of Catachans caught off-guard by orks in camouflage, striking without all the normal ear-splitting cacophony and booming war cries of a greenskin attack. Brant getting his throat deftly cut from ear to ear. The ork with different-coloured eyes.

Aldalon pushed the thoughts away. He wouldn't share his concerns about preternaturally stealthy orks prowling the jungle. Not because he thought his troopers would be afraid but because he wanted them focused on the task at hand, not giving in to the unknown – many good soldiers, even Catachans, had lost their lives focusing on stories and legends instead of what was right in front of them. He needed them to stay sharp but wouldn't let the idea of ghost orks spread.

'All right, Catachans, gather in,' Aldalon said.

The two squads moved in and took a knee in front of him.

'I don't know what attacked Thorn, so everyone needs to be on their guard, but let's be clear here – greenskins are dangerous when they charge in large numbers. They can't take us in the jungle. We are Catachan Jungle Fighters. *We* own the jungle.'

The Catachans stared at him. They didn't make a sound, but Aldalon saw the acknowledgement in their eyes.

'Our next objective is to set up the orks with a feint into an area booby-trapped with the mines Squad Dram collected, wipe out as many as possible before we take the outpost. We'll prep now, rest and then execute the attack once it's dark.

'And, be clear on something else – there are no ghost orks. I do not want to hear nonsense stories designed to scare common Imperial Guard. The Catachan Fifty-Seventh does not lower itself to the spreading of ghost stories. Greenskins are the loudest, most rambunctious, and most feral of the xenos enemies of the Imperium. Whatever they do, we will hear them.'

As if to punctuate his last words there was an almighty boom, a distant explosion from the direction of Outpost Four. Aldalon recognised it as the somewhat muffled detonation of an underground mine. He cocked an eyebrow as he looked at the troopers before him, his meaning obvious: *I told you so.*

The Catachan 57th were the only Imperial unit operating in this area – or at least they were supposed to be – so either the fools at headquarters had decided to send in another or the orks were fighting among themselves. If the greenskins were distracted with some internal dispute, then now would be a good time to act.

'Get ready to move,' Aldalon said. 'Lieutenant Trast, Sappa and Dram, bring it in for briefing.'

The troopers moved off to prepare their equipment. They'd had little rest, some of them none, but Aldalon knew that sometimes you had to push hard. They could handle it. Lieutenant Trast, Sergeant Sappa and Sergeant Dram moved in close.

'We'll prepare the kill-zone where we planned, south sector, central approach, just inside the trees around the Outpost Four clearing. Dram, your squad will lay the demo. I want the mines on det. cord, not pressure triggered. Tonight, you'll execute the feint attack, drawing as much ork attention as possible, pulling them back through the kill-zone. Once you clear the ambush zone you'll establish as far-end security.'

Sergeant Dram nodded. No complaints about being given the most dangerous aspect of the task.

'Sergeant Sappa, your squad will scout the best crossfire sight lines. You'll be the attack element. When the greenskins hit the kill-zone, you'll blow the demo and open fire.'

'Sir,' Sappa said. 'We can handle the feint.'

Aldalon looked at her. He should have known it would be whoever was tasked with the safe job that would complain. These were Catachans and Learna thought she had more to prove than most.

'You'll do as ordered,' Aldalon said.

'Yes, sir.'

'Good,' Aldalon said. 'Get your squads ready to move.'

The NCOs got to work quickly and Aldalon noticed that even the soft-worlder was ready to move out when the others were. He was still lugging his standard-issue pack around but had at least started leaving some of its contents behind. He'd finally realised that despite the instructions outlined in Munitorum manuals and *The Imperial Infantryman's Uplifting Primer* it wasn't strictly necessary to carry spare underwear into battle – though on second thoughts perhaps most of the galaxy's Guardsmen did need some spare undergarments when the shrapnel began to fly.

The Catachan fighters moved to the location Aldalon had determined for the ambush – the south side of the outpost. It was from this direction the main ork force had first attacked the outpost, which meant the defences in that direction were the most damaged. It was where Squad Dram had cleared the minefield and the fence and wall were now non-existent. It served as the most obvious direction for a real attack and provided the clearest retreat for Squad Dram.

At the ambush site Squad Sappa began eyeing their sight lines and preparing camouflaged firepits the length of the kill-zone while Squad Dram dug shallow holes under the wide-leafed ferns and undergrowth to lay the mines.

The entire time this was happening Aldalon had those sharp senses on high alert; he heard the occasional shout from the orks inside the outpost but little other than that. There was no movement; there didn't seem to be any greenskins outside the outpost at all.

The two squads soon reported in. The ambush area was ready. Aldalon looked in the direction of Outpost Four, even though it was hardly visible through the trees.

'See you tonight,' he muttered.

The Catachans left as quietly as they'd come. Just as on their way to the outpost, on their return to camp they encountered no patrols and not even any randomly wandering greenskins. It seemed as though the greenskins were keeping themselves holed up in the outpost now. That wasn't a bad thing; hopefully it meant the few actions they'd taken against patrols and in shutting off the power had forced them to change their behaviour. It was a military rule almost as old as the ambush that whichever force was dictating changes in the other's tactics had the upper hand.

Just as long as tonight, when the Catachans launched their feigned withdrawal, the orks would be willing to come out after them. Aldalon was sure they would. There was only so much the greenskins, or any xenos race, would change their behaviour.

CHAPTER TWENTY-THREE

NOGROK

Nogrok ignored the stabbing from the brambles he hid within. Though ignored wasn't quite the right word because to ignore them he'd have to have felt them in the first place. His hard skin and natural orkish resilience to pain meant he didn't feel the jab of the sharp spines at all as he crouched, motionless, watching the Catachan humies as they moved through the jungle.

Nogrok couldn't keep the grin off his face as he watched. It really was the same sneaky Catachan humies from that stinkin'-hot desert planet – he recognised their boss, the dark-skinned one with that big smashin' power fist on his arm. Nogrok's favourite humies were here just like he'd hoped. He'd killed one of 'em, and now that he was finally in charge he could lead a sneak attack against them, see if he couldn't kill a few more. He wanted to show these humies just how much he liked 'em by sneakin' up and cuttin' their heads off.

Nogrok had scouted ahead, leaving the rest of the boyz back closer to the humie base, not trusting that they wouldn't alert the humies to their presence as they moved with their big clodhopper feet making a ruckus. He had no concerns about the few remaining Blood Axe kommandos with him. Flik, Nukka and Ruktug had grown proper kunnin' but the new Deathskulls he had under his command needed a lot of work to beat some Mork into 'em. Still, in the way of orks everywhere, some of them had already started to adopt the ways of their nob. There were a bunch that were acting like they might take well to sneaking even if they were Deathskulls gitz.

As Nogrok watched them, the Catachans came to a stop. They spread out, disappearing into spots all around the area, and Nogrok realised this was the humie camp. Proper sneaky it was too. All the spots where the humies sat or lay down were hidden with camouflage. Nogrok would have to remember that. He knew about camouflage for yourself or hiding if you were going to jump out and krump something, but hiding a whole camp, that was proper good taktiks.

But now Nogrok Sneakyguts knew where their hiding spots were and the humies didn't know Nogrok Sneakyguts knew. That meant Nogrok had the elephant of surprise. He slowly retreated into the jungle. Time to get his new mob together.

Nogrok moved back to where he'd left his boyz. He spotted them well before they spotted him – at least he spotted the Deathskulls; his kommandos were doing the proper thing and staying well hidden.

'Cor!' one of the Deathskulls remarked when Nogrok emerged from the trees in front of them. 'You just bloody appeared outta nowhere, boss! No wonder you called Sneakyguts.'

Nogrok looked at the ork: Gront, he thought his name was. He hadn't bothered learning the names of most of the Deathskulls gitz before, but he supposed he should now. 'Yeah well, you lot is my boyz now, so we need to get your guts sneaky too. Gonna have to wait on that though coz I been followin' da humies. They were gettin' ready to do some ambushin.'

There were some grumbles about sneaky humies not knowing how to fight – more attitudes Nogrok would have to adjust with some good ol'-fashioned nob teaching by threatening to krump 'em all.

'That don't matter now though coz I seen somethin' else,' Nogrok continued. 'I seen where the humies is hidin.' I seen the humie camp and we gonna attack 'em.'

'Wot 'bout Gutstompa?' one of the other Deathskulls asked.

'Wot 'bout him?'

'Shouldn't we tell 'im if we gonna attack da humies?'

'Nah, listen, we ain't got time. We go now. Wot's he gonna do, be mad we krumped some humies? Warboss Gutstompa can't argue with that.'

The Deathskull nodded. 'Yeah, that's right, boss.'

'We got more boyz than the humies out there and they don't know we is comin,' Nogrok said. 'We gonna use proper taktiks too, so listen careful. My Blood Axe kommandos gonna lead a group of Deffskulls each. They gonna make sure you do your best to not make a bloody racket movin' through the jungle. We gonna surround the humies. We gonna make a circle around the humie camp and move in quiet like. Then we gonna attack 'em from all directions 'fore they know we is comin.'

'But, boss,' another of the Deathskulls said, 'if we in a circle, we gonna be chargin' at each other, ain't we?'

'We ain't chargin,' Nogrok said. 'Remember, you part of Sneakyguts' mob now. We sneakin' in and then we start the killin.'

'Right, right,' the Deathskull said, nodding. 'Got it, got it. But then if we ain't chargin,' boss, when do we yell Waaagh!?'

Nogrok looked at the Deathskulls boy and spoke slowly and seriously. 'We don't yell Waaagh! until you already krumpin.'

The shock was evident on the faces of the Deathskulls, their red ork eyes growing wide at what sounded like complete crazy talk, like utter strategic incompetence being levelled before them.

'We don't yell Waaagh! until we already krumpin'?' the Deathskull called Gront said, voicing the confusion many of them felt. 'If we don't yell Waaagh!, how do the humies know they is about to get krumped by us? How do they know orks is best?'

'They don't know we comin,' they ain't supposed to know we comin,' Nogrok said. 'That's the point of bein' sneaky, ain't it.'

Nogrok looked at the Deathskulls in front of him, focusing particularly on those that, despite his trying to choose the most kunnin', were still heaps more Gork than Mork.

'We is kommandos. You is gonna be kommandos. There ain't many kommandos in orks because most orks ain't good enough. They gonna tell you, you ain't orky, or sneakin' about ain't proper fightin'. They only sayin' that coz they isn't good enough to be with us. They proper jealous.

'What Gutstompa and all them other big bosses don't want ya to know is chargin' in and yelling Waaagh! is easy, any ork wot's green can do that. But we do what only kommandos can do. Every ork knows there is two gods, but they only think 'bout Gork. We is the orks of Mork and he is kunnin' but he is brutal.' Nogrok leant in, making it clear what he was about to say was important, a secret, real proper meaningful. 'You wanna know why we don't need to yell Waaagh! so the humies know orks is the best? Coz when we sneak up on 'em and krump 'em 'fore they know what's comin', then we just showed 'em we is best. We proved to 'em orks is best.'

Most of the Deathskulls stared, but Nogrok saw something flicker behind their eyes. The ork brain was, quite literally, like a sponge and in that way it tended to soak up what it was told without too much critical thinking. It wasn't exactly like one of the speeches the other nobz or warbosses would give about crackin' skulls and cuttin' up whatever they were about to fight, but they felt something rising in them, the same desire to do what their nob was asking.

Plus, Nogrok hoped they were realising that being sneaky was orky after all.

'You wiv me?' Nogrok asked, adding this because now seemed like the time he needed to win over his new crew; probably they needed something quick to cheer at, that might help get some noise out of their system.

'Yeah!'

'We wiv ya, boss!'

'For Nob Sneakyguts!'

The Deathskulls responded as expected and Nogrok chalked this up to good leadership. 'Well,' he said. 'Let's move out and kill some humies.'

'Yeah! Waaagh!'

'Oi!' Nogrok said. The few Deathskulls who'd got a little too worked up went quiet, lowering their heads.

'Sorry, boss.'

'Let's move out and kill some humies,' Nogrok said again, pausing for effect, 'but do it sneaky.'

Nogrok led them through the dense jungle in the direction of the humie camp. He was, for at least a short while, pleasantly surprised by how well the Deathskulls did at moving quietly through the jungle. Of course, he wouldn't call them stealthy. Compared to the Catachan humies or even Nogrok's kommandos they might as well have been firing their shootas into the air, but compared with the standards of ordinary orks Nogrok had to give them credit where it was due.

That was until one of them tripped, cursed, tried to catch himself on a hanging vine which wasn't firmly attached to anything and pulled it down, shaking the whole damn jungle canopy and causing birds to fly squawking from the treetops. When the ork stood back up, Nogrok didn't give him time to look sheepish; he was on him like a flash of green, slamming him back against a tree and holding his bright Catachan knife to the Deathskull's throat. Nogrok felt the gentle push down the length of his knife as the ork swallowed. He could smell the pungent stink of fear coming off the ork. It was a little surprising, but it smelled good, and it felt good to know he could cause fear in other orks now. Nogrok felt the eyes of the other boyz on them. He needed to make an example here.

'What do you think you is doing, you git?' Nogrok snarled, pushing the knife harder against the ork's green throat. 'We is goin' to the humie camp. They probably heard that innit? You do somethin' so stupid as that again and I'll krump you meself.'

The ork nodded. 'Sorry, boss.'

Nogrok pulled the knife away, feeling the ork relax. Nogrok smacked him in the nose with a quick punch just for good measure. 'Don't say sorry, ya git, just do better.'

'Sorry, boss.'

Nogrok punched him again before letting him go and turning away. 'Flik, Nukka, Ruktug. On me. We gonna go recon-o-sance the humie camp. The rest of you, wait 'ere.' Nogrok stopped, turned back and reiterated. 'I mean that. Don't even move.'

The three kommandos joined Nogrok and he led them into the trees further towards the humies. With just the four kommandos moving through the jungle, Nogrok realised exactly how much work he had to do with the Deathskulls.

When they were a short distance from the location of the humie camp Nogrok stopped, crouching down. He squinted, peering through the suffocating green, unable to see the humies but knowing they were there. This was the spot. He signalled for Flik, Nukka and Ruktug to move up beside him. The three kommandos crept through the undergrowth to move in beside their nob. Nogrok pointed, indicating the camp through the trees ahead. The kommandos looked ahead as well, trying to see any sign of movement. Nogrok was sure they couldn't see anything either, but he gave them a moment to take in the area before standing and signalling for them to follow.

When they had rejoined the Deathskulls boyz, who he was glad to see had not moved, Nogrok stopped and turned to his fellow Blood Axes. 'You three see that spot we was at?'

'Dat was da humie camp?' Flik asked.

Nogrok nodded.

'Mork's teef, they is proper hidden.'

Nogrok nodded again. 'You remember where it is?'

The kommandos nodded.

'Reckon we can find our way back, boss,' Nukka said.

'Good,' Nogrok said, coz you three is gonna be me squad leaders, and for me plan to work we need to split up. I need to know you can get back there. Like I said, you is each gonna take a squad of boyz, keep 'em as quiet as ya can and circle round the humies. Then we gonna attack at the same time.

'Flik, your squad gonna come straight on from this direction. Nukka, from round that way. Ruktug, from that way. I gonna take the last group right around and attack from the other side. You're gonna get yourself as close as you think you can without the humies spotting you. It'll take me longer to get into the right position so you lot is gonna wait, and then when you see me lead my squad in to attack the humies, that'll be your signal to get to krumpin' too.'

After organising his new Deathskulls into four squads, which was a little like herding squigs, Nogrok allocated a squad each to himself, Flik, Nukka and Ruktug and sent them off to encircle the humie camp. After his example threatening the Deathskull, the boyz with him moved like they were walking on broken glass – sure, they were hulking great squiggoths walking on glass, but at least they were trying to be careful.

Still, Nogrok gave the humies a wide, wide berth, much wider than he would have if he was moving just with the kommandos. As a result, it took much longer to get into position than it would have had he taken a more direct route.

What Nogrok hadn't anticipated was that despite the Deathskulls trying to maintain some sneakiness, the longer they had to keep it up, the more difficult it got for them. Towards the end of the approach on the humie camp the Deathskulls boyz began to lose grip on their admittedly already very slippery attention span. They snapped sticks, rustled leaves and banged through hanging vines, which shook in long waves all the way up into the canopy.

The final straw was when one of them – it was bloody Gront too – having lost concentration completely and forgotten what it was he was supposed to be doing, actually zoggin' well spoke.

'Oi, boss, are we there yet?'

Nogrok rounded on him, but it was too late. A las-shot cracked through the jungle, blew through the side of Gront's face and hit the tree behind him in a burst of superheated sap.

'Ah, zog,' Gront said, the words even more garbled than usual when an ork spoke because the side of his mouth had been blown open in a cauterised mess. 'Sorry 'bout dat. I forgot about tryin' to be qui–'

Whichever humie had fired through the twisting green of the jungle had obviously corrected his aim because the second las-shot took the top of Gront's head off in a melted burst of boiling flesh and charred bone, leaving the acrid smell of burnt ork floating in the air. Gront thumped back, crushing a fern beneath his large dead mass. Nogrok sighed. He should have known he was asking too much of the Deathskulls gitz to manage a sneaky attack already.

Nogrok raised his Catachan knife and screamed in his most Gorky way.

'WAAAAAAAAAGH!'

CHAPTER TWENTY-FOUR

TORVIN

Torvin sat staring down at the Catachan knife in his hand, the one he'd been given by Corporal Sappa. He turned the knife from side to side, rotating it as he ran a piece of cloth wet with Departmento Munitorum-issued blessed blade-cleaning balm along its length, wiping off the dried blood and the dirt that had stuck to it.

He rubbed his thumb unconsciously at the patches of red still spotting the back of his knife hand too, picking the chunks off with the underside of his fingernail. His hands and arms were covered in streaks of greenskin gore with hard outer husks that had to be scratched off. Unlike human blood, which seemed to lose most of its iron tang as it dried, the smell of ork blood seemed to grow more intense, the blood inside the dry outer shell fermenting and growing rancid. Torvin got a whiff of the acidic stench every time he knocked a piece of crust free from his skin.

'Soft-worlder.'

Torvin looked up at his name – at least the name he'd grown familiar with. Sergeant Sappa was watching him.

'What's on your mind?' she asked.

'Nothing.'

'It's different doing it like that, isn't it?' Sappa said. 'Up close and personal, not at a distance like most Guardsmen are taught to do it. I can see how it might be hard the first time.'

'It wasn't hard for you, sergeant?' Torvin asked.

'Ha. I've lived this life since I was a child.'

'Right.'

'You'll be fine,' Sappa said. 'Get some rest and be ready for tonight's assault on the outpost.'

Sappa turned to walk about, going to check in on the rest of the squad, though Torvin was sure they wouldn't need the same pep talk.

'That's the thing,' Torvin said, almost before he realised he was going to speak. 'I am fine. I thought I'd feel something after that – horror at having killed or elation at having survived – but I don't really feel anything.'

Sappa let out a single, breathy laugh. 'That's the secret, soft-worlder. You think great Guardsmen call upon some deep part of their humanity in war, love for the Imperium or love for the Emperor or whatever, but they don't.

The legendary regiments of the Imperial Guard, like the Catachans, fight with inhuman ferocity because that's what we are – inhuman. The war changes us.'

'What makes us different from the greenskins then?' Torvin asked.

Sappa smiled a crooked smile and shook her head as she walked away. 'You're almost there, soft-worlder, almost.'

As Torvin sat cleaning off ork blood he wasn't sure which was worse, intense hatred for the enemies of mankind or unfeeling coldness.

'WAAAAAAGH!'

Torvin's philosophical musings were interrupted by the very subject matter he was considering: the battle cry of orks filled the air. It seemed the time had come for more cold, uncaring war. The shout had come from the opposite side of the wide Catachan perimeter. The flank in that direction was covered by the troopers of Squad Dram.

'Orks!' Torvin heard the shout and recognised the voice as Sergeant Dram's. 'Breaching cover, twenty yards, my twelve, fire at will!'

Torvin, hidden beneath the low covering of his hole, couldn't see what was happening behind him, but he could hear the eruptive cracks of las-shots and plasma rounds as the Catachans opened fire. He could smell it too: the stench of wet jungle plants instantly burning as leaves, trunks and branches were struck by stray lines of concentrated las-beams. He could even feel it, the faint static buzz as humid air was ionised.

Torvin pulled himself forward until his head and chest extended out from his camouflaged hole. He turned to look. Even in the now clear morning light the jungle was still wrapped in green-hued shadows, but they soon burst into bright life with the streaks of iridescent red/orange las-shot and punches of blue plasma. There was, predictably, an answering cacophony of smoke-billowing, flame-belching, booming ork shootas. Almost nowhere in warfare was there such a distinct difference as between the elegant straight lines of lasgun fire and the eruption of ork rounds leaving their barrels and somersaulting through the air like misshapen cannonballs.

'Squad Sappa!' came Sergeant Sappa's voice from nearby. 'Squad Sappa, gear up and stand to! Break cover and move to support Squad Dram!'

Torvin saw movement coalesce from the hidden places in the jungle around him as Sappa's squad did as ordered, breaking from their camouflaged positions with lascarbines, pistols and Catachan knives in hand, ready to support their fellow troopers in the direction of the ork attack.

Torvin slid back into his hole to grab his weapons. He saw, on top of his pack where he had left it earlier, the fold-worn pict of Melina. This time, as he slipped his Catachan blade into its sheath and took hold of his lasgun, he left the pict behind.

Torvin clambered out of his scrape and to his feet. He saw Sergeant Sappa standing nearby, her lascarbine primed with an audible hum. Poison Guts Fletcha climbed out of a nearby hole. Fletcha hadn't bothered with his lascarbine at all; instead he gripped only his Catachan knife with its blade, even longer and more viciously saw-toothed than most, dripping with some purple poison.

'Come on,' Sappa said as her squad emerged from hiding. 'Support the far line.'

Squad Sappa moved through the trees, weapons up. Those with their lascarbines raised began firing at motion in the trees, but even though it was morning now, it was still difficult to pick out targets through the dense foliage, and their firing slowed.

Torvin raised his lasgun and fired several blasts into the trees as well before realising it was more than just difficult to find a clear shot at an ork, it was also too treacherous; it would be too easy to inadvertently loose a shot at a friendly. The image of Lieutenant Gernson being blown away by Trooper Norsten's shots flashed into his mind.

He lowered his lasgun, slipping the sling over his shoulder, and pulled out his Catachan blade. He was about to follow the others of Squad Sappa who had already made the decision to charge forward and engage the orks in hand-to-hand combat, when the tree beside him burst, showering him with dust and splinters of wood. The booming shot, obviously that of an ork weapon, had come from behind him and the accompanying war cry confirmed it. Torvin stopped and spun, seeing what Colonel Aldalon obviously saw in the same moment.

'Squad Sappa! About-turn!' the colonel roared, appearing like a rolling storm, bursting into view as if the jungle had exploded around him in a hail of shattering glass.

'Squad! Turn!' Sergeant Sappa echoed. 'They've surrounded us!'

Torvin turned to see Aldalon rushing towards the newly attacking orks. His power fist crackled with energy as he roared. Torvin watched as he swung it forward, punching a large ork through the chest and sending a spray of xenos ichor and shattered spine out its back.

Nearby, another trooper – Torvin thought her name was Braker – was not fast enough to turn to the newly arrived threat and a greenskin slammed into her from behind, hacking her down with its rusty blade.

'Soft-worlder!'

Torvin responded to the shout and turned to his right to see Poison Guts Fletcha brandishing his knife as more orks came from the trees nearby. These ones were charging from the side. Sergeant Sappa had been right. They weren't just outflanked by orks, they were completely surrounded.

Torvin glanced back to see Lieutenant Trast, Colonel Aldalon and Sergeant Sappa all engaging orks pouring in from other directions. Beside him, Poison Guts roared and charged at the orks in front of them. Torvin, in an instinctual motion that would have seemed impossible just days ago, maybe even hours ago, charged with him.

One moment he saw Fletcha heading for the enemy and the next Torvin's boots were slamming into jungle mud, his legs slashing through low ferns right beside him. He had seen the Catachans fight orks enough now to know they needed to at least pair up. Fletcha shouted what Torvin thought might have been 'For Catachan!' as he charged. Torvin joined in with a bellowing war cry of his own, but what escaped from his mouth had no meaning. He roared as if he'd known battle his whole life.

Fletcha reached the orks first. He ducked as an ork swung its large-bladed axe, and then launched forward with a thrust of his poisoned knife, jabbing it into the relatively soft flesh of the ork's belly. The ork raised its axe again but stopped, its brow furrowed. Then it buckled forward and vomited hot, red blood and green bile on the ground before dropping.

'One to me, soft-worlder!' Fletcha yelled.

Torvin charged up beside Fletcha and was met by an ork bursting from the trees. It opened its mouth and bellowed something that sounded like the word 'Die!' in a shower of spittle, raising its huge cutta.

Torvin lifted his Catachan blade and slashed at the green-skinned monster. He did not have his pict of Melina in his pocket and in that moment, if time could have been stopped and he was asked, Ted Torvin would not have been able to remember what she looked like, or what his mother and father had looked like, or what it was he thought he liked about Skadi. He couldn't remember anything about his old life because, in that moment, this was home.

CHAPTER TWENTY-FIVE

ALDALON

'Squad Sappa! About-turn!' Aldalon roared as soon as he realised what was happening.

He spun from where he'd intended to support Squad Dram and saw the greenskins thundering out of the trees. They were coming from all directions. All of them were dressed in rudimentary camouflage, black paint in patches or slashes across their face, and where they had been decorated in the bright blue of the Deathskulls, their clothes had been covered in jungle mud and leaves to dull the colour and hide it from view.

Just as Aldalon had feared, the greenskins were adapting. They were learning, or at least, with what Aldalon understood of ork society, there was one ork somewhere that was learning and influencing the others. He thought of that camouflaged ork on Karst, the one who had taken Brant from him. The one with the different-coloured eyes. This was the one, Aldalon was sure of it.

The orks stormed in with a roaring, blustering charge now, but they'd managed to get close enough to launch a surprise attack. They had got close enough that Colonel Aldalon and the 57th Catachan Jungle Fighters were not ready for them. If he weren't about to smash into the whirlwind of combat, the thought that greenskins had surprised Catachans yet again would have been enough to make Colonel Haskell Aldalon nauseous to the pit of his usually rockcrete guts.

'Squad! Turn!' Aldalon heard Learna echoing his orders to her squad. 'They've surrounded us!'

Learna Sappa was strong, as strong as any Catachan, as strong as he had been as a newly minted sergeant, but he heard the panic in her voice. They'd all underestimated the orks.

Aldalon leapt over a series of the low, wide-leafed ferns, each in a single stride. He roared, jumping again as he reached the first ork to come near him. With an audible crackling-hum and a tingling sensation that worked its way from his palm, down to his fingertips and up his arm, Aldalon's power fist burst to energetic life, and he struck with the intensity of all his anger and frustration. His hatred of the orks, his anger at himself for letting them get to his troops – all of it added weight to the blow.

The power fist landed square in the centre of the ork's chest and buried its way inside. He ripped it out with a spray of hot gore and kicked the ork over with his heavy boot.

Aldalon caught Learna's eye briefly before she dashed forward with blade in hand. To one side Lieutenant Trast was engaged in combat and to the other he saw Poison Guts Fletcha ramming his poisoned knife into the belly of a greenskin. Beside him, much to Aldalon's surprise, Trooper Torvin was howling like a mad banshee and slashing at an ork with the blade Learna had given him.

The ork that Torvin hacked wildly at leant back to dodge the blow. He still had to teach that soft-worlder how to fight. If an ork could dodge a blow it must have been blatantly telegraphed. As the ork prepared its own retaliatory swing, Aldalon watched Poison Guts deftly swoop in, deflecting the blow into the dirt, protecting Torvin from the powerful strike.

Catachans were raised from birth to have each other's backs because nothing else on that world would protect them. Still, Aldalon knew that of all the Catachans, Poison Guts would have been happy to see the soft-worlder take an ork blade to the cranium. Fletcha had not allowed that to happen, though.

In return the soft-worlder leapt onto the ork, who was still bent over from the deflected swing, landing on its back. As the ork roared and stood to full height, Torvin wrapped his arms around its neck and held on like a rider trying to break in some wild mount. The ork thrashed, trying to throw Torvin free but the soft-worlder held on, dangling down the greenskin's back. Torvin wrapped his legs around the ork's waist for leverage, shoved his fingers up the creature's overly large nostrils for grip with one hand, and then slashed his blade across its throat with the other.

Blood sprayed out in an arterial fountain before Torvin, still holding on against the creature's now desperate bucking, hacked at the ork's throat again and again until he was through the spinal cord and the greenskin's head hung on by little more than green sinewy flesh. As the dead ork finally collapsed forward, Torvin rode it to the ground.

'That's the way, soft-worlder!' Aldalon heard Learna call from nearby, having also witnessed Torvin's actions.

As Fletcha reached down to him, Torvin pulled his fingers free from where they had been jammed deep in the ork's nostrils and wiped the snotty slime on his trousers before taking the Catachan's hand.

'You can't claim that,' Fletcha said as he pulled Torvin to his feet. 'You'd be bleeding out on the ground if I hadn't swooped in.'

'Groxshit I can't,' Torvin said in the no-nonsense, no-argument way of a Catachan Jungle Fighter before he turned back to face more oncoming orks. Despite himself, Aldalon smiled.

Then he turned his attention, and his crackling power fist, to the destruction of more orks. As a veteran who'd served the Imperium through some forty years and countless battles against almost all the major threats that beset it, Aldalon, even in the centre of carnage, could take in the greater battle in a way that most confronted with the slavering, snarling visage of greenskin madness could not.

Even as he slammed his power fist into the face of one greenskin and then immediately spun to backhand another on the side of its head, caving its skull in with the ferociousness that had earned him the Hell Fist moniker, he scanned the scene. The jungle was as dense with fighting as it was with foliage. Flashes of green-skinned mayhem met streaks of red-bandannaed insanity. It was difficult to get as much situational awareness as he would have liked in the glimpses he could spare, but it was clear to Aldalon that a handful of Catachans – he couldn't be sure exactly how many – were dead. The only positive was that there were clearly more dead orks.

'You lot! We fallin' back!'

Over the clash of weapons, the shouts and the guttural roars Aldalon heard a single ork voice cut through the fray. It was coming from the direction of Squad Dram. For it to be that loud and clear it had to have been the leader of this group.

Aldalon smacked aside an ork that was coming for him, ending its howling war cry as his power fist smashed off its entire jawbone, and headed in the direction of the ork calling the orders.

He sped up as he saw some of the orks begin to pull away. Not all of them were listening though; at least half the remaining orks were still locked in ferocious fighting with his troops and showed no sign of being willing to listen to an order to retreat. Still, the fact that an ork had even ordered a retreat, and that some of the greenskins were listening, was another major alteration in greenskin behaviour and Aldalon needed to see the ork who was pulling these strings. He suspected he knew which one it was, and he wouldn't let him escape. Not after what he'd done.

Aldalon turned to where Lieutenant Trast fought nearby. 'Hold here, lieutenant!'

Trast looked at him as more orks breached the trees. Aldalon felt that same anger, and now Trast was giving him the same look, as when they had been out on reconnaissance together, when Aldalon had lost his composure.

'Sir,' Lieutenant Trast said. 'That side of the perimeter is holding. We need you here, this is where the greenskins are outnumbering us. This is where they could hurt us!'

'We taktikal retreatin,' boyz!' the leader yelled again, and Aldalon decided. He began moving in the direction of the ork's shouts.

'Sir!' Trast called. 'We need you here!'

'I said hold here, lieutenant,' Aldalon said as he hurried away through the trees. Trast could handle that flank of the battle. Aldalon could not let that ork escape him.

'Right, stuff ya then, ya gitz – the rest of ya, come on!'

Aldalon quickened his pace, slamming aside one of the orks. When he burst through a particularly dense thicket of trees Aldalon finally caught sight of the retreating xenos. The one in the centre, the largest of them, turned at the sound of Aldalon careening through the jungle. Aldalon stopped. He and the greenskin locked eyes.

It was him. Just as he'd known it would be. He was looking at the distinctive eyes of the ork that had killed Brant. The ork that seemed to be single-handedly changing the way orks behaved. The ork he was about to single-handedly slaughter.

The ork looked back at Aldalon with what he was sure was similar recognition. To confirm Aldalon's suspicion the greenskin raised its hand, which held what Aldalon immediately recognised as a Catachan blade, and put the point to its forehead in a kind of salute.

'Colonel! Your six!'

Aldalon spun by instinct. An ork was bearing down on him. He ducked to the side to dodge the ork's blow before reaching out and grabbing the creature around the throat with his power fist, squeezing until he felt the pop of the windpipe and the crunch of spine. When he turned back, the ork with the red and green eyes and those that had followed him were gone. The only thing that stopped Aldalon from charging off into the jungle after the mysterious creature was another shout from behind him. A shout that drained his anger in an instant and left him full of a sudden cold.

'Trast is down! Lieutenant Trast is down!'

Aldalon hurried back towards Trast's last position, ignoring the battle around him. His troopers were still locked in combat with the last of the orks who hadn't retreated, but the Catachans clearly had the upper hand now. They would deal with the rest. Aldalon had eyes only for the fallen body of his lieutenant. He dropped to his knees beside him and rolled him over onto his back. He'd been run through with a savage ork blow right in the centre of his chest, his ribs shattered and caved in. The life was already gone from Trast's face as he stared up at the canopy overhead, flecks of jungle dirt stuck to the surface of his unmoving eyes.

'Sir.'

What had he done?

'Sir.'

He would tell himself later, and the rest of the Catachans would believe, that Aldalon had abandoned Trast in that spot because he had full confidence in his lieutenant's ability to hold his own. But in that moment Aldalon knew the truth: he had been reckless in his pursuit of the ork with the mismatched eyes. His anger at all orks, and that one in particular, had clouded his judgement again. This time, though, it had resulted in one of his best and most loyal veterans lying dead in the jungle dirt. The orks had managed to get inside his head in a way he couldn't allow. He was a Catachan colonel. He needed to pull himself together. Anger was a weakness only one step above fear. He was Catachan. There was no weakness in the Catachan.

'Father!'

Aldalon looked up from Lieutenant Trast's body, finally realising that Learna was yelling at him. He wasn't quite sure how long he'd been there, kneeling beside Trast, but the battle was over. He stared up at his daughter for a long moment, too long, before he shifted back into the correct frame.

'Action report?'

'The orks that didn't fall back have been dealt with. The area is secure. Perimeter re-established.'

Aldalon looked around. As Sergeant Sappa had said, the Catachans had not only finished off the orks but had already returned to defensive positions in a standard, albeit tighter, perimeter. 'Casualties?'

Sappa looked at the body splayed out in the mud in front of Aldalon. 'Including Lieutenant Trast, five dead. Two wounded.'

'Who?'

'Braker, Krall, Holler, Krill and' – she paused – 'Lieutenant Trast are KIA. Whirler and Crusel are both wounded but still fighting fit.'

Aldalon nodded slowly and then sighed. 'Get their red.'

Sappa held out her hand. Four red bandannas were clutched tightly in her fist. 'Already done, sir.'

Aldalon reached down and slipped Trast's bandanna off his head, then held his hand out. Sappa laid the rest on his open palm. Aldalon squeezed them tightly, muttering a common Catachan ode to the dead under his breath, and then rose to his feet, stuffing the bundle of red cloth in his pocket. He would carry these deaths with him just as much as he had Brant's, he promised himself that. But this time he would not let it turn to anger, to weakness that cost lives. He would not fail these Guardsmen again. He would not fail in his duty as a leader of the greatest Imperial Guardsmen the Emperor was fortunate to have fight in His name.

He was Catachan Colonel Haskell Aldalon and he would use death as it was intended for the people of Catachan: as motivation to become better, more resilient, more deadly. It was not to be used as fuel for anger or sadness. It was only fuel to be stronger. It did not matter that his son had died. Countless sons and daughters of Catachan had died. He would not let himself be controlled by that any more, nor would he let his feelings of loss hold back his daughter. She deserved the right to be Catachan too; to live, to fight and maybe to die in service of the Emperor, the Imperium of Man and the glory of their world. That was the love he needed to have for her. Letting her be Catachan.

'Catachans, form up.'

The Guardsmen that remained pulled in close to their colonel.

'You can all hear this. You all need to hear this. You all know my son Brant was killed in our last encounter with the orks on Karst. I have let that affect me. I have been fighting angry and as a result I have made mistakes. That was wrong of me. It is not the Catachan way. We fight hard but we fight clear of mind. Sergeant Sappa?'

'Yes, sir.'

'You are right to have accused me of holding you back. As my daughter, as my only other child, I have been concerned for your well-being after Brant's death. But you deserve to forge your path and serve the Emperor however He chooses, whether that be a long life of war or a short one. Effective immediately you are field-promoted to acting lieutenant.'

'Sir, I–' Sappa began, but Aldalon held up his hand. He wasn't sure whether she was going to thank him or argue with him. Either way it didn't matter. The decision was made.

'We've been hit hard by the greenskins, but we are going to finish this now. We are taking back Outpost Four because it belongs to humanity and because that is what we have been tasked to do. The plan remains the same – feign an attack and lead as many orks as possible to be slaughtered like a line of grox in the abattoir.'

The Catachans around him were steel-faced and calm, but Aldalon could feel the anger radiating off them. He needed to harness that and use it to end this fight.

'Lieutenant Sappa, you will be leading the feigned attack with your squad. Sergeant Dram, your squad and myself will make up the ambush element. We're executing now. Any questions?'

The troopers watching on, including newly promoted Lieutenant Sappa and Sergeant Dram, were silent. They already knew the plan of how they would take back the outpost, or perhaps, more than that, they were shocked that Hell Fist Aldalon had admitted fault.

'Good,' Aldalon continued. 'There's one other thing to do before we move out. Soft-worlder?'

Torvin looked up, surprised to be addressed directly. 'Yes, sir?'

'Stand up and come here.'

Torvin did as he was bid, moving towards the colonel until he was standing in front of the watching Jungle Fighters. He walked hesitantly and Aldalon saw his throat bob as he swallowed nervously. He likely didn't know whether he was about to get praised, torn a new arsehole or killed on the spot. Luckily for him it was the former.

'Stop looking like you're facing the firing squad,' Aldalon said. 'You fought well. You're still a soft-worlder but at least you didn't piss yourself this time. You're a soft-worlder who beheaded an ork and maybe, just for a moment, you made a greenskin piss themselves instead. Because of that, you're going to need one of these.' Aldalon reached into his pocket and pulled out one of the red bandannas that had been taken from the dead Catachans. He held it out and Torvin stared down at it. 'Go on, soldier, take it.'

Torvin reached out and took the bandanna, folding it over into a strip and then wrapping it around his forehead, tying it tight at the back. Aldalon looked at him, stone-faced, unsure really whether he had done the right thing.

The red bandanna was a simple object and yet it meant a lot to the men and women of Catachan – it represented what it meant to be more than a simple Imperial Guardsman and to be one of the greatest warriors the Imperium had at its disposal. This trooper from Skadi was not one of those, but in the last battle he had shown growth and bravery, and had stood by Poison Guts – who had threatened his life – as if he were one of them. So, for now at least, he could be an honorary Catachan Jungle Fighter.

Aldalon took in the expressions of the troopers around them. They all watched Torvin with faces of unreadable granite. He worried they thought he was giving that away too easily, but he was relieved to see that when he returned to take a knee, several troopers patted Torvin on the shoulder. Aldalon had headed into the jungle with a mind that retaking this outpost would be a simple matter, an easy guerrilla activity, but he had underestimated the orks – the one with the two-toned eyes, and his ghost orks in particular – and now he needed all the Catachan Jungle Fighters he could get. More importantly, he would not, under any circumstances, let down the men and women under his command again.

CHAPTER TWENTY-SIX

NOGROK

'I sent ya out with way more boyz than that, ya bloody useless git,' Gutstompa roared when Nogrok re-entered the humie outpost. 'I knew ya should never 'ave been made a nob, and don't fink I don't see all the ones that didn't come back are Deffskulls, ain't it? All you Blood Axe sneaky gitz is 'ere. You tryin' somethin' to take over, ain't you?'

A crowd of Deathskulls had gathered, all the boyz that were left in Gutstompa's small warband. Not that there were that many now. Gutstompa reckoned he'd been looting and preparing and waiting on reinforcements to roll down and take the humie city, but as far as Nogrok could see, all he'd done was lose boyz. None of the orks at Outpost Four, even the most intelligent like Nogrok himself, could count high enough, but if they could they'd know there'd been two hundred and fifty-three orks in the original attack against the outpost and now there were sixty-four.

The loss of three-quarters of one's fighting force would be staggeringly unacceptable for any army in the galaxy, but Warboss Gutstompa barely gave it a thought. As far as he was concerned, he was gonna be warboss of a proper Waaagh! He was just waiting for Gork and Mork to send enough boyz his way.

The remaining sixty-four orks gathered around as Nogrok returned, pushing and shoving to get to the front. Gutstompa had obviously riled them up, getting them ready for a fight.

Gutstompa himself stood in the middle of the orks, blocking Nogrok's entrance, his head and shoulders ducked down and hunched forward to fit under the ceiling. His thick metal-framed legs were spaced wide, planted on the grey-painted rockcrete like massive pillars sunk into the ground to support a bridge, or maybe an entire space port.

'I ain't tryin' to take over, boss,' Nogrok said. 'Trust me, I don't want a bunch more useless Deffskulls anyway. The only reason it was Deffskulls that didn't come back was coz it was only Deffskulls what were the stupid gitz wot didn't listen to my orders.'

Warboss Gutstompa growled. 'What orders?'

'I told 'em to do a taktikal retreat so we could get ready for another attack, but dey didn't listen, so now they is krumped fungus for the jungle.'

Nogrok heard shocked gasps from the onlookers. Gutstompa's face twisted in more disgust than Nogrok thought he'd ever seen on an ork's face.

'You ran away,' Gutstompa said, not even sounding all that angry, just shocked or amazed, 'from a fight.'

'No,' Nogrok said. 'I ain't run away, I *taktikally retreated.* It's different, ain't it.'

'Don't seem no different to me,' Gutstompa said. 'You ran away. Orks don't run from a fight.'

'And dat,' Nogrok said, unable to stop himself, 'is why we keep losin'. Orks ain't never gonna be the best if we don't win.'

'Orks is best!' Gutstompa roared. 'Orks is best at fightin'!'

'Orks could be best at fightin',' Nogrok said. 'But da big problem is orks ain't best at winnin'.'

Gutstompa's shock and disgust had given way to proper anger now. 'You is talkin' unorky zoggin' words!'

'No I ain't,' Nogrok said. 'I is tellin' the truth. Us orks could krump the whole galaxy if we used taktiks like the humies or the pointy ears or the fish 'eads. Don't you wanna be warboss of the whole galaxy, boss?' Nogrok was very deliberate in adding this last part because of course Gutstompa wanted to be warboss of the whole galaxy; every warboss wanted to be warboss of the whole galaxy. Zog, every ork down to the scrawniest snotling probably wanted to be warboss of the whole galaxy. It had the desired effect too. Gutstompa was suddenly a lot calmer, at least a little calmer, as his mushroom-brained thoughts turned to galactic domination.

'The Deffskulls you give me needed to be weeded out anyway,' Nogrok continued. 'It's like squig farmin', ain' it. You know how them snotling squig keepers wot breed up the squigs only keep the big 'uns or the fastest or the most tasty? Dat's wot I is doin', boss. The boyz wot got krumped was too weak or too stupid, not strong enough to win. Same thing ain't it? Natural election.'

'I ain't gave you boyz to do whatever natural election you on about, Nogrok,' Gutstompa said. 'I oughta krump ya right now for messin' up me boyz.'

Nogrok, still standing only to the shoulder of Warboss Kazkorg Gutstompa, was nevertheless now larger and bulkier than most of the orks watching on. He pulled himself to his full height and stomped to stand in front of Gutstompa.

'I is Nob Nogrok Sneakyguts,' he boomed – not shouted, but boomed, projecting his voice with orky power. 'They was my boyz, and whether you like wot I asked 'em to do or not, I told 'em to do somethin', they ain't done it and they got walloped coz of it. You ain't got grounds for krumpin' me at all, boss.'

Gutstompa growled again, but this time it was a growl of acceptance. He had made Nogrok a nob and whether he liked it or not, Nogrok was right. If his boyz got krumped for not listenin' to their nob then that was their own stupid fault.

'You are gonna be–'

Warboss Gutstompa was interrupted by an explosion from outside. A concussive blast that reverberated through the walls of the humie base and caused a shower of dust to fall from the ceiling onto the orks standing and watching their warboss confront this new upstart nob.

Gutstompa spun to those orks nearest the stairs. 'Go!'

Most of them looked at him blankly, which didn't much surprise Nogrok because he was sure their minds were as blank as their faces.

'Go and 'ave a look wot all dat noise is, ya gitz!' Gutstompa roared at them.

Half a dozen of the orks dashed up the stairs, and moments later booming shots came from the roof. 'Humies! Humies is attackin'!'

Orks moved in a flurry of excitement like feeding time in a squig pit. Gutstompa moved through the centre of them, shoving boyz aside to push his way through the crowd to the stairs.

'Get outta me way, gitz.'

Nogrok tucked himself in behind the warboss and trailed along in his wake like a snotling following a massive war trukk. Gutstompa ploughed through the gathered orks and charged up the stairs to the roof.

Up on the rampart, Nogrok peeled off and saw the humie attack. It was smaller than he'd expected. Six of the Catachan humies were charging across the clearing. They'd already made it past the destroyed fence, almost all the way to the humie base, because just like every idiot warboss, Gutstompa hadn't left any boyz on watch.

One of the humies was a little further back than the front five, crouching down with a rokkit launcher thing on his shoulder. A rokkit burst from the tube and flew towards the outpost with a long plume of smoke trailing behind it. That explained the explosion they'd heard from inside. Nogrok saw a smoking crater in the wall of the base where the last rokkit had hit and, because humie rokkits tended to go where they pointed them instead of wherever else they wanted to like ork rokkits, he could see the next one was going to hit the same spot.

Nogrok dived to the side, anticipating the result of the impact in a way that few other orks did. The humie rokkit slammed into the wall right at the already weakened point and erupted in a ball of black soot and a ferocious fireball. The wall burst inward, and an entire section of the rampart collapsed in a shower of broken rockcrete, soot, dust and ork swear words. The orks standing above the point of impact were blown to fragments by the concussive shock while most of those nearby were flung off the wall.

Warboss Gutstompa was standing near the destruction of the outpost's wall, but the bulky warboss didn't move his armoured feet at all. The front of the base collapsed in a landslide of rockcrete and debris, but he remained entirely still, staring out at the Catachans crossing the long grass towards him.

It was an orky truth universally acknowledged that bigger is better, red ones go faster and purple is the sneakiest colour. It was also well understood that a warboss could stand in the middle of the most outrageous scene of carnage and mayhem just like this and nothing, not a ricochet, not a fragment of secondary projectile, not even much in the way of splattered gore, would touch them.

So it was that Warboss Kazkorg Gutstompa stood, completely unharmed, with the end of his mammoth boots hanging over the jagged edge of the rampart. Lasgun fire began coming from the humies, zipping into the battlement and the occasional ork forehead. This was when Gutstompa's face hardened and he lifted his own massive shoota.

'Well,' he boomed, 'I can't believe I gotta tell you gitz to start shootin' back!'

The puny humie las-shots with their cracking zaps were joined by the much more satisfying – at least to green ears – booms of ork-built weapons, weapons that some crazed mekboyz had spent as much time optimising for peak noise level as they had for anything related to accuracy.

Nogrok watched the humies as the dirt around them started bursting into the air from shoota rounds slamming into the ground. The humies headed in the direction of a downed Deff Dread that had almost made it all the way to the humie base during the first ork attack. The Catachans dived behind the fallen Deff Dread. It had been blasted full of holes by the big humie guns but was still solid enough for the six Catachans to take cover behind as Gutstompa's greenskins fired down at them.

Rounds pinged off the Deff Dread as the humies huddled behind it. They popped out to shoot their zappy lasers back at the orks occasionally, but mostly the only thing that came from the humies behind the Deff Dread was shouting. They were shouting at Gutstompa and his orks.

'Come on, you green bastards!' Nogrok heard one of them shout.

'We're going to kill you all!' another of the humies yelled as they leant out from behind cover and fired three rapid shots. A Deathskulls boy further down the battlement took one of the shots right in the nose, the front of his face caving in and stuff bursting out the back. That was one of the different humies, the girl ones. Weird how there was two different types of humies. Even Nogrok didn't know why they weren't all just the same, like orks. What was the point of that?

Nogrok watched as Gutstompa finally snapped out of his tough, angry warboss pose and did exactly what Nogrok knew the humies wanted him to. Gutstompa, with the type of brutal roar that only a warboss could muster, leapt from the top of the wall, out over the destruction below, and landed with a ground-shaking thump on the grass. His huge mechanical legs hissed and sprayed as they absorbed the sudden force of his landing.

'WAAAAAAGH! Come on, boyz! Let's get 'em! There's 'ardly any!'

At the call of their warboss, orks began to move. Some jumped from the rampart trying to emulate their boss with varying degrees of success – from those that landed in the rubble and crumpled as their very much non-mechanically reinforced legs snapped beneath them, to those that managed to land on something a little softer and stumble on after Gutstompa.

Most of the orks hurried down the stairs and were soon flooding out of the recently opened hole in the wall. Gutstompa was right that there weren't many humies. Nogrok knew this wasn't enough humies for a proper attack on the base. No matter what Gutstompa might like to believe, humies weren't stupid, especially not the Catachan humies. Plus, Nogrok had watched the humies setting up for an ambush, and this felt a lot like what they might try to do to draw the orks into it.

'Oi!' Nogrok shouted. 'Warboss Gutstompa!'

Nogrok had expected the enormous ork to completely ignore him, but to his surprise the warboss turned back to look at him; maybe being a nob gave him a little more sway after all.

'Wot, you Blood Axe git? I is about to do fightin'!'

'Pretty sure this is a trap, boss,' Nogrok said. 'Da humies are plannin' somethin' sneaky.'

'You da worst nob I ever had. Dere's 'ardly any humies there an' loads of us boyz. If you is too scared to come fight, you can stay 'ere.'

'I ain't scared,' Nogrok called down to the larger ork. 'I'm tellin' ya the humies are settin' a trap. I seen 'em doin' it. You wanna keep dis base, you should shoot 'em from 'ere. Don't chase 'em into the trees.'

'No humie trap gonna stop me, even if dey is tryin' sneaky stuff like you love so much. You stay 'ere and miss da fightin' whateva, but I 'ad enough of ya now. Nob or no nob I'll be killin' you when this is done.' The warboss turned and called to the Deathskulls flooding out of the base. 'Waaagh! Get 'em, boyz!'

As Gutstompa began to shout, Nogrok watched the humies start to move back. They kept the Deff Dread between them and the base, but they kept firing at the orks charging towards them. They were doing a taktikal retreat, Nogrok was sure of it, but this taktikal retreat was different. This was a taktikal retreat where the humies wanted them to follow. Then, as one of the humies tossed a grenade back behind them, they began to run.

'Dey is running!' Gutstompa yelled. 'Charge 'em down!'

The humie grenade rolled over the ground but didn't explode. Instead, it burst into sprays of thick grey smoke, so thick that it was immediately hard to see through. Nogrok smiled. He'd done that when they'd attacked the base. The humies were covering their escape. But they'd made sure the orks had seen the direction they were running. Thick-skulled Gutstompa was leading most of the boyz right into the humie ambush.

Nogrok's Blood Axe kommandos stood around him watching, as still as he was, but Nogrok could tell the rest of his mob of boyz, those Deathskulls who'd actually done what he'd said in the attack on the humie camp, were just about vibrating with desire to charge with the rest of the warband. He could see the muscles quivering under their green skin. He held up his hand. 'No,' was all he said.

'But Sneakyguts,' one of the Deathskulls boyz who seemed the most jittery with the barely contained desire for violence said, 'da warboss is goin'!'

'Da warboss,' Nogrok said, 'is about to get krumped.'

There was audible shock from the twenty or so boyz standing with him – well, the Deathskulls at least; the Blood Axes couldn't have cared less. But for the Deathskulls, Nogrok might have been their nob now, and most of them might have even been coming around to the idea, but he was still lower on the food chain than the warboss and just straight out saying the warboss was gonna get killed by humies was almost as bad as saying orks wasn't the best or that Gork and Mork were weaklings.

'Look,' Nogrok said to the boyz, who'd actually started backing away from him like he was a weirdboy whose head was about to blow up, 'da humies is probably gonna kill all them running down there.' He waved his hand dismissively at the orks running with whoops and howls across the clearing after the humies. 'You 'eard me. I tried to tell the warboss da humies was settin' a trap, didn't I? But 'e wouldn't listen to me would 'e? Runnin' off straight into a trap 'e is. Don't matter how much an ork wanna fight, a dead ork don't do no fightin'. I know most of you ain't never thought 'bout it before, but if you ask me, the first step in fightin' and bein' da best ork is not bein' dead, ain't it?'

The faces of Nogrok's boyz all showed the familiar expression of orks trying to jam a new idea into their mossy brains.

'You Deffskulls is not Blood Axes,' Nogrok continued. 'I know dat. But you is kommandos now and part of bein' a kommando is doin' fightin' a little different. For most warbosses, the thing they is best at is goin' chargin' off to krump stuff.' The Deathskulls nodded. They weren't sure 'bout all the rest of what he was saying but this was definitely true. 'Problem is that sometimes, even though I know it seems 'ard to believe, chargin' in and krumpin' might not be the best thing.' Nogrok tried to continue quickly again before too many ork brains broke. 'Part of our job as kommandos is to do other stuff. We are the orks wot gotta think 'bout doin' big strategiks. Sometimes we gotta try and tell the warboss when we think chargin' and krumpin' ain't the best thing. They ain't always gonna listen to us, like Gutstompa ain't listened to me, but we still try. Then, we do da taktikal stuff, and the most taktikal stuff we can do right now is stay 'ere and hold dis base. We gotta try and stop da humies from gettin' it back. You lot understand?'

Some orks nodded half-heartedly, others didn't look so sure; some still seemed to be bouncing with unreleased fightin' energy. Nogrok sighed. 'We is guardin' dis base or I is gonna smash ya, ya get that right, ya thick-headed gitz?!'

This time they all nodded their agreement with the bigger ork.

CHAPTER TWENTY-SEVEN

TORVIN

Torvin's boots pounded against the ground. He felt his ankle twist as his foot landed in a dirt hole left from the removal of some buried mine. He stumbled, felt the roar of the ligaments in his leg as they were stretched beyond their ordinary limit, but he did not stop, he could not stop.

Orks poured from Outpost Four after them, the largest and most ferocious leading the chase. Torvin didn't risk turning and looking behind him, but he could hear them. They were charging after them roaring their standard war cry of 'Waaagh!' among other more guttural sounds of adrenal rapture like a pack of the slavering ice-wolves that roamed the frozen plains of Skadi - not that Torvin had ever left the city to see them.

Torvin did not run from fear, though. He ran with Sergeant, no, *Lieutenant* Sappa now, and the rest of her squad because that was their mission - to lead the orks into the kill-zone where Colonel Aldalon, Sergeant Dram and the others would hopefully eviscerate them. The rest of the squad was fast, zigzagging, changing direction frequently to make themselves more difficult targets, but it was all Torvin could do to keep up.

The orks behind them were shooting less frequently now anyway, most having drawn their melee weapons and joined the chase. They didn't want to shoot the Catachans from a distance, they wanted to be up close and hit them in hand-to-hand combat where the orks were at their most brutal.

Once, Torvin would have thought that the orks had the advantage over Imperial Guardsmen in hand-to-hand combat too - regardless of what *The Imperial Infantryman's Uplifting Primer* had tried to tell him - but after fighting alongside the Catachan Jungle Fighters he wasn't sure that was always the case. Aldalon had been right: the orks didn't care about the tactical implications of chasing them into the jungle; they didn't care about whether they really did or did not have the advantage in combat.

The orks were enraged, desperate for combat, and were making a huge mistake.

'You all right, soft-worlder?' Lieutenant Sappa called to him as Torvin recovered from his stumble.

'Fine,' Torvin called back, then added, 'And don't call me soft-worlder!'

Sappa laughed as an ork round burst somewhere beside her, throwing a tuft of muddy ground upwards. 'You want me to call you something else!'

she shouted over the sound of the roaring orks. 'You better earn yourself a Catachan name!'

Torvin and Lieutenant Sappa's squad hit the edge of the jungle at a run, plunging into the trees. Almost as soon as they breached the treeline and the dense foliage closed around them, the noises of the pursuing orks quieted, like they'd entered a sound-deadened room. The jungle had enveloped them. For the first time since he'd been on Gondwa VI, even as the trees surrounded him, pressing in with a claustrophobic embrace, Torvin felt that the jungle was not an entity to be fought against, to be feared, to be survived. No, instead he began to feel as he imagined the Catachan Jungle Fighters felt. The jungle was not an enemy. The jungle was a shield. The jungle was theirs, and woe to any enemy who would try to fight them within it.

Torvin twisted his body sideways at almost a full run to squeeze through a gap between two trees. Branches ripped at his cheek, opening a warm gash, but he barely felt it. The thick undergrowth grabbed at his legs in an attempt to trip him, but he pushed through and then found himself, almost by instinct, stepping lightly across it, his boots landing close to the centres of the plants where they were the stiffest, the long, whipping leaves and vines unable to slow him.

Sappa slowed. She began moving through the jungle more carefully than Torvin had known she was capable of. The other members of the squad did the same, and for the first time ever Torvin found himself moving faster through the jungle than the Catachan Jungle Fighters. After a moment he slowed himself too, realising what she was doing, ensuring the pursuing orks did not lose sight of them and followed them exactly along the path they intended.

The squad changed direction slightly, leading the orks down the tunnel-like area of trees that Aldalon had selected for the ambush, a perfect natural funnel into what would be an unnatural barrage of death. Torvin kept moving with the squad as they passed into the kill-zone. No doubt he was imagining it, but as soon as he passed into the area laid with explosives and designated as crossfire zones for those Catachans hiding in dug-in positions off to his left, the air seemed thicker, buzzing with an electric anticipation, as if the jungle here were tense, knowing what was about to take place.

Squad Sappa had slowed enough that Torvin could hear the greenskins behind them. He could sense them closing in. They were bunching up together as they struggled through the gaps between trees and fought through hanging vines. Aldalon had made it clear that at least some of the orks were behaving unexpectedly in this skirmish over Outpost Four, but these orks at least were behaving just as the Catachans had planned, packing themselves tightly together as they pursued the feigned retreat, creating the perfect density of xenos in the kill-zone. Torvin had barely passed through the kill-zone and out the other side into the security zone before the jungle received what it had been nervously awaiting.

Sergeant Dram, from where he had been lying in wait for Squad Sappa to get clear, hit the detonator and, with the pop of carefully laid det. cord, the jungle floor erupted.

There was not one blast but several – at least a dozen, maybe more, each one separated by a fraction of a second but enough that each distinct explosion could be heard running into the next, a percussive series of *boom, boom, boom, boom,* and on and on, linking into a chain of jungle-destroying destruction.

With each detonation the ground above the explosive ballooned upwards, spraying dirt, mud, plants and tree roots out in a spherical shock wave. The released energy stripped leaves from branches, disintegrated moss and vines, and even upended entire trees that were close enough, completely tearing them from the ground. And with the destruction of the jungle came the destruction of the orks.

Those greenskins who had been moving over the buried explosives stood no chance – they were simply shredded, the blasts tearing flesh and muscle from bone and eviscerating it all into sprays of gore that fell back down with the rain of dirt and floral debris.

Those that were a handful of steps away from each explosion were not so universally dispersed but were torn into larger pieces: torsos, limbs and chunks of heads still wearing coverings of shocked green faces all fell with heavy thuds into freshly turned mud. Torvin had thrown himself to the ground to take cover, shielding the back of his head with his arms to protect himself from the torrential fall of dirt, wood and pieces of ork.

Those greenskins who were thrown, injured but still mostly whole, into the surrounding jungle, slamming into trees or other orks or simply sliding across the ground – maybe twenty in total – clambered back to their feet. Despite most of them missing chunks of their bodies that would have been enough of a problem to incapacitate a human, they found what weapons they could – theirs if they hadn't lost them, or those of some ork now blasted into pieces. They turned in mild confusion, looking for something to kill. Most decided to continue on in the direction Squad Sappa had been running. At least before Squad Dram opened fire.

If the explosives had been the single crushing hammer blow, what followed was the precision of a death by a thousand cuts.

Squad Dram and Colonel Aldalon began firing even before the last piece of ejected ork torso hit the ground. Positioned in three different firing dugouts, they opened up with a carefully planned criss-cross of las-fire.

The jungle was lit by as many orange streaks of las-shots as the Catachans could fire from their lascarbines. On full-auto they unloaded the maximum amount of firepower possible, their weapons beginning to overheat in moments and their power packs draining at an ordinarily unacceptable rate – but in this situation Hell Fist Aldalon's orders had been perfectly clear: empty your ammunition and ensure that not a single ork walked away from the massacre.

The still-floating dust and debris lit up in an impressive ground-level display of fireworks as the las-fire cut through it and any falling material caught in its path burned hot and bright. But more importantly for the Catachans, though it was more difficult to pick their targets than they would have liked through the floating results of the explosive carnage, there were still plenty of orks caught in their fire that also burned hot and bright. At least, they melted and were blown open with the instantly cauterising wounds inflicted by las-shot.

When the hail of debris from the explosions ceased and the shooting started, Torvin gathered himself. At this point Squad Sappa was tasked to perform final security detail and gun down any orks that made it through the ambush. The others had made it further to take cover and so Torvin was closest to the ambush area when he turned and grabbed for his rifle. The kill-zone was still partly obscured with floating dirt and soot from the explosions, all alight with the criss-crossing fire from Squad Dram.

Aldalon's planned ambush had gone perfectly. The kill-zone was absolutely living up to its name. Torvin couldn't believe anything would survive the explosions and the web of las-fire that now lanced across the area, but to his astonishment there were several orks coming out the end of the kill-zone towards him.

At the sight of the first ork that came stomping out of the carnage of dust, blood mist and las-fire Torvin's eyes went wide. It was enormous. It was, without any doubt, the creatures' warboss. Its legs and feet, though it seemed to be labouring as one limb dragged with difficulty behind it, were massive and encased in armoured sleeves ringed in pistons, several of which were twisted and mangled from the explosions. One shoulder was wounded, leaving streaks of blood down its chest, as was its face, something which Torvin soon realised was a fragment of ork bone protruding from its cheek. The warboss reached up and pulled the bone free, looking at it as one might examine a thorn pulled from a finger, before tossing it to the ground.

'WAAAAAAAAGH!'

The warboss howled with rage. Torvin was no expert on ork psychology, but this seemed clear enough. The warboss' red eyes found Torvin. He was the nearest target and, from the look in those piercing eyes, the nearest outlet for the warboss' overflowing aggravation. The monstrous ork roared again as it moved towards Torvin.

Torvin rose quickly from a prone shooting position to a drop-knee, knowing he was going to have to be ready to move. He shouldered his lasgun and let loose with several shots. They struck the warboss in the leg, which did nothing but spark off a small abrasion on the thick armour there; the stomach, again striking thick armour plates that had been riveted to the leather-like vest the ork wore, ablating their surface but seemingly unable to penetrate; and the side of the arm – this blew a smoking black gouge in the warboss' flesh, the only shot that did any real damage, and yet the greenskin did not seem to have noticed.

By now Torvin had enough experience fighting the greenskins that it did not surprise him when the ork warboss shrugged off a wound that would have taken a human's arm off. Torvin snapped off a single extra shot, which hit the ork somewhere else on the armour, before he dropped his lasgun, drew his Catachan knife and prepared for hand-to-hand combat with the largest creature he'd seen outside of picts of the Emperor Himself – a figure who was always portrayed as towering over even the primarchs of the Adeptus Astartes. The warboss carried an axe that would have seemed comically large had the creature not been pulling it back over its shoulder preparing to swing at Torvin like it was about to chop wood.

A veteran of the Skadi Second – who was, like they all were, dead now – had once told Torvin and the rest of the new recruits not to be surprised when death came for them.

'Everyone always seems so surprised when they die,' that grizzled salt-and-pepper vet had told them, 'like they thought Saint Celestine or the God-Emperor Himself was gonna appear in a blaze of light and sweep down to save them at the very last moment because they're so damn special they couldn't possibly die. Well, you ain't special, and sorry to say, you're gonna die just like everyone else. Just because that's the body you happen to be ridin' in don't mean it isn't going to explode like everyone else's.'

Torvin thought it would be quite a nice turn of events if Saint Celestine or the God-Emperor Himself did decide to descend on fiery wings and put an end to this ork warboss, but he knew the veteran who'd told him that was right. Torvin was going to die, and he wasn't surprised by this. At least he was going to die having played some small part in helping the Catachans retake Outpost Four.

Torvin stood, taking the best approximation he could of the fighting stance he'd seen the Catachans use when they were preparing to fight in melee combat with their knives. He even twirled the knife around like he'd seen Lieutenant Sappa do – albeit slower and with less flare – because if he was going to go down, he was going to go down like a damn warrior.

The warboss stomped towards him awkwardly, still struggling with its damaged legs, and swung the axe. Torvin, having learned the lesson the hard way once before, did not try to block the warboss' mighty axe swing – it likely would have shattered his arm into a billion pieces and the axe would have cleaved him in half anyway; instead he dodged, diving to the side and rolling.

The warboss' axe continued down, the blade driving deep into the mud. Torvin had intended to take a quick swipe at the warboss as he came out of the roll, but before he could even move to slash at the ork he saw the massive axe swinging back towards him again.

In that fraction of a moment, as the warboss' weapon was coming towards him, the world sharpened. The colours of the jungle, the face of the warboss, so much he would have just called green but in reality was a million different colours, highlights and shadows – bright limes and emeralds, dark green-browns of moss and decay. Spears of light daggering in through the canopy, seeming almost divine, like the lines of blazing glory that would radiate out from depictions of the God-Emperor. The smells were clearer too: the humid damp, the pungent layers of rotting leaves on the jungle floor. He could hear the growling shouts of orks, the cracks of las-fire, the movement of the leaves in the wind high in the canopy. But even with all that it was the axe blade moving unstoppably towards his skull that was in the sharpest relief.

He heard the faint swoosh as the axe cleaved through the air towards him. The blade itself was not sharp; it was chipped and scratched and pockmarked with rust, but it came at him with such force that it wouldn't need to be sharp to split his skull completely in two.

Even with this sudden, almost supernatural clarity, Torvin could not make himself move any faster; he could do nothing but be a passive witness to his own demise as it took place in ultra-slow motion. Maybe everyone experienced this when they died, he thought, the moment of death stretching and stretching until it extended itself out for all eternity – some sort of sick cosmic joke that saw you trapped forever, unable to intervene, as your inevitable death came ever more slowly towards you.

It was not Saint Celestine and it was not the God-Emperor, but something did appear in a blaze of light to intervene – the crackling and sparking power fist of Haskell 'Hell Fist' Aldalon. The colonel arrived as if he'd indeed descended on the wings of a saint and with the vengeance of the Emperor behind him. His power fist punched the head of the axe directly on the edge of the blade as it was carving through the air towards Torvin's face. The crackling energy field and the momentum afforded by the power fist's amplified strength allowed Aldalon to slam the axe to a stop. Aldalon looked down at Torvin.

'Your bravery is noted, soft-worlder, but leave this one to me.'

Torvin did not wait to be told again. He hastily stood, bringing his lasgun to bear on the ambush kill-zone as he backed away towards where the rest of Squad Sappa waited. He heard the crack of ionising air and felt the static-like fuzziness as las-shots flew past him. Squad Sappa firing at the few other orks that had escaped the kill-zone.

They downed them quickly and the eyes of the squad, including Torvin's, turned to the duel between the warboss and the Catachan colonel. Several times the warboss tried to lift its massively armoured legs to use as weapons, kicking out at Colonel Aldalon, but they sprayed sparks and gushed almost arterial sprays of black oil. It seemed the warboss' weapons of choice were too damaged to be of much use and so the ork was left with its still-hideously intimidating axe.

Aldalon recognised this weakness quickly and began sidestepping around the ork to take advantage of its impaired mobility. He dashed forward and back, in and out of the warboss' reach. Every member of Squad Sappa had their weapon raised and aimed towards the warboss.

'Hold your fire,' Sappa said. 'You'll risk hitting the colonel. Besides, he'll take him, I know he will.'

This was no doubt meant to be encouragement, but even Torvin caught the hint of hope in those words, like she was raising a prayer to the God-Emperor, or more likely just throwing it out into the universe hoping it would stick.

Both the warboss and Aldalon carried heavy, unwieldy weapons. The warboss' axe was massive, more than any human other than a Space Marine could handle, and power fists were always difficult for ordinary humans to use, though Aldalon wielded his as though it were his own hand – which if the rumours about the entire inside of his arm being reinforced with augmetics were true then it basically was.

The ork and Aldalon each swung their instruments of war relatively quickly for what they were, but it was still like watching two immense warriors pounding at each other with an unstoppable force and an immovable object. Neither could land a clean blow. Axe struck fist in showers of yellow-and-blue sparks, as forceful strikes from each were not so much blocked as redirected.

In other ways, the two weapons could not have been more different: the warboss with its simple piece of massive metal swung with the inherent strength of its rippling green muscles; the Catachan colonel with his advanced power fist humming with its field of disruptive energy and amplifying his strength to that far above an ordinary human. Still, each combatant recognised that a single impact from either axe or fist would be devastating; they knew that the first to land a blow would likely be the victor.

The warboss swung with the reckless abandon of a disgruntled lumberjack, a wild arcing blow that Aldalon swiped upwards with his power fist. The colonel ducked under the axe and moved inside the ork's guard. His free hand suddenly bore his Catachan knife as if it had materialised from thin air. He drove it with all the strength he had into the ork's side. As he tore it out, letting the serrations do their vicious work, the ork dropped its bottom hand from its axe and grabbed Aldalon's knife hand, pinning the blade inside itself but squeezing tightly around Aldalon's wrist.

'Dis your puny humie hand,' the warboss growled. 'Shouldn'ta used your puny humie hand.'

The warboss squeezed. Even from where Torvin was, he could see the muscles and tendons popping out of the ork's fist, not so much white-knuckled but mint-knuckled. With a growl the warboss gripped harder and pushed, driving Aldalon towards the ground. The colonel buckled as the ork crushed his fist and forced him down. Aldalon dropped to his knees but did not show pain. His non-power fist hand was bionic but the warboss likely didn't realise that. Instead, he growled back at the warboss. He swung a punch with his power fist that the ork parried away with its axe, before the xenos seemingly increased the strength of its grip and slammed its arm down to drive Aldalon into the dirt.

'I am Gutstompa!' the ork roared at Colonel Aldalon as he bent down over him. 'I gonna stomp ya! You is nuthin! You is a puny, weak humie!'

The warboss partly lifted his right leg, but a series of sparks and a jet of hydraulic fluid ejected from the joint, and the heavy armoured leg fell back to the ground. He roared in frustration and tried again. This time, even with more sparks and grinding, Gutstompa managed to lift his leg higher, preparing, Torvin knew, to slam it down on Aldalon. Despite apparently being called Gutstompa, the warboss was clearly aiming to crush the colonel's head.

More orks had come from the kill-zone, drawing Squad Sappa's fire. Torvin was the closest trooper and knew he was the only one who stood any chance of making it in time. He darted forward and drove his Catachan knife as hard as he could into the apparently faulty knee joint in the ork's armour. Something within burst and Torvin was covered with a spray of oil as he fell back.

Gutstompa tried to slam his heavy foot down but the joint sparked and whined and, from the look on the ork's face, seemed to have seized in place. Gutstompa released Aldalon's wrist and bashed his fist down on top of his leg in an attempt to free the joint and make it move. Aldalon rolled to the side and swept his power fist out as he did so, this time as if he were the crazed lumberjack, taking the ork's other leg out from under him and causing the massive greenskin to slam onto his back.

Aldalon scrambled quickly, not even making it to his feet but sliding on his knees towards Gutstompa's head, not giving the warboss time to recover. The colonel reared back and slammed his power fist down onto Gutstompa's face. The ork tried to block, but he was too slow this time and Aldalon's disruption field-encased fist ripped apart the molecules of his flesh and the servo-driven metal cracked his hard skull.

As Torvin wiped at his face to clear away the thick black oil, he saw Aldalon rearing back again and again, punching his power fist down on the warboss' face. Each time, the impact bored deeper into the greenskin's skull and widened the splatter of blood and bone fragments. Eventually, when Aldalon's fist had struck almost nothing but jungle mud three times in a row he stopped. He dropped back onto his heels, his chest heaving with exertion.

Eventually, once his breathing had returned to normal, Colonel Haskell 'Hell Fist' Aldalon stood. He turned and looked at Torvin, who stared back at him. Aldalon wiped sweat, mud and ork blood from his brow and flicked it off his hand onto the ground and then, while maintaining intense eye contact with him, he nodded to Torvin. A nod of thanks and a nod of respect that, even without words, caused Torvin to flush with pride.

Aldalon turned to Squad Dram, emerging from the ambush firing pits, and then, after putting down the last of the orks, the rest of Squad Sappa, approaching from where they'd been set up as security fire-team. When the Catachans had gathered, Torvin could see Aldalon quickly assessing them, then he asked for confirmation.

'No casualties?'

'No, sir,' Lieutenant Sappa replied with a smile. 'At least none without green skin.'

'Excellent. Any targets make it out of the kill-zone?'

'No, sir.'

'Sergeant Dram, everything in there dead?'

'We'll confirm,' Dram replied.

Aldalon nodded. 'Make sure of it. If there's a head attached to anything remotely resembling a torso, you cut it off.'

'Yes, sir.'

'Have you got an estimate of enemy KIAs?' Aldalon asked.

'I'd put us at a good forty toasted greenskins, sir,' Dram said.

Aldalon nodded. He turned to look at Torvin. 'A nice day's work in retribution for your old unit don't you think, Torvin?'

'Yes, sir!' Torvin said, then stopped, confused. 'My old unit?'

'That's right. Don't see much point sending you back to the Skadi Second now we've put in all this bloody effort in getting you to grow a pair. You're halfway resembling a Jungle Fighter now, maybe we'll make a Catachan Devil of you yet. You'll stay with us. Unless you'd rather return to your idiot soft-worlders?'

He thought about Melina. The pict of her was no longer his most prized possession. Now, the most important object he had was something he'd earned, a red bandanna.

'I'll be staying with you, sir,' Torvin said, 'if you'll have me.'

'Very well. Don't make me regret it.'

Torvin stood up straighter. 'I won't, sir.'

And he swore by the God-Emperor Himself he meant it.

CHAPTER TWENTY-EIGHT

ALDALON

Aldalon watched the dumb smile spread across Torvin's face and almost changed his damned mind about letting him join the Catachans. But the kid had stepped up, even Aldalon had to give him that. He wouldn't go so far as to say the soft-worlder had saved him, but it had been fifty-fifty in that fight with the warboss. Torvin had spotted the weakness in the ork's knee and had acted on it, managing to help turn the fight in Aldalon's favour. He was still a soft-worlder, maybe he'd never have the true spirit of a Catachan – what many would call the madness of the Catachans – but he had survived this long and there hadn't been many soft-worlders Aldalon had seen make such a rapid transition from incompetence to showing signs of being a warrior. He'd give him his shot and, if nothing else, more time with Catachans would wipe that idiotic smile off his face.

'All right,' Aldalon said, turning back to the rest of the Jungle Fighters. 'Commendable effort, troopers. Barring that tangle with the warboss, this was a near-perfectly executed ambush. A nice reminder of our Catachan expertise at inflicting surprise death on xenos scum. Once we've ensured every greenskin in the kill-zone has been squashed beneath the Emperor's boot, we're going to move out and execute our main attack on Outpost Four. We aren't sure exactly how many greenskins are left, but given the number of dead here and the intelligence we've gathered it can't be more than twenty. By the time we're done, it will be zero. Is that clear?'

'Yes, sir,' the Catachans responded in unison.

'Good, see it done. We move in ten minutes. We assault as one unit. Extended line across the open. Pull into an arrowhead a hundred yards out and breach the outpost. Left arm, room clear left. Right arm, same to the right. Clear lower level and then move up. I will take point.'

'Sir,' Lieutenant Sappa said. 'May I–'

Aldalon held up his hand. This small mission had taken a turn and it had seen him be more open with his subordinates than he ever had before. It was not the way he had been taught to lead on Catachan, nor something he had needed on hundreds of battlefields previously, but here, the fight for this Emperor-damned outpost had changed him. Once they were gone from here maybe he would go back to cutting off an interruption like this with his ordinary growl, but he knew he owed more to this small contingent of troopers; he owed more to his daughter. This place was different because he had screwed up here, in ways he hadn't before.

'Before you say anything, I understand I've shown both some recklessness and some reluctance to see you, in particular, in danger, lieutenant. I can assure you that isn't the case here. We'll hit this building the right way, clear it out methodically, and I have no doubt you'll be neck-deep in greenskin melee quick enough. I've mended whatever snapped in me – I won't be going off half-cocked, but there's an ork in there that I've got business with.'

The Catachans moved over the ambush kill-zone doing a final sweep for surviving greenskins. There didn't seem to be any, but Aldalon watched as they carried out his orders to the letter. Any ork head, or anything vaguely head-shaped despite cavernous holes and flayed skin and flesh, was cut from its torso or partial torso or even just overly thick neck – you could never be too careful with orks.

If there was one thing that still amazed Aldalon about the greenskins, even after the dozens of times he'd met them in battle, it was just how much their barbaric painboyz were capable of. More than once, Aldalon had hit an ork with what should have been a killing blow – he'd even torn some in half – and then, in some later skirmish, seen what he could have sworn was the same ork, somehow stitched together and sent back into the fray. Well, not so much sent back but willingly throwing itself into the fray. Orks could survive more than most in the Imperium truly understood.

Once the work of ensuring none of these orks would have the opportunity to be stitched, stapled or nailed back together was completed, the Catachans prepared themselves, tending and dressing wounds, giving rifles and blades a quick wipe down with blessed oils, and redistributing ammunition between them. They were down to a single power pack per trooper, but with the tight confines they'd face during their assault on the outpost, Aldalon was sure one each would be enough; they'd have their Catachan Fangs out soon enough.

When they were ready, they assembled again. Aldalon took another look at them, evaluating each in turn, ensuring they were capable of this. He had no concerns about their skill level of course; he was checking them for signs of battle-weariness, physical fatigue and the even more dangerous mental fatigue.

These were Catachans but it was a lot to ask of any soldier to move straight from one engagement to another and then to another with no real chance for recuperation. Aldalon had learned over his career how to spot the signs that his troopers were not fighting fit, or in need of a rest or even a complete rotation out. All twelve of the Jungle Fighters he looked at now were tired, their eyes ringed with purple and heavy with bags. This was natural enough after several days on mission and particularly given how this mission had proceeded. Missions that turned much harder than expected were always the most tiring, and these soldiers looked war-weary. Maybe a less experienced commander would have considered that enough to scrub this attempt at immediately counter-attacking.

Aldalon was not an inexperienced commander, though; he was the regimental commander of the Catachan 57th, a veteran of not just fighting the wars of the Emperor, but of leading men and women into them. He saw through their tiredness to the fiery spark in their eyes, the determination to put an end to this here and now, the glimmer inside them that would fuel their adrenaline for long enough to take back Outpost Four and ensure it would continue to act as the early warning station for Karoo City. They had it in them to make this last push.

Aldalon turned to Learna. 'Lieutenant Sappa, are we ready?'

The troopers stood taller.

'Always ready, sir,' Sappa replied.

'I've admitted some missteps on this mission,' Aldalon said. 'I believe we've all underestimated our foe, but the responsibility lies with me. I should never have allowed us to do that. We have lost Catachans because I was so determined to avenge my son that I made poor tactical decisions. But we will respond in the way Catachans always have, we will avenge the fallen by fighting at our best. We owe it to the brothers and sisters we've lost to finish this.

'Remember, these greenskins are not ghosts. They are flesh-and-blood xenos. They just happen to be a little less stupid than most of their kind. They move well through the jungle, I'll give them that. They fight well in the jungle, I'll give them that too. But you know what I've realised? They fight like us because they're pretending to be us. But they are not us. They are orks. We are the real Emperor-damned deal. We are Catachan Jungle Fighters and we're going to show them why no one in the galaxy ever, ever underestimates us.'

The thirteen Catachan warriors moved out in an extended line, side by side but each separated by several yards. Thirteen was considered unlucky for some, Aldalon knew, but it was only going to be unlucky for the orks today. Aldalon was in the centre, ready to take the point position when they transitioned into arrowhead, six troopers on either side. Farthest to his left was Sergeant Dram, holding the formation there, and farthest to his right was Lieutenant Sappa, doing the same.

They advanced silently from the ambush zone back to the edge of the clearing around Outpost Four. Aldalon had no doubt those greenskins remaining at the outpost would have heard the battle that had just taken place, and the fact that they hadn't charged into the jungle to find out what fight they were missing was more than enough to convince him he was right about the occupants – it had to be the odd-eyed ork and his camouflaged brethren.

Aldalon moved the Catachans further around the perimeter of the clearing to the eastern side of the outpost, not wanting to emerge from the same location they had retreated to. From there they would still be able to make a straight line for the caved-in wall that would serve as their entry point into the outpost.

As they came to a halt ten yards inside the treeline, Aldalon sent hand signals in both directions along the line asking for confirmation from either end that they were ready to move. When the returning signals answered in the affirmative, he stretched his neck from side to side, letting it crack, rolled his shoulders and then armed his lascarbine. The sound of humming lasguns echoed along the line as the others did the same, a call and response sweeter than any Ecclesiarchy choir.

With a nod in each direction, Aldalon stepped forward and then breached the treeline, moving into the clearing at a sprint, keeping as low as he could. The Catachans sprinting across the open grass did not spew some war cry like hammer-headed orks. They were a scalpel; they moved fast, they moved quiet and they would be sharp.

The Catachans were a third of the way to the outpost before the orks started shooting. The camouflaged greenskins that popped up on the rampart to fire at them confirmed Aldalon's suspicions about which of the orks were still here.

As he ran, setting the pace for the troops on either side of him, Aldalon's calm battle-tuned mind, like a carefully programmed cogitator, registered the number of visible orks and the rate of fire of their cacophonous weapons. He estimated the number of orks left at somewhere between fifteen and twenty, about what he'd expected.

The inaccurate xenos fire posed little threat – though of course there was a chance one of the greenskins would get a lucky shot to land true. These orks might have been more tactically savvy in some ways, but it seemed their long-range shooting relied on standard ork tactics: massed fire and luck. Aldalon knew that when they drew closer to each other in their arrowhead formation, the danger increased.

The Catachans sprinted across the clearing. Two hundred yards from the outpost. Boom. An ork shot struck close by. One hundred yards. The oddly harmonic whistling of a tumbling ork round passed overhead. Fifty yards. The Catachans fired up at the battlement, their lascarbines set on fully automatic while they continued running, trying to lay suppressing fire against the orks as they drew closer to the outpost. Even the absolute best marksmen in the Imperial Guard, hell the whole damn galaxy, would struggle to hit the broadside of a grox under those conditions, but accuracy was not a concern. All they needed was a rapid peppering of las-fire that would keep as many green heads ducked down below the battlement wall as possible.

Aldalon stuck his arms back in the shape of a V behind him – the arrowhead formation signal. The Catachans, already anticipating the order at any moment, reacted immediately, closing in sideways and dropping into a staggered diagonal line either side of Aldalon, matching the direction of his arms. They pulled in closer to each other too, the distance between them decreasing from around ten yards to only two or three. Ready to close the gap to less than a yard when they reached the outpost.

Even as they kept up their suppressive fire, a sound down the line told Aldalon that an ork had found luck with at least one of their thundering shots.

'Tacter is down!' Sappa called.

'Leave her,' Aldalon called back. 'There's no time.' Aldalon knew Tacter was wearing a flak armour vest so there was a chance she could have survived the hit. Hopefully she'd been lucky, but they wouldn't know until this was over. Assuming they managed to clear the orks from Outpost Four, then Tacter could be retrieved for medical treatment – until then she would have to tough-out survival like a Catachan.

The rest of the troopers understood. They didn't miss a step, not even looking back as they closed the gap in the formation where Tacter had been. To an outsider it might seem like cruelty, the way the Catachans regularly left their dead and wounded behind, seemingly without a thought. But for them it was the opposite. Being born and raised on Catachan, the cruel thing would be to stop and try to help a fallen comrade. It was cruel to the Catachan who stopped to render aid as they were just as likely to fall victim to the same danger, and it was cruel to any other Catachans you were with, taking away one set of eyes and ears, and reducing fighting capability, making the group even weaker. The weakness of one could get many more killed on Catachan, and that mentality travelled with them to the battlefield.

As planned, Aldalon reached the blown-in section of the wall first and the rest of the troops had closed in tight. There was no need to begin room clearing for orks because, having seen them heading for the breach in the wall, the greenskins were more than happy to meet them at the front door with a very orkish welcoming party.

''Ere we go! WAAAAAGH!'

As soon as Aldalon entered the outpost, the ork calls echoed around him, reverberating off the walls as the xenos rushed down the stairs from the rampart above. Aldalon had barely stepped over the threshold when he met a dozen or so orks in combat.

He swung his power fist in a wide arc, smashing green faces aside, not so much with the intent of killing them all but of clearing space as the rest of the Catachans moved in through the jagged hole and over the rubble, the blades of their knives flashing as sprays of blood began coating the walls like a messy paint job.

The Catachans moved in behind him as Aldalon pushed forward towards the stairs. Each side of the formation swung back out to form a smaller version of the arrowhead as they ploughed in, like a wedge driving into a gap, or an axehead slamming into a split in a log. As the troopers beside him fought in the tight confines of the outpost, Aldalon pressed straight for his target. He would hold the bottom of the stairs as the two sides of the arrowhead split into two teams to clear the bottom level of the outpost, room by room, greenskin by greenskin, to ensure none came down from the upper level.

The fighting either side of Aldalon was ferocious as the Catachan Jungle Fighters tangled with the orks with little space to move. This was the worst-case scenario when fighting orks in hand-to-hand combat, even for the Catachans. They needed to move, to circle around, to have another trooper provide support from the side or rear. If an ork pinned a human in place with no backup and nowhere to move, it didn't matter if you were a soft-worlder or a baby ogryn – the ork's superior strength and insanity in battle meant you were in trouble.

'Hold here!'

'Push up!'

'Take left!'

'Watch your right!'

The Catachans directed each other as they fought. Sappa and Dram barked formation orders but all of them were vocal. A well-trained regiment like this fought and moved as one, each trooper aware of each other just as much as they were of themselves.

Aldalon had the advantage of his crackling power fist and augmented arm, and his initial whirlwind entrance had injured several orks, who were quickly dealt with by the Catachans so that the numbers on the lower level seemed more or less even now. The orks fought with the brutality they always did in close combat, but the Catachans held their rigid structure and that was proving the difference.

The orks, on the other hand, fought maniacally with no consideration for helping the other xenos around them. It almost annoyed Aldalon, all that raw strength and desire to fight; the slightest amount of tactical thinking would make them damn near unstoppable. He wondered if the ork with the different-coloured eyes felt the same way.

'Himrod, on your left!'

Sappa's shout drew Aldalon's attention as well. He turned in time to see Himrod spin to his left. He'd left himself open engaging an ork with Devi and a second of the greenskins had breached the Catachan formation. It roared and plunged its long, rusty sword into Himrod's side with enough force to shatter bone and cave in the side of his ribcage. In true Catachan fashion, Himrod did not scream – though it was unlikely he would have been able to as his lungs had surely collapsed. Instead, even as the ork ripped the rusted blade from his side, he used the last of his strength to shove his own Catachan blade into the ork's throat.

The ten remaining Catachan soldiers drew in closer either side of Aldalon as they overcame the last of the orks in front of them, seemingly the last of the orks on the lower level of the outpost. But, as he had said, they were going to do this right. Aldalon looked at the troopers around him.

'Clear the level, room by room. I'll hold the stairs.'

'Yes, sir,' Lieutenant Sappa replied.

The Catachans moved off, sheathing their blades and raising their lascarbines in front of them. Sergeant Dram took the lead to the left and Lieutenant Sappa to the right. Aldalon held his position at the base of the stairs. He sensed the movement rather than heard it, and even before he turned Aldalon knew what he would see.

There, crouching halfway up the stairs, was an ork dressed in camouflage. Its face was painted with four diagonal slashes of black paint and of course it had one red eye and one green eye. The ork that had killed Brant.

Aldalon's power fist flared to life and with it he felt the flare of rage and anger within him. The same rage and anger that had flooded his better judgement before, that had sent him barrelling into orks without concern for the consequences. The ork on the stairs smiled as if enjoying the sight of Aldalon's power fist roaring to life, as if happy that it'd drawn that reaction.

The ork rose and pointed at Aldalon, and then at itself with obvious meaning. It seemed this ork wanted the same thing – to go toe-to-toe with Aldalon. He gestured for Aldalon to follow and then the greenskin turned and walked calmly up the stairs.

Aldalon felt his power fist arm almost vibrating with the growing energy, a vibration that began spreading to all the muscles of his body. He could feel the rage building inside, could almost see the red haze descending over his vision as he thought about chasing that ork up the stairs and smashing its skull to tiny green fragments. He wanted nothing more than to charge after it, but he realised the ork wanted that too. Did it want to fight Aldalon or did it just want to draw him out of position? What was left of his troops were clearing the rooms on the lower level and if Aldalon left the base of the stairs he would be opening them up to attack from behind.

He would not do that.

He would not let his rage and hatred for greenskins consume his better senses again.

He was Catachan. He would fight smart, he would fight in formation as he had watched his troops do, he would fight to keep other Catachans alive. He looked back up the stairs where the greenskin had disappeared. His blood still boiled but he let his power fist power down. It would not be long. The ork with the different-coloured eyes would keep a few minutes more.

CHAPTER TWENTY-NINE

NOGROK

Nogrok was excited.

It wasn't just normal ork excitement about a scrap, either. The Catachan boss with the power fist was here, and that was a fight worth having.

He knew that sooner or later they were going to meet. After so long as a kommando, krumpin' idiots without an idea in their heads, and finally making it to be a nob, this humie was the humie he wanted to fight. This was the humie he would use to prove himself.

He hadn't wanted to fight the boss humie inside the outpost because he'd already known the humies would be better at that. Plus, the stupid Deathskulls gitz had made it worse by rushin' down the stairs to fight 'em as soon as they'd come through the wall even though Nogrok had told 'em not to. Nogrok had roared at them to stay on the top level and make the humies come up the stairs, but they hadn't listened.

But Nogrok had waited at the top of the stairs. He'd tried one last trick. He knew the Catachan boss wanted to fight him; he'd seen the look in the humie's eyes, like a proper orky look of wanting to fight. He was kinda like Warboss Ripspitta used to be – trying to be scary by keeping his face real still and starin' at everything with squinty eyes.

Nogrok had seen the boss humie go a little Gork crazy before, seen him give into that blood-pumping battle rage, so Nogrok had tried to be proper sneaky and lure him into a fight. While the other humies had gone off to search the other rooms of the outpost, Nogrok had snuck down and got the boss humie's attention. Then some of the boyz could go down and attack the humies while they were searching around – getting them from behind and crushing them between two groups.

It was a good plan and maybe it would have worked on normal humies, but the boss Catachan didn't take the bait, even though he looked pretty mad about it. Nogrok sighed. It looked like they would just have to crash into the humies as they made their way up the stairs, and force them back down.

It would happen soon because even though the humies were searching for other orks down there they wouldn't find any. All that was left of Warboss Gutstompa's warband was up on the roof level with him. Just Flik, Nukka, Ruktug and a bunch of Deathskulls who'd actually demonstrated the capacity to listen.

Nogrok was excited, but he couldn't help but have a bit of a feeling that only an ork really in touch with Mork could get – a bad feeling. Still, he wasn't going to worry about that now because something else had occurred to him. If the orks up here were all that was left of Warboss Gutstompa's warband then the rest had all been krumped, including Warboss Gutstompa – and that meant this wasn't Warboss Gustompa's warband any more. No, now it was the warband of Warboss Nogrok Sneakyguts. Nogrok looked around at the orks on the roof with him. There weren't loads but they were his now. He was warboss.

'Weapons up, cover your angles. Move, move, move!'

The Catachan boss had given up on being sneaky now, just like Nogrok had. There was no point any more. The humies knew where they were, and Nogrok and his boyz knew where the humies would be coming from. Nogrok watched the Deathskulls move towards the stairs.

'Oi!' Nogrok said. 'Get back a bit, ya gitz!'

The few kommandos left were already well back from the top of the stairs because they were smart, not like the stupid Deathskulls. Some of them took steps back from the top of the stairs but others didn't. Nogrok wondered if other warbosses had to deal with boyz not doing as they was told. Then he had, just for a fleeting moment, a little sympathy for Warboss Gutstompa because, he realised, he'd been the ork that never did as he was told.

Ah well. Nogrok was still alive, and Gutstompa wasn't.

'Dis your last chance to get back from the stairs, ya Deffskulls gitz!' Nogrok called, but his heart wasn't really in it.

They probably thought they were being taktikal standing at the top of the stairs, looking down at where the humies would come up. But it just meant the humies moving up the stairs could start shooting them before they had to fully expose themselves.

Bright lasers blasted out from the stairs like a light show. Most went right into the faces of the Deathskulls who'd been waiting at the top. They didn't have a chance. They all dropped, their faces black and burned, the backs of their skulls melted like pitch.

But the humies couldn't shoot the orks standing back where Nogrok had told them to wait; they couldn't see them until they came right out into the open at the top of the stairs, and when the first humie's head popped up Nogrok gave the order to attack.

'Get 'em now!' Nogrok roared. Orks around him began to open fire with completely inaccurate shots, but it was enough to make it hard for the humies to clamber up the stairs. Nogrok raised his Catachan blade and ran at the humies. 'WAAAAGH!'

The orks had managed to pin the humies at the top of the stairs and Nogrok knew they had to get at them quick. If he could get in close to the humies fast, their guns would be no good and they'd have to change to their knives. Hopefully they could catch a few before they was ready to really fight.

But as Nogrok was charging he saw one of the Catachans spot him as a target and raise their laser shoota. Running towards the end of the barrel, it just looked like a bright flash of orange accompanied by a cracking noise.

Nogrok tried to turn to dodge the shot, but he felt an impact on his left shoulder and was twisted to the side. He felt the spreading warmth and tingling sensation in his shoulder that meant he'd been hurt, and then everything down his left arm to his fingers went numb. Pain wasn't that bad. He didn't know why the humies always complained so much when they got shot. He looked at his shoulder and saw the fist-sized hole that had been burned into it, his green flesh gone and a black, gently smoking crater left in its place.

He tried to lift his left arm, but it seemed a little harder than usual and the limb didn't go more than about halfway up. Staring at the hole in his shoulder he could see thin strands of green muscle and sinew trying to pull, but the bone at the top of his arm was sliding all over the place and he was pretty sure that was supposed to go up into his shoulder bit. He didn't know much about the insides of a body, but it looked like some of the bone was missing.

He was going to need a painboy to throw a few teef at, but all the painboyz were dead now. Useless gitz. If he made it through all this, he'd have to stumble through healing it, or replace it with something much killier.

When he looked back towards the fighting, Nogrok saw the boss Catachan coming towards him, his power fist sparkling as bright as loads of squig herders' zappin' sticks. The big humie walked slowly towards him and Nogrok felt a return of excitement about this moment – shame he only had one working arm now.

Around the top of the stairs, the boyz were fightin' the humies. Attacking quickly as the humies came out of the stairs had worked. The boyz managed to catch a couple of the humies off-guard, but it didn't look good. There weren't enough orks left. Even a boss as thick as Gutstompa would have been able to look at this and see they were going to lose to the humies.

Nogrok watched the humie boss comin' towards him and started thinkin' that maybe he better do one last sneaky thing and escape. He was a warboss now – he didn't have many boyz, but he was still a warboss. If he could get out of here, then he could rebuild a warband. He would be Warboss Nogrok Sneakyguts and build a warband that only had kommandos in it. He'd go all round the galaxy and take only orks who understood the importance of taktiks. If he could get a whole Waaagh! of proper sneaky kommandos, he could show not just every ork, but every other thing in the galaxy – humies and pointy-ears and the rest – what orks could really do if they didn't listen to stupid gitz all the time.

First, he had to get himself out of this mess.

Then Nogrok noticed something. Over the boss humie's shoulder he saw something in the treeline of the far jungle. Movement. Not just a little bit of movement but loads and loads. At first, Nogrok thought the humies had called for more humies to come, but when the movement turned into figures pouring out of the trees Nogrok saw that they were orks.

They weren't Blood Axes and they weren't even Deathskulls or any other klan he'd ever seen. They were dressed in animal furs and skins, and none had any armour.

Ferals. That was almost as bad as humies pouring out of the jungle, but he'd needed somethin' to help him escape and it seemed like Gork and Mork had smiled down on him at just the right time. He wondered if Gutstompa had known there were ferals on this planet. Maybe that's what he'd been waiting for. Ferals weren't good for much, but maybe he'd thought he could add them to his warband. Well, Nogrok was boss now so maybe he could use the ferals. Right now though, the ferals were good for a distraction.

'You!' the humies' boss said as he stopped right in front of Nogrok. He lifted his power fist and clenched its fingers. 'You're mine!'

CHAPTER THIRTY

ALDALON

'You!' Aldalon said as he finally came face to face with the ork with different-coloured eyes.

He felt the rage in him, the rage he'd shelved earlier, begin to grow again. This time, there would be no shelving it. He squeezed his power fist and let the energy field build along with his fury. All around him, what remained of Squad Sappa and Squad Dram – far less than he was happy with – were winning the battle for the outpost. What was left of the ork forces were crumbling as the Catachans looked assured of victory.

A commander was never truly freed from the responsibility of command, it was always overhead ready to pour down disaster at any moment like a dark storm, but in this moment Aldalon was as free as possible from thoughts of a greater strategic nature. He thought only of the greenskin in front of him.

'You're mine!'

The greenskin held up its blade ready to fight and Aldalon saw that it was a Catachan blade. Not just any Catachan blade, but Brant's – a hooked end with half a blade of serrations and a long fuller groove.

Aldalon growled and charged the ork, swinging his power fist. The ork was fast, faster than Aldalon had been prepared for, and he dashed backwards out of the way. He slashed out with the Fang and caught Aldalon with the slightest graze along the cheek. He felt a small trickle of warmth. First blood. If this had been a Catachan duel it would be called for the ork. Lucky it was not a Catachan duel, or at least that it was the type of Catachan duel where the loser would not be getting up.

'Sharp cutta, ain't it?' the ork said.

Aldalon ground his teeth together. 'That blade isn't yours.'

The ork smiled. 'I took it fair and square off a dead humie, didn't I? One of you Catachan humies.'

Aldalon growled again. He was ready to kill this ork, but he had to admit he was surprised; this creature knew where they were from. 'Be silent, ork,' Aldalon said, 'and fight.'

Aldalon charged again. This time the ork spun aside as it dodged. It was faster than Aldalon could swing his power fist; he would have to bide his time, get the ork to commit, maybe even take a strike from the greenskin before levelling it. The strength of the power fist always came with this disadvantage of being slow. Often orks overcommitted with their bloodlust in battle, but not this one.

'I'm not just an ork,' the greenskin said after it'd dodged the power fist. 'I am Warboss Nogrok Sneakyguts.'

Aldalon looked at the creature. He was bigger than the average ork but not by much – not really the size of a normal nob and certainly not warboss sized. Aldalon couldn't help himself. 'You're a warboss?'

Nogrok Sneakyguts' brow furrowed. 'Newly promoted since you krumped Gutstompa.'

'Ah,' Aldalon said. If he could get the ork talking, he might be able to surprise him with an attack. 'The one with the big legs?'

'Dat's da one,' Nogrok replied. He kept his eyes fixed on Aldalon as they moved around each other. In the tight confines of the rampart, the ork was slowly but surely increasing the distance between them. 'What's your name, humie?'

Aldalon's eyes thinned. 'Colonel Aldalon, Fifty-Seventh Catachan Jungle Fighters,' he found himself replying, moving to close the gap that the ork kept trying to open.

'Nice to meet you, Aldalon Catachan boss. I been waitin' for this. Us gettin' to fight each other.'

Despite himself Aldalon grinned, though it was humourless. 'Oh, me too, Nogrok. Me too.'

'Problem for me is I ain't gonna win fightin' fair.'

'Glad you understand that, greenskin.'

'I'm hurt. You killed my boyz. I'm in a taktikally bad spot. If I learned anythin' from you Catachan humies it's dat you gotta use taktiks when they workin' for ya and get outta da way when dey ain't. Lucky we ain't got long 'fore the others get 'ere.'

'WAAAAAGH! WAAAAAAAAAAAAAAGH!'

The shouts came from the jungle behind him. The unmistakable sound of ork war cries, the war cries of many, many orks. The continuous sound was accompanied by the booming rhythm of drums, thumping, thumping, thumping. The pounding beat was increasing in speed. The sound of ork shots blasting pointlessly up into the air followed.

Aldalon did not turn immediately, keeping his eye on Nogrok, who had continued to back away. He desperately wanted to close the distance to his most hated ork enemy and strike him down, but he felt the stormy heavens of command opening to pour down that heavy dose of disaster.

'Sir!' Lieutenant Sappa called. 'Incoming orks. Loads of them!'

'Loads is right,' Nogrok said as he continued backing off.

When Nogrok was far enough back that Aldalon did not fear a surprise attack he turned quickly to look behind him. The sight that greeted him was the always terrible green tide. This was the orks at their most dangerous – when they came flooding across the battlefield in numbers both breathtaking and horrifying.

Aldalon's first instinct was that these were reinforcements Nogrok had been stalling for, but these orks were dressed in rudimentary outfits of animal skin, scales and fur. Their weapons were clubs and long pieces of spiked wood rather than edged weapons. Their guns were even more basic than those used by normal orks. Some even carried slingshots into which they had loaded large rocks.

Aldalon had encountered greenskins like these a handful of times before. Feral orks. A civilisation of greenskins that had sprung up on planets previously victim to an ork infestation but appearing seemingly at random many months or even years after the xenos were thought to be cleansed from the world. They were the most basic of creatures, orks that made most greenskins look like scholars of the Administratum or enginseers of the Adeptus Mechanicus. But though they wielded simple weapons and had little understanding of how to wage war they still bore the brute strength of the greenskins, and the numbers that continued to charge from the jungle treeline were astounding.

The feral orks came in such numbers that it seemed impossible that this was some recently sprung-up tribe. There were hundreds streaming from the jungle now, and that meant there were probably thousands of them still infesting Gondwa VI – and despite the commonly cited difficulties with surveillance on this planet, Aldalon could not believe an infestation of feral orks that large could have gone unnoticed.

He turned back to Nogrok and was shocked to see the ork lunging at him. Aldalon caught sight of the Catachan blade in his hand just before it pierced his side, the look of glee in Nogrok's different-coloured eyes. Aldalon felt the hot-poker roar of the serrated Catachan Fang as it buried into the flesh just above his hip. He roared, lashing out with his power fist in self-defence.

Aldalon backhanded Nogrok and sent him flying. The pain in his side screamed again and he saw that Nogrok had refused to let go of the knife. It had torn free as the ork was slammed away, leaving a dangerously open wound in Aldalon's side.

Nogrok crashed into the battlement wall and then rolled back and over, dropping from the outpost. Aldalon growled and moved to the edge hoping to see the ork's broken body, but instead he saw Nogrok looking up at him.

'Kommandos,' Nogrok yelled, 'we is taktikally runnin'!'

Aldalon grabbed for the plasma pistol at his waist to take a shot at the warboss, but Nogrok had dropped something as he fell – a smoke grenade. His view was instantly obscured. 'Emperor damn it!' he roared. That bastard ork was going to get away. He had given himself permission to take his revenge on the creature that had killed his son, and now it had been taken away. The sounds of the charging ferals drew him back – he was a Catachan commander and the situation had changed. His troops needed his leadership.

He turned and shouted to the Catachans still hacking at Nogrok's camouflaged orks, who had heard their warboss' shout and were falling back. 'Let them go. Get to the wall! We have to hold back the ferals!'

Orks may not always listen to the orders given to them, but Catachan Jungle Fighters did. They immediately withdrew from the xenos, finishing those they could before allowing the rest to retreat over the outpost wall and into the thick smoke.

The Catachans hit the wall having already switched from their melee blades to their lascarbines. They set themselves in ready position and peered over the wall. Their faces were steely. Anyone else would barely notice a shift but Aldalon saw the tensing in their shoulders, the pulsing of their jaw muscles, the way they reset their firing positions. It wasn't nerves so much, but a clear understanding that the eight remaining Catachan Jungle Fighters could not face down the hundreds, maybe close to a thousand orks crashing like a wave out from the jungle onto the clearing. Even armed with brains barely evolved beyond common mushrooms they would still wash into the outpost like a tsunami.

Those feral orks who actually had guns started shooting up at the wall. Aldalon knew that the greenskins who'd taken this outpost before, those of this Warboss Gutstompa and now Nogrok, had some rudimentary strategy. As the outpost was the main early warning location for an attack on Karoo City, it made sense to take this location and simultaneously use it as a staging post and deny the city warning of an attack. They might not have been as strategically intelligent as Imperial forces, but Aldalon had no doubt that was the orks' intention.

The feral orks, on the other hand, had no strategic thought. The fighting must have brought them here in this unstoppable bestial horde.

'Hold,' Aldalon said as a staccato of shots hit the outpost wall and the battlement. The small-calibre rounds did little but cause rockcrete dust to burst out in small puffs and their accuracy posed little threat.

'What the hell is this?' Sappa shouted. 'We weren't told about feral orks!'

'I know,' Aldalon said. He bristled with anger that wasn't difficult to direct. There were too many feral orks for no one to know they were here. He didn't think Astra Militarum command or the Departmento Munitorum were aware, and as useless as Major General Nillom was he wouldn't have sent them out here without known intelligence about a massive feral ork infestation. No, he knew where the crowns stopped on this one and when he got back to Karoo City, Colonel Hell Fist Aldalon would be having words with that snivelling worm Governor Misom.

Aldalon's mind, well trained in split-second battlefield analysis, ran through scenario after scenario. He watched the feral orks howling, whooping and growling as they stampeded towards the outpost.

'Pick your targets,' Aldalon said. The handful of Catachans on the wall shifted, sighting down their rifles. 'Fire at will.'

Las-fire began cracking down at the ferals. Not the unrestrained, fully automatic fire of the ambush but single, deliberately aimed shots - each one dropping an ork. The Catachans fired and fired, but it was too much like blowing hard to stop a hurricane.

Aldalon turned to look at the troopers either side of him diligently firing down at the overwhelming green host. If the outpost had been undamaged, if there weren't a gaping hole in the wall and the defensive systems were still online, maybe they could have held the orks at bay and sent a signal to Karoo City. But given the current situation, he could determine no suitable action.

'Catachans,' Aldalon said over the crack of las-fire and the boom of ork shot, 'prepare to move. Fighting withdrawal on my mark.'

CHAPTER THIRTY-ONE

TORVIN

'Catachans,' Colonel Aldalon called just as Torvin was firing off a round, aiming at the orks rampaging from the jungle, 'prepare to move. Fighting withdrawal on my mark.'

Torvin wouldn't admit it, but he was glad to hear Aldalon order their retreat. He hadn't quite mastered the apparent fearlessness of the Catachans, because the sight of hundreds and hundreds of crazed greenskins rushing towards them, even more than the first attack he'd weathered at the outpost with the Skadi Second, was terrifying. He didn't need to be a rookie trooper on his first deployment to know they were as good as left out in a wind-whipped blizzard or, as one of the Catachans might say, as cooked as a grox burger.

Torvin was happy that Colonel Aldalon had apparently skipped the part in *The Imperial Infantryman's Uplifting Primer* about the importance of a glorious and wonderful last stand in the face of overwhelming odds. Torvin had more or less seen one of those already and he was sure every member of the Skadi Second would agree that there didn't seem to be a lot about it that was glorious or wonderful.

Still, despite knowing they had no choice but to fall back in a fighting retreat, Torvin couldn't help but feel a sense of crushing failure. He hadn't noticed when he'd become so invested. He'd trekked out to Outpost Four with the Skadi Second knowing their mission was to keep watch for orks and to hold the outpost, but back then he hadn't cared whether they succeeded in that or not - he just wanted to stay alive. Now though, after being the sole survivor of the Skadi Second and having found a place - something of an awkward place but still a place - with the Catachans, and seeing how hard they fought and the people they'd lost to retake the outpost, giving it up just minutes after they took it back seemed so much like an ironic joke that he couldn't abide it.

'Sir, we can't give up,' Torvin said, as the Catachans pulled their lascarbines down from the battlement and prepared to move.

Aldalon turned to look at him. 'You got eyes in that head don't you, softworlder? You see the thousand feral greenskins down there, don't you?'

Torvin swallowed. 'Yes, sir, but we can't let the greenskins have the outpost, not after all this.'

'That's the thing about war, kid, you can't win every battle and you can't hold every objective. Only a fool or an ork believes you can,' Aldalon said. 'It's simple. If a battle cannot be won, don't fight it, and live to win the next one. But technically you're only seconded to us and this was your post, so you're more than welcome to stay here and shoot as many greenskins as you can before they come pouring inside and rip you apart. I'll be sure to tell the commissar that you certainly weren't a coward.'

'No, sir,' Torvin said. 'I know we can't win here, I'm just saying we can't let the orks have this outpost. I know where the armoury is. Assuming the orks didn't take everything, there are plenty of explosives in there. We should blow this place up. If we can't have Outpost Four then neither can the orks.'

Aldalon stared at Torvin. He could see the colonel was considering. 'What strategic value does destroying this watch outpost have, trooper?'

Torvin shrugged. 'We let a bunch of them get inside then we blow them up. That kills a heap of orks. And as for strategic value' – Torvin paused – 'I don't know, the orks don't get it.'

Colonel Haskell 'Hell Fist' Aldalon actually cracked a smile. 'Well, Throne,' he said. 'That does sound like an awfully Catachan thing to do.' Aldalon turned to the others. 'All right, Catachans, listen up. We're falling back but we're going to go with the soft-worlder's idea because, like he said, the orks don't get Outpost Four. While not necessarily within our mission parameters we're doing it for the Catachans we've lost.' He gestured out towards the rapidly approaching orks. 'Feral orks weren't part of the mission either. Someone has hung us out to dry, so Emperor take them, we're deviating from the mission, but I won't risk more lives than necessary. Torvin, you know where the explosives are – are you willing to be the one to stay behind? You can have one Catachan to assist, everyone else will be falling back. You'll need to find the explosives, lay them and get out before the place blows.'

Torvin nodded emphatically. 'Yes, sir.'

'Sir,' Lieutenant Sappa said, 'I'd like to volunteer to stay and assist Torvin.' Torvin saw Aldalon on the verge of responding, but Sappa continued before he could object. 'You put him under my command, sir. He's one of my squad, so I'd like to ensure he makes it out.'

Aldalon nodded. 'Very well. Lieutenant Sappa and Trooper Torvin will remain behind to set the explosives. The rest of you, down the stairs now and make for the exit. It looks clear to the north, make for the jungle and then we head for Karoo City.' The six troopers who would move out with Aldalon nodded and headed for the stairs. Aldalon turned to Lieutenant Sappa.

'I think I've come to a balance now.'

'How's that, sir?' Sappa replied.

'Between being a Catachan commanding officer and being a father.'

Sappa didn't reply, but her mouth tightened.

'You make it back,' Aldalon said. 'That's an order from your commanding officer because the Catachan Fifty-Seventh needs its newest acting lieutenant officially promoted, and it's also a request from your father.'

Sappa nodded. 'Yes, sir,' she said, snapping up a salute.

'Astra Militarum regulations are clear that any operational battlefield is a non-saluting area, lieutenant,' Colonel Aldalon replied.

'I'm not saluting the commanding officer of the Catachan Fifty-Seventh, sir,' Lieutenant Sappa said.

Colonel Aldalon huffed and then returned the salute. 'Good luck,' he said as he turned and made for the stairs.

'Thank you, sir,' Sappa replied.

Colonel Aldalon did not turn back as he descended the stairs. Lieutenant Sappa watched him until he was out of sight and then continued to stare after him for a moment longer. Torvin felt a little uncomfortable. Most people might have considered that almost entirely straight-faced exchange of salutes to be stony military decorum, but he'd been with the Catachans long enough now to recognise it as the most emotionally charged moment he'd seen outside of the raw chaos of battle.

'Lead the way, Torvin.'

'Yes, lieutenant.'

The pair of them left the rooftop and descended the stairs into the outpost. He hadn't had much chance to take in their surroundings when they'd breached the structure before in their attempt to take it back from the orks. He didn't have much time now either, but as he led Lieutenant Sappa away from the central room and down the corridor to the armoury he at least had fractionally more time to notice what the orks had done in their time here. The walls had been covered with all sorts of graffiti written in blue, red and green paint:

Orks is best

Deffskulls rulez

Kuzz woz 'ere.

Doors had been smashed in and rooms ransacked. The sight did not fill Torvin with hope that the armoury would be untouched when they reached it. Every room had a pile of equipment in the centre: vox communicators, cogitators and displays that had been dismantled. It looked as though the orks had been stripping the equipment for parts, but they seemed to have taken as much care in breaking the equipment down as one could when using a sledgehammer for tooth removal.

All down the corridors and in every room he glanced in, in the corners between the floors and walls and especially in dark places, where it seemed to be spreading out along the rockcrete or tiled floors and up the walls in treelike branches, a mosslike fungus was growing - an infestation that Torvin was sure could not have happened naturally had the outpost been left uninhabited for the few days the orks had been here, even in the humid environment of Gondwa VI.

The further they went into the outpost, the more it was the smell that became unbearable. There was a thick aroma of wet earthiness that Torvin was sure came from the fungus on the floor and walls, but other smells were growing stronger too, stenches of acrid sweetness and what might have been rotting meat but was quite unlike anything Torvin had smelled before.

When they reached the armoury Torvin felt hope rising: the door was open but still intact - maybe they hadn't trashed this room as badly. As they entered the armoury, though, his hopes were dashed. The shelves of ammunition and racks of weapons had been emptied.

'Looks like they've picked most of it clean,' Sappa said, 'but where were the explosives?'

He pointed to the far wall. 'They were over there, in stacked crates. I saw them close to the emergency flares.'

Lieutenant Sappa ran to the wall and began tossing aside empty wooden crates painted in green and adorned with the aquila and labelled DEPARTMENTO MUNITORUM.

'Here!' she eventually called as she tossed a final crate aside, ignoring it as it smashed on the rockcrete floor, and then began pulling one of the bottom crates out by the wooden rope handle on one side. She jammed the end of her long Catachan knife under the lid and used it to lever the crate open. The nails gave and the lid popped off. Inside were several rows of demolition charges.

She laughed. 'Stupid orks. Need to learn to read. Grab as many plastics as you can and let's go.'

Sappa grabbed one of the demolition charges and the roll of det. cord. She planted the explosive on the wall of the armoury, close to a bunch of crates that likely had things that would love to explode, buried the end of the det. cord in the explosive and then started unspooling it as she left the armoury and moved down the corridor. Torvin picked up half a dozen of the charges and followed.

Sappa stopped part way down the corridor and turned to Torvin with her hand out. 'Explosive.' Torvin passed her one and she stuck it on the wall, running the det. cord into it and out the other side before continuing on. As they moved down the corridor, the sound of the orks' wild shouts from outside was growing louder. They must be almost inside.

Lieutenant Sappa increased her pace, letting the det. cord unroll as she ran. She stopped further down, just past the door to the communication room, and held out her hand for an explosive again. Torvin passed it to her and she did the same, sticking it to the wall, connecting the det. cord and then moving on. Ahead of them was the central space of the outpost and just as they were about to reach it, Torvin saw animal skin-clad, bone-pierced orks charge in through the opening in the wall.

'Drop the explosives and hold them off,' Sappa called. 'This'll have to do.'

Torvin did as ordered, dropping the four remaining bundles of plastic explosive to the ground and lifting his lasgun. It hummed to life as he primed it. He glanced at the green indicator on the side: it blinked at three bars out of six, half a power pack of ammunition left.

He stepped forward of where Lieutenant Sappa crouched wiring the final four explosives together, raised the lasgun and began firing. His first shot struck an ork in the side of its head as it charged in, blowing it sideways and giving the greenskin beside it a hot shower of brain matter. The orks all immediately turned in the direction of the shot though and, having noticed the two humans just down the corridor, began charging with clubs and stone axes raised. Torvin's heart was racing, his body screaming, but he breathed as deeply and as slowly as he could. He picked a target and fired. Picked another target and fired. Picked another target and, trying to ignore how much closer they were getting, fired.

Lieutenant Sappa was next to him then, lascarbine in hand, firing as well. 'It's ready. One-minute timer set. We're going to have to fight our way out. That'll give us time to clear the area.' Sappa fired off another shot before she let her lascarbine drop and slid her blade from its sheath.

Torvin did the same, dropping his lasgun and pulling out his knife, but as he watched the orks coming he wasn't sure they were going to make it. It didn't seem possible that two humans could fight through a swarm of greenskins. 'Just arm it now,' he said.

Sappa looked at him and nodded. She hit a button on the remote detonator and the countdown timer started. She left it beside the pile of explosives. 'Move fast,' she said as she rose. 'Don't let the orks engage you.'

Torvin nodded. Sappa looked at him one last time and then charged. She ran directly at the first ork but twisted to the side, sliding past it as she slashed, before moving on. Torvin breathed and readied himself. If he stopped running he was going to die, either at the hands of the orks or in a fiery explosion. So he did the same as Sappa, charging forward, sidestepping the first ork and then dashing the other way to dodge the second. He slashed at another ork and, as he desperately tried to keep moving through the increasing number of xenos, echoed Sappa's cry.

'For Catachan!'

They didn't fight, they simply tried not to be fought. They sidestepped and dodged and ran as fast as they could before the outpost filled with a wall of orks that would be impossible to get through. They slashed at orks that tried to engage them, but only if they absolutely had to.

Torvin knew the clock was ticking on their escape. He battered aside an ork's club as they reached the centre section of the outpost. As Sappa slammed into the door on the northern side of the building, barging through it with her shoulder, Torvin glanced in the other direction.

It was not a rising tide, it was the entire damn sea pouring into the outpost. Hundreds and hundreds of feral orks squeezing their way inside, brawling with each other as they did not find a fight waiting for them. Torvin, for the second time, found himself bursting out the north door of Outpost Four on a desperate escape. This time though, he had one minute to get clear, and as Sappa and Torvin sprinted across the grass, that one minute expired.

Torvin felt the explosion rather than heard it, like he'd been kicked in the back by a planet. He flew off his feet amidst a hot, howling fury. The energetic release of the explosion slammed him so hard that he blacked out even before he hit the ground.

CHAPTER THIRTY-TWO

NOGROK

'Oi, Flik,' Nogrok called up the tree. 'You high enough to see anything yet?'

'Yeah, boss,' the sound of the smaller ork's voice called down from up in the jungle canopy. 'I can see stuff now.'

Nogrok waited a moment, but when Flik failed to explain exactly what stuff it was he was seein,' Nogrok sighed – honestly, sometimes even the best of his boyz was thick gitz. 'Well, ya gonna tell me what it is?'

'Right,' Flik said. 'Sorry, boss, it's just usually you the one doin' the lookin' out, but I guess you don't do dat now you is warboss.'

'Kinda lucky you still warboss though, ain't it?' Ruktug said.

Nogrok turned to look at Ruktug and saw the wide grin on the kommando's face.

'Wot you sayin'?' Nogrok asked.

'Well, we ain't got a base and most of da boyz are dead, and we didn't krump the humies. Ain't much good warbossin."

Nogrok lashed out with speed that even surprised himself and punched Ruktug square in the nose. The ork flew back off his feet with a burst of blood from his face and slammed into a tree, coming to a jolting stop and sliding to the ground. Huh. He hadn't meant to hit him that hard. Seemed there'd been more changes to his size, speed and strength. Ruktug groaned from the crumbled heap at the base of the tree.

'You wanna challenge me already, Ruktug?'

'Nah.' Ruktug shook his bleeding face emphatically. 'I shouldn'ta said anything. It's just, we ain't never 'ad a kommando warboss before. We ain't never 'ad a sneaky boy warboss. You ain't...' Ruktug looked like he was going to say something else but then maybe thought better of it.

'I ain't what?'

'Nothin,' boss.'

'I ain't what, Ruktug?' Nogrok said, sterner this time.

'Well,' Ruktug said, looking like an ork boy who was about to admit to stealing all the fungus beer, 'you ain't, you know, you ain't scary like a normal warboss.'

Nogrok felt a rise of orky rage. 'I ain't scary,' he said. 'I'll show you scary if I 'ave to.' He took a couple of steps towards Ruktug but then stopped himself. He looked at Ruktug, blood flowing from his nose over the black paint on his face. The other orks around him were all wearing various attempts at camouflage and so, of course, was he. He stopped coz, despite being annoyed about it, Ruktug was right.

'You right, Ruktug,' Nogrok said.

'I am?'

'Yeah. I ain't scary like a normal warboss. I ain't a massive ball of muscle with legs I bought from a mekboy or a big suit of armour so I can charge into a fight like a rok smashin' into a planet. I ain't a big tough warboss in dat way, sure, but I ain't a big stupid git either. All dem dumb warbosses think Gork is da best but I is gonna show 'em Mork is da best. You think dem humies was scared of Warboss Gutstompa?' None of the orks answered, probably not knowin' whether he was asking a real question or a wotsit – a retro-oracle question. He turned to Gluk. 'Do you think tha humies was scared of Warboss Gutstompa, Gluk?'

The ork boy shrugged. 'I was.'

'Yeah.' Nogrok nodded. 'You was, but guess wot, dat humie with the big hand? 'E wasn't scared o' Gutstompa at all. Gutstompa just a big idiot. Strong, yeah, but dumb as squig juice. Who do ya think that humie was scared of, Gluk?'

'Uh,' Gluk said. 'Those feral orks wot come–'

'Me, ya git!' Nogrok yelled at him. 'Dat Catachan humie was scared o' me and he was scared o' me for the reasons you sayin' I ain't scary, Ruktug. Da humies scared o' me coz I ain't a big, dumb warboss. I gonna be a kunnin' warboss what fights like they ain't never seen. I'm scary coz I'm different.'

Nogrok leant in close to the orks around him. 'I gonna be a different warboss. I gonna raise a whole warband of kommandos. We gonna be kunnin.' Kunnin' but brutal.'

'Boss!' Flik called down from up the tree. 'I see somethin' you probably want to know about.'

Nogrok waited for another moment. 'Well, tell me then, ya git!'

'Da humies is runnin' away from the outpost and all them feral orks are chargin' inside.'

'I thought you said the humies weren't scared of the feral orks, boss,' Gluk said.

'Shut your squig hole, git,' Nogrok said. 'They runnin' coz they can't win. You saw 'ow many of them feral gitz there were, 'eaps of 'em. Them feral orks are the stupidest of the stupid. They don't know nothin' about fightin.''

Nogrok stopped. Somewhere inside the deepest parts of his mycelium mind there was a bright spark of electricity. It ran along the twisting channels until it reached the mushroom equivalent of his prefrontal cortex, where it merged with a series of other electrical signals and suddenly erupted into an idea. He smiled. Most orks never had an idea, at least not a new idea – most ork knowledge was simply preprogrammed into their genetic code – but every once in a while, in the brain of a particular ork, some factors collided that led to them having the very rare feeling of an epiphany. He'd already thought about making the feral orks part of his warband, but maybe he could do more than that; maybe he could show 'em the way of bein' proper orks. Ferals didn't know anything so maybe he could make all of them into kommandos, convince them that was the proper way of being an ork.

Nogrok's moment of inspiration was interrupted by a booming explosion, and then another, then another, and finally a truly massive boom that rattled his internal organs and caused an uncontrollable reaction of orkish glee.

'Cor!' Flik called from up the tree. 'Da humie base just blew up with loads of the feral orks inside.'

Nogrok huffed a tiny laugh. Good one. The Catachans must have gave them one last sneaky present. 'How many of them feral orks left out there then?' Nogrok asked Flik.

'There was still heaps outside,' Flik said, 'maybe loads.'

'Dat's good then,' Nogrok said.

'It is?' Ruktug asked with a nasal whine, as he'd plugged two fingers up his nose to try to quell the bleeding.

'Yes, Ruktug,' Nogrok said. 'It is. If we gonna build a kunnin' warband we need orks that ain't already thinkin' they know better.'

Nogrok smiled again. He was going to be the first warboss to ever lead a Waaagh! full of properly sneaky orks. A little time was all he needed, and he'd show the Catachans, and all the humies, and everything in the whole galaxy what a Waaagh! Sneakyguts could do.

CHAPTER THIRTY-THREE

ALDALON

Colonel Aldalon crouched in the low undergrowth, peering out between two large, gently parted fern leaves. He felt a tightness around his shin and when he looked down, he saw one of Gondwa VI's multi-limbed serpents coiling itself around his lower leg. Aldalon looked down at it, considering the creature. It was close to ten feet long, green with a pale belly and jagged yellow stripes on its back, with four pairs of legs set evenly along its length that it had tucked up as it wrapped around Aldalon's calf, its muscular body pulsing as it began to squeeze.

Colonel Aldalon poked at it with his Catachan knife. The lizard lifted its snake-like head towards Aldalon and opened its mouth, hissing. From between several rows of small triangular teeth its tongue shot out and opened to reveal another wet, mucus-covered appendage extending from inside the tongue like a blood-sucking proboscis. To most humans this would have caused a panic on an instinctive, primal level. Yet Aldalon's adrenal glands barely fluttered. He was from the death world of Catachan; this bloodsucking half-snake half-lizard was a child's plaything. He stuck his blade point first into the mud and then, with his bare hand, grabbed the head of the creature. It writhed and hissed, its bloodsucking tongue whipping around.

'Now, is not the time,' he said to the lizard before twisting its head around hard, wrenching it a full one hundred and eighty degrees and feeling the spinal cord snap and sever. Then, just to be sure, he continued the twist all the way around as everything in the neck ruptured and the vertebrae ground against each other. The animal's long body squeezed harder with muscle spasms before finally going limp. Aldalon pulled it off his leg and tossed it away into the scrub.

He turned his attention back to the direction of Outpost Four. Aldalon had led Sergeant Dram and the last of the troopers far enough away from the watch station to avoid detection should the feral orks somehow manage to follow them. This meant being back a distance from the edge of the northern treeline. The trade-off was that it was difficult to see the outpost from here, but he could just make out the shape of the rockcrete structure through the curling vines and densely growing trees that stretched for the light above the canopy. It was difficult to make out individual orks, but the general movement of the mass of greenskins was clear enough.

The first of the feral orks had reached the outpost and were charging inside through the destroyed section of wall. They were charging inside and not coming out. The other thing he could not see coming out was Learna or Trooper Torvin. He leant from side to side, trying to find the best sight line he could through the trees.

Aldalon watched the outpost, waiting for Learna to come running across the open ground to the north. He muttered under his breath for her to hurry. 'Come on. Come on.' He even sent his desire to the Emperor Himself, something he had not done since Brant's death. 'Immortal Emperor, have mercy and guide her to safety now so that she may continue to serve you with her life.'

Aldalon had barely finished speaking when the outpost erupted in a massive series of explosions. The first occurred somewhere near the central chamber. Even from this relatively short distance Aldalon saw the flash of light and the first expansion of fracturing rockcrete before the sound reached him with a booming roll like thunder and a buffeting of his eardrums.

The devastation continued as the first explosion rolled into a second and a third. The central section of the outpost had collapsed into a pile of debris, and a column of black-and-grey smoke was rising into the air, but some of the rockcrete chunks hadn't even fallen back to earth when the subsequent detonations followed towards the west end of the outpost, smaller explosions but still enough to blow out walls along the building's length.

Finally, like the cymbal crash right at the crescendo of a rising symphony, the final explosion rocked the jungle as the black sooty burst of demolition charges was joined by the unmistakable detonation of an armoury. It wasn't the first time Aldalon had borne witness to the chaining explosions of an erupting ammo dump – he'd even caused it once or twice himself. Ammunition, explosives, mines, lasgun power packs and missiles all released their stored potential energy with a cacophony of pops and booms that combined to blow the rockcrete structure of the western end of the outpost into little more than rapidly expanding dust. Some of the bigger debris was thrown in high arcs all over the clearing and some even had the velocity to plunge into the edge of the jungle.

Aldalon watched the corpse of Outpost Four as the destruction slowed to smaller blasts and pops as the last holdouts of the armoury supplies gave in to their fate. Of the feral orks who'd been inside the outpost, nothing remained but their component atoms and even those nearby had been vaporised. A wide band of orks had been flattened, many speared through with flying debris, torn apart by the sheer energetic release of the shock wave, or even killed by the flying body parts of their comrades. That was something far more common than people realised. Aldalon himself had seen Imperial Guardsmen killed countless times by pieces of other Guardsmen. They tended to leave that off the recruitment posters and out of the motivational brochures; no one wanted to think about having their skull crushed as the ripped-off leg of their best friend hit them in the face.

The feral orks that hadn't been killed or mortally wounded had stopped and were staring at the destroyed outpost like the children Aldalon had seen when the Catachan 57th had been part of the force that liberated Tyringal from drukhari slavers and the planet had celebrated with an immense display of fireworks over the capital. The children had stared with wide-eyed wonder at the explosions, just as the orks were doing now. At least, the people of Tyringal had celebrated until the planet was completely destroyed by a drukhari dark matter weapon in retribution some six months later.

Aldalon waited as the explosions finally ceased. He waited as the rain of debris ended. He waited even as the dust began to settle and the feral orks started picking over the carcass of the outpost for what might be left. He waited long enough.

'Catachans,' he said, turning away from the destroyed outpost, stone-faced and cold. 'Let's move out.'

The remaining Catachans turned to follow without speaking. Colonel Aldalon knew none of them wanted to be the first to raise any discussion of the heavy price that had been paid today. Aldalon walked into the green of the jungle. Learna had said this world reminded her a little of Catachan, but it was not Catachan, and for all the deadly horror of that world, it was their home. It was their home and Learna would never see it again. Catachan had sacrificed much for this tiny outpost, too much, and there would be more than warping hell to pay for those that had sent them out here with the understanding they were facing a small warband of ordinary orks.

Not only had Catachan paid too heavy a price, but he had also paid too heavy a price yet again. Here, and on Karst, he had paid with his blood kin. He had felt such pride, as any Catachan would, when both his children had made it into the Jungle Fighters. Now, when they had whole careers of distinguished service to the Emperor and the Imperium ahead of them, the orks and the bad intelligence of soft-world fools had got them both killed. Aldalon felt a warmth in his hand and realised he was unconsciously causing his power fist to crackle with energy. He released the tension, knowing the bloodlust and madness caused by the loss of Brant would be all the more difficult to control now that he would have to squash down the grief for his daughter as well. He had to force it down though, he had to bury it deep. Emotion was weakness and there was no room for weakness on Catachan. Although, he was going to make an exception for the emotion of rage when he got back to Karoo City.

The Catachans, even under the circumstances of defeat and loss, moved with their well-practised stealth into the thicker jungle of the valley leading to Karoo City. It was because they were moving so silently that all of them heard the series of clicks behind them. Aldalon held up his fist for the soldiers to halt and then he turned, almost hesitantly, unsure if he wanted to believe it.

There, moving gingerly and not as stealthily as he would have approved of, was Trooper Torvin with a clicker in his hand. He was limping and was supported by – or perhaps they were supporting each other – Learna. They were dirty with grey rockcrete dust and the sooty black of spent explosives. It coated their uniforms and covered their faces, thick in their eyelashes and eyebrows, turning to a wet paste around their numerous bleeding cuts and scrapes. They approached the smiling Catachans, who greeted them with claps on the shoulders and arms.

Colonel Aldalon looked at his daughter and felt a rush of relief of course, but more than that, he felt pride even greater than he had before. She was a true Catachan, a warrior and a survivor. He kept his face as impassive as he could, but he had to admit, it felt good; perhaps there was something to focusing on emotions other than rage after all.

'I'm glad you made it, lieutenant.'

'I told you I would, sir,' Lieutenant Sappa said. 'I was just following orders, and a request from my father.'

To that Aldalon smiled. 'You two can make it to Karoo?'

Torvin and Learna nodded. 'Yes, sir.'

'Good,' Aldalon said. 'All right. Catachans, let's move. There's a politician in Karoo I've got business with.'

CHAPTER THIRTY-FOUR

ALDALON

The crashing tide of feral orks roaring from the jungle and slamming into Outpost Four was nothing compared to the energy with which Colonel Haskell Aldalon entered the temporary headquarters in the reliquary room of the Karoo City chapel. His look alone sent the single guard outside wilting into a puddle of nerves on the floor, and he opened the door with his power fist with all the subtlety that entailed.

The wooden door shattered as he punched his way in, sending splinters scything dangerously through the air. The usual suspects were inside, no doubt awaiting his arrival since he and the remains of the two squads he'd left with had been spotted entering the lower levels of the city. Both Planetary Governor Misom and Major General Nillom stared wide-eyed and pale and with the posture of two men who had unexpectedly answered their daily call of nature. Commissar Redvin, who was made of stronger stuff, had clambered to her feet and displayed a stance more akin to someone well versed in causing others to evacuate their bowels.

'Colonel Aldalon!' the commissar roared. 'What is the meaning of this? You could have killed someone! I will have you on charges immediately.'

'Unfortunately, it appears I did not manage to kill anyone, commissar,' Aldalon replied.

Commissar Redvin had already flicked back her long black greatcoat and was reaching for her bolt pistol. 'Wilful endangerment of the life of a superior officer. Astra Militarum Disciplinary Regulation 416A calls for the commissar present to judge and deliver immediate punishment up to and including death.'

Colonel Aldalon did not seem concerned. 'I'm not the one who should be brought up on charges, Commissar Redvin.' Colonel Aldalon pointed to Planetary Governor Misom. 'He should be.'

'What?' Governor Misom objected in his pathetic squeaking voice.

'You've returned with a fraction of the troopers you left with, colonel,' Commissar Redvin said. 'Are you trying to shift the blame?'

Aldalon felt a rise of anger. 'You want to know why I lost so many troopers out there? The intelligence we were given was that we were facing a small warband of orks who'd overrun and occupied a watch station.'

'Yes,' Major General Nillom replied, 'that was the situation.'

'Have you ever heard the stories of the ghost orks?' Aldalon asked.

'Fairy tales,' Nillom said. 'Stories that arose from scared Guardsmen on Karst and earlier campaigns in the defence of this subsector.'

'So, you weren't aware that a large contingent of the orks that had taken Outpost Four were those the orks call kommandos?'

'Well, I don't see the relevance of that,' Governor Misom said. 'An ork is an ork is an ork.'

'No,' Aldalon said, 'an ork is not an ork. We had already learned that lesson on Karst. The ghost orks are very much real. They are a bunch of kommandos being led by the now Warboss Nogrok, and they are far deadlier in small numbers than any orks I have ever encountered.'

'Thank you, colonel,' Commissar Redvin said. 'I understand you being upset with losing troopers, but I believe we can put this down as a mistake rather than negligence. I'm sure–'

'I'm not done, commissar,' Colonel Aldalon said, cutting the commissar off with her mouth hanging open. 'I'd also like to note you haven't yet asked about the outcome of the mission, Major General Nillom. You see, if I am here, and all my troopers are here, who would be holding Outpost Four?'

'I...' Nillom started, 'I, uh, I assumed we'd need to send a unit out to man it or, colonel, are you saying the mission failed?'

Aldalon smiled, but it was not a smile of warmth or humour. 'Major general, do you think I would be this riled up if the mission had been a rousing success?'

'So, the orks still have control of Outpost Four?'

Aldalon turned to the whiny voice of Planetary Governor Misom. 'Governor,' Aldalon said, 'what do you think we encountered out there?'

'Colonel Aldalon,' Nillom said, 'do the orks have control of Outpost Four or not?'

'No, sir, the orks do not have control of Outpost Four.'

'Ah, good,' Governor Misom muttered.

'Nobody does,' Aldalon finished. 'It has been destroyed.'

'What?' Misom blurted out. 'Destroyed? How?'

'Well, we blew it up to deny it to the enemy,' Aldalon said matter-of-factly.

'You... but... you cannot!' Misom continued to bluster. 'That outpost is of vital strategic significance.'

'Colonel,' Major General Nillom said, 'your mission was to retake the outpost, not destroy it.'

'Well, sir, as if not knowing about the ghost orks wasn't bad enough, there was another even bigger threat out there. We retook Outpost Four, before being completely overrun by an immense force of feral orks,' Aldalon said. He was speaking to Nillom but kept Governor Misom squarely in his sights as he said this. As he expected, Misom's face instantly drained of colour, as it had when he'd first burst into the room. 'We were forced to abandon the outpost and turned it into a baited trap for the orks. Despite the number we killed, there are still a thousand or so feral orks out there in the jungle, possibly more.'

'Feral orks?' Major General Nillom said, and the look on his face was enough to confirm Aldalon's suspicions. He hadn't known. 'A whole force of them?'

Aldalon turned to Commissar Redvin. 'Commissar, our relationship is a little rocky and I know you have no jurisdiction over a planetary governor, so I can't ask you to do much here, but would you mind turning a blind eye to my actions for a moment?'

'That depends on what you are talking about, colonel,' the commissar responded.

'You see,' Aldalon said before gesturing to Governor Misom, 'he knew about the feral orks but has kept it from the Imperium.'

'I certainly did not,' Misom spluttered, 'I-I-I knew nothing about any orks.'

'There are thousands of feral orks in the jungles surrounding your planet's capital. Even the most incompetent, worthless cesspit of an Imperial world can detect a feral ork population of a hundred or less. They aren't exactly subtle.'

'No,' Governor Misom said with all the confidence of a man with blood-covered hands, 'it's, ah, it's because of the planet's, you know, magnetic field. We have difficulty with surveillance and, it's... we didn't know about them.'

Aldalon looked at the commissar. 'Would you mind?'

Commissar Redvin nodded and Aldalon was on the planetary governor in two-tenths of a heartbeat. He grabbed him around the throat with his augmetic left hand and squeezed. The governor made the noise of a terrified mouse.

'You listen to me, you soft-world fool,' Aldalon growled. 'If I grabbed you like this with my power fist and squeezed, your head would pop off like a lanced pustule.' The governor squirmed uselessly like a wet towel flopping in the colonel's grip. 'Why didn't you tell us about the feral orks?'

'I didn't know,' the governor managed, but Aldalon squeezed again and Misom yelped. 'All right,' he pleaded, 'all right! We knew we had a feral ork problem.'

Aldalon let him go. Misom rubbed at his reddening neck. 'Speak.'

'We just...' the governor said. 'We've had several ork invasions over the years and they always seem to come back. Every time the orks invade and we think they are driven off they pop back up again – either more of them come from the void or we have a feral infestation. My grandfather, when he was governor, claimed to have fought off the last infestation without Imperial aid, but when the feral orks started appearing again he was terrified of what would happen if he was openly proved wrong. The Imperium seemed to be less concerned about our planet each time we called for help. Our tithe isn't large enough to warrant endless resources being spent to make sure it keeps coming.'

'Wealth,' Aldalon said, shaking his head. 'You kept quiet about an ork infestation because you were worried about money.'

'You don't know what it's like trying to keep a world going. We are a jungle world, we require much from the Imperium, but if we are infested with orks again and again, eventually the Imperium will give up on us. We resolved to handle it ourselves, and then, well... the lie grew.'

Aldalon turned to Commissar Redvin. 'Satisfied with my concerns enough that you can drop charges against me, commissar?'

Redvin turned from Aldalon to Governor Misom. 'Yes, colonel, very well. You are correct in stating I do not have any authority over planetary governors, but I certainly feel this warrants further investigation.'

'No,' Governor Misom pleaded. 'Please, don't bring the Inquisition into this.'

'Shut up,' Redvin said. 'Not reporting an ork infestation is tantamount to traitorous.'

Aldalon turned to Major General Nillom. 'Sir, I know you believed you were well on your way to clearing the Gondwa System of orks but the actions of the Gondwa VI government have destroyed that notion. At the moment, we've got a three-way war for this world involving us, Warboss Nogrok and his ghost orks, and now these ferals. If we act swiftly, perhaps we can at least keep it that way. If not, I fear things could get much worse.'

'And how could they get worse, colonel?' Nillom asked.

'If Nogrok pulls the ferals under his control he'll be very dangerous.'

'Major general!' A lieutenant entered the room in a fluster. 'Sir, reports of orks approaching the city through the valley!'

Major General Nillom looked blank-faced.

'Sir?' the lieutenant repeated.

Aldalon looked from Nillom to the lieutenant. 'Lieutenant.'

'Yes, sir?' the lieutenant said, turning his attention to Aldalon.

'You tell the city defence the Catachan Fifty-Seventh are on their way.'

----- DEPARTMENTO MUNITORUM FORM 8712/AM/R03 -----

ASTRA MILITARUM OPERATIONS REPORT

CORRESPONDENCE NUMBER: OR-12710735734

TO: High Command, Task Force Devotion of Pangea
CC: Departmento Munitorum – Office of Records – Correspondence Department
Office of the Supreme Commander Ultima Segmentum
Officio Tactica Logistics Division
FROM: Major General Niko Nillom, Officer Commanding Gondwa System Defence
SUBJECT: Gondwa System Defence Update
ENCLOSURES and REFERENCES:

1. Gondwa VI Casualty Report from Skadi Second Infantry and Catachan 57th Jungle Fighters
2. Request Form for Priority Two Transfer of Additional Reinforcements (Eighth Submission)
3. Request Form for Special Order Wargear – Power fist

In the name of the most Holy Emperor of Mankind I, (insert name here) MAJOR GENERAL NILLOM, submit the following report on (insert relevant operation name) THE GONDWA SYSTEM DEFENCE.

Following my last official report (see OR-12710735626) I can update that the purging of Gondwa VI is continuing with all confidence of success.

The Skadi Second Infantry Fourth Platoon had been stationed at watch station Outpost Four on the outskirts of the planet's capital, Karoo City. The platoon encountered high ork resistance to their presence and performed admirably in a final stand in the glorious spirit of the Astra Militarum and in the name of the most Holy Immortal Emperor. All members of the platoon were killed in action. Related: please see my attached request form for additional reinforcements. This is the eighth request for additional reinforcements I have directed to the Officio Tactica. Please respond at your earliest convenience. I praise the troopers of the Skadi Second and would recommend the raising of the Skadi Third Infantry Regiment when next the planet is tithed.

Outpost Four was retaken by the valiant and ever-reliable forces of the Catachan 57th Jungle Fighters, although it is my understanding that it did sustain some damage in the assault. The commanding officer of the Catachan 57th, Colonel Haskell Aldalon, has provided sufficient evidence that there is a larger ork force on the planet than we initially believed. However, I am confident the Catachan 57th can assist the Gondwa VI militia in holding strong as I await further reinforcements to cleanse the world entirely (see again reference 2).

The capital, Karoo City, does appear to be a target of the orks on this world, but we will resist them with the blessing of the Emperor and I myself shall take to the battlefield if necessary. Please see the attached Departmento Munitorum request for special wargear. I would like the blessed privilege of wielding a power fist against the foes of mankind as Colonel Aldalon has shown the benefit of such a weapon in this environment. A small one would be acceptable.

In the Emperor's name we continue this winning campaign.

- - - - - END COMMUNICATION - - - - -

IRON RESOLVE

STEVE LYONS

0700

Guardsman Myer was bleeding again.

He had only closed his eyes for a second. Somehow, however, his mind had drifted elsewhere. He came back to his senses with a jolt. The Chimera in which he was travelling was a relic, its suspension shot. It was only through the press of bodies around him that he had not been juddered right out of his seat.

A dark stain spread across his brand new uniform jacket.

'I told you to keep pressure on that dressing.' Scornful eyes blazed at the young trooper from the shadow of a cap peak.

'Yes, sergeant. Sorry, sergeant.' Myer stiffened his posture. He pressed his hand into the sticky wetness of his right side. Pain lanced through his body. He clenched his teeth to keep a groan from escaping. He took a deep, shuddering breath.

He tried not to think about how much blood he had lost.

He wanted to ask how far they had to go, but that would have looked weak. What was the point in knowing, anyway? They would reach help before Myer died or else they wouldn't. His fate was in the Emperor's hands.

The trooper beside him doubled up in another coughing fit. The sergeant, leaning across the narrow space between them, pushed him upright and ordered him to breathe. The trooper complied, sweat drenching his face. A crimson rash extruded tendrils from beneath his stiff blue collar, cradling his chin. Skin flaked from his cheeks. He couldn't last much longer either. Not if the infection had reached his lungs.

Myer's instinct was to shrink away from him, but this would have meant leaning closer to one of the others. Of the four other patients jammed into the crew compartment, three were victims of the same blight.

His heart soared hopefully as the Chimera juddered to a reluctant halt. A moment later, the roar of its engine ceased. Silence rushed into Guardsman Myer's ears. The sergeant unlatched the rear hatch and shouldered it open.

Myer flinched as bright light flooded the gloomy compartment. Having only left Mordian – the world of his birth, the World of Eternal Night – four weeks ago, he was quite unused to sunlight. It had been night when he had clambered aboard the Chimera. Now, blinding rays streamed through the tangled structures of an alien forest.

'Those who can walk, disembark,' the sergeant ordered. Myer didn't think that included him, but he didn't dare say so. It was easier to try.

His wound flared white-hot again as he levered himself up. He steadied himself with his free hand against the Chimera's chassis. He saw blurred figures through the blinding light, hurrying to meet him. Just three or four steps, he told himself.

He managed two – two faltering, agonising, hunched-over steps – then tumbled forwards out of the back of the vehicle.

He watched the forest floor rushing up towards him. Then a pair of strong arms caught him. He didn't know whose arms they were. His hand fell away from the wound between his ribs, letting blood flow freely from it. It no longer mattered. The stale, recycled air of the troop compartment had been replaced by a warm, fresh, floral-scented breeze. He felt his mind drifting from his body again, and this time he was relieved to let it go.

He had made it, he thought. He was at the command post, far from the carnage of battle.

He was finally safe.

1000

Guardsman Myer was going to die.

The news hadn't sunk in yet, hence his outward reaction to it was suitably measured. He sat to attention, his arms like ramrods by his sides. He felt self-conscious in his flimsy white surgical gown. It rubbed against the knot of stitches and synth-skin holding his side together.

Lieutenant Veimer sat across a cluttered desk from him. 'Anything to say?'

'No, sir,' said Myer. 'I mean, no, sir, I didn't. I wouldn't.'

Veimer didn't look at him. He was tapping at a data-slate, head down, presenting Myer with a view of his balding crown. He had glanced at the young trooper only once, when inviting him to enter the small room and sit down.

Myer feared he should have insisted on standing. He felt like he had walked into a trap. He had let his defences down, feeling grateful to the man whose surgical skills had saved his life. Veimer wasn't just a medic, however. He was an officer in the Mordian Iron Guard. He had rescued Myer only to condemn him anew with the flick of a stylus.

'Name?' Veimer rumbled.

'Lucius Myer,' said Myer, and he reeled off his serial number.

Veimer nodded. The information matched that on his slate. He confirmed Myer's date of birth and age, which was sixteen. 'First tour of duty?'

'Yes, sir.'

'Tell me what happened.'

'We set up camp in the Dirkr Forest, sir. We were told that an ork ship crashed on Kallash some years ago. A feudal world. The survivors were dealt with by the local militia, but–'

'I am aware of the mission specs, Guardsman. Tell me what happened last night.'

'Last night, my squad was clearing a section of the forest. We hadn't seen a xenos in over two days. We thought they must have fled from this–'

'Don't tell me what you thought.'

'No, sir. They had set an ambush for us. It was Guardsman Steinvorst who saw them. Or heard them or smelled them, I'm not sure which. If he hadn't… He shouted a warning. Sergeant Ven Coers voxed for assistance, but the orks were already–'

'Feral orks,' the lieutenant corrected him.

Myer took a breath. He willed himself to remain composed, dispassionate. 'They burst out of the trees ahead of us. They were wielding clubs, and a few had axes too. They came at us, howling and slobbering for our blood. We shot some of them – I think two or three of them – down, but the rest...'

'According to the report, your squad acquitted itself with honour.'

'Yes, sir. We lost one Guardsman. But we held off the orks – the feral orks – until reinforcements reached us. We purged this world of twenty xenos, at least.'

'You must have been afraid. A fresh young recruit like you.'

'Not for a moment, sir,' insisted Myer.

'Concerned for your life?'

'I did my duty,' he restated, with as much conviction as he could muster.

'Sustaining a near-fatal wound in the process.'

'Apparently so, sir.'

Lieutenant Veimer met Myer's eyes for the first time. The officer's own eyes were red-rimmed, slightly distended. He was obviously tired, although he showed no other sign of it. 'Of course, you reported this wound to your sergeant at once?'

'I was unaware of it, sir. At the time. The xenos swarmed us, clawing, biting, slashing, spitting. I was trying to keep them at bay with my bayonet. I don't remember feeling the knife blow to my side. It was only later that I discovered the bleeding.'

'Knife blow?' Veimer raised a sceptical eyebrow.

'I assumed so, sir. It looked like a knife wound to me. The blade, or whatever it was, had sliced through my uniform.'

'And yet, you didn't start to bleed until later?'

'Only minutes later,' said Myer. 'I didn't realise how serious it was, to begin with. I thought I could staunch the bleeding myself. I emptied the synth-skin canister in my medi-pack.'

Veimer made more notes on the data-slate. An agonising minute passed before he spoke again. Myer's side ached and his throat felt dry. He clenched his fists against his hips, his fingernails cutting his palms. He had to keep himself from shaking.

'I have been a field medicae for almost twenty years,' said Veimer, finally. 'I have dealt with numerous troopers – young men, usually – who thought they could escape military service by injuring themselves.'

'Surely no man of Mordian would ever–?'

Veimer spoke over Myer without raising his voice. 'The preferred method used to be to shoot oneself in the foot. Since that became a cliché, cases like your own are more common. You were cut by a xenos blade, I don't doubt it. I have learned to tell the difference, however, between a wound sustained in battle, with the full strength of a feral ork behind it, and one crafted rather more slowly and carefully in the victim's own tent.'

Myer found he couldn't speak.

'My report will state that, in my expert opinion, your wound was self-inflicted,' the officer pronounced. 'You will have an opportunity to defend yourself in front of the Commissariat. For your sake, I hope you are more convincing than you have been today. Dismissed.'

Myer pushed himself to his feet. His head swam. For a moment, he thought he might pass out again. He wanted to argue, to shout, to plead, to lodge a desperate appeal against his fate. Such behaviour would have been indecorous, however, inviting only further scorn; anyway, he still had no words.

'Do you need an orderly to help you back to your bed?' asked Veimer, without looking up.

'No. Thank you, sir. I can manage,' Myer croaked.

The young trooper made his way out of the office, determined to hold himself tall.

Only after the door had closed behind him did Veimer set aside his data-slate and allow himself a disappointed sigh.

As if he weren't busy enough, he thought. It had never been intended that his understaffed, makeshift facility in the forest should cope with a full-scale plague. How much time had he wasted saving Myer's life this morning – and for what? So that he could be hauled before a military court and almost certainly convicted and shot?

He had done his duty, he told himself. It was not for him to question. Still, he found his thoughts veering towards a familiar gloomy place. How many young soldiers like Myer had he tended to in his time? How many of them were alive now?

Those who passed through Veimer's hands were, in many ways, the luckier ones. They had stared death in the face and, one way or another, had survived. He had patched them up and sent them back out to fight. Most, he had never seen or heard of again. How many could have been so lucky a second time?

It might have been better for all concerned had he left Myer to bleed to death.

It would surely have been kinder.

The Dirkr Forest command post squatted in a circular clearing, created by the fire of the Emperor's holy infantry. The largest of its four prefabricated huts had been pressed into service as a medicae ward. Fourteen beds lined its long walls, each of them occupied. As many patients again lay on the floor on mattresses, squeezed between the beds.

Myer had to walk past all of them. His trembling legs would have made this difficult enough. He was quickly aware, however, that every head in the room – save for those of the very sickest patients – had turned to greet his return. Conversations had abruptly ceased.

They knew. Somehow, every one of them knew. Myer tried to pretend he hadn't noticed. He kept his chin up. He stared ahead as if blinkered, avoiding their accusing eyes. The walk to his corner bed felt like a five-mile march.

He lowered himself onto it, at last, with relief. He kept his back firmly to the rest of the room. His mind raced, composing the report he intended to write to set the record straight. He had felt so tongue-tied in front of Veimer, and after all, he had just had major surgery. He could do much better, say so much more, in writing.

Mordian officers loved a good report. When they read his report, they would know he couldn't possibly be guilty of the charges levelled against him.

'Coward!'

Myer thought – or hoped – he had imagined the voice. It had been kept low, a surreptitious hiss. A spit. The background drone of the command post's generatorum outside, behind a thin plasteel wall, had almost drowned it out. He couldn't mistake the spiteful murmur of agreement that rippled along the ward, however.

'It isn't true,' he blurted out, without looking around. 'I didn't do it.'

He hugged his pillow, burying his head in it. He was deeply, overwhelmingly tired. His body demanded sleep after its series of ordeals, but his mind was keeping it awake.

The room was gloomy, windows shuttered against Kallash's harsh daylight. Myer welcomed the darkness. He focused on the steady hum of the generatorum, letting it fill his head. Everything would look better after sleep, he told himself. He would write that report and show everyone how wrong they were about him.

He just needed not to think for a while.

Patterns danced behind his eyelids. He left the ward, with its counterseptic tang, behind him. Instead of going somewhere better, however, he found himself back in the forest. The patterns resolved into the shapes of trees and bushes. Myer was back in his pristine uniform, back with his squad... his old squad, of which he had been a member for so short a time. Back in the darkest moment of his young life.

He knew what was about to happen, but he was helpless to stop it. It was Guardsman Steinvorst – solid, reliable Steinvorst, twice Myer's age but the colleague to whom he felt closest, the one who had been kindest to him – who shouted the warning.

A jolt of terror, as strong as it had been the first time, shocked him awake.

Myer had cried out – only in the dream, or in reality too? He couldn't tell. He prayed he hadn't disgraced himself. He lay still until his breathing slowed to its normal pace. Only then did he dare close his eyes again, but it was no use. As soon as he did, the dreadful image returned: a snarling, savage monster, thundering towards him.

1100

The first time Myer had set eyes upon a xenos, it had been dead.

A distress call had come in from another squad. They had stumbled into a trap - one of the spiked pits of which their foes were so fond - and been surrounded. Sergeant Ven Coers had led her nine Guardsmen through the forest at a run.

Myer had heard gunshots, guttural grunts and screams. He had prayed for the battle to be over before they reached it - and the Emperor had been with him that day, granting his unworthy plea.

Other squads had been closer than theirs. The feral orks had been few, relying on their trap for advantage, and were swiftly outgunned. Ven Coers had prodded a carcass with her toe, nodding with grim satisfaction.

Myer had been on Kallash for only three days, after several weeks spent in the limbo of transit. For three days, he had been seeing threats in every shadow, hearing them on every breeze. The reality was every bit as horrific as he had imagined.

Huge, vicious tusks sprouted from the xenos' jaw. Oversized ears jutted from a misshapen head, amid haphazard tufts of wiry hair. Its eyes, recessed beneath a prominent brow, were open and, even in death, blazed with barbaric fury. Spikes of bone and metal pierced its ears and squat nose, some hung with tiny rodent skulls. The xenos' skin had a sickly green tint, and stinking blood trickled from its wounds like plant sap.

It had taken all of Myer's willpower not to retch.

These creatures were backward, lacking in strategy, no match for the Iron Guard's massed ranks. So comrades and officers alike had assured him. Scant comfort, he had thought, for those Guardsmen impaled upon their spikes. Guardsmen like him.

'The Emperor must like you, Guardsman Myer.'

He recalled Ven Coers' first words to him. Myer had just stepped off a drop-ship, clutching his kitbag. His new squad leader looked him up and down appraisingly, with dark eyes sunk into a shaven granite head. 'Either that or He thinks you need coddling. Do you need coddling, Guardsman Myer?'

'No, sergeant, I do not.'

'You should find these feral orks no challenge, then. It would dignify that rabble to call them enemies. They are but vermin, infesting this forest, requiring us to stamp them out. This mission, Myer, is hardly a mission at all, more like a training session. Your biggest worry on Kallash will be finding ways to keep busy, so that you do not go soft.'

Myer had felt doubtful, but had kept this to himself. He had already picked up a few salient points from briefings and from other troopers' mutterings. He knew that, by all accounts, the xenos' numbers were increasing and that nobody really knew why. How could this be, if everything was going so well? How was it, indeed, that the XVII Mordian Regiment had been mired in this alien forest for months?

And why did the sight of a single feral ork, even dead, fill Myer with fear?

It wasn't that he was a bad soldier.

In some ways, he excelled at it. He had grown up in a military academy. He had mastered the fundamentals of drill by the age of five. His uniform was always crisply pressed, his boots shining like stars. He had done well, if not spectacularly so, in combat exercises and was graded a better-than-average marksman.

His instructors had commended him to the Astra Militarum, as sure as they could be that he would do nothing to shame them.

Had they been able to see into Myer's heart – past the dutiful, disciplined façade he had developed to avoid their undue attention – they might have thought again.

Myer had liked the routine of the academy. He had liked knowing what was expected of him. Whenever he had looked ahead, however, whenever he had thought about the day of his actual deployment, a sense of dread had gripped him.

He had learned about the horrors that awaited him outside the academy walls. He had seen those horrors, night after night, in vivid dreams. He knew this wasn't normal. Duty, discipline, courage – these were the qualities for which his world was renowned, which its armed forces exemplified. The Mordian Iron Guard was respected throughout the galaxy, and they counted Lucius Myer among their number.

He only wished he could be like everyone else.

'Xenos,' yelled Guardsman Steinvorst. 'Eleven o'clock!'

Ven Coers reacted immediately: 'Form up, ready to fire on my command!'

It wasn't the Mordians' way to hide from their enemies. They took to the battlefield in bright blue, embroidered dress uniforms, proud to announce their presence. These ten troopers quickly snapped into two rigid lines, five kneeling, five standing behind them, guns trained on the twitching foliage ahead of them.

Myer scanned the trees from the second rank, standing, his palm sweating into his lasgun's grip. Having not yet seen the threat himself, he hoped his comrade might have been mistaken. He was rudely disappointed. Two days ago, he had seen his first xenos. A dead xenos.

Right now came the moment he had spent his entire life dreading.

The first feral ork burst out of hiding, barely fifty yards from him. The howl that emerged from its throat chilled Myer's blood as it tore through the clinging overgrowth to reach him. Ven Coers gave the order, and las-beams stabbed into the creature's muscular green hide. It reacted as if assailed by stinging insects, attempting to swat them away. It stumbled but recovered itself, its advance barely slowed. Myer squeezed his trigger again and again as the xenos relentlessly closed the gap between them.

It toppled, at last, with an indignant splutter as it hit the ground face first. Already, more of its kind - so many more - had followed its impatient lead. A stampede swept towards Myer, a dozen pairs of eyes blazing, slobber dribbling from a dozen pairs of gnarled tusks. Gaping slack-jawed at them, he gave an involuntary step.

'Back into line, Guardsman,' his sergeant snapped.

Obedience had been drilled into Myer until it was second nature to him. Otherwise, he would have turned and run by now - and the feral orks, with their powerful leg muscles, would no doubt have run him down.

'Switch to automatic fire.' The squad complied with the order, laying down a barrage of sizzling laser light from which even the xenos recoiled. 'I have called for reinforcements. We only need hold off these vermin a minute or two.'

Through the dazzling curtain, another feral ork crumpled. The others continually ventured forward, however, seeking a gap in the Mordians' defences. Already, it seemed to Myer that his lasgun's discharge was weakening. On the full-auto setting, its power pack wouldn't last long. Two minutes had never crawled by so slowly.

'Fall back,' bellowed Ven Coers at last, 'maintaining formation.' Her troopers fell back, one step at a time, in unison.

Then one feral ork pushed its way through their faltering las-beams, and suddenly a stone axe whistled through the air between them. Guardsman Hagvitz ducked under a blow that would have severed his neck - and, though his attacker then succumbed to its considerable wounds, the damage was done. The bright blue line was broken.

The next few seconds were a blur to Myer. All he knew was that the feral orks were on top of him, and he fired his lasgun wildly and lashed out with his bayonet, but their putrid green bodies and blood-encrusted blades were everywhere.

He saw Steinvorst going down and, instinctively, leapt at the xenos that had felled him. It flexed its shoulder muscles and swiped him off his feet with insulting ease. Its axe followed Myer to the ground. He threw up the only thing he was holding to block it. The blow's force jarred the bones in his hands and splintered his lasgun's stock.

His attacker, distracted by a shot to its back, turned its attention from him. He scrambled away from it, but stumbled over Steinvorst's body. His fellow trooper's stomach, he saw, had been slashed open. He was bleeding out, pawing at the air as if for mercy. He was dead, without a doubt, and Myer was about to join him.

Trapped in that hopeless moment, his mind did the only thing it could to spare him.

It woke him up. Again.

***

Myer didn't know how long he had slept.

It didn't feel like long. Food had been placed at his bedside, however – the usual carton of thin gruel, almost tasteless but nutritious – and had cooled. His clothing and weapon had also been returned, laid out across his sheets. Both had been neatly repaired. He inspected his jacket, impressed by some orderly's work in scrubbing the fabric clean of blood and stitching up the tear.

The ward's other patients were asleep or unconscious, or ignoring him. The trooper in the next bed sat up, polishing his gleaming boots, although his arms were mottled by the fungal infection and his chest rattled with every laborious breath.

Myer chewed on his unedifying meal and forced himself to swallow it. It was his duty to look after himself, after all. He thought about his crisp blue uniform and what its return represented. Soon – too soon, within a couple of days, perhaps – he would wear it again, most likely to be marched away from this place by a commissar.

He needed to write that report.

But what then, he asked himself? What if he could convince a court of his innocence? So what if they wiped Veimer's terrible libel from his record? What else would they do then, but return Guardsman Myer to active duty? Send him back out into the alien forest?

The cold food turned to ash on his tongue. He couldn't do it. He couldn't walk out there and face his nightmares again. Every nerve in his body revolted against the idea.

He would rather face a firing squad.

Myer gave in to his body's demands and slept again.

His dreams returned him to the aftermath of the battle, this time.

Salvation had come in the form of three more squads, responding to Ven Coers' call. He had barely been aware of them at first, only knowing that the whine of lasgun fire around him had intensified and that the xenos were scattering.

He had clambered to his feet and, holding his broken weapon together, pumped two feeble shots into a feral ork's back. It had fallen, like its fellows, likely in spite of his efforts. He had shot it again as it lay twitching.

Myer felt a heady rush of relief. He'd had his first real taste of combat and emerged from it relatively unscathed. A few bruises, no more. His fellows were in good spirits too. They counted fourteen dead xenos, while the only casualty on their side had been the luckless Guardsman Steinvorst. This amounted to a palpable victory.

Minutes later, that sense of relief had drained away. Myer scrabbled in the dirt with an entrenching tool, digging a grave for a friend. It had been Steinvorst this time. Next time, it could be Sergeant Ven Coers or Guardsman Hagvitz or Myer himself.

The only sure thing was that there would be a next time.

Myer felt cold, but he was sweating. He shifted his position, and his hand recoiled from something unexpectedly hard and sharp beside him. Sifting through the undergrowth, he discovered a vicious-looking knife with a blade carved out of yellowing bone, embedded in a half-rotten wooden handle. The blade was stained with old blood. It could only have been knocked out of a feral ork's hand.

He picked up the knife. Had he been challenged at that moment, he wouldn't have known what to say. He couldn't explain – or didn't want to acknowledge to himself – what was going through his mind. As it happened, his squad mates were too busy digging, and perhaps too wrapped up in their own introspections, to notice him.

Reaching under his bright blue jacket, he slipped the knife into his pocket.

1200

The xenos should have died by now.

Its green hide was pockmarked with livid red burns. One hand had been sheared off, still clutching its stone axe. Belligerence alone kept it on its feet, howling defiance of its Emperor-ordained fate. Sergeant Katryne Ven Coers vowed to put an end to that.

She let out no battle cry as she charged with bayonet levelled. Her jaw was clenched in grim determination. The xenos lashed at her with the stump of its right wrist, perhaps forgetting that its hand and weapon were gone. Thick gobbets of dark, malodorous blood spattered her bright blue uniform.

She thrust her blade between the feral ork's ribs, up to where the heart of a human opponent would have been. The Emperor only knew how a xenos' organs were arranged, if it had them at all. All the same, her blow had the desired effect.

The creature's eyes dimmed and rolled back into its head. Its body struggled on as if it hadn't got the message. Ven Coers toppled it with a well-placed polished boot. At the same time, she yanked her blade out of its flesh, spraying herself with its blood again.

Silence fell upon that part of the forest.

The Mordians tallied the dead. Eleven feral orks in all, but they had lost three of their own. That might have been acceptable for another regiment, but they ought to have done better and they knew it. They were getting tired.

Even Ven Coers' muscles ached, though she would never have shown it. Her exertions had left her out of breath. She straightened her back, dabbed feral ork blood from her face with a clean white handkerchief and ordered her squad to form up on her. She berated Guardsman Hagvitz for being the last to respond.

They were nine strong now. A fresh-faced rookie had replaced the late veteran Guardsman Steinvorst. Until Guardsman Myer was fit to return to duty, however, they would remain shorthanded. Had it really been less than a week since the latest recruits from the home world had filled their ranks?

None of them had fallen today, though, and that was what counted.

She grunted a few words of condolence to the other squads. Then she left them to bury their comrades, as she led her own Guardsmen back to their assigned sector.

***

Ven Coers had come to Kallash a little over four months ago.

Initially, she had expected to be done here within a few weeks.

The feral orks were more numerous, more persistent, than anyone imagined. No matter how many were uprooted from their hiding places in the sprawling forest, how many the Iron Guard crushed, still more of them seemed to sprout up daily like poisonous weeds. They had recolonised whole sectors from which they had been declared eradicated.

At first, this had been merely frustrating.

Ven Coers had responded to two emergency calls today. These, added to the previous evening's ambush, made three in less than twenty-four hours. She had heard reports of other battles, further afield. The feral orks were gathering into larger mobs, growing bolder by the day – while her own regiment was becoming inexorably depleted.

The fungal infection that had taken hold among them was especially concerning – though, by the Emperor's grace, it hadn't yet touched Ven Coers' squad.

No longer did this assignment feel like a 'training session'.

'Assistance required,' the voice buzzed in Ven Coers' earpiece, then reeled off a set of coordinates. She calculated that they were over a mile and a half away.

Ordinarily, she wouldn't have responded to the call; others were closer. She had a feeling, however, that this time she should. She led her Guardsmen off at double-time. Barely had they taken twenty steps than Ven Coers' instincts were proven correct.

'This is Sergeant Venig, calling anyone in range of my signal.' The same voice again, but strained to breaking point. *'The xenos have a... I don't know what to call it. Three of my Guardsmen are–'* The next words were lost as the vox-channel was flooded by noise, making Ven Coers wince.

For the next twenty seconds, she could make out very little. Gunshots, a metallic grinding noise that was likely interference and a dreadful keening human scream. An officer's voice cut over the clamour, demanding an urgent update, but nobody answered.

Ven Coers ordered her squad to halt. They faced her, unable to disguise the hope in their eyes. The message had come in over a command channel, unheard by them. Ven Coers raised a hand to forestall any questions. The short run had left her out of breath again, and speaking would have betrayed her weakness to them. Her lungs felt raw.

Another sergeant soon reported in. *'We've found them. Sergeant Venig's squad, or what remains of them. Just a few... a few body parts and pulverised pieces of equipment. We cannot yet confirm how many casualties – but we have located no survivors.'*

At an officer's prompting, the sergeant gave his exact location. Ven Coers took out her hand-drawn tactical map of the area and consulted her chrono-compass.

'Sir... The xenos couldn't have done this with their usual primitive weapons. It looks like a tank, or something even bigger, ploughed through here. Trees have been uprooted. Fires are still burning in the undergrowth, and

there... may not be enough left of our people for a burial. No sign of the xenos themselves, but it's plain to see which way they went.'

Ven Coers had heard enough. She cleared her throat and relayed the bad news to her squad, who took it with the stoicism required of them. 'This craven attack, this affront to the Emperor and everything He stands for, will not go unanswered,' the sergeant swore.

A few minutes later came the order she had fully expected.

Her company and one other – ten platoons, five hundred Guardsmen in all – were to abandon their searches of the forest. They were to converge upon a given set of coordinates, which would be updated as they marched. They were to hunt down the xenos that had slaughtered their fellows, and slaughter them in turn. Most crucially, they were to destroy any weapons that had fallen into feral ork hands.

Sergeant Ven Coers' squad was already en route.

They knew what was waiting for them. They knew that, in the forthcoming battle, some of them would probably die. Any qualms they may have had about this, they kept to themselves. They had surrendered their fates to the Emperor upon joining the Mordian Iron Guard. They had their duty and they were not afraid.

An explosion shook the ground beneath their feet. It was followed by the cracks of weapons fire and xenos howls from dead ahead of them.

'Advance and engage the enemy at will!' Ven Coers yelled.

She didn't look to see if her squad was behind her. She knew they were. She burst upon this latest battlefield, her lasgun blazing on full-auto. The feral orks were taken by surprise, and two were shot down before they could even react.

A third – a hulking brute with quivering armour plates lashed to its torso by ropes – came charging right at her. She dived and rolled beneath the arc of its crude axe, its stone blade twice the size of Ven Coers' head. She ended the manoeuvre on one knee, rifle shouldered, and strafed the creature's sneering face at point-blank range. It bellowed as its right eye bubbled and burst but took another heavy, shuddering step towards her.

Her Guardsmen didn't let her down.

Three more head shots from behind and her opponent toppled, landing face down in a simmering mass of blood and brain tissue. The remaining xenos – she counted seven of them – were pinned between her newly arrived squad and one other, making them easy prey. They appeared no better armed than any other feral ork she had encountered. The explosion she had heard had probably been a Mordian frag grenade, smoking their enemies out.

She reported her status tersely into her vox-bead, advising that all was in hand. As feral orks roared and thrashed and died in a deadly grid of las-beams, Ven Coers kept one ear tuned to similar reports from other squad leaders.

'It's here!' She recognised the voice of Sergeant Graf, a member of her own platoon. *'Urgent assistance required. Repeat, urgent assistance required. It's–'*

Another explosion, five times more thunderous than the last one, ripped through the forest. Ven Coers bit her lip. She couldn't let it distract her from the imminent threat. The feral orks in front of her persevered against all odds, one even reaching a Guardsman from the other squad and dealing her a glancing blow from its massive club. It seemed to take an age before the last of them finally succumbed.

She saw the flashes of more detonations through the trees. She smacked a fresh power pack into her lasgun, adjusted her peaked cap and led her squad forward again.

A cloud of dark smoke rolled in around them. It caught the back of Ven Coers' throat and made her cough. Fraught chatter filled her ear. Casualty reports were mounting by the second, but more disturbing were the voices that simply fell silent. *'It's shrugging off our las-beams,'* one sergeant spluttered, in what turned out to be his last communication. *'We need heavy ordnance in here.'*

'Prepare to employ grenades,' Ven Coers cautioned. 'We may be facing some kind of... armoured vehicle.' Even as she spoke the words, they sounded false. A simple tank could not have caused the confusion and carnage she had heard.

A feral ork reared up in front of her, suddenly. She hadn't seen it through the smoke until it was almost too late. Forced onto her back foot, she shot it in the throat, and the creature fell obligingly onto her waiting bayonet. She recoiled from its final, foetid breath as it slid to the ground between her boots.

'Sergeant,' spoke up Guardsman Kramer, beside her, 'do you hear that?'

She tuned out vox-chatter and the dull crumps of further explosions. She became aware of a harsh, mechanical sound, like rusted cogwheels grinding into each other. A familiar sound. It took Ven Coers a long moment to remember where she had recently heard it.

A shadow loomed ahead of her. It seemed to gather smoke about itself. Wreathed in misty tendrils, its shape was impossible to make out. She had the impression of four powerful arms and a squat head perched upon a body many times her height and girth. The forest itself groaned with the creature's passage; and then its head turned ponderously towards her, a pair of fiery eyes blazing at her through the haze, and the monster let out a malevolent hiss.

'Fall back!' yelled Ven Coers to her squad. 'Fall back!'

She pulled the pin of a frag grenade. She was taking a terrible chance. If it hit the monster at this range and rebounded, the backwash would likely kill her. She threw the grenade, then ran for all she was worth. She heard it burst behind her, and a wave of heat and shrapnel washed over her, the latter mostly clattering off her uniform's armoured fibres.

Barely a second later came another, louder, hotter blast, its force lifting Ven Coers off her feet and smashing her into the unyielding ground.

She knew it was her duty to pick herself up and run again, but her head was swimming and she had no strength in her arms. She had to report what she had seen to the rest of the companies, warn them, but she found she couldn't speak. She had to know where her troopers were, if any had been hurt, but she couldn't even lift her head to see.

One by one, her senses slipped away from her, until all she knew was the staccato throb of an engine grumbling towards her and, somehow making itself heard even over this, the relentless percussive drone of metal grinding against metal.

1300

Guardsman Myer woke with a start again.

The sound of gunshots had invaded his nightmares, but this was nothing unusual. Only when he heard them again did he realise that, this time, the gunshots were real.

They were coming from outside. He pulled himself up into a sitting position with his elbows, grimacing at the pain from his injury. His eyes met those of another patient, across the ward and one bed up from his, who was doing the same.

'Want to grab your uniform and gun and get out there?' the trooper sneered at him. He wasn't much older than Myer, but his eyes were colder, harder.

'Maybe,' said Myer. 'If I'm needed. If I'm able.'

The other trooper snorted his contempt. 'You hear that, Sergeant Hartman? Suddenly, the coward wants to leap off his deathbed and defend us from the xenos single-handed. Or he's looking for a chance to run away. Which do you think it is?'

A lethargic figure shifted beneath sheets on a mattress beside the trooper's bed. 'Nothing to worry about,' the figure croaked with an audible effort. 'They'd have sounded an alarm if it were something serious. This is probably just… probably just another…'

He choked on the words and his neighbour yelled for assistance, but nobody came.

Hartman settled down after a moment or two, having kicked his sheets into a tangled mess. Myer could see his drawn face now, shiny with sweat, hair plastered to his brow. He hadn't realised there was an NCO in here. He felt guilty, all of a sudden, about occupying a bed. He felt he should offer to swap – but as the sergeant was clearly infected, he knew that would not have been wise.

At least no one was paying attention to him now.

Hartman had been right too. The gunfire had already stopped. Whatever had happened outside, it was over. Still, Myer suppressed a shudder at the thought that the horrors of the forest could reach so close to him, even now, even here.

'What happened?' Lieutenant Veimer demanded. 'Report.'

Just one squad, ten men, had been left behind to keep the command post secure. Their sergeant snapped to attention as the officer bore down upon him.

'Feral orks, sir.' Veimer couldn't recall the sergeant's name. He had only taken up his post four days ago, one more in a very long line. 'Just three of them, we think.'

'You think?'

'I have Guardsmen checking the perimeter now.' The sergeant nodded towards the nearby treeline, past a single stationary Chimera. Veimer saw a pair of troopers stabbing at the bushes with bayonets. He also saw three feral ork corpses slumped against the officers' mess hut. 'This had none of the hallmarks of a planned attack, sir. I believe the xenos simply stumbled upon this facility and thought they might catch us with our guard down.'

'Even so,' Veimer grumbled, 'someone has been remiss in their duty.'

'Sir?'

'Is there not meant to be a ring of iron around us? Explain to me how a single creature – let alone three hulking brutes like these, hardly known for their stealth – could have slipped past our highly trained troopers unnoticed.'

The sergeant couldn't, of course. 'That's why my squad is here, sir.'

Veimer sighed and accepted the point. 'Be sure to burn those bodies when you're done,' he instructed. 'Downwind of my office, if you please.'

He turned on the spot, surveying his surroundings. His eyes probed the shadows of the forest, half-expecting to find eyes glaring back at him. The command post had no perimeter wall or fence. Its borders were delineated by the parallel walls of its four huts.

To one side, behind the medicae and supply huts, was an almost sheer drop of several hundred yards, a natural defence. Around the three other sides, the alien forest lurked. Veimer shook off the irrational notion that it was closer today than it had been yesterday. Recent reports from the front had given him cause to worry, however.

'There may be more xenos than we imagined, sergeant. I would not be surprised if there were more attacks. Tell your men to be on the alert.'

The sergeant nodded, stiffly. 'Naturally, sir.'

Veimer lingered in the cool, fresh air a moment longer. It assuaged his tiredness a little. He couldn't remember when last he had slept more than an hour without interruption. He had his duty, however. He took a deep, fortifying breath and turned towards the medicae hut.

Its door burst open at that moment and an orderly emerged. 'Lieutenant Veimer,' the young Guardsman panted. 'We've been looking for you, sir. We need you.'

The patient was dead.

Veimer had done all he possibly could. He had performed chest compressions for several minutes, kneeling in the centre of a zone of deadly silence. He had even got his subject breathing again, barely and for too short a time.

He drew the patient's sheets up over his face. He rose to his feet and, in a quiet voice, told the watching orderlies to take the body away. The air of punctured hopes around him was almost tangible. Veimer looked for the dead man's name on his data-slate. He made a note beside it and archived a file.

'We'll hold a service for Sergeant, uh, Hartman outside at sixteen thirty hours,' he announced.

He made a quick tour of the ward. He checked that Guardsman Myer's stitches were holding, took his temperature and asked him how he was feeling. 'Much better, thank you, sir,' the youth replied, a little too eagerly. 'Looking forward to returning to active duty. The way I see it, the Emperor has given me a chance to...'

Veimer was no longer listening. He had no interest in Myer beyond his duty of care to him. His only concern was that the infection that had killed Hartman – and with which the majority of his other patients suffered – had spread no further. The evidence so far suggested it wasn't contagious, but this could change in a heartbeat.

Four other troopers' symptoms had worsened. The face of one glowered with a prickly rash, while another's skin had begun to slough. Veimer upped their drug dosages. He amended the file of each patient with a flick of his thumb, and never met their eyes.

He understood so little about their condition. His investigations thus far had uncovered almost nothing. All he could do was treat them with a standard antiviral, antibiotic cocktail and pray for the best. Some patients recovered, especially those whose symptoms were detected early. Others did not.

He had issued a general warning a fortnight ago. He had decreed that no native flora or fauna should be ingested, nor touched without good reason. Drinking water was always to be purified, even when every test pronounced it clean. Troopers were to protect themselves against insect bites. The tide of new infections had not been stemmed in the slightest.

The latest rumour on the ward was that the feral orks themselves were poisonous, and Veimer had no evidence to gainsay this.

'Sir.' He chafed at yet another interruption. This one, however, came from Corporal Elherdt, his acting adjutant. She had been monitoring vox communications and wouldn't have left her post for any trivial reason. Veimer reeled off a few more instructions to his attendant orderlies. He gestured to the corporal to follow him into his office.

This news, he sensed, would not be for general consumption.

'How many?' asked Veimer, feeling numb.

'That is unclear, sir,' said Corporal Elherdt, 'but in the hundreds certainly.'

'Perhaps even higher?'

'Yes, sir.'

He perched on the edge of his desk, sucking air between his teeth. 'Hundreds, perhaps a thousand feral orks, headed this way. Along with this... this weapon of theirs, which has killed a hundred Iron Guard already. What do we know about that?'

'Not a great deal, sir. No one has seen the weapon up close and survived to make a report. Also, with respect, we can't be sure where the feral orks are headed.'

'We don't seem to know much, do we?'

'Captain Blukher thought it best to put us on alert in case–'

'In case the xenos horde, having put his company to rout, decides to follow the most-trodden paths through the Dirkr Forest. Paths made by our troopers as they fanned out from this very command post. Paths that will lead them straight back here. To us.'

'That isn't quite how the captain phrased it, sir, but essentially, yes.'

Veimer held out a hand. The corporal passed a data-slate to him. He glanced over her record of Blukher's vox-message. She had already outlined the salient points to him.

'The captain, of course, appreciates that we have more sick men here than healthy,' Veimer grumbled, tapping out a brusque reply. 'We are also guarding the only food and drug reserves on Kallash. I'm sure he intends to make our defence his highest priority.'

Elherdt told him what he already knew, what he had read for himself. 'He is pulling back as many troops as he can from the front, sir.'

Veimer handed the data-slate back to her. 'Relay that message to Captain Blukher, corporal. Has there been any news of that supply ship?'

The corporal blinked. If she was surprised by the sudden change of subject, however, she showed no other sign of it.

'What date did we send the requisition form?' asked Veimer.

Elherdt checked and told him. 'The amounts were queried on the twelfth, as we expected they would be, but no further word since then.'

Veimer clicked his tongue. 'Do they think I'd be asking for more drugs so soon without reason? Do they think we fill out their forms for the fun of it?'

'I'll chase them up again, sir.'

'Do so, and contact the Officio Medicae too. Remind them that we are waiting very patiently for their advice and instructions.' He doubted it would do much good. The Administratum was a bloated, lumbering bureaucracy, and its medical arm was inefficient even by its dismal standards. Veimer's dealings with them were a constant source of exasperation to him, as they would have been to any Mordian officer.

What he needed from them was a fully resourced facility, staffed with better-trained physicians than himself. That was what he needed...

Corporal Elherdt saluted, performed a smart about-turn and marched out of the room, closing the door behind her. Lieutenant Veimer sank into his seat, alone and weary.

Hundreds, perhaps a thousand feral orks, headed this way... The approaching army was not his problem, however. His duty was to his patients, and this would still be the case long after this present crisis had passed, this latest battle fought and won or lost.

That was, if he or any of his patients were left alive by then.

1400

Sergeant Ven Coers ran for her life.

Her heartbeat threatened to burst the veins in her neck. The undergrowth tore at her feet as if trying to drag her down. Her every breath hurt. More explosions and cries of horror and pain swamped the vox-net. She had ordered her squad to report in over their channel, but no one had responded. Either they were out of range or they were dead.

Ven Coers should have been dead herself.

She had recovered her senses, sprawled in a prickly bush. She had picked herself up out of it, thorns snagging and tearing her uniform. She had found herself alone. The great engine that had felled her was gone, leaving behind a trail of devastation. It had passed within feet of where she lay, but it mustn't have seen her.

The smoke had almost cleared, but an acrid smell had clung to Ven Coers' nostrils. Ashes had crunched beneath her boots. She had come across three humanoid bodies, turned to ash too. She hadn't been able to identify them, and hadn't had time to search for more.

Footsteps had scampered through the forest around her. She had heard xenos grunts and, a little more distantly, howls. A terrible truth was beginning to dawn on her. Snatches of vox-chatter, once she had found and reinserted her vox-bead, had confirmed her greatest worry.

For the first time in Ven Coers' career, the Iron Guard was in retreat.

And she had been stranded alone behind enemy lines.

She was in an uncharted, uncleared sector of the forest.

There could have been pit traps here or any number of natural hazards. A footfall on the wrong spot could mean a sudden, painful death; but Ven Coers could not afford to be cautious. An army – an army and something far worse – lay between her and her allies. The only hope she had was to find a way around them, and quickly.

She had been running for an hour. She really thought she was going to make it.

She could almost have screamed with frustration as fleshy shapes erupted from the foliage around her. Instead, she dropped into a firing stance as half a dozen squigs came bounding and gibbering towards her.

She had encountered these vicious beasts before. They were squat and repulsive, no more than two feet tall, more head than body, a jumbled assemblage of orkoid limbs and facial features. It was unclear if they were the runts of feral ork litters or a life form in their own right. Ven Coers had come to think of them as a distraction, a nuisance at worst – but that was when she'd had a squad around her.

Squigs were, above all other things, tenacious. She shot one down before it reached her, but the others pounced on her in a flurry of teeth and claws.

She drove her bayonet into the eye of one, cracked the skull of another with her handgrip, but she couldn't shake them off her. It was all she could do to protect her face with her arms. They were tearing her reinforced uniform to shreds, and her flesh would be next.

Her lasgun was prised from her hands. Ven Coers felt for her belt, for a grenade. The last thing she could do was immolate herself and take these foetid aberrations with her, before their touch defiled her further. Her fingers closed around the metal egg.

She heard the blessed cracks and whines of Imperial lasguns.

One by one, the squigs fell away from her, screeching with resentment. Blue-uniformed troopers burst from the trees around her, like the dawn sky banishing the night.

Ven Coers staggered to her feet and kicked the last of her diminutive attackers away from her. The creature rolled, skipped, bounced and landed in a heap. She advanced upon it, ready to throttle it with her gloved hands if she had to. The squig's jaws parted and it vomited out a stream of thick brown liquid, spattering her chest and stomach. The liquid hissed and bubbled and stank as it ate into what remained of her uniform.

Several las-beams skewered the creature at once – and the Emperor knew what gases its stomach secreted, because it burst like a miniature bomb. Ven Coers threw off her jacket and rubbed it in the undergrowth, trying to scrape off the squig's acidic bile and its disgusting guts. Too late to save the garment. She stood in her shirtsleeves, holding the tattered symbol of everything she had ever believed in.

Around her, a Mordian squad was ensuring that the squigs were indeed all dead. Ven Coers nodded her gratitude to their sergeant. She felt ashamed of her dishevelled, defeated appearance. She tried to explain, but instead coughed up flecks of blood. She wasn't sure if the blood was her own or if, worse, she had swallowed some from the bursting squig.

'Your squad?' the other sergeant asked.

Ven Coers shook her head.

'We're trying to make it back to the command post – captain's orders – but these vermin have been nipping at our heels the whole way. Can you walk?'

Ven Coers found her voice. 'I'm not dead yet.'

'The feral orks have... something. Some kind of–'

'I know all about it, believe me.'

'It's out there somewhere,' the other sergeant said, 'running us down one squad at a time. By the time you see it...' He left the thought unfinished. He turned to his Guardsmen and told them to take three minutes to tend to any wounds they had and adjust their dress.

Ven Coers was secretly glad of the respite. She rummaged her medi-pack out of her field rucksack. She dabbed sterilising fluid on her bruises and scratches. Her right forearm itched, and she feared a squig's claw might have nicked her there. She rolled up her sleeve.

What she saw made her heart freeze. A red rash mottled her skin. Squatting in its centre was a livid red blood blister. It seemed to glare up at her, balefully, like some evil eye.

It must have been the squig, she told herself and tried to believe it, *some side effect of its acid spit.* All the same, she checked that nobody was watching her before she sloshed fluid over the blister too, then quickly lowered her shirtsleeve to conceal it.

She tied her jacket around her waist. It might be ruined, but she would be flogged for leaving valuable kit behind, and rightly so. She took a dose of combat stimms from the medi-pack and swallowed it. It would help her focus, steady her still-ragged breathing and refresh her tortured muscles. She had a long and gruelling march ahead of her.

They had been underway – Ven Coers and the new squad to which she had attached herself – for a little under forty-five minutes. They had been harried by several more squigs, but had slain them with creditable ease.

The best news was that the vox-net had quietened down. The withdrawing Iron Guard troopers were outpacing their pursuers. There had been no strained reports of mechanical monsters for some time. The squad leader, Kulm, had even contacted other sergeants, and arranged for their paths to converge.

Their caravan numbered over forty now, and the squigs were keeping a respectful distance from them. They trudged through the forest, beneath a despondent shroud that their proud uniforms and well-drilled formations couldn't entirely disguise.

For Ven Coers, stimms coursing through her veins like lightning, time seemed to have slowed. She was alert to every sight, every sound, every scent upon the cooling afternoon air. Hence, she was first to hear the engines approaching, the first to call out a warning.

Kulm, as the senior sergeant present, brought the others to a halt and ordered them to ready their weapons. He turned to Ven Coers, worried. 'If this is the monster...'

'I've heard enough, seen enough, to know that las-beams won't scratch it.'

'Any recommendations?'

'Only that we stay as still and silent as possible and hope it passes us by,' she answered gravely. 'Failing that, we scatter and pray to the Emperor for our lives.'

The engines were growing steadily closer, however Ven Coers listened for the sound of grinding metal, but heard nothing. The engines, in fact, sounded reassuringly familiar. She almost smiled. 'I think the Emperor may have answered our prayers already.'

The solid, reliable shape of a Chimera came grumbling towards them. Through its billowing exhaust smoke, Ven Coers traced the silhouette of a second vehicle.

As both shuddered to a noisy halt, Kulm stood his relieved troopers down. He marched up to salute the tall, rakish figure who emerged from the tank commander's seat. Ven Coers recognised her own company's Lieutenant Gunderson. He was still a young man, younger than Ven Coers herself, but well respected.

'I can take twenty bodies on this trip,' said the officer in clipped tones, 'including one experienced gunner, if you have one.'

'Understood, sir,' said Kulm, and he set about selecting the Guardsmen to be rescued. Most raised a token protest, of course. Someone else should go in their place, they said. Few of them sounded sincere enough for Ven Coers' liking. She felt her top lip curling in disdain. Had they been in her charge, there would have been the warp to pay.

Then Kulm turned to her and spoke her name.

She reeled from the words, insulted. 'No. No, thank you, sergeant, but I feel I would be best-placed out here, helping to guide these men back to–'

'Sergeant Ven Coers lost her squad, sir,' Kulm interrupted her, 'to that feral ork contraption, whatever it is. It knocked her cold.'

'I feel fine, sir,' Ven Coers pleaded with the officer. 'Fit for duty.'

Gunderson frowned. He bent his knees to bring him eye to eye with Ven Coers. She tried to meet his probing gaze but felt her eyes betraying her, twitching. 'How long ago did you take the stimms, sergeant?' Gunderson asked her.

'Not long, sir. Less than an hour.'

'Let's get you back to base before they wear off, shall we? And get you kitted out with a new uniform jacket while we're at it.'

She bowed her head, defeated. She stepped up into the Chimera and perched on the end of a bench. Someone closed the rear hatch behind her with an emphatic clang. Ven Coers was cut off from the rest of the world, cocooned in metal. She snarled at a Guardsman across from her and ordered him to sit up straighter.

She heard Gunderson clambering into the cockpit cabin and, a moment later, the engine started up again. The Chimera juddered forwards, every hull plate straining as it doggedly inched its way around a tight U-turn. Sergeant Ven Coers voxed a final appeal to her squad, but static was the only response. She had failed in her duty, to them and to the Emperor.

Her cheeks burned with shame.

And that damn itch was flaring up again, engulfing her whole arm in prickly heat.

1600

Lieutenant Veimer heard the engines approaching.

He marched out of his office, through the adjacent ward. His patients had heard the racket too. A few made the effort to sit up, but he ignored their questioning glances.

A pair of Chimeras nudged their way between the command post's huts. They pulled up in the rectangular space that Veimer still thought of as the parade ground, though it hadn't been used as such in many months. Their hatches clunked open, disgorging two streams of brightly clad passengers.

Another Chimera hauled its bulk across the treeline, joining its fellows. A fourth grumbled to a halt alongside the administration and communications hut. Veimer's eyes scoured the forest for more, but he was disappointed. As the Mordian troops formed up, he identified the young lieutenant in charge of them and introduced himself.

'Gunderson, Third Company,' the officer responded, shaking Veimer's hand.

'Are these all the troopers we have?'

'For now. More are on their way.'

'Some of them look exhausted.'

'I prioritised the wounded, those who might not have made the journey under their own steam and were slowing up the rest.'

'The last thing we need is more patients,' said Veimer, pointedly. 'We need able bodies, equipped and ready to fight. We need defenders.'

'Quite.' Gunderson drew his fellow officer to one side, almost furtively. 'The xenos tore through us pretty badly, I'm afraid. They scattered the Third and Fourth Companies to the winds. I'll send the Chimeras back to find as many as they can, but we don't have nearly enough of them. Nor as much time as we thought.'

Veimer raised an eyebrow.

'You haven't heard the latest reports?'

'They don't always reach us here.'

'You're aware that a horde of feral orks–'

'That much, I had heard. I assume they haven't turned from their path?'

Gunderson shook his head. 'In fact, they are moving faster than we expected they would. As if they know exactly where they are going. They also appear – impossible as this might seem – to have swelled their ranks in the process.'

'I was told they numbered in the hundreds,' said Veimer.

'At least twelve hundred, and that's a conservative estimate.'

'Against how many? Fifteen men stationed here, and what have you brought us? About forty? How many more can we expect? Best-case scenario?'

A brawny sergeant marched up to them, snapped to attention and saluted. She addressed Lieutenant Gunderson: 'Parade ready for your inspection, sir.' She couldn't have looked less ready for inspection herself. She was scratched and bruised, her ruined jacket tied around her waist. Her back was as rigid as a plasteel rod, nevertheless.

'Thank you, sergeant. We'll skip the inspection. Have the troops fall out but remain on standby.' Gunderson turned to Veimer. 'Where can they rest for an hour or two?'

'I was forced to repurpose the Guardsmen's billets,' Veimer told him. 'Every bed, every mattress, every inch of floor is taken, thanks to this damn infection. My orderlies and security squad sleep in shifts in the officers' quarters. We could clear space for twenty or so around the edges of the comms and supply huts.'

'With your leave, sir,' the bedraggled sergeant spoke up, 'we could build a shelter in the lee of the longer structure there.' She nodded towards the shuttered windows of the medicae hut.

Veimer nodded his assent.

'See to it, Sergeant Ven Coers,' Gunderson agreed.

He returned Ven Coers' crisp salute. Then, turning back to Veimer, he asked where they could talk in private. The best place, since Veimer had been forced to share his quarters, was in his little office at the far end of the medicae hut. He led the way.

The first of the four Chimeras revved its engine. It juddered back and forth like a penned bull, seeking a route between the huts back into the forest.

Sergeant Ven Coers' voice competed splendidly with the vehicle's clamour. She was bellowing orders at the regimented ranks of Guardsmen on the parade ground. Few of them would get much rest today, if Veimer was any judge. Any free time they had, they would likely spend polishing their shoes or bulling their belts.

'Let me be frank with you, Veimer.'

'By all means, do.'

The officers faced each other across Veimer's hastily tidied desk. Gunderson swallowed his last drop of amasec and pushed the glass aside. 'I have been charged with the defence of this command post. Captain Blukher is determined that it should not fall to the xenos. It would be a terrible blow to morale.'

'However?'

Gunderson took a breath. 'My initial assessment of our circumstances is not favourable.'

'On that, we certainly concur.'

'I have requested, and been granted, reinforcements from the First and Second Companies.'

'Good to hear,' said Veimer with caution, suspecting a catch.

'A force has been despatched and should reach us by twenty-three hundred hours.'

'I see. And how soon will the feral orks reach us?'

'According to our most up-to-date projections, allowing for a margin of–'

'How soon?' Veimer asked again, impatiently.

'The horde will almost certainly be upon us by sunset. Nineteen hundred hours.'

He felt his stomach tighten, though the answer had not been unexpected.

'This post has little in the way of defences,' observed Gunderson.

'It was never expected to need them,' countered Veimer.

'If only we had stout walls around us...' Gunderson let the thought trail off. He knew as well as Veimer did that such wishful thinking was futile.

'Four hours,' breathed Veimer. 'Give me your honest assessment, Gunderson. Do we have the resources to hold off that feral ork horde for four hours?'

'At present,' the other officer confessed, 'we do not. By nineteen hundred hours? Perhaps, if the Emperor wills it.' He paused a moment before asking, 'Do you have another suggestion?'

'I think we must consider a withdrawal. Yes, morale will suffer if this facility burns. I suggest it would suffer all the more were all hands to burn with it. We have a fair stock of explosives. We could mine the huts before we leave.'

Gunderson nodded thoughtfully. 'Let the feral orks take the command post, then raze it to the ground. We could kill a few dozen, at least.'

'But the rest would pursue us,' Veimer sighed. 'Through the forest. At night.'

'Could your patients make that journey?'

'On foot? Not a chance. In a vehicle? A few might survive.'

They were silent for a moment, each pondering the obvious conclusion to that line of thought, neither choosing to voice it. A few lives for many, thought Veimer. As an officer, his duty was to make that call. It wasn't as if he could have saved them, anyway. Not the majority of them. Not for very long.

'We would also need to act quickly,' said Gunderson, 'to keep ahead of the horde. I'd suggest setting out within the hour.'

'Which doesn't leave much time for the search and rescue mission.'

Gunderson nodded, gravely. 'Nor for any of our people who might outpace the xenos to reach this facility before they do. We'd be leaving them behind too.'

Another short, reflective silence followed. Veimer broke it with a sigh. 'There are too few of us. Our enemies would run us down and slaughter us. That's assuming we could stave off the forest's natural predators long enough to give them the chance.'

'I concur. We stand and fight, then?'

He nodded, relieved that at least the decision was made. It felt like the right decision too – instinctively, not only logically. It was likely that Olius Veimer would die tonight. A small part of him quailed at this prospect, but he fiercely denied it. He had been away from the front lines too long. He had lived a long life compared to most, but a brutal end had always lurked in wait for him. Far better, he felt, to die fighting rather than running.

He must have voiced the thought without meaning to, because Gunderson agreed: 'That is the most any of us can ask of Him.'

Veimer's wrist chrono chirruped. He checked the time, pushed back his chair and stood. 'I have another duty to attend to.' He straightened his jacket and donned his peaked cap.

Several patients had struggled out of their sickbeds and into their uniforms.

For one, pale and haggard from the infection, the effort had proven too much. As he tried to lace his boots, he was seized by wracking coughs. The youngster, Myer, limped over and offered to help him, but was batted away with contempt. Veimer stepped in. He hauled the Guardsman's feet back onto his mattress and ordered him to rest.

Eight patients in all preceded Veimer out of the hut. He found himself appraising each of them in turn. If they could walk, perhaps they could also fight.

They followed the sound of entrenching tools striking dirt. Behind the latrines, two orderlies were filling a fresh grave. Gunderson's new arrivals had got wind of what was happening, and they too gathered around. They removed their caps, clasped their gloved hands, bowed their heads. Their buttons, boots and belt buckles gleamed. Few of them could have known Sergeant Hartman, but they respected a comrade. He would have been proud.

With the burial complete, Lieutenant Veimer said a few words. He recounted the salient details of a career, including campaigns fought in and decorations received. He didn't refer to his data-slate. He concluded with a brief prayer to the Emperor, expressing the hope and belief that Hartman's service had earned His approval.

Then the Mordian soldiers stood in silence. Veimer wondered who would pray for them – and him – were they to be slain tonight. Who would be left to bury their bodies?

That was why this ritual was so important, of course. It wasn't just for Hartman. It could have been anyone, any body, lying three feet down in the dirt. The facts that Veimer had memorised about this particular body, he would forget by dawn. By the time the week was done, if he survived, he would probably forget its name too.

The gathering was on the verge of breaking up when Gunderson cleared his throat and stepped forward. Veimer knew what he was about to say, and felt a fleeting irritation that he hadn't been consulted first. His fellow officer was right, though. It was time the troops knew what they were facing. They had preparations to make.

'We have,' announced Gunderson with classic understatement, 'a situation.'

1700

Myer stood at the foot of his bed. He felt cold. He felt alone, despite the buzz of urgent conversation around him. The ward seemed hardly to exist. In his mind, he was back in his tent in the forest, locked in his life's most desperate moment.

A hand clapped him on the shoulder, startling him back to reality. The young trooper from across the ward leered in his face. 'Look on the bright side, Myer. Chances are you'll never face the Commissariat now.'

They had both been at the service and at Gunderson's briefing thereafter, and so wore their uniforms. The other trooper, in fact, seemed perfectly healthy. Whatever malady had brought him here, either he had recovered or he was hiding it well. 'You get another chance to die with honour. It's more than you deserve.'

'That is,' another man put in from his bed, 'if you can resist the urge to run.'

'Try it and I'll shoot you in the back.' Myer's heart sank at the familiar bark, but he made himself turn to face the last person in the world he wanted to see.

Filling the doorway to the hut was the granite form of Sergeant Ven Coers. Myer had spied her outside, but thought he had avoided her gaze. No such luck.

Ven Coers took a menacing step towards him. Her fists clenched at her sides, spasmodically. 'I heard a nasty rumour about you, Myer,' she growled, dangerously, 'but I knew it couldn't be true. I know no Guardsman of mine would ever dare disgrace his uniform, dare to disgrace *me*, by–'

'It isn't true, sergeant,' Myer half-shouted in frustration.

'I see. A big misunderstanding, then?'

'Yes, sergeant.'

'I hope so, Myer. I hope so for your sake – because, this afternoon, I led my squad into battle short-handed. Do you know what happened next?'

Myer didn't know, he hadn't heard, but a tingling dread crept over him.

'We lost them, Myer. My squad. Your comrades. Three confirmed dead. Five missing, presumed dead too. An extra gun could have made a difference. Yes, even one wielded by you. Look me in the eye, Myer. Swear to me that eight brave, loyal Mordian soldiers didn't die today because of your cowardice.'

Myer opened his mouth but couldn't speak. He was paralysed by Ven

Coers' thunderous glare, as much as by the horror of what he had just learned. He was painfully aware that, once again, all eyes in the ward were upon him.

'I... I didn't cut myself, sergeant,' he managed to stammer, finally.

'Then Lieutenant Veimer is a liar?'

'No, sergeant. He... I didn't cut myself. It's a misunderstanding, like you said, and I'm sure that, at my trial–'

Ven Coers cut him off. 'Your trial, Guardsman Myer, already began. You are looking at your judge, your jury and, if given the slightest excuse, your executioner. Officially, you are still unfit for duty. You heard Lieutenant Gunderson, however.' She raised her voice a fraction to address the whole of the ward. 'He requests volunteers – any patient, regardless of condition, who feels able – to assist in the defence of this facility.'

A spirited murmur made it clear that there were volunteers aplenty. Ven Coers returned her attention to Myer, who hadn't spoken up. 'You look able to me. You can stand and walk and wear that uniform. I'm sure you can hold a lasgun.'

The only thing Myer wanted to do was climb back into bed. He wanted to draw the covers up over his head and blot out everything else. He wanted to sleep, to heal, and to know that he was being protected. Ven Coers had backed him into a corner, however. He took a deep breath and, in a loud, clear voice he said, 'I wish to volunteer for duty, sergeant.'

The hint of a cruel smile tugged at Ven Coers' lips.

Another Chimera pulled up outside the command post.

A ragged cheer greeted the ten troopers who emerged from it, blinking in the fading evening light, looking slightly bemused. Sergeant Ven Coers immediately took charge of the new arrivals. Within minutes, they were hard at work alongside the others.

Myer lugged a heavy sack of grain from the supply hut. Most troopers carried two or three at once, but he was wary of reopening his wound. They were wedging sacks together between the huts, binding them with rolls of barbed wire. They were building walls of grain and canvas, as if they could keep out a determined attacker for long.

'Remember,' Lieutenant Gunderson encouraged them, breezing across the parade ground, 'we don't have to win this battle, only prolong it enough. Reinforcements are coming from the north to give the xenos a nasty surprise. One of these sacks might only gain us a second or two, but that could make all the difference.'

Myer dropped his sack into place atop a growing barricade, and turned to fetch another. He passed Ven Coers and felt dark eyes boring into his back. He half-expected the sergeant's bark to bring him up short, but it did not. She could have found no fault with Myer's performance – and why would she? Myer had no fear of hard work.

Troopers were drilling holes through the supply hut's exterior walls, so they could crouch beneath its tightly shuttered windows and fire out of them. Gunderson stood with a data-slate, fastidiously checking off grenades as they were distributed around the command post's four structures. A Guardsman, a stranger to Myer, commented loudly behind his back: 'Don't let him get his hands on one of these. He'll pull the pin.'

He ignored the jibe, although it made him burn inside. So, news of his disgrace had spread. He was hardly surprised. In a couple of hours, it wouldn't matter anyway. He pictured a horde of feral orks tearing through the command post's flimsy fortifications. He swallowed hard and willed the image away.

Instead, he remembered a tent. A tent shared with two other Guardsmen. One of whom had just died in front of his eyes. The other, Kramer, was alive in the memory, almost certainly dead in the present. Myer felt a pang of guilt over this, but angrily suppressed it. He didn't subscribe to Ven Coers' theory that he could have helped, could have saved them. What help had he been to Steinvorst, after all?

He recalled the feel of the xenos knife under his jacket. He had been acutely aware of it, its rough shape pressed against his hip, since he had placed it there.

In the memory, he teased the knife out of his pocket. He turned it over in the dim light of a flickering lumoglobe. He remembered thinking, if only the knife - or another knife like it - had pierced him in the battle. Not a fatal wound, of course, but deep enough. Enough to give him a reason not to fight. An honourable reason.

'Get a move on!'

Someone nudged him from behind. Myer blinked and focused on the sacks of grain in front of him. There were few left now. It was just as well, he thought darkly, that there would soon be fewer mouths to feed. He bent his knees, picked up a sack and hefted it onto his shoulder. He hesitated for a moment, then stooped and picked up another.

Myer sagged to his knees halfway across the parade ground. The pain between his ribs was even sharper than he remembered, making him gasp. His grain sacks landed with a thud, and one burst open. Other troopers turned to look at him, but only one took a step towards him before thinking better of it.

'On your feet, Myer. That's an order!' Sergeant Ven Coers barged through the desultory ring of onlookers. Her polished boots clicked together under Myer's nose. Myer tried his best to obey, to lever himself up, but the effort was agony to him. In helpless appeal, he squinted up at Ven Coers' glowering features.

To his relief, suddenly, Lieutenant Veimer was there. He crouched and tore open Myer's jacket. The shirt beneath was bloody again. Veimer glanced at the spilled grain around them. 'What did you think you were doing?' he demanded.

'Sorry, sir. I just wanted to help.'

Ven Coers' nostrils flared. 'Sir, this is clearly another attempt to–'

Veimer cut him off. 'He's bleeding, sergeant.'

'Of course he is, and how very convenient for him.'

'A court will make that judgement.' With a sharp look at Myer, Veimer added, 'For now, my duty is to a patient in need.'

He clicked his fingers at the two nearest watchers, beckoning them over. Under his direction, they made a seat with their arms and hoisted Myer onto it. He felt ridiculous, like a helpless child.

An orderly rushed up to Veimer with a data-slate. Taking advantage of the officer's distraction, Ven Coers growled in Myer's ear: 'Don't think for a second this gets you off the hook. When the fighting starts, you will be front and centre with the rest of us. I'll see to that myself. I'll prop you up against a sandbag, wrap your hands around a gun and tell you where to point it. I'll nail your damn feet to the ground if I have to.'

Myer clung to his carriers' shoulders as they followed Veimer into the medicae hut. The ward seemed as busy as ever. Though most of its occupants had volunteered to help, in the pinch few of them had been capable. It seemed unjust, then, that they greeted his return with scornful sighs and shakes of the head, when at least he had tried.

He was bundled, not gently, onto his old bed. Veimer rolled up Myer's sodden shirt, tutted to himself and called for a medi-kit. 'You've torn a couple of stitches. Nothing vital. I can have you fixed up in a couple of minutes. In future, I'd advise you to take more care when...' Myer didn't hear the rest.

His eyes had closed and his mind had drifted back to the tent.

He could feel the point of the chipped bone blade, poised against his flesh. He had pressed a little harder, let it break the skin, breathing through the pain.

He had welcomed the pain. It had felt like blessed release. At the same time, it felt like all he deserved. Duty, discipline and courage. Guardsman Lucius Myer had lived his life by those values. He was a man of Mordian, after all. More, he was a member of the Mordian Iron Guard, about to betray everything his uniform stood for.

The pain was his punishment, and he had welcomed it gladly.

He had pushed down on the xenos blade, a little bit harder.

1900

Ven Coers was ready.

She lay on her stomach, propped up on her elbows. Her lasgun was braced against her shoulder, a solid, reassuring pressure. Guardsmen stretched across the roof to each side of her. She peered through her sights, down into the circular clearing.

The last light of the day was dying, the surrounding trees fading into shadow. A heavy silence lay upon the Dirkr Forest command post. The generatorum beside the medicae hut was stilled. All four huts were shuttered, all lights within them extinguished.

The scouts in the forest each voxed in every three minutes. They had yet to sight the approaching xenos horde. Perhaps it had changed direction, after all, and would bypass the command post without ever knowing it was there. Perhaps.

Ven Coers hated waiting. The trials of the day had left her sore and tired, and the plasteel surface beneath her was hard and uncomfortable. Once the fighting started, adrenaline would surely see her through. Right now, her body only wanted to sleep.

She didn't often feel the cold, but the descending night chill made her bones ache deeply. That damn itch had worsened, spreading into her shoulder and neck. She wanted to throw off her new uniform jacket and scrape away the soiled skin beneath.

She tightened her grip on her gun, tightened her jaw too.

Her right hand strayed to a small pouch attached to her belt. Her fingers teased out a bullet-shaped capsule, which she had placed there earlier. She had hoped to save it till later. It would be her third dose of stimms today, and the medicaes warned against taking too much. Her need for the drug was a weakness. She hesitated with the capsule poised over her tongue.

A scout's voice crackled in Ven Coers' ear: *'They're here.'*

She swallowed the capsule and renewed her grip on her lasgun.

The scout gave coordinates for the head of the approaching force. They were almost due east of the command post in its clearing, and barely a mile away.

Lieutenant Gunderson broadcast over all vox-channels. He reminded his troopers of their orders. Ven Coers had heard the speech or variations of it many times before, but still she drank in every word, swelling with pride.

'Remember,' said Gunderson, *'we fight for a higher cause than any individual life. We are fighting for the honour of the Mordian Iron Guard.'*

An explosion shattered the darkness, followed by two more in short order. The scouts had, as planned, hurled frag grenades into the feral orks' midst. The intent was to claim a few early kills, but more to rile the enemy into precipitate action. Where such savage creatures were concerned, this didn't take much. They were only too predictable.

As the echoes of the blasts died away, Ven Coers heard bestial howls of outrage.

The howls drew closer – slowly, inexorably closer – until at last three figures, too slight to be the enemy, burst across the dark treeline. The Mordian scouts. They raced into a gap between two huts, leaving Ven Coers' line of sight. She heard troopers scrambling to rebuild a barricade behind them. Her index finger tightened around her trigger.

The waiting was over.

The xenos horde crashed into the clearing, in another explosion of noise. Las-beams lit the night sky in response. A dozen snipers, including Ven Coers, lay on the comms hut roof. Two dozen were stationed atop the neighbouring officers' mess hut. More barrels protruded through the firing holes in the huts' walls. A dazzling fusillade greeted the unruly mass, and cut down a dozen of their number in seconds.

It was nowhere near enough. Many more just howled and raged, shrugged off their wounds and kept on coming; and, for each that fell, another ten poured out of the forest behind them. The feral orks formed a solid phalanx of heaving green sinew – which at least meant that Ven Coers didn't have to aim her weapon. She switched to automatic, loosing off ten beams at a time, confident that almost all would find a mark.

'Hold the line. Show them that iron does not bend.'

Gunderson's homilies aside, the first feral orks had reached the huts and were pounding at their walls with stone axes. The comms hut shuddered and creaked beneath Ven Coers' stomach. She hauled herself forwards on her elbows, pointed her gun down over the edge of the parapet and pumped beams into a xenos' scalp. She snatched the weapon back as a second xenos took a flying leap at it, trying to grab it from her.

'Deploy explosives on my mark... Now!'

Frag grenades hurtled over the grain sacks stacked between the huts. They showered upon the clearing like hailstones. They plopped into the writhing green mass and there they burst, a hundred fiery blossoms thrusting their way to the surface. The horde was sapped of much of its momentum as some of its constituents were gloriously torn apart, others burnt or blinded, shrapnel tearing scars across green flesh.

A cluster of small bodies extricated themselves from the melee – squigs, Ven Coers apprehended – and sprang towards the far corner of the officers' hut. They had noticed the lack of a barricade there, but lacked the wit to suspect an obvious trap.

Two engines roared to life, amid a sudden blaze of floodlights. Ven Coers made out the rounded prows of a pair of Chimeras, straining eagerly forwards.

A quartet of heavy bolters chattered fiercely, and the squigs caught in their arc of fire were shredded. The remaining few had no time to appreciate their fortune before a heavy flamer blast cremated them.

The Chimeras shot a second volley into the green-skinned mass. Two more appeared from around the side of the comms hut, turning the bombardment into a deadly crossfire. Some xenos, realising that they couldn't reach their tormentors, tried to withdraw to the shelter of the trees. They clashed with others still mindlessly trying to join the battle.

'That's it. We have them on the ropes. Keep up the pressure!'

The feral orks, even those unhurt as yet, were struggling to keep their footing. Some of the survivors had actually turned on each other, fighting with claws and teeth and knives to escape the areas where flames had taken hold. Many were dragged under, to flounder upon the growing heaps of the dead and the soon to be. Their howls of rage had turned to howls of anguish – and never more so than when the xenos looked to the sky to find it dotted with a second deluge of grenades.

Ven Coers began to choose her targets. She aimed for those not bloodied, still straining forwards, those festooned with crude bone jewellery and wielding the biggest, most brutal-looking weapons because these were likely the leaders. As more explosions ravaged the xenos ranks, as more flames licked at their feet and thick smoke rose to obscure the scene, she fired at the bulkiest, most active shapes she could discern.

Her heart pounded loudly in her ears, its drumbeat spurring her to greater efforts. Adrenaline mixed with the drugs awash in her system to form a heady cocktail. She ached no longer, and couldn't have slept if she had tried. She exhausted one power pack, then a second; and, though it was impossible to count kills in the confusion, she never once doubted that she was acquitting herself well.

She was never more alive than at moments like these, she reflected. Her life had purpose.

'Hold your fire.'

The order came as a surprise. Hadn't they been fighting for only a minute or two? Ven Coers' second power pack was near-drained, however, telling a different story. The Iron Guard's weapons fell silent, and the four Chimeras killed their lights. Most of the fires in the clearing had burned themselves out and their smoke was beginning to disperse.

The first cheers were raised from behind the barricades below. More voices soon joined them from across the rooftops. As Ven Coers' eyes readjusted to the gloom, she looked down upon a mass of steaming, green-skinned carcasses. A few of them, but only a few, were twitching, even struggling to rise.

'A commendable performance,' Gunderson voxed in his usual clipped tones. *'We have repelled the spearhead of the enemy force and shown the rest our strength. We must remain alert, however. The xenos will not lick their wounds for long.'*

The Guardsman to Ven Coers' left snorted. 'If the rest fall as easily as their fellows did, bring them on now.'

'Complacency will get us all killed,' the sergeant snapped at him. She voxed Gunderson over the command channel. 'Sir, may I ask if the location of the xenos engine is known?'

'No sightings yet, sergeant.'

'As you know, sir, I had a close encounter with it earlier today. I recommend we keep a supply of explosives in reserve for if and when–'

'Already in hand, Sergeant Ven Coers,' the officer interrupted her.

Ven Coers didn't argue. She had seen the stockpiles of grenades in the supply hut, however. In her rough estimation, half had been used up already. A show of strength, as Gunderson had said – and she couldn't deny that an early taste of victory had lifted morale. Dozens, perhaps two hundred, of the feral ork vermin were dead, with not a single Mordian casualty.

From what she had heard, at least six times as many were to come.

The command post was defended by one hundred and thirteen troopers. Most had been found and brought back here by the Chimeras, of which they had four, the whereabouts of the others unknown. A tenacious few had stumbled out of the forest on foot, late in the evening. Still, they were massively outnumbered. Their guns and bombs gave them an advantage over their attackers, but only as long as they lasted; and somewhere out there was that smoke-wreathed mechanical monster, with guns of its own.

A xenos dug its way out from beneath the charnel heap. Its flesh had been roasted and it dragged a mangled foot behind it. If it'd had a weapon, it had lost it. With a howl that was half-pain, half-defiance, it lurched towards the command post's huddled huts. Had it only been human, Ven Coers might have admired its hopeless courage.

The feral ork crossed the Chimeras' lines of fire, but they sat and watched it in disdainful silence. At last came the order: *'Troopers inside the comms hut only, each take a single shot.'* Gunderson was conserving resources. A single shot from each of twelve snipers, however, was more than sufficient. The xenos fell, but crawled an agonising few feet more upon its stomach before it finally, once and for all, expired.

At that same moment, a noise like no other rose from beyond the treeline. It seemed to expand to fill the night: a horrible, discordant, keening wail, almost bypassing Ven Coers' ears to drill directly into her skull. It was the howling of a thousand xenos voices: a lament for their recently slain and a vow of bloody avengement.

They were letting their enemies know that they were still out there.

2000

'Assistance over here,' Lieutenant Veimer demanded.

He was stooped by a patient, halfway along the ward, in a pool of dim yellow light cast by a portable lumoglobe. The patient convulsed on her mattress, moaning with pain. Veimer was trying to hold her still to inject her. 'Guardsman Myer,' he prompted, sternly.

'On my way, sir.' In fact, Myer was already struggling out of bed. There was no one else available. The orderlies had gone out to fight, alongside every patient who could manage to stand. Every patient other than Myer. He gritted his teeth and clutched his injured side, only partially for show, as he shuffled to answer the summons.

He followed instructions, holding the patient down until Veimer found a vein. He must have administered a sedative, because Myer felt the strength leaving the patient's body; an instant later, she lapsed into a fitful doze.

It was at this moment that the dreadful howl sounded, outside.

There had been relative silence for some minutes, prior to this. Myer had dared hope, against reason, that the xenos had been driven off for good. Then he had begun to suspect the silence, to miss the comforting cracks and whines of friendly fire. What if there was silence, he had asked himself, because there was nobody left?

He would have given anything to have the silence back now.

He met Veimer's tired eyes across the slumbering patient. The colour had drained from the officer's cheeks, making Myer feel even more nervous yet somehow less alone. Or was it just a trick of the yellow light? 'What do you think it is, sir?' he asked in a whisper.

Veimer regained his composure, broke eye contact and stood up. 'If you want to know, Myer, I suggest you try looking outside.'

'I thought you said...' Myer's voice trailed off. He didn't mean to question his superior. When Sergeant Ven Coers had tried to keep her promise, however – when she had tried to drag Myer outside to fight – Veimer had stood up for him. 'I will not have a patient in my charge bullied,' he had said. 'Guardsman Myer is recovering from a very serious injury. No matter how he may or may not have sustained it.'

'As you are on your feet,' Veimer said now, 'you can help me out with a few other tasks. If you feel up to it?'

'Whatever I can do to help out, sir.'

'Between us, we might even keep a few of these people alive until–'

'Sir!' Myer hissed. Veimer frowned at him. 'I heard... I thought I heard...'

The two men stood for a moment, listening. 'Heard what?' the officer prompted.

'It sounded like a growl. A xenos growl. It came from the end of the ward there, close to my bed. Just inside the door.' The disbelief in Veimer's expression made Myer doubt himself. But there *had* been something. There was nothing wrong with his hearing.

The lumoglobe's pool of light had shrunk around him. Beyond it was a world of shadows, barely kept at bay. And from those shadows came a snuffling, scraping sound.

'Who's there?' demanded Veimer. 'Is somebody out of bed?' His only answer was a rasp of laboured breathing and, from one of the mattresses, a very human groan.

Then came a fresh volley of lasgun fire from without, making Myer start. Veimer relaxed. 'Lack of sleep can play tricks on the senses,' he mumbled.

'But, sir–'

'The doors at each end of this ward are closed,' said Veimer firmly, 'and I know I brought no xenos in with me.' He holstered a pistol, which Myer had not seen him drawing. He wished he had a weapon himself. His lasgun lay upon his bed, atop his uniform. He felt defenceless in his surgical gown. And there was something in the shadows, he knew it.

What if it had snuck in earlier in the day and hidden itself? What if it had somehow gnawed its way into the building, through plasteel, unnoticed amid all the day's activity?

Veimer was moving away from Myer, taking his light with him. 'Guardsman Ven Roy has a fractured skull. I need to change his dressing. You can help by... Myer?'

Myer's eyes had alighted upon another lasgun, belonging to a patient. He took a step towards it, reached for it – and, at that moment, a small creature hurtled out of the darkness, slavering and screeching. It flew at Veimer with claws extended. He sidestepped it with admirable reflexes for a man his age, at the same time swinging the one object he happened to be carrying. The lumoglobe shattered against the creature's hide. Its light flared violently and died, scarring a yellow after-image into Myer's retinas.

His fumbling fingers closed around the gun. He snatched it up. He squinted through its sights, but he was blind. Then Veimer's pistol barked; and, in its muzzle flash, Myer glimpsed a leering, inhuman shape perched on a bed frame, tensed to pounce again.

Veimer was still trying to relocate his attacker. His second shot destroyed a laundry basket, bulging with soiled bedding. It was up to Myer alone.

His years of training took over. He couldn't shoot for fear of hitting the officer. Instead, he propelled himself across the ward. Another primal, vengeful howl struck up in that same moment; to his surprise, the sound came from his own throat.

He thrust his bayonet into the darkness, letting instinct guide his aim.

The squig cannoned into him, in the process impaling itself. Its sudden weight almost jarred the gun out of his hands. Myer drove the squealing, thrashing creature into the floor. He felt the spray of its frustrated spittle on his face. He gritted his teeth and, with all his strength, he twisted the blade inside it, one way and then the other. Its gargling, choking whines reassured him that he had found a vital organ.

He pumped three las-beams into the squig's innards, and its struggles ceased at last. He stood over the body for another minute, to be sure. He was out of breath, prickling with cold sweat. He was barely aware of his surroundings – until they were flooded with fresh light.

Lieutenant Veimer had found another lumoglobe. He held it up, surveying the scene. 'Well done,' he said, dryly.

The sight of the dead squig at his feet revolted Myer. He inched away from it. His bayonet emerged from its guts with a sucking, squelching sound. The creature's blood and offal had stained his white gown. He felt elated too, however.

He had faced a xenos – admittedly a small one – and slain it. Best of all, in the heat of the moment, he hadn't felt afraid. Guardsman Lucius Myer had seen his duty and done it. Or was it what he hadn't seen that had made all the difference?

In the darkness, the squig had no longer been a monster. It had just been a target. It could as easily have been a practice dummy.

'I hear you.' Myer wasn't sure who Veimer was addressing. Then he saw that the officer was speaking into the vox-bead sewn into his stiff uniform collar.

'I see. Many casualties?'

Veimer listened for what felt like many seconds, and a deep frown etched itself into his features. Then, quietly, he said, 'I think that is probably wise.' His gaze shifted suddenly back to Myer, who realised he had been staring and quickly looked away.

'Burst any more stitches?' asked Veimer in a mild tone.

Myer felt his tender side. 'Not this time, sir.'

'Then get that stinking carcass out of here, Guardsman. Throw it behind the latrines. We'll burn it with the others tomorrow.'

Tomorrow...

Outside, the sounds of gunfire continued sporadically. It made Myer realise that his personal victory meant little. He was no more likely than he had been to live through the night. The walls of the medicae hut would not protect him were the feral orks to overrun the command post: the squig had shattered any illusions he might have had about that.

Myer had been trying not to think too hard about tomorrow.

'Sir,' he ventured.

Veimer turned back to him, an eyebrow raised.

'You told Sergeant Ven Coers you wouldn't let me fight.'

'I said I wouldn't force you to fight. There is a difference.'

'If you need my assistance, sir, I will gladly provide it. If you can spare me, however, I... think I would like to...'

'Guardsman Myer. I can safely say that, right now, these patients need you outside with a lasgun in your hands more than they need you in here mopping their brows.'

'Yes, sir,' said Myer. 'Thank you, sir.'

Veimer finished making notes on his data-slate and looked up.

Guardsman Myer was struggling with his armour-fibred jacket, wincing every time he reached for the sleeve with his right hand.

The officer felt an unexpected wave of sympathy towards him. With a sigh, he strode along the ward to him and offered assistance. Soon enough, Myer stood in his pristine uniform. The very act of donning it appeared to have made him grow taller – but Veimer had felt his shoulders trembling with fear. To him, Myer looked like a boy dressed in a man's clothing. A boy who hardly knew what horrors awaited him.

Lieutenant Gunderson had first voxed him a second before the squig's attack. Veimer had tuned out his voice, having other concerns, until after. He had taken a moment to steady his breathing, then answered, 'I hear you.'

'Thank the Emperor. I thought we'd lost you too. Listen, Veimer. We just heard from Renvard of the First Company. The troops she is bringing us ran into an ambush.'

'I see.' He had almost surprised himself with his calmness. 'Many casualties?'

'Not as far as I'm aware. Trouble is, there are signs of more xenos in that sector. Spike pits and the like – and somehow the savages have acquired explosive charges and mined the ground with them. What this means is that–'

Veimer knew full well what it meant.

'–progress has been slower than expected, especially now that night has fallen. We can't expect them to reach us before sunrise at the earliest. That's oh seven hundred hours. We're on our own until then. I... don't intend to share this information with the troops.'

Veimer had agreed, 'I think that is probably wise.'

He had found Guardsman Myer staring at him in pale-faced apprehension, and lied to him because it was his duty to do so.

Now, Myer took a pair of scorched bed sheets – from the pile that Veimer had shot at – and stooped to wrap the squig's deformed corpse in them. 'On second thoughts,' said Veimer, 'I'll find someone else to see to that.' He waved away Myer's objection. 'We don't want you lifting more heavy loads, do we?'

'I suppose not, sir.'

'I have better things to do than stitch up your side a third time.'

'I'll be careful. As careful as I can be. I'll prop myself up against a sandbag and just point my lasgun where I'm told to. An extra gun could make the difference, right, sir?'

Veimer nodded. He returned Myer's crisp salute, then watched as the young Guardsman marched out of the hut, thrusting his chin forwards determinedly. As the door swung shut behind him, the officer reflected that he was unlikely to see Guardsman Lucius Myer again. For once, however, he felt he might remember his name.

Then a patient screamed and, thrashing against imaginary daemons, tumbled out of bed. Snatching up a medi-kit, Veimer rushed to his side.

He blotted out the renewed sounds of fighting from beyond the medicae hut's shutters.

He could only try to blot out the treacherous thought that he was wasting his time, prolonging his charges' lives for just a few pointless hours longer. Hadn't it always been that way? he thought bleakly. Tonight was no different to any other night.

He had his duty to do.

2200

There had been no let-up for an hour.

The xenos appeared from the forest, usually a handful at a time but sometimes mustering into larger groups. They charged the command post, slobbering and howling. They fell to the guns of its defenders, but some fell harder than others.

Myer crouched between the officers' and comms huts, behind a canvas barricade six sacks high. It came up to his neck when he stood, so he kept his head down. His knees and ankles ached and he longed to stretch his legs.

'Thank the Emperor for these xenos' stupidity,' a Guardsman muttered. 'If they only had the patience to coordinate their runs...'

'If they did, the Chimeras could take them out twenty at a time.'

The speaker was Myer's new sergeant; he didn't know his name. After he had left the medicae hut – as he had willed his leaden legs to carry him across the parade ground and while his nerve held – he had made for the nearest set of stripes. The sergeant had welcomed another pair of hands and, thankfully, had not seemed to know him.

Myer had prised his gun barrel into a gap between sacks. His view along its sights was restricted to a narrow tunnel, stretching to the trees two hundred yards away. Whenever the shape of a xenos appeared in that tunnel, he squeezed his trigger.

It was like being on the academy target range. If he half-closed his eyes, he could almost believe he was back there. Sometimes he took his shot, took several shots, but his target failed to drop. It kept on coming, growing larger and larger until it filled the tunnel, until it was all he could see. Then Myer felt his breath growing short and his heart freezing with a familiar terror.

For the sixth time – or seventh or eighth, he had lost count – a hurtling body slammed into the sacks beside his head. For the sixth or seventh or eighth time, the impact knocked him off balance. A dislodged sack tumbled towards Myer, but was caught in a tangled loop of barbed wire, suspended above him.

'It has my lasgun!'

The cry went up from the Guardsman to his right. His weapon was being pulled between the sacks, dragging his arm with it. Myer and several others rushed to balance the sides of the unequal struggle. Myer grabbed his comrade's shoulder, pulling for all he was worth.

The feral ork surrendered its prize, suddenly, and half a dozen men sprawled in the dirt. As they fought to disentangle themselves, a meaty green fist burst through the barricade. Its fingers jerked open and closed, grasping for a victim. Myer's sergeant leapt forward. With a hate-filled roar, he speared the feral ork's palm with his bayonet. Myer heard its animal yelp as it snatched its hand away.

The barricade shuddered with two more powerful blows.

Another two xenos had made it across the clearing, and were employing their axes. Two more sacks fell, while several more were slashed open. Grain showered the Mordian defenders. Myer fumbled for his gun as the barricade bulged and threatened to burst. The xenos' blades sliced through the wire binding it together, strand by inexorable strand.

It was just like the last time – his first time – out in the forest. No longer were the xenos held at a comforting distance. They were here, right here, with only the flimsiest of barriers to keep them from his quailing form. A barrier they were swiftly demolishing.

He was helpless to stop them.

He was distantly aware of his sergeant, calling for urgent assistance.

Myer heard the wheeze of a venerable engine approaching, then the chatter of bolters. 'Heads down!' yelled the sergeant, as stray bolts ripped through the grain sacks to whistle past the Mordians' ears.

The sergeant listened to a vox report and grinned. 'One down. The others are actually trying to fight the Chimera... One just brought its axe down on the prow and shattered its head.' A renewed burst of bolter fire followed, then a feral howl, abruptly truncated. 'Now it's lost its own head to match... and that's the third. We're clear.'

He was already climbing to his feet. Myer followed his lead but ducked when, from beyond the teetering barricade, the bolters sounded again. 'The Chimera is staying in place,' the sergeant explained, 'to cover us while we rebuild. So, let's get to it.'

Myer spent the next few minutes hefting sacks and tying wire around them, under the sergeant's direction. He felt the stitches in his side straining, but said nothing. He was careful, however, not to lift too much at once.

Several more times, the Chimera's bolters flared – and twice, its flamer lit the night for an instant. 'See, this is what I meant,' the sergeant grumbled. 'Heavy weapons against two or three xenos at a time is overkill, but they're leaving us no choice. They might not be smart enough to know it, but they're slowly depleting our resources.'

'So what?' a Guardsman scoffed. 'I make it less than half an hour until twenty-three hundred.'

'That's when our reinforcements are due, right, sergeant?' another spoke up.

'So, who needs to count ammunition?' the first continued. 'I say we hit these vermin with everything we have. Kill most of them before the First and Second Companies get here, leave them to do the mopping up.'

The suggestion was met by a general murmur of agreement, but the sergeant said nothing. The barricade was swiftly reassembled – albeit now five sacks high – and Myer retook his position behind it. He had to dig out a new hole for his lasgun.

He heard the sergeant voxing the tank commander. 'Thank you for your protection, sir. We can take it from here.' He was sorry to hear the Chimera grumbling away. Its silhouette left his tunnel of vision and he focused on the treeline, waiting for fresh targets to emerge. His heartbeat was slowly returning to normal.

Was it possible? he wondered. Lieutenant Gunderson *had* promised reinforcements. Myer had been there, at the briefing after Sergeant Hartman's burial. He hadn't realised how much time had passed since then – despite each minute of this terrible night seeming to last forever. Was it possible that this nightmare was almost over? Was salvation finally at hand?

He prayed it might be so.

'Does anyone else hear that?'

The sergeant interrupted Myer's whispered supplications. For a second, he thought his prayer had been granted already. Was that not an engine he could hear? It was approaching from the east, however, from behind the xenos horde, rather than from the north where the other Iron Guard companies were stationed.

Nor did it sound like any engine he had heard before.

It sounded almost broken. It sounded like rusted metal surfaces grinding together.

'Lieutenant Gunderson. Sir. I hear it. The...'

Ven Coers stopped herself from saying 'monster'. 'The engine, sir. The xenos engine.'

'Are you positive, sergeant?'

'As long as I live, I will never forget that grinding sound.'

In contrast, the clearing below had fallen silent, as if the xenos had tired of charging into hails of gunfire. More likely, they had finally found a reason to be patient. They were waiting for the weapon that would ensure their victory.

The stillness was shattered by the Mordian Chimeras. They emerged from their vantage points beside the huts. They took up positions in a row before the command post, defying any enemy to pass. Gunderson was taking Ven Coers' warning seriously.

The troopers beside her had also sensed something amiss. They had all heard reports of the monster and the many lives claimed by it. They exchanged nervous glances, finding no comfort in each other's eyes. They inserted fresh power packs into their weapons and steeled themselves; and they too waited.

'The Emperor be with us,' someone breathed over an open vox-channel.

Another howl went up from the forest, and the trees at the clearing's edge trembled. Ven Coers swallowed dryly and wished she had time to take more stimms.

The squigs came first, dozens of them, leaping out of cover – in some cases, literally flying as if scooped up and thrown. Another wave of feral orks came hard on their heels; and for all the hours that the Mordian forces had fought them, for all they had slain, the xenos seemed more numerous than ever and twice as ferocious.

Ven Coers and the rest of the rooftop snipers fired into the pack. With no grenades to support them this time, she knew it would not be enough. The Chimeras were almost overrun; they employed their flamers to keep the horde at bay, and yet some slipped through with blistered flesh and smouldering hair and attempted to wrench open the passenger doors, to get at their enemies inside.

And then, in a flash of deadly fire, the monster was there.

When Ven Coers had glimpsed it in the forest, through a smoke haze, it had seemed impossibly massive. It had grown in her imagination since, and yet still she hadn't done the thing justice. It was almost as tall as the trees. It towered over the command post's huddled huts, dwarfing the tiny, fragile figures atop them.

It was mechanical, certainly. It looked as if it had been built from a hundred tanks, haphazardly welded together; and yet, as she had noticed earlier, it was vaguely humanoid too. No, *orkoid* was the word. Its crudely carved, square head was clearly meant to resemble an ork, with its low brow, jutting tusks and those blazing red eyes that had burned into Ven Coers' soul once already today.

The Chimeras had been holding back for this moment all night. They made up for their reticence now, spitting out a double broadside of white-hot bolts. At the same time, Gunderson employed the last of the explosives. Most were armour-shattering krak grenades, which made the ground shake as they fractured against their target. Some brave troopers even ventured out from behind their barricades to get a better shot.

Ven Coers' snipers, too, fired at the monster on full-auto. 'Forget it,' she roared at them. 'You may as well shine flashlights at that thing. Leave it to the artillery. Your targets are the xenos, as always.'

Her gaze couldn't help but be drawn to the monster, however.

It was visibly reeling from the concerted assault upon it. Great jets of steam burst from its ragged seams, gathering around it. It sounded as if it were hissing in resentment. Still, its grinding advance across the clearing had hardly been slowed.

In place of feet, the monster had thick caterpillar tracks. It juddered over mounds of feral ork corpses, pulverising them beneath its incredible weight. Four jointed, mechanical arms unfolded, each ending in a black mechanical maw. Each of these four muzzles flared in quick succession, pumping out explosive shells in different directions.

To Ven Coers' horror, one struck a Chimera head-on, with force enough to blast it off the ground and hurl it backwards. It slammed back to earth, its ceramite frame groaning; and when its weapons tried to fire again, they coughed up black smoke instead.

She had no time to worry about it. A second shell cannoned into the hut beneath her, smashing through its outer wall. Flames billowed out of the hole, a few feet below her chin, and more smoke spiralled up towards her.

'Fall back!' she yelled, scrambling to stand. 'Fall back! Get down from here before–'

She never completed the order.

The plasteel roof caved in under Ven Coers' feet.

2300

'Fall back! Fall back! Position B!'

Myer didn't need to hear the order twice.

Crude axes tore through the stacked grain sacks, destroying the work of hours in mere seconds. Feral orks jostled to be first between the huts, which at least slowed them a little. Myer loosed off a full-auto burst in their direction, but didn't stop to judge its efficacy.

He didn't have to feel guilty for running when everyone else was running too. Had he not been aware of the cliff edge to the west, he might never have stopped.

The parade ground was criss-crossed with more sacks and wire, swarming with displaced troopers. The administration and communications hut was lost. It was burning, beginning to fold in on itself. An hour earlier, he had envied the snipers stationed in there, protected by a solid wall. He wondered how many had made it out.

The sky behind the hut was filled with smoke. He thought he saw a shape shifting inside it, but averted his gaze. Whatever had torn through the Iron Guard's defences, he hadn't seen it yet and was fairly sure he wanted to keep it that way.

Perhaps two dozen xenos and numerous nauseating squigs had invaded the parade ground. Some Mordians rallied against them, with bayonet charges. These brave souls, invariably, were hacked down, but they bought their fellows time.

A moment ago, everything had been confusion, so it had seemed to Myer. He realised now that, while he had lain in bed, preparations had been made for this contingency. His fellows were disappearing behind fresh canvas barricades. They pushed the barrels of their guns between the sacks and fired upon their attackers anew.

The Iron Guard's defensive line had been comprehensively broken, but they had swiftly drawn a new one. A shorter line, for sure, and one that left two huts exposed. The officers' quarters were burning now too, undergoing a swift evacuation.

With a start, Myer realised that he didn't know where he was meant to be.

'Where's Position B?' he yelled at a pair of Guardsmen he thought he recognised. They didn't seem to hear him. He sprinted after them regardless, and hunkered down with them beside the silent generatorum.

Four troopers had hauled themselves up onto the metal cylinder. Myer stayed below, squeezing himself behind a still-warm steam pipe that emerged from the cylinder's flat end and plunged into the ground. He looked for a target and started firing.

For a second, Ven Coers was in free fall.

Then she landed, with a bone-jarring impact, in the clearing.

Immediately, she dropped to one knee and snapped up her lasgun. Flames seared her back from the comms hut behind her. Had she not pushed herself away from its collapsing roof when she did, she would have been dragged into that inferno.

The position she had landed in, however, was hardly safer. Nothing stood between her and the xenos hordes. Her only protection was the smoke that billowed around her, concealing her from them. And the mechanical monster was out there, mere yards away from her. She could hear its mechanical grinding, louder than ever.

A shape erupted from the haze. She was almost relieved that it was just a feral ork. Five las-beams, not all of them her own, struck the creature as it charged her. It managed to reach Ven Coers, but its knife slipped from its hand and it collapsed against her, dead.

Another two former roof snipers found their way to her. One was limping, presumably injured in the jump. She communicated to them with urgent gestures. Maintaining a defensive formation – each facing a different way – they inched along the front of the burning hut, as close to the flames as they could bear. The howls of the xenos, their timbre now triumphant, filled their ears between the blasts of powerful weapons. Any of those shells, falling a fraction closer, could have wiped them out before they even knew it.

Ven Coers made out the silhouette of a Chimera, still pumping out lethal bolts. The sight of it gladdened her heart, but being this close to it was perilous. She found the gap between the comms and officers' huts – rather, between the burning shells of both – and whispered her gratitude to the Emperor as she plunged into it.

The barricade here had been destroyed, as she had expected. She signalled her Guardsmen to advance with caution. Feral orks had been this way; therefore, the three Mordians were coming up behind them. If more of the creatures came up behind them in turn, they would be trapped. What choice did they have, though?

Barbed wire snagged on Ven Coers' uniform trousers. She trod on sundered grain sacks – and, reassuringly, on several xenos corpses. Sifting through vox-chatter – the vox-caster had been saved from the flames, at least, as had Lieutenant Gunderson – she tried to build up a picture of what awaited her at the passageway's end.

A desperate battle raged between the huts. The feral orks, stranded in the open while their enemies crouched behind their barricades, were already losing. Ven Coers and the others were still glad to lend their guns to the effort.

One by one, the xenos were cut down by a lethal crossfire. A few, becoming aware of the new arrivals behind them, rounded on them but never had a chance to reach them. One badly wounded, dying feral ork hurled its axe as a last resort. Ven Coers barely managed to duck under it as it came spinning past her head.

As soon as she saw an opening, and mindful of the continuing battle behind her, she led her team forward, warning them to keep their heads down. Apart from anything else, coming from the direction they were and out of the smoke, there was a risk of friendly fire. She looked for an unmanned position behind a barricade.

There came a monumental crash from behind her. She whirled to see a Chimera smashing through the remains of the comms hut. It was sliding on its side, with a tortured screech that set her teeth on edge. She threw up both hands to protect her face from splinters.

The vehicle ploughed through a row of sacks, scattering the troopers behind them. It came to rest at last, a creaking ruin, its underside facing Ven Coers. Had there been any hope of saving either the vehicle or its crew, it was swiftly, cruelly dashed. Flames erupted from the Chimera's engine housing and out of its turret.

Ven Coers' attention had already been dragged elsewhere.

A familiar sound, a nightmare sound that made her spine tingle, crept up on her – and she knew only too well what was coming in the destroyed Chimera's wake.

All that remained of the comms hut now was a skeleton, crumbling to ashes. The massive xenos engine rolled through it as if it were nothing. High up in the sky, its huge head jerked from side to side. Its scarlet gaze swept over the parade ground, which was strewn with burning canvas sacks. It took in the command post's remaining huts beyond this, and the tiny blue figures racing and leaping for cover.

Ven Coers heard the solid, heavy clunks of the monster's guns cycling.

'Fire! Keep firing! Throw everything you have at that abomination!'

Myer screwed his eyes shut and obeyed.

It wasn't as if he could miss a target so large, at so short a range. It wasn't as if his beams were likely to cause it even the slightest harm. It was just that the Mordian Iron Guard had nothing else left. Even Gunderson's voice began to crack as he yelled over the general vox-channel: *'Don't give it a second to fire its weapons again.'*

Myer expected death to strike him at any moment. On some level, he would almost have been glad of it. He had no wish to see his fate coming, however.

'We're going to try breaking into that thing. Are you with us?'

He opened his eyes in surprise. He met the questioning gaze of the Guardsman beside him, but didn't know what to say. He looked past her instead. The xenos engine still loomed over them, as he had known from its terrible racket. Looking directly at it for the first time, he realised that its metal hide was beaten and scorched. He wondered if its movements had always been so clumsy and spasmodic. One of its gun arms was a smouldering stump, while another coughed and sparked uselessly. So, it wasn't invincible, after all.

Myer noticed another detail too: a hatch in the monster's side, close to ground level. 'It's a vehicle,' he breathed. 'An armoured vehicle. There are xenos inside it...'

And suddenly, his comrades' plan made dreadful sense. If they could reach that hatch and prise it open... If they could take the fight inside the mechanical monster, to the flesh-and-blood creatures that steered it and aimed and fired its weapons...

It was a suicide mission.

'I... I...' he stammered. His two fellow Guardsmen were already starting forward. At that moment, however, with a sweep of an undamaged arm and a smug hiss of escaping steam, the monster threw up a curtain of flames between them, forcing them back.

Myer didn't know whether to feel dismayed or relieved.

Then, emerging from the smoke behind the monster – through the burning huts – came the squat shape of the Iron Guard's final Chimera. Vox-chatter had suggested that it had been disabled like the others; nor had this been far wrong.

The vehicle looked in even worse shape than the monster, as if it could fall apart at any moment. Its engine whined and spluttered. Three feral orks clung to its back. They had torn its heavy flamer from its mounting and were hammering dents into its armoured hull.

It remained the most glorious sight of Myer's young life.

Bolters strafed the xenos engine's back. It jerked and thrashed and sparked and stumbled. Only one of its four gun arms could reach behind it, and this was one of the defunct ones. Its cumbersome size became a disadvantage to it as it struggled to round upon its attacker. It fired an explosive shell at a barricade ahead of it, attempting to clear itself a path. Another ten blue troopers ran for cover, but the monster – or rather, the creatures inside it, controlling it – had more immediate concerns.

Reeling beneath the Chimera's vicious onslaught, churning up soil as it fought to regain some purchase, the monster jerked in fits and starts across the clearing. *'That's it!'* roared Gunderson's voice in Myer's ear. *'Just a few yards further, and drive it over the cliff edge!'*

Its pilot saw the sheer drop awaiting it in time. The monster ground and hissed to a tentative halt, poised on the brink. Myer worked his trigger finger with gusto, aiming beams at the monster's massive head. Even if all they did was confuse and blind its crew, there was a chance it might just help.

The monster completed its turn and steadied itself. It snapped up its two working guns, fire flaring in their muzzles. The Chimera, swamped by the monster's huge, black shadow, looked very small indeed – until it roared like a Catachan Devil and surged forwards.

Its prow smacked into the xenos engine and crumpled. Its tracks continued to spin, its engine screaming in defiance. Myer gaped at the scene, too breathless even to pray. The small vehicle strained against the monster for a seeming eternity, the sound of grinding, rusted metal rising to a cacophonous pitch.

Then the xenos engine disappeared over the edge.

The Chimera, unable to stop itself, followed it over, the clinging feral orks leaping from it too late to save themselves. There were few cheers from the Mordian defenders this time; most of them reacted with stunned and exhausted silence. It felt as if everyone present were holding their breath, until they saw smoke rising from beyond the cliff; and only then did the silence diffuse into a collective sigh of abject relief.

'Well done!' Gunderson enthused, from wherever he was currently stationed. *'We have won a spectacular victory today. We have made the home world proud.'* Myer felt proud too, of his own tiny part in the battle. It was a new and very welcome feeling for him – and it was crushed, a moment later, by the officer's next words:

'We ought to have no trouble now, keeping this up until dawn.'

0100

Veimer stood in the darkness of the medicae hut.

He listened to the wheezing breaths of soldiers sleeping and dying around him. He listened to the bestial howls outside and the answering cracks of las-fire.

He pondered on how much closer those sounds seemed than they had before.

The doors at the end of the hut burst open. Sergeant – what was her name? – Ven Coers marched in. She saw the waiting officer and threw up a salute.

'Your pardon, sir. I have orders to–'

'I am aware of your orders,' Veimer interrupted her, quietly.

Ven Coers' eyes twitched. Her nostrils flared as she breathed. She was clearly on stimms; but then, so were two of the four Guardsmen behind her. Veimer might have taken a dose himself, to ease his tiredness, had he been less aware of the side effects.

'I have sixteen patients in here,' he said. 'Two, maybe three, should be able to walk with assistance. We'll take them out first, and the rest in order of how likely they are to survive the journey.' It was a cold but necessary calculation.

Ven Coers detailed two men to guard the doors.

Veimer frowned. 'Is that necessary? Is the enemy really so close?'

'In my opinion, sir. They're bearing down hard on our northern flank.'

He wondered if he had made a mistake. Gunderson had wanted to sacrifice the medicae hut almost an hour ago. *'We're stretched too thinly,'* he had insisted. *'Taken too many casualties, with too few resources remaining. Something has to give.'*

Had Veimer only been resisting the inevitable?

He shook a groaning patient awake and tried to get him on his feet. The patient had some strength left, but was delirious. He kept reaching for his folded uniform and asking where the fight was. A young Guardsman hurried to answer Veimer's call for assistance. They draped the patient's arms about their shoulders and lifted him between them.

They walked him steadily along the ward, into Veimer's office. A side door there let out at the edge of the cliff. It had never been used – he'd had to clear a stack of chairs from in front of it – but it was the most direct route to their destination.

The young Guardsman stumbled on the steps outside, the patient almost slipping out of his grasp. 'Sorry, sir,' he mumbled. 'It's been a long night.'

'For us all,' sighed Veimer. 'All the same, be more careful in future...' A moon slid out from behind cloud cover at that moment, and he looked at the youngster's face for the first time and was surprised to recognise him. '...Guardsman Myer.'

A fire blazed behind the supply hut, at the cliff edge.

A Guardsman was feeding spent power packs into it. It was the least efficient, most dangerous way of recharging them – something Myer had been taught not to do in any circumstances – but also the fastest and the only way available at present.

Myer felt he had passed beyond tiredness.

For a short time following the xenos engine's destruction, the Iron Guard's morale had been buoyed. So, who cared if their reinforcements were delayed; who needed them, anyway? The xenos' attacks had continued unabated, but they had felt desultory and been repulsed with relative ease. Victory had been theirs for the taking.

Now, as the night crawled past its midpoint – its darkest hour – the xenos were growing in numbers and confidence again. Maybe they had never truly lost either. The spirits of the command post's defenders, in contrast, were slowly deflating.

Myer and Veimer hauled their semi-conscious charge towards the supply hut.

They passed behind a barricade, manned by a dozen troopers. From the sound of full-auto discharges and a sergeant's bellowing and cursing, they were clearly under pressure. Myer wasn't sorry to be away from the battle's front lines. He only rued the fact that he was once again under Sergeant Ven Coers' supervision.

Ven Coers came up behind him now, a patient slung across her shoulders, handling the squirming weight with ease. 'Pick up your feet, Myer,' she growled, although Myer was keeping pace with Veimer. 'Lives are depending on you – God-Emperor help them.'

They deposited both patients in one corner of a picked-clean storeroom. One had passed out, while the other curled up on the hard floor, gasping for breath.

'We'll grab some sheets on our next run,' Veimer grunted. 'I doubt we'll have time to fetch pillows or mattresses for them.' He turned and followed Ven Coers out of the hut.

Myer cast a glance back at the wheezing patient. Unlike most others, he didn't have the mysterious infection. He had been brought in late that afternoon, with crushed ribs from a glancing axe blow. He would have recovered, given time. He still could, if moving him hadn't caused a broken bone to puncture his lungs. If the xenos didn't kill him.

It could have been Myer...

Had the feral orks attacked just one night earlier, he could have been the one lying in the dust, helpless, waiting to die. He shuddered at the thought.

***

Myer helped to transfer two more patients to the supply hut.

As he and Veimer returned to the ward for another, the sound of las-fire greeted them. In a series of staccato flashes, Myer saw the sentries at the doors fighting off a belligerent, club-wielding feral ork. One of the Guardsmen planted a foot in its stomach and managed to send it sprawling. As he did so, a pair of squigs forced their way past him.

They scampered towards the new arrivals. Myer drew his gun, but Veimer beat him to the trigger. He slew both creatures with two precise shots from his pistol.

The sentries slammed the main doors shut and bolted them. 'They've broken through our northern perimeter, sir,' one explained to the officer, breathlessly. 'They–' He broke off as something slammed into the doors from outside, making the whole hut tremble.

Veimer motioned towards two empty beds. 'Give us as much time as you can.' The Guardsmen nodded and set about pushing the heavy beds up to the doors.

Veimer snatched up a lumoglobe and held it above his head. He turned on the spot, surveying the beds and mattresses around him. Some patients were stirring as the feral orks hammered at the doors again and again. Others, unmoving lumps beneath their sheets, might as well have been dead already. It was up to Veimer to choose which ones to save and which to abandon. Myer didn't envy him that impossible decision.

The officer chose a gaunt-looking older patient, who was gamely trying to haul himself upright. As Myer attempted to lift him, however, the man pushed him away. 'Don't... waste your effort,' he gasped. 'I won't see another sunrise. All I want now is... to die fighting. Let me... die...'

Myer looked across the bed at Veimer, helplessly.

A shadow passed across the officer's eyes. Then he nodded, grimly. 'You heard the man, Myer. Prop him up and find him a weapon.' To the patient, he added in a kinder tone, 'May the Emperor be with you.'

Myer located the patient's lasgun and did as was bade. He placed it in the man's hands, which closed around it with surprising strength.

From across the ward, two more cracked voices called for their weapons too. Veimer attended to one, leaving the other to Myer. This patient's eyelids were already fluttering and his gun slipped through his fingers, bouncing off the floor. Myer settled for laying it on the mattress alongside him.

Ven Coers and the final Guardsman returned at that moment. Framed in the office doorway, the sergeant demanded, 'What in the Emperor's name is–?' The rest was drowned out by a shriek of tortured metal, as the main doors of the hut were rent from their hinges. Muscular green arms forced their way through the gaps, pushing heavy beds aside.

'Fire at will!' Ven Coers bellowed. 'Don't let those vermin get past you.'

'Belay that,' Veimer snapped. 'We have done all we can here. Let the xenos have this building, for all the good it might do them. Fall back! Fall back! Get out of here!'

Ven Coers looked as if she might argue. Instead, she ushered the rest of the troopers past her, through Veimer's office, out of the back of the hut.

Myer was the last of them. Glancing over his shoulder, he saw Veimer opening a bottle of amasec and emptying it over his desk. Then he dashed his lumoglobe into the desktop. It shattered, starting a small fire, which spread hungrily. The desk was quickly engulfed, and the office - along with the rest of the hut - would no doubt follow.

Myer was horrified, thinking of the patients who would burn in their beds.

Then he heard a tremendous crash, louder than the others, from out in the ward; and, following hard upon this, triumphant xenos howls. He vaulted the steps out into the night, Ven Coers and Veimer behind him. He hit the ground running but faltered after a few strides, turning back. From inside the hut, he heard the familiar sound of las-fire, swiftly silenced.

He had been wrong. He knew now, with dreadful certainty, that the fire would take no Mordian life. Veimer had seen this - to be more precise, he had accepted it - before Myer had. He had done what he had to do.

The feral orks would have their victory, claim a few kills, but they would get no further. Smoke was already seeping around the edges of the hut's closed shutters. They would be unable to follow their prey through the inferno. They would have to turn back - or better yet, thought Myer, clenching his fists as a powerful anger rose in him, die trying.

A strong hand clapped him on his shoulder. Myer knew before he turned that he would find Ven Coers behind him. 'In case you hadn't noticed,' the sergeant sneered, 'the rest of your company are fighting a war here, while you stand staring into space.'

'I know that, sergeant.' Unexpectedly, Myer's anger bubbled up and spilled out of him. 'I've been fighting all night, the same as you have. I've drained every power pack I had and then some. I don't know how many xenos I've killed, I've lost count, but I'll happily kill another hundred or a thousand or more if I can.'

He hefted his lasgun to underscore his point. As his right hand closed about its stock, something felt wrong. The gun felt sticky. Myer looked at his palm. It was red. He looked down at his side. He already knew what he would see - he could already feel the biting pain between his ribs - and his anger drained away as he filled up with dismay instead.

He was bleeding again.

0200

The medicae hut was well and truly ablaze.

A chill western breeze blew smoke and ashes across the former parade ground, filling the forest clearing. This was good news for the Mordians, as it left the xenos groping and choking in the dark. It eased the pressure on them as they rebuilt their barricades and regrouped around the command post's sole remaining structure: its former supply hut.

It also reduced their visibility, however.

Often, the first they saw of a feral ork was when it half-stumbled, half-charged out of the smog, just yards from one of their emplacements.

'Conserve your ammunition,' Lieutenant Gunderson cautioned. *'We can't afford to waste it jumping at shadows. Don't shoot until you see the reds of their–'* He let out a sudden curse, and fired his laspistol twice before breaking the connection.

Guardsman Myer sat behind the supply hut, his back to its wall, breathing through his teeth. Sergeant Ven Coers crouched beside him. 'I swear, if you're faking this...' she growled, but in a softer tone than usual. She could see the blood on Myer's uniform.

Myer rolled up his shirt. 'It doesn't hurt as much as before,' he lied. 'I think the stitches are more or less intact. A fresh layer of synth-skin ought to solve the problem, but I used all mine up when I... when I was first...'

The sergeant grunted and produced a canister from her medi-pack. Myer expected her to hand it over, but instead she set about treating the leaking wound herself. 'Sergeant, I can do that,' he protested.

Other wounded soldiers had been dragged back here, to the only shelter left for them. Some were dressing minor cuts and bruises; others had been seriously hurt by knives or claws or flames or shrapnel. None of them were complaining. They could be proud of their scars, received while facing down the galaxy's very worst horrors. Myer couldn't say the same.

He hadn't just hurt himself with that knife, he thought. Now he was keeping a veteran sergeant away from the front lines, from doing the Emperor's bidding. He didn't belong here, with these others. They put him to shame.

'Don't even think about it,' Ven Coers hissed.

Myer started. 'I wasn't. I... About what?'

'About climbing down the cliff. I saw you looking.'

'I wasn't, sergeant.'

'You'd likely break your neck trying, in the dark.'

'I wasn't planning to–'

'I can read your mind, Myer. We've lost three-quarters of the area we were trying to hold, and dawn is more than five hours away. We're surrounded on three sides by what feels like an inexhaustible army. What options does that leave you?'

'I won't run,' insisted Myer. 'I haven't even thought about it.'

'Then you're the only trooper here who hasn't.'

Myer didn't know what to say to that.

'How does that feel?' Ven Coers' dark eyes flashed up at him. Myer noticed that she was sweating profusely. 'I think I've stopped the bleeding. Can you stand? Here, take my hand.' She held her right hand out to the youngster.

Myer looked at it, and saw a red rash mottling the sergeant's wrist. He tried but failed to hide his shocked reaction. Ven Coers followed Myer's gaze, and hastily tugged the cuff of her jacket sleeve down. 'You said you'd used up your power packs,' she grunted.

'I did,' said Myer. 'Sergeant, I–'

'That's good,' Ven Coers interrupted him. 'That you've been making good use of your armaments, I mean.'

'How long have you–?'

'I see no las-beam burns on you.'

'Does Lieutenant Veimer know? Does anyone?'

'So, you managed to point your weapon at the enemy this time. Even better. Have you been to see Guardsman Ven Roy?'

Myer nodded. He had been coming from the recharging fire when Ven Coers had collared him. He had handed four cold power packs to its bandaged custodian, taking two warm ones in exchange. He had pushed one of them into place, but hadn't fired his lasgun since. There was a chance that, when he did, it would explode.

'Ven Roy's brain is leaking out of his skull,' said Ven Coers, eyes darting to her wrist. 'He can't stand without passing out – and yet he's out here, making himself useful, because that is the Mordian way.'

Myer didn't know what else to say. His wordless, horrified gaze was sufficient, however. 'Tomorrow,' Ven Coers conceded, gruffly. 'Tomorrow, I will report my... symptoms. Tonight, I have – we all have – more pressing concerns.'

'Yes, sergeant,' said Myer.

'Only you and I know about this, Myer, and that is the way it will stay.'

'Yes, sergeant. Only...'

'I know I can count on you to keep a secret.'

'Only... what if tomorrow is too late? I've seen what this thing, this infection, does. Especially left untreated. You've seen it too. And... and isn't it our duty to report any sickness in our ranks? Not just for the trooper's own sake, for the rest of us too.'

Ven Coers scowled and looked away. She didn't speak again for long seconds. Myer began to regret his outburst. He didn't know where it had come from, where he had found the courage to stand up to his fearsome sergeant. Perhaps it was because his sergeant no longer looked so fearsome. She looked pale and somehow smaller.

'You're right,' said Ven Coers in a hoarse whisper. 'It's what I'd tell any soldier under my command to do. But suppose I went to our senior medicae right now? What exactly do you think he could do for me, Myer? We just watched him torch the medicae hut.'

'I guess we did.'

Myer could almost have laughed at the bleak humour of the situation.

Perhaps it was blood loss, he thought, making him light-headed. Either way, he felt an unexpected kinship with Ven Coers at that moment. Before he could stop himself, he blurted out a question he had never asked before: 'But aren't you afraid?'

'Every day of my life,' came the unexpected answer.

Myer gaped.

'You thought my heart was made of stone? You think I feel this filthy disease eating through me and don't care what it might do to me? You think, when an army of xenos is bearing down on me – and I've faced dozens of xenos armies in my time – that I don't wonder what it will feel like to die?'

'I...'

'This morning, I faced that mechanical monster in the forest. I still don't know why I alone survived, when the rest of my squad...'

'I should have been there,' Myer mumbled. 'I'm sorry, sergeant.'

Ven Coers shook her head. 'In all my years of service, I have never felt so helpless. I couldn't have saved them. You couldn't have saved them either. Perhaps it was the Emperor's will to send you here instead, where you can make a difference.'

'Do you really think I can? You think we can win this battle?'

'Every feral ork we kill is one less to blight the galaxy. You say you've lost count of the number you've slain tonight. That's how you know you've done your duty.'

Ven Coers stood up and helped Myer do the same. The muscles in his side protested at the move, but not too strongly. 'Do you have any stimms?' the sergeant asked.

'I was always told not to take them,' said Myer, 'unless absolutely–'

'For me.'

'Oh. Then, yes I do.' Myer shrugged off his backpack. He rummaged his medi-pack out of it and handed over three capsules.

Ven Coers took them with a grateful nod. She popped one into her mouth and swallowed it with some effort. She squirrelled the rest away in a belt pouch. She clapped a hand on Myer's shoulder again, but this time it was a more companionable gesture. 'It's like I said. There's nowhere to run. There never is. You stand and fight because it's the only thing you can do. You, Myer, are as good a fighter as most.'

'I don't think I am.'

'Your problem is, when you aren't fighting, you think too much.' Ven Coers leaned a fraction closer to Myer. She fixed him with eyes that were regaining their spark. Her granite jaw hardened, her lips curling into a sneer. Her grip on Myer's shoulder tightened, almost making him wince. 'So, get out there,' the sergeant barked, 'and fight.'

Another barricade was summarily demolished.

The xenos hacked and tore their way through the grain sacks, as viciously as if they were living opponents. Behind the sacks, however, they faced a very real wall of Iron Guard troopers.

Myer was among them. He had taken one knee in the first of their two rigid ranks. He sighted along his lasgun, waiting as long as he dared. He waited until rippling green flesh filled his vision, almost within his arm's reach.

Then he fired and fired again; and he could hardly miss his massive target.

His third shot pierced the feral ork's left eye, killing it instantly. Its great green bulk collapsed an inch in front of Myer, and a thrill of excitement shot through him. He didn't have time to indulge it. There were plenty more targets. Still, no one – no future defeat – could ever take this victory from him.

He was doing it. He was making a difference.

Another xenos toppled before him, though he couldn't tell if the killing shot had come from his weapon or not. It hardly mattered. When they buried him, when an officer stood over his grave and summarised his military career, this would be remembered. They would say that Guardsman Lucius Myer had been dutiful, disciplined, courageous – and no one would ever know otherwise. No one but the Emperor Himself...

Or maybe they would. Maybe everyone would know – because Myer's fellow soldiers weren't so different from him as he had always imagined. They too had their façades; and if they could appear to live up to the Mordian ideal, so too could he.

Then he remembered his forthcoming trial.

The oncoming xenos tide had been stemmed, for a time, in this small area. Other troopers put the finishing touches to a replacement barricade, the lowest one yet. Myer followed the orders of the nearest sergeant, to pull back and find himself a new defensive emplacement. He lowered himself onto his elbows in the dirt, but his stomach was churning.

'Look on the bright side, Myer. Chances are you'll never face the Commissariat now.' He recalled the words of a fellow trooper in the medicae hut and suddenly appreciated their ironic truth. Myer had just begun to imagine that he might survive this long night, after all. If he did, it would only be to die a less honourable death. No officer ever spoke glowing words over the grave of a coward.

He would be better off if the feral orks killed him.

0300

Ven Coers' lasgun had run dry again.

She suppressed a frustrated scream. She pumped the trigger with all her strength, as if she might jolt out a few more precious shots. She turned to the trooper manning the barricade beside her and demanded he give up a power pack. 'I don't have any to spare,' the trooper pleaded. Ven Coers spat out an insult and reluctantly abandoned her position.

A Guardsman was bandaging a burnt arm behind the lines, and Ven Coers bellowed at him to stop wasting his time and take her place. She stomped up to the recharging fire and barked at its custodian: 'Three more packs now, Ven Roy, and make sure they work this time. The last one you gave me barely had enough charge to light a candle.'

She knew she was being unfair. The stimms were stoking a red-hot anger inside her, which she didn't try to suppress. That fire was the one thing keeping her alert, keeping her alive. Ven Coers embraced the anger, kept it burning.

She barely noticed the itch in her right arm, which had spread to her shoulder and halfway across her chest. She barely noticed the faint rattle in her lungs when she breathed in.

'What in the name of the Golden Throne are you doing?'

A fair-haired young Guardsman knelt behind the supply hut, decanting promethium from a mangled, rusted flamer into a glass bottle. More bottles surrounded him, already half-filled. Their necks were stuffed with canvas wicks. The Guardsman looked up with a start, and Ven Coers recognised him.

'I asked you a question, Litmann.' She gave the youngster no chance to answer, however. 'Is this how a Mordian fights? You know those things are liable to blow up in your hand. Are you trying to cremate us all?'

'Sergeant Kulm's orders, sir, but–'

'Where is Kulm? I have a few things to say to him.'

'–with Lieutenant Gunderson's approval. Any means necessary to buy us more time, is what he said.'

'Oh,' grunted Ven Coers, wrong-footed. 'I see. Well... be careful, Guardsman. If I see flames back here, I'll have your–'

She choked on the words as a sudden commotion flared out on the parade ground. She heard the explosive bark of a heavy weapon, which then cycled with a mechanical clank. Her heart froze. For an instant, she was back in the forest, blundering through a smoke haze, with the shape of a monster looming over her.

It couldn't be, she told herself. *The xenos engine went over the cliff. I saw it with my own eyes. I looked over the edge. I saw it burn. Unless...*

She didn't dare complete the thought. She snatched a power pack from Ven Roy's hand and raced back to her post. She hauled her bandaged replacement roughly out of her way and dropped to her knees behind the barricade. 'What is it?' she demanded, as the xenos weapon clanked and fired again. The ground churned with the impact of an explosive shell, showering Ven Coers with flaming soil and ashes.

'One of the xenos,' a trooper spluttered. 'It must have found a way to the bottom of the cliff and... and salvaged a gun from...' He doubled up, wracked with coughing.

'All troopers, the xenos with the gun is our primary target,' Gunderson commanded. *'It must be taken down at all costs. All costs, do you hear me?'*

Ven Coers attempted to locate the enemy, but couldn't. She risked half-standing to get a better view, peering over the barricade's brim.

She made out the shape of a feral ork, struggling to tame a cannon almost as large as itself. There was no second monster – which didn't mean there was no threat. The creature aimed its weapon in the general direction of the supply hut. It fired, but a powerful recoil sent it sprawling. The shell streaked over its shoulder to be swallowed by the forest. It was as likely to blow itself up as strike a viable target.

The Mordians couldn't bank on those odds, however.

Ven Coers fired, along with fifty other troopers, including snipers on the hut's roof and Gunderson and others inside. The weapon slipped out of the xenos' grip as it crumpled; but at least a dozen others scrambled keenly to retrieve it. The Mordians immediately turned their fire upon these, and several fell. One of the survivors hefted the weapon in triumph, but was swiftly attacked for its prize by another.

'We can shoot these vermin down all night,' grumbled Ven Coers into her vox-bead, 'but one will eventually get its stinking claws on that weapon again. Our only hope is to take it out of action altogether.'

'Agreed,' Gunderson's voice crackled in her ear. *'But we're out of explosives. We've a few artillery shells left, but nothing to launch them. I'm open to suggestions, sergeant.'* He switched to the general channel. *'If anyone is holding back a grenade or two for emergencies, now is the time to use it.'*

'I might have something,' said Ven Coers.

Others had had the same idea. She had to elbow her way through them to reach the young trooper, Litmann. By the time she did, there were few promethium bottles left.

She snatched one out of a Guardsman's hands. 'What do you plan to do with this? You think you can throw it further than that weapon can shoot?'

She swept the others with a scathing glare. It rested on one who had acquired four bottles, tucking three behind her belt. Immediately, she knew what was in this Guardsman's mind. She favoured her with a grim smile, but took the bottles from her anyway.

'Sergeant!' the Guardsman protested.

'How are you holding up?' the sergeant growled. 'In good health?'

'I'm fit to serve.'

Ven Coers pushed up her right sleeve, displaying the infection. 'Then I'd say this duty falls to me.' The Guardsman lowered her gaze. She understood.

She gave up the rest of her stash, and others followed her lead. Ven Coers pushed a bottle into each of her pockets. She used her belt to secure four more to her hips. She clutched four bottles to her chest with one arm, waving the others away. 'This ought to be enough. Hold on to the rest, in case I fail. How long do I have once I light one of these fuses?'

'I don't know, sergeant,' said Litmann. 'It's impossible to say. I'd recommend waiting as long as you possibly can.'

Ven Coers nodded. She searched the debris-strewn ground with twitching eyes. She located a short, stout branch and had a Guardsman fetch it for her. She instructed another to take the last capsule from her pouch and feed it to her. She strode back up to the fire and plunged the branch's end into it. She held the primitive torch up over her head, keeping its flames as far from her bottles as she could.

She didn't pause, not for a single breath. For much of the past day, Ven Coers had felt helpless, at the mercy of powers beyond her own. Now, a pair of troopers ran ahead of her, clearing a path for her. She marched along the side of the supply hut, towards the barricade she had so recently manned. The troopers there scrambled aside for her, tearing down sacks to create a narrow opening.

She squeezed through the gap in the barricade and broke into a run. She heard the liquid in her bottles sloshing. Some of it seeped through the wicks and soaked into her uniform jacket, its stinging smell making her nose hairs curl.

Sergeant Katryne Ven Coers had never felt so powerful before.

Her heavy boots pounded the blasted ground. Smoke clawed at her eyes and teased out burning tears. She ran, half-blindly, for the spot where she had seen the xenos weapon. She heard a ferocious blast ahead of her, and a wave of heat struck her like a physical blow. She lowered her head, set herself against the force and ploughed onwards, as breathless vox-chatter piled up in her ears.

Another barricade, she ascertained, had just been blown asunder. Through clenched teeth, Ven Coers swore it would be the last.

She had banked on taking the command post's attackers by surprise. Only now were they beginning to react to her sudden appearance among them. She could see the hazy shapes of feral orks – more clearly, hear their howls and smell their mossy xenos odour – converging upon her. She couldn't let them steer her from her course.

Finding a burst of speed, she dived between two lumbering creatures. An axe and a club swung at her, the former becoming embedded in the latter. She left the wielders behind her, wrestling for possession of their conjoined weapons.

The next feral ork lunged at her from the right; she twisted away from its bone knife, at the same time thrusting her burning branch into its eyes.

By her reckoning, she had covered half the distance to her target – when the shifting smoke revealed an obdurate green frame planted in front of her. Too late to avoid it, Ven Coers slammed into the xenos with a bone-jarring impact. She felt two bottles shattering and a sharp pain in her shoulder, swiftly washed away by an adrenaline tide.

More importantly, despite its greater bulk, the xenos gave way to her charge.

It was more surprised than she was, howling in confusion. It snatched at Ven Coers' arm but she shrugged it off with ease, leaving shreds of blue fibres and raw flesh beneath its claws. She raced on, the xenos on her heels. Its legs were more powerful than hers, but still she outpaced it. Every beat of her heart felt like an explosion in her chest, as if it might burst at any moment. She feared she might have taken one capsule too many, but she pushed the thought aside.

Nothing could stop her now.

A hurled missile, a stone club, glanced off her temple and staggered her.

She expected the feral ork behind her to pounce on her, but she could no longer feel its hot breath on her neck. It must have fallen to a sniper's beam, she reasoned. She felt a proud thrill that, even here, even now, she wasn't alone. She belonged to the Mordian Iron Guard.

She blinked away a stream of blood from her eye.

Another xenos rose before her, clutching the weapon. Its face clattered with bone jewellery. It wore a necklace of animal teeth around its neck. It had seen her coming, too late to defend itself. By the time it wrestled its ungainly burden around, Ven Coers would be upon it. Already, she could see that the weapon was broken and leaking. A shallow promethium pool formed around the feral ork's feet.

Her torch had burned down almost to her knuckles. She opened her hand and let it go.

She heard the great gun's bark as she tackled its wielder round its midriff; and her whole world erupted into fire.

The feral ork's wiry hair was alight. Its green skin reddened and peeled as its eyes began to melt. An expression of horror was trapped on its monstrous face. The gun was dropped, forgotten, as hungry flames caressed its fractured casing. A distant part of Ven Coers' brain wondered if she would live long enough to witness the predictable explosion.

Her fuel-doused uniform was burning too.

For a fraction of a second, she was a human fireball, like a living embodiment of the Emperor's wrath; and a sound forced its way up through her throat, but it was neither a scream of pain nor a howl of rage against her fate.

The last sound Ven Coers made before she died was a raucous, joyous burst of laughter.

0600

Myer had only closed his eyes for a second. Somehow, however, his mind had drifted elsewhere. He came back to his senses with a jolt.

He looked around guiltily, but no one had noticed his lapse. His comrades were every bit as weary as he was. Their eyelids were drooping, their heads beginning to nod. Even their sergeants' harsh voices, commanding them to keep alert, had quietened down. The Guardsman beside him had fired a shot at shadows, or possibly at nightmares.

Myer shifted his position on the hard ground. His every muscle ached. He gulped in mouthfuls of smoky air to re-energise himself, but choked on them. He almost wished he hadn't given away his stimms. He was almost jealous of Guardsman Ven Roy, with his fractured skull, snoring by the embers of the recharging fire.

Shortly after 0400 hours, Gunderson had called it.

'The battle is won,' he had declared. *'The xenos horde has not only been defeated, it has been annihilated. The cost has been just fifty-three lives – less than half of our initial force – in exchange for many hundreds of theirs, a thousand at least.'*

It didn't feel like a victory to Myer. Not yet.

It was true that the xenos were no longer attacking in force. Their siege was relentless, nevertheless. Not a minute had passed without two, three or four creatures – sometimes just one – hurtling out of the forest, slobbering and raging. These sporadic attempts ensured that no trooper, but for the most wounded, had been able to rest.

Some had made it through the gauntlet of weakening las-beams to batter at the few remaining barricades. At one point, one had thrust a fist between the sacks and seized the Guardsman next to Myer by his throat. It had expired before it could tighten its grip. The next one, however, might be more robust, or just more fortunate.

The long night wasn't over yet.

Another xenos thundered into Myer's sights. He squeezed his trigger and waited to see if it fell or if he needed to expend more power. The routine was familiar by now, perhaps overly so. It was easy, too easy, to let his concentration falter.

No Mordian had fallen in the past two hours, however. No more xenos had made it through their defences to lay a claw upon them. The most recent casualty, in fact, had been...

It had been Sergeant Ven Coers.

Myer swallowed at the memory. It stiffened his resolve, more than any drug could have. His old sergeant had not just turned the tide of battle, she had lighted the heavens. The explosion of the xenos engine's weapon had taken out at least two dozen creatures and pelted many more with molten shrapnel.

Myer knew he could never live up to such an example. All the same, since Ven Coers' death, he was determined at least to survive. He couldn't bear the thought of the command post falling, of no one remaining to record such noble deeds.

Another four feral orks broke cover. He fired at one, then another, until they dropped. He wondered what went through their tiny minds as they made their suicide runs, as they died one after another. Did they think they were heroes, like Ven Coers?

The question was pointless, he concluded. Xenos didn't think as men did. Their sole motivation was the spread of Chaos. They deserved nothing from him but his hatred and disgust. They certainly didn't deserve his fear.

The clearing was strewn with their mouldering green bodies. They stretched past the ashes of the command post's former huts and the razed shells of burnt-out Chimeras, to the treeline and beyond.

It struck Myer, suddenly, that he hadn't been able to see to the treeline before.

The sky was beginning to lighten. A peaceful hush descended upon the alien forest like a blanket – or it may have been Myer's imagination. The sound of his own breathing filled his ears, and his eyelids felt heavy again.

The next time he opened them, some time had clearly passed.

From the east, the first rays of sunrise felt their tentative way through the trees. Somewhere, a bird sent up a cackling call. There were other sounds too, which Myer almost didn't notice at first, so accustomed had he become to them. Sounds of gunfire.

He felt his throat tightening. Had the xenos come up with some new horrific weapon?

'Lasguns,' the Guardsman beside him whispered hoarsely, as if voicing his fragile hope might tempt the fates. 'Imperial lasguns.'

Gunderson's voice over the vox-net quickly confirmed it. *'I've received a communication from the First Company commander. Her force is here and has the few remaining xenos surrounded. They will fight to their last breaths, of course, but they haven't a prayer.'*

Myer held his breath, waiting for a *but*. He didn't dare believe that the ordeal was finally at an end. He had to hear the words.

'This battle is over. Praise be to the Emperor.'

A tired cheer went up. Troopers clambered to their feet and shook blood back into their stiff limbs. Myer did the same, uncertainly at first. It felt wrong to be raising his head above the barricades. His eyes kept scanning the surrounding forest, nervously, and he saw others doing the same. Snipers dropped down from the supply hut roof.

'We can be justly proud of this night's work,' Gunderson crowed. *'This victory was gained in the teeth of impossible odds. This has been the sort of night in which reputations are made, and from which legends are spun. I am proud of every one of you.'*

Everyone was congratulating each other. A few Guardsmen clapped Myer on the back and shook his hand. He recognised some of their faces. One was the young trooper who had lain across from him in the medicae hut. He had shown only contempt for Myer yesterday – as had many of the others – but now this was forgotten.

Yesterday seemed a long time ago.

Gunderson mingled with the crowd, taking hands at random and pumping them enthusiastically. Myer saw Lieutenant Veimer too. He was kneeling beside a semi-conscious trooper with his medi-kit. He looked as tired as anyone else, if not more so, but his work was not yet done. Myer wondered if he should offer to help him, but was glad when someone beat him to it.

Gunderson raised his voice above the chatter. 'Let's clear some carcasses out of the way, shall we? Dump them over the cliff edge for now. We'll clear enough space to lay down bedrolls, so we can all get some well-deserved sleep.'

Before Myer knew it, he was holding a dead feral ork by its armpits, its broken head lolling against his stomach, while another Guardsman hoisted its brawny legs.

His body protested at taking yet more punishment, but his mind was glad of some direction. He felt as if he were living in a new world, one he had not expected to see and hardly dared to think about. He wasn't sure what to do next. It didn't feel real.

He felt a warning twinge from his side as he helped swing the body over the cliff. He watched as it plummeted into darkness. He could just make out the dark, sullen shape of the wrecked xenos engine down there, and shuddered at the recollection of that horror.

He would do what he had always – almost always – done, he supposed. He would follow his orders, do his duty.

The fighting in the forest had ceased.

Troopers poured into the clearing, a never-ending river of blue. They must have marched most of the night, but they held their backs straight and their chins up. Myer felt a hint of awe at the sight of their immaculate uniforms, such as he had felt as a boy when, for the first time, he had seen the Iron Guard on parade. He was proud to count himself among them.

Their senior officer conversed briefly with Gunderson, then began to issue orders.

Most of the xenos bodies were disposed of in short order. A pit was dug to provide the Mordian dead with a rather more dignified burial. There was nothing left of Sergeant Ven Coers' body to place in it, nothing identifiable. Plenty would be said about her over the grave, however; Myer would make sure of it, if no one else did.

For now, bedrolls were being laid out across the old parade ground. Gunderson informed the troopers of the Third and Fourth Companies that they had eight hours' downtime. Myer could sleep for five, he thought gratefully, and still have time to clean and repair his uniform. Sentries had been chosen from among the fresh newcomers, to line the clearing's perimeter. He could hardly have felt safer.

'One more over here,' called Gunderson.

He stood at a corner of the prefabricated supply hut, where it didn't quite reach the uneven ground and was propped up on wooden chocks. A dead squig had rolled into the gap and been overlooked. The officer prodded it with his toe, lips curling in distaste.

The creature came to life and clamped its teeth on to his leg.

An expression of horror crossed Gunderson's face, but was gone in an instant. He snatched a pistol out of his holster and fired. The weapon let out a plaintive whine, its target hardly flinching from its feeble discharge. Though Myer had seen little of the officer during the battle, he had exhausted his power packs just like everybody else.

Myer had already drawn his lasgun, instinctively.

He took four measured steps towards the creature, firing in time with each of them. His beams punched into the squig's distended head, the last at point-blank range. It shuddered and squealed and coughed up stinking blood; and Gunderson tore himself away from it, blood streaming from his leg too, calling for Lieutenant Veimer.

The squig was still thrashing its half-formed limbs, so Myer shot it again. He used up the last of his own dwindling power on it, until it was incontrovertibly dead.

By this time, Gunderson had recovered his usual composure. He limped up to Myer, towering over him. 'Name?' he demanded, in clipped tones.

Myer hauled himself to attention and told him.

'That was quick thinking, Guardsman Myer.'

'Thank you, sir.'

'I have witnessed many acts of heroism tonight, but yours–'

'No,' Myer interrupted before he could stop himself. The officer's eyebrows knitted into a warning frown. 'I... No, sir,' he stammered. 'I'm no hero. Not like... some of the others. I happened to be in the right place at the right time.'

'The right place – the right man – to save my life. This will be mentioned in my report to Command HQ.' Gunderson smiled tightly. 'Whether you like it or not.'

Myer realised that a hush had fallen around him. Everyone, it seemed, had stopped to turn and look at him. This time, however, their gazes approved of him. Even Veimer, poised to bandage his fellow officer's leg, favoured Myer with a curt nod.

He didn't know what to say, so he said nothing. He straightened his back, puffed out his chest and saluted. At the same time, the sun made it over the treetops at last, to bathe the ruins of the Dirkr Forest command post in harsh, white light.

No light had ever been welcomed more by a denizen of the World of Eternal Night.

A brand new day had dawned.

ANOTHER DAWN

Lieutenant Olius Veimer stepped into the cool pre-morning air.

He closed his eyes and took deep, cleansing breaths.

He had worked another night, stitching up wounds and cooling down fevers. His patients were all stable now, with most on the road to recovery. The source of the spore infection remained a mystery, but he had finally found time to work on its symptoms. His latest combination of drugs was showing some promising results.

He enjoyed a rare moment of peace, alone with his thoughts.

He surveyed the five gleaming huts of the Dirkr Forest command post. Even the old supply hut had been repaired and scrubbed until it looked almost new. The five prefabricated buildings outlined an even, pentagonal shape, completed by the razor wire fences strung between them. Behind him, nestled in the lee of the brand new medicae hut, the old, reliable generatorum hummed softly to itself.

Of the desperate battle fought here mere weeks ago, no trace remained. No trace, that was, but for a small monument, erected close to the cliff edge: an enduring testament to the courage of the soldiers buried there.

The roar of an engine intruded upon Veimer's reverie. He sighed to himself, before calling for all available orderlies.

A pair of Chimeras nosed out of the forest, grinding to a halt before him. Their hatches juddered open and the latest contingent of injured troopers clambered out. A sergeant handed Veimer a list of the new arrivals. He scanned the names and accompanying notes, seeing nothing that others couldn't handle.

Most of the new patients were able to walk. The orderlies were taking stretchers to those who weren't. He even had sufficient beds for those who needed them.

He began to think about getting some sleep.

The door of the nearby Guardsmen's billets opened. Five Mordian troopers in dress uniform tramped down a flight of steps. One of them was Guardsman Myer. Veimer had almost forgotten he was leaving this morning. He had certified him fit three days ago, but Myer had had to wait for transport to return him to the distant front.

The troopers reported to the sergeant and, one by one, climbed into the back of a Chimera. Veimer drew Myer to one side. 'I'll be sorry to lose you,' he rumbled. 'Your assistance these past two weeks has been commendable.'

'Just doing my duty, sir,' said Myer, stiffly.

He nodded at the expected response. 'Ever thought of training to become a field medicae yourself?'

'Maybe, sir. I never thought I had an aptitude for it before, but helping out here while I've been restricted to light duties... I have found the work rewarding. So, maybe once this tour of duty is over...'

Rewarding... Veimer recalled a time, not long ago, when he would have said the opposite. He rolled the thought around his mind for a second. He realised that Myer had trailed off and was looking at him, his round eyes betraying an unspoken plea.

It was past time to put him out of his misery.

'As for the matter that brought you here,' said Veimer, 'I believe I may have been mistaken. There were some indications, as you know, that the stab wound to your side was self-inflicted. Having since seen you in action, I am satisfied that you, Guardsman Myer, would never commit such a cowardly act. Am I correct?'

'Yes, sir. I mean, no, sir. Thank you, sir.'

'I am duty-bound to report the incident, of course.'

Myer's mouth twitched in dismay, but all he said was, 'Yes, sir.'

'On this occasion, however, I fail to see what purpose that would serve. Especially considering the report already made by Lieutenant Gunderson, commending you for your bravery during and after the battle.'

The young Guardsman couldn't quite disguise his relief.

'This isn't the end of the matter,' Veimer added, sternly. 'I expect you to prove to me that my faith in you is justified. I hear the feral orks appear much fewer in number than they were, but of course their belligerence has not been dampened one bit. It will be some weeks yet - maybe even months - before this world is cleared of them completely.'

'I know that, sir. I am not afraid of them.'

Veimer raised a quizzical eyebrow, inviting Myer to elaborate.

'What threat could such vermin pose that is worse than what I went through - what all of us did - that night?'

I pray you never have to face the answer to that question, Veimer almost replied, but he chose to hold his tongue.

The waiting Chimera was revving its engine impatiently. He dismissed Myer and they exchanged salutes. Myer scrambled into the back of the armoured vehicle, the sergeant pulling the hatch shut behind him with a final-sounding clang.

Veimer stood watching, long after both vehicles had disappeared into the forest. By then, the new arrivals had been ushered or carried indoors, leaving him alone again.

He thought of the many young troopers he had tended to and sent back out to fight: a faceless army marching through his conscience. Myer was no different to any of them. He had nothing but a lifetime of war to look forward to. Nor could he be lucky forever.

But this didn't make him unimportant.

Veimer, his hands guided by the Emperor, had saved Myer's life for a reason. For every xenos he had slain since then or would slay; for the lives he had saved in turn; and much more. Myer had discovered the person he was meant to be, which was a gift indeed. No matter what befell him in the future, whether he was struck down by an axe today or survived to someday command a platoon of his own, Veimer could be certain of one thing.

Guardsman Lucius Myer would make a difference.

PRISONERS OF WAAAGH!

JUSTIN WOOLLEY

CHAPTER ONE

Trooper Hank Skelton's boot collided with the steel door for the fifth time – a sound Sergeant Major Marcus van Veenan was finding increasingly irritating.

'Emperor's teeth, that one hurt,' Skelton complained.

'You know,' van Veenan said as he sat up on his bunk, 'there's a simple solution to that. Stop kicking the fragging door.'

Skelton ignored him, slamming his boot into the door once again. Just like the last five times, it didn't move. He let fly with another chain of expletives.

Van Veenan hardened his tone. 'I said give it a rest, trooper.'

'With all due respect, sergeant major, I–'

Van Veenan moved fast, pushing himself off the top bunk and landing with a thud on the floor. In two steps he was standing before the much taller Trooper Skelton. Skelton, like most Rotauri natives, was built solid as a rockcrete pillar and much taller than the galactic average. Still, it was the short and stocky sergeant major, with his scarred face and grizzled hair, who seemed to tower over the other man.

'Let me stop you there,' van Veenan said. 'In my many years in the Astra Militarum it's been my experience that when someone says "with all due respect", they're usually about to say something disrespectful. Is that what you were about to do, Trooper Skelton?'

'No, sergeant major. It's just...' The large Guardsman pawed at the stubble growing on his square jaw as if trying to rub away his frustration. 'We're supposed to be killing greenskins, not sitting around like we're their fragging guests.'

'We tried to kill them,' Corporal Alani Trotter said from where she sat nearby. 'In case you missed it, it didn't go well.'

'Why are they even keeping us here? Let me out, you green bastards!' Skelton's frustration rose to the surface again, and he lashed out, kicking the – yes, still immovable – steel door.

'Trooper Skelton.' These words, thickly accented, rolled across the barracks like slowly approaching lava. 'The sergeant major told you to stop kicking the door.'

'Yes, commissar.' Skelton looked immediately sheepish. 'Sorry, commissar.'

Why, van Veenan wondered – not for the first time in his career – could a trooper not just do as they were told without the threat of a commissar to scare the breakfast out of them? Though, he supposed he couldn't blame Skelton for reacting with quivering knees to Commissar Tarna Hardnuss. She had a reputation for being ruthless. Like van Veenan himself, Commissar Hardnuss, 'Hard Nuts' as she was known to the rank and file, was a relatively new posting to the Rotauri First Infantry. Rumour had it she was transferred after decimating her last company following a mass refusal to charge a t'au firing line. Van Veenan didn't know how much stock he put in that, but Hardnuss certainly seemed the type to force her grandmother into battle at the business end of a bolt pistol.

The click-clunk of the door unlocking drew everyone's attention.

'There you go,' Trotter said. 'Good job, Skelton, you got it open.'

'Shut up,' Skelton replied with what van Veenan assumed was the most cutting retort in the enormous Guardsman's vocabulary.

The door swung inward and slammed against the wall.

'Holy Throne, that stinks,' Skelton said, covering his nostrils with the back of his hand.

Any Guardsman who's faced them on the battlefield can tell you plenty about the orks. They've heard the rapturous howls of joy the monsters make as they charge into combat. They've seen them rolling like a green tide over the crest of a hill followed by noisy, clanking, smoke-spewing machines. They've witnessed the bladder-loosening sight of them crashing into the first ranks, their choppas carving through armour and spraying arcs of Imperial blood in every conceivable direction. But there's one thing you don't notice about the greenskins when you're only around them for those moments of battlefield terror, and that is the smell.

Van Veenan knew the smell of battle, the metallic tang of blood, the choking smoke, the heavy sweat of fear and exhaustion. But what floated through the doorway was different. This was the stench of fungal growth, mounds of rotten trash and the rancid scent of ork piss. These were the smells you only got to know when forced to live with orks. Though living with orks was not what the dogged survivors of the Rotauri First were doing. No, these men and women were prisoners. They had been since Rotauri had fallen to an ork invasion three days earlier.

Rotauri had been a quiet agricultural world until half a century ago when vast organic mineral deposits had been discovered beneath the planet's surface. This led to the rapid establishment of several mines and promethium refineries. The Rotauri First was stood up in response to this shift from agrarian backwater to resource-rich backwater.

When the orks eventually invaded, the Rotauri fought with the fury of the Emperor to protect the planet's largest promethium refinery. Unfortunately, having not seen much in the way of combat in the forty years since the regiment's founding, they were unprepared for the sudden appearance of the greenskins. Their hasty defence held for a chaotic eight hours before being crushed, and the several hundred survivors were rounded up and kept captive in the buildings of a nearby Munitorum depot.

Almost every one of the thirty Guardsmen in this particular Munitorum storeroom-turned-barracks leapt to their feet as an ork thumped in through the open door. Stripped of their weapons, there was little they could do against the creature, yet their training as warriors of the Emperor and their instinct to abhor everything alien sparked them into motion. The ork was hunched over, but at full height it would have towered over the average human. Its long arms might have dragged on the floor had it not been carrying a cast-iron pot in front of it. The ork's head moved lazily as it inspected the Guardsmen, pale red eyes piercing out from beneath its enormous, protruding brow. One of its long algae-green ears, which seemed coated with thin hairs, twitched like that of an equine bothered by an insect. The corner of its mouth hooked up in what could have been a grin or a snarl, its long lower fangs tilting in its crooked mouth.

''Ere,' the ork said in guttural Low Gothic as it dropped the pot on the rockcrete floor, 'grub.'

Judging by the smell, which was not altogether better than that from outside, the 'grub' the ork had brought in was the same they'd been served every meal. The orks' attempt at 'humie' food was a light-green broth thickened with grains from Munitorum storage and occasionally garnished with floating pieces of indeterminate meat or fungus.

Trooper Skelton, constantly filled with a bravado that had surprisingly not yet seen him killed, stepped across to block the open doorway. Most young people of Rotauri joined the Astra Militarum to avoid a hard life of working in the fields, mines or refineries. Skelton had joined the Guard because he wanted to shoot aliens, preferably up close and in the face. The ork lifted itself to its full height as Skelton faced it.

'Listen, you xenos scum,' he said, 'you've kept us in here for three days. What–'

The ork's hand lashed out with impressive speed and shoved Skelton in the chest, sending him sprawling across the rockcrete floor. The ork grunted something incomprehensible and then left, slamming the door shut behind it. Even as he was recovering, trying to suck air into his winded chest, Skelton called after the ork. 'Coward!'

Commissar Hardnuss walked forward and held her hand down to Skelton. Even stripped of her weapons and flak armour she still cut an imposing figure in her long black coat with its gold epaulets. Skelton took her hand and pulled himself to his feet. 'No doubt the Emperor applauds your bravery,' the commissar said, 'but unfortunately our current circumstances preclude such a frontal assault.'

'If I can, sir, we have a suggestion.'

The attention of the barracks turned to Corporal Amoa. Beside him was Corporal Amoa. Twin brothers with the same rank in the same company of the same regiment. That had caused van Veenan no end of confusion when he'd first arrived on Rotauri.

Hardnuss turned to the twins. 'Any suggested course of action is welcome, corporal.'

'The last two nights we've been working on a section of brickwork in the back wall,' Corporal Amoa said. 'These buildings were designed as stores, not prisons. We've chipped through the mortar and with a little more work we'll be able to push free a section of bricks. We're thinking we could sneak out tonight, see if we can't make for Flaxton.'

'Assuming it's still standing, Flaxton is ten miles from here. You'll have to move through the forest, stay off the roads,' Hardnuss said.

'We can make it, commissar.'

'No, you won't be doing that.' Lieutenant Tam Pokato turned from where he'd been pacing, attempting to wear standard-issue grooves in the rockcrete floor. 'It's reckless and could bring retaliation down on us all. I have no doubt that the governor will have sent word for reinforcements. More Imperial forces will be arriving to crush the greenskins and liberate us. There's no point making the situation worse. We shall sit tight and wait to be rescued.'

Lieutenant Pokato. Van Veenan had pegged this one within seconds of meeting him. Third son of the governor of Rotauri. Undertrained. Incompetent. Annoying. Van Veenan had seen countless junior officers like him over the years – completely unaware of their ineptitude, craven fools dangerous to the soldiers under their command. The only saving grace to having an officer like Pokato was that he'd likely get himself killed relatively quickly.

'Lieutenant,' Commissar Hardnuss said, 'it is our duty as warriors of the Emperor to attempt an escape, pass word to Imperial forces and do everything in our power, despite our defeat, to harass the enemy.'

Pokato looked from the commissar back to the twins. 'I am ordering you not to attempt an escape. We don't know why the greenskins have taken us prisoner, or how they may react if you're captured. They might kill us all. We will await reinforcements and then take the fight back to the enemy.'

'You cannot order these men to act against their duty,' Hardnuss said.

'I am the ranking officer,' Pokato said. 'I decide what their duty is.'

Hardnuss moved closer to Pokato. Van Veenan could see the bulge in her cheeks as she clenched her jaw. She kept her voice low and spoke through gritted teeth. 'You may be the ranking officer here but let me offer some advice from the Commissariat. I strongly advise you not to order your troopers to cower from the enemy, lest it appear that it is in fact *you* who are afraid. The last thing you want is the Guardsmen under your command to believe you a coward. Actually,' Hardnuss tapped her lip as if in consideration, 'the last thing you want is for a commissar to think you are a coward. That is, of course, punishable by death. But certainly, the *second*-last thing you want is for your troops to believe it.'

Pokato, seeming even paler than usual, took a long moment and then acquiesced. 'Fine,' he said, 'see if you can get word to Imperial forces from Flaxton.'

An hour later, when darkness had fallen outside, van Veenan still lay on his bunk. He was tossing a ball he'd fashioned from his socks against the ceiling, aiming for a small crack in the rockcrete, and catching it on its way down, when Corporal Amoa – he wasn't sure which one – announced they were ready to slide the section of bricks free and attempt their escape.

'Do it,' Commissar Hardnuss said.

Van Veenan tossed his sock-ball into the air and caught it one last time.

He sighed. He'd tried to stay quiet, tried to keep out of it, but he couldn't let these idiots throw their lives away. 'Emperor damn it,' he muttered before he sat up. 'You aren't going to make it.'

'Sergeant major?' Amoa said.

'You won't make it,' van Veenan repeated.

'What makes you say that?' Hardnuss turned to him. 'The Emperor will guide them.'

'The orks obviously want us for something, otherwise they wouldn't have kept us prisoner for three days,' van Veenan said. 'I'd be surprised if there aren't guards and fences around us by now.'

Hardnuss narrowed her eyes at him. He could see that bulge in her cheeks again.

Van Veenan spoke louder, addressing the whole barracks. 'Fifty thrones say they don't make it. Any takers?'

'Sergeant major, that's enough,' Hardnuss said.

'Fifty thrones,' van Veenan repeated.

'Sergeant major!'

'I'll take that bet,' Corporal Trotter said. 'I think they'll make it.'

The air in the barracks was thick with tension. Commissar Hardnuss sliced through it with her heavy accent. 'It's your decision, corporals.'

The twins looked at each other and then spoke in unison. 'We're going.'

'Very well,' Hardnuss said. 'The Emperor protects.'

The two corporals nodded and moved off, others in the barracks patting them on the back and wishing them well. Van Veenan lay back on his bed, tossing his sock-ball at the crack in the roof, listening to the sound of the bricks in the far wall being slid free. The pair climbed through and moved outside.

Not long after they'd left, the residents of the barracks heard a series of dull thuds coming from the exterior walls.

'What is that?' Pokato asked, his voice wavering.

'Bern,' Hardnuss said, addressing a trooper near the spot where the Amoa brothers had worked the bricks free. 'Can you see anything?'

Trooper Bern manoeuvred the loose bricks, opening a small gap to peer out. He fell back from the wall, shocked. 'Emperor save us,' he said, 'it's them. It's the corporals. They're throwing them at the barracks!'

'What?' Hardnuss said. 'What do you mean they're throwing–'

The barracks door burst inward. A single object hit the floor and rolled to a stop. It was the head of Corporal Amoa, though, once again, van Veenan couldn't tell which one. It hadn't so much been severed as ripped from his body. Long strings of muscle and sinew trailed behind it. It stared up through lifeless eyes at the occupants of the barracks. All the Guardsmen, even Commissar 'Hard Nuts,' stared in horror at the head in the centre of the room. Outside, they could hear deep guttural chuckles. The greenskins seemed to find the whole thing immensely amusing.

Van Veenan sighed as he looked at the head. Sometimes he hated being right. 'I guess I'll take an IOU for those thrones, Trotter.'

CHAPTER TWO

Van Veenan woke like a soldier, stirred by the sounds of orks shouting outside. He swung his legs around and dropped off his bunk. Here was one of the small things that revealed whether a Guardsman was a veteran or a green recruit: whether they laid their socks out to dry when they took them off, whether they wrote their blood type on their helmets and boots, and whether they woke instantly, clear-eyed and ready to fight.

The barracks door burst open. The ork that had brought their food the evening before stomped inside.

'All right, you zoggin' gits. Get outside, da boss is ready for ya!'

Nobody moved. Van Veenan surveyed the faces in the barracks. These troops wanted vengeance. Being taunted with the dismembered bodies of the Amoa twins had given them a reason to fight even beyond their sworn duty to Emperor and Imperium. Van Veenan could appreciate that. His allegiance had long since shifted from those giving the orders to those forced to follow them.

Time and time again, van Veenan had seen decisions made at the highest levels cause utter carnage on the ground. What had happened on Rotauri was yet another in a prestigious line of command catastrophes. He, and every one of the remaining Guardsmen from the Rotauri First, were in this position because of the mind-bogglingly stupid plan to assault the ork position before they could establish a secure staging base. Van Veenan had tried to tell headquarters that they should establish defensive formations, that the greenskins didn't need a staging base to begin obliterating Imperial infantry. No one had listened. Now van Veenan's only goal was ensuring that at least some of the troopers left might somehow survive ork captivity, despite the insurmountable odds.

Van Veenan had survived more than his share of insurmountable odds. He'd been told many times that the Emperor had a plan for him, but he was fairly certain the Emperor gave as much of a shit about any one individual as the captain of a battleship cares about a rat living in the lower decks.

The ork growled. 'I said get outside!'

'Frag off!' Trooper Bern, proving himself as suicidal as Skelton, shouted at the ork.

The ork turned to loom over Trooper Bern, and Bern spat in the creature's green face.

Well, that was just stupid, van Veenan thought.

The ork clamped its massive hands on either side of Bern's head and lifted until Bern was hanging in the air, his feet kicking.

'You want to fight Urzog?' the ork said. 'You fink you is 'ard? I is not allowed or else I would snap you in 'alf. Now get outside!' The ork, Urzog, used his grip on Bern's head to fling him towards the door. Bern hit the floor awkwardly and his head hung at an impossible angle, blank eyes staring back over his shoulder. For a moment the entire barracks, including Urzog, stared at Bern's lifeless body.

Even as the war cries grew in the throats of the Guardsmen, van Veenan shouted, 'No!'

Most of the troopers stopped, likely more from the tone of his voice than from any recognition of his authority, but five of them launched themselves at Urzog. The ork swung a heavy fist and battered the first aside. The second trooper threw a punch that connected with the ork's massive jaw. Urzog barely seemed to notice and punched the trooper in the stomach, folding him in half and sending him flying. It was Skelton who struck next. The largest of the Guardsmen, he dropped his shoulder and charged into Urzog, causing the ork to stumble back against the wall. As Urzog shoved Skelton off him, Trotter took advantage of the ork's distraction and slammed her boot hard into his groin. Her kick landed squarely between the ork's legs with an impact that made every male Guardsman in the room wince in empathy. Urzog looked down and growled.

'Wot?' he said. 'You fink that's gonna 'urt one of the boyz?'

As Trotter moved to attack again, van Veenan grabbed her by the arm and held up his other hand to stop more Guardsmen getting involved. 'Emperor damn it, I said no.'

'Oi, what are you zoggin' doin' in 'ere?'

A new ork stood in the doorway. This one was over seven feet tall and broader in the shoulders than the doorway was wide. A nob, by the size of him.

The Imperium had long known ork hierarchy was dictated by size, something that seemed easy for the feeble-minded greenskins to grasp. It was also useful for Imperial snipers because they could immediately tell which orks were in charge – nobs, the orks called them. This nob had a distinctive metal dome on top of its head that looked almost like a steel helmet, but for the fact it was screwed and stapled into its green flesh. The nob looked at Urzog.

'Big Nob 'Ardskull,' Urzog said, 'I is just gettin' these humies outside.'

''Urry up. Da boss is waitin.'

'You 'eard 'im,' Urzog growled. 'Out!'

'Do as they say,' van Veenan said.

'But, sarge–' Corporal Trotter began, but van Veenan cut her off with a stern look.

'Do as they say.'

The troopers made their way outside. Urzog grabbed Bern's lifeless arm and dragged his corpse through the dirt after them. 'Over there,' Urzog said, pointing through the buildings of the depot to what had once been the transport yard. It was now full of hundreds of captured Guardsmen.

Van Veenan saw he'd been right about what the orks had done in the days they'd been inside. The Munitorum depot had been haphazardly converted into a prison camp. All around the perimeter the greenskins had constructed a fence from an assortment of rubble, wood, steel and even whole trees from the nearby forest. It varied in height from twelve or thirteen feet in some places to twenty or more in others. All along the top was an uneven tangle of razor wire, wrapped around jagged steel spikes.

A dozen or more open-sided guard towers had been built around the circumference too, each with a similarly ramshackle appearance and with little thought given to their structural integrity. Van Veenan could see two orks in each tower holding the guns they called 'shootas': horribly inaccurate but if the large-calibre rounds hit their target there was little left to ship home.

As van Veenan began moving through the depot, he realised the dozen or so other buildings used for holding prisoners had all been painted with tallied numbers, presumably so that the orks could differentiate between them.

He turned back to see five tally marks painted on the door of the building they'd spent the last three days in. *Huh*, he thought, *I didn't know orks could count that high.*

Although van Veenan had to admit the greenskins were strange like that. They built their own weapons, manufactured vehicles and could even construct void ships, but most of the time they seemed like they wouldn't know whether to hit a nail with a hammer or their forehead. How they waged interstellar war with their crude but effective technology was one of the great mysteries of the species.

Even the decision to use the Munitorum depot as the location for the prison camp was, if not total luck, strategically sound. It was isolated, but near enough to the promethium refinery that the orks could maintain control of the important resource.

Commissar Hardnuss moved up beside van Veenan. 'You did the right thing in there, stopping them from attacking that ork. We need to pick our moment.'

'I'm just trying to stop more idiots getting themselves killed,' van Veenan replied.

The troopers from Barracks Five moved towards the mustering of Guardsmen in the transport yard. An enormous heavy-lift gantry crane loomed over them and an open-fronted parking bay held a row of Departmento Munitorum transport trucks. Some smaller greenskins – the ones they called gretchins, or sometimes grots – clambered over one of the trucks with blazing blue cutting torches spewing sprays of yellow-orange sparks as they hacked into the vehicle's structure. There were only twenty or thirty of them, where van Veenan knew ork warbands usually had hundreds.

A single ork stood atop a stack of crates watching the gretchin swarming over the truck like flies on rotten fruit. All orks were bizarre, but this one even more so. It was small, probably even shorter than van Veenan, and had arms and legs far skinnier than orks he had met on the battlefield. It had a box-shaped contraption strapped to its back, with a pair of coils extending from the top that intermittently sparked and flashed with arcing bolts of electricity. Each time the bright blue discharge jumped between the copper coils, the ork's drooping ears rose and fell with the buzzing electrical field. Van Veenan had never seen one before, but he'd heard about them – this was a mekboy, the closest thing the orks had to engineers.

'Hurry up. I need these trucks stripped down to lighten them for optimal transport capability. We need to bring back all the gubbinz from the big factory,' the strange ork said. 'I need thermal conductors and those quantum power inverter wotsits, plus all the metal we can get.'

Van Veenan listened to the mekboy with interest. It didn't sound like it'd been smashed in the head with a mallet like most greenskins. It sounded vaguely intelligent.

'I said hurry up, you zoggin' gits!'

Well, mostly.

''Ere,' Urzog said to the troopers of Barracks Five, 'get all lined up like you humies do.'

Van Veenan saw the eyes of the troopers fall on him. He nodded. 'Fall in, parade formation.'

'Excuse me, sergeant major,' Lieutenant Pokato cut in, 'I am the ranking officer here.'

Van Veenan looked at the man. Typical lieutenant. Greener than the orks. But, as a veteran sergeant, van Veenan knew how to play the game. He nodded. 'Apologies, sir, please go ahead.'

'Right,' Pokato said, grabbing the front of his shirt and pulling it down. 'Fall in.'

The troopers did so, most of them still looking towards van Veenan, who nodded as subtly as he could.

Big Nob 'Ardskull made his way front and centre of the gathered Guardsmen.

'All right, you humie gits, shut ya gobs and listen. I is Grut 'Ardskull and I is big nob for the boss round 'ere. I is da boss' most trusted advisor because I 'ave only tried to kill 'im one time. I is gonna keep all of you in line with no muckin' about. From now on you is all prisoners of Waaagh! 'Eadbasha, so look proper smart. Boss!'

'Ardskull shouted towards the supply depot headquarters, a building now adorned with an enormous metal sheet etched with the image of what van Veenan was sure was an ork slamming its head against a wall. When the door opened, the ork that stomped out was even larger than 'Ardskull. Warboss Nok 'Eadbasha clomped down the steps and walked past the gathered Guardsmen. Each footfall seemed to shake the world.

'Eadbasha was the largest ork van Veenan had ever seen. The beastly warboss wore massive metal boots and his arms and legs were enclosed in steel frames, his movement assisted by pumping and hissing hydraulic rams. His armoured torso piece was painted bright red and adorned with an ork skull and crossed-axe motif. His right hand was sheathed inside a vicious power klaw.

More than anything it was the warboss' head that drew van Veenan's attention. It was enormous. His lower jaw was covered by a metal plate spiked into fearsome iron teeth and the top of his skull was horribly misshapen, bulging out in huge lumps and bumps like a sack of the tuberous vegetables they grew on Rotauri.

Warboss 'Eadbasha came to a stop before the assembled Guardsmen. He paused for a moment, his red eyes peering out from beneath that disgusting head, then his metal jaw dropped open.

'WAAAAAAAAGH!'

Orks throughout the camp took up the bellowing call, until the buildings seemed to vibrate. When the war cry died off, van Veenan's ears rang.

''Ow many?' 'Eadbasha said to 'Ardskull.

'Loads, boss.'

'Eadbasha smiled. 'Loads is perfect.'

The warboss cast his gaze over the Guardsmen again. 'I is 'Eadbasha.' The ork's voice boomed out effortlessly over the transport yard. 'You probably think I got a name like 'Eadbasha because I bash 'eads. Well, I do! I bash humie 'eads, I bash ork 'eads and I bash tin can 'eads, but that is not why I is called 'Eadbasha. I is 'Eadbasha because I is blessed by Gork and Mork. If I bash me 'ead I get visions 'bout the future.

'Gork and Mork 'ave told me to gather a Waaagh! The biggest Waaagh! you ever seen. Gork and Mork 'ave told me I 'ave to build a wotsit called, an effigee, and loads of boyz will come to join me Waaagh!

'I 'ad 'eaps of stinkin' grots to build this effigee, but one stupid weirdboy blows 'imself up and kills most of 'em. You humies are my slaves now. You humies are gonna build for me.'

'Eadbasha's eyes fell on the Guardsmen from Barracks Five. He caught sight of Urzog still holding the arm of the recently deceased Trooper Bern and stomped towards him.

Urzog was visibly shaken by the sudden attention from the mammoth warboss. 'Uh, hi, boss.'

'Eadbasha's eyes thinned as he looked down at Bern and then back to Urzog. 'Why dis humie dead? I told ya not to kill da humies.'

'Sorry, boss, 'e wouldn't come out so I grabbed 'im by da 'ead and 'is zoggin' 'ead come right off.'

The warboss stared at Urzog for a long, tense moment and then a look of disgust crossed his features. 'Puny humies. Dey die if ya pull their 'eads off. Dey ain't tough like da boyz. Still, these are my humies. You don't pull off their 'eads unless I tells ya to pull off their 'eads.'

'Yes, boss. Sorry, boss.'

The warboss leaned forward. 'Else I will pull your 'ead off.'

'Yes, boss,' Urzog said, his deep voice wavering in the presence of the larger ork.

'Eadbasha turned to the bizarre mekboy, who was still watching the gretchin dismantle the truck. 'Mekboy Rukaz!'

The mekboy turned. He wore a pair of green-lensed goggles, one lens at least four times larger than the other. He pushed the goggles up and sat them on top of his head.

'Yes?'

'That's yes, *boss*, you zoggin' brainy git.'

Rukaz removed a spanner from his belt, shoved it into his ear and wiggled it around as if scratching an itch. He pulled it out and examined the end. Apparently satisfied with whatever he'd removed, he returned his attention to the enormous warboss. Van Veenan could tell 'Eadbasha was irritated by this obvious display of contempt. 'Yes, boss?'

A throaty growl escaped 'Eadbasha's clenched teeth. ''Ere is your new workers. Put 'em to good use otherwise I'mma 'ave to come back 'ere and give you a right krumpin.'

Mekboy Rukaz lifted the spanner to his forehead and pulled it away in a salute. 'You got it, boss.'

'Eadbasha growled again before turning away. 'Zoggin' smartboy git,' he muttered before calling out orders. 'You nobz get on back to 'eadquarters. Guards, stay 'ere with your humies. Don't kill 'em.'

When 'Eadbasha and the larger orks had walked away, Mekboy Rukaz looked at the gathered Guardsmen. A large zap of blue electricity jumped between the coils on his back and the muscles in his face all seemed to momentarily contract. 'I ain't never used humies before but you must be smarter than the grots, and probably smarter than the other so-called smartboyz I 'ave to deal with.'

'Oi!' Another mekboy looked up from some contraption on the ground in front of him.

'Quiet, Groblok,' Rukaz said, 'I'm the big mek and I'll say what I like about your lack of smarts until you prove otherwise.' Rukaz returned his attention to the Guardsmen. 'What's going to happen is simple. I is going to build the boss his Waaagh! machine and prove that I is the best mek there ever was, and then he can go off and have loads of fights.' Rukaz waved dismissively, as if he didn't care much for what 'Eadbasha had planned. 'You lot just has to do what I says. First, we're getting these humie trukks stripped of everything that don't make 'em go.'

Rukaz started calling orders and soon each barracks had been organised into separate work details. They began climbing over the Munitorum trucks with whatever tools they were handed and started stripping them back to bare chassis and engine. There were several attempts by the more valiant troopers to refuse to work or to use the tools to attack the orks. These brief revolutions were quickly, and messily, put down by the ork guards, until the Guardsmen realised, as van Veenan already had, they weren't going to fight their way out of this.

'So what, sarge,' Corporal Trotter said as she looked over at van Veenan, 'just like that we're not Guardsmen any more, we're damn slaves for the greenskins? The Emperor would rather see us dead than working for the xenos scum.'

'You listen to me, trooper,' van Veenan replied. 'Don't be mistaken, you might be a prisoner but you're still an Imperial Guardsman. We all are. But I've been around long enough to know that the chief duty of a Guardsman is keeping your arse alive. And that's what we're going to do.'

CHAPTER THREE

Over the next few weeks the Guardsmen fell into as much of a routine as was possible amidst the anarchy of the orks. Some days they waited hours before Urzog came to collect them and take them to the transport yard. Other days they were in the yard before Rotauri's red sun rose. Some days they received three square meals. Other days they received nothing. Van Veenan might have considered all this a deliberate confusion tactic by their captors had it not been obvious that mayhem was part of daily life for the greenskins.

Once the trucks had been stripped they were used to carry small groups of Guardsmen on heavily guarded convoy trips to the promethium refinery. There they would pillage power systems, turbines, pressurised tanks and whatever other machinery Mekboy Rukaz had demanded.

The remaining Guardsmen worked in the yard under the scattered direction of Rukaz and the other mekboys. They began bolting, welding and smashing together contraptions with little idea of what they were doing. There were mounds of twisted cabling snaking across the ground, strapped-together powercells humming disconcertingly and piles upon piles of sheet metal being bent and hammered into whatever shapes the meks could draw in the dirt or explain with cursing and wild gesticulation at the Guardsmen. All around them was a constant cacophony of shouting orks, the crashes of collapsing metal and the screams of humans as the greenskins' construction process went horribly, violently wrong.

Van Veenan felt the kick of the rivet gun as he punched rivets into the join along two sheets of metal. For much of the last few weeks it had been easy to think Mekboy Rukaz and the other manic meks had even less idea what they were doing than the Guardsmen. Now though, van Veenan could see their mad vision taking shape. The metal curve he was securing in place was part of a large foot, the matching one being built across the yard. Cables were being laid out in long strands among large steel beams that would make up the legs. The greenskins meant it when they said they were building an effigy: what looked to be emerging from the bedlam was a crude but enormous statue of an ork.

'Oi! Ogbrok! I know it was you wot stole me teef!'

Van Veenan looked up to see an ork storming across the yard. It was dragging a large-headed axe through the dirt behind it. The angry snarl on its face revealed a gummy mouth missing all but two teeth. An ork supervising a group of Guardsmen nearby turned.

'You shouldn't 'ave passed out and left 'em lyin' around then, Rarzug,' the ork, obviously Ogbrok, replied.

'They was in me gob!' Rarzug roared as he ran forward, raising his axe.

Every day van Veenan saw arguments like this break out between the greenskins and erupt into hand-to-hand combat or full-blown firefights; on one notable occasion he had even seen an ork ramming a live grenade down another ork's throat.

Ogbrok reached down and yanked a hammer from the hand of a nearby Guardsman. He sidestepped and Rarzug's wild swing missed, the axe head burying itself halfway into the dirt. Ogbrok swung his hammer, connecting with a brutal impact upon the other ork's cheekbone. Rarzug's face snapped to the side spraying dark crimson blood in a spatter that almost reached van Veenan five yards away. Rarzug stumbled but somehow didn't drop from the blow. Ogbrok slammed into his stomach, tackling him to the ground. When Rarzug scampered to his feet, retrieved his axe and lopped Ogbrok's hand off, the watching greenskins cheered. But it was when Ogbrok began hitting Rarzug in the face with his bare, bleeding stump that they really roared their approval.

With the guards distracted, van Veenan watched a group of half a dozen Guardsmen make a run for a low section in the orks' crude fence. They'd chosen a spot midway between two of the guard towers where the poorly constructed barrier had sagged under its own excessive weight, no doubt gambling on the inaccuracy of ork weapons and hoping they could make it over the fence and into the forest before being unceremoniously blown apart by shoota rounds. Van Veenan had to admit they'd selected the best place to make such a brazen escape. That said, this brazen escape was still incredibly stupid. No doubt a commissar like 'Hard Nuts' had riled them up with nonsense about courage and duty.

Catching sight of the attempt, another group of Guardsmen made a break for the same section of fence. Van Veenan could see the calculations running through the minds of the Barracks Five troopers around him. He reached out and grabbed the back of one trooper's shirt just as they were about to take off.

'Don't,' he said.

Meanwhile, some of the orks had noticed the escaping Guardsmen sprinting for the perimeter. 'Oi! Humies are tryin' to run!'

'They're going to make it, sergeant major,' Corporal Trotter said. 'Let's go.'

'No.' Van Veenan looked at her. The orks in the guard towers hadn't even raised their weapons. They seemed completely unconcerned. 'Trust me.'

The first of the escaping Guardsmen reached the bottom of the fence and jumped onto it. He began scaling the fence, driven into a frenzied climb by panic and adrenaline.

'See, sarge!' Trotter said. 'We should have gone.' Van Veenan could see the disappointment in her eyes, disappointment that seemed to border on betrayal.

The next trooper planted his foot down to propel himself onto the fence and was met by a reverberating boom. The ground ballooned up under his feet in the black sooty explosion of a landmine. The Guardsman who had trod on the mine, plus the five or six nearest to him, vanished in the smoky burst. The explosion threw the remaining Guardsmen near the fence in all directions, most with fewer body parts than before. The air was full of sprays of gore and screams. The Guardsman on the fence was lifted into the air by the shock wave expanding beneath him. When he eventually fell back down, three of the steel fence spikes impaled him through the leg, stomach and chest. He didn't have time to scream.

The sound of orks roaring in approval filled the camp.

Van Veenan turned his attention back to his rivet gun. Corporal Trotter and the other Guardsmen of Barracks Five watched him in silence before they too had no choice but to return to their construction. Commissar Hardnuss approached and crouched beside van Veenan, feigning working on the foot.

'These troopers look up to you,' the commissar said, keeping her voice low. 'That coward Lieutenant Pokato is content to sit around and expect rescue to come for us. That may not happen. I know you've been protecting them in your own way but the troops need a leader willing to do more than wait around and, like it or not, that leader is you. I've given you three weeks, sergeant major, but you have done nothing.'

Van Veenan fired another rivet into the metal. 'On the contrary,' he said, admiring his handiwork, 'I think my riveting skills have come a long way.'

'You need to drop this act, van Veenan,' Hardnuss said. 'You cover it up with your sharp wit and cynicism, but you are afraid.'

Van Veenan looked at Hardnuss. 'Commissar, I can assure you I'm not afraid of the greenskins.'

'I didn't say you were afraid of the greenskins. I said you were afraid. I know who you are, van Veenan, and so, I should remind you, do the troops. Sergeant Marcus van Veenan of the Talissian Guards, sent to the Second Rapture Penal Legion for insubordination after the disaster of Endota Prime. Yet here you are, still alive and back in the ranks of the Astra Militarum, and with a promotion no less. You have survived the penal legions, van Veenan – that is all but unheard of. You must be aware of the rumours that swirl around the regiment about you?'

Van Veenan shrugged as he fired home another rivet. 'I try not to pay attention to regimental gossip.'

'Most believe you blessed by the God-Emperor Himself. Many say you did something so remarkable they had no choice but to release you from the penal legions – single-handedly killed a tyranid queen or rescued a squad of Adeptus Astartes or destroyed an entire battleship of the Archenemy. Others say you escaped from the penal legions in an elaborate and daring scheme.'

'I assure you, commissar, the only remarkable thing I did to earn a pardon from the penal legions was being lucky. I think I just stayed alive long enough that they got sick of me.'

'That may be, but the troops won't believe it. They want a hero. If you can make it out of a penal legion then you can make it out of this – and you can take them with you.'

Van Veenan closed his eyes and sighed. 'Commissar–'

'That,' Commissar Hardnuss cut him off, 'is what you're afraid of. You're afraid of caring about these Guardsmen. I do not presume to know what happened to you during your time in the penal legions but it has clearly warped your view of the Imperium. I could very well execute you for cowardice, but I do not believe you a coward. If duty alone will not convince you to lead these men and women, then do it because it will keep them alive. It doesn't matter whether the rumours are true, sergeant major. They believe you are the hero that can get them through this.'

Van Veenan took a moment before answering. 'Let's say we managed an Emperor's-own miracle and got out of this camp, and then somehow defeated the orks or got off this planet, what then? These troops would just end up chasing down another deadly foe on another worthless planet. I won't lead more soldiers to their deaths, commissar. I'm done with that shit.'

The commissar stared at him.

'I bet you wish you had a bolt pistol after all, don't you?' van Veenan said.

Commissar Hardnuss sucked in a deep breath but, saying nothing, she rose and walked away. Van Veenan began firing rivets into metal with decidedly more force than was necessary.

CHAPTER FOUR

With hundreds of Guardsmen working every day, the giant ork effigy soon came together. The feet, legs and torso went up rapidly, built from a frame of steel overlaid with an incongruous collection of metal sheets, the whole thing wreathed in rickety slopes of improvised scaffolding. As construction of the torso neared completion, the enormous ork was already taller than an Imperial Knight.

The men and women of Barracks Five had spent the last two weeks working on the upper section of the left arm and, having finished their labours, had been locked in their barracks early that evening. The arm would be craned into position the next day. Van Veenan lay on his bunk, tossing his sock-ball at the roof, listening to the troopers discussing the possibility of sabotage.

'It's likely Rukaz will get us to lift the arm,' Corporal Trotter was saying. 'Hook it up to the crane or something. It would be easy to ensure an accident happens.'

Skelton was nodding enthusiastically. 'A little loose when we lock the hook in place, maybe we give the main pin a bit of a cut, and wham,' he smashed a fist into his open palm, 'that arm comes crashing down and stops construction. If we're lucky, it might take out the whole bloody effigy and kill a few greenskins at the same time.'

'No. No way. That's too risky,' Lieutenant Pokato said. 'It's possible we kill or injure Guardsmen, or the orks discover what's happened and punish us. It doesn't matter if we finish the effigy. You don't really believe their insane superstitions?'

'Sure,' Corporal Trotter said, ''Eadbasha is a bloody nutcase but what happens to us when that thing is finished? You think we get retirement and a pension?'

'We don't act recklessly,' Pokato said. 'That will keep us alive.'

'Maybe there's a risk some of us will die, sir,' Trotter said, 'but that thing is being built quickly. It'll be done soon and then we're definitely dead. If you really believe Imperial reinforcements are coming then the longer we slow down construction, the better. My vote is with dropping the arm.'

'I am the ranking officer, your "vote" means nothing,' Lieutenant Pokato said. 'I will make the final decision on any plan that puts the men and women of this barracks in danger.'

'Lieutenant, Corporal Trotter is right. The longer the construction takes, the better – more time for reinforcements to arrive or more time to plan an escape,' Skelton said. 'Right, sergeant major?'

Van Veenan turned to see the Guardsmen looking at him. He thought back to what Hardnuss had said, that these troops wanted him to lead them out of this. What was holding him back? Sure, some of them would die, but Guardsmen died, countless thousands every day. It hadn't stopped him leading troops into danger before. He'd stood beside them as they faced down multi-limbed aliens whose gaping mouths dripped with acidic saliva, he'd made them disobey orders at the risk of instant execution, he'd led penal legionnaires into suicidal charges against blood-soaked cultists. So why wasn't he doing it now?

Because he was tired of never-ending war and he was tired of leading troopers like those around him to their deaths. How many had he seen slaughtered? And yet, he was still here. Guardsmen died. That's what they did. But not Marcus van Veenan. He survived. Time and time again. What on Holy Terra did the God-Emperor want with him? What difference could he make in a galaxy like this?

Van Veenan looked from Lieutenant Pokato to Skelton. 'The lieutenant is the ranking officer, trooper. It's his decision to make.'

Van Veenan saw the disappointment on Skelton's face. It was finally dawning on him, and on the rest of them, that Sergeant Major Marcus van Veenan would not be their hero. Skelton looked away in thinly veiled disgust.

'Yes,' Pokato said. 'At least the company sergeant major is setting a good example by remembering the chain of command. Tomorrow, we lift the arm in place and there is to be no sabotage. Is that clear?'

'Yes, sir,' the Guardsmen muttered.

'Good then,' the lieutenant said. 'Now everyone get some rest.'

After the gathering split apart, Commissar Hardnuss wandered over to van Veenan's bunk. Van Veenan caught his ball of rolled-up socks and looked at her. 'I know what you're going to say, commissar.'

'And you know as well as I what will happen tomorrow,' Hardnuss said.

'What's that?' Van Veenan asked.

'They will sabotage that arm anyway.'

'That's a fair possibility, yes.'

Hardnuss looked at van Veenan with that adamantine stare he was sure commissars practised in depth at the schola progenium. 'You know what the greenskins are building.'

Van Veenan nodded.

'Whatever happens,' Hardnuss said, 'remember that you could have helped these troopers.'

The next day, as anticipated, the troopers of Barracks Five were put to work readying the arm for its crane lift. They wrapped it in enormous slings secured with a U-bolt thicker than a person's arm, a U-bolt that would carry the entire weight of the load.

Van Veenan watched them secure the lifting gear. They huddled together in a way that wouldn't have seemed suspicious had van Veenan not seen Trooper Skelton slip a cutting torch into his pocket earlier. The Guardsmen had arranged themselves to block the view but van Veenan was certain Skelton was cutting through just enough of the U-bolt that it would give way and drop the arm in a cacophony of noisy destruction. When the Guardsmen drew apart, the cutting torch was gone, hastily hidden away.

Van Veenan scanned the yard but none of the greenskins seemed to have noticed. Mekboy Rukaz was busy yelling insulting instructions at a group of Guardsmen who were soldering a wild collection of coloured wiring onto what looked to be a helmet. The other meks were also busy either instructing Guardsmen or working on things themselves. Even Urzog, who was supposed to be watching the troopers of Barracks Five, didn't appear to have seen anything. If there was one benefit of having ork captors it was that, if they weren't engaged in fighting, they didn't have long attention spans.

Van Veenan noticed someone watching though – Lieutenant Pokato. He was standing some distance from the other members of Barracks Five, tinkering with some small contraption, or at least pretending to. In fact, he was standing awfully close to Urzog. When Pokato covered his mouth with his fist and coughed three times, Urzog looked to him and then stomped towards the Guardsmen without hesitation.

'Oi!' Urzog called to them. 'Wot are you humies doin'?'

'Nothing,' Trotter said, 'just getting ready to lift this like Mekboy Rukaz said.'

Urzog's eyes narrowed as he cast a suspicious gaze from the Guardsmen to the straps around the arm. He moved forward and pulled at each sling before he grabbed the U-bolt and looked at it.

'Mekboy Rukaz!' Urzog shouted.

'I'm busy!' Rukaz replied, not looking up from the Guardsmen working on the wired helmet.

'Da humies 'ave been tamperin'!'

Rukaz, suddenly very interested, turned and walked to where Urzog stood holding the lifting lug.

'Look 'ere,' Urzog said, displaying the damaged U-bolt. 'This ain't supposed to be like this, is it?'

Rukaz bent closer to inspect the bolt. He pulled his goggles down over his eyes and muttered to himself. 'High temperature cut through load-bearing structural element.' He lifted his goggles and growled. His head twitched to the side as sparks jumped from the coils on his back. He looked at the Guardsmen. 'Who's tryin' to break my gubbinz?'

No one answered.

'Search 'em,' Rukaz said.

Urzog moved between the Guardsmen. They stood tall, their heads high, staring at Urzog as he patted them down.

Van Veenan looked to where Pokato stood watching the situation unfold. Their eyes met briefly before Pokato looked away. Van Veenan's knuckles grew white as he unconsciously squeezed his hands into tight fists. He looked back to the Guardsmen in time to see Urzog roughly patting his thick green hands down over Skelton's torso.

''Ere we are,' Urzog said, pulling the cutting torch free from where Skelton had stuffed it inside his jacket. 'Wot's this then?'

'Proof,' Rukaz said, reaching out and taking the torch. 'That's wot. Round up the humies. I'm gonna get the boss.'

Within minutes the Guardsmen were formed up in the yard. Mekboy Rukaz and Big Nob 'Ardskull stood before them. Warboss 'Eadbasha stomped back and forth, his hydraulically assisted limbs scratching and hissing as he paced. He was deep in whatever constituted thought for an ork. Eventually he stopped and spun to face the gathered Guardsmen.

'I thought I'd been good to you humies. I ain't let my boyz kill none of you 'cept the ones that tried to escape. It ain't easy keepin' boyz from krumpin' you. Now you tryin' to sabotage my effigee. I should just tell the boyz to smash you all.' Van Veenan felt the buzz of excitement course through the orks gathered all around them. They grunted, fidgeted – some even let out whoops of joyful anticipation. They wanted nothing but permission to do exactly that.

'I ain't gonna do that though,' the warboss continued, the orks' anticipation turning to groans of disappointment. 'Eadbasha paused, scratching at his chin with the end of his power klaw. 'Gork and Mork told me to build this effigee. They can tell me 'ow you should be punished. 'Ardskull!'

'Ardskull sagged under the call of the warboss. When he approached, 'Eadbasha grabbed him by the shoulders. 'Ardskull, with practised resignation, lowered his head and displayed his shining metallic scalp to the warboss.

'Eadbasha reared his head back and slammed his forehead onto 'Ardskull's iron dome. The sound of the impact, which would have been enough to compress a human spine down to the size of an ammo box, resounded through the yard. 'Ardskull fell back, unconscious. Warboss 'Eadbasha was still standing, swaying gently in a circle. His red eyes had rolled back in their sockets. His drooping eyelids fluttered. He stayed in that trance-like state for what grew to become an awkwardly long time. The orks, accustomed to their leader's odd decision-making strategy, waited patiently.

Eventually, as van Veenan began wondering whether the ork was permanently broken, 'Eadbasha's eyes rolled forward again. He shook his misshapen head as if clearing away a daze and then spoke.

'Gork and Mork 'ave spoken to me!'

The orks roared in approval.

'Gork and Mork 'ave told me we need these humies to finish buildin.' We can't krump 'em all but we is gonna teach them a lesson. The humies is gonna fight in the pit!'

The orks roared and began to chant. 'In the pit! In the pit! In the pit!'

The pit, like most ork things, was not imaginatively named. Just outside the prison camp, the greenskins had dug a hole in the ground almost as big as Barracks Five and with walls high enough that it would be impossible to climb out. All around the outside, on storage containers stacked into tiered seating, the orks of Nok 'Eadbasha's warband had gathered to watch the spectacle.

Under instructions from 'Eadbasha, the orks had selected two Guardsmen from each barracks. From Barracks Five they had picked Moko, a trooper van Veenan barely knew, and the giant Trooper Skelton, no doubt because it had been him wielding the cutting torch. Those two, and the other ten Guardsmen chosen to fight, fidgeted nervously under ork guard near the edge of the pit.

The remaining Guardsmen of the Rotauri First sat in a caged section of the seating, made to watch the fighting just like the orks around them – though the mood among the Guardsmen was far more sober than that of the greenskins. Grots with trays hanging from straps around their necks walked up and down the seating handing out refreshments, and the orks greedily grabbed cups of a thick, fermented fungus drink and began tearing into hunks of cooked squig flesh. Some orks had even painted their faces with blue and yellow warpaint and chosen which of the Guardsmen they would root for. They shouted out the number of 'teef' they were willing to wager, and a grot would run frantically over to collect and record the amount. Most of them bet on, as seemed appropriate for orks, 'da biggest humies.'

'All right, boyz,' 'Eadbasha bellowed to the gathered horde. 'I know we been buildin' stuff 'stead of wreckin' stuff but we gonna get some entertainment today. We gonna watch some humies krump each other!'

The orks roared and stamped their feet in a cacophony of appreciation.

'Humies,' 'Eadbasha said, turning to the selected Guardsmen, 'dis real simple. Two of ya go in and one of ya comes out. You keep on killin' each other till there's one of ya left. Got it?'

The Guardsmen didn't reply.

'I said got it, ya zoggin' humie gits?!' 'Eadbasha roared.

The Guardsmen nodded.

'Good.' 'Eadbasha turned to the crowd of orks. 'Let's have some fightin' then!'

The roar from the greenskins was even louder. ''Ere we go! 'Ere we go! 'Ere we go!' they began to chant. ''Ere we go! 'Ere we go! 'Ere we gooooo-oh!'

Van Veenan sat in silence, staring down at the pit. He was tense, his breaths short and sharp, barely able to contain his outrage. There were two targets of van Veenan's anger, and strangely neither of them had green skin. First, he was furious at himself because Hardnuss' words echoed in his head like an annoying itch: *remember that you could have helped.* But most of his rage was directed at someone else. His eyes searched the crowd of Guardsmen and found him – Lieutenant Pokato, that slimy Cerillian mud serpent.

There was little ceremony to the beginning of the fights. The first two Guardsmen were simply kicked into the pit by their ork guards. Van Veenan knew one of them – Sergeant Tuhoe, a veteran with Second Company. The other was a young trooper he didn't recognise. All around them the orks bellowed and roared and chanted. 'Fight! Fight! Fight!'

'Oi!' 'Eadbasha yelled. 'You can zoggin' start now!'

'They can't make us fight each other, son,' Tuhoe said to the terrified trooper opposite him.

When it became clear the humans weren't going to attack each other, the watching orks made their disappointment known. The roars and chants became boos and hisses. Empty drink cups and half-eaten squig legs were pelted down into the pit.

''Ere,' 'Eadbasha said, 'last chance, humies.' He threw two long-bladed knives onto the dirt between their feet. 'Maybe you need some cuttas coz of ya tiny pink hands.'

The Guardsmen remained unmoved.

'You is my slaves!' 'Eadbasha screamed at them. 'You build when I tells you to build and you fight when I tells you to fight! Now, last chance or I'll krump you meself!'

The warboss waited for a moment, tapping his steel boot impatiently on the ground, then, when Sergeant Tuhoe and his opponent did not leap into vicious combat, he growled, a deep rumble that rose angrily from his throat. He jumped into the pit, landing with a heavy thump.

Both Guardsmen stumbled backwards, but Sergeant Tuhoe showed the fighting spirit of a veteran warrior of the God-Emperor, recovering quickly and facing down the towering foe. The young trooper did not have such a strong resolve, and collapsed back from the nine-foot ork. 'Eadbasha reached out and caught the falling trooper by the front of his shirt. The Guardsman quivered in the ork's grip, paralysed with terror, a wet stain rapidly covering the front of his trousers.

Sergeant Tuhoe moved forward, as if there was anything he could do, but 'Eadbasha reached out and grabbed him with his free hand, the three digits of his power klaw closing with mechanical force around the sergeant's torso, pinning his arms to his sides.

'I said dis was simple,' 'Eadbasha roared to the Guardsmen still waiting on the edge of the pit. 'One of you dies or both of you dies.' And, with the assistance of the powerful hydraulic rams encasing his arms, he slammed the two Guardsmen together. They impacted face to face like high-speed mag-trains going in opposite directions on the same track. The Guardsmen's heads didn't crush so much as they burst like bags of bright red liquid. 'Eadbasha tossed the two headless corpses to the ground and turned his blood-covered face back to the Guardsmen. 'Whichever of you humies is the last survivor gets to live – dat's a prize to fight for, ain't it? So fight!'

When the next two Guardsmen in the pit refused to fight as well, 'Eadbasha grabbed a burna from a nearby ork and sprayed them with superheated burning promethium. Their screams were short-lived but horrifying.

It was the third fight when things turned. Van Veenan watched as a Guardsman from Barracks Two – Ratley, he'd overheard Hardnuss say – was dropped into the pit to face off against Trooper Skelton. Both Guardsmen looked at each other and hesitantly glanced up at 'Eadbasha, who was readying the burna for another round of exterminations. Van Veenan could sense the desperation beginning to infect the two in the pit and spreading to those still yet to make their appearance.

Van Veenan leapt to his feet. 'Stand your ground,' he called into the pit. 'Whatever happens.'

Skelton looked up and his gaze met van Veenan's. There was sadness in the huge Guardsman's eyes and something else – an apology maybe, perhaps disappointment. *You're no hero, sergeant major,* he seemed to say, *and neither am I.*

Skelton reached down and picked up one of the long-bladed knives. He kicked the other across the ground to Ratley.

Van Veenan rushed down the tiered seating in long, loping strides, pushing and stumbling through the crowd of watching Guardsmen. He crashed into the cage separating them from the pit and slammed his fists against it.

'Skelton! Don't you fragging raise a weapon against a fellow Guardsman!'

An ork guard was swift to reach van Veenan, punching him right through the front of the cage, buckling the metal around the impact. Van Veenan was thrown into the front row of Guardsmen, his cut face leaking blood. Dazed, he shouted towards the pit. 'Don't do it!'

Skelton waited for Ratley to pick up the knife and then, ignoring van Veenan's shouts of protest, charged at the smaller trooper. He dodged Ratley's weak effort to defend himself and drove the blade hilt-deep into the other Guardsman's stomach. And, in that moment, van Veenan knew the orks had broken them. The moment the soldiers in that pit turned on each other, the orks had won in a way they hadn't even when they seized control of Rotauri: they had crushed the troopers' humanity, reduced them to the same level as the barbaric xenos.

And so it went from then. Guardsman versus Guardsman to the roaring delight of the orks. Few resisted fighting any more and the orks received their entertainment. Guardsmen slashed at each other with the greenskins' cuttas, losing chunks of flesh and entire limbs in the process. When one went down their opponent would leap, taking the fight to the ground and beating or hacking them to death in a brutal display of desperate viciousness. After hours of fighting it was Skelton who overcame all others and was ultimately the last one standing.

He stood in the centre of the pit, his chest heaving. His face and what remained of his once-proud Astra Militarum uniform was splattered with dark, drying blood. The dirt floor of the pit was slick with spilled ichor. Skelton looked up at the roaring orks and hung his head. He dropped to his knees as if the weight of realisation had fallen on him.

''Ere is da winning humie!' 'Eadbasha shouted to the cheers of the ork crowd. 'But before you get your prize dere's one more opponent you get to face as a special bonus for being da toughest. Da ork pit-fightin' champion, Mikrull da Greenest!'

Skelton, physically and emotionally beaten, barely looked up as an enormous heap of bright green muscle leapt into the pit, opened his arms wide and bellowed out an immense, 'WAAAAAGH!'

Skelton grabbed the two cuttas and rose to his feet to face the ork gladiator, but it was evident he was struggling to stand. Wounded and exhausted, he had little fight left.

Unarmed, Mikrull stalked towards Skelton. Skelton swung a cutta at Mikrull's throat, having to reach up at the target above his head, but Mikrull caught Skelton's wrist in his thick fingers. Skelton wasted no time in swinging the second cutta but Mikrull caught that too. The ork held Skelton by both wrists, lifted him into the air and, with a flick of his arms, slammed Skelton face first onto the ground.

Skelton lay immobile in the blood-soaked dirt of the pit. Mikrull roared again and the watching greenskins joined him. He lifted his large foot and brought it down on the back of Skelton's head. The Rotauri First stared in abject horror as Skelton's skull was crushed beneath the ork gladiator's heel. None of the Guardsmen could look away, none except van Veenan, who was staring only at Lieutenant Pokato.

When the Guardsmen returned to their barracks, van Veenan's rage had not abated. He was seething with it, his jaw clenched hard enough that he thought he might crack teeth.

The troopers of Barracks Five entered their now depressingly familiar accommodations with their eyes down. Van Veenan, on the other hand, burst into the building and strode towards Pokato. The lieutenant's eyes grew wide at the sight of the sergeant major, his bloodied face a storm of fury.

'Sergeant major,' Pokato said, retreating in panic. 'What are–'

Van Veenan reached the lieutenant and interrupted him with a stinging right jab perfectly placed on his nose. Pokato stumbled back against the wall and slid to the floor in a jumble of arms and legs. The barracks was quiet, everyone trying to process the day's events, but now it fell into shocked silence.

'Sergeant major,' Pokato whimpered, touching his nose and pulling away his fingers to inspect the blood flowing freely from his nostrils. 'You have struck a superior officer!'

'Oh, Emperor's teeth,' said van Veenan, 'shut your prepubescent face, you treacherous little shit.'

'How dare you! I am an officer and the son of the governor.' Pokato turned to Commissar Hardnuss, who stood a short distance away. 'Commissar, I demand you discipline the sergeant major. This is unacceptable.'

'Ordinarily I would agree wholeheartedly, lieutenant,' Hardnuss said. 'Striking a superior requires severe disciplinary action.' She walked over to where van Veenan loomed over Pokato. 'However, regulations are non-specific about prisoner-of-war situations. Given the strain placed on all of us over the last month I think it's suitable to let this go. Plus there are mitigating circumstances.'

'And what are those?' Pokato asked. 'What possible circumstances excuse the breakdown of discipline within the Astra Militarum?'

'Simple,' Hardnuss said, 'you *are* a treacherous little shit.'

'Commissar!' Pokato blustered. 'This is a disgrace. I am the only officer–'

Van Veenan interrupted Pokato yet again by slamming his boot on the man's neck and pinning him back against the wall. The lieutenant choked and gasped. 'What… are you… doing?!'

'Tell them what you did,' van Veenan said, in a tone that would plant fear in the heart of just about anyone but a Space Marine.

'Somebody... do something.' Pokato's eyes were panicked.

'Tell them what you did.'

'I... I don't know what you're... talking about.'

Van Veenan steadily increased the pressure. Pokato grabbed at van Veenan's boot, but he had little hope of getting free of the veteran Guardsman. 'Tell them you ratted them out. Tell them how you told the orks they were going to sabotage the lift of the arm.'

'No,' Pokato said, his face turning red, his voice mangled from the pressure van Veenan was applying to his voice box. 'I didn't.'

Van Veenan grabbed the uprights of a bunk for leverage and pressed more of his weight down. Pokato began to flail and hit weakly, now almost unable to breathe.

'Tell them how you gave the orks a signal when Trooper Skelton started cutting.'

'You what?' Trotter said from nearby. 'You told the greenskins?'

Pokato shook his head.

'Tell these troopers the truth!' Van Veenan roared, unleashing all the fury he'd carried back with him from the fighting pit.

'Okay,' Pokato rasped.

Van Veenan pulled his foot away. Pokato took a deep, ragged breath.

'Okay,' he said. 'I told the greenskins... about the sabotage... I was trying to protect–'

'Trying to protect what, you conniving bastard?' Trotter said. 'I had friends in that pit. Skelton–' Her voice caught and she couldn't go on.

'You're a fragging traitor is what you are,' another said.

All the Guardsmen in the barracks were looming towards Pokato. His eyes grew even more terrified at the sight of the gathering mob. Van Veenan didn't move. He let the troopers of Barracks Five stalk towards Pokato, who hurriedly stood. 'Stop. Listen. I ordered you not to attempt that sabotage because I knew if you succeeded even more of us would be punished.'

'You're trying to act like you protected these men and women,' van Veenan said, 'but you turned on them.'

'Maybe we should have a fighting pit of our own,' Trotter said. 'You can go first. Against all of us.'

Pokato stumbled as he moved sideways along the wall of the barracks, desperately trying to put some distance between himself and the Guardsmen. He rushed to the door and began banging on it with his fist. 'Help! Let me out!' He bashed the door as hard as he could. 'They're going to tear me apart!'

The door unlocked and swung open. Urzog was standing there. 'Wot is all the zoggin' racket?'

'They're going to kill me,' Pokato said as he hurried out of the barracks, pushing past Urzog.

'Oi!' Urzog yelled. 'Dis humie is runnin'!'

'What?' Pokato said, as he stopped and turned, his voice desperate. 'No, I'm not running. They're going to kill me in there.'

Two orks grabbed Pokato roughly by the arms.

'I'm not trying to escape. I'm the one who told you about the sabotage, remember?'

'You ain't allowed out of your barracks after the door gets locked, humie,' said one of the orks that had hold of him. 'Da boss said it's the only time we's allowed to krump you.'

'Please,' Pokato said, 'they're going to tear me apart.'

'They gonna tear you apart?' the ork said.

'Yes,' Pokato answered. 'Help me.'

'Humies aren't good at tearin' apart. You ain't got strong arms like us boyz. We's show you tearin' apart.'

'No!' Pokato pleaded. 'Stop! You said you'd keep me alive!'

'I never said dat.'

'Urzog did,' Pokato squealed. 'Ask him. We had a deal.'

Urzog stared at the lieutenant and lifted his broad shoulders in a shrug. 'Don't remember.'

The orks holding Pokato looked at each other and also shrugged. They pulled in opposite directions, and with a pop and a squelching tear they ripped off both of Pokato's arms. He screamed, howling in pain and terror and calling out desperately for mercy as blood spurted from each side of his torso. The orks looked at each other again, then beat Lieutenant Tam Pokato, son of the governor of Rotauri, to death with his own arms, howling joyously as they did so.

The Guardsmen from Barracks Five looked on through the doorway.

'Couldn't have happened to a nicer guy,' van Veenan said. 'At least he died like a Guardsman even if he never lived like one.' He turned to look at Commissar Hardnuss. 'Fine then, commissar, I guess you get your wish. I'm the ranking officer now. Let's figure out how to get the Holy Throne out of here.'

CHAPTER FIVE

Van Veenan moved with the mass of Guardsmen making the daily trudge to the transport yard. Six weeks they'd been captives now. Six long weeks working as slaves for the greenskins. But at least van Veenan had focus. He had a mission and whenever he felt himself sliding back into despondency, he just had to remember the way Skelton had looked at him from the pit. That was enough to remind him that he couldn't abandon these troopers, not the way the Imperium apparently had.

Van Veenan approached a group of Guardsmen from Barracks Five. On a nod from him they slowed, slipped their hands into their pockets and turned them inside out, emptying black dirt on the ground. Van Veenan's original idea had been to stealthily dispose of soil by having Guardsmen sew secret pouches inside the bottoms of their trousers, which would be slowly emptied over the course of each day. But the orks had proved so unobservant that dumping pocketfuls of dirt and roughly kicking the piles around was plenty sufficient to remain undetected.

It was still tedious work as they could only move small amounts of dirt at a time, but they'd been doing it for a week straight and with the amount of Guardsmen now involved in van Veenan's scheme, it was startling how much soil they could displace.

Planning for their elaborate escape had begun the night after the pit fights even while Lieutenant Pokato's screams still hung in the air.

'Okay,' van Veenan had explained, 'the concept is simple but will be difficult to pull off. We start a tunnel here in Barracks Five and go straight down, three yards at least. Then we dig a straight shot for a hundred yards before angling back up to the surface. That will bring the tunnel up in the forest beyond the fence. Three yards down should be deep enough that we don't disturb any mines the orks have placed around the perimeter. We'll keep the tunnel small but will still need to reinforce it with wood slats from the beds and shelves, plus whatever else we can take without it being too obvious. We'll dispose of the soil in small batches, which will be the hardest part – other than avoiding certain death if we're caught.'

Just as Commissar Hardnuss had said, most of the Guardsmen believed the stories about van Veenan and they followed his plan to the letter, completely confident that he was guided by the God-Emperor. He didn't have the heart to tell them he was completely improvising. Still, that shouldn't have come as a surprise; he'd been in a lot of unusual situations throughout his career and often improvisation had been the only way out.

After dumping today's soil the Guardsmen entered the yard, walking into the long shadow of the enormous ork effigy that loomed over everything in the camp, a jumble of red and yellow metal panels cut from containers; green sheets pulled from Munitorum truck bodies; and dirty, blackened steel stripped from the promethium refinery. The towering idol was complete but for the lower arms. The angular head, a little undersized for the immense body, was hinged at the jawline and the face and top of the head was folded open. Inside the metallic skull was a chair. Two mekboys, one of which was Rukaz himself, and several grots moved around inside, securing the chair and working to connect and solder a veritable spider's web of wires in place.

Rukaz leaned forward, hanging out of the open head, and yelled to the mekboys on the ground.

'All right, you lot,' he called, 'tell 'em to bring up the weird 'un – and you better get the boss, 'e'll want to see it fire up I 'spose.'

Once Rukaz's order reached them, a group of orks opened the door to a rockcrete bunker ordinarily used to store highly volatile chemicals or ammunition. With a tentativeness rarely seen in the greenskins, four orks entered the bunker while two remained outside with shootas trained on the door. Moments later the four orks re-emerged literally dragging a fifth with them. They pulled it along the ground by chains that were wrapped around it what must have been twenty times, pinning its arms to its side and holding its legs together. The ork squirmed and fought but the heavy chains held tight so that it could do little but flop around like a fish pulled up onto dry land. The ork wore nothing but tattered yellow rags and strapped to its head with a dozen buckles was the colourfully wired helmet van Veenan had seen other Guardsmen making. When, in its desperate thrashing, the chained ork rolled to face the watching Guardsmen, van Veenan saw its eyes were ablaze with a phosphorescent green glow.

'My 'ead!' the ork called out in a pained cry. 'I is gonna blow! Take this thing off so I's can zap somethin'!'

'Bring 'im up 'ere so we can wire 'im into the capacitive amplification unit,' Rukaz called. 'Quickly, you zoggin' gits! Remember what 'appened last time!'

Van Veenan had seen psykers before. Once, when he was still with the Talissian 51st, he'd fought alongside a sanctioned psyker and had watched him manipulate immense towers of flame into swirling vortices and send them out to engulf hordes of slavering tyranids. This chained-up ork must be one of the greenskin psykers, the ones they called weirdboyz. But where the sanctioned psykers van Veenan had seen had been rigorously trained, constantly monitored and covered in holy seals to lend them the resilience of the God-Emperor against the dangers of the warp, the ork weirdboy was physically pulsating with uncontrolled power, ready, like an unpinned grenade, to explode at any moment. Hesitantly, the orks hoisted the weirdboy onto their shoulders and carried it up the scaffolding to the head of the massive construction.

It was hard to see the details from ground level but van Veenan heard Rukaz shouting orders through the screaming and moaning of the weirdboy. They forced it into the chair, strapping it in place with more buckled straps and extra chains. Grots scampered around soldering hanging wires to those spraying out from the helmet. When they'd finished, Rukaz flipped a large lever and with a hydraulic drone the skull of the monstrous ork effigy began to close. Rukaz, the mekboys and the grots hurried out as the face lowered, hiding the still-struggling weirdboy from view.

As Rukaz and his team of assistants descended the scaffolding, the enormous figure of Warboss Nok 'Eadbasha stomped into the yard, orks and grots scampering away at the sound of his hydraulically assisted footfalls. When he reached the ground Mekboy Rukaz completely ignored the warboss. He backed up, his face turned skywards to stare at the head of the giant ork, rubbing his hands together in anticipation.

'Rukaz,' 'Eadbasha said with obvious impatience, 'wot's 'appening then?'

Rukaz turned to look at the warboss. 'We've strapped the weirdboy into the phase-invariant amplifier.'

'Wot?' 'Eadbasha snapped. 'Speak proper, you brainy git.'

He kept it hidden from the much larger ork, but van Veenan noticed the way the mekboy rolled his sharp red eyes. 'The weirdboy's energy is being ampli- made bigger and will shoot out into space so that orks all over the galaxy will feel it.'

'Eadbasha smiled. 'And join my Waaagh! Right. Good. 'Ow is we gonna know if it works?'

Rukaz didn't answer. He just stood watching. Then, the eyes of the ork effigy began to glow with that same light that had emanated from the weirdboy, a bright green illumination that suddenly gave this enormous conglomeration of mismatched metal the eerie sense of being alive. Crackles of energy in curling bolts of emerald ran from the head down the torso before earthing into the ground. The air filled with a faint buzzing and van Veenan felt the hair all over his body stand on end.

'Haha!' Mekboy Rukaz exclaimed. His body jerked with twitches and convulsions as the coils on his back picked up the energy being exuded by the effigy, firing zaps of green straight into his head. 'That's 'ow we know it's gonna work! I told you I was the brainiest mekboy. I knew I could amplify spontaneous emissions out of a weirdboy's 'ead.'

'Yeah, yeah,' Warboss 'Eadbasha said, 'you is a right genius. Now wot?'

'Now we wait,' Rukaz said. 'The signal is being sent out tellin' more boyz to come 'ere, and while that's happening we move on to stage two of construction.'

'Stage two?' 'Eadbasha asked. 'Wot's that?'

'We need to complete the internal fit-out, control and propulsive systems,' Rukaz said. When he noticed the way 'Eadbasha's misshapen forehead furrowed in obvious confusion, he explained, 'We need to make it move.'

There it was, van Veenan thought to himself, confirmation of his and Hardnuss' fears. The ork effigy was not just some enormous statue designed to draw orks from across the galaxy – it was going to be a vast, ambulatory engine of war.

'Yeah,' 'Eadbasha said. 'I know that.'

'Plus we need to fit the weapon systems.'

The warboss' thick green face broke into the widest grin van Veenan had ever seen, showing almost all his crooked teeth and yellowing tusk-like fangs. 'The dakka.'

'Yes,' Rukaz said. 'The dakka.'

While most Guardsmen were in the yard witnessing the ork effigy burst to life with weird energy, inside Barracks Five Commissar Hardnuss and a dozen other troopers worked on the tunnel. Most of the work took place at night, but van Veenan and Hardnuss had taken advantage of the greenskins' inattention to keep a crew digging during the day.

The most difficult thing had been getting through the rockcrete floor. Corporal Trotter and Trooper Williams had been tasked with stealing whatever tools they could to assist with breaking through. They'd ended up with a large rotary-bladed saw and several heavy-headed hammers. The saw had no problem cutting rockcrete but it was slow work and it was loud. Luckily, as more time passed with the orks remaining here in 'Eadbasha's camp and not out slaughtering their way across the galaxy, pit-fighting tournaments among the greenskins had become increasingly common. While the orks drank and roared at one of these pit fights, the residents of Barracks Five used the opportunity to cut through the rockcrete floor in a rear corner of the storeroom. The open square of soil could easily be hidden by dragging a bunk over the tunnel opening.

Tunnel construction was now well under way. Having dug straight down, the Guardsmen had begun work on the long horizontal section. Three troopers worked in shifts in the tight confines at the tunnel face, digging and clearing away the soil with handmade picks and shovels. They loaded a small wheeled cart – also handmade by the Guardsmen – with the dirt they removed. Two ropes were tied to the cart, one coiled up on the floor near the diggers and the other running back to the Guardsmen waiting at the tunnel entrance. When the cart was full, those at the tunnel face would tug on the rope running back down the tunnel. On that signal the Guardsmen at the entrance would pull the cart down to them, empty it out, and then signal for those at the tunnel face to retrieve it and continue.

In this way the tunnel had reached almost thirty yards long and while Guardsmen worked to dig and remove dirt as fast as they could, another group built and installed wooden supports along the tunnel to avoid the roof or walls collapsing.

Commissar Hardnuss stood in the vertical drop at the tunnel entrance, keeping watch and supervising construction. Hardnuss stepped back as the Guardsmen holding this end of the rope nodded and began to pull another cartload of soil down the tunnel. When the cart rattled out of the tunnel entrance, they tipped the load onto the ground and tugged the rope to send it back. Hardnuss set to helping pack the soil into the small pouches that would be distributed among the troops and disposed of during tomorrow's march to the yard.

They were almost finished packing this load when a dull thump came from inside the tunnel, followed by muffled shouts of panic. Moments later one Guardsman, Corporal Tua from Barracks Three, emerged grimy and wide-eyed from the opening.

'Cave in,' he panted, out of breath from a desperate crawl back down the length of the tunnel, 'about twenty yards in. Something gave way. Gemmell, Vercoe and Enoka have been buried.'

'Throne,' Hardnuss said, 'get some shovels and come on.'

She shrugged off her heavy Commissariat greatcoat before grabbing one of the small hand shovels. She all but shoved Corporal Tua aside and dived head first into the tunnel, crawling on hands and knees as quickly as she could into the gloom. The Guardsmen had only managed to secure a handful of lumen globes and used them sparingly, so most of the tunnel was shrouded in darkness.

'Commissar, is that you?' she heard from ahead of her as she reached the location where a pair of troopers were working on reinforcing the tunnel supports. They had a lumen globe with them but the tunnel collapse ahead had filled the air with thick brown dust yet to settle.

'It is,' she responded as she approached. 'What happened?'

'We heard the wood splinter,' one Guardsman said, 'then it all came down.'

'We were working our way along to add more support but we didn't get there in time,' the other added. 'I'm sorry, ma'am.'

She could have told them it was all right, that it wasn't their fault, but she was a commissar and she'd learned long ago that it was best not to let any troopers get comfortable around you – even in this situation. Besides, she feared she was already too late and would not delay further with sentimental nonsense.

'Give me your lumen,' she said, holding her hand out, 'quickly now.'

The Guardsman grabbed it from where it hung on a nail nearby and handed it to her. Without another word Hardnuss hurried into the pitch-darkness ahead. The Guardsmen digging at the tunnel face would have had a lumen globe with them too, but that was buried under collapsed soil now, just as they would be.

As she crawled ahead, the light of her lumen globe fell on the mound of soil marking the location of the collapse. Without hesitation she dropped the globe and began to dig. Corporal Tua was soon beside her, both of them shovelling soil. The dirt, freshly dropped to fill the tunnel opening, was loose and easy to displace, but there was a lot of it and in the tight confines they could only move so much at a time.

It took ten minutes before Hardnuss' shovel blade came to a jolting stop against the brown boot of an Imperial Guard trooper. She and Tua worked frantically in the hot, sweaty tunnel to clear away enough dirt that they could pull the trooper free. But when they did, Hardnuss' fears were realised. It was Trooper Enoka, a stocky woman who had proven a natural at digging tunnels. As they pulled her into the open, they found her eyes wide, brown and black spots of dirt stuck to her unmoving eyeballs. Her mouth was open as if gasping for breath, but all that had filled her throat was black soil.

'Help!'

The call was coming from ahead, muted by the fallen earth but unmistakably originating from the other side of the collapse. Hardnuss shovelled as fast as she could, calling for Tua to hurry despite the fact he was working just as fast as she was. Eventually they broke through to another buried Guardsman, this time barely missing taking fingers off with the end of their shovels – fingers that squirmed, clawing for fresh air. They cleared soil up to the shoulders before grabbing the arms and pulling. Trooper Gemmell came out coughing and spluttering.

'Vercoe's still in there.'

It didn't take long to locate Vercoe, who, luckily, had been on the other side of the collapse. She crawled through the hole Hardnuss and Tua cleared. Her face sank when she saw Enoka's body nearby.

'No,' she said, crawling up beside her and laying her hand on her cheek. 'No.'

Trooper Gemmell looked to Commissar Hardnuss. 'They were... together.'

Vercoe turned to Hardnuss. Her eyes were glassy and red as she fought to keep the tears back. 'This is too dangerous, commissar. We can't keep going. We're barely a third done and it's starting to collapse.'

Hardnuss hardened herself. They all thought of her, as they did most of the Commissariat, as a cold-hearted, uncompromising disciplinarian. The truth was Hardnuss would have preferred to comfort Vercoe. But soft-hearted commissars led to disciplinary breakdowns and even though they were prisoners, she could not allow that. As a commissar she simply accepted that in order to keep humanity safe there were those in the Imperium who had to push more of their humanity aside than others; they had to be Hard Nuts.

She thinned her eyes at Vercoe. 'Unauthorised fraternisation within a regiment is against regulations, trooper. It leads to loss of focus. Now pick up your shovel and keep digging.'

CHAPTER SIX

In retrospect, thinking the orks would build anything this big and not fit it with enormous, bowel-loosening guns was extraordinarily short-sighted. What sort of effigy would the greenskins consider fit for their gods other than one that could be used in war? Two days after the mammoth ork had lit up with glowing green energy, ten greenskin trukks had driven into the camp spewing pillars of grey smoke into the air. Two of them were loaded with smaller equipment while the remainder drove eight abreast, the barrel of an enormous cannon laid across their flat trays. After they were unloaded the trukks left and later returned with the barrel of a second cannon. They returned a third time with housings, support structures and pieces of an immense firing mechanism. Here, van Veenan realised, were the lower arms of the ork.

'It's as we suspected,' Commissar Hardnuss was saying to van Veenan as they stood side by side in the yard watching the trucks roll in. 'This isn't just a transmitter, it's a Gargant – an ork war machine on par with the Titans built by the tech-priests of Mars.'

'I don't imagine the Adeptus Mechanicus would care to have their work compared with that,' van Veenan said.

'No,' Hardnuss agreed. 'But it's certainly of a similar size.'

Van Veenan sighed. 'Yes, and I can't say I'm reassured by the glowing green eyes either.'

Before Hardnuss could reply, a rumbling roar filled the air, louder than thunder and rolling on and on. The sky above them was suddenly alight with an orange glow and the thin wispy clouds began to churn. A void ship was entering the planet's atmosphere – a void ship large enough that it had no business entering the atmosphere at all.

The entire sky appeared to be tearing open. Eventually the roaring, boiling fire parted and the shape of the ship became clear. It was descending to the planet's surface some distance beyond the confines of the prison camp. In the void of space it was easy to forget the scale of the ships crossing against the black, but here, as one attempted to land on the surface, it was a stark reminder of their sheer size. It must have been close to two and a half miles long and resembled an Imperial light cruiser, the long body peppered with arched windows and bearing a distinctive scooped plough at the front. But this was no Imperial ship, at least not any more. The front had been converted to approximate a blue ork skull with its mouth wide open, a gaping maw filled with teeth and two enormous curving tusks. Across the hull were other colourful additions: armour and cannons and skull motifs that could only be the work of the chaotic minds of ork mekboys, minds van Veenan was now all too familiar with.

''Ere comes a kroozer of Deathskull boyz for me WAAAAGH!' 'Eadbasha roared in delight as he emerged from his headquarters.

The massive ork ship dropped towards the surface of Rotauri, the forest below bent under the blast of the descent thrusters, centuries-old trees snapping like twigs beneath a boot. They were here. Whatever fringe science Rukaz had cooked up in his xenos brain had worked and it had brought a massive ork kroozer here in only days.

Van Veenan looked at Commissar Hardnuss. They both knew the situation had escalated. As much as van Veenan was loath to admit it, this had become about more than escape. The wider Imperium needed to know what was happening on this backwater planet. What had started as a relatively small-scale ork invasion had blossomed into the beginnings of a major threat.

'We need to speed up tunnel construction,' van Veenan said to Hardnuss. 'We've probably only got a few weeks until the Gargant is finished and now 'Eadbasha's plan is actually working. We need to work around the clock.'

'We've already had multiple cave ins,' Hardnuss said, 'one of which I had to dig troopers out of myself. We haven't got enough material to reinforce the tunnel.'

'Get each barracks to strip everything they can. We'll build more tunnels and start moving material into Barracks Five.'

'That's a huge risk,' Hardnuss said.

'Yeah, well, I guess it's time to find out whether I really am blessed by the Emperor.'

It was early morning and van Veenan's eyes stung with lack of sleep. One of his eyelids had been twitching for eight straight days and his head had been pounding almost as long. He knew he was at the limit of physical endurance. He'd slept maybe ten hours over the last week and saw from the deep black rings under the eyes of the surrounding Guardsmen that they too were reaching breaking point. But they were close now. So close.

Van Veenan stood at the entrance to the main escape tunnel, helping to pass along planks of wood being brought in from the side tunnels. The escape tunnel now extended about eighty yards out from Barracks Five. Van Veenan had enlisted the help of troopers who'd served as a Basilisk artillery crew to perform range estimation, and their approximation put the tunnel out past the fence but not yet into the forest. Smaller passages had been dug between the barracks until a network of tunnels criss-crossed underneath the camp, allowing transport of material and Guardsmen from any barracks to any other and ultimately into Barracks Five and the main tunnel. 'Honouring the Emperor' was the code for their escape attempt and it would hopefully take place within the week.

Two more ork craft had arrived since the first. One had been another light cruiser, the other a rok – a greenskin 'ship' constructed by hollowing out an asteroid and outfitting it with engines and as many guns as the orks could fit on the available surface area. The rok hadn't so much landed as it had plummeted in barely controlled atmospheric entry, slamming into the surface with a devastating impact. It had come down several hundred miles away at least, keeping the prison camp safe from the shock wave and resultant shower of debris.

Even having made planetfall so far away, the orks of the rok were slowly making their way towards the monstrous Gargant like a teeming mass of pilgrims approaching a holy site. With that, and the other two ships, the population of greenskins had swelled. Most of them stayed out of the prison camp on the orders of Warboss 'Eadbasha, who van Veenan was sure had grown bigger since so many orks had flooded to join his Waaagh! The recently arrived xenos had established a settlement nearby that was rapidly turning into a sprawling shanty town, adding to both the overpowering smell and the amount of conflict breaking out between orks of different clan affiliations.

The eyes of the massive Gargant still glowed and bolts of green lightning regularly shot down its height or arced off to hit the roofs of nearby buildings, or ground out through nearby orks causing them to pop like oversized green pimples. The construction efforts had now moved to the interior of the machine, the massive cannons had been attached to the arms and heavy motors were brought across from the refinery to act as propulsion. Huge electro-magnetic pistons, also pilfered from the promethium refinery, were positioned inside the legs and arms where they connected to massive gears at the joints. A control room was established in the chest section and stairs and ladders were being erected throughout the inside. It would soon be operational.

'All right,' van Veenan said to the Guardsmen working around him, 'let's close up the tunnels for the morning. Pass the word to rotate the day shift in. Twenty pouches of soil back to each barracks and remind them to at least spread it out. I saw half a dozen dirt piles yesterday morning. Let's not get complacent this close to the end.'

The Guardsmen moved back through the tunnel system to their own barracks, where they covered the tunnel entrances, cleaned themselves up as best they could, filled their pockets with soil and waited innocently for the ork guards to lead them to work.

When he arrived at the yard, van Veenan saw Rukaz approaching. The mekboy had his goggled eyes fixed on him and was moving with determined haste. Van Veenan, having never had much to do with the head mekboy, stopped, a little taken aback by the sudden attention.

'You,' Rukaz said when he reached van Veenan, his head twitching as energy jumped between the coils on his back. 'You are some kinda nob for the humies, aren't you?'

'Company Sergeant Major Marcus van Veenan, Rotauri First Infantry, First Company.'

Rukaz lifted the green-lensed goggles up and rested them on his forehead. He stared at van Veenan as he jammed his finger in his ear, wriggled it around and then smelled it with an oddly satisfied look on his green face. 'Long name,' he said.

'You can call me van Veenan.'

'Right, well you listen to me, humie nob van Veenanz, I know you sneaky humies are up to somethin'. The others are too thick to notice but I see you lot skulkin' about with dirt in your keks.'

Van Veenan's heart froze.

'Oh,' Rukaz said, slapping his hands on the sides of his face in mock surprise. 'Da humie is shocked. You think you is real smart but I is the smartest mekboy in the whole galaxy and that makes me proper brainy.' He pointed back towards the Gargant. 'I built that.'

'Well, actually us humies built it,' van Veenan said.

Rukaz growled. 'You know wot I mean. I imagined it up.'

Van Veenan looked at the Gargant. 'Bit small, isn't it?'

'Wot?'

'I don't know, I was just expecting it to be bigger. More guns at least.'

Rukaz growled again. 'You think I'm not smart enough to notice you sneakin' about. I been watching you, van Veenanz. I could tell Warboss 'Eadbasha to go lookin' for your tunnels right now.'

Van Veenan raised an eyebrow. 'But you're not going to?'

Mekboy Rukaz sniffed. His face twitched. He shrugged. 'You better 'urry up and get to the yard, humie nob van Veenanz. You and your humies got to finish my Gargant before you get about your sneakin'.'

Van Veenan stared at the mekboy as the ork turned and walked away. He had the distinctly unpleasant feeling he was now engaged in a battle of wits with a greenskin and was somehow losing.

He thought about his encounter with Rukaz all day. No ork guards came to tear his limbs off or drag him to the fighting pit or toss him over the fence to the gathering orks of the Waaagh! By late afternoon he'd almost driven himself crazy trying to decide what Rukaz's game had been: was he trying to goad him into launching an escape so they'd be caught? Or was he hinting they should escape, helping him because he was pursuing his own scheme against the warboss? Still, by the time the red sun of Rotauri began to set and the sky slowly blended from the white-blue of the day to the pink of evening, van Veenan had decided. He moved among the Guardsmen as subtly as he could and gave them a simple message to spread. Tonight, a full week early, they would honour the Emperor.

CHAPTER SEVEN

'We're only at eighty-five yards,' said Corporal Roha, one of the Basilisk crew who seemed to see distance markers everywhere they looked. 'If we bring the tunnel up we won't have reached the forest.'

Van Veenan knew the thick forest would provide much-needed cover for their escape; having the tunnel exit in open ground was a huge risk. He rubbed his stinging eyes and looked around at the gathered troops, Commissar Hardnuss, Corporal Trotter, Corporal Tua and others who had been instrumental in the execution of the escape plan. He realised something then that he hadn't appreciated during his career as a front-line Guardsman. Something that made him – at least partially – reconsider his attitude towards those in command. The orders that came down from the captains and the colonels and the lord militant generals that had seemed so ludicrous to those on the front lines must have been made under circumstances very similar to this. Risk versus reward. Cost versus benefit. Impossible choices. Did they go now and risk being seen during their desperate dash for freedom, or did they wait, knowing that at least one of the orks was well aware that they were building an escape tunnel?

'We just have to hope the darkness is enough,' van Veenan said. 'Pass the word along, we're bringing up the tunnel.'

And that was what they did. Despite the hesitation he knew they felt, each of them nodded and moved off. The order was passed to the Guardsmen in the tunnel to start digging upwards and breach the surface. Trotter and the others used the minor tunnels to move off to the other barracks, spreading the word that it was time to prepare for the escape.

Commissar Hardnuss turned to look at van Veenan, who obviously wore his concern on his face.

'They know what to do, sergeant major,' she said. 'You've readied them well. This will work.'

Van Veenan nodded. She was right. He'd readied them as best as he could. They knew what to do. Once the tunnel breached the ground, the opening would be reinforced and two ladders sent down the tunnel. A sentry would use one ladder to watch for any ork guards and signal when it was clear for Guardsmen to escape up the other.

Commissar Hardnuss would lead the first group of twenty-five troopers down the tunnel. Then fifteen minutes later the next group would go. Throughout the night, at fifteen-minute intervals, groups of twenty to twenty-five Guardsmen would make their escape. Naturally, van Veenan would lead the last group.

It took a little less than two hours to bring the tunnel to the surface, reinforce the opening and put the ladders in place. In that time, van Veenan made only one alteration to his plan. He would act as watch sentry for the first group. He needed to see them safely away.

The first group of escapees was already in Barracks Five fidgeting with nerves as Corporal Tua came crawling out of the tunnel. He looked up at van Veenan and nodded. 'We're through, sarge,' he said. 'Twenty yards short of the woods, just like we thought. It's a good night for it though, it's dark out there.'

'Thanks, corporal,' van Veenan said. He turned to look at the gathered Guardsmen. 'You all know the plan. When you reach the end of the tunnel, wait for my signal to go. When you go up and over, keep low and make for the trees.' He paused a moment and added, 'The Emperor protects.'

Van Veenan climbed down and began the long crawl through the dimly lit passage. At the end of the tunnel he climbed the ladder and peered out through the hole in the ground, keeping only the top of his head exposed. Tua was right, neither of Rotauri's small moons hung in the sky and darkness lay heavy. The prison camp was bathed in a sickly yellow glow from high lumen towers, but luckily the diffuse light didn't reach the tunnel exit. Van Veenan turned to examine the treeline. It seemed so close and yet dangerously far away. Darkness had wound itself around the trunks of trees to provide the perfect cover – provided they made it there. He turned his attention back to the prison camp, watching for ork patrols. A group of greenskins passed, arguing loudly about whose fist was the biggest, but they never once looked in the direction of the tunnel.

He looked down at Hardnuss and gestured for her to go. She climbed the ladder, looked over to him and, in a moment of human connection he'd never had with a member of the Commissariat, reached out a hand. Van Veenan took hold of it. She locked eyes with him, squeezed his hands with a vice-like shake and nodded. Then she climbed out and, crouching low, dashed away into the thick shadow of the trees.

Van Veenan watched her go, alert for any signal that the orks had spotted her fleeing across the dark ground, and only when she vanished into the thick gloom of the trees did he allow himself to breathe again. He exhaled slowly, calming his nerves. The first of them had made it. They could all make it.

He looked down and nodded for the next Guardsmen to go. They climbed the ladder, up and out, and stalked low across the grass and into the trees where Hardnuss would be waiting. Each time a new Guardsman came out of the tunnel, van Veenan checked the surrounds for any guards, watched the fence-line and listened intently until he was sure they were clear. Then he would signal for them to exit the tunnel.

After the eleventh had made their way across to the trees, he was about to signal the next when he heard the crack of a footfall breaking a twig and the gruff voices of two approaching orks.

'I'll be warboss of me own lot of boyz one day. Won't be doin' any zoggin' patrols then.'

'Yeah, you be warboss of cleanin' the squig pen.'

'Shut ya face. I is gonna work me way up.'

'Go on then, ya git. Challenge 'Eadbasha in da pit. Show everyone you is toughest.'

'I will. Next time there's a pit fight I'll challenge the boss in front of everyone, show 'em dat I should be the boss.'

'Zog off ya will. Pass me dat fungus beer. You 'ad too much.'

Keeping the barest amount of his head visible, van Veenan watched the pair of orks trudge past. They were outside the camp but were keeping close to the light as they patrolled the perimeter. As they moved closer, van Veenan lowered himself down the ladder and with a sudden crack the rung bearing his weight snapped. His feet dropped out from under him but he held tight to keep from falling.

'Oi,' he heard one of the ork guards say. 'You 'ear that?'

''Ear what?'

'A snappin' noise.'

'I ain't 'ear nothin' but you gobbin' off. Now pass me dat beer back.'

Van Veenan exhaled. He pulled himself back up the ladder and watched the bulky shapes of the ork guards disappearing into the dark. He waited at least a minute and then motioned for the Guardsman to go.

The rest of the twenty-five Guardsmen made it out of the tunnel and into the relative safety of the dark woods without incident. Van Veenan watched the trees for a good five minutes after the last of them had gone. There was nothing he could do now. Hardnuss would take command of that group, moving them off on the long march through the forest to Flaxton, where the Rotauri First had been headquartered, and hopefully contact Imperial forces, inform them of the rapidly growing ork threat and request reinforcements. Van Veenan descended the ladder and began crawling back through the tunnel towards Barracks Five, where he would oversee the rest of the escape.

By the time Corporal Tua led the third group of Guardsmen down the tunnel he allowed himself a sliver of belief that they might pull this off. They had been right to put their faith in Sergeant Major van Veenan, and perhaps what some of the troopers said about him being blessed by the Emperor was true after all. Van Veenan's escape plan certainly seemed to have His blessing.

Tua climbed the ladder, keeping watch, and was ready to clear the first of his Guardsmen to make for the trees when he heard the loud approach of two orks. The same two greenskins that had passed just over an hour before were making their way back around the outskirts of the camp. Tua stayed low, remaining patient as the orks approached, waiting for them to pass before sending his troops up and out of the tunnel exit. Unfortunately, the inebriated orks, who must have been consuming fungus beer at an alarming rate, were wandering directly towards the tunnel.

'I is gonna drive the big Gargant.'

'You is not. Only the mekboyz are gonna drive it.'

'I could if I wanted to.'

'You don't know anything about it, you zoggin' git.'

'I is not a git. You is a git.'

'Git.'

'Call me a git again and I'll bloody well krump ya.'

'Zoggin' git.'

The first ork roared and swung a wild, beer-fuelled punch at its patrol partner. The haymaker strike landed awkwardly but was still hard enough to send the second ork staggering directly towards the tunnel exit. It stumbled, tripped over its feet and fell directly into the tunnel opening.

Tua cursed as the ork fell past him and slammed into the dirt at the bottom of the hole. Shocked, the greenskin stood, shook its head and found itself looking directly into the face of Corporal Tua. It took the ork a moment before its red eyes grew wide.

'Humies! Da humies 'ave a tunnel!'

'Shit,' Corporal Tua said. 'Shit! Fall back! Fall back now!'

Even as Tua was screaming at the Guardsmen to retreat, the second ork jumped down into the hole. Both orks grabbed their shootas and began firing indiscriminately at the Guardsmen around them and those still in the tunnel. In that moment, Corporal Tua's thoughts turned to the God-Emperor. He had time to wonder why the Emperor had chosen that moment to lift van Veenan's blessing and forsake them all to their enemy before several explosive shells entered his back and erupted out his chest, opening his torso in a splatter across the freshly dug dirt.

Inside Barracks Five, van Veenan heard the kinetic booms of ork shootas firing from beyond the prison camp. Though the deafening cracks of the ork weapons echoed and bounced off the buildings outside, the sound was unmistakably coming from the direction of the escape tunnel.

These booming blasts alerted not only van Veenan to the discovery of the tunnel but also drew the attention of every greenskin within earshot, including those newly arrived orks in their rickety shanty town – and, of course, not wanting to miss out on some fighting, they came streaming towards the noise.

The troopers who'd been in the tunnel when orks began swarming back the other way came flooding out in a mass of chaotic confusion. They poured like rats fleeing water up and out of the tunnel entrance. Van Veenan grabbed the next trooper that clambered out of the tunnel, a young off-world girl, and spun her to look at him. 'Give me the situation, trooper.'

'Orks found the tunnel, sergeant.' She spoke quickly, her pupils dilated from both the darkness and the adrenaline flooding her body. 'They're coming!'

Van Veenan suddenly found himself pumped full of adrenaline too.

'How many soldiers were behind you?' he said to the red-haired trooper, but her eyes had returned to the tunnel. 'Hey!' He shook her by the shoulders. 'How many were behind you?'

'I was tenth in the line so there's fifteen others behind me.'

Van Veenan turned to the troopers who had escaped the tunnel, huddled together like frightened civilians. 'Stand to!' he roared at them. 'Pull yourselves together, damn it! You are warriors of the Imperium!'

He counted the troopers coming out of the tunnel. There were still ten down there. The howling, roaring war cries of the orks were growing louder. Human screaming soon followed. The orks were on them, tearing them apart in the claustrophobic darkness below ground and any moment the xenos would burst into the barracks. Van Veenan decided quickly.

'You, you, you, you and you,' he said, picking out five of the troopers, 'slide the bunks over the tunnel entrance, put everything heavy you can find on top of them.'

'Sergeant major, there are still–'

'Now, troopers!'

'Yes, sergeant.'

They slid the bunks along the now worn track in the rockcrete and over the hole in the floor.

'Hey!' a voice screamed as the troopers moved the bunks across. 'We're still down here!'

Screams of pain. Squelching of soft tissue. Breaking of bones. The roar of orks reverberated from under the beds, joined by the dying screams of those Guardsmen who'd been trapped with them. Van Veenan saw the faces of those troopers who'd closed the tunnel. He kept his face passive as he returned their gaze. He knew how they felt. He felt the crushing guilt too, probably more so, but unlike them, he couldn't show it.

'You acted under my orders,' van Veenan said. 'I condemned those troopers, not you. The sacrifice of the few for the lives of the many. Now, weigh the bunks down. Quickly now.'

The troopers moved off and began tossing whatever loose objects they could find onto the bottom bunk. It was best to put them to work. He could not afford for them to dwell on what had happened. He needed to keep the Guardsmen in this barracks, and the hundreds of others still in the camp, safe. The orks began smashing against the bottom bunk; he could see their strong green fists pounding upwards, the whole unit lifting with each strike.

'We need more weight,' van Veenan said. 'Get on the bunk.'

The nearby troopers glanced at each other, the sounds of the dying still echoing from below.

The bunk bounced again with the strikes of green fists.

'Now!'

The troopers didn't hesitate again, clambering onto the bottom bunk to add weight. Van Veenan had bought some time, but it would not be much.

'You there,' van Veenan said, gesturing to another group of four Guardsmen, 'we need weapons, whatever you can find that we can swing, stab or poke at an ork. The rest of you, there are loose bricks in the rear wall. Find the removable section and pull them out. Get ready to go but not until I give the word.'

The troopers set about their orders. He could see them trying to ignore the thumps of the orks hitting the bunks, but many of them flinched with each pounding crack.

A pile of what would have to pass for weapons collected on the floor: half a dozen handmade picks and shovels, hammers, an assortment of planks of wood, twisted scraps of metal, and there, on top, the circular saw they'd used to cut through the rockcrete.

Van Veenan walked forward and picked up the heavy saw. He hefted it up, judging its weight and balance. Then he realised the banging had stopped and instead he heard the scraping of the bunks on the floor. Eventually, even orks would realise they weren't getting anywhere by punching whatever was in front of them. Now they were working together to tip the bunks over.

'Are you ready?' van Veenan said to the troops at the back wall. Several of them nodded. He could see they'd removed the bricks, opening their way for an escape into the camp.

'We're going to make a break out into the yard. Once outside you need to scatter. The greenskins are obviously going to be displeased with us so spread out and fight as best you can. We're going to have to hope the orks coming through the tunnel provide some amount of distraction.'

Van Veenan stepped up to the hole in the wall. Behind him, the bunks – the troopers who were weighing it down now off to gather weapons and ready themselves – had started rocking on the spot, closer and closer to toppling over. 'I'll take point.' Van Veenan flicked the safety switch on the saw and squeezed the trigger on the handle. The saw roared to life, shaking and wanting to pull down with the gyroscopic force of the spinning blade.

'Go!' van Veenan called, and he ducked through the hole in the wall. He began moving even before his eyes adjusted to the dark. From inside the barracks he heard the rocking bunks finally tip over and fall with a crash to the floor.

It didn't take long for the greenskins of the camp, already alerted by the sounds beyond the fence, to notice van Veenan and the troopers pouring out of the barracks. When the first snarling ork appeared in front of him, van Veenan wasted no time. He rushed at the greenskin, right into the spittle spray of its war cry, and swung the saw. The blade, its serrated teeth spinning at three thousand revolutions per minute, met the side of the ork's neck and threw chunks of green flesh in a wide arc. Eventually the ork's severed head dropped to the ground. The body fell back, a great crimson flood gushing from the headless neck.

Around him the troopers ran in multiple directions, ork guards thundering after them. Shoota shots reverberated through the night.

The orks coming from the tunnel soon surged out of the hole in the barracks wall. It took a moment for the prison guards to realise what was happening, but when they did the chaos of the night intensified. Warboss 'Eadbasha, who himself strode out amongst the camp, roared orders that the humies be rounded up and any orks from outside the camp trying to kill them be krumped instead.

A group of orks rushed into Barracks Five and tossed several grenades into the tunnel. This killed a number of greenskins still coming into the camp from outside and collapsed the tunnel entrance in a blast of soot and dirt.

The orks eventually corralled the Guardsmen, van Veenan included, into one corner of the camp. Most of them were obeying 'Eadbasha's shouts to not kill the humies, but van Veenan watched as some troopers refused to be recaptured and the orks, perhaps from some vicious greenskin instinct, forgot they were supposed to keep them alive. Most were rapidly caught, tackled to the ground and torn apart amid screams of pain and terror, or were blasted into fragments by the impact of a shoota round, but some of them kept the guards going on comical chases.

One Guardsman, being chased by none other than Big Nob 'Ardskull himself, sprinted towards the edge of the transport yard, where six ork warbikes had been parked. He threw his leg over to mount the black, skull-fronted bike. Two exhaust pipes as thick as a human torso stuck diagonally up behind him. The Guardsman hastily looked down at the handlebars as if searching for how to start the thing. He flicked a switch, gunned the throttle and slammed his foot down on the kick-starter. The bike turned over, puffing smoke and firing briefly before dying again. The Guardsman pressed another button, flicked a different switch and tried to kick-start the bike again but all to no avail. It wouldn't start.

'Ardskull slowed as he approached, the Guardsman now desperately hunting for how to start the bike.

'You ain't orky enough,' the massive nob said before grabbing the trooper by the shirt and lifting him off the saddle. 'Ardskull looked around as if checking the warboss wasn't watching and then smashed his steel-topped head into the trooper's face, caving his skull in. He tossed the body to the dirt and then walked off.

When what passed for order in the camp had been restored, van Veenan stood with the group of Guardsmen rounded up by the ork guards. Warboss 'Eadbasha thumped over in his hydraulically actuated suit, his red eyes glaring at the group of Guardsmen.

'Which of you humies did this? Which is da boss of you?'

Van Veenan stepped forward.

'Eadbasha grunted. 'You is boss?'

Van Veenan nodded. 'I organised the escape if that's what you mean. I'm responsible.'

The warboss grunted and opened his massive klaw to reveal the sharpened edges of the two hooked fingers. Van Veenan's heart began slamming in his chest and adrenaline flooded his system as 'Eadbasha's klaw arm pulled back ready to strike. But, despite every instinct telling him to flee, he stood his ground. He set his jaw and stared at the creature.

The klaw flashed and 'Eadbasha's hydraulics hissed as he swung. As the killing blow began to fall, van Veenan screamed with furious rage at the greenskin. The klaw stopped, just before impacting the side of van Veenan's skull.

'You got gutz,' 'Eadbasha said. 'But you ain't even da biggest.' The warboss grumbled as if that fact was immensely disappointing to him. He turned to two nearby guards. 'Bring 'im.'

CHAPTER EIGHT

The two orks carried van Veenan across the camp, his feet barely scraping the ground as they hustled after the looming, hydraulically powered shape of their warboss. He led them to the bunker where the weirdboy now powering the Gargant had been imprisoned. 'Eadbasha opened the heavy door, the hinges groaning their complaints.

Inside the bunker was a row of steel cages. The orks tossed van Veenan into the first cage, slamming the door closed and securing it with an old-fashioned padlock. 'Eadbasha stepped forward, grabbing the cage door and rattling it to check it was secure. Then he lowered his immense form – already hunched over to fit inside the small domed bunker – and stared at van Veenan through the thick bars. His green lips peeled back over both rows of pointed yellow teeth, each one rotten and twisted like gnarled stalactites and stalagmites in the dark of a cave. Van Veenan could see the defined scratches of file marks where 'Eadbasha had worked to sharpen his fangs even more than was natural.

''Ow many?'

Van Veenan knew what he meant but wouldn't give him the satisfaction that easily. 'How many what?'

A rumbling snarl built in 'Eadbasha's throat. ''Ow many humies sneaked away?'

Van Veenan stared back into the red eyes buried inside 'Eadbasha's bulbous, misshapen head. 'None,' he said. 'That was the first group that tried to escape. I don't know how many your new friends out there killed though.'

That same growl emanated from 'Eadbasha's throat. Van Veenan wasn't sure if it was annoyance, disappointment or disbelief. 'Don't matter. I got a buncha humies left. I got more grots comin' with the boyz joinin' my Waaagh! I ain't gonna krump ya and I ain't gonna krump ya friends neither. You humies is gonna finish my effigee and then you is gonna watch as Waaagh! 'Eadbasha goes off and smashes humies all across the galaxy. All ya humies sneakin' about for nothin'. We smart enough to find ya little tunnel. We gonna make sure your friends can't do nothin' like that again, and you is gonna sleep in 'ere.'

'You didn't find the tunnel. One of your idiot guards fell into it.'

'Eadbasha slammed his huge fist up against the cage with a crash. Van Veenan, despite himself, flinched.

'Eadbasha smiled with vicious glee. 'See?' he said to the guards. 'Even da 'ard humies are scared. It's like they don't even like fightin.' Then he turned, and with the hiss of released hydraulic pressure, stomped out of the bunker, the two orks following like canids trailing after their massive green master. The heavy rust-orange door swung closed and locked.

They left van Veenan alone, bathed in the withered amber glow of the bunker's emergency lighting. The light was enough to see by but little more than that. Van Veenan propped himself up against the bars of the cage and leaned his head back, closing his eyes and feeling the cool of the metal against the back of his skull.

'Humie nob van Veenanz.'

Van Veenan opened his eyes – apparently he was not alone. Through the cage bars he saw the shape of Mekboy Rukaz move out of a dark corner. It took van Veenan a moment to realise that Rukaz was also locked inside a cage, at the other end of the bunker.

'I thought I told you not to go sneakin' about yet,' the ork said. He still had his green goggles propped up on top of his head and wore his strange coiled contraption on his back. It flashed with a pulse of green energy that momentarily lit up the bunker.

'I'm touched,' van Veenan said. 'I didn't know you cared.'

'I don't,' Rukaz said. 'I care whether you finish buildin' my Gargant.'

'Sure,' van Veenan said. 'So, why are you locked in here?'

'I is always locked in 'ere.'

'You're a prisoner too?'

Rukaz didn't answer but in that moment, van Veenan knew he'd been right about the tension between the mekboy and the warboss. Maybe he could leverage that.

'Why does 'Eadbasha keep you locked up?'

'Da warboss is a warboss,' Rukaz said as if that explained it; perhaps in the mind of a greenskin it did.

'Did you get on his bad side? Not that I suppose he has any other side.'

'I is a smartboy,' Rukaz said. 'I do too much thinkin' for 'Eadbasha. They won't never admit it but all them big nobz and warbosses are scared of us that do the thinkin' because they ain't never done any themselves. They don't know how to think. Unorky they call me. I'll show 'em. If I can think up ways of killin' while not gettin' killed that seems like the way to win fights. That seems orky to me. Zoggin' git locks me in 'ere and tells me to stop doin' so much thinkin' when he knows wot's wot about krumpin.'

'Sounds like you should be in charge,' van Veenan said.

'Yeah, I probably should.'

'And that Gargant, the one you built, it should be yours.'

'Should be, yeah.'

'So, why don't you take it?' van Veenan asked.

'He's big, ain't he?'

So, even for what might well be the smartest ork in the galaxy, things still came down to who was biggest. Van Veenan knew he was about to take a step over the line into heresy, and that if he ever got out of this the Inquisition would likely want a word, but, given the situation, he took it.

'What about you help us escape?'

Rukaz chuckled. 'You want me to help you escape? I is already locked up. 'Eadbasha will krump me for that even if I haven't finished his Gargant. You is proper stupid, humie nob van Veenanz.'

'You should be warboss. You should have that Gargant. If you help us escape, we can help you get it.'

'You already been caught sneakin' about. 'Eadbasha is stupid as a brainless grot but he ain't gonna let you do any more sneakin' about buildin' tunnels.'

'We won't be trying that again. We'll fight our way out.'

Rukaz chuckled again. 'Did you get krumped in the head, humie nob van Veenanz? You think you can fight all 'Eadbasha's boyz?'

'No, but if we can get weapons, we can make a surprise attack, blow up the fence and make a break for it.'

'Now you the one not doin' any thinkin',' Rukaz said. 'None of you humies would make it past 'Eadbasha's Waaagh!'

'If we finish your Gargant first, why do you care?'

'I don't.'

'So, will you help us?'

Rukaz scratched the side of his neck. A spark of green between the coils on his back momentarily lit up the space again. 'I is still not sure what's in it for me.'

'You get my soldiers some weapons and we'll kill 'Eadbasha on our way out.'

Rukaz was silent for what stretched into an awkwardly long time, but van Veenan didn't push him. He waited for the green cogs to turn inside the ork's mind. 'All right then, humie nob van Veenanz. I get you some dakka and help you escape, and you kill me da warboss and I get to keep the Gargant.'

'You've got a deal.'

Van Veenan had no intention of letting any orks off Rotauri with that massive war machine. If the opportunity arose, he'd more than happily help kill Warboss 'Eadbasha. He didn't care about what passed for ork politics and who would fill the void left at the top, whether it was Rukaz or 'Ardskull or some other ork, but right now he'd say whatever he needed to get his troopers free.

Van Veenan had been confined to the bunker for a week. It had reached the point where, if they hadn't been bringing him food and water at semi-regular intervals, he might have thought the orks had forgotten about him.

Each morning the door would open and a pair of 'Eadbasha's most trusted ork guards would enter. They'd walk past van Veenan's cell and drop a dish of cold, unidentifiable goop and a small cup of water outside his cage, just within reach, and would continue on to let Rukaz out of his cage. The entire time they were inside the bunker the orks never engaged van Veenan, no matter what he said to them. The guards must have been under the strictest orders from Warboss 'Eadbasha to simply pretend he wasn't there. Then when Rukaz was returned to his cage at the end of the day, they repeated the whole routine with the food and the ignoring.

Strangely, van Veenan had begun to look forward to the return of his bizarre greenskin cellmate. They may have been enemies but at least it was someone to talk to. Each evening Rukaz would give van Veenan a brief update on what was happening in the camp.

Day one: 'All your humie friends look... wotsat thing you humies get... sad, ain't it?'

Day two: 'Some of da humies were puttin' in the nuclear plasma reactor and stupid Groblok told 'em to plug it in the wrong way. They is dead now but it was only a little boom so the Gargant is still okay.'

Day three: 'Another kroozer of ork boyz showed up today. All of them those flashy Bad Moon gitz. Got more teef than brains those Bad Moons.'

Day four: 'Today I stashed away a bunch of shootas, stikk bombs and rokkits in the yard for you, humie nob van Veenanz – enough for about thirty of you. A leg servo fell off the Gargant and crushed loads of your humies though.'

Day five: 'Good news. Only one humie dead today.'

It was the sixth night when Rukaz said: 'Da Gargant is done.'

'What?' Van Veenan said. 'It's finished? But I asked you to warn me when it was almost finished.'

'Yeah. I told you they was puttin' in the plasma reactor days ago. That's the last bit wot goes in. It's been all hooked up now and ready to be powered up.'

'How was I supposed to know the plasma reactor is last?'

'Stupid humie. The plasma reactor is always last.'

Van Veenan breathed out heavily.

'So what happens now then?' he asked.

'We starts up the Gargant tomorrow for a systems check, then 'Eadbasha'll probably start gettin' ready to get off this planet and on with his Waaagh!'

'We can't let that happen,' van Veenan said.

'You is right, humie nob van Veenanz. I is gonna have that Gargant. It should be mine.'

'That's right – it's only fair that after all your work creating such a masterpiece it should be yours.' He wasn't sure whether it was working, but he'd tried to maintain the ork's trust, tried to flatter him and inflate his ego, all the while knowing the first thing he would do, aside from trying to get the remaining soldiers of the Rotauri First out of this prison camp, was his Emperor-damned best to blow that enormous ork monstrosity into more pieces than a gretchin force-fed a krak grenade.

'You is lucky. I heard Warboss 'Eadbasha sayin' he wants you to see it. He wants all you humies to see the Gargant ready to go. Da humies is done after that, he said.'

'We're going to have to attack before that happens. How do I get the weapons you've left for us?'

'You leave that to me. I is gonna get you the dakka. You wait for my sneaky signal and you is gonna know what to do. You just take care of killin' 'Eadbasha.'

Van Veenan thought about Lieutenant Pokato and the deal he'd tried to forge with the orks. He had to believe they'd made deals for very different reasons. Pokato might have wanted the Guardsmen to believe he was trying to protect them, but he was a craven fool just out to save himself. Van Veenan had no doubt he was a fool too, but he would die for these Guardsmen if that's what it took. Still, he hoped his deal wouldn't end with being beaten to death with his own limbs.

There had been no sign of Imperial forces over the last week. He hadn't wanted to enact his ridiculous escape plan – well, his second ridiculous escape plan – without external support, but as usual it seemed like his hand was being forced. He'd hoped Commissar Hardnuss or one of the other escapees had made contact with Imperial forces and they would come roaring in to rain the Emperor's fire of liberation down on the greenskins. That hope had faded more with each passing day and he couldn't wait any longer.

As was proving far too common over his life, Sergeant Major Marcus van Veenan was on an unfamiliar battlefield with no one to rely on but himself and an improvised plan to try to keep those around him alive – and now he could add a shaky and possibly heretical alliance with an ork mekboy into the mix. In all the accounts of famous Imperial Guard soldiers he'd read over the years, none of them seemed to get into situations like this. Or at least none lived to tell the tale.

CHAPTER NINE

As van Veenan was led out of the gloomy confines of the bunker for the first time in a week, it took time for his eyes to adjust to the orange light of Rotauri's high sun. When he reached the yard he saw the ork Gargant looming over the gathered Guardsmen, big-bellied and brutish against the backdrop of the sky.

Even as the giant ork machine stood motionless and silent but for the occasional crackle of green lightning down its mismatched torso, van Veenan could imagine what it would be capable of. He could see it stomping with ground-shaking power over a battlefield, unleashing a torrent of mighty rounds that would tear through every armoured vehicle the Imperial Guard could throw at it. More than ever, with its power to draw untold number of orks to 'Eadbasha's side, the Gargant seemed a threat that could bring the entire sector to its knees.

When van Veenan was led towards the Guardsmen by the two ork guards, he was greeted by the sight of the soldiers of the Rotauri First even more ragged than he remembered. They were thin, their faces gaunt, their uniforms mismatched and dirty. Still, when they saw him most of their faces showed relief. Corporal Trotter clapped him on the shoulder. 'Good to have you back, sarge,' she said. 'Sorry to say you've made it just in time for the end.'

'Don't count us out quite yet,' van Veenan said, keeping his voice low. 'I want you to find thirty troopers who can still fight and quietly gather them here.'

Trotter nodded and nonchalantly moved off into the Guardsmen.

Van Veenan resisted the almost overwhelming urge to pace. He wrung his hands together, desperate to be doing something other than passively waiting. The mekboyz and gretchin moved over the massive Gargant, dismantling the last of the scaffolding, and then began entering the machine to undertake the final stages of preparation. It seemed obvious from the way the orks ignored them that there would be no more work for the humans. They had done the heavy construction. The slave work was finished. The only reason they were still here was likely because 'Eadbasha needed something to test the Gargant on.

Slowly, van Veenan watched troopers moving towards him, giving small nods as they approached. Eventually Corporal Trotter and thirty Guardsmen she considered capable had joined him at the back of the group. They stood around in anticipation, though not entirely sure of what. In truth, not even van Veenan knew precisely what the plan was. He was waiting, probably ill-advisedly, on an unknown signal from a crazed ork mekboy.

Just as van Veenan was thinking Rukaz had either forgotten about him or had deliberately abandoned him, the short mekboy came waddling towards him.

'You,' he said, pointing at van Veenan, 'you is in charge, right?'

'That's right,' van Veenan said, playing along for the benefit of the nearby orks who watched with passing interest.

'I need you to take some of your humies into that bunker and collect the plasma generator power inverter coupling. It's 'eavy, probably you'll need lots of humies.' Rukaz paused, lifted his goggles and performed the most exaggerated wink van Veenan had ever seen. It was so painfully obvious that he was sure they would all be killed on the spot, but oddly none of the orks recognised the gesture for what it was. Apparently stealth and deception, or the detection of it, were not within the ork skill set.

'Right,' van Veenan said, 'got it.' He looked around at the thirty Guardsmen who had already been selected. They knew this was somehow related to their instructions but were understandably confused about what Mekboy Rukaz had to do with all this. 'You at the back here, with me.'

The ork guards, whose eyes had begun to glaze over with the words 'plasma generator power inverter coupling,' watched van Veenan and his thirty troops walk towards the bunker. They shrugged and turned back to the Gargant.

Inside the bunker was a large pile of equipment that had been covered with a green canvas tarpaulin. It was irregularly shaped and seemingly out of place amidst the rest of the neatly stacked supply crates. Van Veenan approached the pile, waiting for the Guardsmen to enter the bunker after him.

'Is that what we're in here to get?' one of the troopers asked.

'I'm hoping so, trooper,' van Veenan said. He reached down and flicked the canvas cover off the pile. He heard sharp intakes of breath from many of the troopers; some of them let out low whistles.

'Yep,' van Veenan said, 'this is what we're here for.'

Piled against the wall of the bunker were at least some of the weapons the greenskins had confiscated after Rotauri had fallen. Ninety per cent of the collection were lasguns but there were several boxes of grenades and a crate of Mars-pattern man-portable missile launchers too. There were far more weapons here than van Veenan had expected. Not that he was complaining.

'Time to gear up, Guardsmen,' van Veenan said and he began with his orders, pointing at troopers as he went, organising them to suit the plan rapidly forming in his head. 'We'll split into three ten-man fire-teams. You eight there run light, one lasgun each plus another to drop with others on the way – you're with me and Trotter in squad one. Make sure you're able to shoot as soon as we leave this building. You ten are squad two, grab as many weapons and grenades as you can carry. The rest of you grab those missile launchers, you'll run as heavy weapons in squad three.'

The men and women behind him did not hesitate; though they must have known van Veenan had somehow made a deal with a xenos, a crime punishable by death, none of them mentioned it. They grabbed weapons, the familiar sound of lasguns priming like a sweet music to them all. They carried the Emperor's fury in their hands once again.

'All right,' van Veenan said, looking at those gathered before him. 'Our objective is simple – we're getting out of this camp and we're taking that Emperor-forsaken Gargant down on the way. You all know the odds aren't good so I won't blow smoke up your arse. Many of us will die. Maybe all of us. Guardsmen die, that's what we do. But when we die, we take xenos with us. We'll show them why Imperial Guardsmen are not to be kept as slaves.' The men and women nodded, steeling themselves, grasping their lasguns and launchers with white knuckles. 'Our attack will be three-pronged.

'Squad one, we'll come out in arrowhead formation. I'll take point. We exit this building in a firing advance towards the yard. We move fast and hit as hard as we can. If it's got green skin, you kill it.

'Squad two, move inside the arrowhead. Your primary goal is to get weapons to as many other Guardsmen as you can. Once you've delivered your weapons, break formation and start a fighting swarm.

'Squad three, you move at the rear. Once the havoc starts, your aim is to breach the fence. The missiles and grenades should be enough to do it. Bust us a hole. Squad one, through all this you stay on me. We're going for the Gargant. All clear?'

There were nods and responses of 'Yes, sergeant.'

'Good.' Van Veenan moved to the door, the troopers behind him readying themselves. He turned back to look at them. 'We've forgotten who we are,' he said. 'We are the Astra Militarum. We are the hammer that crushes the foes of mankind. We've spent all this time fearing the fact that we are locked in this prison with the greenskins, but we've forgotten what else that means. They are locked in here with us. The Emperor protects.'

'The Emperor protects,' they responded in unison.

'Good speech, sarge,' Trotter said. 'Like I said, good to have you back.'

And van Veenan opened the door.

No doubt the orks expected to see van Veenan and the group of Guardsmen exit the bunker carrying a large piece of equipment they didn't understand. What they saw instead were Guardsmen emerging with guns, something they absolutely did understand. Their eyes grew wide with surprise. A nearby ork reached for its slugga, but van Veenan already had his lasgun shouldered. He pulled the trigger and, with the familiar crack of las-fire, an instantaneous beam lit up with a blaze of blue directly through one of the ork's wide red eyes; the eyeball shrivelled away into black goo and the back of the ork's skull blew out with the pressure of superheated fungal brain matter.

A dozen greenskins standing nearby stared as the dead ork landed with a heavy thud in the dirt. After a moment they opened fire with booming shots towards van Veenan's small force. Those orks armed only with choppas began charging, bellowing out guttural roars. The troopers in van Veenan's first squad fanned out in a broad arrow, targeting lasgun fire at the approaching xenos. The second and third squads, as per van Veenan's orders, remained tucked inside the formation, firing out if they could but remaining focused on making it to the yard. Like blood in the water, the sound of shootas and lasguns attracted the attention of the predators all around them. Orks throughout the camp turned en masse at their favourite sound in all the galaxy, the sound of fighting, and none wasted any time in rushing towards it.

The hundred or so Guardsmen left in the yard reacted to the sudden eruption of fighting in various ways. Some scattered, either from fear or from a realisation that they could aid van Veenan by spreading out as a distraction. Others remained where they were. The bravest, or perhaps most reckless, among them attacked the orks. They tackled them in groups of three or four, jumped on their backs, scratching and gouging at their faces and eyes. Most of these desperate assaults ended with the Guardsmen being tossed to the ground and orks battering their heads into pink paste, but several groups of troopers overpowered their much larger foes.

Warboss 'Eadbasha, who with the swelling of his Waaagh! had grown to almost ten feet tall, turned from where he was waiting near the feet of the Gargant and looked in the direction of the rapidly spreading conflict. His red eyes flashed with anger. This may have been fighting, but it was fighting that was interrupting his big moment. He stomped towards the fray, swinging his enormous power klaw. With each powerful arc, the klaw sent a spray of Guardsmen into the air, arms, legs and backs fractured by the impact. Van Veenan saw the warboss coming through the yard. He wasn't interested in the unarmed Guardsmen around him; he was coming for those that had started this – he was coming straight for van Veenan. Van Veenan looked around but could not see Rukaz anywhere. The mekboy had no doubt run away to hide as soon as he'd let van Veenan into the bunker.

Van Veenan shot as he moved, picking targets and firing on them with as much priority as he could in the growing mayhem. In his peripheral vision he caught sight of a Guardsman taking a shoota round in the leg. He fell, his leg torn apart from the knee down. 'Pick up the pace!' Van Veenan yelled as he fired a las-beam into the chest of an ork who ran at them with choppa raised and spittle flying from its wide, roaring mouth. A shoota shell from somewhere hit the ground in front of van Veenan and exploded, bursting upwards, spraying a shower of dirt into his face and momentarily dazing him.

'Sarge!'

He heard the shout from behind him. He thought it was Trotter, but with the noise and confusion he couldn't be sure. 'I'm fine,' he called. 'Triple time, let's go!'

They were almost to the main group of Guardsmen but needed to hurry. They wouldn't stand a chance if they couldn't arm as many troopers as possible. They were already dying faster than van Veenan had expected. Inaccurate they may be, but with massed fire now turning towards the advancing Guardsmen, the orks' shootas were levelling troopers all around van Veenan, blowing limbs off or opening bowels in sprays of viscera.

Van Veenan saw 'Eadbasha sweeping his way through the yard like a tornado. Despite what he'd told Rukaz, he had no intention of trying to take down the rampaging warboss. Van Veenan was not a power-armoured Adeptus Astartes who could go toe to toe with a ten-foot-tall howling green killing machine. No, the heavy weapons team would breach the fence and hopefully some Guardsmen would escape, but more than anything he hoped they would create as much confusion as possible so he could bring down the Gargant before Warboss 'Eadbasha crushed them all between the long digits of his power klaw.

'Squads two and three, execute now,' van Veenan called as their arrowhead formation reached the main group of Guardsmen.

Squad two began running in all directions, handing out or just throwing weapons to every unarmed Guardsman they passed. None of them needed any encouragement to turn their newly acquired firearms on the orks all around them.

'Scatter and fight,' van Veenan roared.

Newly armed Guardsmen shouldered weapons and began firing as they moved. This sudden injection of new opponents drew the orks' attention into a thinly spread attack.

A shoota round struck the ground to van Veenan's left, bursting on impact and covering him with more mud. He dived to the right as another round whistled past, rolled and came up kneeling. He raised his lasgun with practised ease and fired in the direction of the shot. His las-beam struck an ork in the chest, opening a smoking hole.

Around him the mass of Guardsmen in the yard were breaking apart, troopers scattering in all directions to find what cover they could behind the depot buildings or piles of unused scrap. Las-beams streaked outward with flashes of blue in an anarchic display as the fighting rapidly spread across the camp, in all directions, with seemingly no fixed battle lines.

Van Veenan's plan was progressing though. He watched squad three as they ran to take cover behind what had been Barracks Seven, not letting the surrounding mayhem distract them from their goal. Moments after they slammed their backs up against the wall, and with half the squad dropping to their knees to provide covering fire, van Veenan saw first one, then two, then several more missiles fire towards the camp's fence. The first missile fell short, detonating in the middle of a group of gretchin trying to run away from all the fighting. With a burst and a spray of small, squealing green bodies the last of 'Eadbasha's original grot slaves met their undignified end. The second and third missiles found their target and directly impacted the fence, blowing the wooden and steel construction outward. When the next missile struck the ground just inside the fence-line it triggered several landmines just below the surface. Mushrooms of dirt erupted upwards in a tower, and even before the soil and fragments of rock had settled to the ground Guardsmen were already making a break for the exit. Van Veenan silently congratulated squad three before he yelled his order to his own squad.

'Squad one, tighten up on me.' He looked at the squad's six remaining members. He saw a few longing glances towards the now smoking hole in the fence. 'I know the way out is open but that's not our job. Our job is to put an end to the threat here. We're going to get inside the Gargant. We built it, we can tear it down.'

Squad one nodded in unison. 'Yes, sergeant.'

They followed after him as van Veenan ran for the towering ork machine. All around them the camp had devolved into carnage. If there was any focal point of the fighting though, it was the mammoth hole that squad three had blasted through the fence. This was where most Guardsmen were headed and it drew most of the greenskin attention.

Van Veenan and his squad took advantage of the confusion and moved swiftly towards the massive ork war machine. As they were crossing the yard, stray shoota rounds and tumbling ork rokkits cut squad one's numbers from six to four. Just van Veenan, Corporal Trotter and two troopers, Natana and Tereti, remained. Van Veenan hastily corrected that number to three when Natana's head exploded.

As he was urging the last remnants of his squad to hurry, van Veenan heard a rumbling, screaming roar overhead followed by the unmistakable boom of aircraft rupturing the sound barrier. He looked up in time to see six aircraft passing above them. Not just six aircraft but six Imperial Thunderbolt fighters on a low-pass reconnaissance flight. The type of flight van Veenan had seen many times before, the type of flight that meant there was a force advancing somewhere behind them.

Van Veenan felt a sliver of relief at the possible arrival of reinforcements, but they would need to join the fight soon. The men and women of the Rotauri First had deliberately swarmed throughout the camp, causing it to descend into mayhem – and there was only so long they could hold out in the anarchic fighting so suited to the orks.

As he turned to make for one of the Gargant's feet, where he knew there was a doorway, he saw the massive, hydraulically driven shape of Warboss 'Eadbasha stampeding through the fighting, his eyes fixed squarely on van Veenan.

CHAPTER TEN

Commissar Hardnuss rattled around inside the commander's seat of the Leman Russ tank, peering out through the thin reflector sight. She was glad she hadn't refused the helmet handed to her as every time the immense sixty-ton vehicle accelerated, decelerated or abruptly turned, her head hit the turret ring above her in the tight space. Not to mention that without the helmet's noise-cancelling headset, the furious roar of the tank's V12 engine would have deafened her.

Following their escape from the prison camp, Hardnuss and her small retinue of troops had trudged the ten miles to Flaxton. The civilian population, mostly workers at the promethium refinery or families of Guardsmen, had fled at the first signs of the ork invasion and the town was completely empty, the flora and fauna of Rotauri already reclaiming the streets.

From inside the First Infantry's headquarters, Hardnuss had managed to contact the Navy transport *Wings of Endeavour* carrying the Larlo VI Seventh Armoured Rangers. They were one week out but already en route to investigate the loss of communication with Rotauri. Hardnuss had filled them in and provided coordinates for Flaxton to act as a staging ground.

After a week of impatient waiting, the sight of the mammoth Devourer drop-ship descending in a field outside the town was like a vision straight from the Emperor. A yawning beast, the Devourer opened its immense forward bay door, and with a rumbling growl from its throat came the glorious sound of a mechanised regiment firing their vehicles to life.

Colonel Dresner, a tall, wide-shouldered man in command of the Seventh, had rolled forward in his command Chimera to meet Hardnuss.

'Commissar Hardnuss, I presume,' the colonel had said.

'Yes, colonel,' Hardnuss replied. 'I'm very glad to see you.'

The colonel nodded. 'You seem to be missing one of these.'

He tossed an object to Hardnuss. She caught it and looked down at the familiar sight, a gunmetal-grey barrel, a black body emblazoned with a golden aquila – a bolt pistol.

Later, as the tank regiment thundered away from Flaxton, Hardnuss squeezed the grip of the bolt pistol, feeling the familiar weight in her hand. It felt good to wield a weapon of the Emperor again, to have the power to deal out punishment to those who deserved it. As a commissar that was her purpose; she hadn't realised quite how much she missed it when it had been taken away. It was an extra thrill to be in the commander's seat of a Leman Russ, to have the might of the machine to add to her pent-up need to deliver vengeance. Command of this tank had been given up to her by one of the Seventh Armoured Rangers' sergeants so that she could ride into battle with the regiment and use her knowledge of the ork camp to assist their attack.

Her tank was near the front-centre of the forty-strong advance of lumbering, unstoppable armoured vehicles as they drove in an extended line towards the now wildly overpopulated ork shanty town and the prison camp beyond it. The tanks powered through the forest, turning sharply on their rumbling tracks to negotiate their way between the trees, splintering and knocking them down with their thick armour plating when there was no other way around.

As the Seventh emerged from the treeline, forty promethium-guzzling V12 engines growled in unison. And the orks were already waiting. There could be no hiding the advance of an armoured regiment. The greenskins did not need complicated auspex stations or a planetwide vox-network, it was enough for them to hear the ferocious engines ploughing through the forest. When the line of Leman Russ war machines hit the open ground before them, a sight that should have stuck fear and awe into the hearts of mankind's enemies, the orks whooped in joyous rapture. It was not only Hardnuss who felt elated at finally engaging in battle; the greenskins too were at last able to release the frustration that had built up within them.

The orks poured from the shanty town in a green wave, some clambering up onto the roofs of precariously constructed buildings and others hanging out the windows to take aim at the approaching Imperial forces. Seemingly all at once, with no leadership or tactical consideration, the greenskins opened fire. Bullets from sluggas and shootas merely pinged off the thick Leman Russ armour and even large-calibre explosive shells that detonated on impact did little more than leave black scorches over the surface of the tanks.

Despite being sealed within the steel beast with her noise-cancelling headset firmly over her ears, when the Leman Russ fired Hardnuss felt as though she were inside a crack of thunder. The world shuddered but the commissar kept her gaze fixed on the reflector sight and watched the barrage of battle cannon shells from the Seventh Armoured Rangers slam into the ork town. The hastily erected buildings stood no chance under the onslaught and they burst apart in flying debris of wood, rockcrete and sprays of ork flesh. Beyond the exploding town, Hardnuss could see the camp and the shape of the immense ork Gargant standing above it all.

'Colonel Dresner,' Hardnuss said over the vox, patching into the colonel's tank beside her in the line, 'I'd advise watching our fire. We've got friendlies in the camp.'

The colonel didn't reply and for a moment Hardnuss wondered whether he'd received other orders – it wouldn't surprise her to learn that those in the camp were considered acceptable losses. But then the colonel spoke over the regiment-wide vox-channel.

'All units, close fire only. We hit the orks with smash and crash.'

The line of tanks accelerated towards the ork shanty town ready to plough in, their advance all but unstoppable, at least until the first ork tankbustaz emerged onto the field. Several mobs of these large boyz pushed their way through to the front.

Dozens of rokkits were loosed towards the advancing tanks, spinning, tumbling and looping through the air and leaving tumultuous lines of smoke trailing behind them. Most flew in harmlessly haywire trajectories, spearing into the ground or buzzing away into the forest, but a number found targets. These tankbusta rokkits struck the immensely thick Leman Russ armour but their shaped charges punched hard. With explosions that rocked the mammoth vehicles on their tracks, they tore craterous gouges into hulls and several managed to bring tanks to a halt as engines took damage or the crews inside were punctured by spall rupturing off the internal walls.

Commissar Hardnuss watched as the tankbusta boyz brought out bright red squigs, snarling, snapping and yanking at the chains that held them. Each of the wild creatures had bombs and rokkits strapped to their sides and their ork masters released them, letting them bound straight at the vehicles.

Tanks across the line opened fire at the charging squigs with their hull-mounted heavy bolters. The red orkoid creatures began hopping and dashing in serpentine paths to avoid the fire, but those that were hit splattered in sprays of red or exploded as the armament they carried discharged. Any that reached the tanks struck with suicidal detonations, blasting damage in the front and sides of tanks and in some cases disabling the vehicles as they blew their tracks off.

Hardnuss saw tanks, half a dozen or more, drop back from the line as the orks managed to disable them. That still left more than enough of the Emperor's hammers to smash into the ork town and lay waste to everything around them. Hardnuss felt the fully unleashed raw power of the Leman Russ' engine as they crashed through a rockcrete barrier and into the tight, twisting streets.

Tanks rammed their way through ork buildings, killing just as many of the greenskins under their rolling tracks as they did with their heavy bolters. Close confines were not ideal for tank warfare and the need to smash their way through buildings and negotiate the shattered debris slowed down their advance.

Orks swarmed around the slowed tanks, shooting at them from close range, climbing onto them to try to lever open the hatches. Some even resorted to hitting them with choppas. Those vehicles armed with sponson-mounted flamers sprayed the greenskins with superheated promethium when they drew too close.

'Tankbusta bombs,' Colonel Dresner roared over the vox. *'Take down any greenskins with those tankbusta bombs!'*

Hardnuss immediately began scanning the area she could see through the reflector sight and saw a lightly armoured greenskin dashing down the street towards them, a round flat-sided bomb in its hands.

'Two o'clock,' she called down the vox, 'we've got a tankbusta at two o'clock.'

The gunner on the heavy bolter was firing into a group of greenskins descending a destroyed building beside them and immediately began to swing around to target the tankbusta, but Hardnuss could already see he was going to be too slow. She undid the turret hatch and pushed it open. As she emerged from the top of the tank, she was immediately assaulted by the sounds, sights and smells of battle. She ignored it all to raise her newly acquired bolt pistol. She fired three times in quick succession at the ork tankbusta. The creature fell, dropping the tankbusta bomb harmlessly to the ground.

Below her, the tank jerked and began rumbling forward again. Hardnuss bellowed out a war cry to match that of the greenskins around them, firing randomly with her bolt pistol. After so long kept captive, she couldn't help but feel a cathartic release in executing those greenskins that had kept her prisoner. She considered, just for a moment before she banished the heretical thought, whether perhaps humans were not so different from greenskins after all.

CHAPTER ELEVEN

Outside the camp, the complexion of the battle had changed. Van Veenan had seen the reassuring sight of a battle line of Leman Russ tanks burst forth from the trees and slam into the ork shanty town in a thunderous frontal assault. Those orks from outside who had been running for the hole in the fence had performed a rapid about-turn and headed back to engage the newly arrived armoured vehicles.

But inside the camp, van Veenan had more pressing concerns as, with deceptive speed, Warboss 'Eadbasha had caught up with him. The massive ork lumbered across his path, blocking him from reaching the Gargant.

Hydraulic fluid sprayed in a high arc from a hose connected to his shoulders as the warboss leaned forward and roared, his misshapen and bulbous head close enough that van Veenan felt the heat of his breath.

'WAAAAAAAAAAGH!'

'Eadbasha closed his mighty klaw, already dripping with blood, and swung it wildly. Van Veenan lunged forward, right under the arc of the klaw and almost between 'Eadbasha's legs. Troopers Tereti and Trotter both dived to their left, dodging the powerful weapon. Trotter rolled smoothly and lifted her lasgun as she came up kneeling. She fired at the enormous warboss, the las-beam connecting with 'Eadbasha's torso, but it struck a part of his chest encased in thick armour. The surface of the metal burned and became a bubbling black liquid in an area not much larger than a one throne coin. She fired again, moving her aim upwards towards 'Eadbasha's exposed head, but he shifted sideways just enough that the beam caught his iron jaw with a glancing blow, leaving a superheated red line that soon faded into a black gash. Tereti was up and firing too, her las-beam burying itself in 'Eadbasha's power klaw arm but doing little damage.

'Emperor damn it,' Trotter muttered as she prepared to fire again, but by now 'Eadbasha had swung his other arm around. He held a twin-barrelled shoota that looked like little more than a pistol in his enormous fist. Trotter rolled to the side, the concussive blast striking the ground nearby and causing an explosive ringing in her ears. Tereti attempted to scatter too, but was caught as the shot burst at her feet. She was thrown backwards, her standard-issue Astra Militarum boots, and the feet that were in them, nowhere to be seen.

Meanwhile, van Veenan, lying on his back under the hulking warboss, plucked a krak grenade off his belt, ripped the pin out with his mouth and tossed it straight upwards before scampering through 'Eadbasha's legs to clear the blast radius. Thankful for all the practise he'd had with his improvised sock-ball, he looked back to see the krak grenade float perfectly upwards and, with a clink, magnetically attach itself to 'Eadbasha's armoured chest. Van Veenan counted. *Three... two...* 'Eadbasha clamped his power klaw over the krak grenade, but before he could pull it off, it erupted. Van Veenan rolled onto his stomach and covered his head with his hands to protect himself from the explosive debris and the fragments of shattered armour.

After the momentary deafness had passed, van Veenan looked up. His heart immediately sank. Warboss 'Eadbasha still stood. His power klaw had been blasted open, the weapon twisted and missing one of its long, talon-like fingers, and his chest armour was blackened and cracked, but he was still alive, his face full of fury.

'Emperor's teeth!' Van Veenan cursed as he clambered to his feet. A lasgun beam streaked past. Trotter, in her dazed and confused state, had fired again but missed high over 'Eadbasha's shoulder.

Van Veenan lifted his lasgun ready to fire but 'Eadbasha swung his power klaw. Van Veenan took a leaping step backwards, dodging the swing, but the end of the warboss' weapon caught the barrel of his lasgun and sent it spiralling from his grasp. The ork brought his shoota around to aim at van Veenan, who instinctively dived sideways as the barbaric gun boomed, gouging twin craters where he'd been standing. Van Veenan rolled, knowing a follow-up attack would be imminent, but he wasn't fast enough. 'Eadbasha's power klaw slammed down from above him, the two remaining digits impaling themselves into the dirt either side of van Veenan's torso. The klaw sparked, smoked and released a high-pitched grinding as 'Eadbasha closed the damaged appendage. Van Veenan felt the pressure of the klaw squeezing shut, pinning his arms to his sides.

Trotter screamed as she ran at the warboss, firing las-beam after las-beam. Most of them struck the warboss on his thick armour, ablating the surface a small amount but causing no significant damage. Several of the shots struck flesh, though. Van Veenan could smell the burning of ork as las-beams cut into 'Eadbasha's bare arm just above the power klaw, a smell like setting a match to a mushroom. 'Eadbasha didn't flinch, not even as Trotter's final las-beam hit him in the face, burning through one cheek and exploding out the other in a spray of teeth and tongue. As Trotter reached the warboss and desperately swung her lasgun at his legs like a mad lumberjack, 'Eadbasha threw his free fist and backhanded Trotter aside like an annoying fly before turning his attention to van Veenan.

'Should 'ave krumped ya when I 'ad da chance,' 'Eadbasha growled as the crushing pressure of the klaw grew, squeezing van Veenan's arms against his ribs and making it hard to breathe. He was sure his bones were about to snap.

'Puny humies easy to break.'

Van Veenan saw stars burst across his vision. He felt a pop in his ribs, then another and a sudden sharp pain. He couldn't breathe at all now. He knew he was about to be crushed and was disappointed he wouldn't get to go out with a witty one-liner. He seemed to be looking out at the world through a rapidly contracting tunnel. Then, as his vision was fading, the pressure released.

'Eadbasha had let go.

Van Veenan instinctively gasped for air, which magnified the pain in his ribs. He settled for small gulps as he tried to suck in precious oxygen. The power klaw lifted away as 'Eadbasha turned, only to be engulfed by a searing hot torrent of orange flame.

Van Veenan felt the skin of his face tighten; his eyebrows and hair began to curl and burn as the stream of flame roared over the top of him. He rolled to the side several times, ignoring the pain it caused in his ribs, knowing he had to escape the radiant heat. When the flame ceased, van Veenan looked up at what had sprayed the warboss with fire. To his surprise it was not Imperial forces; it was a contraption that looked like an enormous bipedal tin can. The machine, painted black and white and thickly armoured, walked on multijointed mechanical legs. Its four arms had two serrated power klaws, a spinning saw blade and a short-barrelled flamer, smoking from having just fired. Thick exhaust pipes on the back spewed coils of smog into the air. On top of the cylindrical body a hatch was open, out of which was poking the unmistakable green-goggled head of Mekboy Rukaz.

'Eadbasha turned to the mekboy driving the robotic machine. Large sections of the warboss' armour and much of his exposed flesh were charred and melting away after being hosed down with the flamer. He growled deep in his throat and worked his jaw, attempting to speak, but the dark-green skin was blackened and, in some places, completely gone. He persisted though, ripping burned flesh apart as he opened his mouth to howl at the mekboy.

'Rukaz!' 'Eadbasha roared. 'You traitorous git. I knew you was nothin' but trouble.'

Van Veenan was utterly astonished that 'Eadbasha was still standing. Being doused with burning promethium would have left little of a human but charred bone. The pain must have been excruciating. Perhaps it was true that greenskins felt no pain at all.

'Smartest is best, 'Eadbasha,' Rukaz called back. 'It's time da galaxy got to see what us mekboyz can do. I is gonna be mek-boss now. This is gonna be Waaagh! Rukaz!'

'As if,' 'Eadbasha said. 'I is toughest.'

'My smarts make me toughest,' Rukaz said. 'Time for you to see why.'

Rukaz disappeared into his insanely armed Deff Dread, the hatch clanging shut behind him. Moments later the mekboy's can, saw blade whirring and multiple klaws opening and closing, charged at Warboss 'Eadbasha.

'WAAAAAAGH!' 'Eadbasha roared and despite the way his damaged armour still smoked, his power klaw sparked and black hydraulic fluid sprayed from almost every pipe and tube, he charged straight at Rukaz's machine. The gigantic ork and the monstrous machine, both around ten feet tall, slammed into each other with unbelievable force, momentarily spinning like dance partners before separating.

'Eadbasha swung his enormous power klaw and slammed it into the armoured shell enclosing Rukaz, taking a chunk out of the metal and causing the Deff Dread's mechanical legs to work furiously to keep itself upright. Rukaz recovered control and ploughed straight back into 'Eadbasha, knocking him backwards.

Rukaz's smaller power klaws didn't strike 'Eadbasha. They worked surgically, grabbing at pieces of his shoulder armour and bending and pulling them off. 'Eadbasha retaliated by pushing the machine back and then slamming his power klaw down on top of it. The legs buckled but then powered up again. Rukaz went straight back to working on 'Eadbasha's armour. Like the mekboy he was, he was dismantling 'Eadbasha piece by piece.

Van Veenan scampered away from the fighting, grabbing Tereti's fallen lasgun with one hand and Trotter's arm with the other.

'Come on,' he said as he ran for the Gargant. Even as they headed for the massive mechanical ork, smoke began pouring in rising pillars from vents at the back. The eyes still glowed green from the power of the tortured weirdboy but now the head turned, the arms began raising the massive cannons and the whole thing seemed to shift its weight forward, ready to walk. The Gargant was coming to life.

'Emperor's teeth and damnation,' van Veenan cursed, but his words were swallowed by the sounds of rending metal, smashing rockcrete and howling engines. He turned to look behind him and saw the comforting sight of Leman Russ tanks smashing out the back of the ork settlement and towards the camp.

The Gargant groaned and with a discharge of its green energy, the right foot lifted, moved forward and then slammed to the ground in an earthquake step.

The Leman Russ tanks roared as they bulldozed through the fence and into the camp. The cavalry was here to liberate these prisoners of Waaagh! Van Veenan felt immense relief – they wouldn't need to get inside the Gargant after all. That many Imperial tanks would blow the ork's mighty war machine back into its component parts.

And sure enough, with resounding booms that seemed to crack the air in half, tank battle cannons opened up with the Emperor's fury on the Gargant. Van Veenan waited for eruptions of superheated metal to burst from multiple locations all over the Gargant. Instead, what followed was a bright green flash of energy several yards away from the surface of the machine. Wherever a shell struck, a green crackling glow appeared and traced the shape of an energy bubble. Van Veenan's heart sunk. The Gargant was protected by some form of force field.

Of course it was.

Even as shell after shell hit the Gargant, its force field held strong. It lifted its immense weaponised arms towards the tanks. The multi-barrelled cannons started to rotate, slowly at first but quickly gaining speed until they began to fire. The rapid, concussive booming of the cannons was even louder than the firing of the tanks. It was so loud that it may as well have been the only sound in the world. Van Veenan planted his hands over his ears, his eyes began to water and he was fairly certain he would never hear anything again. The orks throughout the camp cheered but van Veenan only knew this because he could see them raising their arms and weapons in the air.

The shots from the Gargant's cannons streaked towards its attackers. The shells struck everything: tanks, buildings, the ground, other orks – it didn't matter, the destruction was indiscriminate. The shells that hit tanks plunged through the armour, bursting them open in explosions of spinning shrapnel.

Van Veenan could do nothing but watch as the Gargant tore through the Emperor's most faithful vehicles with relative ease. The armoured division returned fire, and the Gargant took a small step backwards under the barrage, but the energy bubble surrounding it never failed. Tanks were sheared in half, disappearing in bursts of fire, leaving the shapes of burning Guardsmen to run from the wreckage with flailing arms.

A dozen, maybe two dozen tanks were destroyed in what seemed like an instant. Eventually the armoured assault force broke through and peeled out in a fan, spreading into the camp to avoid the concentrated fire of the Gargant. Throughout the camp the Guardsmen, who had moments ago been fighting so valiantly, dropped to the ground and scrambled for what cover they could find, men and women now trapped in the middle of a war between gods.

As the tanks spread out they unleashed their heavy bolters and flamers at the orks, who ran around in what seemed delirious joy at the battle unfolding around them. Many had flocked to the Gargant and stood around its massive feet cheering and roaring and firing randomly towards Guardsmen and tanks. As the Gargant stepped backwards to maintain its balance under the barrage of Leman Russ fire, it planted a foot right on top of a large gathering of greenskins. Many of them avoided the foot but several others did not, and van Veenan felt an odd sense of pride that the metal sheets he had spent so much time riveting together had just crushed a bunch of orks.

Eventually the green force field flickered under the onslaught, with shells exploding closer and closer to the ork machine's armoured surface, but the damage it suffered was minimal compared to the utter annihilation it was causing. Tanks were still being shredded across the camp. The might of Imperial Guard armour had been added to the fray, but they had done little more than scratch the Gargant's surface.

'Emperor's Throne,' van Veenan exclaimed. He turned back to Corporal Trotter, who like him was doing little more than keeping her head as close to the dirt as possible. 'Trotter, we need to get inside that thing!'

Trotter crawled up beside van Veenan. 'But, sarge, what about that force field? If battle cannons don't get through, what makes you think we can?'

'Look at those greenskins,' van Veenan said, 'moving around near the feet. They're passing through the field as if it isn't even there. It only stops weapons. I think we can make it through too.'

'That's a gamble, sarge. We could get fried.'

Van Veenan looked at her. 'Fifty thrones says we make it. You going to trust me this time?'

Trotter cracked a wry smile. 'Okay, sarge. I'm with you.' She instinctively dropped as a battle cannon shell flew overhead, low enough to whistle through the air. 'I'm trusting you've got a solid plan of how we actually destroy that thing.'

'The head,' van Veenan said. 'There's an old military saying, to kill the snake you have to cut off the head. Or, in our case, we need to make the head explode. Come on, on me.'

Van Veenan rose to his feet and began running towards the Gargant, Trotter right beside him. They fired at those orks in their path, cutting them down with accurate lasgun fire while dashing through barely aimed shots from the greenskins. As they approached the bottom of the Gargant they drew the attention of those orks who had gathered around it. The orks brought their shootas to bear and unleashed a staccato rhythm of fire towards van Veenan and Trotter.

Van Veenan tried to continue on towards the Gargant, firing back and veering randomly to avoid presenting an easy target, but as more and more shoota rounds exploded all around him he knew either he or Trotter would soon be blown to pieces. 'Emperor damn it,' he said as he rapidly changed direction and headed away from the Gargant, making for the cover of a solid rockcrete storage bunker. He and Trotter pressed themselves against the dome-shaped wall of the bunker. Shoota rounds burst in the dirt nearby and several bounced off the roof and flew over their heads.

Looking back through the chaos, van Veenan saw Warboss 'Eadbasha and Mekboy Rukaz still battling each other amid the mayhem. 'Eadbasha was swinging wildly at Rukaz's Deff Dread but Rukaz had managed to tear 'Eadbasha's thick chest armour away, revealing his green flesh.

Growing desperate, 'Eadbasha planted his shoota up against Rukaz's can and fired multiple times. At such close range the shells burst against Rukaz's armour and blasted back to rip 'Eadbasha's flesh too. Rukaz's can staggered, sparks and smoke and what might have been oil or blood pouring from a hole blasted into it. For a moment van Veenan thought 'Eadbasha had won but then Rukaz's can leapt towards the warboss, leading with the buzzing saw blade. It buried itself into 'Eadbasha's now exposed chest, and with a mighty straining of metal and a wailing of pistons and actuators Rukaz pressed forward and lifted the blade. The saw, throwing an arc of blood twenty feet into the air, buried itself deeper into 'Eadbasha's chest until it was completely inside the warboss and still spinning madly, chewing his flesh and internal organs into mince. 'Eadbasha smashed his power klaw against Rukaz's can contraption again and again, denting the top in, long after van Veenan thought he should have been dead. Eventually though, with nothing left inside his chest but blended soup, the warboss fell still. Rukaz lowered the saw blade and the body of Warboss Nok 'Eadbasha, self-described prophet of Gork and Mork, dropped to the ground, dead.

As if the orks had somehow sensed the death of their warboss and the sudden shift in the power dynamic, the fighting throughout the camp lulled;

the greenskins not directly engaged with Imperial Guardsmen stopped and turned to look at Rukaz standing over the body of 'Eadbasha. Blaring through a vox-amplification unit, Rukaz's voice suddenly boomed out over the camp.

'I is no longer Mekboy Rukaz,' he said. 'I is now Mek-Boss Rukaz and this,' he gestured to the Gargant with his bloody saw blade, 'is all Waaagh! Rukaz now! WAAAAAGH!'

Most of the orks joined the roar, but not all.

'I is not fightin' for no oddboy!' a shout came from nearby. 'Ardskull, a huge choppa in his hand wet with human blood, approached. 'I should be warboss. I was big nob!'

'You ain't killed 'Eadbasha though,' another ork shouted, 'Rukaz did. He da boss now.'

'He only killed 'im because he got that Deff Dread wotsit,' 'Ardskull replied, but seeing a lot of the orks didn't seem to agree, he said, 'We don't fight for no mekboy. I is the biggest. I kill Rukaz and I be warboss then.'

'Ardskull rushed towards Rukaz with his choppa raised over his head. ''Ardskull for boss!'

Rukaz dropped back inside his Deff Dread and stomped towards the charging nob. 'Ardskull swung his choppa but Rukaz parried the blow with one klaw. The other klaw shot forward and grabbed 'Ardskull right around the circumference of the metal dome attached to the top of his head. Rukaz's klaw squeezed shut. 'Ardskull howled in anger, but Rukaz didn't relent. The metal dome bent in half, squashing whatever brains 'Ardskull might have had beneath it. Rukaz's saw moved forward and beheaded the ork nob. He raised it high to display to all those orks that watched.

'I is mek-boss!' Rukaz screamed.

'Well,' van Veenan said, 'would you look at that.'

Taking advantage of the momentary confusion, van Veenan hurried to enter through the door at the back of the Gargant's foot and began climbing a set of winding metallic stairs that spiralled up into the legs. Trotter followed close behind, their heavy boots clanging on the metal with every step.

Somewhere near the knee they ran into a mekboy who was dashing around tightening bolts that seemed to be springing loose whenever the machine moved. The ork looked up, its eyes growing wide with the surprise of seeing humans inside the Gargant. It grabbed for a large spanner that lay on the floor nearby, but van Veenan acted first and killed the greenskin with a lasgun shot through the chest.

They continued up, reaching the propulsion system in the bowels of the mechanical beast. Here a dozen gretchin worked to patch leaks of oil and solder together live, sparking wires under the agitated direction of another animated mekboy. Van Veenan held his fist up and then gestured with his palm down, silently signalling for Trotter to stop and sneak past.

They moved carefully and the greenskins didn't seem to notice them until a shout from below drew their attention. It was the familiar shriek of Mek-Boss Rukaz.

'Humie nob van Veenanz!' The ork's voice carried up from the levels below. 'I know you is up there!'

The grots working nearby turned and saw van Veenan and Trotter attempting to sneak up the stairs. Van Veenan shot them a quick teasing smile before he unclipped a frag grenade from his belt, pulled the pin and tossed it towards them.

He didn't need to tell Trotter to take advantage of the distraction and follow as he dashed up the stairs. She was close on his tail, her lasgun raised in ready position, just as aware as van Veenan that the gift he'd thrown to the greenskins was about to make the entire Gargant aware of their presence.

The boom of the frag grenade was followed by a succession of other noises – rending metal, grinding gears and drive shafts smashing around their casings. Van Veenan continued moving, hoping he'd managed to break something important.

They rounded the spiralling stairs and were met at the next landing by several ork boyz alerted by Rukaz's shouts and the subsequent grenade explosion. Only one had a pistol-sized slugga; the other two were armed with choppas. The slugga fired with a loud report and a burst of black sooty smoke as van Veenan and Trotter came into view. The bullet pinged off the wall well wide of the two Guardsmen and Trotter shot the ork through the face with a well-aimed lasgun beam. Van Veenan fired as well, cutting down one of the other orks with a burst to the chest.

The third ork ran at van Veenan with a howling cry, its choppa raised overhead. Trotter recovered quickly, aimed and fired. The las-beam hit the ork in the shoulder, opening a cauterised gash. The ork stumbled somewhat but managed to swing its choppa at van Veenan. Van Veenan dodged back and to the side, but in the tight confines of the stairwell he was forced to raise his lasgun and use it to parry the ork's weapon. He felt the jarring impact as they connected. He managed to deflect the ork's blow but the overpowering strength of the greenskin sent him slamming into the wall, his broken ribs erupting with pain. Trotter fired again and thankfully this time her shot put the ork down for good.

Van Veenan coughed and was dismayed to see blood spray from his mouth across the wall. He wiped his mouth. 'Come on,' he said to Trotter. 'We need to keep moving, avoid close combat with the greenskins if we can.'

They continued, higher into the torso and the workings of the Gargant. They came out into a space where dozens of orks carried immense shells over their shoulders, shuttling them up to the arms to feed the massive cannons. The orks spun to look at van Veenan and Trotter but van Veenan didn't stop, knowing they didn't have time for, and likely wouldn't survive, an engagement with that many greenskins.

Eventually, after climbing a seemingly endless number of steps, van Veenan and Trotter emerged into the control room, high in the chest of the great Gargant. Orks were manning control panels of rudimentary dials and gauges and yelling instructions into a complicated network of twisting speaking tubes. In front of them a large pict screen that had once been erected to provide messages of Imperial support to the promethium refinery workers showed the scene outside the Gargant.

The large ork who seemed to be in command – not only because he was standing in the centre of the room yelling wildly, but also because he wore an oversized peaked cap like some comical impression of an Imperial Navy officer – turned towards them. His eyes grew wide.

'Dey is 'ere!' he called, word of their intrusion having obviously preceded them. Several of the orks rose from their seats but a voice stopped them.

'You sit down. You need to keep my Gargant runnin.'

Van Veenan turned to see Mek-Boss Rukaz stepping off the stairs and into the command room. He turned his goggled gaze to van Veenan.

'Humie nob van Veenanz,' Rukaz said. 'I knew you wasn't going to kill 'Eadbasha and I knew you was going to go for my Gargant. Sneaky humies always bein' sneaky. Don't matter though. I just needed you to start some fightin' for me so I got my chance at taking down 'Eadbasha myself. I showed 'im what a smartboy can do. Now I is boss. I 'ave the Gargant. I is gonna lead the Waaagh!'

'I didn't think you liked fighting,' van Veenan said. 'I thought you weren't interested in conquering the galaxy like 'Eadbasha was.'

Rukaz smiled. 'I ain't said that. I just said I could do krumpin' differently. I showed 'im. Unorky 'e called me. Who's unorky now?'

And Trotter fired. She'd shouldered her lasgun and pulled the trigger before van Veenan even knew she was moving. The las-beam should have struck Rukaz directly in the centre of the chest but instead of burning an immense hole through him, it stopped several inches away, a bubble-shaped energy field momentarily flashing around him; the two coils on his back sparked and zapped in response.

Rukaz smiled again. 'Sneaky humies.' He lifted the shoota-sized weapon he held, aiming it at Corporal Trotter. It was unlike any weapon van Veenan had ever seen, ork-made or otherwise. It was connected to Rukaz's backpack with a series of colourful cables, the barrel ending in three spheres that began rapidly spinning about its axis. They flashed with electrical energy before suddenly erupting with what could only be described as lightning. The blazing arc struck Trotter in the stomach. Her entire body spasmed, her muscles locked in seizure and she dropped to the ground, her skin smoking. Van Veenan instantly knew she was dead.

With a burst of ferocious energy van Veenan rushed at Rukaz. The mekboss aimed his lightning gun at van Veenan but the veteran sergeant anticipated the shot. Even with his shattered ribs and punctured lungs the sudden tumult of adrenaline flooding through him was enough for van Veenan to drop into a tumble. The crackling lash of lightning blasted over the top of him. In that moment he felt no pain as he rolled through and jumped up hard, slamming into Rukaz.

Rukaz stumbled back with the impact. He swung his lightning gun up again but van Veenan was quick enough to get back inside his force field and slam the butt of his lasgun into the ork's face. Rukaz swung at van Veenan with his free hand, the blow catching him on the side of the face. The strike resonated through his skull and sent him lurching to the side, but he managed to keep his feet. Van Veenan had lost count of the number of times he'd been punched in the face – by humans or xenos – and this strike wasn't even as bad as some of the larger human fists he'd managed to get his face in front of. It was almost always a bad idea to engage in hand-to-hand combat with an ork but Mek-Boss Rukaz was not, it seemed, as much of a threat when you could get through his bizarre inventions.

Van Veenan took heart in this and charged once more. He slammed the end of his lasgun into the ork's face again and again. He barely registered that he was roaring, howling with all the fury of the past months as he struck Rukaz with vicious and overwhelming speed. The lenses of Rukaz's goggles shattered under the butt of the lasgun and as the mekboy back-pedalled under the flurry of attacks, van Veenan saw the ork's eyes staring out at him. His reddish eyeballs were wide and alight, not quite with fear but with something like wonder.

Van Veenan managed to push Rukaz back to the top of the stairs but felt his attacks slowing. He was burning through the adrenal fuel that was keeping him going. His arms were growing heavy. As his attacks slowed he expected Rukaz to take advantage and retaliate, but instead the ork stared at him with a smile on his face.

'That was good fightin',' humie nob van Veenanz,' he said. 'You turnin' orky now? You want to join–'

Van Veenan lashed out and kicked the mek-boss as hard as he could. Rukaz fell backwards, almost comically windmilling his arms to try to maintain his balance, but he dropped and tumbled down the stairs.

Van Veenan turned and saw the other orks around the control room staring at him. The greenskins seemed perplexed, at least momentarily, about what they were supposed to do now their new mek-boss had been booted down the stairs. Most of them looked more physically imposing than Rukaz, and van Veenan was not going to risk fighting them, which he was sure would be their eventual conclusion. He took the opportunity to sprint for the stairs; he needed to keep going higher.

Up he twisted through the Gargant, following his nose until he emerged into the head. Before him the weirdboy was still strapped to the chair. The sight was shocking and van Veenan felt a pang of sympathy for the ork. It had shrivelled into a wretched creature. It seemed to have lost all muscle mass and its green skin was tight around the shape of its bones but hung in loose folds elsewhere. Its sunken face was little better than a skull. Still, its eyes and body glowed with the same eerie green energy.

Van Veenan, not giving himself time to think, dashed forward. He began unbuckling the straps holding the helmet to the weirdboy's head. His pursuers sounded close. Once all the straps were loose, he grabbed hold of the helmet and pulled. It came free of the weirdboy's head with a sucking sound, like water down a plughole. Long, tendril-like wires coated in blood and pus popped out from where they had been inserted into the weirdboy's brain. The ork, who had been silent until that point, began to groan.

The orks from the control room reached the top of the stairs and van Veenan turned to face them. Mek-Boss Rukaz emerged and saw what van Veenan had done. This time van Veenan was sure there was fear behind those shattered goggles.

'I guess that means I was right,' van Veenan said.

The weirdboy's groan started to increase in volume. Green energy began bursting from its head and striking the walls with electrical sparks. Van Veenan raised his lasgun and fired at the orks, who had begun running towards the ork weirdboy under the frenzied orders of Rukaz. The orks desperately tried to refit the helmet on the weirdboy's overloading brain. As it became clear they would not be able to contain the eruption, Rukaz growled. His face twisted in anger.

'Humie nob van Veenanz!' he shouted. 'I ain't forgettin' this.' The ork mek-boss turned and scampered down the stairs.

Some of the orks from the control room followed; those that remained turned their attention to van Veenan. He leaned over and lifted the handle he'd seen Rukaz use from the ground. With a hydraulic drone and the whistling of wind, the face of the Gargant began opening. He fired repeatedly with his lasgun to force the orks to keep their distance and then, without thinking – because thinking just led to unhelpful hesitation in these sorts of situations – van Veenan jumped out of the Gargant's head.

He landed on the machine's sheet-metal surface and began half falling, half sliding down its torso. Luckily, the Gargant's portly belly meant that its structure rose to meet him. He hit metal with a jolt, his ribs erupting with pain, blood spraying from his mouth as the air blasted from his lungs. He tumbled over the surface, rolling and falling, and hitting the metal again. Disorientated, unable to determine up from down as he tumbled, van Veenan groped wildly for anything to slow his descent. He managed, perhaps from instinct more than anything, to throw his arms out and plant the soles of his boots on the surface. He slid on his back, his vision wildly twirling and alight with stars. The rubber of his boots slowed him – at least until he reached the groin, where he ran out of metal to cling to and plummeted to the ground.

Landing heavily on his feet van Veenan felt a sudden stab of pain and immediately knew his leg – perhaps both – had broken. His vision swam. He hacked up blood in spurts of spasmic coughing. For a moment, as he lay on the ground looking up at the Gargant, van Veenan was certain his idea had failed or that the orks had managed to secure the helmet back on that unstable weirdboy. Then with an eruption of green energy that spread outwards like a disc, the head of the Gargant exploded. For the briefest of moments the headless Gargant swayed as if that would be the extent of the destruction, but then a series of explosions cascaded down the body of the massive machine and the whole thing began to fall. As it toppled backwards a multi-bladed flying machine emerged from a hatch in the belly, whirring away into the sky as the Gargant collapsed with a world-shaking crash.

It took almost all van Veenan's energy to lift his head and track the smoke-spewing flying machine across the sky. Even if it hadn't had an open cockpit under its spinning blades he would have known who was piloting it. Rukaz flew away from the camp out over the trees, a small contingent of orks and mekboys fleeing after him on foot.

With the destruction of the Gargant and the disappearance of any leadership, the orks collapsed under the continued assault of the Rotauri First and the Larlo VI Seventh Armoured. The remaining men and women of the Rotauri First scoured the camp and the shanty town from end to end, making sure there were absolutely no surviving greenskins. After their experience over the last few months they would not be taking any prisoners.

Company Sergeant Major Marcus van Veenan lay back on his stretcher in the infirmary at Flaxton Barracks. With both of his legs encased in stiff splints he could do nothing but stare at the ceiling. He wished he had some socks to throw.

Van Veenan looked up when Commissar Hardnuss approached; Colonel Dresner was beside her.

'Well, you know they'll certainly tell stories about you now,' the commissar said.

'Emperor save me,' van Veenan replied. 'As if anyone is going to believe this.'

'How are you feeling, sergeant major?' Colonel Dresner asked.

'I feel like I was kept prisoner by orks for several months and then fell off a Gargant, sir.'

The colonel seemed unfazed by van Veenan's response. 'The commissar has told me you planned the escape and have essentially been in command of the remnants of your regiment.'

'Yes, sir. The escape was my plan, though I wouldn't say I was in command of the regiment,' van Veenan said. 'I simply led those that were left, sir.'

'How do you feel about a more permanent command?' the colonel asked.

'Sorry, sir?'

'That ork that escaped, the one Commissar Hardnuss said was called Rukaz, he is the supposed mastermind of all this?'

'More or less, sir.'

'Well, we tracked a small ork void ship leaving the planet. Seems he's escaped off-world. Several other ork ships have entered the system. They seem to be flocking to this so-called mek-boss. He still poses a significant threat to the Imperium.'

'Yes, sir.'

'The Rotauri First is being disbanded as an infantry regiment, sergeant major – the losses were too heavy. The Rotauri Second will be stood up after a tithe. However, I have been granted authority to give command of the remaining troopers of the Rotauri First to you. Commissar Hardnuss has volunteered to serve as unit commissar. You and your troops are to spearhead the campaign to engage the xenos threat and finish off this Waaagh! before it can get started. Congratulations, Lieutenant van Veenan.'

'Sir, I'd prefer not to–'

'I said congratulations, Lieutenant van Veenan,' Colonel Dresner repeated.

'Yes, sir,' Lieutenant van Veenan said, 'thank you, sir.'

'The unit will be officially stood up and transport provided once you and your soldiers recover.'

Once the colonel had left, van Veenan looked over at Commissar Hardnuss. 'See, commissar?' he said. 'I told you something like this would happen if we got out of that prison.'

Commissar Hardnuss smiled at van Veenan. 'Rest up, lieutenant, the Imperium isn't done with you just yet.'

WHERE DERE'S DA WARP DERE'S A WAY

MIKE BROOKS

"Ere we go, 'ere we go, 'ere we go!'

Ufthak Blackhawk, Bad Moon warrior and definite second-biggest in Badgit Snazzhammer's mob, no matter what that zoggin' idiot Mogrot thought, raised his voice in the rolling, rollicking war cry as they piled into the 'Ullbreaker. Outside in the cold vacuum of space, Da Meklord's warfleet was busy crumping the humie ships, but that wasn't Ufthak's fight. Blowing stuff up from a long way off was fine in its way, but he preferred getting up close and personal. Let the gunboyz have their fun: Ufthak was on his way to the *real* fight.

The last few boyz piled in, along with Dok Drozfang and various grots, and then came Da Boffin. A Bad Moon like Ufthak and Da Meklord himself, and one of the warboss' most trusted meks, Da Boffin had replaced his own legs with a single wheel, powered by a fuel made of concentrated squig dung. Ufthak had never worked out how Da Boffin stayed upright on it, since even warbikes needed at least two wheels, plus either a kickstand or the rider's leg – or a kickstand made from someone else's leg – on the few occasions they were stationary. When Ufthak had asked, Da Boffin had just started talking about 'whirly bitz inside it', as though that made any sense.

The last hatch slammed shut and the flyboyz in the cockpit whooped, firing up the engines and vaporising anything immediately behind the shuttle. Ufthak had been on boarding missions before, so he knew what to do: grab on to one of the handholds roughly welded into the walls, and hang on like a grot on a warboar.

The flyboy kaptin stamped down on the lever which released the mag-clamp fastening them to the deck of *Da Meklord's Fury*, and they were away. Immediately, all the boyz who hadn't been in an 'Ullbreaker before went flying back to the rear of the ship, where they were crushed into a painful and indignant heap against the metal bulkhead. Ufthak laughed uproariously as they tumbled past him with expressions of confusion plastered across their faces.

'Ullbreakers got up to full speed quickly, and so it was only a few moments before the G-forces subsided enough for the newbies to untangle themselves from each other and start the important process of working out whose gun was whose. It only took a few moments more for fists to start to fly as they began bad-mouthing each other's shootas.

'If you gitz don't settle down den I'm turnin' dis fing around!'

Boss Snazzhammer stormed down the shuttle, spittle flying from his gob as he kicked boyz out of his way. He was a huge ork, head and shoulders taller than the rest of them, and bedecked in the most ostentatious finery that teef could buy – and, since he was a Bad Moon, he had a lot of teef. There was barely a surface of his armour that wasn't decorated with loot, whether that was medals taken off the corpses of humie bosses, those little bits of wax and paper from the armour of dead beakies, or even some of the fancy gems the pointy-earz wore. In his right hand he carried the massive weapon that had given him his second name: a metal shaft the height of a humie with its legs still attached, with a hammer on one side of the head and a choppa blade on the other. The entire head could be engulfed in a crackling power field with one flick of Snazzhammer's clawed thumb, and Ufthak had seen the boss smash right through a humie tank with it.

The boyz ducked their heads, grabbed their own shootas and tried to avoid the boss' eye. No one wanted to end up like that tank.

'Dat's betta,' Snazzhammer growled. He turned on the spot, addressing the entire 'Ullbreaker. 'Right, we ain't da only 'Ullbreaker wot's flyin' today...'

Boos and jeers.

'...but we got da most important job!' Snazzhammer continued. 'Da Meklord 'imself told me wot we gots ta do, so you all best listen.'

The mob quietened down, as much as they ever would. If Da Meklord had told them what to do, they'd probably better do it. Da Meklord was no ordinary warboss, if there was such a thing: he was Da Biggest Big Mek, and his gear was legendary. He'd gone toe to toe with rival warboss Oldfang Krumpthunda, and after one hit with Da Meklord's shokkhamma no one had found any part of the Goff larger than a finger. Da Meklord's personal force field could shrug off hits from a humie Titan's cooka kannon. His supa-shoota could cut a Deff Dread in half before you could say 'Gork and Mork.' He was what any Bad Moon wanted to be: massive, 'ard as nails and carrying enough weapons and armour to kit out a small warband in his own right.

'Now,' Snazzhammer declared. 'Humies don't got Gork 'n' Mork ta guide dem froo da warp, ta take dem to where da next fight is. Dey gotta use some fancy worky bitz wot dey keeps in da middle of dere ships. Wot we gots ta do is get Da Boffin dere, where he's gonna do some mek stuff. Got it?'

There was a general muttering and nodding of heads, and Snazzhammer beamed. 'Good. Now den. *Who are we?'*

'SNAZZHAMMER'S MOB!' the assembled mass of orks bellowed, Ufthak amongst them.

'Are we da biggest?'

'YES!'

'Are we da baddest!'

'YES!'

'Are we da shootiest?'

'YES!' the mob yelled, and everyone waved their shootas, which were almost all kustom jobs with extra dakka. No one pulled their trigger yet, though, which was good: Ufthak had once been in an 'Ullbreaker where some git with a kannon had managed to crack the flyboyz' seeing-window, and it turned out there was a reason why these things weren't open-topped.

'Dat's what I fort,' Snazzhammer said with grim satisfaction. He reached up and grabbed a handhold overhead. 'Now, everyone hold on to sumfing.'

Ufthak had known this was coming, and reached up with his other hand. 'Ullbreakers flew quick.

There was a shudder as the shuttle's short-range torpedoes all fired at once, concentrating on a small part of the enemy ship's hull to weaken it. Ufthak began counting down.

Five...

Four...

Free...

Two...

One...

He frowned.

Bit of one...

The 'Ullbreaker smashed into the humie ship, its specially reinforced nose cone taking the brunt of the impact and punching them clean through into the interior. The force of the sudden deceleration lifted Ufthak's boots from the floor and nearly wrenched his arms from their sockets, but he held firm. Some of the new ladz who hadn't minded the boss' words enough went flying the other way down the shuttle. One of them collided with a support strut hard enough to snap his back clean in two, much to the disdain of the other boyz who'd managed to remain upright.

'Leave 'im!' Snazzhammer bellowed as a few of them started putting the boot in. 'We got humies ta paste! Get out dere, and get clobberin'!' He aimed a kick at the downed ork's head as he acted on his own words, and his steel toecap hit hard enough to knock it right off. Dark blood sprayed out across the nearby members of the mob, while the flying head caught a lurking grot clean in the chest and knocked it backwards into the wall.

'WAAAAAAAAGGGGHHHHH!'

Ufthak drew his weapons and surged forwards with the mass of green around him. This was life; this was what it meant to be an ork. Enemies in front of him, ladz around him, ammo in his slugga and a good right arm to swing his choppa. What more could anyone ask for?

The fore hatches burst outwards and the boyz spilled out. Ufthak shouldered his way forwards and forced his way through, looking for something to kill.

They'd busted through into a vast chamber of metal, the ceiling of which arched up overhead into gloomy shadow. The walls looked to consist largely of pipes, cables and contact points, some of which spat blue-white sparks, but Ufthak couldn't see much of them. That was partly because of the strange humie machines which loomed throughout the chamber – strange even to him, who'd fought a lot of different humies in a lot of different places – and partly because the humies that crewed this ship had decided they wanted to fight.

They were already swarming inwards, like buzzer squigs converging on an intruder into their nest. Ufthak saw the red-robes and the first flashes of gunfire and grunted in recognition: humie mekboyz! No wonder Da Meklord had his eyes on something fancy; humie tek could do some pretty wild stuff so long as you didn't hit it too hard.

The red-robes slowed, setting themselves to shoot, and Ufthak groaned. Why did humies never want to fight properly? Only beakies ever fancied a real rumble, and they didn't even taste good once you got them out of their armour. The rest of them got close enough for you to smell 'em, then hung back to shoot like Mork-damned Deathskulls.

They also always seemed to think that da boyz would just stand still.

'All right, ladz! 'Ave 'em!' Snazzhammer bellowed, and the mob surged forwards. Ufthak could feel Mork urging him on, and time slowed. His strides seemed to eat up the metal deck beneath him, and the figures in the humie gun line grew larger with each step. He saw an individual barrel track towards him, saw the humie's finger tighten on the trigger, but he took his next step at an angle and Mork smiled on him, because the bolt of spitting energy flew past his head instead of taking him full in the face. The next shot hit him in the shoulder, a white-cold shock that staggered him for a moment, but Ufthak had taken worse in the past, and the humie had gone for the kill instead of turning to run while it could. Not all of its fellows had done the same; some of them were already fleeing in the face of the unstoppable green tide bearing down on them.

Ufthak bared his fangs, bellowed his war cry and cannoned into the humie line with the rest of the mob.

The humie who'd shot him tried to parry his choppa with its rifle; Ufthak gave it respect for the effort but nothing for the execution, because his heavy blade smashed through the spindly weapon and split its torso from neck down to the middle of its chest. Like most humies, it died after one hit, sagging to the floor as he wrenched his choppa free and fired his shoota into what passed for the face of another, although this one was wearing a lot more metal there than most humies did. The metal didn't help it: Ufthak's slugga shots blew its head apart, metal face and all, and it dropped as well.

A humie lunged at him, wielding some sort of spear. The blade buried itself in Ufthak's chest and he bellowed in pain, then booted the wielder in its stomach. It flew backwards, disappearing with a despairing wail into the rolling maul of bodies around Boss Snazzhammer. Ufthak wrenched the spear out – it turned out to be one of the electro-guns with a knife stuck on the end – and threw it after its owner. There was a roar of anger, and Ufthak grinned as Mogrot Redtoof whirled around and clobbered a humie which had had nothing to do with the fact that there was now a knife in his back.

Next to Ufthak, Deffrow had lost his choppa – probably stuck in the ribcage of a dead humie somewhere – and so was using the next best thing: a stikkbomb. He battered one humie aside into the path of Dok Drozfang, who carved it apart with the power klaw he called Da Surjun, broke the skull of another, then wound up and took a swing at a third–

The world went white, very loud and extremely sharp.

Ufthak realised he was on the floor, along with everyone else within three yards of Deffrow. Deffrow himself was on his back, staring stupidly at the handle clutched in his somewhat shredded fist.

'Dey go bang, squigbrain!' Ufthak yelled at him as he got back to his feet. 'Dat's why we frow dem!' Deffrow's idiocy had left him with a bunch of shrapnel in his right-hand side, but it was nothing he couldn't deal with later. The humies, on the other hand, hadn't fared so well. The one Deffrow had hit most recently had taken the brunt of the impact and was now rather red and squishy, and even those further back weren't in a good way, rolling around, wailing and crying like a grot that had swallowed a fire squig.

'Seems like a design flaw t'me,' Deffrow muttered, pushing himself up. He winced and shook his mangled hand, and a finger that had only been attached by a shred of flesh pinwheeled off. 'Ow, dat smartz...'

'Now look what you did!' Ufthak complained at him. 'Dey're running away!' Sure enough, the remaining humies had clearly decided that enough was enough, as they were turning tail and fleeing from the slaughter. Or at least, they were trying to: those of Snazzhammer's mob who hadn't still been picking themselves up because their idiotic neighbour had blown everyone up were jumping on the humies from behind and sending them to see their Emprah. Humies liked to yell about their Emprah a lot, but Ufthak had once heard a bunch of really tough beakies in spiky black armour shouting that the Emprah was dead. With worshippers like this, he could see why. He raised his slugga and shot one in the back, but his heart wasn't in it.

A high-pitched whine grabbed Ufthak's attention. For a moment he thought it was just the after-effects of Deffrow's stikkbomb going off, but then he saw a crackle of blue power, and one of the machines lurched into life. It was a big trukk of some sort, with wheels taller than an ork, and if the blue-crackling thing on the top of it wasn't some sort of gun then he, Ufthak Blackhawk, was a Blood Axe.

'Oh *zog*,' he muttered fervently. 'Boss! You got ya hammer?'

'Don't worry about dat,' Snazzhammer retorted confidently, spinning his hammer and casually decapitating a stray grot with the backswing. 'Dat humie stuff breaks if you look at it funny.'

Ufthak had his doubts. Humies might not be much good in a proper scrap, but their guns tended to be the business. The dirty little gitz also had a nasty habit of aiming, instead of pulling the trigger and letting Gork and Mork decide what would land where, as was right and proper.

The big trukk-gun fizzed noisily, and glowed brighter. Ufthak braced himself: he had a feeling this was going to hurt more than a carelessly detonated stikkbomb.

There was a tremendous sound of tortured, tearing metal from behind them, and a huge shape came sliding across the chamber's floor, careering off humie machines and leaving the wailing red-robes it struck as mere red smears. It collided with the gun trukk, which exploded in a ball of blue fire, and came to a halt. Hatches popped open and boyz emerged, bellowing in anticipation.

'Told you we wasn't da only 'Ullbreaker flyin' today!' Snazzhammer said with satisfaction. He raised his voice in a mocking shout. 'What 'appened to you gitz? Got lost?'

The other mob's boss responded with a rude hand gesture, and Snazzhammer laughed. 'Right, on wiv da job. Boffin! You know where we're goin'?'

Through a lot of doors, as it turned out.

'Beats me how dese humies ever get anywhere,' Mogrot commented, as Wazzock fired up his burna to cut through yet another sealed hatch.

'Dey know how to open 'em,' Ufthak snorted.

'We know how to open 'em!' Mogrot protested, pointing at where Wazzock was dragging a white-hot line down the hatch.

'Open 'em wivout burnas,' Ufthak said patiently. Mogrot was hot squig dung in a fight, no doubt about it, but he wasn't what you'd call a thinker. That was why Ufthak was second-in-command, even though they were more or less the same size. 'Dey're lockin' us out, right?'

'Don't seem too bovvered we're here, den,' Mogrot countered. 'We ain't 'ardly 'ad no one to fight since dat scrap when we got out da 'Ullbreaker!' He nudged a red-robed corpse with his boot, but the mob outnumbered this bunch of humies, and they'd barely been worth the effort.

'Dere's a whole buncha ladz on dis ship by now,' Snazzhammer put in. 'So da humies don't twig wot we're up to. Dey're what da humies call a "destruction".' He raised his weapon and activated the power field. 'All right, outta da way!'

The ladz parted, and the boss stepped forwards. He swung his hammer and, with a *krakka-boom!* like thunder, the burna-bisected door caved in as though it were made of sticks. It revealed a long corridor, wide enough for five orks abreast. A few yards down it were another bunch of red-robes, aiming their guns somewhat shakily at the gaping hole where their door had been.

Snazzhammer lunged forwards, swinging his weapon two-handed by the very base of its handle to maximise his reach. The powered head smashed through their squishy humie bodies and killed most of them with a single blow. The other two turned to flee: Snazzhammer let them get a few steps before hurling his hammer after them, decapitating them both, one after another. The mighty weapon skidded to a halt, slippery with red humie blood, and Snazzhammer turned to look at Da Boffin.

'Def'nitely dis way, right?'

Da Boffin held up a clicking gizmo, and revved the motor of his monowheel excitedly. 'Yup! We got supa-strong warp stuff down da uvver end. Dat's where we needs ta be.'

'You heard da ork!' Snazzhammer bellowed. 'Get to it!' He turned back towards his hammer and began to stride down the corridor. Ufthak was just taking his first step after the boss when the door at the other end of the corridor slid open, not thanks to the destructive activities of some other ladz but with the smooth action of a machine operated by someone who knew how to work it properly.

A huge shape stamped into view, blocking out much of the light behind it.

'Now *dat*,' Mogrot said from behind him, 'looks like a proper fight.'

It was on two legs, but it was no humie. It wasn't an ork, either. Ufthak reckoned it was twice his height at least, and nearly the same across. It sort of looked a bit like a humie Dread, the kind the beakies sometimes had, but not quite. It had two power klaws, the weird round humie ones instead of a proper pointy klaw like any self-respecting ork would have, and some sort of 'eavy shoota looming over its right shoulder.

'Tinboy!' Da Boffin exclaimed with what sounded like real excitement. 'Always wanted ta see one up-close!'

The 'eavy shoota opened up just as Badgit Snazzhammer broke into a roaring charge. He got three strides before his head exploded in a welter of gore and pulverised bone, and he dropped as dead as a swatted squig.

'Zoggin' 'eck!' Ufthak yelled. 'Back round da corner, ladz, sharpish!' The tinboy was tracking its shots towards them, and in the confines of the corridor there was nowhere to take cover. He shouldered Deffrow aside and scrambled back out of the line of fire, and a moment later the rest of the mob joined him, hunkering down on either side of the doorway. More thuds of shoota fire sent gouts of blood spraying across the corridor's floor and over the threshold of the ruined door, as a couple of stragglers got well and truly crumped. As soon as there were no more orks in view, the tinboy's gun fell silent.

'Why'd you run for?!' Mogrot demanded from the other side of the gap. Ufthak found faces turning towards him, red eyes focusing on him. He'd given a command, and the boyz had followed him. The only problem was, he'd told them all to run away.

That wasn't going to wash for long, if he wanted to stake his claim as boss. He had to prove himself once and for all as the bigger ork.

'Dat wasn't runnin',' he declared firmly. 'Dat was a... strateejik wivdrawal.'

'If it looks like a squiggoth, an' it smells like a squiggoth...' Mogrot began menacingly. He drew himself up, fingering the activation switch on his chain-choppa. 'I don't fink you'z proper boss material, Ufthak. Don't fink you should be givin' orders.'

'Yeah?' Ufthak shot back, making a rude hand gesture. 'Why don't you walk over 'ere an' say dat?'

Mogrot growled, deep in his chest, and took one step...

...then paused, frowning distrustfully at the gap between them. Ufthak tried not to look at the same bit of floor, but it was no good. Even Mogrot's brain had remembered why they were hiding in the first place.

'Gimme a grot,' Mogrot grunted, reaching out behind him. One of the mob's hangers-on was seized and passed forwards with a squeak of protest, and Mogrot tossed it into the corridor.

The tinboy's shoota opened up immediately, and the sad, mangled remains of the grot thudded to the floor.

Ufthak cursed inwardly. That would have been *hilarious*, as well as useful. Nothing for it, then.

'We need to kill da tinboy,' he declared, as though Mogrot had never challenged him. 'An' we ain't doin' dat from here, an' we can't get to it ta kill it easy, coz it knows we'z orks, right?'

The ladz nodded. All of that seemed logical.

'Wot you finkin'?' Da Boffin asked, scratching one ear and looking at him thoughtfully as he rocked back and forth on his monowheel.

Ufthak beamed.

'All right, ladz, I'z 'ad a great idea...'

''Ello, I'm a humie!'

Humie spaceships, it turned out, had a lot of decent metal sheeting lying around if you had access to a burna to cut it off the walls, so Wazzock had been put to work. Before too long, the mob had several large chunks, to which they'd strapped the more intact of the red-robe corpses they'd made on the way to the door.

'We'z just humies, walkin' down dis corridor!'

Ufthak's plan was proper cunning if he said so himself, which he did, so that was okay. The tinboy must be able to tell humies from orks, or the humies would never let it walk around their spaceship. Therefore, it stood to reason that if it saw humies in front of it, it wouldn't shoot.

Into the corridor they went, a few boyz behind each metal plate, with dead humies on the front to confuse the tinboy. Simple, but genius.

'Wot if it don't work?' Deffrow hissed.

'S'gotta work,' Ufthak argued. 'I'm talkin' in humie, ain't I? An' makin' my voice squeaky an'–'

The shoota opened up again. The three boyz behind the foremost plate leaned into the impacts on what had suddenly become a makeshift shield, but the metal sheeting wasn't designed to stand up to firepower of that magnitude. One of them came apart as a shell punched right through, and Ufthak suddenly had guts over his steel toecaps.

'Zog it!' he shouted. 'Next plan!'

The boyz hadn't got far down the corridor before the tinboy had rumbled them, but they'd reached Snazzhammer's body. They dropped their apparently useless humie-shields and opened up, pouring fire into their enemy.

Which stopped short of reaching it, swallowed up and destroyed by some sort of force field.

'I've 'ad enuff of dis,' Ufthak growled as another ork was blown apart. He reached behind his back and pulled out what he'd decided he'd call a bombstikk. It was basically half the mob's stikkbombs all taped together courtesy of Da Boffin's toolbox, and by 'basically' he meant 'exactly'. He took a quick two-step run-up and hurled it overarm.

When *that* hit the tinboy's force field it was like Gork himself had stamped on them all.

Ufthak's vision cleared a moment or so before his ears stopped ringing, and he picked himself up and peered down the corridor.

The Mork-damned thing was only still standing, wasn't it?

'Dat woz s'posed ta blow its bloody arms off!' Mogrot yelled.

'Nevamind!' Ufthak shouted. 'It's stunned, innit? Scrag da zoggin' fing!'

He ran forwards, snatching up the Snazzhammer as he passed it. Sure enough, the tinboy was standing wonky, and making confused buzzing noises. Shots began to fly past him from behind, and this time one or two of them raised sparks as they struck home: the force field had been overloaded.

Lenses in the tinboy's face whirred as the machine suddenly seemed to recover itself, and the 'eavy shoota lowered to target him.

Ufthak threw himself into a slide as the big weapon began kicking out shots again, and he felt the shiver of impacts as they chewed up the floor behind him. The tinboy's power klaws crackled into life as whatever tek powered it realised that he was getting close, but it was a shade too slow: it lunged for him, looking to crush him, but he was already sliding between its legs and lashing out with the Snazzhammer.

Which bounced clean off with barely a scratch caused, since he hadn't activated the power field.

'Mork's teef!'

The tinboy lurched around to follow him, alarmingly fast for such a big thing. The 'eavy shoota remained steady somehow, pouring shots into the boyz that'd been following him, but the two power klaws were all for Ufthak. It swung at him again, and he barely dodged back from it, then ducked under the counterswing from the other arm. When the tinboy tried to clobber him on the backswing, he set his feet and swung the Snazzhammer to meet it.

He'd activated the power field this time, and it took the tinboy's arm off at the elbow.

Laughter erupted out of him as the huge thing staggered, its balance thrown off by the sudden lack of weight on one side. The sound of its detached power klaw skittering away across the deck was the sound of his triumph.

Then it punched him in the chest with the other one.

Ufthak had never known such pain, and he'd taken shots from a beakie gun before that had left half his insides hanging out, until Dok Drozfang had stuck them back in and stitched him up once the fighting had calmed down a bit. It was like someone had let buzzer squigs the size of grots loose on his chest, and that was before he flew backwards and hit the wall behind him hard enough to dent it.

He lay there for a moment, vision foggy, as the tinboy turned its attention back to the rest of the boyz. They'd now reached it and were hacking away at it with choppas, blasting it point-blank with their shootas, and were surely going to bring it down any moment now. They didn't need him to help, he could catch his breath.

Any moment now.

'Zog it,' Ufthak muttered, as another boy got pulped by the tinboy's remaining power klaw. 'If you want somefing dun right...' He levered himself back to his feet, ignoring the sensation and indeed the smell of scorched flesh coming from his front, and took up the Snazzhammer again.

'Oi! I ain't finished wiv you yet!'

The tinboy didn't turn around, which was its second mistake, the first having been to not make sure he was properly dead. He ran at its back, crackling Snazzhammer held high, and smashed the axe side into its armour plating.

KRAKKA-BOOM!

The tinboy spasmed and fell forwards, circuits overloading and sparks shooting in all directions. Ufthak forced his own battered body to climb atop it, then raised the Snazzhammer for the killing blow, laughing as he did so. Let Mogrot try to lead the mob after *this*!

He saw Da Boffin raising one hand in apparent warning just as he brought the weapon down for the final time.

Everything went red.

He was on his back when his brain was actually working well enough again to figure out what was going on. He stared up at the ceiling, which looked to be blackened and scorched as though a massive explosion had washed across it. He could hear the sound of ork boots tramping past him, but no one seemed to be stopping to congratulate him on his kill.

A face appeared in his line of sight. It was Dok Drozfang, who was wearing what Ufthak thought of as his considerin' face, which was never a sight an ork wanted to see.

'Dok,' Ufthak managed, although it was surprisingly hard to speak. 'I can't feel me legs.'

'Well, dere's a reason for dat,' the dok shrugged. 'Look down.'

Ufthak managed to do as Drozfang suggested. For a moment, he couldn't work out what he was seeing. Then he realised that it was what he *wasn't* seeing that was the issue.

'Where's me legs?'

'One's over dere,' Drozfang said, pointing out of Ufthak's view. 'Not too sure about da uvver one. Or yer arms, ta be honest.'

'Dat'd explain why dey ain't hurtin',' Ufthak muttered. He frowned. 'Wot about da hammer?'

'Mogrot's got it,' Drozfang replied. 'Said 'e's da boss now, an' no one argued wiv 'im.'

'Ungrateful grots,' Ufthak managed. Air was definitely becoming a problem, which was only to be expected when you looked to be missing the bottom part of your lungs. 'Well, see us off den, dok. No point waitin' – may'z we'll get back ta Gork 'n' Mork so dey can put me in anuvver body an' I can get back ta fightin' again.'

Drozfang frowned. 'Yeah, about dat... Wot if I'z got a better idea?'

Ufthak tried not to let his trepidation show. Painboyz were useful to have about if you needed stapling back up, or a new arm sewing on, but some of them could get a bit 'creative' at times, especially when the patient wasn't in a condition to have much say in the matter.

'Nah, yer all right, dok,' he said, managing a grin. 'Nuffin' ta worry about, is it?'

'Yeah, well, I ain't finkin' Mogrot is da best boss da mob could 'ave,' Drozfang replied, lowering his voice. 'I reckon dey could do wiv da sort of ork wot has da smartz ta plan for a tinboy, an' da gutz ta bring it down. An' if I could fix dat ork up, he might remember da painboy wot fixed 'im, coz I reckon dat ork might be goin' places. Know wot I mean?'

'Wotever you'z finkin,' yer gonna 'ave to do it quick,' Ufthak told him flatly, as darkness began to encroach on his vision.

'Fankfully, da raw materials are at 'and,' Drozfang grinned, and pursed his leathery lips to emit a piercing whistle. High-pitched grunts and swearing heralded the arrival of the dok's grot 'disorderlies,' apparently towing something heavy. They stopped next to Ufthak, and he turned his head to look at it.

It was Badgit Snazzhammer's body. Huge, battle-scarred and untouched apart from the small point of completely lacking a head, thanks to the tinboy.

'Now,' Drozfang said, producing an intimidatingly large cleaver and placing it at the base of Ufthak's neck. 'Dis may 'urt a bit...'

Ufthak hadn't really registered the blow given that, percentage-wise, he wasn't losing much more than he had already. The staples that the dok used to fix his head onto Snazzhammer's neck – which had been 'tidied up' with the same cleaver – only registered as minor pricks of discomfort.

What *really* hurt was the injection.

'You'd be lookin' at a day or so before you'd be up an' about, normally,' Drozfang told him matter-of-factly, as burning agony began to spread downwards from what remained of his neck into what had until recently been Snazzhammer's. The dok tucked his syringe back into his belt. 'But fanks to Dok Drozfang's Healin' Juice, da nerve endin's will connect right up an' you'll 'ave full control in a matter of minutes. Course, dere's always da side effects,' he added.

Ufthak tried to swear at him, but he was too busy convulsing.

The tinboy looked to have been the humies' last real line of defence of their 'fancy worky bitz,' as Snazzhammer had called them. There were a few bodies scattered here and there on the route to the massive double doors from which an eldritch glow was emerging, but little sign of an organised resistance. The alarms going off suggested that perhaps Da Meklord's 'destruction' techniques had been extremely effective. All Ufthak knew was that they weren't helping his headache much.

''Ere we are, boss,' Drozfang said with a grin, gesturing at the one open door. 'Da rest of da ladz should be in dere. Time ta make yer grand entrance.'

Ufthak bared his fangs, squared his – or possibly Snazzhammer's – shoulders, and strode in as though his neck weren't still leaking a bit, and his left leg weren't dragging slightly.

It was a vast space, as big as one of the humies' buildings which they seemed to put up simply to sit in and have a proper good think about their Emprah. However, whereas those had lots of empty space in, perhaps in order for the thoughts to fly around properly, this one was jam-packed full of... stuff, was the only term Ufthak could come up with. Huge metal pillars which gave off a glow that only partially obscured the runes carved into them. Enormous pistons, crackling with energy. Giant wheels larger than his outstretched arms. And yet, despite how impressive it all looked, there was the distinct impression that this place wasn't fulfilling its function. It was heavy with potential, an almost palpable heaviness in the air. It was as though the room itself were yearning for something.

Which probably wasn't Da Boffin and Mogrot Redtoof having a scuffle, but that was what it currently had.

'Gerroff it!'

'I'm da boss, I get ta push da button!'

'Yooz gonna break it, you stoopid–'

'Gonna break yer face in a minute–'

Mogrot, facing away from Ufthak, reared back with the Snazzhammer in his grip, ready to knock Da Boffin's lights out with it.

Ufthak grabbed it just under the head and yanked it out of his grip. Mogrot whirled around, fumbling at his belt for his chain-choppa, but pulled up short when he came face-to-chest with Ufthak. His brow creased in uncommon cogitation.

'Wot da zog...?'

'Sumfin' like dat,' Ufthak agreed, and nutted him.

Mogrot went down. Ufthak winced, and reflected that possibly hadn't been the smartest thing to do with a stapled-up neck, but what was done was done. He brandished the Snazzhammer over his head.

'Anyone else wanna be boss?'

There was a distinct lack of volunteers, as the rest of the ladz took a sudden interest in their boots. They weren't sure if Badgit had got a new head or Ufthak had got a new body, but they weren't planning to argue with either eventuality.

'Dat's settled, den,' Ufthak said with satisfaction. He could almost feel Dok Drozfang grinning behind him, but that was fine. Fair was fair, and he'd see that the dok got his due. A few extra teef passed his way, the occasional 'volunteer' for surjury, that sort of thing.

'You done ya mek fing yet?' he asked Da Boffin, who shook his head.

'Mogrot wanted ta press da button.'

'Well, get on wiv it,' Ufthak commanded him. He wasn't interested in pressing buttons: that sounded like a mek job.

Da Boffin's device was surprisingly small, and was clamped to what looked like some sort of humie control panel. It had three buttons on it: 'STOP', 'GO' and 'MEGA-GO'.

'Wot is dat, anyway?' Ufthak asked.

'Dis,' Da Boffin said gleefully, 'is da Warp Dekapitator. You know how humies choose where dey're gonna fly through da warp?'

'Yeah?' said Ufthak, who didn't.

'Well, dey leave tracks behind in da warp. Sorta like squig trails, only nuffin' like dat,' Da Boffin explained. 'Dese are humie mekboyz, so dey prob'ly came from a humie mekboy planet, where dere's loadsa shiny tek Da Meklord can nab.'

'Right,' Ufthak nodded. Shiny tek sounded good. Da Meklord would get the best, obviously, but that didn't mean there wouldn't be some left over.

'So when I turn dis on, it uses da energy of dese warp engines to cause a katastroffic warp implosion!'

Ufthak frowned. 'Is dat good?'

'Course it's good!' Da Boffin scoffed. 'S'got a lot of fingies, syllables, innit? Like, "grot" is bad, but "Wazbom Blastajet" is good.'

Ufthak nodded. It was a powerful argument.

'Dis ship gets sucked into da warp, right back to da startin' point of da last warp jump it made, and den pops back out again,' Da Boffin continued. 'An' it sucks all da rest of da ships around in wiv it too, includin' Da Meklord's fleet. Job's a good'un!'

He reached out, and pressed the button labelled 'MEGA-GO'.

The control panel sparked. More alarms started sounding, but these weren't the high-pitched whiny klaxons that denoted a relatively minor problem like rampaging, murderous orks aboard the ship. These were bone-deep and throbbing, and bore an inherent sense of panic. If a star could have screamed a warning, it would have sounded like that.

All around Ufthak and his mob, the glowing, crackling parts of the room began to move: slowly at first, then faster and faster. Ufthak frowned. He could have sworn that something apparently solid just passed through something else equally apparently solid.

'Is dat s'posed to 'ap–'

There was a stomach-churning, resonant *bloorp!* and everything turned inside out.

It took Ufthak a few moments to check that his arms weren't now five miles long, or that his stomach hadn't swelled to the size of a planet, both of which felt like they could be viable options. He definitely had an annoying tic in his left eye, but that was less unusual, and he glowered at Da Boffin with it.

'If dat's your definition of "good"...'

Da Boffin held his hand up for quiet. Ufthak was about to clobber him for disrespect when he heard it too.

It was the screaming of tortured metal. And that, Ufthak realised, was not fancy words. It was the voice of actual metal, and it was actually screaming, and the whole thing was overlaid with a bubbling, wet giggle. From outside in the corridor came the slithering thump of something malformed dragging its huge bulk along with nothing more than brute strength and an endless malice directed at all living things.

'Course,' Da Boffin commented, 'dere's always da side effects.'

'All right, ladz!' Ufthak barked, laying about him. The boyz hadn't coped well with the katakrumpic warm diffusion, or whatever it was Da Boffin had said, and most of them were still on their backs or counting their fingers to see if they still had the same amount – which was causing some problems in Deffrow's case, as he couldn't now remember how many he'd started with. A few knocks with the haft end of the hammer got them back into it, however. 'Da entertainment's comin'! Up ya get!'

The other massive door slammed back, and something made of blood and steel and endless hunger squirmed in, all sharp teeth and barbed tongues, and glistening black talons that reached out hungrily for flesh.

Ufthak grinned at it. Time to see what his new body could do.

'On me, ladz! One, two, free...'

'WAAAAAAAAGGGGHHHHHHH!'

PAINBOYZ

MIKE BROOKS

'To properly unnerstand somefing,' Dok Drozfang said, 'ya gotta get into its gutz.' He looked around with interest. 'Mekboyz'll tell yoo da same. Wiv dem, it's engines an' sprockets an' all dat sorta fing. Wiv me, it's all dose wobbly bitz wot's inside a git – tubes an' squishy lumps an' so on.'

'So why're we 'ere, boss?' one of his yoofs asked. He was a young painboy, still wet behind the ears – with someone else's blood – and Drozfang whacked him on the back of the head.

'Because we're in da *gutz*!' he said, gesturing around them. Their surroundings weren't organic, not like those giant bugeye monsters that floated around in space and had all the other bugeyes travelling inside them, but they *felt* organic. The walls were damp and curved, and the passageway meandered back and forth with side passages branching off and occasionally opening out into larger, irregularly shaped chambers, such as the one in which they were now standing. It was as if the whole thing had been carved out by some enormous, burrowing worm rather than constructed. It was dim, too – not proper waving-yer-hands-around dark, but you somehow got the impression that the only light was filtering in through the teeth of something into whose intestines you had unintentionally strayed.

'Honestly, yoo lot gotta learn to pay attention, or yoo're never gonna amount to anyfing,' Drozfang finished.

They were in a spikie nest, and Drozfang had led a mob of boyz, some apprentice painboyz, and his general hangers-on under what passed for the ground here. Spikiez were like scrawniez, in that they had pointy ears – tiny little things, not big, proud, flappy pointy ears like an ork – were about as wide as your arm, and flipped around a lot until you clobbered them, at which point they collapsed like yesterday's breakfast. However, spikiez were *unlike* other scrawniez in that they had a lot more spikes, hooks, and general cutty-things on their armour, and also seemed to take positive delight in butchering stuff.

Drozfang could understand that to an extent: after all, what ork didn't like smashing up some gits in a fight? And more specifically, as a painboy he had a deep and abiding interest in how living things were put together – and, indeed, how they came apart and sometimes went back together again. Combat was just a sort of succession of high-speed, experimental surgeries. Drozfang was dimly aware of some concept that surgery was only really surgery if the other git had agreed to it, but he never paid much attention to that sort of limp thinking anyway. So far as Dok Drozfang was concerned, anyone sleeping, or unconscious, or just looking the other way when he was around clearly wasn't *that* bothered about whether or not he operated on them.

Still, spikiez were a bit more *intense* about the whole thing. They seemed to be more focused on the git under the knife being as unhappy about it as possible. Drozfang didn't see the point of that. Of course, you couldn't let a little thing like the patient screaming and thrashing get in the way of the work, but that was a by-product while you tried to attach your brilliant new Explodin' Arm invention to their shoulder, not the purpose of the exercise. He had better things to do than just spend his time hurting gits for the sake of it. After all, Dok Drozfang's Speshul Steam-Powered Lungs didn't just invent themselves.

'Dis place is *weird*,' said the same yoof. His name was Fingerz, on account of having accidentally stitched one of his own inside another ork after he'd accidentally cut it off while trying to amputate the patient's leg (the patient hadn't needed the leg amputating, but as Drozfang pointed out afterwards, Fingerz clearly needed the practice). Drozfang kept him around because he definitely had the right sort of ideas, even if he currently lacked the skills to see them through properly.

'Yeah, well. It's a spikie place, innit?' Drozfang said airily. 'Bound to be a bit weird.' Still, Fingerz wasn't wrong.

'Dis is, like, a spikie painboy's place, right?' said Wheezer, one of Drozfang's grot Disorderlies, prodding a discarded tool of unclear purpose.

'Reckon so,' Drozfang said, taking a deep sniff, and nodded knowingly. 'Smell dat? Dat's blood, dat is.'

'Yeah, but everyfing here kinda smells like blood,' Fingerz pointed out. 'Da one fing you can say about spikiez is, dey like blood.'

Drozfang clipped him around the ear again, although he took it easy on the yoof and didn't use the hand with the power klaw. 'Not like dis! Dat's *fresh* blood, an' lots of it! All different sorts!'

'So, boss,' Wheezer said hesitantly, with the air of a grot that had the ability to see into the future, so long as the future consisted of getting kicked. 'If some git an' his mates broke into *yoor* place, yoo wouldn't be happy, right?'

Drozfang aimed a kick at him on general principle, but Wheezer dodged backwards with a yelp.

'Course not!' Drozfang barked after him. 'I'd have 'em sayin' hello to dere own gizzards! Da bloody cheek of it!'

'Do ya fink dis spikie's gonna be any different?' Wheezer yelped, from somewhere in the midst of a crowd of ork legs. 'Just askin,' cos yoo're always sayin' we should explore our curiosities, an' dat.'

'*Orks* should explore dere curiosities!' Drozfang snapped. 'Painboyz ain't gonna get good if dey just stick to wot dey already know. Grots don't know nuffin,' an' are only around to hand us da brainsaw, or wotever.' He drew himself up. 'Anyway, so wot if da git don't like it? He's welcome to come an' complain!'

Drozfang laughed, and the other orks dutifully laughed along with him. Still, he thought, he'd better get them moving onwards. Drozfang had come down here out of curiosity, and the yoofs had come with him because they hung on his every word, and the Disorderlies were here because he'd have them scragged if they wandered off without his direct permission, but the regular boyz had tagged along simply in search of a fight. If they didn't find one soon, then they were probably going to start causing trouble, which would impinge on Drozfang's ability to have a good old root around and find out what was what in the world of spikie painboys.

'Let's try dis way next,' he said, pointing in his best leaderly manner, which was to make a decision at random but pretend he knew something no one else did. 'Dere's bound to be–'

He cut himself off as his ears picked up the sound of running footsteps. Well, the uneven gait and ragged breathing made it sound more like hurried limping than running, but it was close enough. Still, it was coming from the direction he'd been pointing in, so Drozfang faced that tunnel entrance with a smug smile, and waited.

The humie appeared and staggered to a halt, squinting in the dim light since humie vision was generally poorer than orks' in darkness. It was also notably lacking an eye, which probably didn't help. It was also lacking a few other things, Drozfang noted with the professional eye – he smirked at his own joke – of a skilled painboy, starting with clothes, detouring around toes, lingering on body fat, and finishing with irregular patches of skin. All in all, it was about as gaunt and banged-up a specimen of humie as he'd expect to see still able to stand remotely upright and move at anything approaching speed.

He expected it to scream, possibly soil itself, and then turn to run as best it could in the direction from whence it had come. Humies didn't like fighting orks, the only exception being the beakies, who were generally well up for a proper scrap and pretty handy at it to boot. As a result, the desperate wail that emerged from this one's mouth was quite within expectations, but the fact it hurled itself at the nearest ork was not.

'Wot's goin' on?' the ork in question asked, confused. He was a Deathskulls nob called Grubsnik, and normally he'd have taken a humie's head off before it could get within arm's reach of him, but this wasn't a normal situation. This wasn't a fight, with wild-eyed humies wielding their little chain-choppas or trying to put your eye out with a stabby-gun; this was a half-dead humie who would have lost an arm-wrestling contest with a snotling. Grubsnik blinked in surprise as the humie bounced off him, staggered back, then launched itself at him again.

'Must be somefing wrong wiv it, in da head,' Fingerz opined.

'Yoo're tellin' me!' Grubsnik said. 'Oi!'

The humie had slapped him in the face as hard as it could – which wasn't at all hard, but that wasn't the point. Grubsnik poked it in the chest and the humie fell onto its backside, but then it was up again, crawling on its knees towards him. It made a lunge and managed to grab Grubsnik's slugga with both hands. For a moment, Drozfang thought it was making a hilariously futile attempt to wrench the weapon from Grubsnik's meaty grasp, but then the humie placed its face right against the muzzle, and screamed.

It wasn't a high-pitched scream of fear, such as Drozfang had heard many a time. Nor was it one of the lung-tearing screams of pain he'd heard far more often, both on the battlefield and in his surgery. This was a ragged noise, non-stop aside from hasty, clumsy breaths – the sound of a creature staring death in the face and demanding that it get a move on.

Still not quite sure what was going on, Grubsnik pulled the trigger. Such was the relative size of the slug to the humie's head, and the proximity of the target to the barrel, its entire skull was blown apart.

Orks were not by nature a particularly contemplative species, but they looked at the corpse for a moment or two, each one trying to piece together what they'd just seen.

'Dat was weird,' Fingerz said in the end, accurately summing up what each of them was thinking.

'I've seen humies wot ain't scared of dyin' when dey're comin' atcha wiv a choppa or wotever,' Grubsnik said. 'Or at least, I've seen ones wot don't *fink* dey're gonna die. But I ain't never seen one wot ackcherly *wanted* to die.'

'Well, lads, wot've we learned from dis?' Drozfang asked brightly. He was answered by a confused silence, and he sighed. Any good painboy needed a solid understanding of cause and effect, but it seemed this lot were particularly slow on the uptake.

'Dat humie obviously fort dere's somefing in 'ere wot's scarier'n us,' he said patiently. Then he grinned.

'An' I wanna find out wot it is.'

The spikiez took one of the gits at the back of Drozfang's party first, just after they'd entered another chamber. They all heard a rapidly receding yell, and turned around in time to see a piece of floor sliding back into place with a notable absence of ork on top of it.

'Wot 'appened to Gaztoof?' someone asked.

Drozfang scratched his chin, looking down. 'Bit weird dat fing didn't trigger when da rest of us walked over it. So woz it a really *slow* trap, or–'

A grot wailed in dismay as it was hauled up into the shadows of the roof by hooked chains that had not, Drozfang would be prepared to swear, been dangling down a moment before. High, mocking laughter rang out from somewhere nearby, and was instantly drowned out by the much deeper, raucous laughter of the orks themselves, because seeing a grot screaming in terror while it was snatched up by an unknown enemy was never not going to be hilarious. Then everyone opened fire upwards anyway, because while grot-snatching by an unknown enemy might be hilarious, the most important part of that sentence was the 'enemy' part.

'Wot wiv dis an' da humie, I fink dey're tryin' to scare us!' Drozfang shouted as he blasted away with his slugga. The roof was lit haphazardly by the repeated sparks and bangs of ork munitions impacting on solid surfaces, but it was very difficult to make anything out. There were shadows moving up there – solid shadows that were not just the results of sudden and shifting illumination – but actually *hitting* one of the zogging things was another matter altogether.

'Why'd we be scared?' Grubsnik shouted back, just before something fell back out of the roof and landed on his head.

It was the grot, neatly flayed. It bounced off Grubsnik and collapsed wetly onto the floor, already dead. If Drozfang knew anything about spikiez, that wouldn't have been their intention. However, if he knew anything about grots, it was that their puny physiologies were unable to deal with much pain, trauma, or indeed anything else. If you took a lung out of a grot, they'd be dead before your hand had left their chest cavity. Try the same thing with an ork, and he'd punch you in the head until you put the zogging thing back. That was why it was important to sedate the patient so they couldn't interrupt you.

'It's wot spikiez do, innit?' Drozfang said in response to Grubsnik, prodding the grot's body with his boot. 'Dey try'n scare stuff, cos dey know dey ain't gonna last long unless half of da uvver gitz run away.' The boyz had stopped shooting now, and were waiting to see if anything else fell down after the grot, but nothing did. Either it was dead and stuck up there, or they'd not hit their target. Drozfang had a feeling it would be the latter, because spikiez didn't tend to hit you from a place where you could hit them back.

He looked around with renewed interest. This chamber was more like what he'd been expecting, with a series of slabs on which the owner could conduct his experiments. He looked the tools over with a professional eye, and sniffed in mild disdain. Overly fancy stuff, in his opinion: lots of wiggly things, and tiny drills, and a succession of skinny knives with long handles, each slightly smaller and finer than the last. Where were the rotating saw blades, and the clamps, and the hammers, or the bits of metal you bolted to some git's leg because the bones were broken?

'Where's da git wot woz laughin'?' Grubsnik demanded, which was also a fair question. Drozfang's eyes landed on a large container in one corner of the chamber – a sort of upright, weirdly shaped barrel in which a spikie could theoretically be hiding.

He pointed at it with one talon of his power klaw. 'Let's try in dere.'

The container was shackled shut by a chain held fast by multiple complicated-looking locks. Drozfang simply snapped the chain with his power klaw, and wrenched it open.

Within stood an upright casket formed of some sort of hard, clear substance, filled nearly to the brim with a yellow-green fluid. Immersed in the fluid was a scrawnie of some sort, its mouth and nose covered by a mask connected to pipes that presumably provided it with air to breathe, its head just above the fluid's surface. The rest of its body was submerged and, Drozfang realised, burned away to the point that he could see the pale flash of bone in places as a thrashing limb came close to the edge. Someone had dunked this scrawnie into acid, given it a mask so it wouldn't suffocate, and then locked it away in darkness.

'Dat don't look like it's laughin',' Grubsnik said after a moment. The creature's eyes, wild and watering from the permanent acid fumes, stared at the two orks with an emotion Drozfang couldn't interpret. Rage? Hope? Despair?

'Nah,' Drozfang said. 'Fink I'm just gonna shut dis up again.' Whatever was going on here wasn't anything to do with him, and he was starting to get the impression that he didn't want to know either. Why kill the scrawnie when it was probably on its way to dying anyway? On the other hand, why let it out when the only thing scrawniez were good for was killing? It was very confusing, so he decided to ignore it. The scrawnie thrashed a bit more as he closed it away from view, but so what? It had been thrashing anyway.

'Right, ladz,' he said, turning back around. 'What we're gonna do now, is–'

A shot rang out, with a sound like some large beast gently clearing its throat, and one of Grubsnik's boys – Badlug, Drozfang thought – jerked backwards as something struck him in the shoulder.

Orks might not be particularly contemplative, but the time saved on thought was usually put into action. The assembled boyz did not pause to wonder who was attacking them now, or why; they went straight from hearing the shot to replying in kind, opening up with their combined weaponry down the tunnel from which the attack had come. A barrage of slugga and shoota fire of varying calibres struck back, accompanied by at least one rokkit, which corkscrewed off and exploded somewhere out of Drozfang's sight.

This meant two things. Firstly, none of the other boyz paused to see what had happened to Badlug – that was between him and Gork and Mork, in any case – and so none of them saw his body stiffen up as it rapidly began to fuse into some sort of crystal. Drozfang watched in fascination, tinged with disgust, as Badlug became an orkoid statue within the space of a couple of seconds. Dying was fine, but dying like *that*, trapped in your own body so you couldn't even swing a choppa at the thing what had killed you – that was downright *unpleasant.*

Secondly, none of them were looking the right way when a horde of creatures came piling out of one of the *other* tunnels, and slammed into the back of them.

These weren't your regular spikiez; these were bigger and bulkier, their faces obscured by smooth masks. Their bodies were criss-crossed with scars and packed with slabs of muscle, with swollen backs and protruding spines, extra arms, and, in one or two cases, even extra heads. They drove into the boyz in a tide of thick-bladed cleavers and studded clubs, giving voice to no war cries other than sibilant hisses and whistles.

Against many enemies, the sudden and unexpected attack would have led to an immediate collapse, but orks lived for battle. The mass of boyz turned with a roar of delight and set about their attackers with choppa and slugga. Drozfang was already charging in with Grubsnik at his side, and the first swing of his power klaw nearly cut one of the new spikiez in half. Then he was into the thick of it, stabbing and punching and cutting, driving his klaw into chests and firing his slugga at point-blank range, feeling bones crack and flesh tear under his blows. This was what it was about! A proper scrap, none of this stab-from-the-shadows nonsense. He took a cleaver in his right shoulder, which stung, but he headbutted the spikie responsible in the face, denting its mask, then blew its spine out with his slugga.

'Oi!' Grubsnik bellowed from beside him, then clobbered the thing he'd been facing. 'Bloody git just stabbed me wiv its *fingers*!'

Beyond the shoulder of Grubsnik's collapsing assailant, Drozfang caught sight of another spikie at the tunnel mouth. This was a cadaverous, many-armed thing with lank hair and sunken eye sockets that hovered above the ground somehow. Drozfang knew a boss painboy when he saw one, and he pointed his power klaw at it.

'Is dat da best yoo've got?' he roared merrily as another enemy warrior fell to Grubsnik's ladz. The spikie painboy cocked its head to the side as though curious, then gestured with one thin-fingered hand.

The floating monstrosity that hit them from the side was like nothing Drozfang had seen before. It had a curved, bladed carapace, two monstrous, fleshy arms that terminated in long mechanical tentacles, and a dragging tail section of further writhing limbs. It seized a couple of boyz before they even knew it was there, but instead of throwing them aside into the walls or tearing them apart as Drozfang might have expected, it simply held on. Within a moment or two they had literally *withered* in its grasp, falling from its grip as drained husks that were barely recognisable as having ever been orks.

'Nope!' Drozfang said. 'Not havin' dat!' He was fine with the notion of getting shanked or blown up, although he'd still try to avoid it if possible, but this was a death in which he was entirely uninterested. He opened up with his slugga at the spikie painboy, more out of the principle of the thing than anything else. They were both probably as surprised as the other when one of his rounds hit it, and even more so when something sparked and fizzed, whatever was holding it in the air abruptly cut out, and it collapsed in a tangle of mismatched limbs.

'C'mon, ladz, follow me!' Drozfang bellowed, surging forward. The boyz with him, always happy to be led into a charge even if they were technically already fighting someone, began to move like a boot pulled out of deep, sticky mud - slowly at first, then suddenly coming free with unexpected momentum. The floating monster got two more - a yoof called Wurrgit and a Disorderly whose name Drozfang couldn't remember, if he'd ever known it - but then they were out of its reach and thundering back the way they'd come.

Towards the grounded spikie.

Its legs clearly still worked, but not with the usual scrawnie speed, because it was still staggering to its feet when Drozfang seized it by the scruff of its neck without breaking stride. It hissed at him and lashed out with its various limbs as he ran on, but a solid smack to its head seemed to daze it.

'Wot's dat for?' Grubsnik demanded, pounding along beside him.

'Might come in handy,' Drozfang replied.

'If dat's a joke cos it's got lots of hands-'

'It ain't!' Drozfang snapped. He was fairly sure of the way out, but he wasn't *completely* sure. There were obviously some very unpleasant ways to die in here, but so long as he had hold of the boss, it seemed far less likely that he'd get caught up in anything *genrul*, so to speak. He was a painboy, but he was still an ork, and fighting was in his blood. Get a bit of space around them, away from any traps, and so that floating tentacle thing couldn't come at them unexpectedly, and then the boot would be on the other side of the face...

'Hold on, ladz,' Grubsnik wheezed suddenly, starting to stagger. 'I ain't feelin' so good!'

'We ain't got time to dawdle!' Drozfang protested, but the rest of the boyz were already slowing and peering at their boss, albeit with curiosity rather than concern.

'Zog it, dat *itches* where dat scrawnie got me!' Grubsnik said, scratching at his side as he stumbled to a halt. 'Wot da...?'

Drozfang's instinct was to carry on and leave Grubsnik to his fate, but his inquisitive painboy nature took over. He turned and pointed at Grubsnik's ladz. 'Which one of yoo gits had da rokkit launcha? Shoot da roof of dat tunnel we just came froo, bring it down! Dat should slow 'em a bit.'

The ork in question turned around with a grin and fired towards the sound of pursuit. Orks weren't known for their accuracy in general, but a roof was a hard thing to miss, and the rokkit struck home with a satisfyingly thunderous explosion. Drozfang did for a moment question the wisdom of causing a localised cave-in while he was still technically under the ground, but as piles of blasted rock – or something similar, anyway – crashed down, he found to his satisfaction that the collapse ended well short of where they were.

'No need... for dat,' Grubsnik managed, waving a hand feebly. 'Just gotta... catch me breath...'

He breathed in, and kept breathing in. His chest began to swell, then his entire torso started to expand. His clothes began to tear. The straps that held his breastplate in place snapped one after another, sending buckles flying.

Then his skin started to rip, and *still* he kept getting bigger.

Drozfang wasn't quite sure exactly when Grubsnik died, and indeed when he stopped being Grubsnik and started being simply a mound of greenish flesh, but the whole process didn't take long. Within about twenty seconds, it was over.

'Well, dat was nasty,' Drozfang said into the silence. 'Sorta funny, but def'nitly nasty.'

'Boss!' Wheezer shouted urgently, and Drozfang realised that the spikie painboy was stirring in his grip. It went for him with a hand of needled fingers, aiming for his chest, but Drozfang caught the git's forearm between two prongs of his power klaw just before the dangerous digits struck him.

'Dis wot I fink it is?' Drozfang asked, as the spikie hissed and thrashed, trying to either stab him or get itself free, and completely failing on both counts. It was a wiry little thing, but he had no problem holding it still. 'Dis da same sort of fing wot got Grubsnik?'

He activated the power field on his klaw, and severed the scrawnie's limb. It hissed again, seeming more bothered by indignity than pain.

'Wheezer, put da hand in da bag,' Drozfang ordered. 'Might need to take a look at dat later. Yoo ladz, yoo're wiv me now.'

Grubsnik's former mob looked at each other, but none of them argued. Drozfang was, after all, the top dok around, which meant both that he had a certain amount of influence and that you didn't want him annoyed at you when you needed patching up.

'As fer *yoo*,' Drozfang continued, addressing the spikie, 'yoo're a nasty piece of work, an' no mistake. But y'know, to properly unnerstand somefing–'

He drove the talons of his power klaw into the spikie's chest and belly, impaling it. It felt *that*, all right – fair shrieked, it did. Drozfang grinned toothily at it.

'...yoo gotta get into its *gutz*.'

MAD DOK

NATE CROWLEY

1

Ghazghkull Mag Uruk Thraka, the Prophet of Gork and Mork, who left worlds ablaze in his boot prints, was dead.

There wasn't much arguing with that, since his body was hanging in a hundred pieces, on a rusty scaffold as high as a Stompa's chin. But that was all right, as far as Dok Grotsnik was concerned. In fact, he reckoned the human Blackmane had done him a bit of a favour, by removing Ghazghkull's head. He'd been asking the boss for permission to remove it himself for years, after all, saying that the best way to fix all his wonky bits would be to just... *switch him off* for a bit, and get 'em all done at once.

But since Ghazghkull's counter-offer had always been that he should do the same thing to Grotsnik (without the fixing or the putting back together afterwards, mind), the dok had come to terms with the fact it probably wouldn't ever happen.

But then along had come Blackmane and his mob of beakies - chop, clang, whirr, splat, *thud* - and here Grotsnik had found himself, with a blank canvas to work on at last. Letting the corners of a rare grin begin to work across his staple-puckered face, the dok looked up at the jungle of chains which bore the bits of the Prophet, and flexed his talons in anticipation of the work ahead.

They were good hands, these new ones: extra-nimble ones from his private stash, which he'd grafted on fresh that morning. And while they were still a bit fuzzy under the talons from barrel-mould, and itchy where his blood was still finding its way through the dead bits, Grotsnik knew they were ready to work wonders.

And what wonders they would work. He had big plans for the rebuilding of the boss. Plans so big, in fact, that he couldn't see the whole of 'em at once, just bits here and there. Still, the dok was sure inspiration would show him the way, once he'd started cutting. That was how it had always been, during his truly great works.

It was certainly how it had been on the night of his *greatest* work, all those years ago: the night when he'd first operated on the ork who would go on to become Ghazghkull Thraka. Under the leaky patchwork of that squighide tent, with just that bucket of third-rate tools to work with, Grotsnik had forced the whole galaxy to reconsider what an ork was capable of.

And now? Well. Now he was going to do it again. But bigger. And better. And with *much* fancier kit.

Inside the ferrocrete dome he'd claimed as his lab, deep down under the big human *kafeedral* where the boss had been felled, was enough weird machinery to bring *anything* back to life. Stacks of generators ringed the edge of the vault, exposed coils alive with sizzling blue discharge sparks, while banks of pumps and bioreaktors chugged and hissed and gurgled with every fluid the dok had been able to get his hands on. That was just the start of it: Grotsnik had spent years hoarding machines that looked like they might do interesting things if you attached living things to 'em, and at last he had an excuse to get the whole lot out to play with. And so, every few minutes, a new pile of crates appeared with a bang and a sizzle of dirty yellow light, as they were *tellyported* down from the belly of his medikal frigate in orbit.

Then there was all the meat-bits. A row of cages held packs upon packs of all the painboy's staple squig breeds, from bulbous transfusion squigs to saggy-faced skinlender-squigs, as well as a few mobs of hysterical, shrieking snotlings. Beneath them, a second, worse row of cages held a load of captured beakies, with their eyes and jaws and hands taken off so they couldn't cause trouble. Grotsnik wasn't certain what he'd actually do with 'em, since their blood was about as much use as piss in an emergency. But at the very least, they'd give him something to drill holes in while he was thinking.

And there, of course – well, *everywhere* – was Ghazghkull.

With all the bits of the boss suspended around the dome, Grotsnik was reminded of one of those *horrereys* the human meks made, in service to their pointless obsession with how fast stuff spun round in space. The bits of armoured gristle were like brooding green planets, he reckoned, orbiting the massive slab in the middle of the dome, where Ghazghkull's head sat looking way angrier than anything dead should've been able to.

The dok hobbled over to the slab then, until his torso was level with the dark green cliff of Ghazghkull's face. He admired the yellowed jags of his tusks, reflected in the glassy surface of the Prophet's good eye. Then he poked the eye, just because he could. The head retained its bloodied scowl of fury, but nothing happened.

The boss could be as angry as he liked, Grotsnik figured, letting his grin stretch into a great, giddy leer as realisation dawned. Because right now, the boss was dead. More than that though, he was a patient. And patients *never* got a say in what happened during surgery. *Medikal effix*, the humans called that. It was one of their rare good ideas.

Grotsnik ran a talon over the web of rope-thick scars covering the patient's hide, and as he saw how many had been left by his own blades, he snarled with pride. This was *his* monster. And how well he had done, under the circumstances. Every bolt he'd hammered into the boss over the years, every bloodpipe he'd stapled to another bloodpipe, he'd had to get permission for, from Ghazghkull himself. He'd had to cheat and sneak his way to every creative flourish. And still, he'd created a masterpiece.

Naturally, all the underbosses would've said the boss was the work of Gork and Mork. But Grotsnik had never seen either of 'em show up with a spanner.

Ghazghkull might have been the *design* of the gods, sure. The dok would give them that. But Ghazghkull was *Grotsnik's* work. All Gork and Mork had ever contributed to their Prophet, for all their holy clamour and barging, had been a beakie-forged bolter shell to the skull. The dok had been left to figure out the rest, and he'd done *mirikals.* But it had all just been practice, for the work in front of him now. And in the hours to come, he was finally going to show Gork, and his big idiot twin, just how much room he had found to improve on their work.

What new feats might the boss go on to rack up, Grotsnik dared to wonder, now that his creator was free to flex his art muscles without constraint? How many more planets would he swallow up with war, and make fit for orks to thrive on? The dok looked up past the scaffold to the dome of masonry above, and pictured the stars beyond it turning green one by one. A whole galaxy, claimed for orks by Ghazghkull... and by Grotsnik too, if you thought about it properly.

The dok thought about it very properly, until he found it was too big a thought to keep inside his brain. So, since he was grinning anyway, he vented it all in a big, mad roar of a laugh, which filled the dome just as thoroughly as his authority. At last, if only for a little while, his genius was free to burn out of control. *No gods, no warlords: just Grotsnik.*

That wasn't a bad note to get started on, the dok thought. So he fished his oldest scalpel from his belt – the tool he'd made the first cut with, the night Ghazghkull was created – and leaned in to begin the operation.

11

Just as Grotsnik's blade was about to meet flesh, something heavy and wet smacked into the flagstones next to him. A spatter of small, viscous gobbets followed, coating the left-hand side of his body, and as they began to slither down the grooves of his knobbly musculature, his grin shrivelled into a mean, crooked grimace.

'It was that one what dropped it,' a voice squawked down, from the top of the scaffold. But Grotsnik's immediate interest was in what had been dropped. He looked to the floor where, just as he had expected from the sound of the splat, Ghazghkull's heart lay in several ragged pieces.

It was going to have been Ghazghkull's heart, anyway.

Alongside the bits of the Prophet's original body hung around the dome, there were a lot of bits from other orks too. Some, Grotsnik had been saving for years, putting them on ice whenever he'd found himself operating on a patient too thick to notice the lack of a few ribs or a kidney. Others, to the dok's amazement, had been donated, as word of Ghazghkull's fall had spread across the trenches of Krongar.

This had been the route by which he had acquired the heart. A titanic but simple-minded Goff known as *Got-So-Angry-He-Tried-To-Fight-Himself*, had come to Grotsnik's lab just days before, ducking under the lintel with an expression that made Grotsnik instinctively reach for his chain-scalpel. He had presumed the giant had come to hurry the work, via traditional Goff motivational methods. Instead, the hulk had simply prised a broad slab of armour from the centre of his chest, before reaching into the shell-wound which the carapace had covered, and tearing free his heart with a rubbery snap. *For the boss,* he had mumbled as he had handed Grotsnik the organ, before slumping to his knees and passing out.

It had been a first-rate heart, Grotsnik thought, as he watched its ruptured mass quivering on the stone – the kind of organ he'd once have sold half his tools to acquire. Now it was just more meat for the squigs, however, and he supposed he'd have to modify the fuel pump off a truck instead. But before Grotsnik could even register the disappointment he felt, it had transmuted itself into anger, and his gaze had snapped to the gantries high above, scanning them for the likely culprit.

He did not have to look long. Awaiting his gaze were a cluster of grots in stained overalls, all frantically jabbing fingers of mute accusation at each other.

Behind them, the winch which had been conveying the heart towards its socket swung to and fro forlornly.

Grotsnik found he did not care which of the snivelling things had dropped the organ. He wanted, very much, to shoot the lot of 'em, if only to dodge the tedium of listening to them blame each other. And any other day, he would have done just that. Indeed, his hand was already reaching for the slugga at his hip to do some killing. But a muted boom from beyond the dome above, and a trickle of dust from its apex, checked his arm before he could level the weapon's sights. Because this was not any other day.

Ghazghkull might have fallen, but the battle wasn't over. Up there, beyond the dome, hundreds of thousands of orks were still fighting a vicious defence against Blackmane's Space Wolves. The beakies' boss had been thoroughly gutted in the process of getting Ghazghkull's head off, but rather than calling it evens and moving on, his lads had reacted by getting really, *really* upset.

The orks weren't winning.

Privately, Grotsnik had even started to wonder if the orks were *losing.* Ghazghkull's forces had, by now, been driven entirely into the crypts beneath the kafeedral. They were trapped there. And with every day that went by, they were being driven deeper and deeper, to the makeshift command bunker and the dok's lab at its centre. Even if it felt ungodsly to think about it, Grotsnik knew that if that load of grey-armoured nutters pushed all the way down before he could get the boss up and running again, they'd be done for.

'Mightn't even have that long,' Grotsnik muttered to himself through his tusks, as he glanced at the heavy blast doors sealing his laboratory off from the rest of the bunker. When he'd set the place up, he had hoped the doors would give him a bit of quiet to fill with the noise of his own work, but he'd soon been disabused of that notion. From the tunnels outside came a constant, discordant racket of bickering and roaring, which grew louder by the hour as more orks were forced down here, and as they got closer and closer to breaking Ghazghkull's Big Rule, by coming to blows.

From the sounds of the current bout of hollering, *Finds-Bullets-He-Has-Not-Lost,* the Deathskull lieutenant who was meant to be in charge while the boss was 'recovering,' was moments away from unleashing his fists on Urzog, the Goff chieftain who considered himself to occupy the exact same role.

The idea of being nominally in charge – like the idea of not fighting whenever you felt like it – was a Ghazghkull thing. Usually, if a boss got so much as mildly brainshot, that was that: he'd be done for, and the next biggest orks would slug it out for the job. It was a testament to the Prophet, Grotsnik supposed grudgingly, that the underbosses were waiting at all for him to recover.

But they wouldn't wait forever. One way or another, whether by angry humans or angrier orks, this miserable little burrow of theirs was going to get torn apart. Unless, of course, Ghazghkull came back to will it otherwise.

There was too much work to be done, Grotsnik knew, for him to afford a few shot grots. It was a pure case of what he knew as *straight-line-thinking,* and it made him *miserable.* He hated it, more than anything, when he was forced to reason himself out of what he knew was the *right* thing to do. It felt… alien. Made him think of all the bones he'd had cracked in his youth, all the blades he'd taken, for being *unorky*.

His habit of straight-line-thinking was why they'd called him *Mad* Dok Grotsnik, back on Urk, and it was why they'd treated him like second-hand squig turds. But eventually, as he'd grown older and nastier, he'd developed a knack for this weird, ungodsly cunning. He'd learned to use it to his own advantage, and soon, the cracked bones had started to belong to other orks.

'Who you gurner shoot then?' asked one of the grots on the scaffold, breaking the dismal fog that had settled on Grotsnik's brain, and prompting him to scowl upwards again.

'None of yer,' growled the dok, finding a new ceiling for his already extraordinary hatred of grots, and he drove all thoughts of the burst heart from his mind. 'Too much work to do. But if I were any of you – and thank Mork I ain't, you rotten, degenerate gits – I'd set to getting a new zoggin' heart for the boss fixed up, from anything in the Big Pump Store.'

Grotsnik turned then, with only the quiet splintering of a clenched tusk giving away how much fury he'd made himself swallow, and began stalking back over towards Ghazghkull's head. He'd just got to wondering why he couldn't hear the anxious, moist rustling of a pack of grots getting to work, when the question came.

III

'Is there any real point to it though, boss?'

'You *what?*' Grotsnik said, in a voice like a knife-tip glinting in the dark, and stood stock still.

'Well... is there any point in working, now?' repeated the voice. It was reedy and nasal, just south of a full sneer – and worst of all, without a trace of terror in it. Grotsnik spun round to its source, baring his fangs and narrowing his good eye, only to find... another grot. It wasn't as if he'd ever bothered giving his orderlies proper names, given how long they tended to last, but he'd always thought of this one as Drippa, thanks to the thin strand of mucus which seemed perpetually suspended from its gristled promontory of a nose.

'You're going to have to *explain your reasoning* there, Drippa,' replied Grotsnik, not doing much to stop his hand reaching for the slugga again.

'This place is done for sooner or later,' said the grot, clamping a miserable twist of fungus trimmings between its fangs, and lighting the tip with a sparky-stick. It took a vicious little wheeze, shrugged, and spoke its next words through a thin cloud of rancid brown smoke. 'And we all know you're a miracle-doer, 'cos you tell us all the time and all. But... well. Look at 'im, boss.'

With only a waggle of its broken-and-reset jaw, Drippa dipped the tip of its smoke-stick towards the mute immensity of the dismantled Prophet, and grimaced uncertainly.

'Even if we had a whole year to work,' said the grot, 'you honestly reckon the boss is coming back from *that?*'

The dok wanted to roar that he *very much did reckon that.* But when he did, he found that his jaw had fallen open in shock, so he just made a noise like something dying from a massive and sudden blow to the abdomen.

The shock hadn't come from the way Drippa had spoken to him, since basic disrespect from his minions had long been no surprise to the dok. Just as other orks had always looked down on him, grots had never treated him with the same rightful, undiluted terror as they did other orks, no matter how many acts of extreme violence he conducted either in front of them or upon them. It was like they saw him as nothing more than an especially big, strong, nasty grot.

But for all Grotsnik hated that, he was at least used to it. No: the thing which had struck Grotsnik like a mortar barrel across the brow was the fact that Drippa – disrespectfully or not – had made a good point.

Every grot came out of its hole knowing straight-line-thinking. It was natural to them, which was a big part of why it was such a shameful trait for an ork to exhibit. And in that one little question – 'Is there any real point?' – Drippa had demonstrated just why proper orks held such common contempt for reason. Because too much straight-line-thinking, if you weren't careful, could lead to the unorkiest thing of all. It was a concept so wrong, Grotsnik only knew it as a human word: *dowt.*

And now, to his horror, his brain was awash with it. As his eye flickered over the scattered armour plates, muscle chunks and limb ends that currently made up Ghazghkull Thraka, Warlord of Warlords and Prophet of the Gods, more and more dowt rushed in through it. It was a flood, and the boulder of rage which had been growing in his mind sank down into it, dissolving into nothing. Then, as he carried on staring, slack-jawed, at the suddenly impossible scale of the task, Drippa carried on.

'S'just not gurner happen, dok. Beakies are at our door, bosses at each other's throats, and the big boss is in bits. S'no blood in him. No...' The grot flailed its arms, as if groping for words big enough to describe what it was thinking. 'No *Green* in 'im.'

Grotsnik found a spark of rage at that, even in the murk of the dowt. Because even though he considered the gods idiots, that was *blasfermy,* that was. The Great Green was bigger than gods. It was bigger than every ork and grot and snot and squig stacked together, and nobody but the Prophet had a say in what did and didn't have the Green in it. Grotsnik didn't respect much beyond his own abilities, but he respected that.

'Zoggin' *wretch!*' he barked, lunging a pace forwards and prompting Drippa to skitter three back. 'Who do you reckon you are, then, to be the sayer of that?' With his heart thudding, and the seams on his wrists splitting as his hands clenched into killing-claws, Grotsnik felt a reassuring surge of orkiness, and pressed on without questioning it. With every step he took towards Drippa, the shadow of his confidence swelled. Indeed, by the time he gripped the creature by the throat and lifted it, spluttering, into the air, Ghazghkull's resurrection felt like a near certainty.

'You don't know *nothing,* bin-git!' hissed the dok, snatching the tattered roll-up from Drippa's teeth with his spare hand, and taking a vicious drag of his own, before discarding it. 'You think this is beyond *Grotsnik,* do yer? Think you've seen the extent of what he can do, in the clawful of stinking, cringing years you've spent in the world? Have you forgotten, *grot,* that I've brought the boss back from the Great Green once? Never woulda *been* a Ghazghkull to begin with, if it weren't for me bringing him back to life, back in that tent on Urk.'

Drippa's thin lips writhed over its rotten fangs, as it wrestled to draw enough breath to speak. When it did, Grotsnik couldn't believe what he was hearing.

'It... wasn't you though... was it?' gargled Drippa. 'You just... killed him, operating. Was... *Makari* what brought him back to life.'

The only reason Drippa didn't die then, is because Grotsnik was too distracted hating someone else. Makari. The grot who had dragged bodies for him back on Urk. Or rather, the thing that grot had become, out in Grotsnik's corpse-yard, as they had tried to prise the adamantium plate from the skull of the dok's freshest failure. Because while Makari had been the grottiest grot who had ever skulked out of a hole, they'd also been... something else.

Grotsnik didn't know what that was. Makari had always insisted they were just the Prophet's banner-waver. But the dok knew better. He knew Makari had been granted visions by Ghazghkull. Visions and secrets, and some weird, unknowable connection with Ghazghkull that should've been Grotsnik's. That little scrap of gristle had always stood between Grotsnik and his creation. And while he couldn't prove it, he swore Makari *talked* to Ghazghkull – nudging him here and there, and always keeping Grotsnik from seizing the control which he knew would have made the Prophet unstoppable.

The banner-waver had died at the same time as Ghazghkull, in the scrap with Blackmane up top. But that didn't do much to reassure Grotsnik. Makari had died plenty of times before now. The dok had even killed them himself, once. But the little turd-scrap *came back*, every time – even though everyone knew grots were too rubbish to live more than once. Grotsnik couldn't figure it out in the slightest. And if there was one thing he hated more than grots, it was puzzles he couldn't think his way through.

'Makari's dead,' barked Grotsnik, throwing Drippa into a bank of sparking capacitors, 'and so's their name. They was a thief, is all they was. Got that? It was *me* what brought Ghazghkull back, and that... chancer just happened to be standing in the right place when it happened.'

'If you say so, boss,' croaked Drippa, wincing as it tried to sit upright. Grotsnik lurched towards the little ingrate, intent on giving it a further pasting. But as he did, he became aware of the dozens of watery, beady little eyes fixed on him. The only thing grots enjoyed more than watching their own rise up against their masters was watching them get beat back down, and it seemed that Grotsnik's entire horde of orderlies had gathered to watch the show.

The dok's fists itched, and not just because they'd recently been someone else's. He knew it was right for Drippa to die. But he also knew – somehow – that this was the moment that everything yet to come hinged on. There was another lesson he could teach here, besides the ever-reliable lesson of fists, that might save Ghazghkull, the battle and the whole of the Waaagh! He didn't know how. He didn't even know what the lesson was. But the dok trusted his brain well enough to know it wouldn't have piped up for nothing.

There'd be something there, if he just started talking. *If.* And that was what it came down to, he supposed. Would he be a proper ork and beat Drippa to mush? Or would he be Mad Dok Grotsnik?

'Listen up, you puddles of squig-pus!' shouted Mad Dok Grotsnik, glaring all around him at the grots assembled in the shadow of Ghazghkull's lifeless bonce. 'You're going to work yourselves to squigmeat, every last one of you. You know why? *'Cos I says so*. Something's only impossible, you see, if

Grotsnik ain't done it yet. And since the boss *is* coming back – and it's gonna be me who brings him – then *this ain't impossible.* Got that?'

There was a faint flicker in the dark, as a swarm of grots looked at each other in frantic incomprehension. But it didn't matter, because this time, not even Drippa was stupid enough to speak up.

'But before we get to work,' added Grotsnik, as his mind finally worked out what the masterplan was, 'I'm going to tell you a story. It's not one I've ever told anyone. It's not something anyone ever saw, besides one other ork. And it's why you're going to work your snot-green arses off, once I'm done. Because guess what? There was another time Ghazghkull died, after the first. And that time, there was no Makari to get in the way. I brought him back, all by myself. *And this is how it happened.*'

IV

It happened not long after the boss invaded Armygeddon for the second time. We were down under the ocean, sneakin' up on Tempestora Hive in a great big fleet of *submersibbles.* And of course, I know yous lot weren't even spores back then. But you know what I'm talking about, don't yer? I've seen the little scrawlings you do in places you think I won't see, in glyphs you think I can't read. You pass down your little... *histreys,* and so you know what happened well enough. At least, you think you do.

Oh – and before any of you gits tries to say otherwise... those submersibbles? My idea. Oh yeah, I know very well everyone says it was Orghamek. But who do you think grew all of Orghamek's brains, eh? And who got 'em to play nicely together? Yeah, that's right. Grotsnik. So anything he invented counts as my idea, 'cos of *intallectual propatee.*

Still, it's not all bad that I don't get the credit for the subs, 'cos they weren't exactly our best work of the war. They did their job and didn't sink, sure. Two-thirds did, anyway. But I swear by Gork's bloodied boot-nails, you've no zoggin' idea what it was like on board those things.

We'd welded 'em together from scrapped human tankers in the wastes up north, bulked up with armour plate that the voidboys cut off the hulls of the kroozers in orbit, then dropped straight down through atmosphere. It was tough stuff, all right. But it was leaky as a Blood Axe cipher – in the end, we gave up trying to weld all the bullet holes shut, and just packed 'em with scrap metal and squig resin.

Then there was the heat. You've not got the know-wots to understand this, but spaceship metal's meant to work best surrounded by loads of... nothing, yeah? Put it under the sea – 'specially a boiling hot, sludgy sea like Armygeddon's – then stick one of Nazdreg's mega-reaktors in the arse end, and you've basically made yerself a moving kiln full of thousands and thousands of orks. We was boiling alive in those things – up to our knees in soupy bilge slime wherever we went, blistered all over from the reaktor leaks, and only eating tins of whatever humans we'd managed to round up and render down during the rush to get the Mork-snicked things built.

That's not even starting on the squigs, neither. See, thanks to a snarl-up with the first landings, half the Goff Dread-mobs the boss had ordered for the Big Boat Attack, ended up halfway across the planet, wonderin' where the sea was. And what did we get instead? A whole karrier full of Beastsnagga warbands, complete with their stamping, farting, biting squigs. Worse still, 'cos the boss' sub was the biggest, it ended up with the biggest squigs. So we had this giant barn filling a full third of the hull, packed with tank-sized turd factories. Let's just say it didn't help with the smell, right?

Anyway. I'm only telling yous all this, so you can get an idea how... *worked up* we all was, after what felt like forever chugging along at the bottom of that 'orrible sea. You think you've seen orks spoiling for a fight? Not till you've seen 'em packed inside a hot tin for days on end, you haven't.

It was that bad, even Ghazghkull weren't above it. Dunno whether it was the heat, or the radiation, or the poison I'd been injecting in his neck because I wanted to see how mad he'd go, but his headaches had been getting worse and worse the whole time. It'd got to the point where he wasn't getting any words at all from the gods during 'em, they were just roaring right into his brain, making him thrash so hard he left dents in the walls. Gork's grin, though – it got so bad I even laid off the poison in the end, just in case he thrashed so hard he made a hole and sank us.

Before we left, the Prophet had stood up on the battlements of the flagship's peekin'-spire, and he'd sworn to every ork there that he'd personally lead the charge, once we'd crossed the ocean and beached at Hive Tempestora. The cheer was so zoggin' loud, after he said that, I wondered if they'd hear us in the bleedin' hive itself, all the way across the sludge.

But when, at long last, the day of the landings arrived, I went up to Ghazghkull's throne-chamber to check on him, and found him in the rottenest state I ever saw. He was twitching, and snarling, and he couldn't seem to go three squeezes of a timer-squig without his whole body going rigid and shaking like a Deff Dread's drill arm. It was like nothing I'd seen before. I'd definitely gone too hard with the poison, but there was something more than that, too. Like something had grabbed him by the head, and wouldn't let go.

Now, I've never been one to *under-esty-mate* my own work. Especially a piece of work so killy as Ghazghkull. I knew what kind of punishment the boss could take, 'cos I'd dished enough of it out to his brain, and even taken proper notes. But it looked like here, at last, was the limit. One look at the boss that day told me all I needed to know. He was, in my medikal opinion, *proper busted,* and there was no way he was gonna be leading any charges at all, unless they was charges face first into the sea.

Naturally, I had a plan. I reckoned I could loosen some of the pressure in Ghazghkull's skull. Knew I could, in fact, 'cos I always left a few screws overtightened in there, just in case I ever needed an excuse to get in his head for a bit. He'd need a full overhaul of his headmeat, soon enough. But I figured a quick tune-up, finished in time for the boss to give his big pre-fight speech, would be enough to get him through the day. So I told Ghazghkull that I needed to operate.

Didn't go down well. Lucky for me, he was in such a state that the punch only clipped me, cracking my left arm, and then burying itself two tusk-lengths into the steel of the chamber wall. Still, I knew I couldn't let that put me off. I *needed* to get inside that skull. 'Cos if I didn't, and Ghazghkull went ahead and led the invasion anyway, it wouldn't take the underbosses three kidney-beats to realise their Prophet was cooked in the head.

Well... desperate times, yeah? What can you do? Well, this is what *I* did. After a quick breather to steady myself, I told the boss he was being an idiot, and that he needed the op done there and then.

The second punch didn't miss me. Or at least, it wouldn't have done. But Ghazghkull never finished it. He launched himself towards me, all full of murder, then stopped dead halfway with his face gone slack, and fell to the deck like a sack of anvils and steak.

Seeing him lying there, not even twitching... Well, it was almost like I couldn't see him at all. My eyes was taking him in, all right, but my brain wasn't having any of it. Dropping flat for no reason? That just... didn't happen to Ghazghkull. But there he was, dropped flat. Don't think I could quite grasp what'd happened, to be honest. Same way you lot would lose the plot if, oh I dunno, I *paid you,* or something.

'Cos of what a mindbuster it was, it was a good long while before I worked up the nerve even to go over and poke the boss. And for all my surgical know-wots, poking was all I could think to do, for a while. Eventually though, I heaved the boss' face off the floor, and wished I hadn't. There was blood pouring from his nose, his ears and the corner of his good eye, and even leakin' out from the edge of his metal skullplate. Now, as an expert in bleeding, that told me all I needed to know. The Prophet'd got so angry, on top of the state his head was in anyway, that some part of his brain had just... burst.

That was just... that. Burst brain. And if he hadn't been dead when he'd hit the floor, he definitely was by the time I'd worked out what was going on.

The boss was dead. And wouldn't you know it, at *just that moment,* the shouting-boxes roared into life all down the inside of the sub, and started blarin' out a message from the lookouts up top in the peekin'-spire. They'd seen the target, hadn't they? Just visible through the smog on the horizon, lurking like a git-nest in a marsh, was Hive Tempestora itself.

And that meant that, in the time it'd take you to refill any of those lymph tanks over there, the whole fleet of subs would be ploughing up out of the water, beaching 'emselves on the slag-drifts of the shore, and grinding over any human defences like soil-gits under a boot. When that happened, every ork, on every sub on the fleet, would be waiting in the holds chanting the great war chant, ready to follow the Prophet into battle. Even before that, now that the hive had been sighted, they'd be expecting the boss to show up down in the musterin' chambers, to give his big pump-up speech.

Only... his brain had burst.

There wasn't even time to panic. I knew, right then, I needed to snatch up every moment of time I could possibly get my gristly hands on, to have a hope of *resussertatin* the Prophet before we hit the beaches. That meant someone needed to cover for the boss down below, playing for as much time as possible. And I knew just the someone.

That's not good, Biter had said, when they'd climbed up through the hatch into the throne-chamber, and clapped eyes on the stone-dead Ghazghkull. Typical Biter.

They're all zoggin' weird, the Blood Axes are. But Biter – or Taktikus, as they'd called themself back then – was something else. They'd just become the chief Blood Axe *genrul* on Armygeddon, after shanking their predecessor during a raid behind human lines, and they was probably the weirdest ork I've ever come across. Actually *likes being around humans*. Fought with 'em once, they says. Still betrayed 'em in the end, mind. But they're a creepy git however you look at it.

Unfortunately, they're a clever git and all. And in that moment, they was the only ork on that rotten boat who I reckoned had a chance of seeing Ghazghkull dead, and not completely losing their mind. So in that moment, they was the most precious thing in the world to me. Straight-line-thinking, yeah? Anyway, once they'd got a grip on the situation, I sent them down to where the speech was due to be held, and told them to think up some zoggin' good reasons for the boss not being there.

So that was one problem dealt with, at least. Later, I found out exactly what Biter had done to keep the troops busy, and I will grudgingly admit it was a *masterpiece* of a lie. They'd said Ghazghkull had left the sub to fight a sea monster, because he'd got too annoyed with being cooped up below decks. They'd even had mines detonated just outside the hull, so it sounded like there was a fight going on out in the sludge. Bought me a lot of time, Biter did, with that little ruse.

Not enough time, though. Working like a grot trying to wall up a gap in a gnasher-squig pen, I'd opened up the whole of Ghazghkull's bonce, and laid it out in bits on the floor of his throne-chamber, all the while hoping nobody walked in on me. It was a miserable situation for brain surgery to begin with, what with the dim red emergency lights, and the stench of the squigs and all. But it got worse, fast.

When the subs at the front of the fleet burst through the defensive perimeter of the human sea wall, the hive's defenders scrambled their bombers, and started filling the sea around us with depth charges. They launched too late to actually cause much damage, mind, since the subs were wrapped up in spaceship metal after all. Think they only managed to sink a couple of dozen boats, if I remember right. But the rocking of the hull, and the constant zoggin' concussion waves from the blasts, really tested my detail work. For almost every bloodpipe I managed to close up in the boss' knotted great ball of a brain, it seemed another got tore open when an explosion knocked my hand.

Still, what I lack in precision, I've always made up for in speed. I was makin' progress. And as we passed under the bombardment, I got every rupture in the Prophet's brain closed up. I even charged it with a few gobfuls of my own genius blood, so it'd have enough juice in it to think with, once I got his hearts started.

And I swear, for all that I hate both of the gits, thank Gork and Mork I managed to get his skull bolted together, with just an instant to spare, before our keel hit the beach.

'Cos when I say beach, I'd be better off saying junkyard. Weren't a grain of sand to be found there – just piles upon piles of smashed-up human machinery, eaten through with rust, and with all the gaps filled in with jagged chunks of slag from the foundries upcoast. The sound of it, as jags and snags tore through the sub's belly like squiggoth claws, made it feel like being stuck in the inside of a dakkajet turbine.

As the sub ploughed all the way out of the water and started grinding along under its own weight, I thought we was going to be shook to pieces. And if I hadn't had the massive dead weight of Ghazghkull to cling onto, I would've been smashed to splinters against the walls. It was a grim old ride, that. Sometimes, you know, I wonder how many more mobs might've made it out onto the beaches, if we'd thought to put handholds in the troop bays.

I couldn't believe how long we kept on skidding. But then, I s'pose a ship the size of a small city, sat on a nuclear turbine going at full blast for days, is gonna build up a bit of momentum, isn't it? Still, gravity's such a hard old brute that even ork hardware can't outlast it. In the end we came to a long, rattling halt, and after one last massive groan of metal, and a crack of the central girders for good measure, there was silence.

Gork knows how many of the other subs got shredded to bits on the way out of the sea, or broke in two once they had to take their own weight, but I could see the little red lights on the wall of the boss' throne-chamber pinging green as the survivors reported landfall, and it looked like it was probably more than half of 'em.

Not bad, I know. Weren't gonna last, though. Already, the silence'd been broken by the drone of the human bombers, as they wheeled back round out at sea to take another run at us. And this time, we were sitting targets, with no sludge to hide under.

I heard the rattle and crack of the flak turrets on the sub's tail opening up, but then they stopped again, one by one – no doubt as the gunners took slaps across their heads from their bosses. Why? *'Cos Ghazghkull had said he'd start the attack.* That was how it had to go; so far as every last ork in the fleet saw it, that was how the gods were going to give us our win. And if that meant losing a few more subs, while the boss chose the perfect moment to strike? Well, that was just the way things went.

All well and good, only the boss' heart wouldn't start. I'd tried squishing it with my hands. I'd tried getting the spare one going first. I'd tried sticking the sparky end of a sliced-through cable into the middle of it. I'll be honest, I'd even tried battering it with a wrench, just in case. But the zoggin' thing just sat there between the boss' ribs, cold and rubbery, refusing even to twitch.

The bombs were falling now, of course. But I had to keep trying. So, with my making-things-bigger goggles on and a glow-squig between my teeth, I pushed my head right inside the Prophet's chest for a proper look. At least it was a break from the smell of squig turds.

I don't really know what I expected to find in there. But as it turned out, I was in luck. The problem was stupidly simple, actually. Shining my light through the walls of the boss' main bloodpipes, I saw the biggest one coming out of his heart was all blocked up. I spent a good while squinting at it, trying to work out what it might have been, when I remembered I'd injected him with molten plastek a few days previously. Supposedly, it'd been a cure for the rashes on his neck – which I'd also caused, with a swab dipped in used reaktor coolant – but really it'd just been a bit of spite on my part. For a moment there, I almost regretted having done it.

Especially when something started cutting its way through the wall.

As soon as I managed to pull my head out of the boss, I saw sparks flying, and I knew that the fierce, white-orange square drawing itself slowly across the inner hull could only mean one thing. We'd taken so long to invade the beaches, *that the zoggin' humans were invadin' us.*

Before that moment, I'd been coming up with a dead elegant plan for clearing the boss' bloodpipes. But that had to go down the drops sharpish: this was no time for fancy surgery. Knowing I'd have to go with my gut, I stopped any sort of straight-line-thinking, and solved the problem like any good ork.

That'll do, I thought, spotting a skinny, jagged little banner-pole sticking up from Ghazghkull's shoulder armour. Twisting it off with a neat little snap, I peered back into the boss' open chest, poked my tongue between my tusks to make my aim better, and jabbed him right in the *ventrikular arteree* with the sharp end.

Two things happened at once, then. There was a big, gurgling pop from Ghazghkull's heart as it unclogged itself and started beating, and a massive hollow clang from behind me, as the cut section of hull fell through. The whole chamber filled with smoke, and I had to use my rivetgun blind to close the incision, accidentally putting two bolts through my hand in the process. But I closed it, and as I swept the worst of the muck from the seal, I could feel the thud of the boss' heart through the skin.

Which was just as well. Because standing in the hole in the wall were three massive beakies. I'd spent so long in that miserable, dim red light that they were just black outlines against a wall of blinding white. But there's no mistaking a beaky when you see one – those big pretend shoulders, that tiny little head, those big ridiculous boots: they're all a dead giveaway. Still, it wasn't the most welcome sight in the world, right then.

I was squinting down the barrel of one of their chunky guns, I remember, trying to remember how good beakies could see through smoke, when I heard it. The best sound I'd ever heard in my life, even though it was just five words.

'Move out the way, Grotsnik.'

V

'Now obviously,' said Grotsnik, his stitch-riven chest puffed out with pride, 'there was a lot of fighting still to come, after that. But as far as I'm concerned? *That* was the moment we won the invasion of Tempestora Hive.'

'Yeah,' said Drippa, its face entirely motionless, earning it a scowl from the dok. 'Great story, boss. Just got one question, though.'

'Oh, did I miss something?' hissed Grotsnik, nostrils flaring, as he towered over his nonplussed audience.

'Just one thing, yeah... the pole.'

'What pole?'

'The one you fixed the boss' heart with. You said it was a banner, right?'

'I... think you... yeah.' The dok snorted, taken aback. 'What's that got to do with anything?'

'Do you remember what was... on the banner, at all? Like, a picture or sumfink?'

'Uh?' grunted the dok, his long, scarred face crunching up in bafflement. But then, as some mean little detail fell into place, deep within the algal folds of his own mind, realisation set in. His lone red eye, furrowed into a smouldering volcanic crack with concentration, flared suddenly in shock, and his mouth gaped in wordless exaggeration, as what had seemed such a trivial detail at the time swelled to monumental importance.

'Was it that banner?' asked Drippa, a mean strand of mucus swaying across its sharp little grin, as it extended a claw towards the mountainous shape of Ghazghkull's torso in the gloom.

There, screwed into a socket high up on the boss' fortress of a shoulder, and glinting weakly where endless bullet-strikes had hammered and holed it, was indeed a tattered metal banner. And on its lumpy surface, copied faithfully from the copy of a hundred previous copies, was the design that had first been daubed in the Prophet's own blood, back in the yard behind Grotsnik's own medical tent.

Makari? Makari? Makari?

The name echoed in Grotsnik's head, like a drumbeat, coming from every direction at once. *Is this it?* he thought to himself, as the full misery of the truth continued seeping through his skull like ice water. *Am I finally, properly, going mad?*

But Grotsnik was not going mad. Or if he was, it had nothing to do with the name he could hear being shouted, over and over again. Because the name, he heard now, was being repeated in the same, unmistakable voice whose bellows and barks had underscored Grotsnik's work for some time now. It was Bullets, somewhere outside the laboratory's door. And there was, in fact, a drumbeat underlying it. Something like a drumbeat, anyway: a wet, thudding crack, just a moment or two after each repetition of that hated name.

Makari? Crack! Makari? Crack! Makari? Crack!

Despite the many, many other thoughts clamouring for space in Grotsnik's mind, then, he could never ignore the evidence of somebody else getting know-wots wrong, and he clicked his tusks in contempt.

'The zoggin' *moron,*' he muttered. 'He's trying to find them, isn't he? Trying to find a new Makari. Goin' along a line of grots, I'll bet, and braining 'em when they don't respond.' The dok shook his head mournfully, and absent-mindedly gathered a spanner from his belt. 'Doesn't he have the wits to realise it was always the boss' *touch,* brought the little bin-git back, not just the name?'

'We've still got the Prophet's old hands...' said Drippa, nodding conspiratorially towards a hopper at the back of the dome, stacked with hunks of leathery green flesh. 'Wonder if they'd still work?'

Grotsnik the ork opened his mouth to roar abuse, with fangs bared and talons arched. But Mad Dok Grotsnik said nothing, because he was doing *straight-line-thinking.* The grot, for all its attitude, was correct. There was one factor that had been common to both incidents of Ghazghkull's resurrection, it turned out. And yet, it was absent from this attempt. For all that he hated Makari, he knew that – as a scientist, if not as an ork – it was his duty to suffer them once more.

He took a long look down at Drippa the grot, and narrowed his eye. Was there a similarity there? No. But it didn't matter: the little sods looked different every time. But the attitude? The spiteful, smug piety? Oh, yes; on that front, Drippa was more than halfway there already. It'd make a perfect test subject.

Drippa had been about to say something, but didn't get the chance before the ork's arm swooped down and picked it up bodily by its ragged, greasy ear.

'Congratulations, Drippa,' announced Mad Dok Grotsnik, a smirk of triumph finding a foothold on his face again at last. 'You're about to pioneer an entirely new field of research with me. I suggest you start thinking godly thoughts.'

He turned, then, to the rest of the lab's grot workers, who had been beginning to disperse in disappointment, now that it looked like further violence was unlikely.

'And you lot?' boomed the dok, his eye gleaming with reflections of arc lightning from the capacitors. 'Fetch the boss' old hand, and pulley armature three. We're going to do a little experiment.'

'How's that gonna help?' screeched a miserable specimen at the back of the crowd, with a feeble shrug. 'Bringing the Prophet back's still impossible.'

'Foolish grot,' grinned Grotsnik, turning his wild gaze to the ceiling once more, and the green stars which shone, concealed, behind it. 'Something's only impossible, you know, if the Great Green ain't willed it yet.'

THE ENEMY OF MY ENEMY

NATE CROWLEY

Nestor blinked away ash-brown rain and tried to imagine, for the fourth time that day, the words with which he would accept his promotion.

The scene was clear in his head: the immense basilica, drenched with light and cheering, the warm kiss of metal as the laurels were set on his brow. But the words would not come. He stood dumbstruck, gaping like a fool before the glaring statues of his forebears. Could he not even muster a little dignity here, in the safety of his daydreams?

Something gave way beneath his boot and he stumbled, dashing the image from his mind. It was the chest of a Guardsman – some unfortunate wirecutter, sunk in the mire and plastered over with battlefield filth. Nestor retched as the stench billowed up from the carcass, but soon steadied himself. The last thing he needed was to lose his stomach in front of Phocus.

'General Pyrrhus?' chirped the younger officer from behind Nestor, his voice a perfect facsimile of loyal concern.

'I'm well, Colonel Phocus,' he growled, straightening himself and scraping the worst of the muck from his boot. 'Just acquainting myself with the mood among the troops,' he added in a mutter to himself, before setting his jaw and looking forward.

Cavernam Tertius was a bloody mess. A mining world that had never lived up to the hopes of the explorators, it had been a dreary backwater even before it had been visited by war. Now, it was little more than a cesspit. But with the segmentum shipyards ever hungry for ore, it was a cesspit which the Mystras VIII, the Golden Eighth, had been consigned to defend for the last ten miserable years.

Frankly, it was madness to stay. Nestor had often, to his dismay, calculated the cost of defending the world: the squandered ammunition alone almost outvalued the meagre ore shipments it guaranteed, while the human disbursement did not bear considering.

Fortunately, the Departmento Munitorum, in its star-spanning majesty, had no appetite to consider it. The immense bureaucracy dealt with arithmetic on a stellar scale, provisioning wars on fronts light years long. On that measureless counting board, Cavernam Tertius was just a drab speck, a bead on the abacus of some lowly, cable-faced wretch. Nestor and all the men and women of the Eighth – of every other regiment in his battlegroup – were insignificant figures, liable to be swept away in a carried digit.

Of course, this would all be bad enough, thought Nestor, if the enemy had some desperate need to take this world. Some relic they were sworn to recover, or a holy city they would give everything to possess. Indeed, *anything* that could be denied them by the stalwart defenders of mankind. But this was not the case. As Nestor gazed past the water running from the brim of his cap, at the jagged earthworks and belching smokestacks of the enemy lines, he knew the awful truth: they were just here for *the fun of it all.*

Despite it all, Nestor managed a tight little smile for himself as he resumed his trudge through the bog and signalled for his staff to follow. The stalemate was about to end. And it was going to end in a fashion that nobody – not the drones of the Munitorum, nor the brutish cretins waiting in the trenches ahead, and certainly not that conniving bastard Phocus – could have foreseen. No, this appalling little war was going to end on *his* terms. And in the slim eventuality he didn't end up a drinking companion to that poor wirecutter in the mud, it would be the making of his name.

'Lord General Militant Pyrrhus,' he murmured under his breath as he reached the agreed spot. *'Lord General Militant Pyrrhus,'* he repeated, rattling through the words in the same way his men would invoke the Throne before a big push, and closed his eyes. He let the warm light of the basilica linger behind them for a moment, then opened them and thrust his arm into the dull, brown sky.

'*Pax!*' he cried, and let the white rag bunched in his fist unroll into the drizzle.

A long moment of nothing passed – nothing but the sound of the rain, tapping on his epaulettes and spattering the shell-crater puddles. Nestor stood with his head back and his chest out, ready to be split by a bullet, but none came.

Then the xenos appeared. They rose from nowhere, as if from beneath the sludge, unfolding from their haunches until they towered over Nestor's party. Seen through binoculars, they had always seemed crooked and hunched – awkward, scurrying things. Up close, however, with little more than a lasrifle's length to keep them at bay, they were monsters.

It wasn't their size that was so intimidating. Nestor had dealt with renegade ogryns that would have outmassed these things twice over, and for all their bulk, they had just been bigger targets. No, there was something innately threatening about the xenos – something more primally awful about their proportions. Their gangly, sinew-bunched arms, the blunt enormity of their jaws, made them something out of a child's night terrors – things that wanted to reach out of the dark, pull you away and gobble you up...

Luckily, it took more than monsters to rattle the Golden Eighth. Before the beasts had even risen past their knees, Nestor heard Vatatze's hellgun power up with a shriek, and the old NCO had leapt out in front of him in a firing crouch. He was grateful as ever for the staff sergeant's reflexes, but a firefight now would doom them.

'Stand down,' cried Nestor to Vatatze, waving a hand at the long rifles slung on the backs of the xenos. 'They're snipers. If they'd wanted us dead, they've had this whole bloody walk from the trench to put holes in us.'

'It's just a ploy,' added Phocus, uninvited, to the whole of the cohort. 'They're trying to put the wind up us while we wait for the parley, is all. Don't let the brutes get in your head!'

Nestor was furious at the colonel's interjection. To be talked over in front of his staff was bad enough – but in front of the bloody xenos? The little turd just couldn't wait to step into his boots, could he? He considered a reprimand, but this was not the time.

Besides, it was hard to concentrate on anything with those dull red eyes regarding him. The beasts had not moved since rising from the mud. Even with Vatatze's hellgun sweeping across them, they had just stood there, staring with expressionless curiosity, like predators behind plasglass. Nestor hated to admit it to himself, especially after Phocus' little speech, but they *did* put the wind right up him.

Particularly uneasy was the fact the enemy was fielding snipers at all. Every tactical codex Nestor had read suggested they preferred to fight at close quarters or, if firearms were involved, via wild onslaughts of mass automatic weapons. The Cavernam posting had soon revealed otherwise. After the first few heads had popped with no enemy in sight, Nestor had quietly amended his manuals, and the men of the Eighth had kept their heads well below the trench parapets.

Examining the sniper closest to him, he wondered how they had never been spotted in the field – especially now, when his party had been walking almost within arm's length of them. The creature in front of Nestor was a good head taller than him, and it was by no means the largest of the group: the one standing a few feet to the right must have been half the size of a bull grox. And although they wore long sniper's cloaks, they were little more than gaudy rags, covered in wild splashes of colour like a fool's mockery of his own regimental camouflage.

'Staff sergeant,' said Nestor softly, beckoning the scowling woman to his side, 'am I losing my eyesight? Look at the colours on those cloaks, and tell me how in the name of Holy Terra we didn't see these skaffers a mile off.' Vatatze shrugged and wrinkled her scarred brow, running her eyes across the line of xenos with a look of contempt.

'Beats me, general. I dunno – you know what they say in the trenches, though.'

'Hmm?'

'Word is they're born like that, sir. They grow underground like fungus, then just pop out from the puddles, gear and all. That's why we send 'em back there, sir. Doing 'em a favour.'

Nestor replied with a grunt of grim amusement, then fell silent as he noticed, to his immense discomfort, that the sniper was trying to catch his eye. The beast had clearly caught him frowning in consternation at its cloak, and had dipped its head to stare right into his eyes. And although the leathery wasteland of its face was impossible to read for human emotions, he could have sworn on the aquila that it was giving him a knowing smirk.

Withstanding the urge to shiver, Nestor tore his eyes away from the monster, and looked towards the xenos front line. Aside from the usual plumes of smoke from engines and cook fires, the enemy trenches were still eerily quiet. The wind was picking up now, the rain smacking against them in fat streaks, and Nestor felt a cold stab of doubt. There was still no sign of the enemy commander. What if it wasn't coming at all?

After another minute of unbearable silence, the men began to murmur. Clearly, they were beginning to have similar doubts. He would have to put a stop to things before he was undercut by Phocus yet again. Turning his back to the bestial snipers while Vatatze stared on at them, Nestor straightened himself to address his soaked-through comrades, radiating parade-ground confidence despite his clenching guts.

'We give it ten minutes from here,' he decreed, making a point of glancing at his timepiece, 'and then we make a controlled retreat to our lines. Colonel Phocus will lead, while Staff Sergeant Vatatze will bring up the rear with me. Until then, we wait in silence. Am I understood?'

'Very clearly, general' said a voice as low and rumbling as distant shell fire, and Nestor felt his shoulders stiffen. Spinning on his heel, he scanned the wasteland for the source of the voice, but they were still alone with the snipers. Then the voice came again, this time with a guttural chuckle, and Nestor's eyes shot to the largest of the beasts. In their savage hierarchy, leadership was determined by size alone ('large means in charge' was the mnemonic drilled into the marksmen of the Eighth) so surely it was their leader? But the hulk stood sullenly silent.

'I'm here,' said the voice from a few feet to the left, and Nestor could barely believe the evidence of his eyes as they flicked to its source – it was the sniper who had smirked at him, calmly addressing him in serviceable Low Gothic.

'And may I say,' it continued, the words bubbling up from deep in its boulder chest, 'what a pleasure it is to meet my adversary in the flesh at last. Shall we... make parley?'

Negotiations were brief.

After the enemy commander had revealed itself, 'refreshments' had been called for. A bark from one of the snipers had summoned the atrocious, scampering slave-creatures of the xenos, who had come boiling from some rathole bearing trestles, boards and cans of stinking meat. With the bizarre feast set up, Nestor's party of eight had taken their places across from the eight xenos, and each side had begun weighing the other up. Phocus had been paired with a vile creature whose left side was a mess of scar tissue and leaky hydraulics; he looked at the thing like he had a mouthful of battery acid. Vatatze, meanwhile, had her elbows on the table, offering a mocking grin to the mountain of green meat opposite, as if she were at ease in the regimental mess. And across from Nestor was the xenos commander.

The thing seemed absurdly proud to be offering its 'hospitality,' making a long, rambling invitation to the humans to partake in the food and drink available. As the oration lumbered on, it became clear how doggedly rehearsed the creature's opening lines had been, and how limited its command of Low Gothic really was. Nestor couldn't help but curl his lip. This was no aberrant mastermind; it was just another beast, foolishly aping the customs of its enemy in the hope some quality might rub off.

Needless to say, nobody touched the food – not even the xenos. By the time the parley began, the tins of charred offal were sodden: sad tokens of civility, awash in rainwater.

Next, their host introduced itself. Intercepted transmissions in the early days of the war had forewarned them of its name: in the alien tongue it was *Eats-Face-Of-Face-Eater*, and so 'Face-Eater' had become the common parlance among the ranks of the Eighth. But in its own head at least, the alien had apparently cultivated another identity.

'I... am Colonel Taktikus,' it announced, gesturing proudly at itself with a leathery green claw, and Nestor had to stifle a laugh. This thing called itself a colonel. Now he looked closer, he saw its chest was covered in dented, rusty medals – meaningless things hammered from scrap metal, and looted Imperial insignia on loops of wire. Then, his amusement turned to pure misery. This savage clown, for all its buffoonery, had been the mind keeping him in stalemate for the fading years of his career. His greatest achievement, his entry in the annals of the line of Pyrrhus, was to be the equal of a barbarian playing at soldiers.

As if to hammer home the mockery, the brute's retinue began chanting. While the creatures seemed insensible to most words in Low Gothic, the name of their commander had drawn an instant and explosive reaction.

'Kurnel Taktus!' bellowed one of the other xenos, hammering the flimsy table with the butt of an axe, and the rest joined in. 'Kurnel Taktus! Kurnel Taktus!'

As the aliens roared, Nestor winced at the stink. Whatever weird chemistry boiled away inside them made their breath nearly unbearable. The smell was somewhere between penal battalion wine and the deep mildew of canvas stored in the damp, with undertones of promethium fumes and rotten meat. It was a relief when Taktikus finally silenced them.

'Colonel... Taktikus,' acknowledged Nestor with a sigh, swallowing his distaste. 'I am General Nestor Pyrrhus–'

'–commander of the Mystras Eighth,' finished Taktikus, 'and director of the Astra Militarum battlegroup on Cavernam Tertius. I know you.' The alien stumbled over the High Gothic terms, but spoke at least with confidence in their meaning.

'Well then,' answered Nestor smoothly, 'if you know so much, I dare presume you will know why we're here now?'

'You are here to offer peace,' said the brute, with what was definitely a smile this time.

'On the contrary, my good colonel. We come to invite you to war.

'Allow me to elaborate,' said Nestor, as the group of soldiers and monsters huddled over the table in the rain. And so he did.

The doom of Cavernam Tertius had announced itself on a day like any other in the long, grinding war. The Basilisks at Ferghal's Wood had cut short the dawn bombardment of xenos trenches on the Blackpine Front, citing a missed delivery of shells. The colonel from the 318th Dolmen Blackhands had voxed yet again, requesting the rotation of his men to the rear, and the damn Belisarians were demanding engineers and heavy weapons platoons from the Eighth, after a night raid had nearly made it into their trench on the Dunrust Salient.

'It's the same story every bloody day,' Nestor cursed to Vatatze, his knuckles tightening the sheaf of reports into a grubby crumple. 'I spend every waking hour telling these boneheads they can't have the things they need, and if I'm lucky, I get to squeeze in the time to be told the same myself. Throne forbid I ever get five minutes to fight a war.' Vatatze said nothing, but that was fine – this was their ritual. He would wear himself out ranting about the day's frustrations, and she would lean in the doorway, inspecting the glowing tip of her lho-stub and occasionally cursing in solidarity.

'Oh, and speaking of which,' Nestor continued, in a tone of sarcastic brightness, 'word's in from the Munitorum on those reinforcements I requested. Guess what?'

'Hmm?'

'Not coming. Again. Just reams of platitude and bloody scripture, imploring me to do more with less, in the Emperor's name.' Nestor made the sign of the aquila in a way a commissar would find deeply questionable, and threw the papers to the floor. 'Frankly, it's getting to the point where I'm not sure why I bother asking. We're old news.'

Vatatze nodded her agreement, and aimed a wad of spit into his waste paper basket. Everyone knew their war was a footnote. The massive xenos migration from which their enemies had split was now light years past Cavernam, and deep into the sector interior. Having smashed through the redoubt at Perikal IV, it was now dangerously close to several vital worlds, and was soaking up appalling quantities of materiel as a result. As such, when the bureaucrats did see fit to send something to Nestor's half-forgotten little conflict, it always came as a surprise, and was almost never what he needed.

'Hey, general,' Vatatze quipped, 'remember the horse guys?'

'Ugh, don't remind me of that.' The last big bolstering, two winters past, had comprised a bulk carrier bearing seventy thousand horsemen from a feral world, who had been handed lasrifles en route, and who had gaped in astonishment at the first tank they had seen.

'They didn't exactly turn the tide of the conflict, did they, staff sergeant?'

'Nope. Horsemeat made for better rations though.'

Nestor laughed then, as he only tended to with Vatatze, and found the strength to continue working through the day's pile of unfulfillable requests.

After another hour, he put down the papers and rubbed his eyes, feeling a creeping thirst gathering. His glass of morning amasec was down to a fingernail's depth, dwarfed by the stack of requests he had yet to read.

'What do you reckon, staff sergeant – would a second glass constitute a problem, or just a habit?' There was no reply, which was odd. Vatatze was always game for opening a bottle: along with her brutally dispassionate sense for logistics, it was what made her such an invaluable NCO.

'Staff sergeant?' he repeated, but there was still no answer. Nestor looked up to find Vatatze staring at a roll of printouts that had just been handed to her by a trembling courier. Her face was as grey and still as stone, which, on an officer who considered leading a charge across no man's land to be a reasonable afternoon's recreation, was not a good sign. Wordlessly, she walked over to hand him the papers, before uncorking the bottle of amasec and taking a deep, joyless pull from its neck.

'Tyranids,' Nestor said in a husk of a voice, ten minutes later, after reading through the astropath's report for the third time.

'Aye,' Vatatze said, with a bleak smile. There was nothing much more to say. The tyranids would end the war on Cavernam. They were, almost always, the enders of wars. The arrival of one of their swarms put a full stop on a conflict, a vicious inkblot that pooled and spread, erasing all that came before and after. They were profoundly alien, incomprehensible to a degree that made the monsters in the opposing trenches seem brotherly by comparison. They had no insignia, nor logistics, nor language, nor tactics. Just teeth, and claws, and numbers that beckoned giddy madness.

'The Blackpine offensive, the crossing at Tahl's Rest, the Dunrust Salient... None of it means a damned thing any more, does it?'

'No, general,' Vatatze replied, pouring him a wounded man's measure of amasec.

'The war's over, isn't it?'

'Yes. Yes it is, general.'

He drank, and his thoughts turned grey. Against the constant, miserable drizzle of the campaign, he had always cupped a flickering hope in his hands. A hope that one day he would outmanoeuvre the xenos, that he would find a way to rout them despite their numbers, and be immortalised as another genius in the line of Pyrrhus. But the tyranids, the Great Devourer, had eaten that future. His only option now was to pull as many civilians as he could off-planet, with as many troops as the carriers would hold, and flee in disgrace.

'How quickly can we evacuate?' he asked, mouth dry. But as Vatatze began rattling off a plan based on her almost preternatural memory for planetary statistics, he found himself not listening. A thought had come to him – one that made his head buzz with the rising tide of the amasec. An idea so preposterous that it offered only glory or immediate death – both of which seemed preferable to the options currently on the table.

The tyranids were so alien as to make his monstrous enemies seem brotherly. And he would require a tremendous number of troops to have even a hope of staving them off. The sort of numbers which the Munitorum had denied him for ten years. The sort of numbers, in fact, which his enemy had in abundance...

'Staff Sergeant Epiphania Vatatze,' he announced, knowing the use of her hated forename would stop his comrade in the middle of her tally of civilian populations.

'General Pyrrhus, sir?'

'I may have just solved all our problems. Bring me whoever knows most about enemy communications, as many logistical specialists as can get here in the next hour and another bottle of amasec.'

'And Colonel Phocus...?' Vatatze added, her shrapnel-pocked face creasing into a smile as she pre-empted his thoughts.

'...can stay blissfully ignorant in his bunk until it's too late to complain. I'm sure he'll have his own view of things, but if the bloody tyranids don't make a case for unilateral action then I'm not sure what will.'

'So... you offer me death?' growled Taktikus, picking a sprig of mycelium from between greying tusks as it ruminated on his words. The other xenos had grown bored during Nestor's explanation of the incoming tyranid swarm, but now they hunched forward, sensing the challenge in their leader's response.

'I always offered you death, Taktikus. But so far, to your... credit, you have been unwilling to receive it. Now, however, I fear the tyranids may have an overwhelmingly compelling proposition for us both. What I can therefore offer you, in the light of this development, is a longer and a better fight against the tyranids... If you make war alongside me.'

At this, the brute gave a long and thoughtful rumble, working a claw into the rotten corner of its maw, as if trying to winkle out the logic of the situation. But Nestor knew there could be only one outcome. While Taktikus' warband were peculiar in their obsession with Imperial doctrine, they were still beasts at heart. Beasts that valued the potential for bloody conflict above all other things. Victory, to them, was incidental – any resources and territory acquired through a fight were secondary to the fight itself. It was why they had stayed committed to a stalemate on Cavernam for ten years, despite full knowledge of how poor a prize the planet would make. Now, that mad alien logic would at last work in Nestor's favour. Given the choice between a war on two fronts that would be over in days, and a war on a single front that might last a month, the ugly green knot of Taktikus' mind could only flex towards one conclusion.

'If you know death certainly is,' said Taktikus, Low Gothic beginning to fray with the effort of concentration, 'why look for fighting together us? Surely... no difference, us or tyranid?'

'Because we are sworn to defend this world in the name of Holy Terra,' said Nestor, segueing smoothly into the lie. 'And if we can hold it for even an hour longer through allying with your forces, then we honour the Throne, even as we die.'

Amusingly, this was almost the logic Colonel Phocus had espoused when he had been informed of the looming tyranid threat. A vainglorious, pious bore, the man had been itching to die for the Throne the moment he had heard the news. The only difference was that he wouldn't countenance an alliance with xenos scum. As far as he was concerned, the only way forward was to evacuate as many civilians as possible who couldn't hold a lasrifle, then go down fighting both sets of xenos. To even consider alternatives, in his mind, was heresy.

But then, Phocus was not the battlegroup's general. By the time he had been let in on the plan, with the swarm just days away, there had been no time for extended debate. Nestor's word, for once, had been law.

Crucially, what neither Phocus nor Taktikus knew was the real goal of the proposed alliance. This was no case of delaying the inevitable. It was a chance to achieve the impossible. While Nestor was by no means certain of the maths, he had an inkling that with Taktikus' horde at his disposal, there was a slim chance the tyranids (whose already vast numbers he had exaggerated in his report to the beast) might in fact be beaten back.

And if such a miracle was to occur, Taktikus' forces, after being fed into the meat grinder of the front line, would be so weakened that Nestor could sweep them from the face of the planet. He would be remembered as a defensive mastermind on a par with Dorn or Invictus – and Phocus as the boneheaded naysayer who had tried to impede him.

All it relied upon was for Taktikus to seize the big shiny bauble it had been offered, and give in to its genetic thirst for a big scrap. The enemy commander might have surprised him with snipers and a penchant for language, but there was no helping the nature of the beast. Nestor was certain of the outcome, even as the guttural words emerged in a puff of stench.

'So be it,' boomed Taktikus, and let loose a string of battered consonants in its native tongue. 'An alliance, of orks and men.'

The beast stood to settle the deal, and Nestor allowed himself just a moment to shoot Phocus a look of pure dominance before he too rose from his seat. But in the brief moment his head was turned, chaos erupted on the other side of the table.

The creature to Taktikus' left – the towering hulk that Nestor had at first taken to be the xenos leader – had gone berserk. Letting out a bowel-loosening roar like a Leman Russ trying to power its way out of a quagmire, the beast drew a monstrous axe from its back and dashed the table before it into splinters.

'No fight with mans!' it bellowed as it lunged forward, and for a heartbeat Nestor wondered if he was about to meet his end in the most shockingly simple betrayal in the history of the Astra Militarum. But then, just as suddenly as the beast had erupted, it was smashed sideways by a blur of deep green muscle – Taktikus, moving with terrible, animal agility. The two creatures fell to the mud in an explosion of limbs, and the rest of the xenos contingent began baying in excitement.

The strength of the larger beast was horrifying to behold, but for every blow it landed, the smaller xenos delivered three. The speed, the *ruthlessness* of the thing, was shocking to witness, and left Nestor with no doubt as to how it maintained authority over its larger fellows. After a furious scramble, Taktikus had the big xenos in a headlock, and a fist wrapped round the largest of its tusks. There was a wet, tearing crack, and the fang came loose in the colonel's hand. Then, without a moment's hesitation, the tusk was jammed once, twice and three times into the giant's neck, springing torrents of thick blood.

Then it was over. Dropping the blood-black tusk in the mud, Taktikus stood back up and sauntered over to the table.

'Forgive the major, general,' it said, wiping its hand on its striped cloak and extending it. 'Their mouth... gets them in trouble sometimes.'

Nestor shook the creature's great, cold brick of a hand, and caught Phocus scowling from the corner of his eye. Maybe, he thought, these beasts could teach him a thing or two after all.

Less than a week later, Nestor was stood on the turret of his command tank, watching mycetic spores streak through the evening sky.

It was a rare clear evening: Cavernam's clouds, having parted grudgingly like theatrical curtains, now wallowed in the sun's weak, orange light as the spores carved fierce gashes in the gulf between them. High up, where the sky faded to deep indigo, smaller puffs of light signalled the destruction of further spores by the planet's defences. It was all rather beautiful, thought Nestor, although he suspected it was mildly heretical to do so.

Of course, any prettiness would not last. This was just the start. The leviathan vessels of the tyranids were already deep in the system's gravity well, but would still take weeks to arrive. Nevertheless, they had launched a vast swarm of spores on a hard burn ahead of them, like the slithering feelers of some corpse-pile crawler. Spiny pods grown on vicious biorockets, their only purpose was to slam into the planet, then peel open like rotten fruit to disgorge their innards.

They had no targets, nor any strategy. Wherever the pods landed, their occupants emerged, marshalling in instinctive packs deep in the wilderness. Reports were rife of abominations glimpsed on the edge of searchlights, and Nestor had seen snatches of grainy footage from the scout platoons, the layers of fibrous husk sloughing away, the chitinous shapes clawing themselves clear of sacs of shock-absorbing gel. Needless to say, they were already running short on scouts.

And still the pods came. For now, they were still able to shoot down most of them. Cavernam's orbital defences had been augmented by the two frigates attached to Nestor's battlegroup and then – after much negotiation – by *Big Animal*, the appalling warship that had originally brought Taktikus' forces to Cavernam, which had spent years skulking in the icy rubble at the system's edge. Still, it would not be long before their torpedoes were outnumbered by their targets, and as the brood-ships lumbered closer, vomiting a swelling stream of pods from their bellies, orbital space would have to be abandoned entirely.

But while this stage of the defence held, the race was on to bed in for the ground war to come. Most of the main population centres were being evacuated and laced with mines, while the combined forces of the xenos and the Astra Militarum were deploying in rings around the loose triangle of hive-cities deemed defensible. Restructuring a labyrinth of opposing trenches was proving to be a logistical nightmare, but the sheer earth-moving potential of xenos muscle was staggering. Given shovels and simple charts, the beasts – who of course had been offered the outer line of defence out of supposed courteous deference – had thrown up towering earthworks virtually overnight.

A Chimera column rumbled past on squeaking wheels, like beetles beside the bulk of *Thriambos*, Nestor's ancient Baneblade. Drawn-faced troopers on their flanks threw salutes up at his turret, although Nestor couldn't be quite sure if they were for him or for the vehicle itself. Older than his own family line, the gilded colossus had been with the regiment since the breaking of the gates of Krax Prime, and was decorated all over with statuary and inscribed scripture. Nestor caught himself sneering at one of the sculpted lions that adorned the cupola, and sighed with self-disgust. Was he so bitter as to be jealous of a tank? Purging the thought, he found a salute for the men, along with what he hoped was a stern, fatherly smile. Throne knew they'd need the encouragement when the Great Devourer came.

He doubted Taktikus would be having any such problems with morale. While Nestor's forces were digging in with a grim, tight-lipped anxiety, the xenos lines were alight with revelry. As they rotated from trench duty, the brutes roared and wrestled by the light of bonfires, choffing down rancid meat and bellowing along to what was either music or engine noise. There were rumours that the gunners on *Big Animal* had turned the orbital defence operation into a drinking game. As far as the xenos were concerned, the eve of annihilation was a festival of pure joy.

For the most part, their lines and the humans' were as separated in distance as they were in mood, as there was no easy cooperation between the two forces. Nestor's soldiers hated the beasts they had been fighting for years, and the beasts in turn had nothing but contempt for their fragile new allies. Nestor had been forced to make examples of several officers who had refused to collaborate, and he imagined Taktikus had done the same in his own alarmingly direct fashion.

Tonight, the alliance would face its first acid test. The miners' barrack-town of Low Digbeth, separated from Imperial lines by half a continent, was due to have its occupants emptied into the hold of a bulk hauler before it could fall to the swarm. What's more, its former defenders had been recalled to headquarters three days previously, leaving only the town's former besiegers to oversee evacuation. As far as Taktikus – and indeed Phocus – knew, this was a strategic oversight on Nestor's part. Privately, however, it was a tray of meat left before a sitting hound: a test of obedience. If the xenos could resist the sport of a perfect massacre, it would put all dissent to rest among Nestor's staff. If not...

'Savage Rush,' said Colonel Phocus behind him, as if conjured by doubt. Nestor was so startled he almost failed to question the non sequitur, but mastered himself enough to give an inscrutable grunt as he turned to face the younger man.

'Savage Rush,' repeated the colonel, turning a well-worn green hexagon between his gloved fingers. 'Pelekys, seventy-fifth edition – *If a greenskin token is within six spaces of a civilian token in a sector with no more than eight command points,*' he recited, '*it automatically moves to the space and gains three materiel.* Surely you remember the rule, general?'

'Of course I remember,' snapped Nestor. How could he not? Like every other alumnus of the Mystrasian Academy, he'd played that bloody wargame over and over, with its appendices and its token stacks and its insistence that the Adeptus Astartes were the solution to every damned problem. It would be just like Phocus to resort to it now. 'I remember it as well as you do,' he continued, 'but I fail to see its relevance now. Unless of course you're coming to resolve a rules query, in which case I'd ask you why in the name of Holy Terra you're mucking about with bits of card when there's an actual war on.' To this, Phocus gave an oily smile of false deference.

'I suppose it is a rules query of a sort, sir. The rules, of course, being distilled from thousands of years of combat experience, not to mention the tactical insight of Lord Guilliman himself. Quite simply, general, they tell us what to expect from the enemies of the Imperium, and to prevent disasters such as the one which may be about to unfold at Low Digbeth.'

'Disaster? Do you *question my decision?*' spluttered Nestor, incredulous at the youth's patronising tone. The thing Nestor hated most about the man was his inability to be properly insubordinate; he always had to come at it from an angle.

'Do you question the nature of the enemy?' came the reply, loaded smoothly as a shell into a greased barrel, beneath a cocked eyebrow. Nestor's mouth hung open, half in outrage at Phocus' challenge, half in horror at the truth of the question. He had left ten thousand civilians in the hands of ruthless monsters, based entirely on intuition, and against the wisdom of the primarchs themselves. Was he mad? Struggling to form a reply, Nestor was almost relieved when Vatatze appeared at the hatch to interrupt the discussion. When he saw her face, though, his heart sank even further.

'It's Low Digbeth, sir,' said Vatatze, with uncharacteristic alarm. 'The xenos have opened fire.'

'Get me a live feed now,' bellowed Nestor over the din of *Thriambos*' command deck, as junior officers scurried frantically across his path. If this was going to be the end of his career, he'd at least go out shouting. The vehicle's comms officer was rummaging desperately at the thicket of controls beside the strategic display unit, mopping sweat from her forehead with a braided cuff as she tried to bring up a secure link. It was hellishly hot inside the tank at the best of times, but the crimson situation lights made it seem to swelter like an oven. Nestor was glad of this at least, as it would disguise the anxious sweat pouring from his temples.

If Taktikus had gone rogue this early, they were all doomed, and yet Phocus stood watching proceedings like a man waiting to be served a feast. The sod didn't even care about death, so long as he died in the right. As the display unit's holographic surface crackled to life, he craned forward, squinting for vindication in the resolving static. Sound came first, and it was all Nestor could do not to cringe – from the tinny speakers came the brutal clatter of crude gunfire, the raucous howl of xenos laughter, and under it all, the thin screaming of children.

Nestor put his hands on the table's edge and sagged forward, his head drooping. He was just clearing his throat to resign his command, when the image snapped into perfect clarity. At the table's centre, a child wailed in the dirt, clutching a wooden doll to its chest. Lumbering towards them, pitted blade in hand, was a xenos warrior in a fighting crouch. Nestor stared at the image, unwilling to be seen looking away from what he had done, and bit a hole in his lip as the monster snatched the child up by the scruff of the neck.

Then, the unthinkable happened.

Barreling in from out of shot, right into the space the child had occupied just a moment ago, came a monster. A *real* monster, with limbs like knives and a face (if that *was* its face) like a mass of writhing intestines. It chittered and reared, lashing out with a barbed tail so quickly that Nestor couldn't follow the motion. Then the end of the thing's tail was severed and flopping on the floor, and the ork's boot was on its neck, stamping down with a liquid crack. And that was that. The brute set the child aside with a motion that might generously be called tender, and sprinted out of view, leaving only a trail of viscous footprints and a receding bellow. With eyes as wide as Nestor's, the child ran for safety.

'Horus' *teeth*,' swore Vatatze, to a room too shocked to even register the blasphemy. Phocus simply gawped, as if he had been slapped in the face.

'Well then, colonel,' said Nestor quietly, feeling strengthened by the rumble of *Thriambos*' ancient reactor as it travelled up his arms. 'Rather looks like the rules of the game need updating, doesn't it?'

Nestor swept his eye over the immaculately modelled contours of the strategic map, and let half a breath hiss slowly between his teeth. He counted off the units arrayed round the hives for the fifth time, but still could not find the weakness he was sure in his bones he had missed. Despite the sick dread that rose up from his guts each morning, the war was – for an apocalyptic last stand, at least – going well.

The fall of Low Digbeth had signalled an earlier start to the ground engagement than even the most paranoid of his staff had predicted, and yet still they had been prepared. Within hours of the xenos-led evacuation, creatures had begun rushing from the wilds like ants boiling from a hole, and by the first night the trench-lips had been piled with twitching corpses. Things had only intensified since then, but the lines were holding. Even where they faltered, the sheer ferocity of the defence had ensured that every inch of ground cost the tyranids kilotonnes of biomass.

Nestor looked to the drab grey spires of Primaris Hive, where nearly half his forces were concentrated. Ghostly figures hovered over the model, offering mute reports of the city's efforts to forge shells from its remaining ore stockpile, while blinking lights signified fresh deployments of artillery in the rear lines. The whole edifice twinkled with defiant life.

Two days ago, he had been prepared for the lights to go off altogether in Primaris, replaced by the virulent purple of infested territory. The city had been caught in a vicious claw, hammered on both sides by waves of tyranids, and denied reinforcements by the eruption of burrowing horrors among the supply lines. The situation had teetered on the very brink of collapse – and then the xenos had swept in. They had come out of nowhere: an armada of ramshackle vehicles driven at maniac speed, carving straight through the western pincer of the enemy advance like spilled plasma. With the tyranids reeling, the Third Karakum Airborne had been able to launch a mass drop operation, securing the ground taken by the xenos, and relieving the siege.

Such strange synergies had boiled up over several fronts. In the mudfields at Dunrust, the tyranids had been stopped in their tracks by the mad, clanking war machines of the xenos, pinned down by hydraulic claws while human sharpshooters finished them off. At Thar's Bluff, the enemy's grotesque living artillery had been swarmed by xenos slave creatures, erupting from tunnels as a line of Imperial armour had advanced as a distraction. Time and time again, human precision and xenos ferocity were being boiled up into a brew stronger than it had any right to be.

As the two forces had realised this, their long-term enmity had begun to express itself as brash competition. Where humans held trenches next to the xenos, kill tallies were kept on tall wooden boards, while in Ferghal's Wood, where the aliens' exotic artillery had been pooled with Imperial batteries, the bombardiers were engaged in constant one-upmanship over the reload speed, the accuracy, and even the volume of their guns. As far as Nestor was concerned, this was to be encouraged, as it gave his troops something to do other than imagine death beneath a swarm of writhing nightmares.

Before his own thoughts could sink too far in that direction, he was distracted by a shout of protest from across the bunker.

'Filthy skaffing greenskin!' barked Vatatze, as the brute sitting opposite her shook with growling laughter. The xenos, one of Taktikus' retinue, was a crookbacked mess of scars and metal plates that – so far as Nestor could tell – fulfilled its species' archetype of 'grizzled NCO' as thoroughly as Vatatze did for the human race. The two had been engaged in a game of dice for the best part of an hour, playing for lho-stubs and coming up with increasingly profane ways to accuse each other of cheating.

Glancing at the staff sergeant, with her face riven by shrapnel from a xenos grenade and her prosthetic arm gleaming, he saw someone with every reason to put a blade in the creature across from her. And yet, despite all the cursing, she was wearing the same fierce, weights-room grin as she might in human company. That was the astonishing thing about infantry, he mused, as the pair of bruisers set into another exchange of insults. No matter what world – or species – they came from, if you gave them a shared enemy and a way to cheat each other out of smokes, soon enough they'd end up willing to die for each other.

Yes, there had been mutinies. And yes, there had been examples made of those officers who would not cooperate. By and large, however, you could almost forget the members of the alliance had been locked in a brutal trench war for the last decade. On the xenos side especially, there was simply no grudge – while they viewed their new comrades with a mixture of amusement and contempt, they had regarded the war as fantastic sport, and had no scores to settle.

For the more bitter human troopers, this was perplexing – it was hard to hate an enemy that didn't hate you back, after all. And when it became apparent how recklessly enthusiastic the xenos were to die for the cause, they had been stumped altogether. Nestor would have called the aliens' attitude suicidal, if it wasn't so carefree: as far as they were concerned, a violent death was just the ultimate culmination of good living, a mindset that the soldiers of the Astra Militarum could only regard with awe. When a platoon of Taktikus' self-styled 'kommandos' had lured an advancing swarm into an abandoned smelting plant and then overloaded its reactor, creating a fireball six miles across, the hives had shaken with human cheering.

While Vatatze had adapted surprisingly well to this new madness, Colonel Phocus had collapsed entirely. Vindicated by the events at Low Digbeth, Nestor had relegated the upstart to logistical command, where he could be lord and master of biscuit crates and promethium barrels. Of course, the man still droned on about the risks of trusting the xenos, but it was increasingly obvious he was just bitter. And with Phocus exiled from the war room, Nestor found his droning easier and easier to ignore.

It was then that Nestor noticed Taktikus playing with the war map. The ork commander – which had awarded itself several more bottlecap medals since the start of the defence – was pushing a model tank around the Dunrust Salient with a sinewy claw, making contemplative engine noises as it went. Nestor sighed.

'Taktikus, that's the Nineteenth Cambrian Heavies, and they belong in sector six – could you please put them back?'

Taktikus snapped its gaze from the table with eyes that made Nestor's scalp prickle, and he found his hand darting towards his sidearm before the beast's glare softened.

'Apologies, general,' it rumbled, putting the tank company back in place. 'I was... ronternating strategy.'

'Of course, we all have our habits,' conceded Nestor. 'But perhaps you'd like to share your thoughts with me? And it's "contemplating", for future reference.'

Taktikus made the growling noise Nestor had come to translate as 'let's agree to disagree', and gestured for a slave creature to bring food. After inspecting the repast – some sort of dreadful, charred bird with feathers still attached – the xenos commander took a great bite from it as if it were a piece of fruit, and raised a finger.

'Have you considered...' it said through a grim mouthful, puffing itself up with parade ground pride, '...a full charge at the enemy, with everything we've got?'

Nestor shut his eyes momentarily, after catching Vatatze stifling a laugh from the corner of his eye. Taktikus had already asked the question four times that *day*, with subtly different phrasing each time, and it was beginning to test his patience. Regardless, Nestor took the time once more to explain why, in a frantic defence against an enemy that was coming from everywhere, a massed charge wasn't always the wisest course of action. The brute nodded along, soaking up every word, with its reverence for Imperial tactics that was almost as endearing as it was pathetic. When Nestor finished by gently suggesting a xenos airstrike on the armoured beasts gathering in the hills north of Secundus Hive, however, Taktikus surprised him.

'A capital idea,' agreed the alien, nodding sagely. 'But doomed to fail.

Many spitters in those hills, you see.' With this, Taktikus mimed the action of the enemy's anti-aircraft batteries, and shook its head sadly.

'Instead,' it enthused, snatching up an Imperial bomber wing from an airfield by its elbow, 'airstrike from Imperial bombers – more boom, general – with ork planes flying low and light to soak up spit.' Concluding with a sweep of the model over the hills, and a series of explosion noises that it clearly thought sounded dignified, it replaced the bomber delicately, and grinned over the table at Nestor.

Nestor could only smile back, if a little uncertainly. Although it had been expressed with characteristic crudity, the plan was a solid one, revealing a surprising understanding of Imperial assets, and their place in a combined arms operation. At moments like this, when the creature's walnut of a mind cracked to reveal a kernel of insight, Nestor could almost respect Taktikus. It almost made him feel less of a fool for being the alien's equal for all those years.

As he voxed through the order to air command, Nestor felt a twinge of sadness. They might yet actually win this war – and if that happened, it would *almost* be a shame to wipe the xenos from the face of the world.

Nestor was dreaming of the basilica and the laurels again, when the hammering started. Although he knew he was dreaming, he was furious at the interruption, and tried to shout for it to go away. What came out was something between a croak and a murmur, and the vision began to collapse. All of a sudden, the hands bequeathing the laurel were huge and green and calloused, and the laurel itself was a mass of wriggling gut. The banging continued, and Nestor tried to scream, but his lungs were empty.

'Ugh,' he gasped as he awoke, bolt upright and drenched in sweat. Rubbing a hand over his itching stubble, he glanced anxiously around the dim red confines of the room, swimming in confusion until his brain caught up. He was at his desk, in his cabin on *Thriambos*, and it was day twenty-five of the invasion. Or was it day twenty-six?

The hammering came again, and he jerked round to the cabin door as he realised it was urgent, and real.

'Wuh... Come in,' he blurted, trying to sound awake, and rubbing his eyes with the coarse fabric of his uniform cuff.

'It's locked,' said Phocus from outside, and Nestor gritted his teeth as he got up to let him in.

'What do you want?' he growled as the colonel stepped into the cramped, sweat-stale cabin. It was some small consolation that the younger officer looked every bit as rough as him, with red-rimmed eyes and a week's worth of straw-coloured beard on his jaw.

'You're making a mistake,' said Phocus.

'I beg your pardon?' asked Nestor in a hollow whisper, daring the man to say more.

'You've doomed yourself,' answered the upstart, and Nestor struggled to reply. After all, he was probably right.

What Nestor had come to think of as the war's honeymoon period, when the enemy had just been a mass of chitin to be pulverised by the guns of the alliance, was long gone. The civilian evacuation was over, while the Naval blockade had been forced to retreat out-system, leaving the planet entirely encircled. There would be no reinforcements now, even if some miracle transpired in the halls of the Munitorum. Something in the bellies of the tyranid vessels was curdling the warp, trapping Cavernam deep in shadow. From now until the last body dropped, the planet was a cage in which they were locked, with insects swarming between the bars.

'You know I'm right,' pleaded Phocus, causing Nestor's blood to surge in his veins. 'There's been no signal from Secundus Hive since the breach last night, and Primaris might last, what – another three days? We've only got ammunition left because we're running out of hands to fire the guns. The Belisarians are gone, general, and the Eighth itself is down to two-thirds strength. How long–'

'Good riddance to the Belisarians,' spat Nestor. 'All they ever did was beg for kit. And of course we're losing men, you bloody fool – we're fighting a war. Besides, we have the orks!'

'General, sir, with all respect, we can't rely on those... beasts. I'll admit they're tough as tank treads, but they're *not our troops*. This is a game of numbers, General Pyrrhus, and they have more bodies they can comfortably lose. If the balance tips, and they smell our weakness–'

'So don't let the balance tip, *colonel*. We keep the orks in the teeth of the enemy, and make sure there are Imperial bayonets behind them when we run out of tyranids.'

'Nestor, please,' cried Phocus, forgetting his manners, 'this is... this is a fantasy. This is madness. I tell you as a loyal officer of the Eighth, there's another way.'

Nestor's vision throbbed crimson at its edges. Even now, at the height of the battle that his life had led to, this wretch dared to question him. There was no second option – they would fight with the orks, and by the Throne, they would win. It needed to be real. It was the possibility Nestor had staked everything on, and which would see his name last ten thousand years, as the brightest in the line of Pyrrhus, if it came to pass. This war *could* still be won, and he'd be damned before he let some snivelling career officer drag him from what little rest he could gather to tell him otherwise.

'*Another way?*' roared Nestor, surging forward and pinning Phocus against the doorway. '*Doom?* I thought that's what you wanted, *boy*. A noble death in the name of the Emperor? A chance to put on your shiny officer's cap and go down under a hill of monsters?'

'I said you've doomed *yourself*, you old fool,' hissed Phocus between gritted teeth, with a flash of sympathy in his eye that caused Nestor to waver. 'I'm ready to die in the Emperor's name, general. We all are. And I'll be the first to concede that we'd all have died sooner if you hadn't made parley with that... *thing*. But events are coming to an end now, sir. And you've still got a way out of this. A way that could save billions of lives.' Nestor squinted in disbelief, his hands falling to his sides as he wondered if he was still dreaming. After a steadying breath, Phocus continued.

'There are still ships, general. Fast clippers, message carriers, capable of slipping through the net and making it out-system. What we've learned in this campaign - the data we've gathered, the insights we've gleaned on both sets of xenos - could turn the tide when the tyranids hit the rest of the sector. The Golden Eighth won't make it, sir, but you might... And you could save a hundred worlds.'

'Colonel Phocus, what exactly are you proposing?'

'There's a clipper fuelled and loaded on the east pad, sir. We can have you on board before dawn, with all remaining aircraft scrambled to cover the launch. Leave Cavernam to me, sir - let me die here. I can overload the hive cores, make a quick end for the troops, and put a hole in the tyranid ranks as we go. It's... all we can hope to do.'

Nestor stood motionless, his mind tumbling. The thought that he could be away from here, out of the stifling heat of the tank and the moronic discourse of the map room, in a matter of hours, was intoxicating. The thought that he could leave this awful world, this awful war, behind. For a brief moment, he wanted it more than he had ever wanted anything.

But then he caught sight of his grandfather, stern face sculpted in gold, in the cornice above the door. *Last of the line of Pyrrhus*, said the old man, *fleeing the battlefield at the darkest hour. Leaving a lesser, more cunning house to raise the flag come dawn. Coward.*

'Intriguing,' said Nestor, deathly calm. 'And what if the situation should happen to improve once I am gone, Phocus? What if you beat the tyranids back, and wipe out the last of the xenos? What then? I suppose that would leave me as a lone deserter, a collaborator with xenos, and you...'

'No!' yelled Phocus, raising his hands. 'We can't win this war! And the xenos, Taktikus, they're not what you think. General, please - even if we *did* win-'

Phocus was silenced then, as Nestor smashed his nose sideways with the butt of his laspistol. A second blow caved in his front teeth, and a third to the back of his skull sent him crumpling to his knees. The colonel raised shaking hands, trying to mumble more lies, but Nestor's boot sent him sprawling into the corridor. He fled, limping like a beaten dog, leaving Nestor drawing ragged breaths and waving his gun like a club. From the bridge at the passageway's end, *Thriambos'* command crew stared on with horror, and Nestor stared back, before closing the door with a shaking hand.

When the rage had subsided enough to allow speech again, Nestor lifted the receiver of his desk's vox-rig, and dialled it to an encrypted frequency that only he knew. Holding a palm to the side of his face to keep his grandfather's from view, he listened to the growling static that rose from the endless synaptic chatter of the tyranids, and waited for the other side to pick up. When it did, there was a brief silence, followed by a curious grunt.

'*General,*' said Taktikus, like a host welcoming a guest to dinner, as gunfire rattled in the distance.

'Taktikus,' acknowledged Nestor, his voice hoarse. 'I require your counsel.' There was another pause, in which he swore he could hear the commander's leathery skin stretch into a smile of delight.

'*You... honour me,*' said the alien, clearly taken aback. '*Have you considered... a full charge at the enemy, with everything we've got?*' Nestor couldn't help but let out a bleak laugh at the response, but Taktikus continued unfazed.

'*The Devourer prepares itself to feed, general. It has sent a new creature. A very big monster, with a big, big mind, on the northern plain. It will come here, and eat us up like grots. But with your tanks...*' said Taktikus, with a twinkle of intrigue, '*we could punch through. Fight our way to the middle of the swarm, before tyranids can adapt. With the iron of Taktikus, the gold of Pyrrhus. We fight through, and make meat of it! Meat to share!*'

Nestor had never heard Taktikus manage such a long speech in one go, but every word was like nectar.

'And what happens if we do, Taktikus?'

'*The swarm dies. We win the planet. We win the war. Together. But it will need... everything. Every tank. All bombers. And in space. Every gun, all the boom. The ork way.*'

'The ork way...' mused Nestor, his mind racing. If he pulled this off, he would rewrite rules of war that had stood since the Emperor had walked. Maybe he would even spare Taktikus; he would grant him vassalship under the flag of Mystras, and create a fighting force the likes of which had never been seen. Golden light, tinged with green, now rippled at the edge of vision.

'So be it,' he breathed, sounds of glory ringing in his ears. 'Prepare your vehicles, Taktikus, for we charge at dawn.'

Nestor experienced the battle in flashes, as if in the throes of a fever.

He stood at *Thriambos*' turret hatch, soot-streaked rain lashing his face, as he signalled the charge. He felt the machine-spirit howl beneath him as the ancient vehicle advanced, the rumble in his bones as the great gates opened. All around him, the dying city sang a hymn of steel, a battle dirge from the throats of a thousand engines. Armour from a dozen worlds advanced, every hull crowded with grim-faced troops, while among them weaved the rattling, smoke-belching vehicles of his ally.

The orks were glorious, in their own way. Even if they were born in mud, as the men liked to mutter, they came into the world without fear, without a moment's doubt of their right to *win*. Without any of the drills or the decorum or the endless bloody *manuals* of the Astra Militarum, they were everything a soldier could hope to be. To fight alongside them was not just an advantage; it was a thrill.

He screamed into the wind as the first chitinous bodies cracked under the treads, shook his fist at a sky that swarmed with horrors. *Thriambos* was a ship afloat on a terrible sea, a mass of shrieking things that covered the world from horizon to horizon. They scrabbled at the sides and boiled up onto the hull, but he picked them off with his sidearm, cursing them as they fell back into the morass. Spittle flying from his mouth, he beckoned them on with wild taunts.

He saw tank after tank die, ripped open by the claws of abominations or simply pulled down beneath the gibbering waves. Bombers plunged screaming from the sky, drowning the darkness of the plain in holy light as their payloads went up. Their death-flashes rippled across an ocean of teeth; a galaxy of unblinking eyes.

At some time point in the fugue, Vatatze came to him on the tank's parapet, face etched with worry. She waved her steel arm at the orks massing at the back of the Imperial column, babbling words he could not hear through the thunder of glory. The words did not matter; how could her words weigh anything, against the voice of war?

Dawn came like a sabre, cleaving black clouds to sear the world with golden light. In that first brightness he saw it, distant and dim with haze: a beast like a mountain, moving with the slow threat of a glacier, lowing a challenge deeper than an earthquake. Reckoning he could lock eyes with the thing across the miles, he lifted the blade of his grandfather and slashed down with a shout that echoed in the voices of orks and men alike. As *Thriambos* surged forward, he stared ahead at the behemoth as if his gaze could sear its hide. There was no need to look back now, no need to glance around like a trench-hole rat trembling at imagined threats. The enemy was ahead of him, Taktikus was at his side, and they were unstoppable.

New stars blazed in the morning sky, erupting from the bellies of dying voidcraft. Fumes pounded in his lungs, and he was deafened by the rapture of war. Trembling officers brought him reports, but he shouted them away, exalting in the moment. He had been bred for this, had dreamed of this, had lived every crippled moment of his life in the shadow of this incandescence. As *Thriambos*' main cannon fired again and again into the wall of flesh ahead, he felt as if it were his own will, the will of his line, conjured into fire.

When at last the hide of the beast cracked, when its innards spilled in a steaming avalanche and it boomed its death-cry, it was as if a clap of thunder had gone off in his head. All around him, men screamed in sudden agony, and the world seemed to twist and shriek. Blinding white consumed his vision, followed by deepest black, and he watched the golden hull of the tank streak by in flashes, as if lit by strobe-light, as he fell from its turret. The ground met him with a lung-crumpling thud, and he waited for the swarm to fall on him, but there was only silence.

All around him were the twitching, ruptured bodies of the enemy. And above them, even as vision faded, he fancied he could see it. Descending from the heavens was the laurel itself, offered by the hands of his forebears. His triumph.

Nestor woke on his side, listening to the wind. Opening his eyes to a murky world, he blinked away stinging muck until it came into focus. All around him, convulsing weakly like crushed insects, were the bodies of the tyranids. And moving among them, putting blades through skulls with the methodical rhythm of harvesters, were orks. Some way off, the gore-blackened hull of *Thriambos* steamed under a clear sky.

Despite the tranquility of the moment, he felt a surge of panic down his spine at the sight of the vehicle. Of course – he had fallen from the hull! He tried to stand, but his arms would not move; they were lashed together behind his back. Filling his lungs to call out, he fell into a coughing fit, which made his eyes water again. When they cleared, Taktikus was kneeling beside him, admiring Nestor's sabre as he wiped ichor from its blade.

'General, you're awake,' said the creature, in a tone of pleasant surprise.

'Taktikus...' croaked Nestor, voice raw from the battle.

'Are you going to ask me what happened? I thought... you would have guessed.'

'The tyranids...'

'All dead now. Or... scattered.' Taktikus searched for words, but resorted to mime instead, of an exploding head and creatures running to and fro. 'Big head bang. *Sigh... kick*, I think you say? Knocked you out, and most of your troops. Not orks though... Thicker heads.' With that, the xenos tapped a claw to the side of its cinderblock skull, and grinned.

'And then?' said Nestor, head pounding as realisation dawned. To his astonishment, Taktikus looked almost sheepish, like a vast child caught red-handed in an act of minor theft.

'Well, I betrayed you, of course. The charge, with the tanks. It was... you know... a trick. We held back and... we got you.'

There was an awkward silence, and the xenos grumbled, before continuing. 'You didn't think...?'

'No,' said Nestor, trying to hide the lie. 'I had... planned the same.'

'It was an excellont campaign, still.'

'It was an excell*ent* campaign, yes, Taktikus.'

Another long silence followed. Taktikus looked curiously at Nestor, and Nestor looked at Taktikus, who was no longer the nightmare hobgoblin he had first met in no man's land, nor the clownish oaf who had played with model tanks in the war room. No, while his betrayer had plenty of each aspect, it was also something else entirely. He supposed that *alien* might be the right word for it.

'I suppose the lesson,' said Taktikus, with a faint glumness, 'is something about knowing your enemy? Hmm. Reminds me...'

Then the beast issued a string of throaty barks in its own tongue, and Colonel Phocus was dragged from *Thriambos*' shadow, led on a rope by a dull-eyed hulk.

'Now this one,' said Taktikus, indicating Phocus with a flick of a claw as the man glared at Nestor through a swollen eye, 'he *knows* his enemy. He was a sharp one. In fact, I'm going to keep him.' It was only then, as Nestor figured out what was about to happen, that his heart truly deflated.

'Colonel Phocus,' said Taktikus, with an odd air of ceremonial solemnity. 'Please tell the general the big Imperial rule about negotiating with xenos?'

'Don't,' mumbled Phocus through broken teeth, and spat blood on the ground.

'Good,' said the alien, nodding, and handed the man Nestor's sabre. 'Now, teach the general his lesson.'

Phocus trudged forwards, under the inquisitive gaze of the ork. Sighing with what he suspected was relief at last, Nestor closed his eyes and waited for the sabre's kiss.

ABOUT THE AUTHORS

Mike Brooks is a science fiction and fantasy author who lives in Nottingham. His recent work for Black Library includes the Warhammer 40,000 novels *Warboss, Brutal Kunnin, Da Big Dakka, Harrowmaster, Huron Blackheart: Master of the Maelstrom* and *The Lion: Son of the Forest.* He has also written the Horus Heresy Primarchs novel *Alpharius: Head of the Hydra,* the Necromunda titles *Road to Redemption* and *Wanted: Dead,* and the Warhammer 40,000 titles *Rites of Passage* and *Da Gobbo's Revenge.* When not writing, he plays guitar and sings in a punk band, and DJs wherever anyone will tolerate him.

Justin Woolley hails from the bottom of the world in Tasmania, Australia and is an author of science fiction and fantasy. In his other life Justin has been an engineer, a teacher, and at one stage even a magician. A long-time fan of Warhammer 40,000, he has written the novel *Catachan Devil,* the novellas *Prisoners of Waaagh!* and *Long Live Da Red Gobbo,* and the many short stories including 'Redemption Through Sacrifice' and 'Night Shriekers'.

Steve Lyons' work in the Warhammer 40,000 universe includes the novellas *Iron Resolve, Engines of War* and *Angron's Monolith,* the Astra Militarum novels *Death World, Ice Guard, Dead Men Walking, Krieg* and *Siege of Vraks,* and the audio dramas *Waiting Death* and *The Madness Within.* He has also written numerous short stories and is currently working on more tales from the grim darkness of the far future.

Nate Crowley is an SFF author and games journalist who lives in Walsall with his wife, daughter, and a cat he insists on calling Turkey Boy. He loves going to the zoo, playing needlessly complicated strategy games, and cooking incredible stews. His work for Black Library includes the Twice-Dead King duology, the novel *Ghazghkull Thraka: Prophet of the Waaagh!*, the novella *Severed* and the short stories 'Empra' and 'The Enemy of My Enemy'.